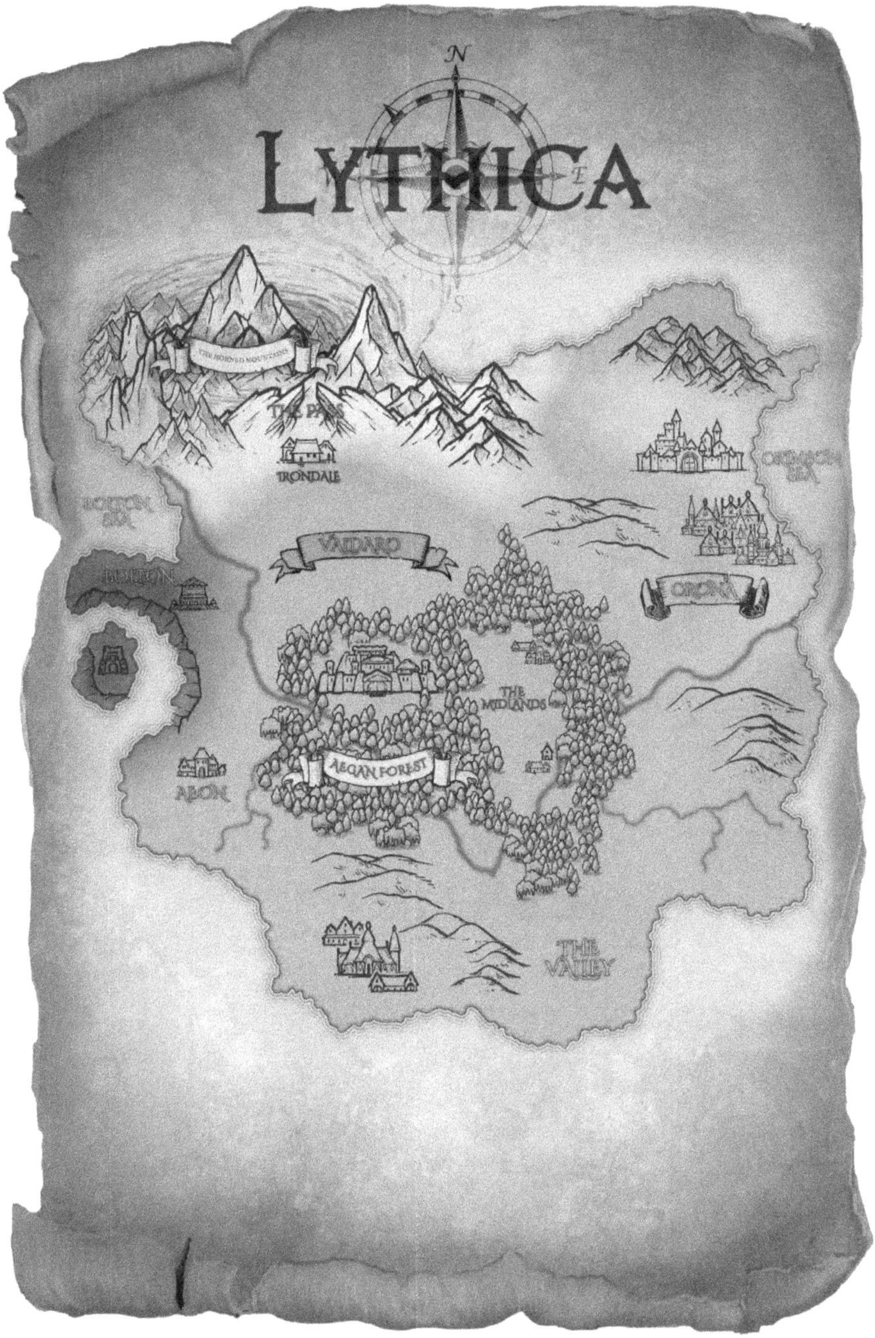
LYTHICA
N
E
S
THE HORNED MOUNTAINS
TRONDALE
VAIDARO
THE MIDLANDS
AEGAN FOREST
THE VALLEY

VALDARO

H. B. ELLIOTT

Acknowledgements

It has been the biggest struggle trying to find the words to express my gratitude for all the people that have helped make my dream a reality and bring this book to life. If I had an endless sea of pages, I still don't think that it would be enough.

When I was fourteen, I learned about the excavation of two bodies that were found together in an eternal embrace. Found out that they were never separated and that they died during a time that whatever story they had must have been one just as beautiful and just as tragic as Romeo and Juliet. Finding out that they were found just a short distance away from Mantua was even more intriguing. Thus, my infatuation and longing to know their story began. I've since written poetry, had them tattooed on my body and even dreamt about them because of how often they crossed my mind. I suppose we all want to know...what happened to them? Of course we'll never know the real story, but I finally decided that they deserved one. So this book was born. The bones of the individuals that have haunted me for years now have faces...names...and a tale that I hope somewhere up there, makes them proud.

To my readers...I want to thank you first. You guys are the reason that books like this have hearts that beat. I hope that you can fall in love with this story and these characters the way that I did, and that their journeys inspire and heal you. We all go through so much, even in a fictional world. I wrote this book to let you know that even in the deepest darkness...there is a light of hope.

To the authors, editors and avid booktokers...I want to personally thank all of you for all your support and encouragement. Thank you for the wisdom and the push that kept me sane through all of this. Your appetite for the written word is truly ravenous and I'm here for it. I couldn't have made it this far without all of you. Here's to many more stories and conversations, collaborations and brilliant ideas! I can't wait to continue this journey with all of you!

To my husband, Jeremy...you're my Crown Prince that was bound to my soul. My light in the dark. That pillar of strength when I need it, and the stronghold that protects me and these kids. Thank you for always being that for me. Thank you for putting up with my long hours leaning over this keyboard, and for helping me with all my ideas. I adore you. You're my everything. This book wouldn't even be possible if not for the love you give me. I love you right back.

To my son, Christian...baby I'm amazed at the devotion and the involvement that you've given to this story. You've been my sidekick through this entire process with your brilliant mind and your perfect little heart. I'll always remember every time you sat next to me begging me to read whatever I'd written that day. I know that the characters in this book mean just as much to you as they do to me, and I'm so glad to have been able to give this to you. I want you to always follow your dreams while you've watched me chase after mine and know that I'll be your sidekick too, cheering you on wherever you go. I love you so much "Sawad" !!!!

To my daughter, Beckett...you're going to be the FMC of your own story and you're going to kick just as much ass. I hope that one day when you're old enough to read this book, you understand that you always have and always will have the strength to conquer anything in this world, and that sometimes princesses can have a short fuse too. Thank you for putting up with all the times throughout this process that I've had to sit you next to me with dolls and crayons so that I could make this happen. I owe you big time and I plan to settle that debt. You and your brother are my reason for living and I love you more than anything in this world.

To my mom, Kelly...I'll let you and Jeremy battle it out about who's my biggest fan. I want you to know how much I love you, and how much your unrelenting praise and support has meant to me. The things that you've endured and come out on top of has given me so much inspiration and drive to overcome things in my own life. As you read this story I hope you always remember that at the end...you stood tall and you're still standing and I'm so proud of you, Mama. Since day one, you've spoken this book's success into existence and wouldn't let me doubt myself for a second. All the times you've reminded me how proud you are of me...they mean so much. All the moments I read you parts of these chapters and the hilarious reaction you gave me. I'll never forget them. You've always had such a creative, artsy mind and I think I get that from you. Thank you for being my rock and my mother. There is truly no one that compares to you. I love you to the moon and back! (Another reason the moon and stars were such a big part of this story...) Luna loves ya.

To my dad, Melvin...Daddy I'm so grateful for all our second chances. I'm so grateful that even though we've had our differences, we're still together and you've been part of this journey with me. Thank you for your support. Thank you for all the long distance calls and the reminder that the love for your kids, while it can be tough and painful...can still cleave through all the hard stuff and be so rewarding. I'm glad for it. I'm glad I have you. And I love you so much!

To my sisters, Erica and Nicole...yall's crazy asses make my life so much better. I really don't know where I'd be without you. Erica, I thank God every day for blessing me with you. Thank you for listening to me talk endlessly about this book over bottomless pots of coffee. Thank you for always believing in me and talking me through mornings where we set up goals for us both to reach before the end of the day and always pushing me forward...well—shoving me is more accurate. I've always envied your confidence and your "go get 'em" attitude. I strive every day to channel that, I know it's in our blood somewhere. In a world full of heavy, dark shit...you're my Paxe. And I'd gladly raise my sword for you. I love you shunk! Nicole, no matter what life throws our way I'm so glad that little red-headed spitfire was born into my life. I'm grateful I had the opportunity to wipe that behind that now shakes in my face just to put a smile on it or make me laugh. Your energy is unmatched and I don't realize sometimes how much I need it. I love you!

To Ashley Dickens...I'm so happy that fate brought us together. You are by far one of my dearest friends and if this book ever has any success it will be because of all your tireless editing and the time that you've taken for me to help my dreams become this reality. I couldn't have done it without you and I can't tell you how much I appreciate and cherish our friendship and all the support you've given me not just now, but ever since we met. I don't deserve you, Ash. There isn't anything better than having a friend bound to you through book pages and fate. I love you!

To Jaimi Cerrato...another one of those amazing people who found the time in their busy lives to comb through my misspellings, grammatical errors and rookie mistakes while also creating unbelievable character art that I know damned well I couldn't do if I tried. I'm so grateful to have another bookish friend to talk literature with and start a journey that will hopefully last a lifetime. Thank you for all that you do!

To Cheyenne Brigham...you're a warrior in your own right. Thank you for all your advice and your support while I started this adventure. You deserve every cent you make through your hard work and you inspire me to push harder and write better. I'm so glad we found each other! When we both make it big, I hope we never forget where we started and continue to lift each other up. Thank you for everything!

To Maureen McGrath...my English teacher in my senior year of high school. I bet you never expected to be mentioned in here, or have a character named after you...or that I even remembered your name. I hope this finds you, and you read this story and know that if not for you and all your guidance and the stellar job you did when you taught me how to forge words like weapons...I'd never be a published author. I can still see the passion on your face when you read Macbeth out loud and the way your eyes lit up with the name Edgar Allan Poe. I got here because of you. Thank you for being unapologetically yourself. You were one of those teachers I'll never ever forget. Oh...and I still know you weren't telling the truth when you said you didn't mud wrestle for charity! *wink*

To Ashlyn Farrow...even though we've gone our separate ways and our lives are worlds apart, I want you to know that I love you. I still remember passing a spiral notebook back and forth between classes when we were just a couple of kids with dreams of sending our poetry out into the world. Then years later, those notebooks were laptops on a kitchen table with bottomless coffee mugs and music and laughter and we made a promise to each other that one day people would read our shit, and know we did that. I remember one night in particular when I wrote the poem about Valdaro and you told me that I needed to write this damn book one day. You poked and you prodded and you believed in me. Here it is Ash. It breathes. And to think it all started with a dream and a pen on a Starbucks cup while we listened to Ville Valo. I hope I made you proud. I love you beepy boppy! Your turn.

To "The Author's Point" publishing team...thank you guys so much for everything. Thank you for your patience and persistence in helping me reach my goal of getting this book out by the end of 2023. Shane, Demetri, Daniel...Miss Alice. I don't have enough words to describe my gratitude for all you've done. Shane, I know that you told me that mentioning any of you in these acknowledgements was unnecessary, as I'm a published author...but you're so wrong. Because of all of you, I was able to do this–and do it on a budget, still making an impossible goal. You all made magic happen and I can't thank you enough for all of it. So glad I clicked on that website. I'm looking forward to working with you all with many more books in the future!

And finally...to my editor. Maria. You're such a damn goddess. I can't believe we're finished with this book, and I'm gonna miss waking up in the mornings to your messages about how much I've ripped your heart out and pieced it back together with every chapter you've finished. I want you to know that it takes a person of unbelievable strength to work as hard as you do while also being a mother and taking care of the ones in your family. It's something I understand completely, having done it myself. The fact that you did that while also knocking out countless hours editing these chapters from your home on weekends that you should have been spending with your mother and your little one...I truly don't deserve you. You have a special place in my heart. You're my feisty Varuna. I hope that we'll keep in touch. You're the reason my very first novel will make it out there. Thank you so much. From the bottom of my heart.

...For Jeremy, Christian, and Beckett...
The greatest loves of my life.
You hold every piece of me together.
I love you.

For the lovers that traded pieces of their souls...knowing one simply cannot live without the other.

In Loving Memory
Justin Christopher Elliott
May 7, 1985 - October 30, 2023

"Because reading is for smart people...and you're not the brightest bulb."

We love and miss you brother...and none of us will be that bright without you in the world.

DISCLAIMER:

This book contains situations of domestic and sexual abuse, graphic violence and brutality, mentions of murder/suicide, slavery, profanity, and explicit sexual situations that include blood-letting and mutilation. While this is a fictional story in a fictional world with fictional races...the topics listed above are very real and in no way reflect my personal views or beliefs. Your mental health is *so* very important. Reader's discretion is strongly advised.

This story is based on a real couple found buried together in Valdaro, Italy, many years ago. It is a re-imagined tale depicting Valdaro as a world in itself. Any references to the Italian language or culture are in respect and honor to the real lovers...who inspired me for so many years and made this story possible. I hope I gave you both a story worthy of your tragic beauty. You deserve it.

PLAYLIST

"Dynasty" - MIIA - (Ch. 1)
"Lovely" - Lauren Babic & Seraphim - (Ch. 7)
"Panic Prone" - Chevelle - (Ch. 10)
"Lost in Paradise" - Evanescence - (Ch. 14)
"Little Girl Gone" - Chinchilla - (Ch. 15)
"Comatose" - Skillet (With Violin Intro) - (Ch. 17)
"Carry You" - Ruelle - (Ch. 22)
"Dark Side" - Neoni - (Ch. 24)
"Saturn" - Sleeping At Last - (Ch. 25)
"Good Enough" - Evanescence - (Ch. 38)
"The Death of Peace of Mind" - Bad Omens - (Ch. 40)
"Chasing Cars" - Tommee Profitt & Fleurie - (Ch. 42)
"Hands in the Sky" - Straylight Run - (Ch. 44)
"Anything But Love" - Apocalyptica - (Ch. 45)
"Silhouette" - Aquilo - (Ch .46)
"Nothing and Everything" - Red - (Ch. 47)
"Part That's Holding On" - Red - (Epilogue)

Contents

CHAPTER 1

UNTIL DEATH

In my nineteen years, I've never grown used to my love-hate relationship with mirrors. The way that they make you think too much or threaten to have you longing for something... or someone... brings a smile to your lips or a tear to your eye. Then there's that awkward feeling of catching the glimpse of a scar or two in your reflection that has your mind swimming in all kinds of memories: the good and the bad. Today, however, my eyes are on that woman staring back at me with her deep green eyes and flowing chestnut hair. The color passed down from her father but delicately woven with the faintest tint of red from her mother. My body has changed so much in the past two years. I'm realizing now that the woman I'm becoming...the one I see in that glass, looks so much like my mother. As busy hands finger through my hair, twisting and twining it into a long braid behind me, I stared at my figure, getting lost in thought.

"You do look a lot like her, Arienne," said the soft voice over my shoulder as she met my gaze in the mirror my handmaiden.

Her name was Paxe, and while she was employed by the royal family from a very young age, she was also my best friend. My only friend. We grew up together in this castle, her mother Isabelle, having been an aide to my own. Being a queen's aide was a prestigious occupation and one that was fought over by the wealthy Valdarian nobles. They would practically raise their daughters on an education solely focused on waiting on royalty hand and foot. But Isabelle wasn't from a well-known family. In fact, she had no known next of kin other than her seven-month-old baby at the time and had found work as part of our household staff. That was how my mother met her the night she found her bloodied, beaten, and still trying to prepare supper in the lower floor kitchen. She took pity on Isabelle and her small baby girl and gave her the opportunity to provide for and protect her. I was born about a year and a half later, making Paxe just a couple of years older than me.

The Valdarian race is neither Fae nor human. Not immortal, but can live to be over two hundred years, all without losing a great deal of our youthful appearance. But the more potent feature about our race is that in our twentieth year, we come into a special ability, and a genetic level of power. Some Valdarians have significantly less according to their stature. My father, King Loren, was the most powerful sorcerer Valdaro had seen in centuries. His magic came from the very heart of our world nearly two thousand years ago when Valdaro's first king was gifted it by the gods for proving himself worthy to rule over our people. It had since been passed to the eldest heir, each transfer stronger than the last. In a royal bloodline, a pure, direct Valdarian heir would receive raw, unfiltered power upon the death of their biological father. In a long line of kings, the power my father possesses has been built upon and passed down for hundreds of years. In the very rare event that a father dies and passes down his power to his heir before their twentieth year, that power is dormant until the moon rises on the night of their *Ventus,* or twentieth birthday—a day usually followed by lavish celebrations among wealthy Valdarians as they receive their abilities.

In just a few months, I'll be having one of my own, and I've been eager to learn exactly what kind of magic will be awakened in me. Each of us, different and unique, will wield our own power. Some are mages that can heal, while others can control elements and weather. Paxe, for example, had a way of reading your mind or, rather...feel it. If you were heartbroken, she could feel your anguish while unintentionally listening to whatever accompanied it in your mind.

She was so young when my mother died that she had very scarce memories of her. She couldn't really tell me stories of what she was like, or the small things she did to comfort Paxe as a small child. We both relied heavily on the oil painting I had relocated from the Great Hall into my chambers and the stories from the household staff that had been around since my mother married into this family.

It goes without saying that talk has dramatically changed throughout the long years. Stories gain small details that were most likely never true, and different accounts of the day I was born become blurry and questionable. But nonetheless, the one detail I was certain of, by *all* accounts, is that my mother never got the chance to hold me in her arms. I wondered, as I smiled back at Paxe in the mirror, if she was at least able to see me before her jade eyes had closed forever.

"I think she did, milady," she whispered, flashing a sympathetic smile.

"Don't call me that." I smirked, nudging her with my elbow. We both glanced up at the painting and the small brass plate centered at the bottom.

Her Majesty Queen Lucinda of Valdaro.

"I wonder what she'd think of me if she knew I didn't want this life?" I dryly said as I smoothed the green fabric of my dress down my abdomen.

"I would think that most any female your age is bound to have that thought cross her mind at one point or another. Royalty is, after all, a tremendous responsibility that you're born into, and it would be highly unlikely that everyone born without options would be happy about it. In other words, she's your mother. And I'm sure she would have understood exactly how you feel." She dropped the braid gently down the front of my left shoulder and turned me from the mirror to face her. "Just be grateful that your mother didn't *choose* to leave you to ponder it all on your own. And in any case, because of the kindness that she showed my mother and me, the two of us will always have each other," she smiled as she straightened the bodice of my gown.

I knew what she meant, and she was right. Paxe and I would never have been in any way close to each other had it not been for my mother's compassion. Isabelle and her baby, being more of a liability, would most likely have been thrown into the cold without having any family to turn to. I suddenly felt ashamed for what I said when she mentioned that Mother didn't choose to leave me. Isabelle had. Although I was too young to remember it, she had chosen to take her own life when Paxe was only four years old. With both of us now without mothers, the elder staff in the household pleaded with my father not to separate us, and all took great pride in raising us—particularly Vetta, an elder of the palace who was once aide to my paternal grandmother. I often thought of her as such. Her demeanor and her gentle, yet oftentimes stern position. I never knew any of my blood relatives aside from my father. Never knew if they were even still alive. As we grew up, we learned only what we were permitted to. For me, it was always strength...power. For Paxe, my father's only gift to a lowly, orphaned palace rat was my company and to be trained how to earn her keep.

"I'd ask you why you seem to be so sentimental this morning, but that would be fruitless. I can understand why you're nervous, but it seems impossible for you to ever keep your feelings to yourself," Paxe said, turning away and slowly walking to the small vanity by my window. Her light footsteps were barely audible, and she always moved with such subtlety. She was well-trained. It stirred this small fury inside me that this beautiful creature, whom I dearly loved, would live her life like the humans do, a life of servitude. And even with the small favor of being a royal aide and living in a castle, my friend would never truly have a fulfilling life.

"Ari, for the love of the gods!" she slammed her palms down on the vanity and leaned over, bowing her head.

"I'm sorry! Come on, though. Everybody has thoughts. It's not as if I have any control over them." I paced quickly over behind her, wrapping my arms around her middle. "You still love me anyway." I chirped, resting my chin on her shoulder.

"You had better be glad I do...you heathen, princess nightmare." she scoffed.

"I accept that." I grinned.

"I do wish you could hear....*my* thoughts." Her tone sounded mischievous as she raised her head, tilting her chin toward me.

"Oh?" I replied with intrigue. "Got something to tell?"

"You need not fret over my dreadful, unfulfilling life. We both know I've always been determined to live as I wish. That said..." she blushed.

"Wait," My mouth dropped open. "You sly hussy. You have a lover!" I exclaimed, slapping her arm in excitement.

"Would you shut your mouth?!" she giggled, slapped mine back, and then reached for a small crested, gold box. I impatiently snatched it from her, pulling my mother's emerald pendant from it and opening the clasp.

"I know how to put on a necklace. Now spill." I said. She turned to face me, leaning against the vanity as I fastened the jewel around my neck.

"You remember Perla Fauci? That girl that's commissioning the gown for your Ventus?"

"I do... it's a woman? A human woman?!" I gaped.

"Gods. You are such a fool. No. She has a brother. Lakan."

"Lakan Fauci, the blacksmith." I couldn't close my mouth.

"The blacksmith indeed." she beamed, and I started to see the tiniest beads of sweat starting to sparkle at her dark blonde hairline. Her matching eyebrows danced up and down, and her grin nearly reached her icy blue eyes.

"How have you been able to sneak around with a human boy? And for how long? And why am I just now hearing about this?!" I crossed my arms in disappointment. She paused and did the same, but the smile didn't leave her lips.

"Look, to be fair...we only kissed...well, a lot. For a few weeks now, until last night."

"I honestly had no idea you were seeing anyone," I confessed.

"Ha! I know. You didn't suspect a thing, and I was careful to pay attention anytime you were around me to get a feel for you and see if you'd started to notice." I started to feel sympathetic again. Something that important was happening right under my nose, and I was too wrapped up in my own feelings to see it.

"Stop. Don't do that. I didn't want you to know just yet. I know what consequences could become me should anyone, especially your father, find out that I'm fraternizing with *human filth*. But as I said, I'm alive. And as long or short as that life may be, I do plan to actually live one. The way I wish to." she reached forward, grabbing my hands. "I'm telling you about this today, not just because...well," she grinned and continued, "But because, my darling friend...royalty or not, you have the same choice. Your predicament may be a bit more complex, but your life is yours, Ari. I love you. You might as well be my sister and whatever you decide, I have your back."

I had so many questions and while I was worried about what could happen to Paxe and the danger this put her in, I was also happy for her. Happy that she was strong enough to fight for the right to live the way she deserves and that she's found someone to love. Love from anyone other than me was something she'd never known. It was something that felt so far out of reach for us both, as it's never been a privilege we were set to have.

"I love you too. Sooooo...?" The corner of my mouth crept up.

"So?" She echoed.

"Are you going to make me beg you for details? Or should I just start rattling off every thought about what a human might be like in bed?" I laughed.

I've never seen Paxe truly bashful before. This was certainly new territory that I was undoubtedly determined to explore. Her face flushed the loveliest shade of red, and even her chest began to match the pale rose color of her dress.

"Oh good grief, Arienne!" she started, moving uncomfortably off the edge of the vanity and heading back over to the gilded mirror to inspect herself. She dabbed the sweat at her brow and flashed a half smile. "It wasn't in bed. It was...on the wall," she cracked, breaking into sheepish laughter. I gawked at her as she covered her mouth with her hand, her face turned to watch the shock of her audacity on my complexion. "Don't look so baffled! He's a blacksmith. Strongest arms you've ever felt," she snorted.

"In any case, *Princess*...today isn't about me—plenty of time to talk about my blatant disregard for rules and gravity later. I'm supposed to be getting you ready for this meeting." She settled her delicate hands on her hips.

The Valdarian lands were situated on the far west side of a small continent called Lythica, with no one ruling north or south. Only Crona lay to its east. Our neighboring king and queen were perched in a castle, only a bit smaller than ours, and like my parents, had a single heir. A male. Luca. He was barely a month older than my dearest Paxe, and like Valdarians, they had power. Lots of it. Sorcerers and mages just the same. Only my father was impossibly more powerful. He was also known for his cruelty and ruthlessness, making him incredibly dangerous but highly respected.

I hated him. Despised him with every fiber of my being. I also knew that he, without a doubt, hated me right back. I was the only heir to his power, a female who looked nearly identical to the wife who never loved him and reminded him of her every day. Mother was said to be a quiet, kind female with the voice and beauty of a siren. She was poetic, wrote music, and had all the qualities of perfect peace, according to anyone who had ever known her, and could....or would...tell me stories about her. Some have said that was her ability. Peace. Tranquility. Something that would never break the surface in Valdaro.

When I was born and my mother died, my father was left with no other heir to be taught and drilled with his brutality. I was not to be like her. I was to be trained to battle if necessary, to govern our lands with a sword and a whip. I was to learn how to torture, punish, and produce an heir of my own to carry on the legacy that Valdarian blood was better than anything. More importantly, I was required to learn how to put humans in their place. To let Cronian subjects have a short leash and press the Midlands between our realms to near crushing, like a prison. Suiting, as the Midlands was human territory. A way to make sure they never get out or expand. To brutalize and punish them for only existing. It must be eating my father alive to know that I'm nothing like him or the ruler he hopes me to become. I'm my mother. And while participating in his training, as if he gave me any other choice, I was going to devise a plan to put an end to his tyranny or die trying.

Every five years, my father would hold the dreaded "meeting" with the royals of Crona to discuss their cooperation and system of keeping the human race subdued. The humans were allowed to grow food and produce healing remedies for themselves as long as they didn't dabble in any medicine that would surpass what their simple, mortal bodies should possess. That was considered witchcraft, and the only ones permitted to use sorcery of any kind were the sorcerers themselves. It was punishable by death and a cruel, slow one, at that.

They could also weld armor and weaponry, but only for our kind. There were humans with all sorts of simple talents, just like Cronian and Valdarian subjects. They were all permitted to use those talents to sustain themselves as long as Valdarian patronage was priority. Thus, making it easier for our kind as well as theirs to mingle and create chaos. It was absolutely forbidden to blend the races, as doing so resulted in the worst kinds of consequences for humans and Valdarians alike. Some were tortured and killed. Women were raped, beaten, and sometimes forced into slavery.

Any child born of a union between our kind and human was to be slain at their birth while the mothers watched. The absolute most cruel punishment there was for giving life to something so impure. In my fourteenth year, I was forced to witness it. I've logged that night in my memory as the worst day of my life. Not just because of the horror that was forever branded into my mind but because I was punished too. I didn't watch that innocent child come to its end alone. There was another young human at my side.

His name was Gideon. He was handsome by human standards, and we had met a couple of years before when Vetta had taken Paxe and I on our weekly trip to the markets. I was only allowed to leave the castle with the two of them, and only after I had completed, and aced my sparring, archery, and swordplay lessons. To be honest, I learned to enjoy them. I was proficient. Even if I had days when I was lax or aloof with teenage fantasies, it was promptly beaten out of me later. I became quite good at staying focused after that. One day, in the markets, a young human boy caught my attention outside the butchery. He was sitting on a barrel, legs dangling carefree under him, carving one of the most beautiful cedar arrows I'd ever seen. I strayed from Vetta and my friend and mindlessly walked in his direction, fascinated by his skill.

The arrow was a milky shade of light brown, intricate swirling designs weaving their way all around the shaft. He had used red hawk's feathers on the fletching and some type of smooth, white quartz for the head. It was a work of art. The tip gleamed like his golden hair, which was closely shaved at the sides but crowned by a tight braid that extended from his forehead to the base of his neck. I think he may have been just as beautiful to me simply because he was forbidden. I asked the young human to name his price for the arrow.

"My father says I can't sell until I'm old enough. Sorry," he replied.

"That's too bad. It's really stunning. How old is old enough, boy?" I asked.

"My eighteenth year," he shrugged.

I politely waved and started to make my way back to Vetta when I felt a soft tap on my shoulder.

"Princess...take it—a gift. I may be too young to sell, but I'm at least a gentleman. I'm honored that you find it worthy of something you'd use," he bowed slightly at the waist and presented the arrow to me. I couldn't have been more than twelve, and I was infatuated. With the arrow, yes, but also with this fragile human thing that had shown me kindness and didn't look any older than I.

From that day on, I cherished that little cedar twig. I used it in every archery lesson, and in the months that followed, Gideon and I became close friends. He taught me a little every visit while Vetta and Paxe did the shopping. After a while, I became quite good at making little masterpieces of my own. He let me keep the ones that I finished and I stopped using the one he gifted me in my lessons. Instead, I found a spot to display it in my chambers. Before I could get a handle on my adolescent feelings, two years had gone by, and our weekly visits started becoming a huge risk of sneaking off and getting caught being young and reckless. We snuck off one afternoon and ducked into a storage shelter where Gideon's father would hang the hides from the animals he carved up. There were no windows, save for a small opening from the back that had no glass, so that the animal skins could tan. Gideon closed the door and touched his forehead to mine, his hands taking my waist. I wrapped my arms around his neck and tilted my head to kiss him. He didn't put up a fight. We knew it was wrong and that it could get us killed, but perhaps there was some way the gods would let me have him?

That kiss was the turning point in my youth. His lips crashed into mine with a fire threatening to burn this world to ashes. I'd never felt that way in my entire existence, and I let his hands travel wherever they wished. I must have thought about that moment every night for months, and it felt better than I could have ever imagined. We were lost in that euphoria until the shelter door swung open, and to my horror stood my father with his guard. There was only one reason that the Valdarian king would be somewhere like this: to find me. Someone had betrayed us. I never found out who. Most likely, a human who had already suffered this exact thing and wouldn't let the daughter of the king that butchered their children have this for herself. I couldn't blame them if I wanted to.

My father beat Gideon nearly blind in front of his father, who was helpless to save him. I wasn't exempt. I was publicly beaten right along with him, lest anyone think that they're safe from his wrath. He dragged us on foot back to the castle, to the lowest level, and threw us both in cells adjacent to each other. There was a woman screaming in pain. We listened to her for what seemed like a century, and the only thing I could do was sob and beg Gideon to forgive me. He stared at me from across the hall and never said a word.

Finally, my father appeared again between us, dragging the bellowing woman along the floor. Now it all became clear...she was in labor.

"You shame me, daughter," he said between gritted teeth. "Do you know who this is?" he pointed a finger down at the young Valdarian mother. "This. This is one of our kind. The worst of them." His voice was low and sinister. She scrambled for air, as it seemed her baby could be born at any moment. He dragged his boot across her breasts and fit the sole over her throat.

"Please, my lord! Please spare us! I'll do anything!" she pleaded between rattled breaths. He squeezed her small neck between his foot and the floor, and she clawed at it with all her remaining strength. How long had she been down here like this? What happened to her partner? Tears tore down her face toward her ears, and mine followed suit. This was unbearable.

"This could have been quite an attractive noblewoman. But she sealed this fate by getting impregnated with human trash. So, this is what you want, daughter? This is the path you want to choose for yourself? This...this is what my power will be passed down to—a naive, pampered imbecile. You're too much like your mother. It's time to teach you some obedience."

The dying woman on the floor began to turn a shade of purple. She was still struggling, her cinnamon hair branching out across the cold stones. He lifted his foot from her throat, and without warning, he began thrashing his heels into her swollen belly. Both the young female and I wailed. Our screams were the most agonizing sound as they echoed off every surface of the dungeons. Gideon was on his knees, a sheer haunted expression on his face. I begged my father to stop the savage attack, but it seemed to be worse with every word that came from my mouth. He finally slowed, his foot coming to rest again on the bloody floor. The broken female lay nearly motionless, and I was almost sure he'd killed her until she risked a final comfort to her infant and raised her trembling fingers to her womb.

"Shouldn't be long now. Take this whore back to her cell. Chain her arms to the wall, and let that abomination come out on its own. She is not to touch it. If it lives, you're to finish it off and leave it at her feet," he ordered, nodding his approval to his guards to take her away. I couldn't stop myself from vomiting on the floor. The king sneered down at me in disgust and waved a finger to Gideon's cell. Two guards unlocked his door, dragging him out into the hall and to my father's side. I was shaken with fear of what would come next.

"Do you think you love her, boy?" My father coldly asked, turning to face my friend. "You think that love gives you a right to put your filthy human hands on her body? To put your disgusting mouth on her skin? Let me ask you...if you do, in fact, love her...do you not respect her enough not to bind her to a fate such as the one I just showed you?" He directed Gideon's attention to the blood at his feet. I could faintly hear the remnants of the tragic young female crying from somewhere close by. Gideon said nothing as he humbly accepted whatever the king was about to do. He never lifted his head. I saw tears fall from his face onto the floor.

"Nothing to say, boy?" He asked, unsheathing a sword from his side.

"Father! Don't!" I pleaded, gripping the metal bars of my cell.

"Be honorable at least, you filth. Hold your arms out in front of you. Show me your kind has a shred of dignity, or die right here." Gideon slowly moved to obey him and lifted his face to meet the king's evil half-smile. He straightened his spine and tried to steady his breathing, tears pouring from his sapphire eyes. "Good man," the king said. Gideon dared one sorrowful glance toward me as I started to sob, and there was a quick flash of light and the sound of metal tearing through flesh. I squeezed my eyes shut as Gideon screamed in agony, both his hands thudding lifelessly to the floor. If my father allowed him to live, he would never carve another arrow. He would never use his artistic skill or shoot a bow again. Never touch me or anyone else for the rest of his days. A sinister punishment indeed.

I couldn't breathe. The guards dragged Gideon back into his cell and slammed the door shut. I'd never cried so hard, and all I could hear over my heaving was his own as he growled in pain. My father turned toward me, cleaning his blade with the front of his tunic.

"As for you, daughter...I do hope that you understand the only reason you live tonight is because your worthless mother was only able to secure one heir to our bloodline. She was handpicked, by my mother and father, to ensure its purity. Our future now depends upon you, and you insist on being a selfish whore, wasting privilege to be fucked by the lowest vermin this world has to offer."

I silently swore to myself I would kill him. If it were my last dying act, I would make this son of a bitch pay dearly for this. He continued, "If all you wanted was a taste of intimacy, you should have just asked." The two guards opened my door and entered my cell, closing it behind them and smiling deviously at me. My eyes widened in terror. "Keep it quick, but make sure she gets the message. She'll sleep here tonight. Sweet dreams, daughter," he said with a smirk as he began to stroll down the long hall and out of my sight.

I backed up against the cell wall in panic as the guards started taking off pieces of their armor and inched toward me.

"No. No, no, no. Don't touch me!" I cried. It was no use. What was I going to do to hold my own against two full-grown, armed Valdarian males? They grabbed me, ripping at my dress, taking turns holding my arms against the wall. They stifled my screaming with cloth from gods know where, and for the next few hours, I was beaten, raped, and thoroughly violated. At some point, I gave up the fight and lay there, numb and utterly broken. I kept my eyes on Gideon, my cheek pressed against the cold stone. He lay there, almost the same way, keeping his arms tucked into himself, a blank expression on his face. I don't know if I fainted or if exhaustion finally had its way with me, but when I awoke, I was grateful to be alone.

They left me there, cold, naked, and unconscious. I woke, curled into the fetal position in the corner of the cell. There were scraps of my clothing strewn around me, and every part of my body hurt. The cell smelled of mold and blood. I lifted my head from the floor, my hair sticking to it in some places, and to my face in others. I winced as I tried to push myself up with my weak, bruised arms and reached for my tattered gown. Hot streams began to trail down my face as I tried to cover myself with what was left of the dress. I pulled the torn fabric around me as best I could and looked around my cell, hoping to find anything else of use. There was nothing. I saw tangled wads of my hair on the floor, and the only sound I could hear was taps of dripping water echoing through the space. An image of Gideon's tears hitting the stone flashed across my mind. Gideon. I jerked my head towards his cell, and he lay there, still and silent, with his back facing me.

I couldn't tell if he was breathing. I wasn't sure I was even alive. I softly called out his name, but no answer. There was no screaming or crying from the mother down the hall. This is what human life was like. This is the fear these people lived in, day in and day out, all because they were born a bit more mortal than we were. Just because they were simple and powerless? If anything, it only made me care more for their kind. My heart was torn to pieces. I pulled my knees to my chest and cowered like a beaten dog in the corner of my cell. There was no organization to be made of all the thoughts running through my head. I let the tears invade and rested my head on the wall.

I woke again sometime later to the sound of my cell door screeching open. My eyes were swollen, my lids heavy, but I made out the blurred image of two females.

"Oh, Ari..." one of them whispered. She was crying. Paxe. That meant the other would be Vetta. Maybe they were being punished, too, having to come down here and see all of this. To help me in my sad state, knowing that they probably could have stopped me from being so careless. Paxe knelt before me, her slender fingers covering her mouth. Vetta moved around her and silently helped me to my feet. She gently wrapped a thick, soft robe around my shoulders and said nothing as she put a hand on my back and started directing me out of the cell. I padded slowly into the hall over the blood, now mostly dry over the floor, wincing when I saw Gideon's bodiless hands lying just by the door. I peered around the bars of his cell across the hall, Vetta's restraint not allowing me closer.

"He's gone, mi'lady. Don't look...don't look. Walk with me," she pleaded softly. Paxe joined us, gently leading me away.

My breath started to catch in my throat, and a broken sob tore out, turning into a fight for air as if I were drowning. Looking back at him, I put up a struggle as they nudged me down the hall.

"I'm so sorry..." Paxe wept as she rested her forehead on my shoulder. We made it to the end of the long hallway, and I caught a glimpse of someone in the corner of my eye. Another cell. I abruptly stopped us all and looked over. A female, sitting against the back wall, one arm chained above her, the other bloody, and shredded, cradling a tiny baby in her lap. Her small white shift was bloodied and ragged, her knees bent, and her head bowed, resting on her chained arm. It was her. She had defied him. Tore her skin nearly off to free her arm and deliver her own baby. Whom she did, in fact, touch and hold...no matter what the bastard had said. By the color of their skin and the lack of movement, I knew they were both dead, but seeing them lit a fire inside me.

Be her. Die for it if you have to. Don't let him take anything else from you. End him.

Little did my father know I *would* learn a lesson that day. Just not the one he intended. Not a lesson from him, but from the two...no...*three*...brave souls in this hall that gave up their lives for freedom...for love. I knew then that it wasn't just the humans that suffered, but all of us. This was why I was born. This was what I was meant to do. To fight until I found a way to deliver us all. As if my sudden epiphany was an unspoken request from their broken bodies to avenge them and right this wrong, I quietly promised...

"Until death."

CHAPTER 2

GAME. SET. MATCH.

Who in Valdaro taught Paxe to apply counter paints? It was all I could do to keep still as she tried... and failed... to outline the corners of my eyes with the small coal stick. I shut my eyes and did my best to keep my flustered thoughts to myself lest she get a whiff and paint me into a fool for spite.

"OWWWWW, Paxe! That is NOT my eyelid," I wailed.

"Sorry... I'm sorry, I know. I'm terrible at this. Perhaps just hold the corner and tug it a bit toward your ear, and I could try to draw it from the other side?"

"Or *perhaps* we could just smudge it off." I rose from the chair at my vanity and nursed my burning cornea. "I really don't see the point in this anyway. I don't look like a jest on a day-to-day basis. And to be frank, I could care less what any of them think."

"Well, I think it might look worse now if you try to take it off. You're the artistic one. Do you want to try to do it yourself? We don't have long now, Ari. Your father expects you to be seated in that room in half an hour, and Vetta said they were already here."

"I know. I heard her. She looked almost excited about it, though I can't for the life of me figure out why," I said, dabbing the moisture from beneath my eye.

"I know why. You and I are like her long-lost granddaughters. She's excited for you to meet Luca. She thinks he's a good match for you."

"Why? Because he's the only royal that's an option? What other choice would I have? That doesn't make him a good match. He's probably just as arrogant and insufferable as any other entitled brat with a crown on his head," I spat, snatching the stick from her hand.

I walked to my mirror and took Paxe's advice, pulling my eyelid to the side as I began to draw. She stood quietly behind me, arms crossed, watching me carefully correct her mistakes. *It's actually an improvement. I should wear this more often.* I found her starting to smile back at me in the mirror.

"Yes, you should. But I wouldn't say it's an improvement. You're a beauty all on your own, my friend. In any case, I can see why one would put forth the effort. It's a bit fun, and I can feel how it's jolted your confidence."

I straightened, admiring my work. "You'd make an excellent informant, you know? Your talent for invading someone's privacy seems genuinely wasted." I joked.

I didn't even have time to laugh before she kicked her foot lightly behind my knee, causing it to buckle and my hand to swipe a nice fat black line across my cheek. My mouth gaped open.

"Oh my— Paxe! Look at....oh my gods." I dropped everything in my hands and scrambled around for something to wipe it off. My horrible friend erupted in laughter, and I couldn't help but join her.

"Come here! I'm sorry," she said, still viciously laughing at how ridiculous I looked. "Let me fix it. I'm so sorry. That wasn't supposed to happen." We turned to face each other, and it just got worse. She took one look at me and exploded. Her laugh started with a burst from her pursed lips and continued with a silent heave that had her bowed over, gripping her stomach with one hand and bracing herself on my shoulder with the other. I snorted in response, my only sound a soft clicking in the back of my throat.

There was a sudden swoosh as my chamber door swung open, startling us both. Vetta stood with her hand still gripping the long handle, an unamused expression stamped on her face.

"What in the world are you two doing?! Your father will blow this castle apart if you're a second behind schedule, Arienne! You think this is a joke?!" She scolded. Paxe and I both stiffened and turned toward her. "Oh, for the love of..." she stomped over to me, licking her thumb and wiping at my face. She pinched and patted at my other cheek.

"...Ouch?" I griped and rubbed over it with a raised brow.

"I'm old, girl. Back in our day, that was the trick to rosy cheeks. Unless you want them to think you mouthed off to the wrong caretaker?" She raised both hers right back.

"No, ma'am."

Vetta was a plump, shorter female who looked as if she were once very lovely in her prime. She had a naturally glowing complexion and very striking light brown eyes. I was never sure how old she actually was or what her hair color used to be. It was gray now and almost always under a thick, white head cover that draped down to her shoulders. She looked intently at me, and I swore I saw a flicker of emotion in her eyes. Her palm grazed my face, and the sting from the coal liner Paxe stabbed into my eye faded almost instantly. White mage.

"I'm positive whatever ability you possess in that body isn't punctuality. Get going. Both of you." She said, turning to the side and extending her arm toward the door. We made a move forward and breached the doorway when Vetta called my name. I looked back over my shoulder. "You look just like your mother." We exchanged smiles as Paxe and I headed out the door and down the short hallway to the stairwell.

The stone steps were seemingly endless on most days. It's a long walk from the main part of the castle to my room on the far west end—a walk I've dredged through thousands of times before. Over time, I've developed a habit of mindlessly trailing my finger across the walls through familiar divots, cracks, and small insignificant imperfections in the stone. They served as landmarks of a sort through the past few years, similar to how one would recognize a small area that stood out on a road or in the forest, letting them know they were getting close to their destination. As we hurried down the steps and through the halls, I suddenly realized that today was not that kind of day. My finger grazed the distinct rough edge of rock-hard mortar that jutted out between stones and, in the happiest of accidents, took the shape of a tiny feline.

It reminded me.

Hissifus. I haven't seen him all day. And how are we already this close to the Great Hall?

Paxe's arm sprang out in front of my middle, stopping me short.

"You're about to step into a dragon's mouth, and you're thinking about your cat?" she fired. I pointed nervously at the small, unintentional statue.

"It's my landmark. It looks like him. So, yes. And why are you avoiding the second part of my thoughts? Is another one of your gifts teleportation? Because I don't remember half the trek down here." I shut my eyes and bit down hard on my lip. She stepped in front of me and took my shoulders in her hands.

"Clear that mind out, Ari. Back straight, chin up, shoulders down. You owe them nothing. Remember, it's you that comes into power greater than they'll ever have. You are the future. Don't forget what I said. Your life is yours, Arienne Genovese. Walk in there and make me proud."

I stared at her for a long moment before it really sank in that she was right. My life was mine. But so was hers. So was Vetta's. So was every person in our world that depended on me to change all of this one day. I am the future. *Their* future. I smiled as I straightened myself, trying to wear a false image of complete confidence like a costume before I took my first step toward the massive double doors a few feet away. I approached two guards standing on each side of the doors, the one on the right acknowledging me with a nod. He moved in and pushed the heavy oak door open, standing still and silent as I stepped through.

The difference in the temperature of this room hit me like a wave about to rob me of oxygen. Any colder, and I would bet you could see puffs of your breath clouding in front of your face. The king is in a mood. It took every ounce of my energy to stifle an eye roll. One guard was placed at every corner. I fought off a shiver, focusing on my posture as I started down the center of the room. The Great Hall was an enormous space that resembled a ballroom. It had a wide floor that centered between two tables that were nearly the length of the room. There was a horrible red-orange carpet that ran down the center. It was plush and thick under my heels as I walked. The walls were lined with narrow slivers of stained glass windows with no particular decoration, just shards of color that were abstractly tempered throughout. The ceilings were high and unpainted, with huge, round chandeliers lined with candles as thick as my arm. In the back of the room was a dais that expanded wall to wall, the back wall housing a large fireplace, and on the floor before it sat a much fancier table, perpendicular to the others. There were three large chairs situated behind it and one at each end. In the middle chair sat my brooding father, his fingers interlocked and resting on the table. I reached the platform perhaps a bit too quickly, pausing in front of him as if awaiting orders. I suppose I was.

"You look well," he murmured, eyeing me carefully.

"And you," I replied. I battled the urge to move, uncomfortable with his stare but never breaking eye contact. His eyes held a haunting spark inside them, near glowing around a deep amber color. It was obvious just by seeing them how much power coursed through him. It's hard to imagine that anyone wouldn't be intimidated. I wasn't sure how much time had passed before he finally spoke again.

"Have a seat, daughter. They'll be joining us in a moment."

"Where will you have me?" I asked.

"West end."

I dutifully made my way to the chair, the guard in the corner stepping out to pull it back for me. As I sat and started to get still, the air seemed to get icier.

"Are you alright?" I asked awkwardly. His face turned toward me.

"Is there a reason I shouldn't be?"

Yes...I'm going to rip your bloody throat out.

"Not that I'm aware. But whatever has your mind at unease is going to cause a snow flurry in here." I gave a shy smile, hoping to gain some small level of trust between us. Miraculously, he smirked back.

"My apologies. I didn't notice." He said softly. He didn't break his gaze as a raging fire suddenly ripped across the fireplace behind him.

"Ah....very nice," I chuckled, nodding my head in approval.

"You know why the king and queen are bringing their son this time." Not a question.

"I do." I nodded again. Smile gone.

"Do *not* disappoint me, Arienne." He warned.

Now it made sense. He was worried that I would stain his proud image—the most feared ruler our world had ever seen. What a pity it would be to show off your unwanted daughter while she makes an utter fool out of you. He must have been really worried to be putting off that level of cold.

Good. I suppose I struck more of a nerve than I thought. Bastard.

"I never planned to, my Lord. I assume I'm dressed to your satisfaction?"

"A beauty. Truly," he replied. Both our heads turned to the sound of the doors opening again.

King Tidus entered first. He was as handsome as I had expected. Tall, olive-skinned, with a dark, clean-cut beard that matched his short hair. I hadn't seen him when he and his queen visited our lands five years ago. I had been injured badly during my...punishment. Vetta, along with the rest of the palace staff, had been given strict orders not to heal me in any way and they had no option but to comply. I had been left to recover on my own. It had taken weeks. They had never brought the prince to their meetings before today. He and I were only children and, up until now, had no reason to attend. Behind him came his lovely wife, Ayla. She was stunning. Her hair was long and black as a raven's feathers. It shined the darkest shade of blue in the light. Her eyes were near white, like pure crystal sitting in her skull, and her pale skin was just as luminous. She moved with perfect grace in a scarlet gown that matched the shade of her lips. She was escorted by what could have been mistaken for her fraternal twin—eyes, hair, and skin nearly identical to his mother. The only difference was the long stubble of facial hair that lined his mouth and chin. His hair wasn't neatly trimmed like the king's but tied back in a small knot behind his head. Luca.

My heart thundered at the sight of him.

Gods. Why couldn't you be hideous?

My father extended his arms in welcome. The royals approached us smiling as they bowed in response. Luca glanced toward me upon straightening, and I looked away. I felt heat on my cheeks, and I couldn't tell if it was from embarrassment or just flat-out anger. Part of me wondered why I should be angry at all. It wasn't his choice any more than it was mine. It wasn't as if we hadn't known this day would eventually come our entire lives. I suppose as a child, I just felt like I had more time. I suddenly felt just as violated as I had the night Gideon died.

King Tidus stepped up the dais and rounded my corner of the table. He bowed politely and offered his hand. I took it nervously. He raised the back of my hand to his lips, gently kissing it.

"Princess Arienne. An honor to finally meet you." He glimmered, releasing my fingers.

"Likewise, your Highness." I smiled.

He walked a few steps to the seat between my father and I and promptly sat. I watched intently as Luca led his mother to her seat, pulling it for her as she situated herself on the opposite side. He turned back, taking the one at the end...across from me. I fidgeted with my fingers under the table against my lap, trying hard to remember Vetta's drilling about posture and etiquette. My father's voice broke my concentration as he started the conversation.

"Friends. Good to have you at my table again," he greeted, turning in Luca's direction. "Young prince. Welcome to Valdaro. I hope you find it as beautiful as we do." Luca smiled gratefully at him.

"Thank you, your Highness," he replied, turning his attention to me. "Very beautiful indeed."

I know I had to have turned at least five different shades of red. That voice. It was deep and primal, yet had a smooth rasp that could send any female to her knees. I softly cleared my throat, adjusting the braid at my shoulder. My father smiled, undoubtedly catching his response like a fish in a grizzly's maw. The room at least felt a great deal warmer. Or perhaps it was just me.

"I like that. Straight to the point." My father grinned, relishing in my humiliation. "Arienne? Meet your betrothed. This is Luca." He gestured toward him with his finger.

I was so stunned I couldn't speak. Couldn't take my eyes off my father's smug face. I didn't even realize my mouth had dropped open. Of course, I knew this meeting would at some point come to this subject, but I should have half expected it to be the one thing my idiot father was known for—torture. By the time I realized I had bested my counter paints with my shock and disorientation, it was too late. I had single-handedly butchered my poise.

"Arienne," he repeated. His tone was familiar. It threw me straight into the past. For a few agonizing seconds, I was back in my cell. The screaming. The blood. The pain...*them.*

Be her. Die for it if you have to. Don't let him take anything else from you. End him.

I lowered my head and took in a deep, calming breath. Slowly, I raised it and looked up at Luca through thick lashes. A smile tugged the corners of his mouth.

"A pleasure...my Lord." I said, my voice as icy as the air around us had started to become again. Our king was getting pissy. What to do? The queen's graceful nature shattered in an instant.

"Enough." She spat firmly. "It's an ugly business, arranged marriages. We all know it. But it doesn't always mean it has to be uncomfortable." My father snapped his head to her, and she gave it right back. "Your majesty. If I may?" He leaned back in his chair, resting his elbows on its arms. She continued, "When I was young, I felt very similar, Princess. The day I met my future husband, I didn't let him off easy either."

"I can attest to that. She tried to kill me." Tidus said, expressionless.

"I threw a fork at you," she snipped, completely dismissing his intrusion and pressing on. "I was angry and bitter about it as well. It's your right. *Both of you.*" She looked at Luca and then back to me. "You may hate each other in the end, but would it not be wiser to educate that decision by getting to know one another? Strong rulers are built on strong relationships. You can't build a relationship by throwing the bricks at each other. You must match them up together and fill the cracks as you go." Luca and I locked eyes for a moment, and he nodded in understanding.

"You make an excellent point, Ayla." My father finally said, leaning forward and looking at the Cronian king. "I propose this. The prince stays here in Valdaro until the evening of Arienne's Ventus. Four months should be plenty of time for the two of them to...bond."

He glanced at me. "At the Ventus celebration, we'll announce the engagement, and should he wish to return to Crona afterward, he may visit whenever he likes until the wedding. Does that suit everyone?" He asked, looking around the table.

I wanted to burst into tears. Who was going to say no? It was already bold enough that the queen interjected as she did. While it seemed her intentions were good, in doing so, she had now sentenced me to spend the next four months *not* enjoying what little freedom I had.

"Would she be allowed to visit me as well, my king? In Crona?" Luca asked. I'd be lying if I said it didn't absolutely shock me. I believe we all felt that way, as the four of us now looked at my father in anticipation. The king pursed his lips and after some thought, settled on his answer.

"While I can accept that your mother and father are a strong match, I don't believe in love. Prove me wrong young prince, and I'll allow her to travel to you if she wishes it. Have we all come to an agreement?"

King Tidus wasted no time in answering for us all.

"Agreed. Thank you, your majesty," he said earnestly.

My blood went cold. I was willing to bet my life that my father wouldn't dare put a smudge on his image. He would never have told the king and queen of my costly mistake. Letting a human boy put his hands on me. I knew then that if they'd asked about my whereabouts at their last visit, he most definitely would have come up with some lie. Which meant that they had no idea what happened to me that night and how he had just taken his golden opportunity to torture me further, knowing that Luca would be hard-pressed to convince me to love him.

I'm going to savor every second of watching you die.

"Then it's settled. Luca, if you're confident in your task, why don't we have a bit of fun? A little wager of our own." My father smiled wickedly at him, and I saw flashes of panic in the king and queen's eyes.

"My Lord?" Luca replied nervously.

"If you can prove that my daughter loves you by the night of her Ventus celebration, then she's free. I'll give my life...and my power. She can take it as a wedding gift. My lovely daughter would love nothing more than to see me perish." My eyes widened, and my father smiled at me like a demon as he continued, "I'll add a sweetener. Arienne can finally prove her worth to my crown by smiting me herself."

Something isn't right. You wouldn't offer me your own life.

"You—you want her to kill you, your Highness?" Tidus's voice was shaky.

"I want to awaken the beast that sleeps within her. The pieces of me she tries so hard to bury. I will live a long time, but not forever. I need my only heir to grow herself a spine." He never took his eyes off me. "You want your mother, little dove? Deny me, and you'll find her. If your prince can't prove that he made you fall for a lie before the moon shines on this land that evening, you'll be the one to die."

And there it was. Cunning, ruthless coward. So afraid of not being able to leave this world in ruin. I realized what he proposed would end my life before my abilities would be allowed to snap into place if Luca accepted his offer. He knows something. The king and queen sat, still as death, as they waited for one of us to respond. I stood from my seat and faced my father, effortlessly channeling Paxe's advice to me in the hall.

"How do we know that this won't be a trick, Father? That you won't bind some sort of loophole that keeps you alive should we succeed? They may think they know you, but you're right. I carry a part of you in my blood....and if you're making a bargain, there *will* be blood. You despise me. You'll protect yourself." I stated coldly. The room seemed to darken, and my father leaned forward.

"No tricks, daughter. I'll make this easier for you. If you truly love this boy, then your *love* should be strong enough to break the binding magic of our agreement. If you win, that magic will end my life. In turn, should I be the victor, your heart stops at moonrise. Do we have a deal?"

"I'll make that deal." Luca said, standing. He looked at me cautiously and then at my father.

"Good man." My father smiled, rising from his seat and walking toward the prince.

Good man...

My mind flashed back to the last time I heard those words come from his mouth. I was, again, facing another man making bargains in my stead. I had the sinking feeling that, somehow, this was too simple. It would already be a difficult task, but I had so much doubt that this would end well for anyone. It didn't end well for Gideon—human or no.

My father extended his hand to Luca and began explaining the process. The two would join hands, and my father's binding magic would seal the contract, locking everything into motion and starting a ticking clock of what could be the last four months of my life. I felt like I could vomit. Luca's mother looked as if she felt the same. I didn't dare look at Tidus. They both knew what my father was. We were making a deal with the devil, and all of us were too afraid of what could happen if we didn't.

I watched as Luca and my father took hold of each other's wrists. A pale blue vine of light began to circle around Luca's fingers, snaking its way up to meet the amber-colored light dancing around my father's. The magic intertwined between them, traveling to their elbows and hissing as it finally flashed and disappeared. It was done.

"Splendid." My father grinned, loosening his grip on Luca's wrist. "Your beloved can show you out. Get you better acquainted with your new home...and your new bride-to-be. I have other pressing matters to discuss with your parents. We'll arrange to have your belongings brought to Valdaro."

Luca firmly held his gaze, his jaw clenching. They glared at each other for a moment before Ayla reached over to rest her hand on her son's arm.

"Luca." She whispered.

He took a few seconds before looking down to meet her eyes, and she softly tilted her head to the doors. Her message was clear. I was frozen in my stance, still reeling in my thoughts, as Luca slowly turned and stepped in front of the table. He offered his arm and waited for me to join him. I sneered at my father, knowing full well that he could read the hate in my eyes. Without a word, I raised my chin and gathered myself, my heart about to leap from my chest as I stormed past Luca onto the ugly carpet, making my way quickly to the doorway. The guard in the corner tried to keep my pace as he bolted toward the doors to open one for me.

"Don't bother!" I yelped through my clenched teeth. He paused, stunned, as I approached him angrily. "Move!" I shouted. I could feel my arms trembling as my rage boiled over. I checked him hard with my shoulder, pushing past him, and I was amazed at the strength my adrenaline supplied when I took hold of the long handle and ripped the heavy door open, slamming it as hard as I could behind me. It made a near explosive sound. The two guards outside jumped, each one reaching for their swords as I stomped loudly between them and into the hallway. I stumbled back when I heard a familiar voice call my name. My head snapped toward the sound.

Paxe hurried to my side with a face full of worry. I felt furious tears begin rolling down my cheeks as she gripped my arm.

"What happened?! Are you alright?" she pleaded. I shrugged her off and started towards the open palace entrance across the hall.

"Don't tell him where I am, Paxe." I sniffled, quickening my steps as I exited the castle.

"Tell who?... Ari!" Her voice echoed behind me. I ignored it, making my way to the forest.

CHAPTER 3

THE MEETING PLACE

Valdaro was lush and green during the spring and summer months, especially in the forests that surrounded nearly all of our castle. It was almost as if these trees grew to protect our palace like a fortress with thick stone walls. If they only knew that the enemy dwelled within it, not out there.

To the south, beyond Aegan Forest, was the Diamond River. It sliced our lands in half and stretched from where the sea kissed the mountains down towards our castle to hug the southern edge of the treeline. It then snaked its way back north, up through The Midlands all the way east through Crona, ending at the Crimson Sea where Luca's castle stood, creating a diamond-like shape across the continent. The land south of our palace was mostly flat, and the soil was rich. Valdarians named it "The Valley." It was where they lived and farmed everything from food to livestock.

The castle was nestled in the center of our side of Lythica, with the Bolton Sea a few hundred miles to the west. The Midlands to our east and the Horned Mountains to our north which were barely visible from my home. The mountains were never inhabited, as they were surrounded completely by perpetual darkness and a howling snowstorm that kept anyone and anything from its jagged white peaks. Some Valdarians believed that the gods cursed them many years ago to be sure no unholy being would ever reach that close to the heavens. To my knowledge, no one who ever tried to test that legend was seen again.

Of course, there was plenty that I had never been allowed to see. I had never traveled to the sea or past the forest's edge to the Valdarian villages. I had only ever been *allowed* to go with Vetta and Paxe to the markets which were built in the clearing of the forest on the castle's eastern side near the Midland territory. The markets weren't far from where I currently was.

I had quickened my steps into a run after my soul had been purchased at the meeting. I knew that Paxe would know exactly where to find me, not just because of her ability, but because I had told her all about this place when Gideon and I would sneak off to look for resources we'd use to make the arrows...among other things. Just outside of the market area was a thick brush of trees that hid a narrow path, cut to make quick access to the river. At the end of the path was a secluded grove blanketed by a thick canopy of trees that leaked broken rays of incandescent sunlight over a twenty-foot waterfall. It was truly a sight. Large stones and logs were covered in shades of soft green moss. A few yards to the right of the path was a tiny, circular meadow crowned with large trees and carpeted by thick grass and violets. Tiny Mecardonia peeked through the purple flowers like drips of yellow paint everywhere.

I imagined that if my mother were alive, she would've loved it here. I couldn't fathom a more peaceful place than this. Or a more beautiful one. My emotions ran high with everything barreling through my mind. I wished I could talk with her. Wherever she was, perhaps it was better to let my father win this bargain and join her. It had to be better than staying here. I stumbled into the meadow, my knees shaking as I lowered myself down to sit on my heels. I tried earnestly to steady my breathing, but it was useless.

Let it out.

I buried my face into the skirt of my dress and screamed, took a heaving breath, and did it again. The third ended in a sob that was relatively quiet, considering how it started. My head raised, and I noticed small black smudges on the fabric across my lap—the liner.

"Oh...gods." I sniffed, wiping pointlessly at the black streaks beneath my eyes. My palms hit my thighs as I squeezed my eyelids shut, sighing loudly up at the sky. I kept them closed and tried to calm myself, focusing on the roaring of the waterfall and surrounding woodland animals. A small meow caught my attention and I tore my eyes open.

"Hiss?" I called. A twig snapped at my side, followed by another tiny mew, and my little companion pranced over to greet me.

"Hissifusssss. Where have you been, my love?" My heart spilled over as his dainty paws invaded my lap. I went straight for his fuzzy ears, leaning over to let him nuzzle my face. All my sorrow was suddenly gone. It was as if my mother heard me and sent him to deliver the comfort she couldn't give.

Hissifus was the most extraordinary creature. One of the most beautiful oddities of nature I had ever seen. He was born with chimerism, leaving one side of his body black and the other white as the moon. The black half of his face was green-eyed, and the white half an icy blue with a distinct, perfect line from his little chin to the tip of his tail. He had found his way into the castle kitchens as a small kitten when I was only ten years old. I had talked Paxe into stealing pastries for us and she came back with him and a bowl of milk instead, explaining how the kitchen staff was hysterical, thinking he was some kind of ill omen. He and I were fated after that day. If it weren't for this loyal little gift from the gods, I'd never have endured the trauma of what my father had done in my youth. He never left my side for a moment, especially when I needed him.

I smiled at the sound of his gentle purring, cradling him like an infant. His midnight paw pressed against my lips as he raised up and started trying to clean my face with his rough tongue.

"You know what, sir? You're absolutely right." I said, wrapping my fingers around his foot and kissing the pads of his toes. "Let's wash this off."

I sat him down on the grass and lifted my skirt from the ground as I made my way over to the river bank and searched for a dry place to sit. I found a long, flat rock and knelt, cupping the cool water in my hands and splashing my face. I scrubbed at it vigorously until I no longer saw color on my fingers when I pulled them back. Hissifus hopped onto a fallen log beside me and started meticulously licking himself.

"I can't believe I let her put this on my face." I ranted, cleaning the rest of the rosy-colored stain from my lips. My little fluff paid me absolutely no mind, continuing his thorough bath. I dipped my hands under the water and started rubbing my fingers together.

"Not that it made any difference anyhow. The bastard made me look like an idiot without having to paint it on. You should have seen the look on Luca's face. He probably thinks me a fool. Gods...I shouldn't have walked out on him like that. I suppose there are worse males to marry out there." I scrubbed harder. "He's gorgeous, of course. Looks like he could snap me in half. And when he speaks, his voice is like a siren's song, luring you to your death."

Hissifus straightened, looking over my shoulder warily. He yelped in warning, hopping down from his perch to investigate, and I closed my eyes in dread.

You've got to be joking.

I stood and slowly turned to see Luca standing there, arms crossed and smiling at me. I wished someone would just put me out of my misery right here in this river.

"A siren's song?" he grinned. I put my hands on my hips, glaring at him.

"She told you, didn't she?" I snapped.

"The servant? Yeah...she did."

It was innocent, and I know my reaction was uncalled for. He didn't know. But something about his response set my skin on fire, and I wanted to beat his flawless face in. I started coming for him with my finger drawn like a dagger, ready to strike its target.

"She is *not* a servant, and you'll watch your mouth!"

He threw his hands up in defense, backing up a step as I marched closer, paying no attention at all to my surroundings. I took another strong step forward and felt an abrupt tug on my dress. It caught the sharp point of a broken branch jutting out from a log, ripping the fabric and slicing through my ankle. I fell quickly, swearing as I braced myself for the impact. Instead, I found myself suspended over the ground, held steady by Luca's arms.

"Shit... are you alright?" His eyes wide.

I should have thanked him, but my pride married my anger, so instead, I decided it felt better to push him. Embarrassed, I forced him back perhaps a bit harder than I had planned and I almost felt remorseful at the shock that mauled his face.

"Don't touch me!" I growled. I leaned on my other leg, tearing my skirt off the branch and ripping through the material. My ankle felt like it had been stabbed with a white-hot poker. I didn't even look at it as I limped back over to the meadow and plopped down onto the grass. I felt Luca's eyes on me and I tried my best to ignore it. I stretched out my injured leg to calculate the damage, not surprised to see it badly bleeding. I sighed deeply and pulled my knees to my chest, propping my elbows and palming my face. Hissifus ran his concerned little body back and forth across my back.

"I'm sorry. Look...there's no reason for us to get off to a start this bad." I heard his footsteps becoming louder as he cautiously approached.

He did not.

"A start this bad?" I replied, annoyed. I dropped my hands and looked up at him, pinching my brows together. "We just met, and the first thing you did was sell my soul! To my *father!* Do you truly expect me to try to accept that I'm going to be forced to marry a male I don't know when his first order of business is to look at me like a meal and make bargains with *my* life?!"

"First of all, I looked at you knowing you're to be my wife, and I *complimented* you. Respectfully. And second, I never planned to make any deal with your father. When it became clear to me that he was doing this to put you in danger, yes...I accepted. I did it to protect you." His voice was calm, and I could tell he was trying to soothe me.

"Protect me?" I scoffed.

"Yes! I'm about to become your husband. My sole purpose is to protect you Princess, and I'm prepared to die for you if that's what it takes. That's the reason I was born. *For you.* To love you and to keep you safe."

"None of that matters now. He's already won this game. You should just stay away from me Luca, and enjoy Valdaro until you're free to go home." I turned my face forward, refusing to look at him again. His words threatened to break my heart into pieces. He actually sounded like he might be a decent male. Someone out there is deserving of him, but it isn't me.

"Why?" he asked, kneeling beside me.

"You don't know what kind of monster you're dealing with. He made that wager with you because he knows I won't be able to love you. He was telling you the truth when he said he didn't believe in love, but that part was just wordplay. My father knows exactly what he's doing. He wants me dead, and now he's sealed that fate with binding magic. *His* magic. There's no one in this world more powerful...I'm done."

"Why wouldn't you be able to love me? Are you cursed?" He asked.

"Cursed? With magic?"

He nodded.

"No."

"Alright then. So, he's dug his own grave."

What the hell is he talking about?

He stood, and I watched him walk over to the scrap of my dress that hung from the jagged branch, snatching it off and taking it to the river bank. His boots splashed in the shallow water and he bent over to wet the cloth. He wrung it out and started making his way back to my side. I was hypnotized by the almost blue color of his hair as swatches of light danced around the top of his head. He knelt before me this time, eyeing the blood that was becoming sticky around my foot. He looked up at me under his thick eyebrows, and I felt like I could choke.

"May I?" He asked softly. I moved my foot toward him and he took it gently, peeling the ragged hem of my skirt away from my skin. Hissifus pounced over from behind me, watching him carefully. "Hey, cat," he said, being careful to only dab away the blood around the wound.

"His name is Hissifus," I murmured. A low chuckle escaped him, but he never looked away from his task. "Are you a healer?" I continued.

"Sadly, white magic wasn't my gift." He began folding the scrap into a long, makeshift bandage and paused to glance at me. "This might hurt," he warned. I nodded in approval and he laid the cloth around my ankle, carefully wrapping it. I watched him reach up behind his head and pull a long leather string, and his black hair unraveled, cascading over his shoulder like the waterfall we sat near.

"What is your gift?" I winced as he tied the strap tightly around the cloth. The side of his mouth raised slightly, but he never looked back up.

"I'll say this, Princess. I will never use it on you unless it's needed...or you ask me to."

I was intrigued, but I decided against pressing him for answers. I wasn't planning to get to know Luca, and asking questions would just make this whole situation more difficult. He must have read it in my expression when he eased my foot back down and looked at me. The hint of a smile he had was gone. His unbound hair started to fall around his face as he stared at me. I couldn't stop myself from staring back. This male was devastating.

Don't make me fall in love with you, Luca.

He stood slowly and started exploring around the meadow, taking everything in and admiring the light as I sat quietly watching. His back was turned toward me while he watched the waterfall, and I admired a few things of my own. He wore a black tunic that matched his father's, and they paired them with close-fitting dark gray trousers...which he wore extremely well. His hair nearly reached the middle of his back, and it almost changed his entire appearance when it was loose and free to move with the wind. I was not of any help to myself at all.

"If Crona has places such as this, I've certainly never seen them," he finally said, breaking my impolite thoughts. "Is the entire forest this colorful?"

"I wouldn't know," I replied.

"Not very adventurous?" He asked, facing me again.

"Not permitted." He looked as if I'd slapped him.

"What do you mean?"

"I mean, I'm not allowed to go anywhere. Truthfully, I'm not even supposed to be here."

He leaned against the nearest tree and looked me over, sliding his hands into his pockets. I crossed my arms and locked eyes with him, tilting my head and prompting him to say whatever was on his mind.

"So, how did you find it then?" He asked, a single eyebrow raised.

"Next question." *I said I wasn't going to do this.*

"Don't do that. Tell me."

"No," I said a bit more forcefully.

"Why? You think I'll run and tell your father?"

"Please do, Prince, if you think he'll kill me faster." I spat.

"I would never do that to you, Arienne. And whatever you think you know about me, you're wrong. Your father is a cowardly brute who preys on everyone and everything weaker than him. He doesn't deserve power of any kind, least of all the power he was gifted. Yes. I know who I'm dealing with. We all know, Princess. The whole world knows, and so do the gods."

His words were a jolt. If I'd kept a journal, I would swear he'd read it.

"The gods? What are you saying?" I asked, nearly begging him to tell me more.

"No, no. How did you find this place?" He smirked.

"Oh, you're such a—fine." I shook my head and looked down to my lap, where Hissifus was now napping peacefully on his moon side. I freed my arms and started stroking his ebony fluff. "When I was younger, my father allowed me to venture out with my caretaker and my handmaiden, Paxe, every week, but only once for a few hours, and only around the markets."

"Paxe...she was the one that I met in the hall? The *not* servant?" He asked.

"Yes. She's like a sister to me."

"So what? You two would go play in the woods together when you weren't supposed to?"

"No. I met a boy...a human boy." I admitted. I couldn't look up to face him.

"I see. You were sneaking around."

"It wasn't what you're thinking. Not at first, anyway. He was my friend, and he taught me things. The path you took down here? He cut it himself to make things easier for humans to get water. He was resourceful and talented. I learned to create things from materials we scavenged from these woods. We called this our "meeting place," and once a week we took refuge here. Many humans know about it now, but most have stayed away for a few years now." I decided not to let on too much more than that. It should have been enough, but of course...

"What happened to him?"

Hissifus stretched in my lap with a loud purr. I took too long to answer.

"He died."

I think it registered with him finally all the details I was sparing. He was quiet for a few moments, probably trying to piece it all together before speaking again.

"We should get you back to the castle to tend to that ankle."

What? No prying?

"You're probably right. With any luck, they haven't yet finished in the

Great Hall." I agreed. I shifted around, disturbing Hiss's slumber, and he reluctantly flopped off my legs. Luca stepped forward to offer his arm and I took it, raising up and steadying myself. He put a hand at my back and leaned down, scooping me up in a swift movement. Stunned, I threw my arms around him and gasped.

"What are you doing?! I can walk!" I insisted.

"Yeah, that's not going to happen, Princess." He said, rolling his eyes and moving toward the path.

"Put me down, or I swear I'll—"

"You'll what...impale me with that little finger?" He grinned.

"You are a jackass."

"I've been called worse. But a jackass would make you walk..."

If my stare was a weapon, I could have put a gaping hole through his face. He looked forward, navigating the path but glancing at me occasionally. I forfeited and silently thanked him. Hissifus lazily trailed behind.

"Don't do this, Luca," I said softly, turning my face forward.

"Do what?"

"Your mother is a wise female. Your parents seem like they actually do care for each other. What she said makes a lot of sense, but please don't try to get to know me. Just because we're the sole heirs doesn't mean we're supposed to be together." He stayed quiet for a moment, pausing to look around. I pointed to the left, and he followed my lead. His hair brushed my face as we moved to the forest's edge, bypassing the markets. It was soft, and he smelled of leather and spice with a hint of lavender.

"They do love each other very much actually. They love me even more. I can't begin to imagine how it must feel not ever knowing your mother." He said apologetically. I started to realize that he seemed to know a great deal about me already, and I was second-guessing my decision not to interrogate him.

"You don't get to speak of her, Prince." I frowned. He stopped walking and looked down at me. I kept my eyes on the ground.

"Why not? Do you feel she doesn't deserve it?" I said nothing and pressed my lips tighter. "Look at me, Arienne." I did. "My parents are excellent rulers. If you want to know the truth, they're beloved in Crona, and we keep a tight lid on that fact so that your father doesn't feel threatened and have our heads. I can understand your bitterness, perhaps even your resentment towards me. You're right to feel as if I'm the spoiled little prince that has everything that was denied you. No one could ever blame you for it. You were never given the love you deserve, and I suppose that's what brought you to this idea that you're to be denied it until the day you leave this world." Heads were turning in the distance. Humans and Valdarians alike started to grow curious about our heated conversation.

"Could you please keep your voice down? We're gaining an audience." I glanced around.

"What do you care? From what you've told me in the past hour, you're giving up and planning on letting your father have your life. You don't want me to speak to you, and you don't want to share anything with me. You aren't cursed with magic, and so that tells *me* that the only obstacle in the way of what you want most is yourself. Unless I'm reading this all wrong, and you have something different up your sleeve? How am I doing so far, Princess?"

You clever, arrogant...beautiful...prick.

"I do." I fired.

"You do...what?"

"I do have something else up my sleeve. That something never included you! That is until you decided to make deals and started throwing explosives in all my plans!" My eyes started to itch at the corners.

"Are you going to let me in, Arienne, or make me work for it? I don't think you understand, so I'll repeat myself as many times as I must. I'm here for *you.* Tell me how to help you get what you need, and I'll do it." A single tear sank slowly down my face.

"I'm going to kill him," I whispered. His eyes were so piercing I swore he saw through my soul. He swallowed, his jaw tightening as he watched that tear drop from my chin.

"Then kill him. The only thing that's changed in whatever plan you started out with this morning is having me by your side." He replied. His voice low and comforting.

"Well...aren't I the lucky one?" I rolled my eyes, trying to lift some tension and redeem myself.

"Oh, you have no idea," he smiled and started moving again.

"You're not going to leave me alone, are you?" I asked, already knowing the answer.

"I'm not going to force you to love me, Princess. That will be entirely your choice. But if I'm stuck in Valdaro for the next four months, then *you're* stuck with me."

"You're in for a very droll vacation," I smirked.

"Oh, on the contrary. We're going on a little trip together. We can start with the rest of this forest tomorrow." He chirped, keeping his face forward and ignoring my reaction.

"I just told you I wasn't allowed to go anywhere."

"You were at that meeting, were you not? He said I would have to prove that you loved me before you could travel to see me in *Crona.*" His smile turned devious.

"Luca..." I opened my mouth.

"He didn't say anything about having to prove that to travel elsewhere." He glanced down at me. We were closing in on the castle entrance now and attracting attention from practically everywhere. I'm sure it was a pitiful-looking sight—the damsel in distress being carried in by the hero. I had severed any intention I had of being the tough one today.

"You're smarter than you look, Prince." I smiled.

"Does this mean you forgive me, Princess?"

"I guess we'll find out. It doesn't sound like you're giving me much choice." I tried to cover the flutter of excitement in my voice.

"Can I ask you something before your friend comes to collect you?" He slowed his pace.

"That depends. Is it something you're willing to take a blow to your face for?" I asked. He twitched his mouth.

"I feel like I've earned a pass. I did just meet you after all, and in the span of a good hour, I've saved your life, treated your wounds, and carried you nearly a mile." He said.

"Fair. Go ahead." There was a long pause, and I thought he'd changed his mind before he finally asked.

"You really think I'm gorgeous?" He lit up with a smile that showed all of his teeth. I flushed, rolling my eyes back as far as they'd go.

"Gods," I replied. Not an answer, no, but enough to tell him the truth. A soft laugh rumbled through his chest, and somehow he managed to pull one from me.

"I meant nothing but respect when I said you were beautiful today. I want you to know that. But I also wanted you to know..." He stopped walking and looked me in the face. "When I went after you in the forest, I had no idea what I would say to you. Then I saw you washing up in the river, talking to your cat. I could barely hear you from the path, but I started smiling right then. When I got closer, I made out the parts you were saying about me, and if I had felt badly about the way I came off at the table it was long gone after that."

"That's what you wanted me to know?" I asked.

"That...and that when you turned around...you took the breath right out of me. I didn't think you could be more beautiful."

I couldn't think of a single word to say, so I stared. Way too long. We were mere feet away from the entrance, and a part of me wanted to wrangle out of his arms and run. But then...the other part wanted to stay right there. Maybe forever.

Snap out of it, fool.

"It was most definitely not my idea. The counter paints," I stuttered.

"Good. Don't think you have to wear them on my account. You've no need for them."

When I thought I might die if this conversation went much further, my savior burst through the doorway looking as if she might go with me. Paxe nearly ran towards us. She wore a mixed countenance of guilt and concern, but I know she was eager to feel me out and talk about what happened.

"Ari?! What in the world have you done?" She said, looking down at my bandaged ankle.

"I'm fine. I just need Vetta."

"Look at this dress!" She pulled the ripped remains up and scowled at me.

Luca gently lowered me to my feet, keeping an arm at my back for good measure. I locked eyes with him again, ignoring my nosy friend.

"Get some rest, Princess. I'll see you tomorrow." He said softly, allowing Paxe to lead me inside. A light nod was my only response, and I leaned on her, turning away and limping forward. My head was flooded with thoughts.

"Oh...yes. You have a lot of explaining to do, *Princess,*" Paxe said, rolling her eyes with a wide smile. I hung my head in dread as she led me inside and started the long, horrible trek to my room.

CHAPTER 4

RED RED WINE

The sun set quickly enough over Valdaro that it seemed even it had seen enough of this day. Paxe had made good on her word on the way up when she agreed not to say a word about everything I knew must have been pummeling her through my heart and mind. She did not, however, hide the wave of various expressions from her face. Vetta was busy with household laundering when we first arrived back at the castle, so I had been stuck with my splintered new battle scar for a while. Paxe talked me into a hot bath and drew it up for me as I sat down at the end of my bed.

I tugged the remains of my skirt to the side and stared down at the bloody green bandage that was now beginning to brown. My eyes caught the leather strap from Luca's hair more than once. Whatever fight I had in me earlier was hushed to a dull flame as my head spun relentlessly with different parts of our conversation. I kept recalling little things he said that stuck out like that blasted branch that made me look even more like a deranged idiot.

Then there were those eyes. One couldn't even call them blue. I supposed they were gray or almost silvery and seemed to turn other achromatic shades in different light. The color of his hair made them stand out even further, especially when it framed his face. Anything he'd want you to feel seemed to be demanded by them. Or perhaps it wasn't just his eyes, but him entirely. From his hair to his body, to—

"Gods, will you stop?!" Paxe interrupted as she leaned against the small door frame to my bath chamber. "Honestly, if you're not ready to talk about today, then I should probably let Vetta finish you up tonight. You know I don't have any choice in what I hear, and I'd rather hear it from you...not that stubborn head." I fluttered my eyes closed and laid back onto the dark blue duvet. Probably a mistake. Now I just wanted to exist under it.

"I'm sorry..." I mumbled.

"Sorry for what, mi'lady?" She smiled. I raised my head to scowl at her, not moving another inch of my body. "I thought that might get your attention. Listen, I just don't want to intrude on your thoughts. I need you to know you *can* actually talk to me. I was really worried about you today. The way you stormed out of here...I just..." she looked down and softly shook her head. "And I'm sorry for telling him where you were. I know that's your place."

"He wants to go back tomorrow," I said, dropping my head back to the mattress. It sank lower this time, fluffing around my pounding skull.

"Are you going to go with him?"

"Should I? I mean, I've never been anywhere other than the meadow. I'll be no help in navigating any of that forest." I said.

"You know that's not why he's asking. Why would you pass up your first opportunity to get away from this place? And with someone who looks like that, no less?" She asked.

"Thank you, friend. I'm not at war with myself at all over that last bit." I rolled my eyes. I couldn't see her, but I knew she was studying me, trying to figure out how to talk me down. My head rolled to the side, and my mother's soft eyes met mine.

Tell me what to do, Mother.

"Okay," Paxe said, walking over and grabbing my hands. She pulled hard and raised me to sit. "Come now. You've had worse days than this."

I felt defeated. She didn't even need to hear my thoughts to know it; it was clearly written all over my face. She gave me an understanding nod and turned to the side to help me to my feet. The few moments of comfort I found hanging on the end of my bed quickly fizzled out as my ankle began to stiffen and throb.

"I have something for you. Get yourself in that tub, and I'll be back in a moment." She urged, making sure to see me into the doorway. I nodded, and she hurried out of the bedroom door. I struggled over to the steps of the bath and was happy to find it warm in the chamber.

A large fire crackled away in the fireplace close by, the soft glow of the flames dancing across the bath water. I pulled at the shoulders of my mangled dress and slipped my arms free, pushing them down my middle. It dropped in a heap to the floor, and I stepped carefully over it, simultaneously pulling my shift over my head and tossing it to the side. I took two slow steps down into the bathing pool and winced.

Damned heinous tree.

The water was so warm. Determined to feel some kind of triumph over this day, I ignored the sting and sank into oblivion. It felt amazing, and already I could feel tension starting to ease away as I gently swam to the seat that lined every side of the pool, my thighs finding purchase on the corner closest to the doorway. I sat for a moment willing my limbs to relax, before I attempted to lift my injured foot and remove the bandage, carefully detangling the leather strap and pulling the bloody scraps from the water. I sat them down and let my neck rest on the edge, laying my head back on the cool stone. It was a perfect balance of temperature.

A soft meow rolled behind me, and Hiss crept into the room, followed by a smiling Paxe who carried in a large bottle of aged Valdarian wine and a dainty silver goblet. She was the hero today.

"Where...did you get that?" I nearly leapt from the seat, forgetting my ailments momentarily. She gracefully spread her skirts beneath her, sitting down by the side of the bath. She made to hand me the goblet, and I promptly snatched the open bottle instead, pressing it to my lips and savoring every drop that spilled out.

"I should have guessed the cup would be senseless." She smiled. She leaned the rim towards me, and I couldn't help but raise my brows.

"*Paxe*...I'm surprised at you. You never drink." I said as I filled it up. She took a large gulp, then another...and another. My statement rang true on my face, my mouth gaping open as she finished it off. "Clearly, I've been missing some things here lately. Do explain yourself, drunkard." I grinned as I turned the bottle up again. "This have anything to do with *Lakan*?"

"I was given this as well." She replied, completely dismissing my question. She reached into her apron pocket and handed me a folded piece of parchment. I paused and looked at her nervously as I stared the little note down like it would grow teeth and snap at me. She took the bottle from my hand, replacing it with the letter, and refilled her cup.

"What is this? And given to you by whom?" I asked, slowly unfolding it.

Today was rough. Tonight will be better. Enjoy the wine and my stupid letter.
...Also...wear pants and appropriate shoes tomorrow. My arms hurt.
~Luca

My face was splattered with wine after Paxe exploded, nearly choking in laughter. I forgot that I didn't need to read it out loud, and I couldn't stop my giggle as I wiped at the side of my face with my wet hand. Hissifus was startled and bolted from the room.

"I'm so sorry!" She cackled, setting the goblet down and failing her attempt to stop laughing as she grabbed a small towel and tried handing it to me. I set the paper down beside her and submerged, coming back to smooth over my hair and propping my elbows over the edge. I folded my arms.

"So he sent the wine?" I asked. Paxe had finally calmed herself and scooted the bottle back to me.

"Earlier, when I came to get you, he sort of...sent me a thought?" She said, creasing her forehead.

"*Sent* you a thought? How?" I asked, gripping the neck of the bottle.

"I'm not sure. He must have known somehow that I could feel them? He made it clear he would have me deliver this to you. I went back down to meet him." I took a large swallow and looked back at her, slightly frowning.

"So they put him downstairs? Where is he?" I pressed.

"Actually...he's..." she paused, smiling.

"He's...?" I nodded, waving the side of my hand in an urge for her to continue.

"In the room below you." She finished. My stomach fluttered. "Look...I'd be lying if I said I didn't like him, Ari. Arranged or not, you have to admit he's quite charming."

"Sure, but I'm trying to wager if I can trust him. He said some things today that he may not have noticed I caught, but did. I feel like he knows something I don't, and let's face it...that's not a surprise, but will this *something* be in my favor? Or is this just another one of my father's cruel antics?" I argued.

"No. It isn't. I'm sure you didn't notice after your adventure in the woods today, but the whole castle was freezing after the king and queen left. Not to mention, shortly after their departure, every stone in the building shook as if the palace itself was enraged. He's angry. I don't know for certain, but I think it was because he thought he had you pinned, but then Luca..." She paused.

"Luca found a loophole. The loophole that I accused my father of injecting into this arrangement." My eyes widened at the affirmation. "Luca mentioned today that his mother and father knew who they were dealing with. That the world knew, and so do the gods. He also told me he was born for me. I have this feeling that's connected somehow, and he may not have meant to say any of it aloud." Paxe looked toward the fireplace and stared, deep in thought. I drank a bit more wine. "I can't read your thoughts, friend." Her attention found its way back to me.

"I think you should go with Luca." She held up a finger. "Before you say anything more, just consider this for a moment. Let's assume that, whether he meant to or not, what he told you holds water. What if Luca *was* born for you? What if that means that the gods are sending him here to stop your father? It would make this all very...sensible."

I blankly stared past her as I chewed my bottom lip and stewed on what she said. That stew began to simmer, and I felt the stab of anger starting to pierce through the wine that was starting to make me slur. If she was hearing me, she didn't say so.

"No. As much as I want that to be true, it isn't. He can't be stopped." I said quietly.

"You don't know that, Ari. Why don't you ask them yourself? Or start thinking of how you'll ask Luca over the next few weeks." She muttered. The small window across the chamber started to bloom with pale moonlight that swirled through like milk in the steam and glow from the fireplace. All my life, I had been fascinated and often comforted by the moon. Now it was a constant reminder of my fate if I didn't strategize a way to accept that there was a chance Paxe was right and Luca was revealing some truth here. She acknowledged the thought and softly smiled. "The moon isn't your enemy, lovely girl. If you decide not to sulk in this room or take your frustration out on the training ground, then I would let this male show you the Valdaro you've been missing. Don't start by demanding answers. *Enjoy this, Arienne.* Give him a fair chance. After all, if you don't, the alternative will be that I lose you in four months. I refuse to let you give up." Her eyes welled with tears.

"She'll do no such thing." A grandmotherly voice bellowed from just outside the chamber, startling us both. Vetta then appeared in the doorway with a large towel in hand, stopping short when she spotted the alcohol resting between us. Her eyes darted back and forth, and she shook her head in disappointment. "I'm going to skin you both alive." She said, reaching for the bottle and snatching the goblet from Paxe's small hand.

"Come on, Vetta, it was a gift." I pleaded as I extended my hand, knowing full well she wouldn't return it. She clanked the items onto the washstand and gestured for us both to stand up as she made her way past Paxe and over to the steps of the bathing pool. We obliged, and I started wading over to meet her.

"Since when do you partake in this nonsense, girl? I'm not daft enough to believe Arienne drank this much on her own." she glared in Paxe's direction. I smiled to myself, waiting for answers she had earlier refused as I stepped up and accepted the towel. It was warm and pleasantly soft against my skin.

"I thought it would be a more comfortable way for Ari to talk about what happened today...unwind a bit." She lied. I rolled my eyes at her, wrapping myself in the towel, and Vetta held me steady under my elbow as I limped carefully out of the water. Paxe avoided all eye contact with the two of us, scrambling to collect my clothes from the floor.

"That's a nasty one for sure," Vetta said, examining my angry gash. "How did this happen?" I panicked for a moment, not wanting to implicate myself, and looked at the wadded dress in Paxe's arms. To my relief, she reacted quickly, carrying it to the bedroom. I knew if Vetta noticed the large tear on my gown, she'd suspect I was somewhere I shouldn't have been.

"I grazed it falling off of the east garden wall. There were tools out there, and I didn't see them." I knew she didn't buy a word.

"I see you've learned nothing since getting caught near the Midlands. Though, I hear permissions are about to change." She scolded as we started my pitiful journey to the bedroom. Word usually traveled a lot faster through castle attendants when my father was in a fit.

So everyone knows.

Paxe stood waiting near my vanity with a nightshift and a brush. Her face was wary as we came toward her. Vetta had very little regard for my modesty and wasted no time pulling the towel from me and beginning to dry me off. A fire had been started near my bedside, but it did little to save me from the chill of the night air creeping in from the open window.

"I take it Father didn't suspect that the prince was laying a trap of his own at the meeting?" I asked, treading carefully.

"He certainly didn't, and no one really knows how he figured it out before the two of you returned this afternoon. We suspect it was magic, but who knows what he plans to do to combat it." She answered, pressing my hair between the towel. "It was clever, but I do feel he'll be seeking some retribution. You and your prince should be on guard."

"He's not my prince. He's just as I am, a product of royal customs without any free will." I flatly replied.

"Be that as it may, he's a strong young male who, so far, has made a deep impression on us all. He was brave to test your father, and he went after you in the *woods...*" she paused,

tilting my chin up and meeting my eyes. "...when he didn't have to. I have no intention of allowing you to damper your future. You're going with him tomorrow." Paxe helped me into the nightshift, and I began to secure the shiny white ribbon that closed the front. "Paxe, arrange her pillows and leave the small silver one out for her ankle. And get the warming pan for the bed. I'll tend to her over there." Her tone lightened as if she sensed the conflict in my heavy heart.

My friend stumbled a bit as she rounded the bed, pulling the duvet down and fluffing the pillows. I watched her through my peripherals while also keeping my eyes on Vetta, who was now brushing my hair. We jumped as the loud ringing of metal sounded through the room. My head jerked toward Paxe, who disconcertedly retrieved the empty copper warming pan she dropped from the hearth. She had too much to drink. My hand went to my mouth as I stifled a snorting laugh.

"Gods, girl! Have you no pride?!" Vetta exclaimed, looking at her as if she couldn't be any more obnoxious. "Finish that and get to your room. Don't even think of asking for relief from your oncoming headache in the morning. That goes for you too, Princess." She griped, leading me over to my very inviting spot on the bed. Paxe filled the pan with the smoldering embers and fastened the lid, placing it under the blankets. They both helped me into position and adjusted my sore leg onto the firm, decorative pillow. We exchanged mischievous grins with one another while Vetta prepared to start her mending, and she leaned over to kiss my cheek.

"Goodnight, mi'lady." She bowed, turning to leave.

"Straight to bed, you." Vetta chimed.

Paxe swayed the whole way to the door, her footsteps immortally silent. She smiled at me through the opening as she closed it gently. I carefully pulled the blankets over the rest of my body so as not to disturb Vetta's process. I started to feel the bite of her healing magic as her aging hands hovered over the wound.

"This cut is a bit deep. I'll be finished in a few moments, but it will probably take the rest of the night to close. Perhaps I shouldn't have been too hard on you over the wine. You may need it tonight." She said in deep concentration. "There's tiny bits of wood or bark all throughout this, and they may be a little painful on their way out."

Vetta's healing abilities were renowned through Valdaro. Her age amplified the effects, as well as her skill. While she was nearly always successful, the healing wasn't painless and sometimes took a long while, depending on its severity. Her fingers relaxed, and she took another careful look at her work. Seemingly satisfied, she rose from the bed and wobbled to the bath chamber, fetching the bottle and bringing it to my bedside table. She held Luca's note in her other hand, a slight smile forming across her lips as she read it. She glanced at the wine and then at me, waving the paper like a small flag.

"I wouldn't be so sodden about your predicament, child. He seems very light and easy to be around. I'm surprised it isn't a breath of fresh air to someone who has suffered as much as

you have." Her voice was soft and tender, and I felt cared for beneath it. She sat the note down on the table. "Get some sleep. Summon me if you need anything." She smiled sweetly as she left.

My eyes were so heavy and I assumed that it was because of the tedious series of events that rattled my nerves today, but mostly from the alcohol taking a firm hold on my body. The body of which felt as if it were sinking slowly into a dark ocean, weightlessly. I succumbed to the peaceful escape, letting my lids fall shut and savoring the feel of the billowing plush around my face. I didn't want to think about anything anymore tonight. I let my mind turn off and finally drifted into a deep sleep.

I shifted uncomfortably after a sharp pain shot from my foot and radiated to my knee. I felt a heaviness lingering near me, and my body bloomed with sweat. I wondered for a moment if I could be fevering from this blasted thing, but remembered Vetta warned me that this could turn out to be a long night. I peeled my eyes open and realized I had turned on my side. I was facing the fireplace, and my nightstand was in front of me. But...so was something else. It took a few seconds for my eyes to adjust, the light from the fireplace had dimmed down to nearly nothing, and panic waved over me when I realized it wasn't a something...but a someone.

I quickly raised to get a clearer perspective and started reaching for a small knife I kept tucked between the wall and my mattress. I felt it, gripping it hard and thrusting it in front of me, and prepared myself for whatever would follow.

"Who are you?! What do you want?!" I demanded. In the dim light it was challenging to make out the features, but I saw a young man with his back turned toward me. He had broad shoulders and stood impossibly still, and I wasn't fully convinced that maybe Paxe hadn't been fooling with me and, in her drunken stupor, left some statue in here to scare me out of my wits. That was until I made out a very familiar detail about him, and the hairs on my neck stood on end.

His hair was closely shaved at the sides, and a braid ran down the middle...touching his shoulders. I blinked furiously, thinking maybe I myself had drank too much tonight, and my mind was surely playing tricks on me. But I was certain I recognized him.

"G–Gideon?" I stuttered. A drip of sweat trailed down my back. I couldn't move. He slowly turned, revealing a face I hadn't seen in five long years. One that haunted me every day. My heart shattered, and I lowered my knife.

"Princess. You've really grown into a beautiful woman. It's good to see you." He said quietly. My eyes filled with tears, and I shook uncontrollably.

"How? How are you here?" Then I asked the most predictable, stupid question. "Are you a ghost?"

He smiled at me sweetly, and the moonlight from my window painted his face a pale blue color, the fire light creating an orange aura around his silhouette. Now I didn't feel as stupid for asking. He didn't look real. "I'm not a ghost. You don't have to be afraid of me. I'm not here to hurt you. I came to talk to you." He said consolingly. His attention turned from me to my bedside table, and he smiled as he plucked a cedar arrow from a small display. "You kept it." He said, examining his handiwork.

"Of course I did. I will...forever." I said unsteadily. "There are so many things I want to say to you." Tears started to run down my cheeks.

"You don't need to. I know what you want to say. I came to tell you something." He said, coming near to sit next to me. He ran the back of his finger down my face, wiping it dry. It wasn't until then, I realized that I had to be hallucinating. Gideon's hands were still attached to his arms. I looked at them in awe, and my breathing quickened. None of this was possible.

"Tell me what?" I asked. My chest was heaving up and down.

"I don't regret a single moment with you, Arienne. You're a truly special girl. I wanted to tell you the answer to your father's question. When he asked me if I thought I loved you? I did. It was worth dying for, and I'd do it all again." My mouth went dry.

"You didn't have to tell me that. I knew you loved me." I replied.

"I tried to convey it when I looked at you. After he put me back in the cell and released his dogs on you..." I squeezed my eyes shut, recalling the most horrible night of my existence. His hand cupped the side of my face, and I opened my eyes, meeting his stare. "I died of shame. I couldn't do anything to stop them from hurting you, and I turned away. It was shameful, and I took my punishment for that. I deserved every second of it. You didn't. That woman didn't, and neither did her baby."

"I did deserve it! It's my fault! All of this was my fault. You'd still be here if I had never spoken to you in the markets that day." I wept.

"No. None of this had anything to do with you. Your father is the one that's at fault. For a lot more than you know. He's the one to blame for the way we all have to live, Ari and I came to tell you to stop blaming yourself and stop him. I heard you that morning. She heard you too." He said.

"Who?"

"The woman in the cell. You promised us something, remember? Until death." *Until death...I remember.*

"I was a fool, Gideon. That promise was made in heartbreak...and anger. I can't stop him." I said, defeated.

"Yes, you can. You have to. Our world depends on it." He pushed.

"How?! How do you kill the most powerful sorcerer in the world?! I don't even know what my abilities are! He's made an unbreakable bond, sealed with magic, that will ensure I don't even get them! What power do I have to stop him?! Tell me how!" I shouted angrily.

"With this." He calmly replied, teetering the arrow between his fingers.

What?

"Take this with you when you journey with the prince. Everything will reveal itself in due time. If you never listen to another thing in your life, then listen to me now. I know you don't trust Luca. I know you feel powerless, and I understand. But you can trust me." He said.

"What are you saying?"

"I'm saying that I know your prince is trustworthy. You need to stay close to him. Let him teach you all the things I wish I could have. Let him love you, Ari. Go with him, and take the arrow with you. Don't let it out of your sight. You can end all of this, but not alone. Promise me again." His voice was desperate.

"How do you know all of this? What is it that you want me to do? I don't understand." "You don't understand *now*. But you will. Promise me that you'll give him a chance. If you don't do it for yourself, then at least do it for me. Do it for our people. Deliver us...promise me."

I thought about it for a long moment. I took in every inch of his face, somehow knowing I would never see it again. I felt an ache in my chest from my broken heart, and I had no idea where to start putting all the pieces back together. I knew that, if nothing else, I owed him this. I looked at him and gathered myself.

"I promise."

He smiled and handed me the arrow. It was suddenly my greatest treasure.

"I need one more favor from you before I leave."

"What is it?" I asked warily.

"I need you to forgive yourself and let me go. Give your heart to someone else that's worth dying for. The way I did with you." As if my heart couldn't break any further. But what he was asking was genuine, and he was right. It did no good to be in love with someone who was no longer here, and nothing would bring him back. It was time to say goodbye.

"I promise, Gideon," I said tearfully. He pressed his forehead to mine and then raised from the bed. He started toward the door, and I called on him one last time. "Gideon?" He looked over his shoulder. "I loved you too." I smiled.

He smiled back.

"I know."

And he was gone.

CHAPTER 5

GETTING TO KNOW YOU

Harsh morning sunlight stung my eyes as I lazily opened them. I was surprised to feel this comfortable considering how much I drank last night, and wondered how Paxe was faring. I felt warm and rested as if none of it had ever happened, and I had to assume it was because Vetta's magic had been hard at work. I rolled to my back, sinking into the massive pillows, and glanced down at my exposed ankle. Exposed indeed. My nightshift had ridden clean up my thigh. I lifted my foot, turning it to each side, and was pleased to see only a faint, rosy line. It was slightly tender when I moved it but not painful at all. Still, it would be wise to nurse it today and refrain from straining it too much when I—

Gideon.

I sprang up into a sit, searching frantically for the arrow he told me to take. My hands raced around pillows and tore through sheets and heavy blankets. Nothing. I darted my head toward the fireplace, finding it gray and dusty. My eyes flickered to the nightstand and there it sat; untouched on its display beside the bottle Vetta left, and Luca's note. I thought I must be mad. I had to have imagined it all. Gideon was never here. My heart sank, and I leaned back on my hands, staring blankly at my lap. A soft knock sounded at my door, Paxe pushing in, carrying a stack of folded clothes.

"Morning. I brought—Ari, what's wrong?" She asked as she rushed over to my side. I tried to keep my thoughts to myself, almost embarrassed to hear what she'd say. But I also wanted to know what she would think about what happened...or didn't happen in the middle of the night. "What's happened?" She asked again, growing concerned.

"I—I think it was just a dream," I answered. I lost control of my mind, and images of him sitting where she now sat, wiping tears away with hands he no longer had, started filtering through my head. Her face turned pale, eyes widening as she looked into mine. She glanced over at Gideon's arrow resting on the table and then back to me. Our silent conversation was interrupted as Vetta waddled through the door.

"You're awake. Good. I came to see how everything was shaping up." We both looked in her direction, and Paxe met my eyes again with a look that let me know that we weren't finished talking about this. Vetta approached the other side of my bed where my mother's portrait hung. She leaned over, taking hold of my foot and turning it to the side. "Ah. You're a fortunate one. I expected it to be a bit less pretty. Make sure you take it easy on that today and pull your shift down, girl. Your backside is the last thing I want to see this morning." I obeyed, ignoring the giggle that escaped my friend.

"Should I stabilize it?" I asked.

"I don't believe that's necessary, but wear the boots you train with. That should be enough support to let you know if you're doing too much. Let's get you dressed, and I'll bring up some eggs and coffee...for the *both* of you." She narrowed her eyes at Paxe. "Be quick about it. The prince is already having his breakfast in the kitchen downstairs."

"He's eating in the kitchen?" I asked, puzzled.

"He insisted on it. Now, up. I want you dressed when I return." She said on her way out the door. Paxe quickly tiptoed after her, peering through it to make sure she was gone before latching it shut. She leaned back against the door, her arms behind her as her hands rested on the handle.

"So he visited you. And told you that you could trust the prince?" She asked quietly. I started easing off the bed, shuffling through the stack she left and unfolding the pair of brown leather leggings.

"It's not possible, Paxe. Gideon is...he's dead." I sadly said as I sat on the edge of the bed, pushing my foot through the leather.

"I know, Ari. But have you never heard of loved ones visiting you in dreams?"

"That would require one to believe that it was a visit and not something that I dreamt about because he was on my mind yesterday." I pulled the thick material up over my waist and began securing the thin leather laces.

"Well, I believe in it." She retorted. "And he believes in you." I slipped into a close-fitting ivory blouse with oversized sleeves that stopped at my elbows and tied. The muslin shirt was light and comfortable, perfect for a hike through the woods.

"So you're suggesting I take this as a message? From someone who we both know isn't real?" I replied. She walked over, picked a brown corset up from the duvet, and turned me to face the nightstand. I held my arms in front of me, and she helped loop my arms through the thick shoulder straps.

"You don't find it a bit ironic that what he said to you last night is a perfect response to what we were discussing in the bath chamber? And then you have a *dream* just a few hours later about him, giving you a clue as to what could possibly be the end of this nonsense?" She snapped, pulling the laces tight behind me. I collected my long hair from around my neck and tossed it forward, letting it fall over the front of my shoulder.

"I don't know what to believe anymore." I sighed.

"Humor me then. Take the arrow with you. The worst outcome is that you're right, and I'm wrong, and nothing happens." She spun me around and put her hands on each side of my face. "I know what else he said to you. He's right. As hard as it is, it's been five years. You have to let him go. Make some room in that heart for someone who might repair it for you."

I smiled and softly closed my eyes for a moment, nodding in agreement. I opened them when she dropped her hands from my face and started straightening the top of my corset. She kept her eyes down and grinned, and I became curious about what she found amusing.

"What?" I prodded.

"I was just...wondering. That's all," she smirked.

"Wondering what?"

"I was wondering where these big...*things* came from." She laughed loudly, gesturing suggestively at my chest. I dropped my jaw and slapped her upper arm. "Look! Your corset hardly fits over them!" she continued to crack, and my face flushed in humiliation.

"Would you stop?!" I begged.

"Go to the mirror and let me do something with that hair." She laughed. I padded over, standing in front of it, and realized she was right. Not that it was anything to be especially proud of. I found them mostly an annoyance. They were bigger than most females, but I didn't consider them huge, just slightly above average.

Paxe stepped between me and the mirror and decided to start my braid higher. This time it began between my part and the tip of my ear, weaving intricately down the front. She tugged at the plaits, fluffing them and making the braid itself plumper and my hair appear thicker. It was actually really beautiful.

"You're getting really good at this. I love it." I smiled.

"Perla has been teaching me some new techniques. She wore hers like this not too long ago, and I begged her to show me how. I've been looking forward to trying this on you," she said, pulling a few loose strands to frame my face.

"You two spending a lot of time together?" I asked, a little jealous.

"Nah, she's around sometimes when I meet Lakan."

"You still haven't told me anything about that," I said, crossing my arms.

"I know. I'm sorry. I feel like every time I think it's safe we're interrupted by something. I'm trying my best to be careful." She apologized.

"Maybe you won't have to be careful much longer." I looked at her as if I were the older sister swearing to protect her sibling. "I'm going to fix this, Paxe."

"I know you will." She moved behind me again and tied a strip of leather loosely around my neck, fitting it into a bow and turning it so that the bow draped down my chest.

"What is this?" I asked, placing my fingers over it.

"It's Luca's hair strap. I grabbed it last night off the floor in the bath chamber. I thought it would be an easy conversation starter for you." She smiled at me in the mirror. I smiled at her in return.

"You think of everything."

A few minutes later, Vetta had come in with breakfast as promised. We had a quick bite, and then I was helped into my boots. They came to my knees, and the soles were reinforced, making them perfect for today. Vetta had me walk around a bit to be sure they would suffice and then sent me out to meet

Luca.

I started down the long stone steps, trailing my finger across the wall in its usual place until I reached the hall. I found him leaning against the left side of the castle entrance with his hands in his pockets, staring at the world outside. His outfit looked mostly the same as yesterday, only not as fancy. Dark gray pants, black boots, and a loose black shirt with long sleeves. It seemed a bit warm for what he was wearing, but the material of his shirt looked thin enough. I supposed he must have had more ties for his hair. It was in a loose bun behind his head this time—a less formal version of the knot he had before.

I walked slowly, approaching him from behind. He must have sensed it, turning around to face me. He bowed slightly at the waist, smiling at me in greeting.

"Morning, Princess."

"Morning," I said shyly. His eyes went straight for the makeshift necklace, and a small part of me was cursing Paxe when I realized she didn't just mean for this to be a conversation starter for obvious reasons, but also the truth that betrayed her jokes about my...development.

You trollop. I'm going to kill you.

"You look lovely." He said, clearly recognizing it. "New accessory?"

"Went with the outfit." I shot back. He pressed his lips together in a tight smile as if he were trying not to laugh at me. My eyes caught the neck of his shirt where a small cut in the fabric was made to be secured by laces, but was left open, revealing a dusting of chest hair. Enough that I swallowed unnervingly.

"So does the red complexion." He snickered.

"Are you going to be like this all day?" I spat. This was not the conversation I expected to start. He put a hand to his chest.

"I'm sure I don't know what you mean." Another cunning smile. He offered an arm. "Are you ready to indulge in your first day of freedom?" I was about to answer when—

"No! No, she's not!"

Paxe came barreling down the hall carrying a plethora of things in her arm. A canteen, one of my swords, a hunting knife, my bow and quiver, and a brown shoulder bag full of fruits and bread.

"Here," she said, panting and handing us both different items. "If you're going that far into the forest, you should take this with you." Luca grabbed the bag last and threw it over his shoulder while my friend bent over, trying to catch her breath with her hands on her knees. I knelt down in front of her, grinning as I let on in my mind that I had caught onto her devious little scheme with the hair strap. She raised her head and glared at me. "Not sorry." She snipped.

"Are you okay?" I giggled.

"Too much wine last night. Thank you, by the way, your Highness." She smiled at Luca.

"Please. Just Luca. And you're welcome."

"Ah. Well, I...can't really call you that, but thank you for that too." She blushed.

I patted her shoulder as she stood with her hands on her hips, earning me a nice eye roll. Luca and I exchanged nods and turned to leave. I got a few steps out into the sunlight before I remembered something important, and I turned back to see Paxe wearing an excessive grin.

Oh, good gods. Get it together, you floozy.

"Can you find Hiss and coax him to my room with a bowl of milk? I don't want him trying to follow me that far into the woods, and I haven't seen him since he ran off last night."

"No need. He's already in the kitchens eating Belinda's fish stock. I've got him. Go. Try to have some fun, and stop worrying." She shooed me out the doorway.

We walked for a while in silence, and I watched his facial expressions as he took in the beauty of this day. There wasn't a cloud in sight, the sun was bright and warm, but the day was mild and a light breeze blew the trees outside the castle to and fro. There was so much greenery and flowering plants in our part of the land. I was used to seeing it; it was all I'd ever known, but I understood his fascination with everything and being in a new place. It made me wonder how different Crona must be from Valdaro. We neared the markets, and with that area being a little familiar to him, I decided to distract him with my questions.

"What's it like where you live?" He almost seemed surprised I asked. He glanced at me and then up at the towering trees.

"Not like this. I apologize if I seem a bit taken aback."

I shook my head.

"Don't. I understand." I paused. "You do...*have* trees, don't you?" He let out a hearty laugh. It was the first time I'd ever heard it and truthfully, it was adorable.

"Yes, Princess. We have trees. They just don't look like this. Crona is more of a coastal place." I tried to picture that, but it proved difficult. A frown started to creep its way through. He must have noticed if the abrupt pause in his walking was any indication. His hand brushed against my upper arm and I looked at him.

"I'm sorry. I wasn't thinking. It wasn't my intention to make you feel—"

"Stupid?" I finished. I pushed forward, leaving him behind and starting past the tailoring shop and the vegetable market toward the tree line. He jogged up behind me and tugged my shoulder, turning me to face him.

"Hey! Please. I didn't mean it that way." His tone was apologetic. "I know you don't particularly find my company appealing, but I wish you'd allow me a fair chance." We locked eyes, but I said nothing. "Please? I've been looking forward to doing this with you." I waited another moment and then slowly nodded, accepting the apology.

"Let's get going." I shrugged, walking again. We rustled through the brush and started on the path, scaring a small brown rabbit that scurried across. Luca pointed, and his mouth turned up at the corner.

"See? Things like that don't happen where I'm from. It's mostly just birds." he smiled.

"The map in the castle study must be wrong."

"What do you mean?"

"Well, it puts your castle right on the water, so I can understand that it must be a different climate, but what about the rest of Crona? The parts that aren't close to the water, like say...further west or south?" I walked slowly before him, not looking behind as I led us closer to the meadow.

"Good question. The lands surrounding our castle are fairly dry and not very grassy. At least until you get closer to the river. I've only been as far as the western half, crossing the Midlands to get to Valdaro and only as far south as the river allowed." He answered.

"Why's that?" I asked. I started to hear rushing water.

"It wasn't because I wasn't allowed to, just more that I never had much reason to go," he said.

"So is the river just...out in the open?" I continued.

"You could say that. It's a lot greener there, but it's not surrounded by forest like this. It's a bit more rocky as well. It's a beauty of a different sort."

We reached the waterfall, and I stopped to wonder if I should venture further on my own or just wait for Luca to decide. My heart started thudding a little faster, and I became anxious.

Well...this is it. Is it too late to turn back?

Luca walked around, studying the options as I tried to quiet my head. I stepped into the river and dipped the canteen under the water to fill it. He passed behind me, walking to the side of the waterfall and peering into it. I knew once we crossed over that my life would be different. One could say I've waited for this for as long as I've been alive, and you would think I'd be leaping over it and running to my freedom.

So why am I so hesitant?

Luca started waving me over, and I slowly obeyed, every step slower than the last. I had never been that close to the falls and if he found something it would be new to me.

"The rocks behind the waterfall run clean to the other side! We can cross here!" He yelled over the roaring of the water. I finally reached the place where he was waiting and extending his hand.

"Luca...I don't think I can do this." I frowned. He hopped off a large rock and landed near me with a confused expression.

"What do you mean?" He asked.

"The king is angry about this little snag you found in his deal. He feels threatened. I haven't seen him since I left the meeting that day, and he never called on me to scare me into hiding. Vetta even mentioned that we should be on our guard as he may seek retribution." I warned.

"Then we stay alert. It was his own fault for underestimating us both." My brows scrunched together, and I stared at him as if he were daft.

"Underestimating us both? The last time I considered going against him, he nearly killed me. He would love nothing more than to see me rot. What reason would he have to underestimate me? I've cowered under him ever since. Now you've pissed him off, and this whole thing seems far too easy. He wouldn't just hand over my freedom. Everyone thinks I'm supposed to be some hero but other than some sword training and knowledge of a few weapons, I have *nothing* to offer this world!" I shouted.

"You don't know that. You've never been allowed to figure it out. The way I see it, you have two choices. I told you this yesterday. You can sit by and let him continue to torture you and our people, or you can use that hate to end him. To end him the way you told me you wanted. You're not alone, Arienne...you have *me*. Let him have his retribution. This whole world is against him seeking the same thing. I'm not going to force you to do anything that you don't want to do, I believe I was clear about that, but I hope you'll reconsider and trust me. You don't belong to him anymore."

The wave of emotion and recollection of my promises to Paxe and Gideon made me want to cry...or scream. It was true, I had all these dreams and ambitions to do whatever it took to stop him and bring life back to this world, but I just didn't feel like I had the power. Luca stared at me like I had said the words out loud but said nothing and patiently waited for me to make my own decision. I appreciated his reservation. My eyes flickered to the red hawk feathers standing out against the rest of the arrows that rested in the quiver over his shoulder. I reached over, pulling it slowly out.

She didn't let me leave without it.

"That's exquisite," Luca said, admiring Gideon's arrow. He made a move to hold it, and I jerked it away.

"Don't touch this." I jabbed. He retreated and raised his hands. "Let me carry the quiver and my bow. I'll trade you the sword." I offered.

"Okay?" He agreed, confused. He started taking the weapons off to switch them with mine. "Is it tipped with poison or something?"

"No. A story for another time." I vaguely replied. I handed him the sword and took the quiver, placing the arrow back inside and throwing it on my back.

"Does this mean you'll go?" He asked.

"I've made promises I intend to keep. Lead the way." I said firmly.

He gave a proud nod and made his way back up the rock, turning back to offer his hand again. I took it this time, and he pulled me up to meet him. I bumped against his chest, and he braced an arm around my waist, keeping me steady. Our faces were far too close. We looked at each other for a moment, and my belly churned with nerves. I broke our stare, clearing my throat and wriggling out of his arms. He gave a slight smile and turned away finally, making his path behind the waterfall. I followed closely behind, trying hard to shake off the rush of what his body felt like against mine.

We cleared the other side and stepped into the mud of the riverbank. I trudged forward, wiping my boots in the grass, and turned to look across the water, my eyes focusing on the flowery grove of trees. Luca stepped behind me.

"You did it. First steps into your future." He said softly by my ear. "Now walk away, and let's start living it." I was uncomfortable with his proximity but invigorated and no longer as afraid of what may happen.

Luca took my hand and started leading me through dense pockets of shrubs and wildlife. We were silent, in awe of everything we were both seeing for the first time. I didn't let go of his hand and decided that I was accepting of that. I tried to keep the words of my dearest friends close to me and let Luca be the prince he came here to be.

Give your heart to someone else that's worth dying for. The way I did with you.

I stared at the back of Luca's head as he continued walking, completely unaware of the commotion in my mind.

Make some room in that heart for someone who can repair it for you.

I smiled to myself, grateful to have the very few people that believed in me and showed me love. They wanted what was best for me just as much as they wanted things to change. I owed it to them but realized I also owed it to myself. I made another silent vow to be strong, take the risks, and push forward until the storm had passed and we could all live. Truly live.

"Let's play a game." I finally said, ending our silence. He stopped walking and looked over at me, intrigued."

"A game?" He echoed.

"Yes. We'll call it *Getting To Know You*. Ask each other questions, and we answer honestly. But...both of us must supply an answer before the next person asks their question." I pecked.

"I thought you didn't want to get to know me?" He smiled.

"I'll make the first round easy." I returned, dismissing it. "What's your favorite thing to eat?"

"That's definitely easy." He grinned as he started forward again. "Pickled pelican eggs."

I halted and gaped at him.

"That is absolutely grotesque!"

His laugh roared through the forest. "It isn't! Have you ever had them?" My brows perked up, and I shook my head.

"Negative. And I won't!" I replied with a smile. We pushed on.

"We'll see about that when you make it to Crona. Tell me yours."

"Oh...Panettone. It's a bread Vetta makes on special occasions. It's sweet and perfect if you dip it into fresh coffee."

"Ah...sweet tooth. I should have guessed. I do enjoy a good mug of coffee, though. Your caretaker barely had enough left this morning to take to you and your friend." That reminded me.

"Oh! I meant to ask you about that, actually. Vetta said you ate in the kitchens this morning. Insisted on it. Why?" I prodded.

"Not your turn, love." He laughed. I rolled my eyes in response.

"Fine. Go."

"What ability are you hoping to get on your Ventus?" He asked.

Damn. Good question.

"That's a good one. I've probably thought about this millions of times. Wait—is this a fair question? You already have yours." And it hit me. *He has to answer honestly about his gift.*

"You have to tell me." He grinned.

"Ugh...okay. After a great deal of sifting through ideas and realizing no one has this particular ability, I thought it would be amazing if I could fly." I answered bashfully. I thought he'd think it foolish, but he nodded.

"You're definitely right about that. I used to think that very thing as a young boy." I waited for a moment, and when he didn't start addressing the subject of his abilities, I began to stare at him, hoping he'd catch on. "I know you're curious about it, Princess. I do plan to tell you when the time is right." He said without looking at me.

"No, no! You have to tell me. Remember?" I spat.

"I just don't think our first outing together is the opportune moment." He continued.

"You asked the question. It would appear that you do think it's the opportune moment...*Prince.*" I pulled my hand away, stopping and folding my arms. He finally obliged and moved closer, sliding his hands into his pockets and glancing down at the bow in the hair strap around my neck.

"I can manipulate your feelings. It's not an extravagant gift, to be honest, but it has proven itself very useful in times of need." He admitted.

"That's why you said you wouldn't use them on me unless they were needed?" I asked.

"Or if you wanted me to."

My mind started to zero in on how many things that could mean, and it triggered a brief moment back in my room the night before. *Perhaps it wasn't just his eyes, but him entirely.* I felt almost angry, wondering if he had been manipulating me this entire time.

"But have you?" I demanded. He looked at me sharply, and I realized my tone sounded accusatory.

"No, I haven't. But you've already seen an example. That I can tell you." He moved closer.

"And what's that?" I asked.

"You may have noticed my father didn't do a great deal of talking at the meeting. I can only work with whatever you're currently feeling. I can't make you feel anything. But I can use what you feed me to either intensify it or shut it down completely. My father despises yours, and he was growing increasingly anxious upon arriving. I used my ability to bring him down and calm him. Keep him quiet so he wouldn't say anything ridiculous. My mother is fierce at times but very level-headed and has a way of controlling a conversation. I meant what I said. I'll never use it on you unless it's needed. It was needed with my father." He finished.

"So when you said if I wanted you to...?" I pressed. His gaze turned sultry, and I started to sweat, quickly realizing exactly what he implied. "Oh..." My face heated, and the butterflies in my stomach turned into a stampede of elephants. He held his hand out, smiling, and took mine gently, moving us forward again.

"Your turn, Princess." He gushed.

CHAPTER 6

SQUALL

We walked for hours in conversation, occasionally stopping to admire some of the treasures of creation offered by the forest. After my moment of defeat in forcing Luca to tell me about his gift, I decided to keep any other potentially damning questions to myself for a while. We talked about our friends, our hobbies, and almost anything else that would keep the topics light and innocent, and I was a little surprised to admit to myself that I was actually having fun. Enough fun that I barely felt tired from all the strenuous hiking. I was sure it put us miles away from the castle by now...which got me thinking.

"Luca? You didn't happen to bring a map of this forest along on this little excursion, did you?" I asked. He was squatting at the base of a huge, mossy oak whose roots had created a large opening that resembled a doorway, and I supposed he was looking for its tenant.

"A map? No. I wasn't aware there was one," he replied, his head still poked into the hole. "What do you think lives in here?" I whipped my entire body to face him.

"Wait. Luca. You brought me out here knowing full well that I have no idea what lies beyond that river bank, and you didn't think to bring a map?" I asked. He stood and turned casually, not seeming at all like he was worried.

"As I said, I wasn't aware a map of the forest existed. The tree line to the other side has to be close by," he shrugged.

"Luca!" I shouted, throwing my hands to my hips. "If we're not going in the right direction, this forest circles our castle! We may not find our way out for a while yet, and if I'm reading the sun's position correctly, we have about two or three hours before we're in the dark!"

He looked around, ignoring my panic, and raised his hands.

"It's a gorgeous day. We'll find our way out, don't worry. If we don't make it back by nightfall, then we'll find a spot to rest until morning. Everything will be fine," he said calmly.

I wasn't so calm. In fact, the notion of wringing his lovely neck was the only thing I could think about. "You're not bothered at all by the idea that we might spend a night in the woods?"

"Not at all. Look at how beautiful it is out here. Just imagine how it would look in moonlight," he smiled.

"Yes. Lovely thought. And have you ever done it? I sure haven't." I argued.

"No, but that doesn't mean we can't enjoy it as much as the rest of this day. This is what I meant by living the rest of your life, Ari. Not everything will go according to your plans; sometimes, those make the best memories. We'll be fine. I won't let anything happen to you." He soothed.

I had to take a moment to let his words season my mind. He did have a fair point, but it didn't diminish my unease. He smiled softly, once again reaching out his hand.

"You're right," I smirked, taking his hand and moving to examine the big hole in the tree. "So...did you find your goblin?" His answering smile was brighter than the beam of late afternoon sunlight that speared through the top of the oak.

"Now, that would be a sight," he chuckled.

Our playful banter was interrupted by a distant rumble that we could hear...and feel. It started low and seemed to be quickly growing as if it were...moving. The ground beneath us trembled, and I was overcome with dread.

"What is that?" I whispered in terror. He didn't reply as his hand squeezed mine, and his head darted around, looking for a predator. He pulled my sword from its sheath as the sound grew louder. Closer. "Luca..." I said, raising my eyes to the canopy above.

The trees I could make out furthest from us looked as if they were being pushed by an unseen force in our direction. The sunlight suddenly grew dark and ominous, and the rumble became a deafening roar as whatever was coming for us shot through miles of forest and sounded like it would make itself known at any moment.

"Get behind me!" Luca ordered, pulling me to safety between his back and the large tree trunk. The forest shook, and I glanced over his shoulder in time to see a wall of rain and leaves of every kind consume everything around us. The wind blew Luca into me, and my body crashed into the oak, robbing my lungs of a scream. He dropped the sword to the ground and spun around, wrapping himself around me and tucking my face into his shoulder. He shielded my head with one arm and held me tightly with the other, ducking his chin over the top of my head. The brutal rain stung my arms as I broke them free, gripping the back of his shoulders. He leaned us in closer to the trunk as the sudden storm howled around us.

"What is this?!!" I screamed over the thrashing of wind. He held me tighter as he tried to lift his head to look around. His dark hair whipped his face, tearing free from its bind. I dared a look up at him, and he met my eyes.

"It's some kind of squall!" He yelled down at me. Water poured from his nose and chin, splattering my face as I squinted against the elements.

"What do we do?!!" I yelled back. We both couldn't have looked more helpless, and there was nowhere to run. Luca's eyes caught the big hole in the tree, and his eyebrows shot up in victory.

"Get down! Try to get in that hole and see how far you can stand!" He belted.

"Are you kidding?!" I replied. A sudden crack of lightning blew the ground apart in every direction close by, and I lost all control of myself. I screamed loudly, holding onto Luca for dear life.

"Go, Ari! It's all we've got!" He said, squeezing me back. "I'm gonna go down with you! Bend your knees!" I started lowering slowly, and he loosened me a little, allowing me some shelter so that I could turn around and climb into the nook. The tree was massive enough to fit us both on either side, but as I tried to stand, my head bumped against spongy, rotten wood. I sat, crouched as far as I could get to the left side, and tried to make room for Luca to crawl in to the right.

It was a snug fit. He struggled to get himself through the opening and took a few moments to shift around, adjusting his back to rest against the far side. We were both drenched and panting, looking at one another in shock as the wind raged and the rain blew into the open entrance.

"What just happened?" I asked, breathing loudly.

"I take it things like this don't normally happen here?" Luca replied, ringing out his hair.

"I've never seen anything like this. Ever." I answered, staring cautiously outside the tree. Thunder crackled again loudly, and I jolted backward, pressing in further against the wood.

"If that's true, then maybe it won't last very long," he said. The storm intensified like it was taunting us, and my eyes widened.

Father. It's my gods-damned father.

"Luca...I'm so sorry," I said softly, pulling my knees up close. He did the same, widening them as he rested his arms on each knee. He studied me for a moment.

"Sorry? For what? The weather?" He asked, confused.

"Yes. I think this is the king's doing," I replied. I refused to look at him and suddenly felt like the biggest fool. I was right about it being too easy. He was going to make this as difficult for me as possible. I'd never be safe. I'd never be happy. I'd be stuck in this miserable existence until he finally killed me.

"Hey," he called. I didn't respond. "Arienne, this isn't your fault." he continued. I looked up at that.

"Yes, it is!"

"No! It's mine. I shouldn't have pushed him for one. And two, I should have listened to you before we crossed the river. You were right. You do know him best and in the worst way. I'm to blame for this. It's me that should be apologizing to you."

I wanted to cry, but anger started to boil inside me like a pot about to spill over. I hated that awful bastard. He's taken everything from me. I just wanted to go ahead and bury myself under this tree.

Don't let him take anything else from you. End him.

"I hate you," I shuddered. My rage started to take control of my limbs.

"What?" Luca asked, a surprised look on his face.

Tears began to well in my eyes, and my skin crawled with heat. I leaned forward, getting on all fours, and dropped my bow and quiver from my back. Luca startled backward, trying to gain some kind of understanding of what I was about to do. I blocked out all thoughts other than every memory I could recall of every time my father had ever hurt me. Every time I missed the mother I never had. Every time I had taken a beating or was starved for days in my room for not being what he wanted me to be. I was done.

I crawled out of the hole into the raging storm, barely feeling the battering rain and debris that grazed my body. Luca shouted from the tree, and I couldn't make out a word. All I could hear was the wind...and my rage. I grabbed my sword from the ground and stood firmly against the cyclone that seemed to have a singular target. Me.

"You piece of shit!" I screamed, my other hand fitting around the hilt and swinging the sword into the rain. My feet danced in familiarity with all the training I was coached, and my blade found true with every thrust of my arms. "I HATE YOU!... Gods, I fucking hate you!" I cried, battling my way through endless sheets of rain and wind. Luca came out of the tree watching in awe as I annihilated my invisible foe. "You're no king! You miserable, mindless fuck!" I swung again. "I'm going to put a blade through your fucking face!" I thrust forward, the end of my sword stopping short against something solid.

I stopped in panic, my first clear thought being that I may have just killed Luca in my fit, but then a bright light flashed before my sword, and an ethereal-looking woman stared back at me, my blade gripped tightly in her large hand. Her eyes were pure white, and she was unusually tall. Her hair looked as if it were made entirely of vines and blooming flowers, and her skin was like bark. She looked like she had been carved right from the forest itself. Luca's arms wrapped around me, jerking me away.

She tossed the sword into the air, catching it by the hilt with her hand, and sliced through the rain, turning the blade with her curious-looking body and knocking the storm back. It ended in the same way it began. The wave of nature cast itself with her movement, bursting through the forest behind her. She lowered the sword and turned the upper half of her body toward us, scraping the ground with the blade's tip. I couldn't move and wasn't sure if she was the reason, or if Luca and I were frozen with fear, or awe...or both.

"You are the king's daughter, are you not?" She asked. It was as if a dozen beautiful voices harmonized together to exist into one being.

"I am," I answered. My legs were shaking. She turned to face us completely and stepped forward. Luca's arm squeezed tighter.

"I am Elowen. You may release her, Prince. No harm shall come to either of you."

Elowen...Goddess of nature. Holy sh—

"Do I have your word, my lady?" Luca asked boldly. She dipped her chin and stabbed the sword into the ground. He gently freed his hold, but I stayed close.

"Your father dares to use *my* power to harm? In my dwelling, no less? He will pay a price. Only I am permitted to smite life with nature. His violation will come with great consequence," she affirmed. I made a step toward her, taking a knee and bowing my head.

"Are you going to kill him, your Grace?" I asked.

"Is it not your wish to end him yourself? It certainly seemed so a moment ago." I stared at the mud.

"I don't possess the power, mi'lady," I said quietly.

"Stand, youngling," I obeyed and held my head strong. "To conquer evil, your intention must be pure. I can feel your hate, Arienne Genovese of Valdaro," I stiffened. "As I have declared, your father must be held responsible for his repeated misuse of power. The gods have grown weary of his offenses. We have chosen you, Princess." I stood in disbelief.

"Chosen me for what?" I asked nervously.

"The king's power was gifted to a worthy Valdarian many years ago. Your father has been the first to abuse this gift with his malice. We did not intend for these abilities to be used in cruelty and fear. It is to be revoked. We have chosen you for this task," she explained.

"With respect, your grace. I have no way to stop him. Unless you're bestowing some sort of ability on me?" I placed a hand to my chest.

"What you ask cannot be given to you by my own hand. The transfer of power that great must be unanimous among the gods. Should you be willing to accept our request, you must have an audience with each of us. Each time, you shall receive a blessing that, when used together...will allow you victory over your father."

I swallowed hard.

"How will I know where to find them?" I asked. She smiled softly and turned her attention to Luca. I looked over my shoulder toward him.

"You will stay with your betrothed. He shall guide you to your next destination. I shall supply you both with protection from elemental woes. The only resolution to this task will be that you complete it together."

I stared at Luca, watching as his expression sank. He knew exactly what I was about to ask. "You knew. You've known this whole time?" I rasped.

"The sea goddess has visited the king and queen in Crona. It is where she resides. Your prince was to journey to you and nothing more. Her blessing was sealed into the binding between them on the day that you met. Your father has since detected her magic and is now projecting his own fear. The only beings that best him are the gods." The goddess answered for him.

Vetta said they suspected it was magic that betrayed the loophole to him.

"I only knew what my mother would tell me, Arienne. She told me that the gods were going to punish him. She didn't say how they would do that, only that I would have to go to you and take my place as your husband and to protect you at any cost. As I told you I would." he added.

"And all the bull about being here to *love* me? That was part of your plan Luca?" I snapped angrily, betrayal and hurt starting to take aim at my heart.

"Princess," Elowen interrupted, demanding my attention. I looked back to her peculiar face. "Love is earned. It is planted like a seed and grows much like the forest with nurturing and the appropriate climate. It is fate that brings you to one another. The love will come with growth." she finished. I slowly lowered my head.

"I'll accept, your Grace." I offered quietly.

"Very well. Bring me the arrow you hold in your quiver," she replied.

My head shot up in surprise at her request, and her own nodded in the direction of the hole in the oak behind us.

Gideon really did visit. This can't be real.

I turned to find Luca pulling my weapons from the hole. He held the quiver out towards me, and I pulled the cedar twig from the bunch. He studied me carefully, and our eyes met. He looked almost hurt or sorry...I couldn't tell which. I ignored it and turned back to make my way to her, still having difficulty believing this wasn't all a dream. I approached her with my palms up and the arrow resting across them, presenting it to her with a bow at the waist.

"Before I begin, I must first warn you. Hate begets hate, youngling. The love for your people and for the ones close to you will be the only true weapon you have against your father. For if you come for him with that loathing in your heart, it shall match his own and render these blessings useless. Take this opportunity to heal. Love is a power that he does not possess. Evil cannot conquer evil. Do you still accept?" She asked.

"I do." I answered.

"Very well," she said as her hand hovered over Gideon's arrow. It lifted from my open palms, and a flickering green aura began to surround it as it floated between us. She started to speak in ancient tongue, and the light became brighter for a brief moment before it snapped through the shaft, painting the carved designs a dark green color and falling back into my hands. "It is done." she said.

"So...I have to shoot him with this?" I asked, examining the piece.

"His powers will subside after he is struck with all the blessed weapons. This will leave the king defenseless and as mortal as a human. The final blow will be yours to determine for yourself. I wish you good fortune on your quest, youngling. Should you succeed, your reward shall be great." she looked to Luca, who was still standing behind me. "For both of you."

"If she is to kill him, my lady...will she inherit his power as she gains her own abilities? Or do the blessed weapons vanquish the entire future line?" He asked.

"The king's power will be diminished until it manifests into the eldest heir following his death. Once the weapons have been used on his body, the king will no longer wield any power of his own. It will lie dormant within him until his heart beats its final thrum," she answered. My entire body drooped in relief. She gestured toward the sword, still standing strong in the ground. "This sword will be the next weapon to be given its blessing. Take heed. The god of the Bolton waters is a cunning sort. I bid you farewell, Princess." A whirl of wind and leaves spun around her, followed by a hiss of flashing light, and she vanished.

The sun peered through the forest in hues of orange and deep rose. It was setting. I stood in deep concentration, recalling everything that had just happened, my eyes fixed on the sword in the dirt. I raised the arrow to my chest and pressed it against my heart. It was clear now that there was indeed a way to rescue our world and our people. I'm not as weak as I've always been taught to believe. I had just accepted a bargain with the gods.

"Ari..." Luca called softly behind me. I closed my eyes, not ready to have the conversation I knew would be inevitable, as it seemed we were going to be stuck in this forest through the night.

"Don't call me that, Luca," I answered, nearly whispering. I opened my eyes and stepped forward, jerking the sword from the ground and turning to meet his face. "We need to gather dry wood. Take this and help me make camp." I ordered, handing him the blade.

A rush of wind swept across from behind me, revealing dry ground. I looked up at Luca, his hand still raised in front of his face as he had tried to shield it from the sudden change. He began to lower it, and his eyes reflected a flicker from where they were now staring behind me. I turned to look and found a good-sized fire crackling where the sword had been in the ground. I couldn't keep the smile from etching across my lips.

Elowen.

"Thank you, mi'lady," I muttered. A flock of martins burst forth across the limbs of the towering oak above us, chirping in reply.

CHAPTER 7

PAWNS

The warmth of a fire built by a goddess is inexplicably different than any other you could ever feel. You don't have to add logs or poke it around. There's no smoke or foul smell. Best of all, I was almost positive it wouldn't get any smaller or go out until morning; as it was controlled by the mother of all nature herself. I found great comfort in her promise of protection as I sat cross-legged, staring into the flames.

"Looks like you, when you waged war on the rain," Luca joked, handing me a plump orange from the bag that Paxe had packed for the road. I looked at him, puzzled, taking it from his hand and averting my eyes back to the fire. "The way the flames dance around each other? It was amazing the way you moved today. Your form is really impressive."

I didn't respond and began peeling the orange, pulling small pieces from the pulp and throwing them into the blaze. I could feel his eyes on me. "What is it, Luca?" I said without looking up.

"There's an easier way to do that so that the peel comes off in one long piece," he pestered, chewing a mouthful of bread.

"I don't care," I continued peeling.

"Look, can we talk about this? Or are you going to spend the entire night pissed at me for things that are clearly out of our control?"

I broke the orange apart, tearing out a wedge and popping it into my mouth. I knew it may have been because of how hungry I was, but it was the juiciest, most amazing piece of fruit I ever tasted. "There's nothing to talk about," I said over my food.

"Mmhmm," he said, rolling his eyes and looking away.

"What? Say it." I fired.

"No. It's fine. Enjoy your dinner." He took another bite off of the loaf. I can't explain why but it made me angry. Right now, he was the last person I wanted to be stuck in the woods with. I plucked another wedge and dramatically threw it between my teeth.

"Typical." I mumbled under my breath. I chewed vigorously.

"What is?" He asked. I shook my head and dug out another piece. He shot up angrily and towered over me, then leaned down and snatched the wedge from my hand, throwing it in his mouth. He mocked my chewing, as well as the scowl I was wearing on my face, crossing his arms and widening his stance.

"What is wrong with you?!" I yelled, jumping to my feet.

"You tell me, *Princess!* You're the one keeping track!" He bellowed back.

"I didn't come here to fight with you every other minute!" I stepped closer.

"No! You came here to *protect* me! Right?! To save me from big, bad dad?! Now I know what you meant that day at the meeting place, Luca! That the gods know who he is, and then you put on that little show saying that you weren't going to force me to love you, and then I find out that's not why you came here at all!" I argued. He matched my inch forward.

"Yes, I did! I did come here to protect you, and it wasn't to rescue you from your insane father! It was to help you rescue *yourself! So what* if the gods want to help us? I thought you'd be happy to have their help! We were going to be married regardless of all of this and we both knew that before I ever stepped one foot in your kingdom, Arienne! I meant every word I've ever said to you!" He snapped.

"Except all the shit you *didn't* say, Luca! You didn't mention that the only reason you're here is because I'm the pawn in this game with you and the gods! Why didn't I deserve to know I was meant to be used? I could have handled it! I've been used my entire life!" I screamed, pushing against his chest and trying desperately not to drop my orange. He retreated a step from the impact, tilting his head to the side and narrowing his eyes.

"We're both pawns! We're both being used! And I would have told you when I thought you'd stop fighting me every step of the way, any time we were alone. But all you've done is shut me out! Every time I think you're trying to let me in, you trail off and find another reason to hate me. I expected that when we first met, Ari and I told you on our way back to the castle that I'm not the spoiled little prince you think I am!"

"Prove that," I planted my knuckles on my hips.

"Haven't I? I've been supportive. I've been understanding. I've told you I'll die for you if that's what it takes. I've complimented you, I've told you I would give you time to love me on your own. I've even decided that I would back off, and just be here to see this through and let you have your space if you never loved me at all! But..." he paused. He turned away and fisted his hair with both his hands, the bread crumbling and hitting the ground.

"But..?" I continued. His hands flew to his sides as he whipped around and stormed mere inches from my face.

"But I can't fucking stay away from you!" He looked straight into my eyes, and I swallowed. "I can't do it. I can't stop looking at you...can't stop reaching for your hand. It's like my skin has its very own need to touch you." His jaw tightened. "You wanna know the part that baffles me even more? It's only been two days since I first laid eyes on you."

My heart thundered and, as angry as I was, every part of my body wanted to betray me and...

Do it, Ari. Take him.

Our noses nearly touched and I could feel his breath fanning across my chin. My own breathing was becoming quicker as I leaned in a little further. He stilled, and I could gather that he was leaving me in complete control. He was keeping his word.

Kiss him, stupid!

My heart raced, eyes locked onto his and for a moment I remembered that he could feel it. He can manipulate it. He promised only to do it if I wanted him to. I almost asked him, but my heart didn't feel ready. We barely knew each other. I slowly backed away and he watched in silence. The glow from the fire made him look like a god himself, and it made it so much more difficult. I backed up another step, not knowing a single thing to say and feeling just about as stupid as I did remorseful. He seemed to read it on my face and turned himself back around, bending down and picking up the mostly salvageable loaf of bread from the ground.

"You made me drop my bread..." he grumbled, dusting it off. I smiled slightly, although I knew he couldn't see it.

"I'm sorry." I said quietly.

"Don't be. I'm still eating it." He replied, blowing the crust and biting into it. I grimaced.

"I wasn't talking about the bread," I replied, as he turned around chewing. His mouth curled up at the corner.

"I know."

I lowered myself back to the ground, crossing my legs and bringing my half-squeezed orange into my lap. My adrenaline was still leaving my fingers and limbs to tremble as I tore another piece from the fruit. Luca made his way closer, joining me to sit. I reached over to offer him the wedge.

"You want some orange to go with your dirt?" I joked. He smiled as he took it and offered me a piece of the bread. "Yeah, no thanks," I passed. "I am sorry... I don't mean to be so defensive, Luca. I never had any other choice but to build a wall around myself. I shouldn't be holding you responsible for that."

"I told you at the meadow. I can understand that." He pulled the cork from the canteen and took a swallow. "I'm sorry for losing my temper. The truth is, no one has ever really pushed me to that edge before...the way you do? I'm not used to feeling that way around a female, if I'm being honest," he admitted, looking over at me.

"How many... females... have you been around?" I asked, immediately wondering if I wanted to know the answer. He smirked in response, taking another bite from the loaf.

"Why don't we play your game again and I'll share as much as you're willing to?" he smiled. My heart started to sink into my stomach.

He deserves to know.

"Okay... I'll play. But I have to be sure. Are you ready to talk about the hard stuff?" I asked. I clung foolishly to the idea that I was ready myself. This wasn't Paxe, and he couldn't read my thoughts. All the things I share would have to come out of my mouth.

"I'm ready. Is that your first question, then?" He asked, raising an eyebrow.

I nodded. "It's fair. If I'm understanding this right, you're asking how many females I've lain with?"

"You don't have to tell me if you don't want to," I interjected. I knew deep down that my real reason was because I was throwing my wall up again.

"No, no. Rules are that I have to answer, right? It's not as many as you're probably thinking—there were only two," he replied, offering me the canteen. "My first time was before my abilities took hold, and it was with a Cronian girl about a year younger than me. I had just turned eighteen and a few of my friends talked me into it. She worked at a tavern in our city that her parents owned. We knew each other fairly well, and they lived above the tavern. She took me up there and... you know." He looked toward the fire.

I turned the canteen up, drinking a large gulp. My lips made a sucking sound as I pulled them off the mouth of the bottle. "So, you didn't enjoy it?" I smiled.

"No, I did. I didn't really have anything to compare it to. Although, I had heard that it definitely wasn't her first time. Most girls just wanted to have *lying with a prince* under their belt." He rolled his eyes.

"Oh, please!" I laughed, rolling mine. He jerked his head toward me.

"What? It's true! All my friends had done it before. I was the little virgin prince. She took me up there and it didn't really last long, at all. Afterwards, we all left and the first thing she did was go brag to her sister." He looked annoyed.

"And you didn't brag to your friends?" I argued.

"No, actually. I left them behind to go talk to my mother. I knew she'd most likely be pissed, and she was. But I felt... dirty. Like I had done something wrong and she's a female... the one I trust the most. I mostly just wanted her advice." My eyes fell to the remains of the orange in my lap. I tore off another piece, chewing it slowly. "I'm sorry... I probably shouldn't have—" he stared.

"No. You should. She seems like an amazing mother, and I actually love hearing you talk about her. It's as if I have this odd opportunity to create happy memories with mine, even though I never knew her." I looked up and smiled. "So... what about the other female?" I asked, eating another piece. I could have sworn he blushed. It was hard to tell against the firelight.

"The other was... very different. My mother had said that I should never give myself to anyone I don't have those kinds of feelings for and reminded me that one day my heart would belong to you." I swallowed. "She said I would be a fool to risk such a thing when royals have no choice in who they marry, and I'd only be making it harder on myself if I can't be with that person."

"So, you loved her?" I asked.

"No... I don't think it was love at all. I lusted after her. She was a palace aide, and... phew." I fidgeted around uncomfortably as I popped the last piece of orange into my mouth. "She wasn't so much beautiful as she was just..." he paused, trying to think of a good explanation.

"Slutty?" I offered.

"Yes," he nodded. "She carried herself like she worked in a brothel. We spent weeks exchanging... suggestive looks. But then one night, I woke up to find her absolutely naked, and sitting on my bed. It only happened one time. My mother never said so, and I never asked, but I'm positive she sent her away." He chuckled.

"How old were you?" I asked, intrigued.

"It was a few weeks after my Ventus." He replied, reaching for the canteen. I was hoping he'd elaborate, but when he didn't, I fished for a bit more.

"So, that time was better?" I asked. He looked embarrassed, but nodded and smiled as he looked back at the flames. "It was after your Ventus. Did you use your *gift* on her?" I grinned. He laughed loudly and turned his whole body to face me, resting his arms on his raised knees.

"It's driving you mad, isn't it?" he laughed.

"Well, I'm just curious!" I giggled.

"I did. The first and only time I've ever used it, intimately." He smiled. A few moments passed in silence before he finally asked, "So... now you know. What about you? How many *males* has the princess had in her bed?" He coaxed. I felt the color drain from my face, and our lighthearted conversation took a nosedive.

"...Two..." I quietly answered, staring off into the darkness. He sensed the fluctuation in my mood and called my name quietly. I looked at him.

"You don't have—" he started.

"Rules, Luca." I said, cutting him off.

"Your human boy?" He asked softly.

"No, actually."

He scrunched his brows together, confused. "I thought you said—so you didn't actually lie with him?" he asked.

"No. His name was Gideon. I met him when I was twelve. He made the arrow that the goddess blessed. I wanted to buy it from him when I saw him carving it in the market outside his father's butchery. He gave it to me as a gift, and over time he taught me to make my own. We were very close, and after a couple of years it became a regular habit of going to the meeting place, sitting too closely and holding hands. But then, that one afternoon, we lost control and he finally kissed me. It was unfathomable and reckless. And we paid a huge price for it." My eyes began to water.

"Your father killed him for kissing you?" He asked.

"Not at first. He found us, and dragged us into the street. He beat Gideon in front of his father. He beat me too. Then he made us walk back to the castle and threw us in separate cells in the dungeon." Luca's face turned serious, his jaw twitching as he clenched his teeth together.

"Ari, you don't have to tell me any more. Perhaps it would be better if you didn't." He said. His voice was lethal.

"I'm going to. You deserve to know why I'm like this, Luca," I said, determined to say it out loud. "This is the first time I've felt strong enough to tell anyone about it." He stared at me quietly. "There was a pregnant Valdarian woman who was in labor in the hall...my father dragged her between us, telling us that she had become that way because she had lain with a human. I knew very well what happened to those children, but he made us watch. He kicked her in her belly, over and over...and over." I started to weep quietly. Luca moved closer, placing a hand on my knee. "And then he took her away, and pulled Gideon out into the hall. He forced him to hold his hands out, and he cut them off for touching me." I sniffed.

"He did it in front of you?" Luca asked. I nodded, my face squinching as I silently cried.

"He left his hands outside the door of my cell on the floor and tossed him like soiled laundry back into his cage, and then he told me..." I hesitated. "...he told me that if all I sought was intimacy, all I had to do was ask." Luca's face turned feral. I squeezed my eyes shut, not able to look at him as I finished the last part. I took a deep breath and kept my voice calm. "He let the two guards into my cell, and told them to make sure I got the message. They had their way with me for hours before they left me there, naked. I woke up and tried to call out to Gideon, but..." I shook my head slowly. "Paxe and Vetta were allowed to come down and get me later that next morning and I realized that he and the woman with her baby were both dead. Gideon bled to death, and I'm assuming she must have as well. I vowed to kill my father that day. No matter what it takes." I sighed, feeling proud that I got through it without breaking into sobs or shutting down.

Luca trembled with anger. I could feel it soaring through him as his fingers seemed to get tighter on my knee. "Who were the guards?" he asked. His voice was low, and dark as the night that swallowed the forest. I looked up at him, wiping beneath my eyes with both hands. He looked like he could explode.

"Don't bother," I breathed.

"I'll kill them. I'll rip them apart, and make them choke on their own—"

"They're dead, Luca," I interrupted, putting my hand over his. "I told you. You don't know what kind of monster you're dealing with. My father had them tortured a few days after my assault. He ordered Vetta not to heal me in any way, and when he found out how badly I had been injured... he killed them. Paxe told me that she overheard some of the other guards around the castle talking about how he told them to *keep it quick...* and they disobeyed." I finished.

He moved his thumb and covered my fingers. I looked down at our hands. "Ari..." he stared at me. A tear fell from my eye, splattering the top of my hand. He tipped my chin up with his free one, and I reluctantly met his gaze. "Please, let me hold you." My breathing became rapid with bottled-up emotions, and I nodded as the tears became rivers down my face. He pulled me forward between his knees and into his body, wrapping his arms tightly around me.

I finally shattered, sobbing loudly into his neck. He squeezed me tighter, reaching his hand to the back of my head and gently swaying from side to side, like a mother singing lullabies to a small child.

"Shhh..." he whispered, his cheek pressed against my head. His stubble grazed the tip of my ear, and I gripped his shirt in my hands. "Nobody will ever hurt you again. I told you. You don't belong to him anymore," he soothed.

"Do it, Luca. Please?" I sobbed.

"Do what, love?"

"Use your magic. Make this stop. I'm done," I begged.

I realized then that asking him to use his abilities on me could mean much more than pleasure when it counted most. I knew that getting this out would be one of the hardest things I ever accomplished, but I didn't expect the heartbreak of reliving those awful memories to be worse than when it actually happened. I succeeded. I gave those memories a voice. Now I needed them to stay in this forest, or burn in this fire forever.

The faces that haunted me began to flash through my mind. First, Gideon...with his perfect smile and his genuine spirit. Then, the nameless red-headed beauty that defied everything and held that small, hybrid infant. Its tiny little hands curled around her finger, leaving this world with its heroic mother. I couldn't breathe. Images of my scraped feet stepping into my bathing pool, and the way I cried alone as I tried to wash my own blood from the inside of my thighs.

The images started to blur, and a calmness washed through me like warm water, starting at my head and traveling through my arms and torso. My lungs began to slow, taking in more air. My body went limp and I relaxed into Luca's arms. I rested the side of my face against his collar bone and breathed deeply.

"How do you feel, Princess?" He asked softly. His neck pulsed close to my forehead and I smiled slightly. I could smell his hair and the scent of his body, combined with rain and the smell of trees.

"Amazing," I breathed, relaxing my grip on his clothes. He chuckled as he adjusted us both to sit comfortably. His arms softened and he leaned into a small tree close to the fireside, reclining us, but still holding me close. He stayed silent for a while, no doubt processing everything I had just said. I wondered for a moment if he was planning a clever demise for my father, but my mind refused to let me think about the sorry bastard. It had to be Luca's magic. I couldn't form a single upsetting thought.

"It's kind of poetic." Luca muttered, staring at the woods beyond.

"What is?" I whispered.

"That the goddess blessed the arrow your friend made for you. You're going to put that thing in his heart. That's a well-deserved ending to Gideon's story, don't you think?"

I smiled. "Yes.... yes, it is."

"What you just did was so brave. I'm honored to be a pawn with you." He looked down at me, and my eyes fluttered closed. "Sleep, Princess," he whispered, stroking my face with his finger.

He leaned the back of his head against the tree, and it wasn't a moment later we both gave into fatigue, sleeping peacefully under the moon and a blanket of ever-watching trees.

CHAPTER 8

THE WAY BACK

Dawn broke over the forest, bringing with it warm, balmy sunlight and the chatter of nearby birds and small animals searching for their breakfast. My puffy eyes fought me as I tried to open them, and I looked up to see Luca sleeping winsomely against the tree. The fire was out. In fact, there was no evidence that it ever existed at all. No remnants of burned wood, no piles of ash. Not even a scorch mark on the ground it raged on all night.

My body was warm and still wrapped in the protection of Luca's strong arms. I hated to wake him, but I knew we had to start moving if we were to ever find our way back to the castle, to prepare for our next excursion. I wasn't even sure how one would travel to the Bolton Sea as it was a good many miles from our palace. My head slightly ached from my mental breakdown last night, and I dreaded the awkward moments that I'd be having today, following my revelation.

I raised myself carefully from his chest, watching his face closely. No movement. I reached for his arm that was rounding my back and thought to lift it off with my hand. That thought blew apart as he jolted awake, startled, and fell on his back to the ground.....taking me along with him.

Oh, for the love of the gods...

He stared up at me, shocked for a moment, my braid falling close to his face. I hovered over him with the same expression as I held myself steady with my palms and forearms. Our faces were dangerously close and I could feel the elephants starting to stomp through my stomach again.

"Morning," he said, smiling.

"...Morning," I repeated. "Umm...we should probably get going." I started to move off, and Luca grunted like he was in pain. "What?" I asked, looking him over.

"Can you be careful?" He winced. His knee was raised beside me. "Your leg is..." I looked down and realized my body was still between his legs and putting a bit too much pressure on certain areas. I cleared my throat, not able to stop the red from gracing my cheeks.

"Oh...I'm...I'm sorry," I paused, realizing where his hand was. "If you take your hand off my rear end, I could probably move." I shot him a glare.

"Oh!" He yelped, throwing his hands in the air. "I didn't...I—"

"Save it, your Highness," I smirked as I lifted myself off and stood, reaching my hand to help pull him up. He smiled as I helped him to his feet.

I surveyed our camp, noting the weapons and the leather bag in the entrance to the big opening in the oak tree, where Luca and I had taken refuge the day before. The canteen was nearly empty and lying near what used to be our fire.

"We need to get to the river to fill that jug. How far do you think we are from it?" I asked.

"Not sure. You want to start retracing our steps? Perhaps, we can find a few spots we stopped to look at on the way. They stood out before, they should again, right?" He answered, gathering his hair. I remembered he lost the strap to tie it in the storm yesterday. I stepped closer, pulling the loose end of the leather bow at my chest. It fell free and I handed it to him.

"Here. This is yours," I smiled shyly. "Good idea, though. I'll get our things."

I walked over to the tree, grabbed the bow and quiver and made sure that the blessed arrow was secure before throwing it over my shoulder. I started to reach for the bag and jumped backward when I realized it was moving.

"Luca!" I yelled in panic. He ran over to investigate as he finished tying his hair behind his head.

"What the..." he said, slowly reaching to poke the leather. The flap flew open with a black and white blur, and we both nearly left our skin. Hissifus scurried around, seemingly just as surprised, with a small rolled-up bit of parchment tied to his neck.

"Hiss!" I shouted, clutching my hammering chest. "What in the world are you doing out here?!" I knelt down to calm him, and he nuzzled my legs. I carefully untied the string and rolled out a tiny note.

I sent him out to look for you after you didn't come home.
Don't be angry.
If you're alive, I'm going to kill you.
You have me worried sick.
Follow him back if you're lost.

-P-

I grinned as I scratched his ear and stood to face Luca, who was blundering through the bag. "I think he was looking for something to eat," he said, looking over to the paper. "What is that? A map?"

"Better. Paxe sent him to find us so we could follow him back home," I chirped. I sheathed the sword and handed it to him, feeling a bit more confident that we'd be back before we had to endure another night in the wilderness without supplies. He stared at me quietly, hooking his thumbs into the front of his pants until I became annoyed. "What?" I barked.

"I just wanted you to know that I'm...I'm really proud of you. And wanted to thank you for confiding in me last night. I weathered that pain with you until I took it away, and I know it hurts," he said consolingly. I stilled. "We have a long way to go, and I thought it would be better to tell you now, than for you to feel like there's a heaviness hanging over us the whole way back."

"Thank you," I smiled. "For everything, I mean." I pulled my loose hair behind my ear. He looked at my bare collar, smiling. I followed his eyes. "Really?" I asked.

"I'm giving the strap back to you when we return. I quite like the idea of you wearing something of mine. To be truthful, it made me feel like you may actually be a little fond of me," he grinned. I stepped forward, and he winced as my fist hit his shoulder.

"Let's go." I snickered, turning towards the direction we had come from a day earlier. I started walking and Hissifus trotted left. "Hiss, this way," I called. He made no indication that he was paying me any mind. Luca made his way behind him, looking over at me.

"I think he wants to go left," he said, digging into the bag over his shoulder and pulling out a couple of apples.

"But this is the way we came," I argued, as my finger pointed the other way. He tossed the apple over and I caught it, watching as he turned to follow my little navigator.

"See you tomorrow then." He said. His tone was cocky, and the bite he took from the apple was loud.

This male.

I rolled my eyes and hopped down the shallow embankment, catching up to them and joining Luca at his side. He looked over and smiled as he chewed, throwing an arm around my shoulder. Hissifus sniffed around with his tiny nose in front of us and I watched his dainty, two-toned backside sway back and forth.

"He's an extraordinary little creature. If he gets us back to the castle, I hope you realize I'm rewarding him with an entire chicken." Luca said with complete seriousness. I laughed, nodding as we followed close behind. "How did he end up with that coloring?"

"He was born with it, and it's extremely rare. He's a very special little fellow," I proudly smiled.

"He certainly is. I've never seen anything like it. He's as individual as you are. You make the perfect pair." I would have taken it as rude if it weren't for our conversation last night, but I knew he meant it respectfully. "Rare, *and* beautiful," he finished. I blushed as I bit into my breakfast.

We walked for a couple of hours, talking about this and that. It was still late morning when I recognized the sound of water. My eyes popped with the realization that we really did take the longest possible route to where we spent our evening. All of that, and we never even made it close to the forest's edge, where the villages must have been.

"Unbelievable." I muttered, admitting my misjudgment. Luca laughed under his breath. "All this looks very familiar. There's no way we got that far off track. We were here!" I argued, taking in my surroundings.

"Or we just started here," he grinned.

The water didn't sound very far off, which got me thinking about our next conquest. Elowen mentioned that the god of the Bolton waters was a cunning sort. But the first blessing was for Luca to use to create an obstacle in my father's plans. It was gifted in the form of unseen magic from a *sea* goddess.

As I'm not a very practiced religious individual, and Bolton was a long distance from us, I found myself pretty empty when it came to knowledge about the god we were to meet next. What would he have us do? Would he test our character or loyalty? I'd most likely fail in that. I never prayed, and never offered anything to the gods since I was very young. Even then, it was because I was told to by my caretaker or other devout staff.

"Hey, Luca?" I slowed. He stopped and turned to acknowledge me. "Who is the god of the Bolton Sea?"

"He's called Nero. God of strength and power," he answered.

"Is he wrathful? Devious? What should I know about him?" I continued.

"I imagine he could be wrathful if one went against him, but I don't think anyone would be that foolish. Well...your father being an exception," he pocketed his hands.

"So he isn't a water god? He's of the sea, isn't he?"

"Well...he is, to an extent. Nero forges ancient weaponry from volcanoes beneath the Bolton waters. Only select mortal and semi-mortal beings are gifted or rewarded such a thing. He's not born of the water, but of the molten world underneath. He's a blacksmith." He finished, eyeing me closely.

"A blacksmith?" I repeated, shocked. He nodded. There was one person I knew who could tell me anything I wanted to know about a blacksmith, and she was waiting impatiently for me at the castle. I started making a mental list of things to ask her when we returned. "Good. I may not be as unprepared as I imagined," I smiled. I walked past Luca, and he followed, continuing onward to find the river.

"You know someone?" He asked curiously.

"Not well, but I know someone that does," I answered, trying not to give away any of Paxe's dangerous secrets. Hissifus pattered on before us, and the water began to sound a bit louder. We cleared some familiar shrubbery and hiked up around a dense gathering of skinny trees, and I was nearly ecstatic to see that waterfall. Across the river, my eyes caught my sacred purple and yellow meadow and movement over by the right where Luca had first seen me washing counter paint from my face.

A young, pretty human girl with bright blonde hair and a red gown was filling pails of water by the river. I was surprised to see her. No one hardly ever came this way to the river after Gideon was killed. Most stayed away out of fear, and others out of respect. They usually took a path further up the river to the north of the markets for their water. She startled and looked up at us, dropping the pails and spilling them both. I recognized that face.

Perla. Well, if that isn't a sign from the gods.

I waved from across the bank, trying to convince her that I meant no harm. Humans shied away from me a great deal of the time following my public shaming. She nervously waved back and I made my way to the waterfall to cross.

"Who is that?" Luca asked from behind me. I started climbing the edge of the rock bridge, hoping she'd wait for us.

"Her name is Perla. She runs a tailor shop with her mother. She's the one designing my dress for my Ventus celebration," I answered as I pulled myself up. He wasn't far behind me as we slipped behind the falls and out the other side.

"She doesn't look very thrilled to see us," he observed.

"She's human. They're never thrilled to see me."

I gathered that he caught my implication after what I had explained to him last night, so he didn't press further. He wound around me and offered a hand to help me down. Hissifus looked like a brat, choosing not to risk wetting his precious paws on a set of mossy stones that we, for certain, would have slipped on.

Luca held firm to my hand after I hopped onto the river bank, obviously worrying that it bothered me that she was afraid to talk to us. We awkwardly approached one another and she smiled sweetly, bowing at the waist. Her hair was tightly braided and crowned around the back of her head, twisting into a lovely knotted spiral that looked like spun gold. Paxe was right about her talent with styling.

"Your Highness," she addressed, straightening herself. "I'm sorry. You gave me a fright. I didn't expect to see anyone." She looked at Luca cautiously. He gave her a polite smile, and extended his free hand to greet her.

"My name is Luca. My apologies for the intrusion. We're on our way back to the castle." She gently took his hand, shaking it.

"Luca...oh you're the—" she paused, retreating her hand and bowing into a curtsy. "I'm so sorry, please forgive me. I didn't know what you looked like, your Majesty." Her voice sounded like she was terrified. I had just about had enough.

"Perla...please. It's alright. No one even knows we're here. May I help you with those?" I asked, pointing to her empty buckets. She turned to look at them and started to rush over.

"Oh...uh...that's alright. I don't usually come down here, but this spot is closer to the shop than the other one. My mother needs it to dye some material," she explained, picking them up and dipping one into the river. "I hate carrying them when they're full." She dipped the other.

"Shorter walk," I nodded, picking up the first pail. Luca grabbed the other, and she wiped her wet hands on her skirts. "After you."

"Thank you," she smiled, starting toward the path.

"Perla... since you're out here, would you mind if I asked a few questions on the way back?" I asked. She dipped her chin.

"Of course," she replied as she fell into step beside me.

"Do you know a lot about your brother's work?" I started. Her face grew with worry and I wondered if she knew that Paxe confided in me often. She seemed hesitant to answer, probably for fear of exposing my friend. "There's a well-known blacksmith I'll be meeting soon and I could use any helpful advice."

She softened. "I see. Well, I'm not sure how much I can tell you to expect, your Highness. Lakan is a very dedicated smith. He does say that certain weather affects his work on occasion. In the winter months, he tends to stay there longer hours to keep the shop maintained at a level temperature." She offered.

"What kind of weapons does your brother produce?" Luca cut in from behind. She smiled bashfully at him and then pulled her attention back to the path.

"He specializes mostly in tools; axes, plows, and such. He's been commissioned weaponry, of course, and his blades are spectacular. He does lovely work in his hilting, and they can be lucrative, but sometimes resources can be hard to find for decoration," she tilted her head. "He's been known to dabble a bit in valuable metals when they're supplied for a commission, or if he's fortunate enough, he purchases some to design jewelry and sell." She finished.

"I imagine it's a taxing profession on the body?" I asked, trying to think of any sort of trial the god might ask me to participate in. I came up extremely short.

"For a beginner, I suppose it could be. Lakan has been practicing this art for years. He's quite passionate about it, but I have seen him exhaust himself with his tempering a time or two." She smiled.

We neared the thick brush at the end of the path and Perla seemed nervous about being seen with us outside the market. I understood, and we slowed to hand her the water pails. Luca's demeanor struggled; with his raising and manners, I could tell it was killing him to let her walk the rest of the way with the heavy buckets.

"I do appreciate the help. Thank you, both," she bowed. "Princess, you should stop in and check on your gown when you get a free moment. I'd love for you to see how it's coming. I'd be happy to answer more questions for you... if you have them."

In the comfort of the store. I get it.

"I'll do that," I grinned. "Thank you again for humoring me. I know it must have seemed strange, but I don't know the first thing about smithing. This meeting is going to be important, I just want to feel prepared." I explained.

"I understand. Perhaps you could visit Lakan. He'd most likely be more helpful than I ever could. It might also be useful to look around his shop. I'll tell him you might visit." We exchanged farewells, and she walked hastily into the market. Luca and I gave her a few minutes before coming out of the tree line. Hissifus, of course, didn't wait. He trotted onward, leaving us behind.

"I can visit him if you'd rather not," Luca offered as we passed by the market. I raised my brows, nodding in gratitude.

"That would be wonderful," I said. It truly wasn't that I didn't want to be around, but the idea that I was invading Paxe's private life stung and I would rather hear whatever she was comfortable telling straight from her.

It wasn't long before we reached the entrance to the castle and I was relieved, but also a little sad. Part of me felt a little more drawn to Luca after all this, and while I knew I'd see him soon enough, as he stayed in a room just beneath mine, I still didn't like the idea of letting him go.

Oh no...he's growing on me.

Paxe wasn't in the doorway to greet us this time. Luca stopped in the same spot as the evening he had carried me in, turning me to face him. He untied his hair, and his long ebony locks fell around his face.

"Here," he said, looping the leather strap around my neck. "I like this better right here." His fingers brushed against my chest as he tied it into a loose bow and I fought off a shiver. "I want to say something, but I'm not sure if I should." He dropped the bow to my skin and flicked my chin with a finger.

"What is it?" I asked as I moved a bit closer. I couldn't even help myself. I started to wonder about what he had said in the woods. How he couldn't stay away from me, and his skin had a need to touch mine. He smiled down at me, looking me straight in the eyes. This definitely wasn't helping.

"I'm going to miss you tonight, Princess," he admitted, his voice low and as smooth as melted chocolate. I decided that was about what I felt like, and the elephants came back to ravage my stomach. I didn't even think about what I was saying before I blurted out my response.

"I'm going to miss you, too."

WHAT?! You fell right into that...fool.

Before I could come up with a clever idea to take it back, he pulled me into an embrace I wasn't expecting but completely surrendered to it as his arms wrapped around my shoulders and our foreheads met. My arms instinctively found their way around his middle. His breathing began to match my own. In fact, I could actually hear my heart thrumming as I started to leak weakness against the urge to kiss this male.

"Ahem..." a voice interrupted from the doorway. He smiled and closed his eyes. "I uh...hate to break this up, but the king wishes to see you both in the castle study," Paxe said with a side smile. I gently pushed out of his arms and briefly met his stare before looking at her with humiliation. It didn't even register that she had just told me that my father had summoned us, but when it finally did, my body locked in worry.

"Why?" I asked, nervously turning to her and stepping in her direction.

Her eyes looked as if she were just as apprehensive as I was. She wiped her palms on her apron in unease.

"Not sure. He told us to make sure that we delivered the message as soon as you returned. Hissifus had come in without the note and I knew you must be out here somewhere," she answered. Luca twined his fingers between mine, and Paxe made sure to notice it as she glanced at me and grinned bashfully. "Should I take your things?" She asked with a tone.

"Can you actually just put them in my room? I don't want them to go back to the armory," I replied, countering her intrigue. "You don't have to go with us, I'll see us both to the library," I resolved. She dipped into a quick curtsy and started shouldering all the weapons. As she turned to walk back, I called out to her and she looked over her shoulder. "Thank you for sending Hiss. You're my hero." I smiled. She reciprocated it.

"Don't think I'm letting you off easy, mi'lady." she winked as she continued through the doorway.

We were a few steps behind her and made a right, past the doors to the Great Hall, and down the corridor to a sharp curve that veered right again and past an entry to the stairs that led up to the castle attendant dormitory. Across the stairs on our right was a set of double doors that were guarded, indicating that the king was inside. I exhaled deeply and Luca squeezed on my hand.

"Don't worry," he said as we slowly approached the doors. "Stay close to me and don't let go of my hand. Let him shake himself up about it. He still believes you'll never open up to the idea that you can explore how you feel, remember? If what I just felt from you outside means anything, then you're already proving him wrong." He said.

"It does." I said, looking over. He stopped us in front of the doorway as the guards pulled them open.

"Then, he's already losing his own game," he smiled. I noticed the glimmer of affection bouncing in his silvery eyes. I had basically just admitted that I was having second thoughts about keeping the wall between us standing. Had it not been for Paxe's urgent message, I'm positive I would have given in to the war I constantly fought with my heart...as well as my body. "Let's go," he said softly, as he led us into the room.

The castle study was a small chamber, closed in at the back of a vast library that housed hundreds of books that dated back centuries. The same ugly, orange carpet from the Great Hall dragged between rows of shelving that reached the ceilings on either side. The aisle through its middle was wide and small tables were placed at every other end of the large shelves, until a small reading area opened up at the back, situated around the study that was encased in stained glass windows, but had no door. It was well lit with many wall sconces around every corner and several more in the study itself. The candlelight bounced beautifully through the abstract color on the glass as we neared the study doorway.

My father was seated behind a large oak desk in the middle of the chamber, writing on several different pieces of parchment and surrounded by several stacks of aged books. He didn't look up from whatever it was he was doing to acknowledge us as we stood at the threshold.

"I'll be with you in a moment," he said, busily scratching a quill on the paper. I glanced at Luca, who never took his eyes off the king and I wondered what he was thinking. My father signed the bottom of one of the pages, dropping the quill in the pot of ink and sitting up to recline with his mouth in an open smile. He slapped his palms on the table. "Ahhh...daughter. I see you've returned in one piece. Do come in... both of you."

I gripped Luca's fingers tightly as we inched into the study. The king leaned back in his chair, resting both elbows on the arms of the seat and joining his fingers across himself. His eyes trickled down to our locked hands and then to my face. I tried desperately to keep my expression collected, but my heart was pounding.

"Seems the two of you are getting better...acquainted," he smiled. Luca's pep talk was doing very little to ease my nerves, as it seemed my father wasn't bothered at all by our closeness.

"You wanted to see us?" I said flatly.

"I did," he replied, leaning forward and resting his hands on the edge of the desk. "I've recently been informed of some...*activity* that needs to be addressed. I thought that since you are to be married soon, and it looks as though your life may surpass my own, after all..." he nodded to our hands. "Perhaps it's time for you to start getting accustomed to your duties as a future queen." His expression was pure evil.

"I'm not killing anyone for you." I answered.

"I'm not asking you to," he grinned. The guards from the door stepped in from behind us and he nodded toward them. "Bring her in." He ordered.

They turned and walked back down the carpet to the library's entrance. I stared at my father in disgust, fearing who he meant and praying to the gods I would be wrong. I swallowed hard and gave every ounce of my effort in stopping myself from ripping the head off his body. My worst fears came true as the guards returned with Paxe in tow.

CHAPTER 9

LITIGATION

The air thickened, and every pull from my lungs was a struggle as the two guards held each of Paxe's arms, which were bound behind her. I could see the horror in her face as every thought from every mind in this room was bombarding her own, and she was realizing their reasoning for her arrest. I turned to my father, releasing Luca's hand and pounding my fists on the desk.

"What is the meaning of this?!" I shouted. "Release her right now!" He didn't budge, and his sinister smile grew wider. "I'm not going to beg you. She's done nothing. You'll release her...now!" I demanded.

"If you care so much for her, then you should have warned her about what happens when you whore around with a human," he leaned forward. "You know all about that, don't you, daughter?" He whispered, looking toward Luca.

"If your plan is to degrade me with that, he already knows what you've done," I argued. He raised his eyebrows in surprise, looking at me and then again to Luca, who was trembling with rage.

"Oh! So, she's told you? Good. Then you understand, young Prince, why we're all here," he turned his attention to me again. "The princess was not exempt from her judgment and repercussions. This one won't be either. You'll be carrying out her punishment," he said, once again leaning back into his chair.

"No. I'll do no such thing." I replied, turning to Paxe and reaching for her. The guards pulled her back and her eyes were pleading with mine. "Let go of her!" I yelled.

"You'll not touch her until you're instructed to," my father calmly said behind me. I turned around. "You'll do this or suffer right along with her. Do you truly want that a second time, my daughter?" Luca finally broke, stepping forward and throwing his arm in front of me.

"Over my dead body," he sneered. "She is my betrothed and no longer your concern. If you lay a hand to harm her, you violate a bond bound with magic and I'll kill you myself." Luca promised with absolute certainty. My father laughed loudly.

"You're a clever prick, little Prince. I do love that about you. She must have really ridden you blind in the woods. Tell me daughter...was he as satisfactory as the two I sent into your cell?" He laughed. Luca held me back, unphased by his attempt to strike a nerve.

"Don't give him an ounce, Arienne," he said calmly.

"Princess! Please. It's alright..." Paxe's voice rang out. "Your Majesty...you brought me here for judgment. What will you have her do with me?" She asked boldly. I stared at her in shock, my eyes beginning to burn in anger and heartbreak.

"It has been brought to my attention recently that you and your human have been seen multiple times in unfavorable situations. You know the penalties for it. You've lived in my home since you were a young child, and did so only out of my sympathy. The punishment for your actions are usually bestowed together...but the vermin you contaminate yourself with seems to have disappeared. Tell me where he is, and I'll grant you leniency." My father said.

"I don't know the human you speak of, sire." Paxe lied. She was going to die to protect Lakan. I should have known. She's spent her entire life protecting me.

"You're a fool to believe I won't have you ripped apart and made an example of. Tell me where he is!" He demanded again.

"What proof do you have of her indecency? There is no judgment in hearsay!" I belted. "I was punished with Gideon because you caught me in the act. A true king does not pass judgment such as this without a solid thing to credit it! Dozens of witnesses can tell you they saw me fly this morning, but it doesn't make that the truth!"

"Is it not proof enough that the Fauci boy is hiding?" He countered.

"You'd hide too if you thought someone was coming to kill you. Truth or no." I said firmly. He stared at me as if I could drop dead.

"Well...I suppose there's only one way to know, isn't there? Throw the whore in the dungeons until we find the boy. He'll be questioned alone. With me. If he so much as gives away a single shred of guilt, the two of you die...a public execution," he said. I stopped breathing. "In the meantime, you and your prince can go looking for something that can prove their innocence. You had better pray that you find it before I find *him.*"

"And if we do?" Luca asked.

"If you do, and it's validated then I'll release her. But you all should know," he looked at Paxe, "Innocent or not, your time in this castle is over. I've had enough of seeing your face here." Paxe's lip began to quiver, despite her attempts to appear strong. My heart split into. "Get her out of my sight." I locked eyes with her, hoping she could read me.

I love you...this isn't over. Don't you dare give up!

The guards jerked her away and began pulling her through the library. I nearly lost my composure as I watched her every step until she was through the double doors. I turned back to face my father who looked very pleased with himself.

"You have nothing on her. You're doing this to hurt *me.*" I trembled. He said nothing, and only smiled. He looked like a snake that was coiling around its helpless dinner, taunting it as if it had any chance. "What happened to you?" I whispered, shaking my head slowly. His face changed, dropping into an icy stare and the room began to darken and feel the same.

"Get out," he said, with a voice like death itself.

Luca wrapped his arm around my waist, turning me and leading me quickly through the library. I shot one last look over my shoulder.

"If you touch her I'll fucking end you!" I promised. Frost began to bloom over shelves and onto books, traveling toward us as we walked away. Luca nearly lifted me from the floor as he sped us up and pushed through the doors. We slammed them shut behind us and hurried down the corridor toward the Great Hall.

"We need to leave, Ari." Luca said, as we charged toward my side of the castle, nearing the stone steps. "Go upstairs, pack everything you need. Meet me at my chambers in an hour." I stopped at the entry to the stairwell.

"I can't leave her!" I cried, beginning to panic. "He'll hurt her. He'll do something to hurt her." I shook as I leaned against the wall. He grabbed me by my shoulders and looked at me. A familiar calm began to take over, and my breathing eased.

"He won't. And staying here won't save her. We need to get to Bolton. I'm not naive enough to believe she's not truly in a relationship with a human and I know you're trying to protect her. But Ari, if we can't get anything to prove she's telling the truth, it's only a matter of time before he finds him. Our best shot is finding Nero and blessing this sword." He pleaded.

"What if he finds him before we get back?" I asked.

"We're taking care of that before we leave," he assured me. "Go get what you need." He brushed my stray hair away from my face. I nodded, as I turned to head up the stairs. "Ari?" He called. I looked back. "Find cat...bring him too. I have an idea to keep him safe."

He's going to make it hard not to fall for him.

I rushed upstairs, skipping over a few in my haste and burst through my bedroom door to find Vetta already packing a large canvas bag. Her eyes were red and misty as they met mine in surprise and it was obvious she'd been crying.

"Vetta!" I exclaimed, throwing my arms around her. She hardly ever showed affection, but today, she held me like I was her own child. "They took her," I said, crying over her shoulder.

"I know, my dear one," she soothed, rubbing across my back with her hand.

"I have to see her." I said as I pulled back to look at her. She took my face in her hands.

"Nothing will happen to her. You have my word, child. I've taken care of you both since you were born. Right now I need you to gather your wits and trust the gods." As many times as I'd heard her say to trust the gods, the look in her eyes felt different. I stepped back, lowering my brows while keeping eye contact.

"Vetta...what do you know?" I asked, growing worried about the answer.

She stilled and seemed overridden with guilt.

"Everything, Princess. You will too...in time." She confessed. I suddenly became furious, fed up with all the secrets and being kept in the dark. I grabbed a small vase from my vanity and hurled it to the wall. It exploded into tiny pieces and Vetta jumped in shock.

"No! People are dying! Lives are being traded! Mine included! Everyone I care about is being ripped away from me! What are you not telling me?! I've been sheltered from the truth my entire life and now I'm supposed to be the one to end it all? Why me, Vetta?" I shouted. She wobbled over to my bed and sat, staring at the floor.

"Because, my girl...your mother sacrificed herself so that you could." My eyes widened as I glanced at my mother's portrait. Before I could ask what she meant, she continued, "Your mother traded her life to the gods in exchange for the king's revocation of power. She offered you to be the deliverer of our people. Of our entire world. She knew you would have Paxe to grow with, and I swore to protect you always. When Isabelle passed, the bond between the two of you grew stronger and you were inseparable. Paxe knows nothing. And the gods paired you with the prince to help you through it. The two of you are joined souls; each one meant for the other, as a gift from your mother so that you would never be alone."

"So the feelings I have for Luca..." I started.

"Are real. As are his for you. Every part of your soul is in need of its other half. That's why the bargain your father made was a foolish one. He knows nothing of your mother's sacrifice or the fact that he sealed his own fate as you and the prince are destined to love each other." I stared at the wall in disbelief.

"Does he know that?" I asked.

"He doesn't, Princess. All Luca knows is that he was to come here for you. You can trust him. I vowed to raise you and care for you, and having been that person all your life, I've grown to love you as if you were my own. You two girls are the children I could never bear. Your future with him is a gift, and it is a gift Paxe would never have. As hard as I tried to keep her from seeking out love in the wrong places, she's headstrong and determined. She'll be the same in that dungeon. Go to the gods. Bring back those weapons. We'll all be here to help you when you come home. We're all with you, Arienne and so is your mother." She finished.

I leaned on the wall near the bath chamber doorway, crossing my arms and beginning to sweat with frustration at all the things that Vetta had just told me. My mother died giving birth to an offering to the gods...me. Luca was my soulmate and I hardly knew him. I was part of a thrown together prophecy to end a tyrant who happened to share my blood. And worst of all, Paxe was under this castle about to rot in a dungeon, all because she didn't want to spend her life without love. Even if that love had cost her everything.

"I'm not leaving without seeing her. Luca needs me to meet him downstairs in an hour. Help me." I begged. She looked at me with a sad smile and nodded her head. She lifted herself from the bed and walked to my vanity, taking my mother's pendant from the box and placing it in my hand.

"This belonged to your mother. It's blessed with her magic, and was left for your protection. Take it with you. I've packed clothes and blankets for you. Gather everything else you'll need and I'll go to the kitchens to pack food. When you finish, find me by the gate to the dungeon. You'll have to make it a short visit but I'll make sure that you see her," she said softly, kissing my cheek and making for the door.

I clasped the long, emerald pendant around my neck and it fell over Luca's leather strap and down into my shirt. I started throwing necessities and random items in the bag, fitting my weapons in last. When I felt satisfied, I pulled the rope drawstring tight across the canvas, tying it in a thick knot and racing for the stone steps. Once I made it to the hallway downstairs, I checked Luca's bedroom. He wasn't there. I raised the long shoulder strap over my head, crossing it over my body and made my way to the dungeon.

Vetta was waiting as promised with a large saddle bag filled with food and water. She reached for my things and I sat them on the stone floor. The lone guard by the door nodded to Vetta and opened the gate to the long hallway. I stared him down warily.

"Be quick, your Highness...or it'll be both our heads," he warned. I hurried through the gate and down the hall, frantically searching every cell.

"Paxe?" I whispered loudly. I heard commotion toward the middle and caught a glimpse of her profile through the dim light. She waved her hand through the bars.

"Ari?! Ari, I'm over here!" She waved. I jogged over, taking her hands. "What are you doing here? You shouldn't have come," she wept, gripping my fingers.

"Well, I did. I can't leave you down here." I said.

"No, you can, and you will," she said as she placed a hand on my face. "I focused on Luca's thoughts in the study. I know what the gods need you to do. You're going," she ordered.

"I can't. What if he finds Lakan and I'm not here?" I started crying.

"He won't, Ari. I need you to trust me. Go to Bolton. End this. Vetta will keep me safe." She replied tenderly. I remembered Vetta's words to me in my room and Paxe's eyes lit up with realization. "Your mother?" She asked.

"Yes. There's so much I need to tell you," I replied. A tear crept down my face. I unclasped the pendant and closed her fingers around it, covering her whole hand with my own. "Put this on. Vetta told me that my mother's magic is inside it. She left it for my protection. If I am to go, then I want you to keep this close, and keep it hidden." I said.

"But this is meant to protect *you*," she argued.

"I have Luca. I have the gods. If what they're all saying is true, then I'm confident they'll all help to make sure we succeed. Now, put it on." I replied. She secured it around her neck, dropping it beneath the breast of her dress.

The gate door screeched, and Vetta stepped into the hall to warn me that our time was up. I looked at Paxe, terrified that this would be the last time I saw her.

"No, Arienne. Don't. This is not the end. You have to go." She pushed gently on my arms, moving me from her cell. I hesitated. "We will see each other again...I promise. Go. Do what you were born to do," she smiled.

"I love you." I wept.

"I know you do. I love you too...go."

I squeezed my eyes shut and wiped at my face, refusing to look at her as I turned away and ran to Vetta at the end of the hall. As the guard rushed me out of the dungeon and locked the gate, I could faintly hear Paxe crying to herself. If this would be the only chance I had of making my father pay, then I'd do this. Vetta helped me with my bags and we began as fast as her stubby legs were able, making our way back up to meet Luca.

"You put the food in a saddle bag," I pointed out.

"Yes. There are horses waiting for you both at the far west end of the castle," she panted. "When you're ready, ride west until you come to a small village called Aeon. You'll be greeted by an elderly man named Frances. He is my brother, and he'll give you shelter for as long as you need." We neared Luca's room.

"I didn't know you had a brother." I said.

"I've not seen him for many years. We keep contact with each other as best we can. He'll make sure you get to Bolton." I looked at her as we stopped in front of his door.

"Does your brother know about me?" I asked.

"He knows everything. He's waited to help you for a long time," she confessed. I leaned in to hug her and she tightly squeezed my shoulders.

"...Thank you Vetta." I said, closing my eyes.

"I wish you the best, my girl. I'll pray every day for your safe return." Luca's door swung open, and he smiled in condolence as Vetta released me. "The world depends on the two of you. Keep her safe, your Highness," she said tearfully.

Luca took the saddle bag, and shouldered it with his own. Hissifus hobbled out of Luca's room between us looking as if he were with child. Vetta and I stared at Luca in surprise, and he smiled bashfully as he shrugged.

"I promised him a whole chicken," he said.

Vetta chuckled loudly, patting his shoulder and shaking her head. "Get going," she said as she kissed my cheek and motioned toward the Great Hall. I bent down and picked up my tubby cat, cradling him in my arms.

"You are a worthless traitor." I smiled, feeling comforted by his tiny nose as it nuzzled across my face. He purred softly and snuggled into me as I carried him through the hall. We quickly exited the castle, leaving Vetta behind as she watched on. "Vetta said there are horses waiting for us on the west end." I said, looking over to Luca.

He strode beside me nodding. "There are. We have to take cat to the meeting place first." My face scrunched in confusion.

"The meeting place?" I asked.

"Elowen agreed to watch over him for you until we get back, so that he won't be in danger at the castle." He smiled. Warmth filled my insides as I came to the realization that this was the reason he hadn't been in his room earlier on. My replying smile made his eyes spark in satisfaction. "I also found Perla and met her mother in their dress shop. My father sent people to collect her brother and hide him in Crona. He'll be protected in my home until it's safe to leave." I stopped and my mouth dropped open.

"So, your parents will hide him in secret? Paxe is safe?" I asked, as my eyes watered.

"And will remain so." He smiled.

I wrapped my free arm around him, pulling him into me carefully, so as not to squish Hiss. He gently hugged me and planted a kiss on the top of my head. I sniffled in relief, knowing my mother's amulet and Vetta's careful watch would be enough to hold my friend, until I could get her out of that prison.

"Thank you so much." I whispered.

"We need to go, love," he breathed into my hair as he softly pulled away, keeping an arm around me as we headed for the forest.

The meadow seemed so much more alive than when I left it earlier this morning. The colors seemed more vivid, and the swatches of sunlight brighter as if it were enchanted. I supposed it was now that the goddess was babysitting my most precious creature. A soft breeze circled around us as I knelt down to say farewell to my furry child, and it gave me peace of mind. I lifted him to my face, kissing into his fluffy neck.

"I love you," I smiled, setting him gently into the grass. "You better behave or the goddess won't feed you." His mismatched eyes studied me closely as if he knew exactly what I was saying. "You stay here." I wagged my finger at him and he meowed as if in response.

"He'll be alright. He ate enough to last him a week." Luca grinned. "I wouldn't be surprised if he slept it off until we got back."

Hissifus rolled back into the vegetation, his paws flopping back and forth in the air. He seemed happy, and content and it was enough for me to turn away and trust that he was in good hands. We traveled back to the castle, continuing to its west end and finding the horses exactly where Vetta said they would be. A stable attendant greeted us as we approached. He seemed fairly older and kind. He helped load our things onto the horses and didn't do a great deal of talking.

Luca stepped up behind me as I ran my hand across the mare's smooth white coat, petting her neck and admiring her beauty. She was milky, with a healthy mane and strong legs. Luca's horse was also suited to him. A black stallion with a single white strip down his nose.

"This one here is Alice. She's a good girl. Yours is called Bjourne," the attendant said, pointing at Luca's stud. "They both have recently been shoed, bathed and well fed. You should have an easy ride until Aeon," he smiled.

"How far is Aeon?" I asked.

"It's a full day's ride, mi'lady. If you go now without making many stops, you should be there by this time tomorrow." He replied.

"Is it safe to camp if we don't?" Luca asked.

"It is, my Lord. Though you need to make sure you're prepared. There isn't anything for a long way hence, other than grassland."

Luca looked at me assuredly. "Ready, Princess?" I nodded, and he helped me up onto Alice's back. I situated myself in the saddle, and took the reins while Luca mounted his horse. I stared back at the castle, getting lost in my thoughts when Luca spoke again. "Shall we?"

"Let's ride." I answered, shaking the straps.

"May the gods be with you both. Safe journey," the attendant smiled as he waved us off.

Our horses started forward, picking up speed as we left the castle grounds and headed into the lands beyond.

CHAPTER 10

DISTANCE

The vast expanse of grassy fields upon leaving the castle was exactly what the stable attendant had described. There were small trees scattered here and there—large rocks sitting by themselves in random places; long blades of grass that jutted out all around us, and a faint beaten trail that we hoped was made by the wear of travelers as we rode along it. Vetta had thankfully packed a map in my things, but there was no road drawn on it that I could see—only a single village between my home and Bolton.

To our right, far off in the distance, we could see the Horned Mountains; the darkness above it was unsettling and ominous. I was thankful we weren't any closer to them. They made my whole body feel as if it were crawling with unseen insects. Our pace was fast and steady for much of the start of our journey to Aeon, which according to the map, seemed to be a halfway point to the sea. We had just started to slow down to give the horses a chance to rest, and I pulled the map open again.

"If we keep riding, it looks like there's a small lake close to Aeon. We could stop there and water the horses?" I stated. "They'll probably need it once we get that far, but it's hard to tell exactly how far everything is from each other on this map."

"Let's see how we feel when the lake comes into view. If you're tired by the time we get to it, we can camp there for the night, but if not, I agree we should stop and let them rest either way," Luca replied, reaching for the canteen tied behind him. I folded the map and slid it into a side pocket on the saddlebag, turning my gaze back to the mountain range. "Are you alright?" He asked.

"Define alright," I replied, still looking right.

"You've been a little quiet since we left the castle grounds. We've been riding for almost three hours." I didn't respond. "We've got a pretty long ride if you want to talk about it," he pushed. I looked forward at the empty fields ahead.

"I saw Paxe in the dungeon. Vetta got me a few seconds with her, and I can't get it out of my head." I said sadly. He looked at me but didn't reply. He was here to listen. "I feel like she's safe. Even more so now that you did what you did. I gave her the pendant my mother left me to protect her, but I hate the thought of her spending possibly *weeks* in that place. I don't have words for how grateful I am to you, Luca."

"You don't need to thank me. We're all in this together, Princess. All of us have our parts to play, and we all want to see him fall. He'll pay for everything he's done. She seems like a very strong-willed female. I can tell how much the two of you care for each other," he replied.

"Besides Vetta, each other has been all we've ever had. She's like a sister to me. I know that's why he wants to use her to hurt me." Luca was quiet for a moment.

"Where is her family?" He asked. I shook my head.

"She doesn't have any family. Before my mother fell pregnant with me, she had gone into the kitchens one night while everyone was preparing supper, and there she met Paxe's mother. Her name was Isabelle and she worked in our castle. She had already given birth to Paxe...I think she was only a few months old. Vetta told me that Isabelle had been beaten pretty badly that night. I've always assumed it was by Paxe's father. Anyway, she was there helping while the baby played around the floor, and my mother couldn't let it go. She gave her a position as her aide and kept close eyes on her and Paxe, up until I was born. After my mother died, Isabelle didn't have anyone to tend to and I think she went back to being just general help. When Paxe and I were toddlers, one of the guards saw Isabelle leap from an upper floor window. There was nothing they could do for her. Vetta has taken care of us ever since." I looked over and found his face drawn with sympathy. I smiled at him.

"What?" He asked.

"She would absolutely hate the look of pity you have right now," I giggled. He scoffed, nodding in understanding.

"She seems tough, Ari. I don't think you need to worry about her. You said your mother's pendant would protect her. Is it blessed?" He asked.

"Mmhmm," I hummed. I started thinking about what Vetta revealed to me in my room and my conscience got the better of me. "Luca...I think there's something you should know. Perhaps, I should have said something before we left for Aeon." I started. He looked at me with intrigue.

"Why do I get the feeling that this isn't something good?" He asked nervously.

"To be honest, I'm not sure how I even feel about it. I suppose... I wouldn't call it bad, but it also could change the way you feel about moving forward." I turned my face ahead again.

"Gods...what is it?" He asked again, and I could see through my peripheral that he kept his eyes focused on me. The amount of time I spent thinking about how to explain it must have felt like an eternity for him. I sighed loudly.

"When I went upstairs to pack, Vetta was already there doing it. I was obviously upset about Paxe's arrest, and I cried on her. She told me to trust the gods, and I asked her what she knew that she wasn't letting on..." I paused, nervous about how he'd react.

"...And?" He continued. I sighed again.

"And she said she knew everything. I got frustrated after she told me that I'd know *in time*...and I broke an old vase on the wall."

"You're worried I'm going to find out you have a temper?" He laughed sarcastically. "You've gotten physical with me twice, and not in a good way," he smiled. I rolled my eyes.

"No, Luca. I'm struggling here. I really don't know how to say this," I pleaded.

"I know, I'm sorry. I guess I'm struggling too. You've got me really nervous. Whatever it is, you don't have to worry. I'm not going anywhere," he assured.

"I wouldn't promise that just yet," I argued, shaking my head again.

"Then maybe you should just say it," he said firmly. I wasn't very fond of the tone he had then. It got me a little fired up, and so I ended up spitting it out a bit more forcefully than I had intended.

"Fine. Vetta told me that my mother died in sacrifice to the gods and that I was the offering she made. The gods will wield me as a weapon against my father, as per their agreement. But she also made sure that I would never be alone..." I paused. His face turned wary. "The gods have joined our souls. When you said in the forest that you couldn't stay away from me and that your very skin had a need to touch me...I believe it's because your soul is aching for mine. It makes sense to me now why I also seem to have such a hard time fighting off my attraction to you. By their standards, you and I are fated to love each other." I grew quiet.

"Why would you think I'd leave you because of this?" He asked. I shot my face toward him, tugging my reins and stopping us. He did the same.

"Because... Luca, yet again, it gives you no choice! It gives *us* no choice! And I don't know exactly how it will make you feel to know that your feelings for me aren't your own. I'm not completely against this myself, but I'd be lying to you if I said that it didn't bother me, that allowing myself to love you would also just be part of their big plan. Neither of us get to make any decisions for ourselves. It's like this shitty map in my bag! Follow it as best you can, and hopefully, you'll get to where you need to go!"

In my frustration, I didn't realize how much my words could sting, but they seemed as though they did when I looked into his eyes. He looked hurt, and I immediately wanted to kick myself for the way it came out. His jaw twitched and he looked at me under his brows. I swallowed hard as I watched him tap his heels against his horse, and Bjourne started trotting forward, leaving me behind. I decided against calling out for him and kept a slower pace behind them, not wanting to make it any worse.

We rode that way for a couple more hours until the sun began to dip lower in the sky, painting it a beautiful gradient of orange and purple. A blanket of small puffs glowed in bright yellow over the horizon, and I caught their reflection, beaming off a small body of water off the path to our left. We had made it to the lake before dark. The idea of setting up camp started to seem desirable as my body continued to feel more and more worn out from our night in the woods and the grueling ride. Not to mention, the emotional turmoil I faced when we returned to the castle earlier today. A hard sleep was desperately needed.

Luca strayed off the path in front of me, riding into a sprint toward the lake and I followed. The banks surrounding the water were mostly dry; it looked like the lake had been receding for a while. There was a single scrawny tree near it, which appeared to be the perfect size to tie the horses for the night. I dismounted Alice and led her to the water's edge; she drank heavily. Luca was busy unloading bags from his own horse near the tree, and I gathered that he had decided camping was a good idea as well. He certainly didn't ask my opinion. I couldn't blame him for being upset with me but as many arguments as we'd had since we met...this definitely felt worse than any of them. The oddest part was that he didn't even actually fight with me, and I still felt as if someone had thwacked me in the heart with a sledgehammer. As much as I'd wished he'd just leave me alone before, now it just felt unbearable.

He dutifully ignored me as he walked over to water Bjourne and started removing my things, shouldering as much as he could carry and walking them back to the tree. I wanted so badly to say something or help, but I couldn't muster the courage. The saddlebag full of food was the only thing left on Alice's back, and I plundered through it, digging out two large carrots that I assumed Vetta had left to feed the horses. I stepped between them, holding a carrot in each hand, and they graciously accepted. I turned back in time to find Luca pulling the saddlebag off and carrying it to the camp. No longer able to shake the feeling that I was being useless, I started poking around the shore, looking for large rocks to use for a fire.

I brought as many as I could find up to the tree where Luca was setting up a small tent and began placing them in a circle. I looked around for any wood we could burn but came up empty, so I started climbing the tree. I hoisted myself onto a sturdy enough branch and managed to break off several good-sized pieces that I thought may hold us until we turned in for the night, and dropped them to the ground below. As I hopped out of the tree, I glanced towards Luca and my breath caught sharply in my throat.

Holy mother of—

Luca's shirtless back was turned toward me as he busied himself with the tent that was now nearly finished. I stared at every muscle that twitched as he secured ties and wiggled stakes to be sure they were sturdy. His skin was damp with sweat, as was his hair, with loose pieces from his hair strap stuck to his neck. His stance was magnified without the oversized shirt, and his back stood proudly over a perfectly sculpted backside, which to my irritation, was still covered with dark gray pants. He started to turn, and I quickly looked away, pretending to be busy setting up wood in the stone circle. The sky was darkening quickly and I made my way toward the shore to fetch the horses, needing to put some distance between us and gather myself.

I took a few deep breaths as I led the horses back to the tree, tying them off and peeking around the narrow trunk as Luca expertly lit the fire with flint and dried grass. As the glow became a bit brighter, my eyes caught something peculiar. A small round symbol, hidden beneath what tiny amount of chest hair he had. It looked familiar, but I had trouble placing where I'd seen it before. It almost glistened in the light as if it were wet, dark blue in color and placed right over his heart. I looked away, pulling off the tree and scrunching my eyebrows together, as I racked my brain trying to figure out why I felt like I should know what I was looking at. I had nothing.

Luca managed to dig a tiny pot from the bags, filling it with some stewed beef and potatoes that Vetta had sealed into a glass jar. He placed it in a flat spot on top of the fire and let it warm while he fished out two tin mugs and some flatware. I came from around the tree to the fire and stood, crossing my arms and looking into the pot.

"Umm..." I started. He didn't look up. "How long until it's ready?" He shrugged, finally meeting my eyes. He still looked upset.

"Not long. Five minutes, maybe," he answered, holding my stare for a moment before looking back down and stirring the stew.

"Can we talk?" I asked. He didn't respond for a moment, continuing to stir.

"Not right now," he said simply. His voice was low, and loose strands of his hair dangled into his face. It took all my effort not to plead with him and tell him how sorry I was. No longer feeling hungry, I moved around the fire and stepped into the tent, grabbing a towel out of my bag and pulling off my boots. I reached back to pull the strings of my corset, loosening it and taking it off. I threw it back into my bag and finished undressing as I wrapped myself in the towel and stepped barefoot out of the tent, passing Luca and making for the lake. I didn't bother looking back, but I could feel his stare as I walked into the darkness. It cloaked enough of me, as the moon hadn't fully risen, to drop my towel and step into the water.

I waded in and the water felt warm at first but began to cool a bit as I continued about waist-deep. I released my braid and shook it out as I submerged. I closed my eyes under the water for a moment and let out a frustrated scream that I knew would be muted and kept secret by the dark lake. Feeling a little more relieved, I stood, taking a deep breath and palming back my wet hair. I swam for a while, enjoying the peace and quiet, and floated on my back, trying to ignore the tension between Luca and me. I watched the moon travel higher into the heavens, and as beautiful as it was, it still felt like a giant clock looming over me—I may have just doomed myself with the only way to stop it.

Why am I so damn stubborn? How did you even know I'd actually love him? How am I to even know if these are true feelings or just this elaborate game you set up for me? How could you just strike a deal like this and leave me here to do this, all on my own? What should I say to him? Can you even hear me, mother?

As if in answer, a bright star trailed across the sky. The water around me shimmered in its image and a tingle of overwhelming peace covered my body. My eyes widened in amazement and I lifted myself from the water. I breathed loudly and covered my mouth with my hand. I grabbed a handful of my hair, rang it out and started wading to the shore. I stepped out, grabbing the towel and squeezing it around my locks before wrapping it around myself, quickly making my way back to the camp.

I approached the slowly weakening fire and noticed a tin cup filled with stew and a spoon resting on one of the large rocks to keep it warm. The flaps of the tent were unrolled, draping over the entrance. I moved them aside, stepping into the tent, and found Luca sleeping quietly on his side, with his back turned toward me. He had laid out blankets and set my bag on the far left side of the tent for me. I got to my knees, pulling out a short nightshift and checking behind me to make sure I hadn't disturbed Luca before removing my towel. I wrapped my hair in it one more time, squeezing as much water out as I could, before I slipped the shift over my head, pulling my long wet hair from beneath it, as it fell comfortably around me. Luca was silent and unmoved when I checked back over my shoulder. I left the tent as quietly as I could, clutching a blanket and going out to retrieve my supper.

I folded the blanket over once and placed it on the ground as I grabbed the tin cup and sat on my knees, wondering how long it would take him to forgive my forthrightness from earlier today. A deep sigh escaped me as I spooned some stew into my mouth. As I chewed, I realized that my body was screaming for nourishment that I was denying it yet again, stressfully unaware that I hadn't eaten anything but an apple this morning on our way back through the woods. So much has happened in the course of a few days that it felt like it had been months instead. A man that I was starting to feel deeply for, I barely knew...but felt like we've already been through so much. I couldn't talk to Paxe about anything that's happened or get her romantic advice, as she was caged up like an animal back at home. I had no one to turn to and no ear to spill secrets in, and I started to really miss arguing with the male that slept peacefully in the tent. I mouthed another spoonful and my stomach gurgled over it, attacking like a rabid dog.

A rustling sound from behind me broke through my sulking, and Luca appeared carrying the remains of the stew in the small pot. He circled the stones and tossed some dry grass and a couple of pieces of wood in the fire, setting the pot on top. I tried not to look at him as I stirred a potato around in my cup. He came and sat next to me on the blanket, spreading his legs and lifting his knees. His shirt was still missing, and now, so were his boots. His hair fell around his face and down his back, completely unbound. As hard as I tried to keep my mouth shut, my mind kept screaming at me that he had come out for a reason.

"Did I wake you?" I asked softly. He shook his head, keeping his eye on the growing fire.

"I wasn't asleep," he admitted. My belly fluttered at the thought of him possibly seeing my naked body, but I reminded myself that Luca was a respectful individual with morals. He leaned forward to grab the pot and set it down quickly on the blanket as he shook his hand around and cursed under his breath. He took the spoon from my hand as he resumed his previous position and started refilling my tin cup with the stew.

"It's okay, I'm not that hungry," I said, holding my hand up to stop him. He continued to fill it to the rim and stuck the spoon back into the cup.

"Your stomach says otherwise," he reprimanded, resting his arms over his knees. I blew the steaming spoon gently and took another bite.

"...Thank you," I mumbled into my cup. He stared into the fire and nodded. He kept quiet as I slowly ate as much as I could stomach, finally lowering my cup to the ground beside me. "I'm sorry, Luca." I said as I looked over at him. He turned his head and his eyes went straight for mine, and the look he gave me was pleading. It reminded me of the way Paxe's eyes looked in the study, and if I thought I couldn't feel any worse, he proved me wrong.

"Sorry for what exactly, Princess?" He asked in a low tone.

"I obviously hurt you, and it wasn't my intention. I just wanted to be honest, but it came out wrong." He shook his head, not breaking our stare.

"No, I think it came out the way that you meant it. There's nothing wrong with that. I just think that our perspectives are completely different." The firelight glowed on the side of his face, catching his eyes and making the whole situation more uncomfortable. I suppose it was what I deserved.

"Different, how?" I asked.

"It doesn't sound to me like you're ready to hear mine," he said simply. My eyebrows scrunched.

"I've waited all evening to talk to you," I said.

"That doesn't mean that you're ready, Ari." He replied, his eyes seeming sadder.

"Tell me anyway."

"If I do, then you have to promise not to say a word until I finish," he offered. I narrowed my eyes.

"Okay." I agreed, leaning on my left thigh and supporting my weight with my hand as I turned my body to face him.

"Before you went upstairs and found out about your mother, you held my hand the entire way through the castle. Before that, you stayed close to me the entire way back through the woods...and before that?" He paused. "Before that, you spent an entire night in my arms, and I didn't feel as though that was much of a discomfort to you." His gaze grew deeper and I swallowed hard. "Then we get out here and you tell me about the gods joining our souls and how you weren't completely against the idea but that it bothered you that being with me was just part of the plan." I started to open my mouth and he tilted his head. I closed it, pursing my lips.

"It seems like what bothers you the most is that you think, because all of this is sealed in prophecy, that we don't have a choice in how we feel. You even said specifically that my feelings for you aren't my own. I'm not saying that I don't see your point, but let me be clear about mine. I've known that my marriage to you would be chosen by someone other than me... my entire life.

I understand that you didn't have the luxury of growing up with parents that could show you that an arranged marriage isn't always a terrible thing and that love does grow if two people that are suited for each other are put together." He turned his body to face me.

"Just because we're soulmates...just because we'd be married even if the gods had never bound us like this...it doesn't mean that my choice is invalid. Nor does it mean that what I feel for you doesn't belong to me. If I had the choice to marry a dozen other royals, Arienne...I would *still* choose you." An entire doorknob started to grow in my throat, and I fought hard to swallow it down as his eyes stared through my soul.

"When you told me that your mother had handpicked me for her daughter so that she wouldn't be alone...the only thing that came to my mind was that I wished so much I could thank her for giving me the greatest gift of my *life*. I thought about a little boy still pissing his pants, who ran around in a castle by the sea. An infant that could barely walk, with drool hanging from his chin...completely unaware that a life had just come into the world that was going to change everything, and *I get to love her.*" His eyes began to turn glassy, and my urge to cry was nearly unbearable.

"Don't you understand? We *do* have a choice. No matter what's written in the stars. I chose you the moment you pointed that finger at me in the woods and started firing off that smart mouth. The moment you trusted me with your darkest moments by that fire and let me finally hold you for the first time. You've been my choice before I ever even knew what you looked like, how your hair smelled, or the way you make me want to burn this entire world down just to be near you every time you look at me. I would tear anyone, limb from limb, for even thinking of harming you or breaking your heart, and that was precisely the reason I made that deal with your father without an ounce of hesitation." He shook his head gently.

"But, when you told me how much it upset you when you found out the real reason we're together, it made me realize that everything I thought you were beginning to feel before you went into that room, wasn't real for you, at all. It's alright, I do understand. I know that it has little to do with me and everything to do with what's happened to you. I know that love takes time and I'm more than willing to be patient. I told you that I would be here with you through all of this, even if you never love me and... I meant that. I *still* mean it. I want you to be happy. I want you to find joy in your life, even if it never comes from me. I want *you*. But yes...it did hurt to find out that even after what we've already made it through...you still don't seem close to wanting me." A tear left my eye as I shook my head and reached for his hand. He pulled away.

"It's okay, Ari. Honestly...I don't expect you to just yet. I'm an adult and I can weather a little blow to my heart. This isn't your fault. I just need a little time to shake it off...alright?" He leaned forward and took the side of my face in his hand, staring into me as if the hardest thing he could ever do was get up and walk away. But he did just that. He stepped into the tent and the ache that had taken over my chest grew into a deep trench of emotions that I'd never felt before. Every feeling I thought I'd had about Gideon seemed like a mud puddle compared to what I suddenly realized I felt now. The short distance between where I sat and where Luca was now seemed way too far apart...and it was killing me.

"If you know, then tell him. It's time," a soft female voice I didn't recognize, spoke softly in my mind. I looked around for the voice, finding nothing, until my eyes looked towards the sky and another star fell...slowly and consolingly as if it understood my heart completely. Everything Luca had said was right. Everything, except one detail.

I do want him. I've never wanted anything more in my life.

I didn't waste a second more, deciding that I was done being afraid of taking control over my life. Home was far away from me. My cruel father was far away from me. Everything that had happened to me was to stay in my past...where I had declared it would, the night that I said it all out loud. This was my life. He was my gift...my soulmate. And if we had only known each other for a few short days, then so be it. These carefully laid plans could go belly up, and a few days might be all we'll ever have. I silently nodded to the sky and stood, turning to enter the tent.

Luca sat against the right side in about the same way that he had been sitting next to me out on the blanket. His elbows were propped on his knees, and his fingers were buried in the thick black hair that crowned his forehead as his face raised up to look at me. I stepped in front of him, kneeling down and taking his hands into mine. I looked him in the eye and slowly shook my head.

"You're wrong," I said softly. "I know I'm difficult, Luca...but you're wrong. I do want you." I climbed into his lap, my nightshift slightly riding up my thighs as I rested them on each side of his. He put his hands on each of my shoulders and leaned backward, trying to stop me.

"Ari, you don't ha—"

"No, Luca...look at me." I interrupted, taking his face into my hands. He did, and my heart raced as I leaned forward, my right hand stroking his stubble and trailing my thumb across his bottom lip. I didn't ask him to kiss me. I tilted his chin up and softly placed my lips to his, never taking my eyes from him. He kissed me back and my body trembled with nerves. Our foreheads pressed together and our breathing shuddered as his right hand pushed my hair back and rested on my face.

"How do you feel?" He whispered against my lips. I closed my eyes.

"Like a fool," I replied. "I'll never fight this again, I'm so sorry. I was angry...and scared." His fingertips grazed my jaw.

"And now?" He asked, our breathing becoming heavier.

I pressed my body against him and claimed his mouth, no longer able to control myself. I breathed in deeply through my nose, and his left hand dropped from my shoulder, tugging the material of my shift with his movement as his arm wrapped around my back and pulled me closer. Our kiss grew intense, my hands reached around the back of his neck and I could feel his body heating against me. I had only kissed one other man...and only once. I remembered how it felt, and I thought back then that the fire between Gideon and I was something real. It may have been, but I was suddenly second-guessing everything when what I felt in this moment far surpassed anything I had ever experienced before. He slipped his tongue into my mouth, and I lost all my senses when I tasted him.

My body reacted almost wholly on its own and I raised myself higher, deepening our kiss and tasting him again. The front of my gown was never secured with the laces, and the weight of the material pulled it down my shoulder, exposing it...and a good portion of my right breast as it dropped. Luca's hand moved from my back to my thigh, gripping it firmly, just underneath my bare cheek. His other hand tilted my head backward and he broke our kiss as he leaned into my neck, breathing into it. I felt the combination of his lips as well as his tongue as it traveled from beneath my chin to the side of my neck...and then further down to my collarbone. I exhaled sharply, lowering myself back down into his lap, and felt the bulge in the front of his pants harden against me as I came to rest on top of it. His teeth closed together gently on my skin in response and I gasped, involuntarily gripping his hair.

I felt an irrevocable need beginning to pool at the apex of my thighs, and my body shook with its desire to be touched. My head fell forward and our eyes met, both of us finding it difficult to breathe. He lifted me from his lap and laid me down on the blankets, resting himself on his side next to me, and leaning over my body. I raised my head to kiss him again and he let me, taking the side of my face and gently leaning in to guide my head back to the ground. His soft hair brushed against my breast, which had fallen completely out of my shift, and my nipple stiffened at the sensation and exposure. I reached up and tucked it behind his left ear, and we existed in that kiss for a few long moments. It was still a bit forceful and passionate, but also tender, and filled every hole that my father had ripped through my heart...holes that I thought could never be repaired.

Give that heart to someone who might be able to repair it for you.

I did. Right there. I felt a rush of emotions as the full acceptance of my decision registered with my very soul, and I thought I could cry. Luca stopped and stared down at me as if he felt it too. His gray eyes turned brighter and a smile I'd never seen him wear before began to take shape across his face.

"I think I may be in love with you, Luca." I said breathlessly.

He pressed his head against mine, closing his eyes and breathing heavily.

"I swear, I just *felt* you say it before it even came out of your mouth," he replied. His fingers trailed down the side of my neck and over the leather bow still draped over my chest, stopping between my breasts and resting over my pounding heart. "This is mine?" He whispered.

"It's yours," I breathed, kissing him again. It started slowly, but became crippling. I almost choked with desperation for him when his lips left mine and he lowered his head, kissing softly where his fingers had been. My chest heaved up and down as his hand cupped the lower part of my breast and he kissed the inside, working his way up and taking my nipple into his mouth. I closed my eyes as my fingers fought their way through his hair, and my skin tingled; an unfamiliar feeling began to gather between my legs.

"...Luca...are you using magic on me?" I gasped.

"Of a sort..." he whispered, continuing to roll his tongue over my nipple. I took in as much air as I could—the feeling became moist and another one began to build in my lower belly.

"Is this part of your gift?" I choked. He snickered through his nose and hummed over my breast as he sucked at the side.

"Not the one you're thinking of," he continued.

I raised my knee, growing increasingly restless as the sensation became stronger, and my heart felt as if it would explode from my chest. I had no idea what was happening, only that I needed to be touched. There. Right now. I grabbed Luca's hand at my breast and slowly pushed it down my middle. He didn't seem to need any further direction as he lightly trailed it further down and then up to my raised knee, gently pushing it to the side and spreading my legs further apart. His hand curled beneath my knee and traveled further up in an agonizingly slow movement. He raised his head, giving me a smoldering stare as every nerve in my body felt as if they were up in flames. His fingertips drew nearer to where I needed them most, and I couldn't breathe.

Gods...I'm going to die. I'm going to die.

He laid his fingers softly over my entrance, dipping them slightly inside and slowly dragged them up, touching the very heart of my pulsing need. My mouth opened and my eyes widened in the sudden intrusion of, undoubtedly, the most amazing feeling my body had ever experienced. I grabbed Luca's arm, gasping for precious oxygen as he slowly circled that spot, occasionally grazing over it and burning me alive with the victorious half-smile that graced his lips. He moved his mouth over mine, slipping his finger between my folds and slowly up inside me, catching the moan that tried to escape my lips in a devastating kiss. My back arched off the floor, and I clawed the skin on his shoulder as he slowly drew his finger out, and added a second, pushing them back inside, his thumb resting over the spot he had just left.

I moaned loudly into his mouth and he released it, allowing my head to fall back and claiming my neck with his teeth as he moved his fingers in and out of me. I closed my eyes and lowered my brows as I fought valiantly against my lungs that seemed as though they were ready to give up. My body started to tense and the sensation that had been building felt twice as potent. I thought my heart might fail me as he quickened his pace and snuck up to my ear lobe, tickling the tender skin behind it with his stubble. My other hand gripped his hair tightly, and he released a sharp breath against the shell of my ear.

"Luca!" I started, helplessly. "...Luca I can't...I can't breathe." He twisted his fingers slightly in response, curling them inside me and pressing his thumb firmly against the most sensitive part of my body. I nearly screamed as I gave in, and a tidal wave of absolute euphoria tore through me.

"Let it go, love," he whispered against my ear. "Look at me." I turned my head and our eyes locked, the silver fire in his stare throwing my body into deeper waves of bliss. His hand moved with me, through every last one of them as our breath mingled. I finally closed my eyes, whimpering softly as he kissed me again. He retreated his fingers, pulling them slowly out and spreading my slick arousal over my center. My legs quaked right along with the rest of me as my release robbed me of the last of my air. Luca kissed across my jawline gently as I panted, slowly beginning to calm. I lowered my knee as he pulled my shift down to cover my lower half and then reached up to do the same for my breast. "Come here," he said softly as he rolled onto his back and reached for me.

I accepted the invitation, turning on my side and laying my head on his chest. He took my hand and pulled my arm onto him, resting it in the center of his chest and trailing his fingers up and down my limb. His other arm held me snugly against his body. I'd never felt so much at once...nothing good anyway, and I struggled to figure out what to do with it. He leaned down and kissed the top of my head, my body still trembling against him.

"Are you alright?" He asked quietly. I didn't open my eyes as I laid there, and a smile crept across my face.

"Define alright," I joked, perhaps a bit too soon. He chuckled against my hair and I couldn't help but giggle myself as I didn't even feel in my right state of mind. "What the hell just happened to me?" I asked.

"That?...That was the result of being treated the way you should always be treated," he replied.

"With the help of your abilities." I chimed. He laughed.

"No. I told you I'd only do that if you asked me to, remember?" I raised my face and looked at him, puzzled. "That was all you. Natural." I opened my mouth, but nothing came out. "That's the way it's supposed to be. One day, I hope to show you more." He stared into my eyes for a moment and then kissed me softly. "Rest, love. We probably don't have long until morning."

I sank back into his body, hardly able to keep my eyes open. His hand found mine and I raised my palm to his, turning it slightly and interlocking our fingers. I closed my eyes, lazily smiling to myself.

".....Luca..." I whispered.

"Mmm?" He grunted.

"...I love you."

He pulled me in closer, squeezing my hand.

"I love you too, Princess," he whispered back.

CHAPTER 11

THE MORE YOU KNOW

I woke that morning hardly any different than how I had fallen asleep, save for my bare leg that I had flung over Luca's. The sun was out—it was fairly bright as it broke in through the flapping entrance to the tent. It was quite windy and the material that sheltered us rattled back and forth. I wondered how late it must be but outright refused to move, as the exhaustion in my limbs was still very present. I had never felt more peaceful as I woke up for the second day in a row in his arms. Luca was a quiet sleeper. As I raised my face to look at him, I couldn't help but think that he reminded me of the way an infant would dream...if an infant had the body of a god and facial hair.

I smiled as I watched him and started to reflect on everything that had happened last night. All the things he said...what we had done. The fact that I completely surrendered my heart to a male that I had met only days ago... and was absolutely fine with it.

I must be barking mad. And I don't care.

I wanted so badly to talk to Paxe and drink wine in the bathing pool, sharing secrets and all the details that make you blush. I missed her terribly and wondered how she was doing, and whether Vetta was able to keep her comfortable. The look she'd have on her face when she filtered through all my thoughts would probably be hysterical. After this experience, I fully understood why she'd risk it all for Lakan. Everything was beginning to become clearer, and in some strange way, I felt...older or perhaps, a bit more adult. I wasn't sure.

I ran my fingers over his hard stomach, trailing across the fine line of hair that traveled up to his chest and spread out across it. I watched his breathing and traced around the small design I had seen the night before. He stirred a little, stretching and slowly opening his eyes.

"I know we can't...but I could exist here for the rest of the day with you, doing that," he yawned, bringing his arm back down around me. I smiled up at him. Everything felt different today, and I knew that after last night, it would, of course, never be the same. Either way, I agreed that I didn't want it to end just yet.

"Would you settle for a few more minutes?" I asked in a sleepy haze.

"Well...twist my arm," he smiled, situating his other arm behind his head and staring down at me. I felt over the symbol again, still not knowing why it seemed so familiar. I looked back down at it.

"What does this mean?" I asked. He stayed quiet. When it became clear that he didn't want to answer, I looked up again to find him staring at me nervously. "....Luca?" My expression turned grave with worry. "What's wrong?"

"Nothing, love. Everything is perfect. Why don't I explain that later?" He offered. I could tell by the look in his eyes that he was nearly begging to put this conversation off. Truthfully, it only made me more curious and now anxious as well. I let it go and softly nodded.

"Okay..." I smiled. "Can we talk about something else?"

"Of course. What's on your mind?" He asked, his tension easing when I changed the subject.

"Well, everything really. I'm just confused about some things. I was hoping to get some clarity," I said, feeling my cheeks tingle with sheepishness. I don't know why, but I felt a little embarrassed about my lack of knowledge when it came to any kind of intimacy. I knew that he understood and would never judge me, but it still felt awkward to discuss.

"Ask me anything," he smiled. I felt hesitant for a moment but decided to get the most obvious question out of the way.

"Last night, you told me that what happened to me was a result of being treated well. I follow, but I've never felt like that in my life. Don't you dare laugh..." I raised myself onto my elbow to look at him.

"I would never," he smiled. "What do you want to know?"

"I thought something was wrong with me. I couldn't breathe and it just kept getting stronger...I...I thought I was dying." His grin was ridiculous, but he didn't laugh.

"No, quite the opposite. Though I can think of worse ways to go." He pulled his arm from behind his head, and barely touched the skin at my neck. His fingertips brushed lightly down to the open laces of my shift and between my breasts. I shuddered. "How does it feel when I touch you like this?" He asked in a low voice.

"It tickles a bit," I smiled. He raised himself up and leaned closer, his lips barely brushing against my ear lobe.

"You know that's not what I mean," his voice turned sultry as he whispered against my skin. I started breathing deeply as his fingers moved slowly over the thin fabric of my shift, down my middle. "What about now?"

"I can feel it again..." I breathed, pressing myself against him. He moved his hand away from where I was hoping it would go and turned my face to kiss me.

"That's your body letting you know it's pleased and it wants more. The more it gets...the more that builds. Eventually, it releases itself..." He kissed me again. "...and calms back down." He laid back down, putting his arm back under his head and smiling at me. I left my mouth open, sneering at him like the monster he just proved to be. "You look flushed." He chuckled. I shook my head slowly.

"You prick," I snapped, elbowing his side. He grunted but continued to laugh under his breath. "How do you know what to do?" I continued curiously.

"The same way you knew where you wanted my hand to be when you pushed it down."

Fair enough. That makes sense.

"It didn't hurt me at all when you..." I started bashfully, not knowing how to finish that statement. "...when you were inside. I didn't expect that." His smile grew wider.

"I'm glad...and I could tell. But you should know...my touch may feel one way, but if *I'm* inside you, I can't promise that it may not hurt a little." I swallowed. "All joking aside, Ari..." His face became serious. "...physical intimacy was never supposed to feel the way that it felt for you your first time. You have nothing to be ashamed of, and trust me; I have absolutely no problem spending days making that up to your body. You deserve to know what real intimacy feels like."

I beamed at him, truly grateful that out of all the people in this world, the one that was chosen for me was this one. I didn't even feel like I deserved him. My wrecked existence was never his burden to bear, but he did it anyway, with so much pride. My heart felt full for the first time in my life. He sat up, kissed my cheek and reached into his pocket, pulling out a leather strap.

"As much as I wish we could stay, we should get going," he frowned as he gathered his hair behind his head, tying it loosely. "I'm going to go feed and water the horses and let you get dressed." He said, grazing his thumb across my chin and scooting over to fetch his boots. I watched every muscle in his back and arms as he pulled them on. He smiled over his shoulder as he stood, bending forward to leave the tent. He gave me a wink on his way out, and I waited until he was out of view before I plopped onto my back, covering my mouth with my hand and grinning like a mischievous child.

When I finally forced myself to get motivated for another long ride, I took into account the blustery weather and opted for leather leggings again, black ones this time, pairing them with a form-fitting dark blue tunic with long sleeves. Not having Paxe or a mirror handy to braid the hair away from my face, I twisted my long curls in a loose spiral behind my head. I tugged the leather bow free from around my neck and tied it snugly around the bun, testing its security with a wiggle for good measure. I started packing our blankets and clothes and double-checked my bag for the weapons, just in case they decided to grow themselves legs and flee. I found Luca's black muslin shirt in the corner of the tent and started to put it inside his bag, but involuntarily brought it to my nose instead. My heart fluttered and I lowered the shirt back down, rolling my eyes at myself.

Yeah...you've got it bad. How did this even happen?

Knowing he hadn't had his chance to get dressed to leave yet, I laid the items on top of his bag, grabbing my own and shouldering it as I stepped outside. Luca had picked up everything that had blown around. I noticed that he had shaken out the blanket I had left outside last night and draped it over one of the branches of the tree. He was over by the lake with the horses, washing the small pot and the tin cups. I sat my bag down and collected the blanket from the tree, folding it small enough to fit back into it. Now that it was bright enough to get a better view, I looked around at where we found ourselves. It was a beautiful day, but a bit brisker than the day before, and it looked as if a storm was making its way towards us from back home. My mind flashed back to the squall in the forest, and I wondered if it was just the usual weather that accompanied the transitional month between spring and summer, or my father's short fuse.

Luca walked the horses back up to meet me by the tree, and gave me a thorough inspection with his eyes. He smiled as he tied the horses off, and I made my way around him to start loading Alice up with my things.

"You look beautiful," he said. I didn't look up as I focused on what I was doing but smiled gratefully in regard to the fact that the entire mood was so much better than the last time we had been out here together. He popped in and out of the tent busily as he made quick work of disassembling it while making sure to finish loading everything up in the meantime. By the time I had finally finished securing the rest and was stopping to take a drink from my canteen, he was joining me with our rolled-up shelter, wearing a shirt nearly the exact color of mine. I swallowed down my water, wiping at my mouth with the end of my sleeve as I slammed the cork into the jug and studied him with a side grin.

"Lovely color," I laughed. He brushed his hands down the front of his garment, looking down at it with an arrogant smirk and annoyingly admiring himself. It fit close and showed off the perfect mold of his torso and broad shoulders. The material was a little thicker than mine, but soft and pliant with long, loose sleeves and a low neckline.

"I thought so, too," he replied. I rolled my eyes and started tying my jug to the saddle. He reached into the bag of food and pulled out a small loaf of cinnamon bread, tearing it in half and handing one to me. "Ready to ride?" He asked as he took a bite. I nodded and took notice of the difference in his handling of me as he helped me up onto my horse. He released the ties from the tree, climbed into his saddle and we started towards the path that was now harder to see as the wind blew the long grass in every direction.

"We're going to have to pay closer attention to this today, or I feel like we'll end up turned around like we were in the forest," I pointed out, riding next to him and taking in our surroundings.

"I checked the map while you were getting dressed. As long as we keep the Horned Mountains to our right, I feel confident we'll reach Aeon before nightfall, but we should keep any stops to a minimum," he assured me.

"What about that?" I asked, looking over my shoulder at the dark clouds gathering behind us. He looked at the growing storm and then back to me, smiling.

"Ride like the wind?" He shrugged.

"That's comforting," I grinned as I bit off a chunk of my bread. He laughed and mimicked my eating, which, in my opinion, was overly dramatic.

"What is with you, and how I eat my food?" I asked, obnoxiously chewing just to spite him. "You did that in the woods when I was mad at you." I reminded him.

"I find it incredibly endearing," he chuckled.

"Why?" I mumbled over another large bite.

"Because you don't eat with the etiquette of a princess. Not that I've seen anyway, and it makes you that much more attractive to me," he smiled.

"That's because I'm not eating at some formal event. Thus far, I've only eaten out of a bag with you." I laughed.

"Well...I'm going to have to resolve that. I promise to make sure we eat a real dinner together in this town or in Bolton," he paused, taking another mouthful and mulling over something in his mind. "That's the reason I insisted on eating in the castle kitchens," he admitted. I had forgotten all about it.

"Oh! Yes! You never did answer me about that. So what...you eat in there because it's less formal?" I asked, trying to finish my breakfast.

"That and I hate dining alone. It's always bothered me. Back home, meals with my parents were always very animated. As I got older, it became a time for us to talk and laugh or just generally spend some time together. Of course, there were some meals I was getting my bollocks handed to me, which could be uncomfortable. Especially, if my mother was pissed over something stupid that I'd done. But that wasn't often," he smirked. I rolled my eyes.

"Yes, I'm sure." I snickered. "But weren't you in the kitchens by yourself that morning?" He shook his head.

"No actually. Your caretaker was there, as well as a few of the kitchen staff. They're quite amusing company, particularly the older attendants. They told me stories about you and Paxe when you were children and it was pretty adorable," he raised his brows as if he was surprised.

"Adorable, how? What did they say?" I prodded, praying it wasn't something humiliating. He grinned and looked forward, straightening our alignment with the path.

"Just that the two of you enjoyed putting each other up to causing mischief. You, especially."

I giggled under my breath as I thought back on simpler days with my friend. It made me miss her that much more. "She was older than me and always a lot more inclined to accepting a good dare. But she got me into my fair share of trouble too," I admitted.

"I can relate. I had a friend that visited me often as a child. My mother became ill after I was born and was never able to have more children. She didn't like the idea of me growing up without a companion, and she made sure to remedy that as I was growing up. We broke a lot of things," he laughed.

"What was his name?" I asked.

"Michele. He actually ended up being a lot better looking than me when we got older. He matured a lot faster than I did, and he was the first of us that laid with a female. He was probably the one who pressured me the most the first time I...you know...at the tavern," he said.

"What happened to him? Does he still live in Crona?" I continued.

"He actually does. He married a female he had been seeing about a year ago. They have a child, and he's an exceptional architect." I quieted for a moment.

"Do you want children?" I asked, growing nervous if it may have been too soon. He stared forward for a moment and his expression seemed to dim before he looked over at me with a side smile.

"I do. If the gods will it," he smiled. "You?" I looked away, feeling an ache in my chest as I thought of all the horrible memories of my youth.

"It's hard to imagine myself as a mother. I don't know that I'd be able to give a child something that I didn't have," I replied sadly. He reached across for my hand and I took it.

"Hey..." He said softly. I met his eyes. "Don't diminish anything about yourself. You'd be an amazing mother. Want to know why?" He asked. I nodded slowly. "Because you carry the strength of your *own* mother. You carry her will and her sacrifice. You carry all the love she couldn't show you, although it's been buried under a mountain of anguish. I've felt it. You'd be incredible." He squeezed my hand and released it. Thunder rumbled faintly in the distance behind us and we looked back. "Time to pick up the pace. Are you ready?" He asked.

"Absolutely. You promised me dinner," I smirked.

"Ah...if you want it tonight, then you better ride hard, Princess," he said playfully, quickly realizing how it sounded. "I—I didn't mean..." He retracted, beginning to flush. I laughed loudly, kicking my heels at Alice's sides and taking off in front of him. He gawked as I passed by.

"You're blushing, Prince!" I yelled, picking up speed and enticing him to catch up as I leaned forward, raising my rear from the saddle. I looked back to see him gaining on me and smiling devilishly as he shook his head at my tease. I laughed as I turned my face forward, foolishly underestimating Bjourne's stamina and feeling the sting of a small slap to my left buttock as Luca raced past, howling in triumph.

He did not.

My mouth dropped open and I rushed forward to catch him as we tore across the grasslands for Aeon.

CHAPTER 12

AEON

The sun began to set, and it seemed we had very little time to spare before our gain from the oncoming storm would be over. We rode quickly toward a tiny village that was slowly starting to twinkle with lights in every window. As we slowed and trotted into the quaint little town, its occupants were busy closing up market stands and preparing for their evening. Children were being called into their homes, and vendors were securing their goods with large canvases to protect them from the incoming weather. The streets within were worn cobblestone, and the clacking of hooves was everywhere. It was simple here and rather peaceful—it warmed my heart to witness a place that was seemingly undisturbed by my father's merciless rule.

"Did your caretaker mention where we could find her brother or what he looks like?" Luca asked, looking around at faces that were curiously taking notice of us as we stopped near the emptying market square.

"No, she only said that his name was Frances and that he'd been waiting to help me for a long time," I replied.

"That's not a great deal to go on," he said, becoming irritated. "We've probably got about half an hour at most before we get wet, and these horses need to rest up."

An elderly woman stepped outside her home across the street and called out to us, waving an arm to come toward her. We dismounted and tied the horses to a hitching post that was nearby and made our way to greet her.

"Good evening, dears. Are you just passing through? I don't recognize either of you," she said sweetly. She was clearly Valdarian and had to be over a hundred years old based on the aging of her skin.

"Good evening," I smiled, taking her hand gently. "My name is Arienne, and this is Luca. We're here to meet a man named Frances. Do you know him?" I asked. Her eyes widened.

"Arienne? You're the Princess?" She asked, bowing at the waist. "My apologies, your Highness." She turned to Luca, bowing again. "And to you as well, Prince Luca. My name is Gretchen, it is an honor to meet you both." I put my hand on her shoulder as she straightened herself.

"Please, there's no need for formalities. We don't want to cause a stir. Vetta is my caretaker and she told me to seek her brother when we arrived. I'd rather people didn't know about who we are, if that's alright." I pleaded softly. She looked surprised.

"Oh, my dear." She started, steepling her wrinkled fingers. "Everyone already knows of your visit to Aeon. Many have been anticipating it now for much of the day," she said apologetically. I raised my brows.

"...Oh..." I replied. "I didn't know that. I'm sorry, but we had to camp last night and got a late start to the morning." Luca smiled at her, and then at me. I gave him a look, daring him to say something smart.

"Oh no, Princess. Don't apologize. It's well over a day's travel from your home to here. You both must be in need of a warm bed and a hot supper. Please, gather your horses and lead them back. I'll be happy to take you to Mr. Lombardi," she said. We thanked her and walked hastily back to the hitching post as the lightning flashed nearer to town. Luca placed a hand on my back as he led me across the street.

"I really hope there isn't a parade outside in the morning," I said, dreading the attention.

"So what if there is? It didn't seem like she was trying to warn us that anybody would be upset that we're here," he shrugged.

"The last thing I need is for the news to get back to my father that we're here for any other reason than finding proof of Paxe's innocence. He'll grow suspicious of whatever we're doing out here if he finds out we're not looking for it." I replied with a little more serious tone.

"You're worried he'll do something to her," he realized.

"I'm certain he will, and I can't risk that," I said, untying Alice's lead.

"Well, let's not assume anything just yet. Maybe if we make it clear enough to Miss Gretchen, she'll spread the word, and they'll tone it down," he said, reassuring me.

"I hope you're right." I replied. We led the horses back across the street where Gretchen was waiting. She started walking as quickly as she could manage through the town square and down a street to our left, while we followed her closely.

"My entire life, I wondered what you must look like all grown up, Princess, and if I may...you're a lovely young lady. Much like your mother." Gretchen complimented as she walked between us.

"You knew my mother, ma'am?" I asked. She fluttered her eyes and smiled.

"I didn't have the pleasure of knowing her, but she's very beloved throughout these lands. She was a beautiful soul. Very kind, and I hear she had a talent for singing," she answered.

"I've heard that as well." I replied.

"You don't say much, do you, your Highness?" She asked, glancing at Luca. I scoffed.

"Oh, he says plenty." I laughed. Luca grinned at us both.

"Forgive me, ma'am. I'm just enjoying the sights." He answered.

I spotted an older male lighting lamp posts with a long metal rod up ahead. He hadn't seen us before Gretchen lifted her arms and waved them around.

"Frances! Frances, your guests are here!" She called.

The male turned toward us and stared with an almost longing look across his features as he started walking toward us, extinguishing the flame from the stick he carried. It didn't take long before he reached us, and Luca and I dipped our chins in greeting. He didn't look as I expected. Taller and thin, unlike my grandmotherly caregiver, but he favored her in many ways. He didn't look older than Vetta either, which came as a surprise to me. He wore simple clothes consisting of a bland-colored pair of brown trousers with matching suspenders and a darker brown shirt that was rolled at the sleeves. He was aging too, but not nearly as much as the sweet female that stood beside me.

"Your Highness...have I waited many a year to meet the likes of you," he said kindly as he took my hand and pressed his lips to the back of it. "Welcome to Aeon." He bowed slightly at the waist and turned to Luca. "And this must be our future King. Very pleased to meet you," he said, shaking his hand. Luca's entire demeanor changed at the remark, but he remained polite and smiled uncomfortably. I tucked that bit into the back of my mind to address later. The wind began to pick up around us as we exchanged pleasantries, and I watched a few pairs of shutters close on the houses lining the street. "We'd better get these horses to shelter. There's a stable around the back of my home just at the end of this street here," he pointed toward a dead end and reached for the lead in my hand.

"Miss Gretchen, may I walk you back to your home?" Luca asked. She smiled in surprise.

"Why thank you, your Highness, but I can manage on my own. Don't let my youthfulness fool you, I've been around for a long time yet," she laughed.

"I insist." Luca grinned, offering her an arm. She patted his shoulder and accepted it, and he handed me his lead as they turned back. "I'll meet you there, love," he promised and escorted her slowly the other way. I followed Frances with the horses toward the stables and he gave me another onceover as we walked.

"I would say sir that I've heard a lot about you, but Vetta didn't tell me she had any family. I apologize." I offered, desperate to settle my awkward tension.

"Ahh...no need for apologies, Princess. That was always the plan," he replied.

I couldn't help but feel a bit unnerved by that response as everything here lately seemed to always come back to 'the plan'. I didn't even think about what I was saying before my words left my loose tongue.

"Yes. The plan. Always the plan." I rolled my eyes, and regret hit me like a slap to my face. "Oh...Mr. Lombardi, I—I'm so sorry I didn't mea—"

"It's quite alright mi'lady. You have every right to feel that way. Anyone would, and we always knew that you'd need support when the time came for you to know the truth. You let it out," he chuckled.

"So...you mean to say that everyone has known about what my mother arranged all this time?" I asked. He nodded slowly, looking ahead.

"The world has long awaited the day when you would be old enough to fulfill your destiny, Princess. We all have patiently waited with it to help you bring an end to its suffering. I do hope that you can one day forgive those who love you. You see...if the King had any knowledge of what was to become of you, I imagine you could understand what he would have done to stop it. The secret we've kept has also kept you alive," he explained.

I suppose I hadn't thought of it in that sense before, and my irritation subsided. We approached the stable and he led Alice into a stall that was readied for her arrival with fresh hay and water. He gestured at the stall beside it and I took Bjourne to his hard-earned bed. We didn't say anything more as the two of us rushed to relieve them of their saddles and baggage before the rain set in.

"I'll take your bags, Princess...you can leave the food and canteens until morning," he said as he hung the saddles on the wall. I, in turn, handed over Luca's bag, opting not to part with my own. He smiled politely in understanding, and the rain started pattering on the ground outside as he gestured to the back door of his home. We jogged across the small yard and he opened the door for me as I hopped inside.

The back door of Frances's house opened up into a good-sized kitchen area with a small wooden table against the wall and a brick oven that was the expanse of the entire back wall to the right. There was a small stone island in the center for preparing food, and old pots and dried herbs hung from the ceiling above it. Directly beside the back door on the left, was a washing basin sitting beneath a small window that looked out to the stables. Across from where I stood at the back entrance was a doorway that appeared to lead into a living area and I could see a glow coming from it that indicated a fireplace was lit inside. He closed the door behind us as he sat Luca's bag on the island and shook off the rain.

"This is quite cozy." I smiled as I admired what I could see.

"Thanks very much, Princess. It isn't a castle by any means, but it's comfortable," he said. I let my bag fall to the crease of my arm and turned to face him.

"Mr. Lombardi...if I may ask just a small favor of you?" I started.

"Of course."

"Would it be alright if we all agreed to drop the titles? Luca and I were really hoping for a little discretion upon arriving, and Vetta is working hard to keep my best friend safe. Knowing what kind of person my father can be, I'd feel so much better if—"

"That won't be necessary," a voice like an angel cut in from the doorway.

Oh my gods. Oh my gods it can't be.

My eyes grew wide and immediately began welling with tears as I stared in shock at the old male. A massive smile etched across his face and he nodded in the direction the voice had come from.

I turned slowly to see Paxe smiling at me tearfully, stretching her arms wide to welcome me. My mouth opened and I couldn't get a word out as I dropped my bag to the floor and leapt into her arms. We cried loudly and I held her tight enough to choke off her air supply as she laughed through her tears.

"How?" I wept, leaning back to get a good look at her. She looked different. Her hair was braided almost the same way as she had done mine a couple of days ago, and gone was the pale rose attendant's attire she usually wore in the castle. She had replaced it with dark leggings and a deep red tunic, with a single rosebud embroidered at the base of her collar. I hadn't seen her look so...normal, and she was twice as lovely.

"There's a lot to explain, I'm afraid," she replied, cupping the side of my face with her hand and thumbing away a tear. "I told you to trust me," she smiled.

A knock at the door interrupted our tearful reunion and Frances opened it. Luca stepped inside, dripping from every part of his body. If I thought that male couldn't get any more attractive...once again I was proven wrong.

"Thank you, sir," he said, standing in his growing puddle. "My apologies for the —" He stopped short as he took in the face of the female embracing me. "Gods...what have I missed?" He asked in shock.

"Luca," Paxe dipped her chin, smiling.

"Let me fetch you a towel, your Highness." Frances scurried past us.

We all stood silent for a moment looking at one another.

"Storm's here." Luca said awkwardly. I snorted first and Paxe followed suit, while he grinned at us and we laughed like delirious fools.

Paxe studied us both, glancing back and forth between us before she finally came to a conclusion.

"Something is different," she said, eyeing Luca the longest. He and I exchanged glances at each other, and then thankfully, Frances returned with a large towel.

"Here you are. I'll show you to your room so you can get out of those wet clothes, mi'lord." He grabbed the bag from the kitchen island, and Luca followed behind him as we stepped out of the way of the door.

"Get your stuff...you and I are in a room across the hall." Paxe said as we turned to follow them up a short flight of stairs across the living area.

The upper level was a U-shaped hallway with a bathing room that met us at the top and was centered between a bedroom on either side. Two other smaller bedrooms sat adjacent to one another further back. Paxe opened the door to the room on our immediate right while Frances showed Luca into the other.

"I'll make us some supper while you all settle in. Please let me know if I can help with anything. I'll be right downstairs." Frances bowed, heading back down the stairway. We thanked him graciously, and Paxe took my bag into the room. Luca stood at his doorway and I at mine, both of us looking at each other as if being apart tonight was an unwanted surprise.

"I know..." He said, as if reading my thoughts. "Go...I'm going to get washed up. Talk to her. I'm not going anywhere, love. Take your time, and

I'll see you downstairs, alright?" He gave me a gentle nod toward my door and smiled sweetly. I returned it, refusing to turn away until he closed his door. Paxe met my eyes as I turned to face her, arms crossed and smirking at me. I latched the door shut and stood there quietly, wondering which one of us should go first. The rain roaring against the roof was the only sound until she finally broke the silence.

"Something has happened between you two since I saw you last," she said, narrowing her eyes.

"What makes you think that?" I asked bashfully.

"Well, before the dramatics in the study with your brute father, I noticed a lot had changed. I clearly interrupted something when I came to get you after you returned from your...*night*...in the woods," she grinned. I rolled my eyes.

"Alright, first of all, nothing intimate happened in the woods. Second of all, I—" I paused and looked at her with utter confusion and a sudden shock of realization. "Why are you asking me?" I lowered my brows, and she raised hers as she nodded her head.

"I was wondering if you'd be able to tell before I told you myself," she started as she took a seat on the edge of the bed.

"Alright...we're starting with you. How did you get here? What happened?" I asked, rushing over and sitting next to her. We turned to face each other, and she grabbed my hands.

"Vetta realized after you left that your father had no intention of touching me unless Lakan was found before you were able to prove my innocence, but he also had no intention of giving me food or water...or practically anything else I'd need to survive down there. So, she went to him and somehow managed to convince him to release me for a price." Her face looked weary.

"Your abilities..." I answered for her. She nodded slowly.

"He agreed to let me go, but I was to be banished from the castle and surrounding areas in Valdaro. In truth, I shouldn't even be in Aeon, but Vetta assured me it was safe until I could find passage to Crona. He summoned me to the Great Hall and asked me to make my decision. He told me that if I chose to leave, I would have to surrender my abilities and my Valdarian heritage and become *as human as my worthless lover.* If Lakan is found, it will cost him his life. For me, it wasn't a very difficult decision. I know that Lakan and I would both die if he was found. It does me no good to sit in a dungeon and wait for my execution if there was any chance I could be free. So, I gave it up." She lifted her chin high and took a deep breath. "And I'd do it again, Ari—all of it. Being with him has been worth every second." She finished, staring a hole through me. "So don't you dare pity me."

"Paxe...do you know where Lakan is?" I asked.

"I don't. I was hardly able to get a message to Perla to warn him before the guards took me to the study. One of the staff warned me first when I was on my way to take your things upstairs," she said. Her voice began to crack with heartbreak. I leaned in close and forced her to look me in the eye.

"He's safe. Luca's father sent for him. He's hidden in the castle in Crona." Her eyes grew wide and began to water as she dropped her mouth open.

"He's...Did Luca..do this?" She finally broke. I smiled and pulled her in close, holding her tight as she wept. "I don't know how I'll ever repay him, Ari. You don't know how much this means to me."

"You don't owe anyone anything. You repay it by living your life. Do you understand? Promise me that you'll grow old...have children..." I trailed off, thinking back to the conversation I had with Luca before we left this morning. "How long will you stay here?" I asked. She leaned back, holding my hands.

"I'm not sure. I'd like to stay for a while. I don't want to leave you just yet...although it may not be wise to stick around for too long. I feel as if the King believes I'm already on the way to Crona. Where else would I go from here?"

"Yes...but if he knows that I'm here, he may suspect you too. Don't risk too much Paxe. You made it out and at a great cost." I said.

"You're right. I suppose you can't have anything good without having the worst of it drag along with you."

No shit.

"When you were arrested, Father mentioned you being caught multiple times in unfavorable situations...how many times have you been with Lakan?" I asked. She looked at me as if reading my question in five different ways.

"Now is about the time I *would* start missing my abilities. Why do you ask?"

"You said you were being careful. Who would have seen you?" I wondered.

"I really don't know. We *were* careful. Perla was really the only person who knew where we were, and I don't think she'd out her own brother. Although I can't rule out that someone didn't spot us if we weren't paying close attention. We only laid together once, but there were several other times that we had done...other things. I suppose it could have been anyone. Perhaps someone that wanted to be in the King's good graces? I guess it no longer makes any difference. The damage is done." She watched me closely as I stared at the floor.

"Did you lie with him?" She asked assertively. My mouth turned up at the corner, and she opened her mouth.

"We didn't. But last night...a lot happened, and some of it I still don't really have an explanation for." She scooted closer and took her boots off, lifting her knees up and waiting for me to start spilling the secrets I had been dying to tell her.

"Tell me everything," she said eagerly.

And so I told her. She stayed quiet as she listened to everything I was throwing at her about how my mother had our souls bound to each other, the things I said to Luca and our silence throughout the ride to camp. I told her about the signs in the sky and the female voice that spoke to me, which I was positive was my mother's. I explained everything Luca had told me by the fire and how it made me nearly wild with my need to have him close to me. She flushed a shade of red when I told her about our kiss and what it became only minutes later. Her face was twisted with deep thought when I mentioned the moment I told him that I thought I could be in love with him and he had stopped to tell me that he could feel it before I spoke the words. I told her about the next morning and how I had asked Luca about the symbol on his chest, and he avoided it as if it were something awful. I finished with our conversation about having children before we outran the storm that was still raging outside. I knew that it was all a great deal to take in, and I let her think on it for a few moments before I became impatient for whatever ideas or advice she had about everything.

"You must think I'm mad." I sighed as I plopped onto my back and stared at the ceiling. She crossed her legs and stared down at me, shaking her head.

"I don't think that at all. You said your mother had your souls bound by the gods...I can't imagine what love like that could feel like. Ari, I'm not sure I can imagine how you managed to fight it off that long being around him for that many days. After what you've been through...I'm so proud of you for actually allowing your heart to open up like that. It took a great deal of strength," she said softly.

"The minute I did, though. He...he knew it as soon as I knew it." I looked at her.

"It must be the bond between you. It's the only thing that makes sense. Perhaps it knew it was accepted." I thought about that for a moment.

"What about the tattoo?" I asked, hoping she'd have an answer.

"Do you think you could draw it?" She asked. I nodded, and she scrambled around the room for something to use. She flattened a bit of parchment she had torn from an old book out across her leg and handed me a chunk of coal from a bucket by the fireplace. I made do with what I had and did my best to draw her an example. She turned it and brought it to her face to get a better look. Her eyes narrowed and she looked at me.

"What? Tell me. Do you know it?" I asked, beginning to worry.

"Ari...this is the seal your father uses on his letters. I've seen this on everything he's posted out. It's your crest for your family's bloodline." She looked at me cautiously and my heart sank. "If Luca didn't want to talk about it then I fear..."

"He branded him." I finished for her. My body began to shake with anger and fear. She laid her hand on my shoulder.

"Arienne," she started, dropping the paper and turning my face to hers. "You don't know what it means. It may just be something that he has to wear until this wager with the king has been fulfilled. Don't make any hasty conclusions yet."

"If it's nothing, then why wouldn't he tell me about it?" I fired.

"Because he may not have been willing to ruin your tender moments together with any mention of your father. Neither of us could blame him for that. You're going to promise me you'll wait and let Luca bring this up on his own," she said firmly.

"I need to know, Paxe." I pleaded.

"And you will. When *he's* ready. Luca, so far, has treated you with respect. He deserves that from you. Promise me." She looked at me like a mother scolding her child. I stared back at her for a moment and nodded slowly.

"You're right." I whispered.

"Say it."

"I promise." I said.

The smell of food crept up the stairs, and my belly ached with hunger. Paxe raised from the bed, picking up the paper and moving to the fireplace. She started a small flame with it and tucked it underneath fresh, dry logs. They began to catch, and she stood and turned around.

"Take that hair down...let me fix it before we go downstairs," she smiled. I knew she was trying to be a comfort to me, and I let her. It was going to prove difficult not to think about what we had figured out about Luca...especially when I saw him again. To think that anything that pertained to my father was stained on his skin made mine crawl.

Give me another reason to slit your throat, you snake.

Paxe sat behind me as she pulled my hair down, fingering through it and handing me Luca's hair strap. I held it tight and began to tense with worry.

"So...do you want to talk about what happened in the tent last night?" I could hear the smile on her face as she started a braid that felt like it was crossing my entire head in the back. I smiled to myself.

"It was...incredible. I didn't realize my body could feel like that." I admitted.

"When it actually happens, I think you'll be surprised how much more you can feel. Physically and emotionally. I'm curious about that."

"Which part?" I asked.

"The joining of two people spiritually bound to one another. I would assume my heart would burst from the emotional aspect of it."

"Did it hurt?" I asked curiously.

"Hmm....I wouldn't say that it hurt. It was a little uncomfortable at first, but we were in the moment, and I didn't really think about it as much as I needed to have him. I think it may also have a great deal to do with how you position your body when it happens. I was...against a wall." She laughed.

"How does one even manage that?" I giggled.

"What do you mean?" She curled around my shoulder to the side of my face and continued to laugh. "He held me up...you know...by my thighs. It was actually amazing. I felt a sharp pain, but then...it was over, and after that, I'd never felt a more satisfying thing in my life." She leaned back and started braiding again.

"What things did you do before?" I asked.

"Well...I told you before, we kissed a lot. There were a few times that things became a bit more intense, but I'll be honest. He never did what Luca did with you. He did touch me, but he never felt inside of me. I'm sure that was a surprise," she snickered.

"That is an understatement." My face heated, and I put a hand over my eyes.

"Aside from that, I did take him into my mouth once," she said. I turned my head and gasped at her and she jerked my face forward again as she laughed proudly.

"What do you mean?!" I demanded. "How did you know to do something like that? You're so...ugh!"

"I didn't. I had touched him, and it...became ready? I just wanted to kiss him there, but it turned into something other than what I had originally intended. Nonetheless, it ended well," she finished. I couldn't believe what I was hearing, but it didn't stop me from wanting to hear more.

"I feel so stupid. I don't want to seem like I have no idea what I'm doing when it does finally happen, although it's the absolute truth." I turned as she tied off the braid.

"Ari...trust me when I tell you... you don't need to worry about that, nor should you feel stupid. Everybody has a first time, and nobody knows what they're doing. I'd be worried if you weren't curious about it. But I don't have any doubt that when you and Luca decide that it's time...it will be unforgettable." She smirked as she kissed my cheek. "Don't get any ideas that it's going to be tonight either. You're rooming with me." She patted my shoulder. "Let's go find your prince."

We got up and started downstairs. We slowed a bit as we listened to Luca and Frances singing in the kitchen. I recognized the tune as an old sea shanty we used to hear the older attendants sing as they completed chores around the castle. We smiled at each other as we crept farther down and peeked into the room. They were cooking together and acting like old friends. I felt so grateful that the formal address seemed to be over. I silently thanked Luca for that.

Paxe started singing loudly with them as we walked into the kitchen doorway, and Luca spun toward her without missing a beat, smiling and handing her a bottle of wine. I stood in the doorway watching them, and the warmest feeling came over me. Frances happily bellowed lyrics as he sat a large serving dish with a roasted chicken and buttered vegetables down on the island. I laughed through my nose as I watched Paxe take a heavy drink from the bottle while turning herself in circles around the island. Luca continued to sing as he made his way over to me, taking one of my hands and looping an arm around my waist. He pulled me close to him and started spinning us around quickly across the floor. Paxe and Frances started clapping in rhythm, singing louder as I threw an arm around his neck and stepped in time with his movements. They finally finished in a long, loud note as he dipped me toward the floor and lifted me back to him, pressing against me firmly and touching our heads together. Their clapping drowned out for a short moment, leaving us in what I would hold forever as one of the most bittersweet memories in my life. We smiled at each other as we let the world back in, and he slowly released me from his hold.

"Ahhhh, friend," Paxe grinned, throwing an arm over my shoulder. "I really like him." She passed the bottle to Luca, who raised it in gratitude and lifted it to his mouth to drink.

"I'm flattered, but I fear I may be a bit too old for a youngster like you!" Frances yelled from the island. We all broke into hideous laughter and made to gather at the table.

The evening was spent riding out the storm, drinking together and finally eating an actual meal. The chicken was savory, paired with the tender vegetables, and my company was the best in the realm. We laughed at stories Frances shared about Vetta as a youth, realizing that she was tough on us because she was just as mischievous. Paxe told embarrassing tales of stupid things we did under her care, and Luca shared a few of his own. For a few hours, I felt like I finally had a family, and my heart was the most content it had ever been. I wished my mother was here to share it with us and I could get to know her. It didn't dampen my mood, and we eventually finished the bottle, as well as one other, and decided it was time to call it a night.

Frances went on about how he wasn't as young as he once was and needed a time-out. He finally rested peacefully on the threadbare sofa in the living area by the fire. I covered him with a blanket that I found draped over a small chair in the corner, and we all helped each other stumble up the stairs. Paxe cheerfully face-planted into her pillow, and I giggled outside the doorway to our room, turning to face Luca.

"I don't think you'll have to worry about a crowd tomorrow. I spoke to Frances about everything. He promised to make sure that everyone knows," Luca said.

"How long should we stay?"

"Well, the sooner we make it to Bolton, the better. But now that Paxe is somewhere safe, if you want to spend a few days here, I can completely understand. It might be exactly what we need. We've been on the move for a few days. Enjoy this time, love. I'm elated to see you so happy."

I pulled the bedroom door to a crack and lowered my voice.

"She's safe for now...but I'm not sure how long she'll stay that way if my father finds out she's here." He lowered his brows.

"Did she escape?" He asked warily. I shook my head.

"Vetta talked him into agreeing to release her, but he's taken her abilities and banished her from Valdaro."

"I see. I'll get word to my father. I can have someone here to take her to Lakan in a couple of days. You should warn her not to use her name around town until then."

"I never should have pushed you away." I sighed. He lightly pinched my chin, leaning down to kiss the top of my head.

"You'll find I'm a resilient guy," he smiled. "Rest. I'll see you in the morning."

He pulled away and turned to walk to his room. I opened my door and started to walk through it, stopping and looking over my shoulder.

"Luca..."

"Hmm?" He turned.

"Thanks for the dance." I smiled.

He bowed and ducked into his doorway, smiling as he softly pulled it shut. I went to the bed, pulling my boots off as I walked and eased in beside Paxe, who was already snoring. I smiled to myself and thanked the gods for everything I had as I wrapped an arm around her. The rain had softened outside, and lightly tapped at the small window as my eyes grew heavy. I closed them, and it wasn't long before a deep, restful sleep took over.

CHAPTER 13

WHO WE ARE

Paxe and I awoke that morning to the smell of breakfast being prepared downstairs. The rain had moved on, and a cooler morning glistened behind it as the sun made diamonds out of the drops that rested over everything I could see out of the bedroom window. The small town started to lazily wake with people readying for their day. Vendors set up shops down the street, and the shutters I saw closing last night began to open, one by one.

"It's so peaceful here," Paxe muttered over my shoulder as we looked out. "I could stay here forever."

"I'd like to explore around today. Want to go?" I turned my face to look at her. She seemed nervous about the idea.

"It probably isn't wise."

"Luca offered a good point last night while you were drooling on yourself." I nudged her in the middle with my elbow. She winced, looking at me curiously. "Don't use your name. Nobody should recognize you. I would use that to your advantage and enjoy a little freedom."

"That *is* a good point. The only ones that will be recognized will be the two of you."

I turned to face her.

"I told him what happened. He's sending word to King Tidus to see you safely to Crona. It may take a few days, but I think you can relax," I smiled reassuringly.

"Ari...he really is amazing. Prophecy or not, he's no doubt sent by the gods."

The gods...

"I need to know anything you can tell me about Nero," I remembered, almost forgetting why we were here.

"I'm afraid I won't be much help. You know I'm not very well versed in religious details."

"Luca said he was a blacksmith. I found Perla by the river before we made it back to the castle and she offered a little information about what Lakan does. Is there anything else you could add?"

"Not really. I've watched him work before, but mostly in lust," she scoffed. "Why don't we ask Frances? If everyone has been waiting to help you, then he has to be knowledgeable in whatever you might have to do."

"You're right," I nodded. "Let's get dressed.

I pulled off my tunic and searched my bag for something warm and comfortable. I found a soft, cream-colored knit sweater and put it on. It hugged my bust but was loose and almost fuzzy as it draped around my middle. Paxe looked equally satisfied with her choice in a chunky, pale blue ensemble similar to my own. I didn't fuss much over my hair as it was still neatly braided behind my head. We pulled our boots on and headed downstairs to find Luca and Frances already eating together at the table. They promptly stood, offering us their seats when we entered the kitchen.

"Morning ladies. I've made eggs and some ham for everyone. Grab a plate and help yourself to as much as you want," Frances said politely, gesturing towards two empty plates on the island that were sitting next to the steaming food.

We didn't waste any time making for the stone surface and accepting his offer. Luca stood across from me at the island, looking much more casual than usual, in a dark heather long-sleeved top that he left open at the neck and some black trousers that matched his regular boots. His hair was down and a little damp. I assumed he must have bathed this morning before coming downstairs. Paxe glanced at his chest while loading her plate. She gulped loudly, smiling down at her food. I elbowed her in the side as she moved past me, laughing under her breath and walking to the table to sit. He took her place beside me as I scooped eggs into my plate.

"I have to go into town and make some arrangements to get a message to my father. If you need me, I won't be far away."

I turned to him, nodding, and mouthed a quiet 'thank you'. He smiled sweetly as he kissed my forehead and dipped his chin to Frances and then to Paxe, who waved in thanks with a mouth full of food. Frances headed for the back door, opening it.

"I'll run out and speak to the locals for you, sir," he said as he stepped outside.

"See you soon, love," Luca whispered, following him out and closing the door behind him. I took my plate and went to sit with Paxe. She sat there, chewing and shaking her head at me.

"Gods! That is an attractive damn male. I can't get over the way he *looks* at you. You have so much more reservation than I do, friend." She forked another mouthful, still shaking her head. I snorted as I started eating and she pointed her fork at me. "You laugh. But that look he just gave you, and that body language? That *body*." She rolled her eyes back.

"Would you stop?" I laughed.

She leaned in, stopping mid-chew and widened her eyes.

"Have you seen him naked? I have to know." I slapped her upper arm. "Ari, have you?!" She pushed as I turned two shades of red.

"No, stupid. Just...without a shirt. I told you that."

She leaned back and continued her chewing as she studied me.

"How big is he, I wonder?"

"Paxe!" I shouted, banging my elbow on the table. She broke into a hard laugh and a bit of egg flew out of her mouth. I finally lost my composure and we were back to acting like idiots, barely able to catch our breath as if we were still passing around a half-empty bottle of wine.

Once we finally recovered from our hysterics, we decided to lend a helping hand to Frances, and tidied up the kitchen area. Paxe cleaned the dishes in the basin, and I pushed a broom across the floor. He came through the door a few moments later, shocked to see us working.

"Mi'lady, please you don't have to do any of that. Let me finish that for you." He reached for the broom handle, and I moved it away.

"It's the least I can do for your hospitality. Please let me. It's the most normal I've ever felt." We smiled at each other and he nodded in understanding. "Can I ask you a few questions? There are some things I'd like to know."

"Of course. Shall we sit?" He gestured to the table.

"I'll make us some coffee," Paxe chimed in from behind him, grabbing a small pot and filling it with water.

"The cloth I steep it with is in a cabinet behind you, and the percolator should be around there too, dear." He pointed at a waist-high wooden cabinet against the wall.

We sat together at the table while she fumbled around the kitchen, and I palmed my hands together as if in prayer.

"Please tell me that you know something about how I'm supposed to prepare for Bolton. I met Elowen in the forest outside the castle, and she warned me that Nero was a cunning sort. I know he's a blacksmith, and I have little understanding of what they do, but I'm worried that if he gives me a task to complete, I'll know nothing of how to accomplish it."

"Well...the god of the Bolton Sea is, as you know, a pillar of strength and power. It may come down to a test of your strengths. That was the way with the trials of the first king. According to old legends about his gift of power to your bloodline, the gods deemed the first king worthy of a small portion of their power. That gift was a decision unanimously agreed upon by them after they sought out a lesser being to take over rule and help govern the people of our world, while also protecting them and their lands. Very few felt up to the task, and it didn't sit well with the gods. They feared that they'd be left without many options in who would be the best fit for such power."

Paxe moved to the island, pouring the pot of hot water over the coffee and intently listening as he moved his attention to include her.

"The few that attempted to prove themselves to the gods were then presented with choices. And based upon their choice, they either drowned themselves in their greed and ended up getting themselves killed, or they would make the mistake of abusing what they had collected from the gods through their trials and were left to pay that price with their lives. The idea began to look less and less promising to those brave enough to try, and for a long time, there weren't any more motivated prospects. Rifts between races began, and many battles were started among Valdaro and Crona. The

Midlands weren't yet established, and people from all over the world couldn't happily coexist with one another. There was no order. It became utter chaos everywhere, and many lives were lost."

I lowered my brows.

"So, the Midlands weren't always human territory?" Frances shook his head.

"The Midlands were only human territory many years ago when your father inherited the crown. He collected humans from Valdaro and forced them to only be allowed to live amongst themselves, between our lands, claiming that they were a vermin of races. Mortals with no known power, unlike Valdarians who had it in spades, and Cronians who possessed lesser power—but were still carriers of magic within their blood. Your father forced a great many humans out of Crona and banished them to the Midlands, but the king and queen have never agreed on his rule. There are still humans known to live in those parts of the world, most likely hidden or keeping a low profile under the protection of the royal family in Crona. Every five years, they travel to your home to meet with King Loren, and he keeps a close eye on the way they rule their kingdom. For many years, they've been under the agreement that a very small portion of their human population be allowed to stay where they are, but your father forbade any blending of human and inhuman races and keeps close track of that. The king and queen present a detailed census at these meetings, and King Loren will seal his approval if all ends well when they meet."

Paxe poured mugs of coffee and came to sit between us at the table.

"So, by his approval, you mean the number of humans in Crona dwindles down to near nothing?" She asked as she moved our cups towards us.

"Not necessarily. Humans are allowed to reproduce amongst themselves. Just not with any race above them. And as long as the number of humans in Crona stay at or below a number that the king is satisfied with, he'll approve. If not, a number of human families will be dragged to the Midlands where he can control them himself."

I felt as if I'd be sick.

"So, what was it like before the Midlands were established? What happened with the first king?" I asked.

"The first king was the only Valdarian in long years that became weary of the way the world was falling apart and wanted to try to complete the trials of the gods. His wife and only son were killed by zealots in one of the many fights over who should govern the lands. He succeeded, making it farther than any other before him. He traveled to the highest peak in the Horned Mountains and was given a choice; immortality or a raw power given by the gods themselves to reign over the world. His choice was made without any hesitation or thought. He chose power. They tested him a final time at the top of the mountain and asked for his reasons for denying an opportunity to live forever. He told them that immortality would never be pleasing to him if he had to live an eternity never being with his family, and he only wanted the turmoil to end. He begged the gods to take his own life if it would fix the chaos below. It pleased them. They found him worthy of that power because of his offering, and he was gifted it, as well as the first crown ever forged to rule. The mountains were sealed off by the gods from that day forward. The first king eventually took a wife to produce an heir and established another royal family to take care of the other side of the world, and it has been that way for centuries until your father began to abuse their power."

"Now he's pissed them off," Paxe grunted.

"Indeed," he nodded, drinking from his mug. "The world is beginning to fall back into misery, and it was never intended for that. They plan to put an end to it before everything that the first king has built upon crumbles."

"But all the people who tried to win the favor of the gods were male. Is that right?" I asked.

"That is true, yes."

"How am I supposed to do this?" I threw my hands into the air, frustrated. He reached for my hand.

"Because you're not alone, child. Your betrothed was born with a purpose...just as you—you complete the trials before you, *together*."

Paxe and I exchanged looks.

"Sounds to me like you're much more than soulmates. Both of you were born to save the world," she smiled. "And *that* means...that you no longer have to burden yourself with the weight of feeling like this was always on your shoulders alone."

"But can these trials kill us?" I asked.

"That's highly unlikely, Princess. I don't think that the gods would risk that if they want to see the king fall."

At least, that made me feel a little better. I would stand with Luca, face whatever they asked and be confident that as long as my other half was with me, it would all prove worth it in the end. Not just because of a prophecy but because it's who we are. We're the chosen, born to bring light back to the world. Frances offered a knowing smile.

"What?" I asked, noticing his expression. Paxe glanced between us both.

"Have you any idea why your prince's name is so significant?" I shook my head. "Luca means *bringer of light*."

My eyes widened. "Luca..."

"Forgive my intrusion mi'lady. It's my gift."

I'll be damned...he read my mind...Luca...Luca is just as much a part of this as I am.

"Frances does...does Luca know this?" I asked. He gently shook his head.

"Ari, you have to tell him the truth," Paxe cut in.

"I will.... when the time is right... I will."

"The prince has always been accepting of his role, Princess. His only concern that I've read since meeting him... has been you. Be good to him. He cares very deeply for you…. it's a rare thing. Precious and fragile. There isn't much in this world as important as the love between the two of you. Protect and cherish it at all costs. The grief that the first king felt for his beloved is the love that started it all. It's the key to undoing great evil," Frances said purely.

"And it's the answer to your question," Paxe added. I shot her a confused look, and Frances raised his brows in agreement.

"What do you mean?" I asked.

"Your strength, Ari. If Nero's trial is to test your strengths…I'm willing to bet the strength of a love bound by your souls is the answer. That means you and Luca have a lot more bonding to do."

"Paxe, you're brilliant."

"Feel better?" Frances asked. My answering smile was anything but slight. "Good. You need a break. I spoke to a dear friend of mine this morning. She's an unbelievable confectioner. She's waiting to treat you two girls to a mountain of sweets when you're ready. There are all kinds of things to do out there and lots of people that would love to meet you. Go have some well-deserved fun. I'm going to head out and tend to the horses today. I'll be here if you need anything." He stood, turning to the door and grabbing a floppy old hat from the wall. He made to leave and tipped it to us, smiling as he left.

Paxe and I ran upstairs, grabbing a pouch full of coin and racing each other out the door like children. We spent the rest of the day enjoying the breezy weather, eating way too much sugar and meeting gracious locals who all wanted us to stop by for tea or poke through their shops. For the first time in my life, I was able to spend a day not caring about a single thing other than keeping company with my best friend and enjoying myself…and I could definitely get used to this. Anything I would have to endure to have this every day, forever, and to bring it to the rest of the world, would be absolutely worth it.

Luca met us in the square during the later afternoon hours and walked around with us for a bit longer before we headed back to Frances's house. Each one of us carried armfuls of ingredients, hoping we'd make it back before he finished lighting lampposts, so we could surprise him by cooking him dinner.

The night was merry and cheerful, and Luca's disposition definitely showed that it felt like home for him. I was happy to provide that comfort, knowing it may be a long while before he ever experienced that kind of time with his family again. We were each other's family… for now—the four of us. I was desperate to keep our moods light and have some fun, enjoying the company for as long as Paxe would stay.

That was nearly two weeks later, as correspondence between Luca and his father was taking much longer than expected. We didn't want to risk interception of their messages and be faced with whatever consequence would come after. We had finally received word from Crona twelve days after he'd requested escort for Paxe, and his father assured us that the route they'd be traveling would be safe for her. They'd be here in about four more days of us receiving his letter. I was thrilled that she was to be somewhere secure and I knew she'd be in good hands, but my heart saddened that our time together in Aeon was coming to an end.

The evening that we had received word from King Tidus, Paxe and I sat on our small bed, cross-legged, talking over a handful of playing cards. She laid one down and narrowed her eyes at me. I smiled deviously.

"You sure?" I asked. She studied my face for another moment.

"I'm sure you're *bluffing*," she grinned. I laid my cards out over hers. "Damn! That's three times now. I don't want to play anymore...you cheat." She griped, pushing them toward me.

"I don't cheat, you're just too trusting. And that's not a horrible thing, it just means you stink at card games," I laughed.

"No, I don't! I beat Luca a few times earlier today."

"Luca is a saint. He threw those games," I grinned. She opened her mouth in defeat. "Don't be upset. He just wanted you to be happy," I chuckled.

"Both of you can plant your royal lips on my derriere."

I couldn't staunch my snort as I started stacking the cards to put them away. She stretched across the bed, lying on her side with her head propped up on her hand. I tucked the cards into a bedside drawer and joined her.

"We only have a few more days. I wish you didn't have to go," I said sadly. She sighed and gave me a half smile. "I'm sure you're ready to throw your arms around Lakan, though. I can't imagine the wait has been easy for you."

"It hasn't. I've noticed it seems a bit too easy for *you,* though."

I scrunched my face.

"What do you mean?" I asked, earning myself an eye roll.

"You and Luca have barely touched each other in the past week. Ever since Frances told us about...well...everything, shouldn't you be getting to know him on a more...*personal* level?"

I swallowed hard.

"I hear what you're saying, but everything just feels..." I trailed off and stared past her.

"Feels...?"

"It feels odd to me still," I sighed, meeting her eyes again.

"Odd in what way? You're having second thoughts about him?"

I drew my brows together, pondering on how to explain my latest conflict. "We...had that moment in the tent. I was sure everything I was feeling was real. I'm sure that it is, but I feel unsure about most everything else." Her confusion trampled her face.

"I don't follow. Actually, everything you just said makes me curse my lack of ability to feel whatever it is you're trying and failing to put into words. Just say it. Let me help."

I exhaled deeply and scratched at the corner of my eye. "I...I told him I loved him, Paxe. After what? Three days? It feels so soon, and I'm worried I may have been ahead of myself. I didn't even know things about my physical anatomy that I should have at least been a little in tune with, but wasn't. I felt a lot all at once and now..." I closed my eyes and shook my head.

"Now you don't know if you love him?" She asked quietly.

"It's not that...but I guess...it is? I feel like I do. Every time I look at him, my heart feels like it's going to fly right out of my chest. I even notice that sometimes when he stands close, I'm holding my breath. My muscles feel loose and weak any time he touches me. I feel like it's love, yes. And what's more unnerving is that I gave him my heart that night without a second thought. It isn't that I'm thinking I've made some mistake, but I kind of feel...like my heart seems more ready now than the rest of me. I'm not sure what to do."

"Have you considered just trying to *follow* it for once? The way you did the night it happened? Maybe it's less about what you think you should do and more about what your heart is leading you to do. The heart wants what it wants. If that want is Luca...satisfy it." She inclined her head.

"I don't know how," I frowned.

"You know...I think that's your issue. I believe you're more concerned with the idea that you won't know what to do or that you won't make him happy. Here's a thought. *He already is.* Luca is happy just to be near you and help you through whatever fate has set before you—both of you. Now you know the truth, Ari. His role in this is just as heavy as yours, and that makes you *equal*. So...free yourself of the worry over the mechanics of everything and let your body react to what your heart feels. Trust me on this. They work very well together."

I laid on my back and thought about everything she was saying. As usual, she was right. The only thing standing in my way was my own insecurity. I had no reason to be worried and I knew that. While it didn't do much to stifle my fear, I knew all I needed was that push I felt when I picked up that sword in the forest and battled my father's raging storm. That feeling of being fed up with not acting on my feelings and the things I wanted out of my life. When I heard my mother's voice in my mind, I walked into that tent and took what was mine. For some reason, that push felt so distant from me. That was until a physical push sent me dropping from the side of the bed and onto the floor, the unforgiving wooden planks thudding loudly under my weight. I shot my attention back up to the bed to see half of Paxe's face staring over me.

"What the hell?!" I screeched, rubbing at my elbow.

"Get out," she snickered, leaning back and sprawling her entire body to cover the small bed as I slowly got up from the floor.

"What?" I asked as I glared down at her. She turned her face toward me and grinned.

"I'm sleeping here tonight. You're going to go talk to Luca...alone." She wagged her brows.

"No. I can't. I don't think I'm ready fo—"

"I didn't say anything about getting intimate. That may or may not happen on its own." She sat up and swiveled her legs around the edge of the bed to face me. "You need to talk about everything. The truth about what Frances said...and how you feel. You need to be honest with him about all of this, Ari. He deserves that. Whatever happens after, is up to the two of you. I have a couple of days left here. I'll be here for you if it goes wrong." Her smile sharpened. "Or if it goes right."

"I—" I couldn't think of anything to cleverly object to her. Not that it would make any difference if I did. It seemed her choice was made. She'd lock me out of this room either way.

"Change your clothes. Put on something dismantling."

I scoffed and turned away. "*Dismantling?* Be serious. I don't have a single enticing thing if that's what you're implying. I didn't exactly pack for a romp. And I don't plan to have one," I sneered.

"Here," she started, plundering through an armoire in the corner of the room and pulling out a dark red, sleeveless nightshift. It was short and thin, but not very provocative, and the material looked soft and comfortable. She threw it at me and I caught it, holding it up to look over it. "Wear that. If the talking goes sour, I'm sure he'll turn his mood when he sees you in that one."

"I don't suppose there are any more pieces to this shift?" I glared at her.

"Not a one. But I do have a satin dressing robe you can wear around it. Yes?" I nodded, and she pulled a deep green dressing robe, with the same embroidered roses from the tunic I remembered her wearing the day we arrived in Aeon. She handed it over and gestured for me to start changing.

"These roses. You have them on a lot of your clothes," I pointed out as I started changing into the items.

"Lakan." She bent down and started gathering my discarded laundry. "He'd leave me a rosebud every time he wanted to meet. Perla started making garments of her own design and put them on several things for me. It's comforting."

I walked in front of a small mirror that sat atop a dresser on the opposite end of the room and tied the robe around myself. It was lovely, and the fabric felt slick against my skin. She appeared behind me and untied my braid, shuffling my long loose curls to fall over my shoulders. I felt pretty. I'd never worn anything like this before. A strange calm settled in.

"How do I look?" I asked nervously as she smiled at me in the glass.

"Like trouble." Her lips curved up at the corners. "Go...tell me all about it tomorrow."

I took a deep breath and made for the door. Paxe crept up behind me and shoved me through it, I turned back just in time for her to lock me out and leave me to my nerves.

Shit.

I looked at Luca's door as if it had grown fangs. Every step towards it seemed to suddenly feel like uncharted territory, and I gulped down every curse that wanted to fly from my mouth at Paxe for making me do this in barely any clothing. I knew damned well that I would in no way appear confident enough to wear something like this just to talk. I inched closer to the door, raising my knuckles to knock and hesitating. I turned for a moment to try to duck back into my room, but I knew Paxe would never open that door.

I breathed deeply, and without giving myself any more time to flee, I knocked softly three times.

CHAPTER 14

LIGHT

"Come in."

My heart thrashed against my ribs as my prayers for silence from the other side of the door went unanswered. I turned the doorknob and slowly cracked the door open to find Luca sitting in bed, shirtless, with his hair unbound and a large book in his lap. He looked up from his tome, and his eyes traveled over me as I padded into the doorway, snicking the door shut behind me.

"Hey..." He started as I slowly moved into the room. It was hardly different from ours, except for a soft green rug on the floor beside his bed. "This is unexpected, are you alright?" He folded the corner of a page he was reading and closed the book, placing it on the bedside table.

"I'm fine." I pulled some hair behind my ear and gripped my upper arms, smoothing across the material of the dressing robe nervously. "I was hoping you were still up."

"I was reading a little about the trials of the first king. Not really much in the way of help yet, but I'm still hopeful. Are you sure you're alright? You seem...tense."

"Well...maybe a little. But yes, still fine. I was wondering if we could talk for a bit?" I shrugged. I had made it to the rug on the floor and stood there awkwardly, not sure where I should go. After he had touched the most intimate parts of my body, one would think I'd be comfortable at least sitting next to him, but I couldn't bring myself to make a move.

"Of course. What's on your mind?" He thankfully gestured for me to come sit on the bed. I didn't miss the gaze he tore over what I was wearing as he slid over and made room for me to sit on the edge. We faced each other, and I looked him over before I wrestled my choice of words.

"Do you...have your parents kept things about this prophecy from you growing up?"

"Things such as..." He asked cautiously.

"In the past few weeks, I've started realizing just how much about my life I haven't been told about. Things people have kept secret from me, especially in the sense that I was born to...save the world, I suppose." I rolled my eyes. "But...I've recently learned that perhaps you've been just as kept in the dark about things as I have, and I want to know what you know." He drew his brows together.

"About you?"

"No, about yourself. And about us." I met his eyes.

"I'm not sure what else there is to know. I know now that I was born to be with you. To help you and to make sure you succeed."

I shook my head slowly. "I don't think you were just born to be with me and help *me* succeed, Luca."

His face seemed to pale. "You said you recently learned something? What do you know?" He asked in a low voice.

"Frances told me about your name."

"My name?"

I nodded. "Luca means *bringer of light.* He said that you were born with a purpose, the same as I. Paxe says that makes us equals. The trials of our strengths may be in union. How strong we are *together.* I'm guessing that was something you were never told."

He didn't respond for a moment and stared down at the end of the bed. "No, that is definitely news to me. Bringer of light...I suppose I've never thought of—" He snapped his attention back to me.

"What?" I asked, fidgeting with my arms again.

"Light..."

"Okay...light? What about it?"

"I've never thought of names having any sort of meaning. Your mother...her name was Lucinda."

"That's right. What about her?" I became nervous and leaned back a little.

"Lucinda...means light. Do you think there's some kind of connection?"

My mind raced and I felt almost dizzy at the thought of all these pieces that were starting to come together but never forming a real answer. It frustrated me. "I don't know."

"How did you find out what my name meant? You said Frances told you? In what context?" He leaned forward and demanded my attention without even trying. I looked at his eyes again, the swirling of gray and silver tones deepening as he seemed eager for me to continue. It ebbed whatever frustration was starting to build and I relaxed under his stare.

"Frances is a mind reader. He sort of...intruded on my thoughts."

"What thoughts, exactly?" He asked.

"We had listened to the story of the first king, and his grief over his beloved wife and son...the trials he faced, and the choices the gods offered. He told us about how the Midlands were started and the small amount of humans that are allowed in your kingdom. By the end, I had thought that no matter what happened, we'd face it together because we were the chosen ones meant to bring light back to the world...the way the first king had. That was when he told me about the meaning of your name."

We were both quiet and in concentrated thought for a few long moments before he finally spoke again.

"I feel like it all connects somehow. It's something we can research in the next few days. I'm glad you told me." His voice was low and didn't sound as if he were sure if it made him glad or upset.

"I'm sorry," I whispered, rising from the bed. He grabbed my hand and tugged, stopping me. I slowly sat back down.

"Sorry for what? You didn't do anything wrong."

"I didn't mean to upset you. That wasn't my intention. I just—I know how it feels to find out that things have been kept from you. I thought that you deserved to know the truth." I glanced at his tattoo. He followed my eyes and stared into me deeply, his expression grim.

"You didn't upset me, Princess. You deserve to have the same." His thumb slid over the back of my hand and he took a deep breath, exhaling slowly and briefly closing his eyes. "The mark...it appeared when the magic that bonded around our wrists was completed...the day I wagered with your father in the Great Hall. It took me a moment, even after my mother ushered me to leave, to let go of his hand. He knew that I felt it...it burned across my skin and filled every vein in my body with magic so strong, I couldn't think of one way it could ever be broken. I wanted to say something, but it was obvious neither of my parents knew what had transpired, and I wasn't sure what would happen if they lost control. I feared for their safety around your father...and yours too, until you stormed out of there, and I realized how strong you were. I debated on telling you about it several times since then, but I couldn't bring myself to. Then in the tent, when you asked me about it...I couldn't bear the thought of ruining your day with the truth. I've been trying to work up the courage to tell you ever since, but Paxe was here, and everything was so...peaceful. You were happy, and I couldn't take that from you." He looked at me sadly, his breathing quickened as I stared back at him. He knew what I was going to ask next.

"What did he do to you, Luca?" I asked, my tone laced with fury.

"The magic was fast. It was knowing...and direct. It filled my body and locked into place. It didn't hide anything when it hit me. I saw a split-second vision. I was with you in a meadow with purple and yellow flowers. The moon was full, and you were crying. There was a bright light, and...."

I swallowed back the knot in my throat.

"And...?"

"If we win this bargain...your father's heart will stop at moonrise. You'll be safe. But..."

No. Gods...no.

"Don't you dare." He stilled as I cut in. "You won't. I'm not going to let this happen." My eyes pricked with tears of rage and heartbreak. I felt its betrayal as one of them shot quickly down my cheek. He reached up and wiped it away with his finger, and I took his hand, pressing it to my cheek and leaning into it. My body shook with anger.

"It's going to be alright. No matter what the outcome. If the vision was a glimpse of what's to come...I'll be with you. I can't think of a better way to die. I'm not afraid." His eyes sparkled in the dim light, becoming more vivid as they welled with tears. They looked like mercury dripping into an ocean, and I was bewitched.

"Did you know the meeting place when you came to find me there?" I trembled as he nodded in response. "Then we avoid it at all costs. It won't end this way, Luca. He'll never take you from me. The gods must know. They'll know what to do."

"I'll never leave you. I need you to understand that...even if this can't be undone. I vow to be right beside you, Arienne. Until death."

A wave of shock and pain went searing through me at the uttering of those two words. "What?" His responding expression was unreadable.

"Did I say something wrong?" He asked.

"How did you know about that?" I moved his hand from my face.

"Know about what?" His eyes were wide, and some part of me believed that he had no idea what I was talking about.

"Until death." I narrowed my eyes.

"I'm sorry...I don't understand."

"When Paxe and Vetta led me out of the dungeon, I vowed to avenge...it was my promise. I said those exact words. Five years ago."

His face lined with understanding, and he inclined his head.

"I see... I didn't know. You did tell me that you vowed to kill your father that day. The night that you told me what happened, I don't think you ever mentioned exactly what you said. Forgive me." I shook my head.

"No, no...I—I think things are becoming a little more clear to me now." I moved closer. "I need to be honest with you, Luca. I've still been at odds with my heart lately." I tried to ignore the hurt that flashed in his eyes, but it was unmistakably there.

"You weren't ready..." His statement was more as if in question. I squeezed at both his hands.

"I questioned it, but only a little. I spoke with Paxe about it earlier to try and understand my conflict. I'm beginning to."

"I tried to tell you that night in the tent that you didn't have to, Ari. I meant it when I said I would wait for you and that it would take time. I've felt a bit of distance between us in the past two weeks, and I'm fine with giving you the space that you need."

"I don't need space."

"Arienne..." He pulled his hands gently from mine, and something in my chest ached. "Elowen warned you in the forest about this. Whatever grows between us takes nurturing...the right climate. We have everything we need, but you can't force something to spring into life. You can't expect anything strong to grow in something that casts as much of a shadow as your father has on your life. It needs—"

"Light..." I whispered. He stared longingly at me, and I wanted so badly to touch him. "Luca...I meant what I said in the tent. My heart is yours. I want you so badly and I feel like my body and mind are chasing after what my heart wants. That's the war I'm fighting. I'm afraid...I'm afraid, and I don't know why. I feel like I'm going to disappoint you. I don't want that, especially after knowing the truth."

"Disappoint me? How?"

"I'm not...I don't have any experience in love, Luca. Or anything close. I thought what I felt for Gideon was love. It wasn't. He died for something that may not have even been real. Now my father has branded you with a curse to do the same to you, and the worst part is that even if I wanted to claim I didn't love you and die in your place...I couldn't. I damn you by loving you—just like Gideon." Tears tore down my cheeks. I stood and turned away, walking to the window and holding my arms tightly. I didn't try to hold back the silent cry and took a few moments to think of something to say. I looked out over the flickering lights of lamp posts that were burning down the little side street.

After a few moments, I caught a glimpse of Luca's reflection behind me in the window. His hands softly brushed down my shoulders and he leaned in, moving my long curls away and exposing my neck. I felt the heat of his breath across my skin as he pressed his lips at the base. He trailed light kisses across my shoulder, pulling aside the smooth material, and then returned up my neck to my ear lobe. I closed my eyes and leaned into his touch, wiping the moisture from my face.

"I would die a thousand times for you. You couldn't damn me if you tried. My heart is yours. My life is yours. My soul...is yours," he whispered, kissing behind my ear. "If you truly mean that you're mine, I'm happy to spend the rest of my days giving you every part of me. Any time with you...right here...is worth it."

My breathing slowed, becoming deeper, as his lips brushed the shell of my ear and his hands pulled the ties of my robe apart. It fell open, and I glanced at our reflection in the window as he tugged the shoulders down and it slid down my bare arms. I released the hold on them, letting it drop to the floor and pool at my feet. His fingers lightly trailed back up my arms, and I tilted my head to give him better access to my neck. He took it slowly, kissing it and sending chills through my body as he nipped at the soft skin with his teeth.

I reached into his hair with my left hand and turned my face toward him. He closed the space between us and pressed me to his firm body. My other hand reached behind to touch him and landed against his bare thigh. Heat pooled in my lower belly as I moved my hand higher, realizing there was nothing there to remove.

Gods give me strength...he's naked. Has he been naked all this time?

The tip of his nose brushed my cheek, and I laid my head back. His eyes met mine and I swallowed. If I'd been afraid of being ready, I wasn't any longer. I gave him a slow nod, and he seemed to understand exactly what I meant. He turned me around to face him and pulled me in close, taking my face in his other hand and breathing deeply.

"Tell me what you want, Princess," his voice breathy and smoldering.

I moved my hands down his sides, resting them on his hip bones and leaning in until our lips barely touched. "Kiss me," I breathed. He obliged, pressing into me and moving us back until we were up against the window. He raised me up to sit me on the sill and I spread my legs to fit around him, inviting him closer as he deepened our kiss and his hard length pressed against my belly. I struck my palm against the glass to raise myself higher and he stopped me, breaking away and lowering himself, as his hands took my thighs and pushed my shift up higher. He kissed down my neck and over my chest. He knelt down and continued trailing his mouth up the inside of my thigh, inching closer to where an ache was beginning to ravage my center.

He pulled my legs over his shoulders, and I leaned against the window as his mouth grazed the apex of my thighs. My breathing was heavy, and my heart thrashed as I looked down and watched his tongue slide through me, moving up and slowly tracing around the throbbing spot at the top that I was desperately praying he'd taste. His eyes flashed up at me with a look in them that took my very breath. He softly took the delicate skin between his teeth, flicking his tongue across it and sucking me into his mouth. I jerked back, laying my head against the glass and biting hard on my bottom lip to keep myself from crying out. That familiar feeling of release crept up on me fast.

His tongue moved over me with expert skill, as if it was more familiar with that area than I was. My eyes rolled back, and I snapped them shut as I knotted my fingers in Luca's hair. I couldn't help the reaction of my body, my hips writhing as he continued. I felt the pressure starting to build and dared another look down at him. His smile demanded my body to let go and I fought it with everything I had. That was until he sucked me into his mouth again and slid his fingers inside of me. My other hand slapped against my mouth as I moaned as quietly as I could manage. It felt unbelievable, but I couldn't shake the need I felt for *him* to be inside me instead. That said enough for me. I was going to have him tonight.

His fingers moved in and out of me, and I knew I wouldn't be able to fight it off much longer when I started losing my ability to catch my breath. My legs began to tremble and I pressed them closer together. He moved faster, and my back arched off the glass. A wave of raw, undiluted pleasure racked through my body and I fisted his hair as I gasped for breath. My breathing shuddered in shallow bursts as I slowly relaxed and laid back against the cool glass of the window. He slowly pulled his fingers from me, and I felt my arousal drip from my body onto the floor as I fluttered my eyes closed and tried to calm my breathing. He kissed the insides of my legs and slowly rose from the floor, leaning in to press his lips to my neck. I could feel every inch of him against me. Part of me was exhausted...the other was starving for him.

"I'd give up everything to make you feel like this every day... for the rest of our lives, Arienne..." His whisper fanned across my neck. My body tensed and began to reheat as if it was already prepared to leave everything that had just happened behind and start over completely.

I wrapped my shaky legs around him and placed my hands on either side of his face, kissing him deeply and tasting myself on his tongue. It only fueled my desire, and I let my body handle all my control. I dropped one hand down his chest and sank it further down, feeling every movement from his labored breathing to his hard muscular stomach reacting to my touch. My fingers met resistance when I finally felt the velvety skin of his length, and I wasted no time wrapping my hand firmly around it. His breath caught in his throat, and he pressed his head to me, breaking our kiss and brushing his lips against mine. I gently took his bottom lip between my teeth and slowly stroked my hand.

From what I could feel, he was intimidatingly well endowed. My fingers couldn't touch together around him, and I knew I had moved my hand several inches and still hadn't reached the tip. A knot gathered in my throat and I swallowed hard. I wouldn't back down tonight. Everything I had in my grasp was mine. I wanted to make him feel what I felt. I wanted to watch him come undone the way that I had. Hear every sound he made as I took him into my body. I wanted it now.

"Take me to bed, Luca," I whispered into his mouth. He hesitated and gripped the underside of my thighs. "Take me." We both struggled to breathe, and I wrapped my arms around his neck. He lifted me from the windowsill, and I hooked my legs around his hips. He walked us over and sat me in his lap, leaning his back against the wooden headboard.

I straddled him, crossing my arms in front of me and leaning back as I pulled my nightshift over my head and threw it to the floor. Not one part of me felt ashamed or bashful about bearing everything to him. His eyes took in every inch of me as he brushed the hair over my shoulders. It cascaded down my back, leaving my breasts open to the cool air. He lightly trailed his fingers across them and my nipples hardened at his touch. His eyes were on fire as they met mine.

"You...are devastatingly beautiful." His voice was low and breathless.

I raised up and leaned over him, taking his face in my hands and claiming his mouth with my own. His hands gripped at my hips as I positioned myself and felt the tip of his cock graze my entrance. I felt it twitch as I began lowering myself onto him, my body stretching to fit him inside. A sharp inhale left us both as I sank farther down and I held my breath, squeezing my eyes shut and dropping my mouth open at the sudden shock of slight discomfort.

"Breathe..." He shuddered, taking my chin in his fingers. His other hand moved to the small of my back and I took his advice as he guided me back up, and then farther down. The sudden pain started to ease into something indescribable as I repeated my movement until I had seated myself completely onto him. My hair fell into our faces, blowing back and forth with our shallow, wild breathing. He tucked it behind my ear and gripped the back of my neck, closing his eyes and cursing under his breath. My heart skipped beats, and a wave of emotions flooded my senses as I moved slowly up and down his entire length. He opened his eyes to meet mine, and a low groan escaped his mouth.

So, this is what it feels like...being in love.

I kissed him again, tenderly at first, but growing ravenous as if everything our bodies were experiencing wasn't enough and demanded more. We listened...picking up the pace and getting louder, no longer caring if we woke the whole house. Every time he made another sound, another fire ignited in me and I followed it wherever it was going.

Paxe had been right. I was afraid for absolutely no reason. This was everything. *He* was everything. I wanted to kick myself for being so stupid. He wrapped his arms tightly around me and I did the same around his neck. He lifted us up and leaned onto his knees, holding me steady and thrusting into me, our faces buried in each other's necks. Our bodies began to stick together, becoming damp with sweat. Heat began pooling low in my center, and I begged him not to slow down. I let my head fall back, and he pressed his forehead to my chest, his movements fluid and deliberate. I gripped his hair in both my hands.

"Harder..." I begged, barely audible over the sound of frantic breathing.

He laid me down at the end of the bed, never pulling himself from me and braced his weight with one strong arm by my shoulder. His other hand lifted my chin, and he rolled his hips more forcefully between my legs. I arched off the bed, raising my legs on either side and pushing him deeper with my heel on his lower back. He growled into my neck and drove into me faster as I dragged my nails down his slick spine. My body began to shake with the need to release. He responded to it, flipping his hair over the shoulder he leaned on, and pressed his mouth to mine. I took it greedily, pulling him close as he slammed into me harder. I felt him pulsing inside me, and it sent me over the edge. I moaned loudly into his mouth, lifting my head from the mattress and shaking violently as he spilled into me. He trembled as I smoothed his damp hair away from his face and looked him in his silver eyes.

Neither of us could get a word out as we took each other in for a long moment, breathing heavily and realizing everything we had just done. Completely exhausted, we kissed again, and I dropped my head back to the bed and tried to catch my breath. He slackened down into my arms and laid his head on my chest, my hands finding purchase in his thick hair. His fingers trailed lazily down my side as we lay there in silence for a while. I could have laid there forever. If it weren't for his occasional touch across my skin, I would have thought he had fallen asleep. I couldn't find any will to close my eyes with everything racing through my mind as I stared up at the wooden planks in the ceiling.

"Did I hurt you?" He asked quietly against my chest. I giggled softly.

"Not at all."

He raised up to look at me, his brows drawn together.

"What's so funny?" He glared down at me. I snorted.

"Did I hurt *you?*" I laughed, trailing my fingertips down the semi-bloody scratches down his back. He tried and failed miserably, to look over his shoulder at them.

"Absolutely not. But you're welcome to try again," he smiled. Something about it heated my cheeks and I raised my brows.

"Oh?" I said, my tone challenging and seductive. I moved my hips slightly, knowing he was still buried inside me, and he flinched.

"Careful, Princess...you'll wake him," he warned.

"Good..." I whispered, leaning in to kiss him again.

The fire between us ignited again, and we raged with it several more times throughout the night until the tendrils of dawn started peeking in through the bedroom window. The misty blue gradients of early morning turned into bright, balmy sunlight and it illuminated our tangled bodies, uncovered and peacefully resting in each other's arms. I winced at the unwelcome morning and tucked my head underneath Luca's chin. He softly kissed my forehead and rested his lips there, tugging me closer. Neither of us were in any rush to move.

When we finally stirred, I turned my face to the window and gathered that it had to be nearly noon. I could hear the faint sounds of happenings through town outside. I shuffled around and Luca smiled lazily at me.

"Paxe is probably wondering where you are. It's late."

I scoffed. "Paxe is the reason for my scantily clad knock at your door last night."

"Remind me to buy her a gift," he grinned, stretching his arms and bringing them back around me. "Tell me...how do you feel?"

"I'd be lying if I said I didn't feel different...somehow," I said softly as I fixed my eyes on his lips. I traced my finger along his bottom one and he bit down on it gently. "I can't figure out now why I was so afraid."

"You were incredible..." He pressed his lips to my palm. My heart warmed.

"I don't ever want to be without you. The first king...his wife. I can't imagine your soulmate being ripped away...I'm going to stop this, Luca." My throat bobbed, and I fought back unshed tears. He leaned in and kissed me.

"I'm not going anywhere, love," he whispered. "Don't worry about it right now. You need to eat." I shot him a confused look.

"Eat?" I asked. He smiled as he raised himself up and sat at the edge of the bed.

"And hydrate. I'm going to get you something."

"Just sit on a plate for me...real fancy like," I grinned. His back faced me, completely marred from my assault, and I flushed at the recalled images of my nails digging into his skin.

"No, you heathen," he snickered. He pulled on some dark gray trousers and stood to tug them up to his waist. I drank in every scandalous inch of his naked body in the light. He turned as he tied the laces at his front and smiled as I bit down on my lip.

"Keep doing that...and neither of us leaves this room for the rest of the day." His eyes turned dark as I crawled to him and raised up on my knees, tugging him forward by the waist of his pants. "Gods..." He whispered, almost accidentally. He leaned down into my kiss and I pushed him backward, stepping off the bed and breaking away as I walked past him towards the door and not breaking eye contact. I hooked a finger into his waistband and snapped it against his skin. He hissed through his teeth and watched me walk naked out the door and towards my bedroom. He appeared in his doorway before I completely closed mine, and I gave him a sinister smile as I clicked it shut. "I've created a gods-damned monster."

CHAPTER 15

BLOOD

The next hour was spent washing up and reluctantly getting dressed as my muscles groaned in protest at everything I tried to do. Luca made a small breakfast and some strong coffee and we ate together at the table alone, no sign of Paxe or Frances anywhere, other than a note she'd left on the stone kitchen island that I nearly spit my coffee out reading.

When you two pigs are finished grunting and sleeping it off...
Come find me.
I'm at Mary's confectioner's shop, trying to eat off my lack of restful sleep.
Thanks a lot...love you.

-*P*-

"She has a way with words," Luca laughed, shoveling eggs into his mouth. I giggled, folding the note and sticking it in my pocket.

"I'm going to miss the hell out of her." I said sadly.

"We'll all see each other again. When it's safe."

"What are you going to do for the rest of the day?" I asked curiously.

"Now that you mention it...I need to go talk to someone about where we can stay when we get to Bolton. We need some more supplies too before we leave in a couple days."

"So, are we leaving the day Paxe does?" He shook his head, standing and gathering our plates as I downed another cup of black coffee.

"I think we should leave the day after, though. From here, it doesn't quite take an entire day to get there. The earlier we leave that morning, the better."

"You're right. Is there anything I can help you get while I'm in town?" I stood, wincing at the cramps in my legs. He grinned over at me.

"Maybe stop by an apothecary...get you something to tend to those sore muscles?" He winked. I slithered around the island and backed him into the wall.

"Watch yourself, Prince." I pressed my body flush against him and he slid his hands down the smooth leather on my thighs. His smile turned adorable. "What are you smiling about?"

"I get to love you," he whispered, kissing my temple. "See you soon. Go find her before she gorges herself. I'm going to clean this up before I head out."

I tore myself away and headed out the door, towards the street and I saw Paxe heading back to the house. I smiled bashfully at her and she scowled at me before breaking into a wicked grin.

"She lives!" She laughed, throwing up her arms and being overly dramatic. I rolled my eyes and slapped a palm to my face.

"Gods...would you stop?"

We were a few yards from each other when unsettling screams started ringing off in the distance. I lowered my brows and she turned to look, the usual clacking of hooves on the cobblestone streets thundered instead. My stomach turned with dread.

Royal guard. He found us. Fuck.

"Ari..." Paxe panicked, throwing her attention to me.

"Hide! They may not be here for you. Let me handle it. Go now. Get in the stable and climb to the loft. Wait there and don't make a sound." I motioned for her to hurry and she raced past me towards the stable. The guard was spreading out through the square ahead, several of them heading towards me. I looked around for my father, but thankfully, didn't see any sign he was with them. I stood my ground as they approached, taking their helmets off and the leader inclining his head in greeting.

"Your Highness...you're difficult to recognize in peasant clothes," he sneered. I didn't react. He stared me down and after a moment decided to dismount his horse. "Where's your prince?"

"Right here," Luca answered from behind me, his tone lethal.

"Ahh...Prince Luca. I'm to bring you both back to Valdaro to speak with your king." His arrogance dripped from every pore.

"We're not going anywhere. Except where we plan to go. My father knows about our plans to travel. As long as we're on Valdarian territory, I'm free to go wherever I please. If you came all this way without a message to deliver, I'm afraid you wasted your time," I said forwardly.

"He thought you might say that. He wanted us to remind you that your friend might suffer grave consequences for your failure to comply. I urge you to heed his warning." A cruel slash spread across his smug face.

"He was not to touch her until we brought back proof of her innocence. Unless you're telling me he's located the human she's accused of bedding," I countered.

"Cute. I'll give you one more chance to tell me the truth, Princess."

"The truth about what?" I narrowed my eyes. Luca drew the sword I had in my bag upstairs and stepped in front of me.

"Take a step towards her and I'll hang you by your bowels," he uttered with a voice cold as death. The other guards dismounted and fell into formation behind their leader who kept his stupid grin and fixed his eyes on me.

"You're going to stand behind your lie and try to pretend you don't know that the filthy slut was stripped of her power and banished from our lands? The king received word that you and your prince were here, accompanied by a female named *Isabelle*. Not to mention, your hospitality being given to you by a woman who raised you both. We know she's here and we'll find her. Come quietly and I won't give her the same treatment you got in that cell...with a lot more than two tiny cocks." He split a grin that showed all his teeth.

"Say another word in disrespect. I dare you. She's your future queen." Luca readied his sword, his knuckles white around its hilt.

"Luca..." I laid a hand on his shoulder. "It's alright." I turned my attention calmly to the prick that was desperately trying to unnerve me. "All the shit I've been given about what happened to me is getting old. I'm not afraid of my past. If you think that you're going to get anywhere by throwing it in my face...again, you've wasted your time. She's not here. And if you're telling the truth, then I hope she got as far away from this shithole as possible. I do have an attendant named Isabelle. She's a resident of Aeon. If my father wants an audience with me, he can leave the protection of his big shiny castle and come speak with his daughter. I'm no longer his prisoner and I won't be going anywhere with you. Now leave."

"A resident of Aeon...tending to you, and bearing the name of her whore mother? You insult me." He jerked his head in order. "Search the house."

"What's the meaning of this?" Frances called from the stable as he walked up from behind me. My heart hammered against my chest and I suddenly wished I had something to protect him with.

"Give her up, Lombardi. Where's the girl?" The guard asked as the rest of them started spreading around the house, kicking the back door in. I was so glad to have had the sense to put her note in my pocket. I tried to think of anything else that would betray her in the house, but couldn't think of anything. Frances stepped beside me and offered a confident glance.

"The only lady in my house is the princess."

"If you're lying old man, you'll die today." The guard's attention moved behind me toward the stable and I did my best to hide my sudden urge to vomit. "Bring her here."

Luca turned to look and I kept my focus on the guard when I heard heavy footsteps creeping closer. Frances looked at him pleading, as if begging him not to open his mouth. From behind the horses, I could see a stout female walking toward us from the square.

One of the men brought Paxe forward and she said nothing as she looked at the leader. She showed little fear, and I tried desperately to read her expression and figure out what they knew that I didn't.

"Who are you?" He asked as he approached her.

"My name is Isabelle," she answered quietly. He looked her over and narrowed his eyes, turning toward two other guards for clarity. They shook their heads as if they didn't recognize her.

"If you know where the fugitive is, you had better tell me. My patience is growing thin. One of you is coming back to the castle today." He looked at us both. The guards that searched the house joined us and went back into formation as the stout figure in the street came into better view.

Vetta?

"I didn't come home for retirement to see you royal lot, every day. If you don't wear a crown or you weren't invited, then I'd appreciate very much if you'd stop scaring old women and children and take your pompous rear ends back to Valdaro," she said firmly as she waddled around the horses and smiled at Frances. "Brother, you look well."

"Welcome home," he smiled. She turned to Paxe.

"Izzy? Why are you here? Your mother is waiting," Vetta lied. I couldn't have been more confused. "Mary said you've been little help since the princess came into town. I'll not tolerate that, girl. Get to it. I've wiped her behind since she was a wee child. I'll take it from here. Go home."

"I don't think so," the guard leader snapped. "What are you playing at?"

Vetta gave him a cross look. "I'm old enough to be your grandmother. You'll watch your tone. I'm caretaker to two girls in that castle that are no longer there. I'm playing no games. I've done my duty and I'm coming home. The last thing I wish to see is a bunch of guards causing havoc in my town. There's no wrong being done here. The princess has been given permission to travel Valdarian lands with her betrothed. Mount your horses and be gone."

The leader sneered at her and pulled a bit of folded parchment from a satchel at his side. He unfolded it and held it up to Paxe's face. It was a drawing that captured her likeness in every way. I held my breath.

"She doesn't fit the description, sir," a shorter officer offered.

What is happening?

"Fine. But the princess has been requested nonetheless." He threw the parchment to the ground. "You'll ride with me, your Highness." He said, turning to face me. "I'm looking forward to having that ass bounce in my lap. You may even enjoy it enough to slide those pa—" His disgusting execration was replaced by a sickening gurgling sound as I moved like lightning, jerking the sword from Luca's hand and slicing through his throat. His eyes grew wide with panic as he clawed at his neck, desperate for a breath. There were none coming.

Everyone flew back from me. Everyone but Luca, who watched proudly as I kicked the leader to the ground and stood over him with a leg on either side of his writhing body. I squatted over him, my chest heaving up and down as I thrust the sword into his groin, pushing it upward into his body and twisting it, skewering him like a shrimp.

"Shut your disgusting fucking mouth." I pulled the sword out slowly, watching the other guards look on in horror as the snake below me finally stopped moving. I stood, blood spatter across my cheek from the spray of his throat, staring at them. "Does anyone else want to try and force my hand? I may not be queen...but as a princess, I rank much higher than you. Take this piece of shit back to my father and leave us alone. Let him know that if he tries another thing...I'll make sure his suffering is long and grueling. Now get out." The guards stood in shock for a moment, none of them making a move. I lowered my voice and spoke with absolute promise, my tone ice cold and unfamiliar, "You have until I clean this blade to move him and clear out before hanging each of you by your bowels starts becoming more and more appealing to me." I smoothed the flat side of my sword across my cream-colored tunic, the blood a stark red against the white.

Two of the guards reluctantly grabbed their leader's lifeless body from the ground and draped it over his horse. The guard standing nearest to Paxe stepped towards me, raising his hands in surrender.

"Your Highness...I'll report back to the king. For what it's worth, the sergeant had it coming. You don't deserve the treatment you've been delivered. When the time comes, I'm proud to be in allegiance to you." He bowed at the waist, turning to the men who were mounting their horses and glanced over at Paxe. "Be more careful," he whispered. She inclined her head nervously at him, and he walked to meet the retreating officers. I looked over at her and she met my eyes. My hands shook and I lowered my head, dropping the sword to the ground and turning to the house. Luca rested a hand at my back and guided me silently to the broken back door.

We didn't speak to each other as we hastily made our way through the kitchen that was now ransacked, through the living area that was equally littered with overturned furniture, and up the stairs into the bathing room. I didn't bother to look into either one of the bedrooms, fearing I'd lose all control of my rising temper if everything we had was ripped to shreds. He closed the door to the small space and finally turned me to face him. I looked down at the blood on my tunic and hands, turning my palms up as I shook with nerves and rage.

I just killed someone...I took someone's life.

"Arienne..." Luca started, calmly. "Look at me, love," he gripped my shoulders.

"I can't," I shuddered.

"Please...look at me." I shook my head, hot tears raced down my cheeks.

"I killed him, Luca."

"If he had laid a hand on you, I would have killed him anyway. It no longer matters which one of us got to him first. Look at me." I raised my head but didn't look him in the eyes. His thumb wiped across my cheek, staining it with blood as he rested his palm on the side of my face. "Ari..." I finally met his gaze. His eyes were calming and completely understanding. "Don't blame yourself for this. If I'd not been here and he'd taken you...he—" His grip at my shoulder grew tighter. "I'm glad. The way you handled yourself...your life. The people you love. Your judgment was earned. You were justified. And I'm glad for it."

"You don't understand...I killed him. I enjoyed it." My voice cracked with emotion.

"I know. I felt you."

"You didn't calm me. You let me kill him."

"I did calm you. You tried calming *me* when I did. You seemed like you had a better hold on your emotions than I did with my own, and I didn't expect you to grab that blade from my hands. By the time I realized what you were doing, it was too late, but I wasn't sorry. Your form was effortless and you moved like a warrior. You took control, and you protected yourself and the people that mean the most to you. I've never been more proud in my entire life. You don't have a single reason to be sorry for what happened."

"I'm not sorry! That's the worst part... I'm not sorry at all. Watching him bleed...feeling the muscle give under my blade...twisting it in his body...it *fed* me. For a moment I was my father, Luca! What I just did...he's tested me. He said in the Great Hall that he wanted me to grow a spine. He wanted me to kill. He sent that bastard here and he *knew*," I started to feel the push of deep sobs in my throat. Luca looked at me as if he were starting to understand where I was going. "I told him in the study I wouldn't kill anyone for him. He's breaking me. I just fell right into his snare. I sent back proof on that horse that he won this round with me." I heaved and the sobs finally tore out. "I don't want you to be proud! I want you to be angry with me... I want you to tell me that I should have known better!"

I shoved him into the door, pushing him away from me. He leaned against it, watching me, too stunned to speak. My rage boiled over and I growled with the deepest hate for my father and my limbs took on a life of their own. I slammed my fist into the mirror, shards of glass exploding from its center. I turned to the wall, breaking potted plants on shelves, and tearing them down. My knuckles tore open with the next blow I landed against a stone inlay in the wall behind me, and Luca had finally had enough, wrapping his arms around me in restraint and forcing me to look at him.

"Arienne! Stop it... Stop! You want to take your anger out...take it out on me. You're hurting yourself." I tried to wrangle free but he held me tighter. "Stop."

"Let go of me!" I screamed, tears soaking my face. He paused and took a step back, freeing me. He patted his chest.

"Hit me," he growled, breathing heavily. I stood there, glaring at him and my body shook.

"Why?" I said through clenched teeth.

"I'm softer than a stone wall, and I can handle it. Hit me. Beat the shit out of me."

"No."

"Afraid?"

"No."

"Then stop acting like it. Hit me."

I landed a solid punch to his middle.

"Not hard enough. Hit me again." He tensed, and I got angrier.

"Stop goading me, Luca. Just get out and leave me be," I snarled.

"Not going to happen. If you're pissed, then hit me again." He stepped closer.

"Don't... Get out!" I shouted. He shook his head and moved in another step. I hit him again, harder this time, and he groaned, but moved forward one more time. I saw red, and unleashed everything I had, until I realized my betrothed wasn't my enemy. He stood there, taking every blow and waited patiently for me to fizzle out before he spoke.

"Ari..." He whispered, looking at me as if it tore him apart to see me this way. I panted loudly and leapt into him, crushing our lips together. Our kiss was violent, and we hit the bathing room door as he lifted me up and held me. I reached down to his chest, tearing his shirt open and dragging the scraps down his shoulders. He turned and sat me down on the wash stand, throwing his shirt to the floor and ripping my tunic apart, without ever breaking our kiss.

I shrugged it off, and we tore at each other's clothes until we were both fully naked. My legs wrapped around him and he thrust himself inside me, without warning, and I cried out, hooking an arm around his neck and bracing myself against the wooden table with my other hand. Feral growls rang out between us through ragged breaths, over the harsh sound of our bodies slapping against each other. He picked me up and pinned me against the wall, gripping the backs of my shoulders and slamming into me faster. Every movement was punishing and hard. He reached up with one hand gripping me by the hair and pulling my head back to bite down on my neck, sucking the skin harshly, while he pounded himself against my body.

My nails sank into the back of his shoulders and we both made ungodly moans as release tore violently through us...first with Luca, and ending with me. He looked up at me scrambling for air, and I put my hands on his face.

"I'm so sorry..." I whispered breathlessly. "I'm so, so sorry," I touched our heads together. "Forgive me."

"No...forgive *me*." His breathing staggered. "I should have cut him down...not you."

"I shouldn't have hit you like that. Did I hurt you?" I looked down at his chest, angry red spots splotched across his skin. It made me feel terrible. I looked back up to find him grinning. "Luca...this isn't funny. Look at your body."

"Regardless of whether or not you enjoyed your kill, you were in a state of shock...you needed an outlet. I'm happy to be that for you. I'll wear a few bruises with pride. My Queen packs a mean punch. I'm more than impressed. If anything, it makes me love you more." He kissed me deep and spoke into my mouth, "You're incredible."

He moved me from the wall and laid me into the small tub, filling it with warm water, and nearly overflowing it as he sank into it behind me. I leaned back against him as he bathed me, washing blood from my face and hair and carefully removing tiny shards of the mirror from my busted knuckles. We tried to clean up as much of the destruction from my outburst as possible, throwing all the broken glass into a bin and replacing the shelf to its home on the wall. I looked around, thoroughly disappointed in myself, and wondered how I was going to explain it all to Vetta and Frances. I hoped I hadn't destroyed anything special to them.

Luca pulled his pants back on and wrapped the remains of his shirt around me as we finally emerged through the door to find Paxe leaning against the door jamb of our bedroom with her arms crossed, smirking and shaking her head.

"Are you alright?" She asked, softly. I nodded. Luca turned me to him, holding me close and kissing the top of my head.

"I love you," he whispered into my wet hair. I closed my eyes and buried my face into his bare chest, lightly touching my fingertips to the welts I'd left on his body.

"I love you." I pressed a kiss to his damp skin and looked up at him.

"I'm going to talk to Miss Vetta. See if she'll forgive the bathing room and be willing to take a look at your hands." He looked at Paxe. "How bad was your bedroom? Anything missing?"

"Not that I could tell. The knife and arrow are still safe. Just a bunch of clothes strewn everywhere, but I've cleaned them up. I—I umm...straightened your room too, Luca. I hope that's alright."

"Of course. Thank you," he smiled. I gulped at the realization that she probably heard everything that happened in the bathing room.

Gods help me.

I shot Luca a look that said as much, and he grinned in response as I turned to my room to find clothes and he started down the stairway. I took notice of Paxe's expression when she caught a glimpse of the marks I'd left all over his bare back. I hurried into the room to hide my face from her and she shut the door behind us.

"Ahem...friend," she started. I ignored her as I plundered through the rickety old drawers of the dresser against the wall, pulling out a snuggly oversized gray sweater that was almost the color of Luca's eyes. I dropped the tattered shirt off my shoulders and heard her take in a sharp breath behind me. I turned to look over my shoulder.

"What?" I asked as she stood gawking at me.

"Gods, Ari...your back looks almost as bad as his does."

I moved a few steps over to the small mirror and turned around to see. There were a few long red marks from the wall, and heat flushed across my cheeks. I could see her head shaking in the mirror. "It's not that bad."

"It looks like a dog got ahold of your neck," she smirked. I pulled the sweater over myself and snuggled into its soft feel as it fell across my thighs. I grabbed a pair of knit leggings and pulled them on next, pulling my hair from the collar of my sweater and walking to the bed, sitting carefully. "Do you want to talk about what happened out there? I'm worried about you." She came and sat next to me.

"Did you hear our fight?" I asked quietly, staring forward.

"I did....among other things," she chuckled softly through her nose.

"Am I right?" I asked as my lip quivered a little. She let out a long sigh.

"I think you both are... if I'm being honest. He has a very good point too. Before you lashed out, I would have thought the same as Luca. The fact that you enjoyed killing a monster doesn't *make* you one. He may have been worse than the kind of sick, demented pieces of shit that violated you. Imagine the safety of your people, Ari. Not what your father set up to trap you into doing. There's no telling what kind of justice you just gave to females he's hurt before. Consider that. Forgive yourself. Move forward. It's all that you *can* do." She put a gentle hand on my back. Tears fell slowly from both my eyes.

"I can imagine the victory he'll feel over me when that body gets back to the castle."

"If he was smart, he'd take it as the threat you intend it to be," she offered.

I thought back to the afternoon and images of his face and the blood spilling from his throat played back through my mind. Then I remembered the picture of Paxe that he threw to the ground, and the officer that tried to comfort me afterwards. My brows came together and I looked over at her.

"What's the matter?" She asked, concerned by my expression.

"Why didn't they recognize you? And why did that officer tell you to be more careful, as if he *did* recognize you?" I asked, my tone almost angry.

"Frances found me in the stable and gave me the necklace I had worn here. Your mother's amulet. He told me to put it on and assured me it would give me protection from anyone that meant me harm. He said that Vetta had sent word that she was on her way home and would be here to see me off before Luca's father collected me. She was aware of the royal guard, and he said that she warned him that I was to give the name I had been using in Aeon, and *only* that name. My only hope was to trust that there was a reason and when they didn't recognize me, I assumed that her amulet cloaked my true identity."

"And the officer that swore his allegiance to me? He seemed to know it was you," I pressed.

"He did. His father is your training instructor. His name is Mischa and he used to have a fondness for me when we were younger. I never really gave him any affection in that way but it was obvious that his heart showed no ill intent towards me. The magic in her pendant must have sensed that. I'm forever grateful that he didn't give me away. I hope he lives long enough for me to thank him." She seemed melancholy. "I feel I've caused so much unneeded friction in everyone's life. I wish this was all over."

I felt terrible for ever seeming angry after hearing what she'd said. I pulled her close and laid on her shoulder. "I love you," I murmured gently. "You could never be a burden to me. I'm going to miss you so much...but I feel like you'll finally have some peace in your life when you get to Crona."

"I love you too...I can tell you this though," she started, "It will sure be nice when I can sleep without hearing a couple of rabid animals ripping each other to shreds in the next room." We both broke into explosive laughs and she hit me in my arm.

"You did this...it's all your fault," I snorted, shoving her. She gaped at me.

"All I did was give you something to wear and lock you out of this room. The rest is between the two of you. And I can't wait to hear how the sweaty handprints came upon the bedroom *window*. Here, I thought you were so afraid of not knowing what to do and you give Aeon a peep show and tear down the entire house." She heaved a hard silent laugh, gripping her stomach and leaning over.

We caught our breath and I stared off, recalling every moment of the night before. A small smile tugged at the corners of my mouth and I bit down on my lip. "I didn't realize how amazing it could be, Paxe...being with him, like that...it's—" I paused. "My body...my heart...I can't get enough of him now."

"I'd ask if it hurt, but it seems that does the trick for you." She laughed. "But really...that male is so in love with you. It makes me so happy to know that he's with you when I can't be. I have no doubt that he'll do anything to protect you and keep you safe." I frowned and looked at her, "What is it?"

"The mark on his chest...he told me the truth. Father cursed him to die with him at moonrise on my Ventus, if we win this wager. He's trying to take him from me." Her face went pale. "I'll die if anything happens to him. I don't want to live another day if he's not in the world."

"Ari..." She wrapped her arms around me. "That's not going to happen. Push it out of your mind. Don't let that be a stigma on what you and Luca have together. Enjoy each other...be together. Love him. The gods told you that the reward would be great for both of you. They'll fix this. Have faith."

"If I kill the king before the Ventus...do you think it would break the curse?"

She released me and thought hard about it for a moment.

"You know...that actually...that makes a lot of sense. Have you told Luca about this?"

"Not yet, it crossed my mind only a moment ago. If my father dies and the power is transferred, perhaps it voids the binding magic between them. Nothing about that bargain mentioned not trying to rid the world of each other before the Ventus. It hasn't stopped him from trying to hurt me." My eyes widened with hope.

"He's underestimated you," she smiled. "I think we all have."

A knock at the door interrupted our conversation and Vetta came into the room with coffee and looked at me with an expression Paxe and I must have seen thousands of times before. This time without her normal dress of servitude. "You have some explaining to do, child."

"Vetta...I'm so sorry," I raised from the bed as she handed Paxe and I the steaming mugs. "I don't know what came over me. I'll replace everything." She swatted the air and gestured for me to sit back down.

"I'm not talking about the house. You two girls have damaged enough things in your short lives to drive anyone mad, but all that can be fixed. It'll give Frances something to do. What I do want to understand is why your prince looks as if he fought off a bear in the woods."

Paxe's coffee exploded from her mouth and she covered it with her hand. I turned thirty different shades of red. Vetta leaned in and moved my hair from my neck, inspecting the bruising and bite marks, and rolled her eyes.

"Gods have mercy," she grumbled. I swallowed and opened my mouth to speak. "No need, child. Passion is a strange thing. But I must say...I've never seen two people so in love." I felt warm, touched by her approval and smiled up at her. "Let me see those hands." Paxe moved to the other side of the bed as Vetta sat, and I put the mug down on the bedside table, allowing her to examine the torn flesh of my knuckles. She looked up at me and met my eyes, gently squeezing my fingers. "I can heal the body, but the heart will take time. Are you alright?"

"I'll be fine," I whispered, leaning in to hug her. She rubbed my back and patted it twice and I winced. She pulled away and looked at me crossly. I gulped. The back of my sweater tugged away from my skin as she leaned forward and looked down the collar at my back. Paxe giggled from behind me and Vetta shook her head.

"Lay back, child...good gracious. I've never..." She scolded as I obeyed, ignoring my friend who was still snickering beside me. "How that could be pleasurable to anyone just evades me. I suppose, that's why they use the expression *crazy in love,*" she smirked to herself, placed a pillow in my lap and started mending my fingers. I closed my heavy eyelids and drifted into sleep before she had even finished.

When my eyes opened again the room was dark; a weakening fire burning in the small fireplace. It was quiet and I was alone. I stared into the shadows of the ceilings and flexed my fingers. They were stiff, but not very sore. I glanced at the window and wondered how long I had slept and where everyone was. Images of the brute that I slaughtered, flashed in my mind and I shivered with anger...no...not anger...

I jolted up from the bed and charged for a chamber pot sitting on the floor. I pulled my hair back and hit my knees, retching into the pot with vigor. I saw my father's wicked face, his mouth curved into a sinister half smile and I squeezed my eyes shut, heaving into another violent purge. I coughed loudly and tears dripped from my eyes as my body tried desperately to rid itself of unpleasant imagery. My breath caught in my throat and I gagged once more, bowing my back and emptying the rest of my stomach into the pot. I coughed harshly and spit.

The bedroom door swung open and Luca's knees hit the floor beside me, taking my hair and pulling it back in his hands. "It's alright, love." Paxe and Vetta entered a moment later.

"What happened?" Paxe asked in a panicked voice as she knelt in front of the pot.

"Out of the way, you two," Vetta said, waddling toward me in a long nightgown. Paxe sat on the bed and Luca moved behind me, as she slid the pot over and crouched down in front of me, taking my face in her hands. She lifted my face to meet her eyes. "She's in shock. Luca...hold her steady. Paxe, get her hunting knife from the bag and bring it over here.

My vision blurred and my body began to shake as Vetta wiped her hand across my face. A thin sheen of sweat started enveloping me. Paxe handed Vetta the knife.

"What are you doing, Vetta?" She asked, her eyes wide.

"Light that lamp on the table. Luca, give me your hand." They both did as they were told, and Vetta cut a large slit into his palm. He grunted, leaning back and pulling me to his chest. My breathing grew heavy and more images flooded my mind. I had no control over them. I saw flashes of Gideon's hands hitting the floor and the two guards that raped me. One laughed in my face while the other thrusted into me from behind. An angry sob tore from my throat and I growled in pain, chest heaving, as Vetta sliced through my opposite hand. "Put them together and use your magic, boy. Hold her close. Give it all you got."

Luca's bloody hand met mine, gripping it tight as he turned us to lean against the side of the bed. My back pressed into his chest and he nuzzled into my neck, his other arm wrapping around me and tugging me in closer. "I'm gonna make it go away, Ari...just breathe."

I felt the moment our blood merged. We both jerked back into the bed, sharply inhaling, and an intense sensation began blending itself into my body. I felt as if my soul reached for it, chasing it down to wherever it was leading me, and his magic intensified. I could hear his voice, but knew somehow that he wasn't speaking out loud.

"Leave her. She is mine," his voice echoed through my mind. *"We are no longer two, but one."* More disgusting images of my brutal assault in my cell struggled through me. He tightened around me, breathing heavily, as if he were seeing everything I could see. Bloody handprints on cold stone, one of the guards forcing himself into my mouth and making me choke on his release. My father slamming my body to the wall in a hallway with his magic when I was a young girl, breaking my arm under his force as punishment for taking sweets from the kitchen. A tiny lifeless baby, lying cold in a dead female's lap, as her arm hung from a cell wall. *"Come back to me. Come home."* A flash of warm light cornered my vision and my soul turned to it. *"Come to me, love. Fight. Remember me."* I tried to block out any other

images, replacing them with his face. Visions of the moment he first looked at me at the long table in the Great Hall, my body against his chest as he carried me down the path. *"Keep going."* I remembered how it felt kissing him for the first time in the tent and the way he looked at me. Images of our bodies writhing together as he made love to me...the way it felt waking up in his arms. I ran to the light and it became brighter the closer I got to it. My inner voice cracked as I finally reached it.

"I love you, Luca." The light took over, surrounding me, and I bathed in its calm. It was a feeling so intense my body drooped in his hold. I felt like I was floating in a sea of utter peace and tranquility. I stayed there until the snap of his magic retreated and reality pulled me back into the world. I gasped as if I had just emerged from a body of water and I was back in my room, in the comfort of my prince's embrace. He looked at me, beads of sweat coating his forehead. We breathed in time with one another, our bleeding palms dripping onto my gray sweater.

"What was that?" I whispered.

"Us..." He answered, his voice low and smooth. We both looked at Vetta, who sat there smiling at our hands that were still in a strong grip.

"Indeed. A blood union with your soulmate connects you both in a way that's unmatched. Should we leave you to destroy the rest of the house, or do you think you have enough control over yourselves to let me mend those slashes?" She smiled.

Paxe stood behind her in awe. "I've never seen anything like that before. How did you know it would work?"

"I didn't." Vetta answered, proudly raising from the floor and grabbing the chamber pot to empty it out.

I turned in Luca's arms to face him and looked into his stare. "I heard you. I heard you like you were there with me. Wherever *there* was."

"I know. I *was* there...I love you, too." He pressed a chaste kiss to my head. "You're incredible."

"You keep saying that, but I'm starting to wonder if it's the other way around. I saw it. I saw your light," I said, feeling the same calm that surrounded me in my fevered fit.

"This is remarkable," Paxe said softly. She handed me a clean, long sleeved blue shirt. "I'm so glad I was still here to bear witness to that. That's not something anyone could soon forget."

"Hold yourself, girl. Don't get blood on that clean shirt. Give me your hands," Vetta cut in, wiping the blood from our open palms with a wet linen. "Did you tell her about the message yet?" She turned her attention to Luca. He shook his head as Vetta's fingers hovered over the slashes that were slowly closing together.

"What message?" I asked, watching in awe of her healing magic.

"Luca's father will be here in the morning with the men that are taking me to Crona. He's going to escort me himself," Paxe answered. I looked at Luca and he smiled.

"He's looking forward to seeing you."

"How late is it?" I asked.

"Probably close to midnight by now...why?" Luca answered. I looked at Paxe sadly, and she tightened her smile in understanding. This was our last night together.

"Vetta...I know you don't approve...but..." I started.

"There are four bottles of wine downstairs. Frances is already waiting for you drunkards." She griped without looking up, as the cuts smoothed into faint purple lines across our palms. Paxe put a hand on her shoulder.

"It would be a tremendous pleasure...if you'd allow me one night to get absolutely inebriated with you," she grinned.

Vetta rolled her eyes. "You'll be on the floor, child, before you ever get near the amount I can put away." I dropped my mouth open and Luca chuckled.

"I thought you didn't drink?" I gawked. She released our hands and motioned for me to change my shirt.

"I don't. Not in front of anyone. But tonight, being in my own home, celebrating my retirement and sending you both off to become adults...I'll make an exception," she smiled as she turned and headed for the stairs. Paxe and I squealed with shock and excitement.

The rest of our night was spent much like we had with Frances. We played card games, danced and sang horribly, and drank to excess. There was hysterical laughter, tales of mischievous acts from our childhood...and Vetta's. Kisses stolen from my betrothed, whenever I got the chance, and the feeling of comfort you can only get from family. I was grateful. My heart felt full. Even if the morning would prove hard, as I'd watch my best friend leave to travel across the continent...tonight would be one to keep close to me forever...for so many reasons.

CHAPTER 16

BOLTON

The morning came much too fast, all of us dragging with a little more than an hour's rest and the hard realization that a knock at the door would sound soon, and King Tidus would arrive to take Paxe home to Crona. Luca helped Vetta in the kitchen, preparing sustenance after our loud night in the room, and checked every so often to search for his father outside the house. I could tell that he was looking forward to seeing his father. I wished so badly that I could say the same about mine. I vowed that the next time I came face to face with him, the life would drain from his eyes.

With Paxe's grand exit, brought ours as well, and Frances prepared Bjourne and Alice for our leave. He packed them down with the food and supplies that Luca never got the chance to go get after the events that transpired yesterday. It felt odd to be leaving Aeon, especially now that Vetta was home for good. I wished I could spend a few more days with all of them. I reckoned we had been here long enough though, and there was still so much ahead of Luca and I, having no idea what future meetings and happenings awaited us.

I stood at the bed Paxe and I shared, folding various items of clothing and packing them neatly in her bag. She stumbled around miserably from lack of rest and too much wine. I stared out the bedroom window watching rain tap the glass. It was a dreary day...fitting of my mood.

"Why don't you ask Vetta to spruce you up? The king is going to get one hell of an impression from you," I grinned, desperate to lighten the situation. She scoffed, pulling more clothes from her armoire in the corner.

"As if he probably doesn't already think I'm a pain in his ass?" She grumbled.

"Wow," I giggled. "You need coffee in a haste. What's wrong? Other than the obvious."

She walked to my side and placed her clothes in the bag. "Nothing. It *is* the obvious. I'll miss you...terribly. All of you. I've grown to really like Luca as well. I'll miss his drunken singing." A smile tugged at her lips. I pulled her into a tight hug and rested my chin on her shoulder.

"This will all be over soon. Then we'll be together again. Truthfully, I'd be happy living here in Aeon and never setting foot in that castle again."

"The simple life, hmm? It does suit you. But you're our future queen..." She pulled back to look at me, a hand on each of my shoulders. "And you haven't seen all there is to see in the rest of this world yet. Neither have I, nor has Luca. I'm betting there's a lot more adventure out there than this sleepy little hollow. Now is our time to go find out. You have a responsibility to your crown, and building a new life with Luca after all this, and healing our lands...that's what we look forward to now." Her eyes filled with tears. "Luca is right...you're incredible. You're going to make one hell of a queen, Arienne."

I pulled her in to hold her tightly and we quietly cried with each other, savoring the last few moments before commotion began downstairs. I pulled back and we looked at each other wide-eyed. "They're here." We broke away, scrambling to primp ourselves before turning to rush downstairs.

Both of us wore a long, plush braid down our left shoulder and form-fitting tunics suitable for long travel. Mine was emerald green, and Paxe's a soft lavender, with her ever-present rosebud at the collar. This one in particular, was white. She looked beautiful, and I knew Lakan would be happy to see her when she arrived wearing their symbol of affection. She let me go ahead of her, shying away from the idea of formally being introduced to a king that wasn't violent. I understood exactly how she felt—the same nervous feeling fluttered in my own stomach as we stepped through the living area and into the kitchen.

Four impeccably dressed royal aides stood next to the fire near the stove, Vetta and Frances softly making conversation with them at the end of the island. Luca and his father stood next to each other, meeting our attention when we entered. Luca was glowing with pride as he beamed at me, loose strands falling into his face from the knot he had tied behind his head. King Tidus grinned in adoration, inclining his head and giving his son a firm slap on the back in approval. The king approached me, taking my hand and pressing it to his mouth. We slightly bowed to each other in greeting.

"Princess...it is a pleasure to see you again," he smiled. Luca leaned against the island with his hands as he looked on, staring tenderly at me as if he were more than happy to show me off like his greatest treasure. It made my heart melt.

"And you, your Highness. Thank you so much for taking care of her," I smiled.

"This must be Lady Paxe." He slid his attention to her as I stepped aside, Luca claimed me with an arm around my waist as she stepped forward and dipped into a curtsy.

"It's lovely to meet you. I'm Tidus, Luca's father."

"Thank you, your Majesty. Lovely to meet you as well," she said as a slight blush of pink grazed her cheeks. I couldn't blame her. Both of Luca's parents were strikingly attractive.

"If you'll give us just a few moments to stretch our legs, we'll be heading out. Hopefully, the rain won't chase us back through. I'm afraid it's going to be a long ride. We're traveling south of the forest, crossing the Midlands and following the river back to Crona."

"Any trouble on the way, Father?" Luca asked.

"None so far, but we'll need to keep a low profile. We've only told very few about our travel so as not to provoke King Loren. The only ones aware are the ones we'll be taking shelter with, and even so... we have protection. You'll be safe mi'lady. I give you my word." He gave Paxe a comforting smile and turned towards Luca and I. "My queen sends her love to the both of you. She misses you very much, son. She's looking forward to having Paxe around for company. It's been far too quiet without your mouth," he smirked.

"Will I be tending to her majesty?" Paxe asked. The king turned to her in surprise.

"Of course not, child. You are a guest of our home. Guests are meant to enjoy themselves. I do understand that your life has been mostly servitude, but you'll have plenty of time to adjust to your new freedom. When you're ready to venture out, we'll help you. I do know a stubborn, very hard-laboring individual who has been biding his time waiting to see you again. Let that be your main focus for now." Paxe's eyes watered.

"I don't know how to thank you," she said, her lip trembling.

"By living your life. Cronians, Valdarians, humans...we're different, but we all have hearts that beat all the same. Each one is deserving of happiness. That's what we believe. Leave the deliverance to these two." He nodded toward Luca, who looked down at me and gave me a side smile. "That said...is there anything else I can help you with before we start off for the southern lands, Princess?"

"Actually...Luca was going to inquire about where we'll stay when we reach Bolton. He wasn't able to go yesterday... there were—issues."

"So I've come to understand. I received word that your father didn't take your answering gift very well, and if I may say so...it brought a smile that didn't leave my face for quite a while. You're a force to be reckoned with, it seems. I'm proud to have you as part of our family, Arienne." He reached into his front pocket, pulling out a bit of parchment. "There's no need to make arrangements. The queen did so. This is where you'll stay. She hoped that by now you'd likely want to stay together. There's a royal suite close to the temple where you'll meet Nero." He handed the paper to Luca.

"He didn't take my gift well? What happened? If you don't mind my asking?" I asked inquisitively. The king ran a hand through his ebony hair and Paxe shivered.

"Rumor has it, his rage took down several walls in the castle," he grinned. "He must not have expected the surprise." Luca and I exchanged looks.

"I see," I answered, feeling much better about my assumption that my father had sent the savage guard to test me. That also meant that I was wrong, and I had taken my frustration out on Luca, and the bathing room, for nothing. I laid a hand to his chest, looking at him as if asking for forgiveness and he put his hand over mine. A whole conversation being had without words.

"I've missed something," the king chuckled. Paxe followed suit.

"Oh, it's nothing you aren't used to Father. She beat the bloody sin out of me, is all." Luca grinned at me, and then at his father. The king laughed loudly, and so did the four men standing close by.

"Maybe that's why I'm fond of you, Princess. My queen is also a feisty one. It just makes the relationship all the more interesting. Don't feel badly about it, we quite enjoy getting our bollocks handed to us by our wives. You need not worry about my son; he's tougher than he looks."

That's an understatement.

A small sting of embarrassment nipped at my face, and I laughed it off, scratching at the back of my neck bashfully. I looked over at Paxe, who was studying the king's every movement. "Why don't we run upstairs to get our bags? I need a quick word before you leave." She nodded, and the king inclined his head. Luca kissed my fingers and led me a step towards her.

"I'll help secure them when you bring them back down. Be quick, love. We should be getting on the road as well," he smiled. I hooked my arm through hers and we moved up the stairs. When we'd reached the landing at the top, I whispered near her ear.

"Stop staring at the king like he's a pastry covered in chocolate." I nudged her ribs.

"I can't help it," she whispered back, fiercely. We shut the bedroom door behind us as we made our way into our room.

"He's a married man and you have to travel with him...probably for several days. And what of Lakan?" I argued, quietly. She drew the straps of her bag together in a jerk and turned towards me.

"Everything I feel for Lakan when I picture him is exactly the same...perhaps more so, now that I've been without him this long and I've had to hear the sounds of your insane lovemaking for the past two days," she stilled and crinkled her brows. "Actually...I don't feel as strongly now as I did when we were downstairs. It's almost as if—" She looked up at me.

"Oh no...his gift," I suspected. "Gods...all the more reason to do what I brought you up here to do. Drop the bag...come here," I said as I dug my mother's pendant from my pocket. She stood before me and glanced down at the gleaming emerald in my hands.

"Ari, don't. You need this to protect you out there." She pushed my hands away. "I can't accept this." I placed a hand on her face and forced her to look at me.

"I told you in the dungeon...I have Luca. I don't remember ever hearing that my mother meant this for only me. If it protects you, disguises you, or keeps you from betraying your own restraint from magic, then you're going to wear this. Don't take it off for a second, do you understand?" She nodded and I placed the necklace over her head, dropping it down the bust of her tunic. "I need to know you'll be safe. The king's word, or no." We locked into a tight embrace and I felt my emotions starting to give way again.

"I love you," she whispered over my shoulder. I squeezed my eyes shut and fought back tears.

"I love you too. So much." We reluctantly broke our hold and looked at each other. "Let's move." We grabbed our bags and took deep breaths as we reached the cozy kitchen and found it empty. Everyone had gathered outside under the shelter of the stable. Paxe headed out the door to meet them and I paused, turning to look at the house as if I'd never see it again, and recalled our time together. I let loose a deep sigh and stepped quickly into the rain, closing the door quietly behind me and jogging over to the stable.

Luca laughed merrily with the royal aides about gods know what, and the king conversed quietly with Frances, admiring Bjourne and securing Luca's bags. Vetta was fastening a dark brown, heavy traveling cloak around Paxe as I approached.

"Here, child," she tossed another dark blue cloak into my arms. "You'll need to put that on. It doesn't look as if this weather will cease anytime soon." I dropped the bag from my shoulder and flung the material around myself, draping the large hood over my head. My movement caught Luca's attention and he excused himself as he walked towards me.

"You look..." He stared, a smoldering look in his eyes as he trailed them over me.

"Incredible?" I rolled my eyes. He started fastening my cobalt buckles and chuckled through his nose.

"I was going to say mysterious... Like some witch about to spell me with—"

"Keep your tongue in your mouth, son," King Tidus interrupted, cutting him off with a firm hand on his shoulder. I couldn't stifle my snort. "Although I'm so glad to see the two of you in a much better state of companionship. I wasn't too sure about it after the meeting at the castle." He smiled at me.

"I—I'm so sorry, your Majesty. I was so..." I couldn't think of a single thing to describe my temper when I had stormed out of the Great Hall that morning.

"Angry...it's perfectly understandable, my dear. Luca's mother was the same. She threw things at me and unapologetically told me where I could go. She still denies this, but I know for certain that she tainted my wine that evening with something that made me retch for two straight days," he laughed.

I remembered her boldness at our meeting and the way she took complete control of the conversation. She even had my father leaning back in his chair, surrendering to the command in her voice. It was inspiring. "She seems like a strong female. I do remember her saying that she threw a fork at you," I giggled.

"Nearly took my eye out. But she was no match for my princely charm at the time," he winked. I looked at Luca, who rolled his eyes, answering the question before I could ask.

"He means he won her over solely on his gift. Beguilement."

"That's not true. She wanted me. She just had trouble because of her own gifts," he smiled.

"And what gift does she possess?" I dared ask.

"Fury," they both answered together. We all laughed as Frances approached, taking my bag and promptly loading Alice with it.

One of the royal aides brought Luca a heavy black hooded garment that was more of a coat than a cloak with Cronian insignia stitched in silver on the lapel. He shrugged it on and looked every bit the role of royalty as his father pulled on one of his own with a fancier design. They pulled their hoods up and the fluttering in my stomach grew stronger. I decided it was best to direct my attention back to Paxe, who was nervously patting her speckled gray horse.

"Looks like it's time. As much as I want to just tuck you into my bag, I feel we should tough this out and make it easier on ourselves," I said, gripping her fingers.

"Show them the strong type?" She smiled. I nodded. "I'll not say farewell. If you need me, you send word. When the time comes, I'm happy to help you bring him down. I'm never too far to come back for you, *mi'lady*." She nudged me softly. I growled as I rolled my eyes.

"Tell Lakan I owe him for setting this unintentional plan in motion for your freedom. He deserves whatever favor you're about to bestow on his poor human body," I laughed.

"Oh, I'll hear none of that from you...you insane maniac," she scoffed. Tears started invading us both, and we shook them off, hugging briefly and tearing ourselves away as one of the aides helped her onto her horse. Vetta stepped up beside me.

"You take care of yourself, child. There's always a place for you in Aeon." She smiled softly at Paxe and turned her attention to me. "For both of you. If, for some reason, we don't meet again, I want you both to know you're like daughters to me. I'm forever grateful to the gods that I was blessed to be your caregiver."

I pulled her into a hug, and she kissed my cheek. "It won't come to that. We'll see you again." My throat bobbed against the ache of emotions that kept trying to break through.

"And here we were trying to be tough," Paxe sniffled as she swiped at a rogue tear. Frances led Alice up to my side, and Luca stepped up from behind me, brushing the back of his knuckles against my spine. I turned to him as he gestured for permission to help me onto my horse. I looked back to Vetta and Paxe, then nodded once. He leaned in to press a kiss to my forehead and raised me to the stirrups with his strong arms.

I situated myself in the saddle while the king and his men mounted their horses. Luca was last as he shook Frances's hand and raised himself up onto Bjourne's strong form.

"Frances..." I called, and he turned to face me. "I'm truly grateful for your hospitality and your friendship. I'll miss you," I smiled. He tipped his floppy hat to me and bowed slightly.

"It was a pleasure being in your company, Princess. Safe travels to all of you." Our horses started into the misty rain, and Vetta and Frances stood close together, waving as we began trotting forward down the wet cobblestone street.

I rode beside Paxe and smiled under my hood as she wobbled uncomfortably on her saddle. She cut me a glare that said, *"Go screw yourself,"* as I giggled at her inexperience.

"You gonna be alright?" I asked playfully.

"The last time I rode a horse was as a small child. Don't patronize me," she warned.

"You'll get it. Whisper sweet nothings into its ear and he'll be nice," I chuckled, earning myself a hand gesture.

We came into the square, the townspeople opening their doors and waving at us. Some of them bowed and others, as we spread out, began yelling, *"Long live Queen Arienne!"* My heart thundered as I took in all the hopeful faces, and Paxe looked at me, dropping her mouth open in awe.

Luca rode in, stopping beside me and staring out at the crowd gathering around the sides of the streets, none of them bothered by the rain that began to fall a bit heavier. The few voices yelling turned into a sea of chanting that got louder as I put a hand to my chest. I looked at Luca, and he met my eyes, smiling. He pulled my sword from his side and handed it to me by its blade. I took the hilt and stared down at the weapon as it gleamed with rainwater. Someone had cleaned it and did an immaculate job. King Tidus trotted in between Paxe and I and I turned my face to meet his.

"Our world depends upon you, Princess. We're all here for you. I shall send word when we've made it to Crona safely. Be strong, be courageous and love one another." He struck his fist to his chest and held it there. "For our world!" He inclined his head and I dipped mine in return. I shot Paxe one last glance, and she put a fist to her chest as well—the royal aides following suit.

The growing crowd chanted louder as I looked back at Luca, who already had his fist at his heart.

My gods...

I faced the crowd riding alone further into the square and slowly raised my sword into the air. The chants erupted into a symphony of cheering and a tear rolled down my face. The cheering quieted as I opened my mouth to speak.

"May the gods ride with me and keep my feet swift!" I bellowed. "May we all rise against tyranny and smite evil with love! I vow, as your future queen, to bring you peace! I vow to end your suffering as I have suffered with you! For our lands...for our families...for our world!" I thrust my sword higher into the air. "Until death!" I slammed my fist to my heart as the crowd cheered deafeningly. They began to chant with a fist over their hearts and their other pumping the air... *"Until death!"* They flooded the streets, carving two paths to direct us. One to my left toward Bolton, the other towards the town entrance to the grasslands.

I grasped at the reins, held my sword steady above me and kicked my heels against Alice's sides, riding to the left with Luca following close behind. Paxe and the king split away from us, riding the opposite way with the aides. The crowd cheered and waved as we barreled through the exit and picked up speed through the rain. We began crossing more grassland and followed a path that wasn't as faint as the one we'd taken into Aeon. I finally tucked the sword into the large bag behind me and looked over at Luca. He looked at me with deep pride and mouthed an "I love you." I whispered it back, although he couldn't hear it. We smiled at each other as I raised in the saddle and we tore across the grass.

Our horses seemed eager to move quickly and we didn't slow until they showed signs that they were tiring. It had been over an hour of riding full strength and I was surprised that we hadn't slowed sooner. The rain had finally stopped and the sky was blanketed by thick, fast-moving clouds as we continued forward.

"How long do you suppose the ride will be from here?" I asked, weak from my lack of sleep.

"Hard to say. Do you want to camp, or do you think we should keep going?" Luca looked me over, assessing my strength. "I can set up quick if you're tired."

"I'd rather get there and rest in an actual bed, but it's difficult to judge the distance. I'm alright... I think I can make it." I raised my canteen and drank heavily from it.

"What happened back there...I—" He started. I looked over, shoving the cork back into the mouth of the bottle. "I'm so proud to be yours, Arienne. You looked heroic and even I felt the hope you gave those people. My father watched you like his own gift was compromised. It was amazing to witness." He looked at me with a fierce stare. "I'm so proud."

"I didn't expect that at all. We've spent weeks with them, and everything seemed so natural and relaxed. I've played with their children and eaten in their shops...I never thought anything about it. Seeing them all chanting like that...it touched my very soul," I responded quietly.

"Hearing them chant your vow...especially after our conversation and the things I witnessed during our blood union. It sent chills down my body, seeing you become something infinitely stronger."

"You're right. I think it awakened something in me." I stared forward.

"Your people are with you. I remembered Frances saying how beloved your mother was. I think you wear that crown now. It's difficult not to see you in a different light."

"Is that a bad thing?" I asked, looking over at him again. He stared at me as if the only thing keeping him from taking me off my horse and laying me down on the grass was my permission.

"Not in the slightest." His voice had an edge to it that sent heat to my cheeks.

"Why do you look as if you could rip me apart?" I smirked. He jerked his face forward, adjusting himself in his seat.

"I should think you already know the answer to that question, my betrothed." He smiled and didn't bring his attention back to me.

"Does your father know that we…" I failed to finish my question and he cleared his throat, looking down and fidgeting with the reins. I cocked my head to the side. "Oh gods…you talked about it, didn't you?" I palmed my face as he scoffed.

"Don't think for one second that I'm not aware of your indiscretion with Paxe. It's really no different with males," he laughed.

"Is that the reason he seemed so proud of you when I came downstairs?" I gawked.

"You misunderstand…he was proud of *you*," he grinned.

"What? Why?"

"Because you remind him so much of my mother, and he adores her. He asked me if I pushed you too hard but I assured him that I left you completely in control of the pace you set for your healing and warming up to the idea of being together. Our first joining was a difficult leap for you… that, in my opinion, you conquered and slayed." He smiled over at me.

"Well…thank you, your Highness," I blushed.

"If you keep looking at me like that, I'll set up camp right here," he warned.

"Oh? Trying to conquer and slay me?" I straightened, dropping my hood. He watched every shift of my body as if his control were slipping away bit by bit.

"Gods give me strength…" He grumbled, tugging his trousers at the crotch and looking forward. I giggled at his discomfort of the bulge starting to show below his waist. My heels tapped, and Alice sped up. He cursed as I passed, shaking his reins and clicking his tongue.

We rode swiftly throughout the remainder of the day, stopping only a few times to feed and water the horses. The cloudy sky darkened quickly as I finally caught an unfamiliar smell in the air, and the landscape seemed to subtly change from thick grass to mostly rocks.

"What's that smell?" I asked as I surveyed the area. Luca smiled with familiarity.

"That…is the sea. We've made it."

We traveled through a pass with towering cliffs on either side, ushering us into Bolton. The rock was dark and almost shiny as we cleared the other side. We stopped and looked out over a large city carved into a massive cliff edge, the sea licking violently at its base. Lights were shining everywhere and far in the distance was a small island that housed a huge monumental structure that flickered with, what looked to be, torches all around. I nearly cried at the sight of it.

"This is extraordinary. Is this what it looks like in Crona?" I said while staring off in wonder at everything.

"No, Crona isn't a cliffside. The city and the castle are both built over flat beaches. Our buildings are round in shape and most are bone white, with turquoise paint. Almost like the day to this night." He gestured at the black rock, "Or *cat*, with his stark contrast in his fur."

Hiss...I wonder how he's been.

"You think Hiss is doing alright?" I asked sadly.

"I have no doubt. Elowen seemed very happy to oblige. She is, after all, a goddess of nature and he's quite the creature. Perhaps, I shouldn't have mentioned him, I'm sure you miss him terribly."

"I do, but...my mind has been otherwise occupied as of late," I grinned.

"Shall we? I'm eager to see more of this place. It's very impressive. Michele would weep at the architecture."

"Yes, let's," I answered as we moved forward through a cave opening with flat ground. It led into the city, opening a short ways down and revealing the streets at the base of the huge expanse of the cliff. More streets and houses stacked upward, becoming more lavish and elegant near the top. There were shops and clubs, and the smell of food cooking from eateries filled my senses as we passed.

Not many stopped to pay us much mind as we snaked up the cliffside. We assumed any royal suite purchased by a queen would be somewhere near the top and hoped we were right as we inched further up. I counted five levels until we finally came upon a huge onyx building jutting out over the sea, that had an elegantly covered entrance and a long, torch-lit passageway into a courtyard with interesting looking trees, carefully trimmed shrubs and a large fountain in the middle, featuring a statue of Nero.

I admired the artwork as we rounded the fountain. The figure was very masculine and the god raised a huge hammer in one fist and a sword in the other. A young male who was nicely dressed walked out to meet us as we reached the front entrance.

"Good evening, Mi'lady," he bowed. "Mi'lord." We dipped our chins at him in response. "My name is Alister. Welcome to Bolton. We're happy you're here, and his grace is much looking forward to your visit. When you're ready, I'll be happy to escort you to your suite." Luca and I exchanged looks as he dismounted and came over to help me off Alice's back.

My legs felt spongy and sore from the ride, and exhaustion settled into my body. Alister assisted in untying our bags from the horses and shouldered mine while Luca did the same with his own. We followed him inside and my breath was stolen by the beauty of the foyer. Walls of polished black stone towered in a cathedral-like, open space with fountains splashing on each side and a huge shining staircase that curved to the upper floor. Large crystal chandeliers hung down from the high ceilings and glittered across the shiny surfaces of the room. Elegant sconces were placed every few feet apart along the walls and paintings of sea monsters from my childhood books were placed between them. It was the most lavish thing I'd ever seen.

"I apologize for the stairs. I know the two of you must be weary from travel," Alister said as he led us up.

"It's quite alright, I've nearly forgotten about it after seeing all of this. It's really beautiful here," I offered, still looking at every luxury.

"We take great pride in it mi'lady. I'm honored to be the one to show you both around." We approached a huge set of ebony double doors with silver handles that resembled hammers at the end of a short corridor. Our attendant pulled them both open and we walked behind him through a short hallway entrance into an enormous, well-lit suite that looked much like the foyer, decorated with similar paintings and lush plants, tastefully placed at the corners.

Directly across the large room was an open entryway that led to an equally large balcony that could be closed off for privacy with thick velvet black curtains. On the wall to the left of the balcony was a good-sized canopy bed with sheer drapery that swayed lightly in the breeze coming in from the sea, which was pleasantly audible even from where we were standing. We stepped further inside onto a plush deep gray rug, turning to see a sunken bathing pool that was bigger than our bed. The water was steaming and smelled as if fragrant bathing oils had been added, awaiting our arrival.

"It smells like lavender," I said softly, closing my eyes and breathing it in.

"Yes, mi'lady. We added it to help you both relax after your journey here. The water is hot, so use caution. It's fed from a freshwater volcanic hot spring beneath us." He directed our attention to a long, narrow table against the wall to our right. "We've gathered plenty of refreshment for you, but should you need anything else, ring the bell with the cable hanging by the door. We'll assist you promptly."

Luca and I examined the table that was artistically stacked with fruits of all kinds, breads, cheeses and several different meats. There was wine and a pitcher of water with sliced oranges and strawberries floating at the top. Wine glasses and dark ceramic cups resembling black and white marble lined a shelf above the table, next to stacks of plates and eating utensils.

Am I dreaming? And people think living in a castle is luxurious...

Alister walked next to the bed, lighting an oil lamp on a gorgeous vanity with a mirror that bled elegance with ornate carvings framing the glass. On top of the vanity were bottles of oils and perfumes and soaps for bathing. "Please accept these as our gifts, Princess. They were handpicked for you to use and take with you after your stay." He opened a door in the corner and gestured for us to follow. "In here is where you can keep your belongings, and we've provided some attire for the two of you as well as various accessories. Those are also gifts from Master Nero."

We walked into a large closet filled with tailored suits, formal dresses, silk bedclothes and robes, as well as very expensive-looking shoes and a few casual pieces with light, thin material, appropriate for weather by the sea. We dropped our bags to the floor and looked around in awe.

"This is...overwhelming," Luca said, eyes wide and mouth open as he continued to thumb through some of his new clothes. "Thank you very much, and please extend our gratitude to his grace."

We stepped back out into the bedroom and Alister turned to face us, placing his hands behind his back.

"Can I get you anything before I leave you to get settled in?" He asked politely.

"Actually, I was going to ask...when are we to meet with his grace?" I asked. He smiled and extended a hand toward the balcony. We walked out, and he followed and the wind blew the rogue strands of our hair away from our faces as we neared the banister.

It was breathtaking. The moon wasn't quite full and its light peeked through the clouds, glittering across the dark water. The small island we had seen before seemed much closer now, and the temple where Nero resided was in better view. Alister pointed to it.

"That there is the temple of Nero. In two days, you'll receive a formal invitation to join him. When it's time, I'll take you to our private dock down below and our boatman will ferry you across. Take some time to rest and tour the city. Everything for the two of you is of no charge by command of his grace, and he wishes for you both to enjoy yourselves."

"Thank you, Alister. You're really something," I smiled. He bowed with a hand behind him and bid us goodnight as he slipped back inside and out of the door in what seemed like mere seconds. I stepped forward and looked out at the sea, a small tear creeping down my face as I watched the beauty of the inky waves churning toward the cliff and crashing against its steep face. Luca's arms wrapped around me from behind and pulled me close. He rested his chin on my shoulder and I snaked my arms around his.

"What's wrong, love?" He whispered, kissing away the tear from my cheek.

"Absolutely nothing," I smiled. "It feels like something I'm going to wake from at any moment and I'm afraid to close my eyes. I've never seen the sea before."

"If you think this is beautiful, wait until sunrise." He turned me to face him. "This isn't a dream. When you do wake in the morning, I'll be right here with you...always." He took my hands to his mouth, kissing each of my fingers.

"Until death?" I whispered. He put a fist to his chest and pressed his head to mine. "I love you."

His hand grazed the side of my face and he pulled me into a deep kiss that we decided would stretch on for several long moments now that we were finally alone and unbothered. Even after our playful conversation and Luca's unfortunate timing for desire during the ride here, that kiss didn't feel at all sexual, but perfectly intimate and satisfying. For once in my life, I was supremely happy and far from home, where the monsters couldn't get to me. It seemed we had the protection and favor of the god of strength, and no fool, even one as big as my father, would ever dare test a deity. We were safe and free to be together... to enjoy each other until it was time to start back on the parts of our destiny that would no doubt challenge us later...but not right now. Right now, there was only us and my heart was content with that.

"Let's get you a hot bath, yes?" He asked softly. I nodded with an adoring smile, and he led me back inside, walking into the closet and leaving me some privacy to undress.

I stripped down and laid my traveling clothes across a long ebony ottoman at the end of the bed, then stepped slowly into the steaming water. It was still very hot and extremely soothing as I took the last two steps into it and was surprised at its depth when it nearly reached the underside of my breasts. I took a deep breath and submerged, palming my hair back as I came back up and savoring the feel of the heat on my tired muscles. I swam to the side against the wall, seating myself with my back against the edge and lying my head down against the warm black stone. It didn't take long before I gave in to exhaustion and fell into sleep.

I woke to the sounds of the sea and gulls outside, calling to each other as a warm breeze fluttered over my skin through the open entrance to the balcony. I opened my eyes and was relieved to see the comfort of our room wasn't some fantasy I had dreamt up. I was naked, and Luca was pressed against my back, sleeping as peacefully as he always does, with an arm wrapped tightly around me. I gathered he had found me completely out by the time he'd reached the bath and took me directly to bed. My hand slid across his arm, and I rolled backward, stirring him awake.

"Morning, Princess," he whispered, smiling sweetly at me with his eyes half open.

"I'm sorry," I said, tucking his hair behind his ear.

"I'll not accept apologies. My evening was perfect. We were both exhausted." He pressed his lips to my shoulder. "I pity the men that will never have a chance to wake up with you in their arms."

I leaned in and kissed him and then turned my face to the balcony. The sun was finally out, and I raised myself to sit. "Is it late?" I asked, looking back down at him.

"Still early, but we've missed the sunrise. Want to go see Bolton in the light, love?" He raised from the bed, wiping the sleep from his eyes. The light in the room cast itself around his solid body and I watched his every move as he walked into the closet.

"You're a stunning example of a male, Prince. Truly," I called as he disappeared from view. I heard him laugh from the closet as I stepped off the bedside and walked to the table with food. I took a cup from the shelf and poured the infused water into it, a piece of orange splashing into the top. It tasted lovely. Luca came up behind me in a silky black robe and held one out for me by the shoulders. I lowered my cup to the table and slipped my arms inside, tying it off at the waist after I wrapped it around me. I still wasn't convinced I wasn't dreaming. "Taste this." I offered him the drink and he sipped it, raising his brows and taking another swallow until he had emptied it. I poured two more and handed him one of his own, making sure a strawberry or two fell into our cups this time as well.

"Let's go outside." He hooked his arm around my waist, and we stepped out onto the balcony, the sunlight stinging our eyes as we paused at the banister.

Bolton was even more stunning and alive in the daylight. The waves churned below us in a deep blue, instead of moon-kissed darkness, and boats drifted out into the distance. The sounds from the city below sounded much like the chatter in Aeon, but busier. Seagulls scattered around loudly, looking for anything they could scavenge below. Paxe, as usual, had been right again. I thought I could have lived comfortably in the countryside, at that little cottage at the end of the street, but Bolton was also somewhere I could picture staying forever. If Crona was anything like this, I figured it must have been hard to leave behind.

"Does it feel a bit like home?" I asked, looking up at him as he took a sip from his cup. He lowered it and nodded, staring over the sea. The salt air left a slight curl in his thick raven-black hair.

"It does remind me a lot of home. It feels good to see the sea again. So much is different here. I'm looking forward to exploring the city a bit." He smiled down at me and promptly lost his grin when he met my stare. "What's the matter?" I leaned into him and looked back out over the ocean.

"I feel like you've been dragged away from home because of me. You had a life there and a family that loves you...friends..." I trailed off and he tipped my chin up with his finger.

"Hey...while I did have all of that, I was never dragged from anything. You were always going to be my life, Arienne. If you need clarification from either one of my parents...or even my friends about how much I looked forward to meeting you... then you can ask them when I take you to Crona. I've always been ready to leave. Don't ever feel like you've taken anything from me. You've given me more than you could understand."

I wrapped my arms around his middle and tucked into his chest. He held me tightly and rested his head on top of mine. "I don't deserve you," I whispered. He squeezed tighter.

"Then we're both undeserving, love." He pulled back and looked at me. "Enough of this kind of talk. Let's try on some of these clothes and see what the city is like." He kissed me softly, and we padded back into our room.

It didn't take long to tear through our closet before I settled on a thin, comfortable sleeveless ice blue dress. The top was two overlapping pieces of material that bunched together as they crossed over my bust and gathered at the waist. The skirt was airy and smooth and swished over my thighs, falling just above my knees. I slipped into matching flat slippers and stepped out into the bedroom to find Luca dressed casually in a soft gray knit shirt with short sleeves, hugging every part of his body with perfection and showing off the corded muscle in his arms. His trousers were the normal dark gray that I loved, which always pleasantly accented his toned behind. He tied his hair off in a loose, messy bun and looked every bit the relaxed opposite of royalty.

"You look gorgeous," he grinned as he gave me a onceover. "Come here...there's something missing." I walked over and he slid his hair strap, I was sure I'd lost around my neck, tying it loosely and letting the bow fall down my chest.

"Oh, where did you find it?" I beamed, touching over the leather with my fingers.

"I've had it for a while around my wrist. You never noticed?" He asked. I shook my head. "I even had it on the first night that we..." He trailed his fingertip along my skin, tracing the neckline of my dress.

"I see," I smirked. "Forgive me...I was a bit distracted." My cheeks flushed and he offered me an arm.

"Mi'lady..."

I took his arm and we went downstairs. The attendants greeted us and ensured our horses were being well cared for. We were asked if we wanted transportation by carriage into the city, but we declined. Our plan was to take in all the sights and activities on foot and spend the entire day out...and that was exactly what we did. We shopped around, ate lunch at a small cafe in the harbor, tasted different wines and expensive liquors, and met with tons of locals who were eager to shake our hands and offer us things. It would take some getting used to. I wasn't familiar with so much attention.

By the time the sun began to dip into the sky and marry itself with the ocean, we were making our way back to the harbor, hoping we could watch the sunset together. We found a tavern bustling with patrons that sat right over the water. The barkeep had reserved a spot for us on the outdoor patio that was secluded from the rest and had a spectacular view. Luca ordered us fresh seafood, and expensive wine and we dined together, savoring each other's company while watching the sun turn different hues as it sank into the water.

"I finally did it," Luca grinned as he sipped his wine. I drew my brows together.

"Did what?" I asked, reaching for my glass.

"Took you to a meal...alone. I'm sorry you had to wait so long for this."

"Don't be ridiculous. It was worth the wait. Today has been amazing. I've never been so happy," I smiled. Music played in the tavern, and he looked at me longingly. He scooted back in his chair and stood, offering me his hand.

"Dance with me?" He asked sweetly.

"Absolutely," I answered, taking his hand and raising from my seat. He led me beside our table to the open space and took my waist, pulling me closer. We relaxed into a sway and started turning slowly to the music, eyes locked and lips barely touching. "I'm not used to dancing with you without your boisterous singing and quick spins," I grinned, and he chuckled through his nose.

"It's not that kind of night," he said in a low voice. I slowly cocked my head.

"Oh? What kind of night is it?" I asked curiously. He smiled, lifting our hands and twirling me around. He brought my back flush against his chest and continued to sway as he nuzzled into my neck. His arms settled around my waist, and I placed one of mine over his, the other reaching up, and my palm sliding across his hair as his stubble tickled my skin. I leaned my cheek to rest on the side of his head.

"I don't think I could spend another day without you near me, Arienne," he breathed against my skin. "I've fallen so fucking hard for you." His hold around me became stronger and something urged me to nearly cry at the desperation in his voice. "Please."

"Luca...what's wrong?"

"Will you let me hold you like this until morning?"

"Of course I will. Are you alright?" I turned in his arms and looked at him. His expression was etched with fear. I couldn't, for the life of me, figure out why, after the perfect day that we'd had, something was wrong.

"I'm perfect. Let's go back," he said softly as he kissed the corner of my mouth.

"Okay."

We left the tavern and didn't say much as we walked hand in hand back up the cliff to our temporary residence. Alister was back this evening and bowed as we arrived. We headed upstairs and into our room. Luca led me into the closet and pulled on a cream-colored set of night pants while I found a two-piece set of short dark blue pajamas with black lace around the hem. I thought seeing me in something provocative might change his sudden drop in moods, but he only looked at me with the same strange stare, as if I was going to vanish before his eyes. I wrapped my arms around his neck, and he was trembling.

"Luca, please tell me what's going on. Why are you shaking? Would you just talk to me?" His hands rested on my hips for a moment before reaching under my thighs and hoisting me up to hold me. He walked us out to the balcony and carefully put me back on my feet, tugging me in close and brushing the hair away from my face.

"Do you love me?" He asked, his tone serious. I furrowed my brows.

"You know that I do."

"Tell me when you realized it. Don't say the night we camped out by the lake. It was one of the best nights of my life, but you told me you'd never fight it again. You knew before. When?"

I slackened my arms, pulling back to get a better look at him. His eyes remained desperate and burned with that silvery gleam that singed every nerve. I decided against asking why he needed my answer this suddenly and seemingly out of nowhere.

"I had this...strange feeling when you carried me in the woods after I slashed my foot open and you patched me up. It was like something fell into place that had been missing my entire life. I knew it couldn't be love. I had just met you only moments before. But then, when I got upstairs that night, I laid across my bed and I—I couldn't stop thinking about you. Paxe obviously still had her abilities, and she called me out on my thoughts when she drew my bath that night."

"Was that—"

"No. But after I got into the bath, my eyes kept catching the tie from your hair that you had wrapped around the bandage, and then she gave me your note and the bottle of wine. It was like every one of my senses pulled my attention back to you. She convinced me the next day to go with you into the forest and the night we fought, it took every ounce of my strength not to kiss you. I think I may have figured it out right then but my heart didn't feel ready to accept that as the truth. When Paxe caught us at the castle entrance after we made it back, you held me and told me that you were worried about saying something."

"That I was going to miss you."

"Yes. When I answered, my words flew from my mouth before I even thought about saying them. It wasn't because I didn't mean it...it was because I *did*. I knew right then that I loved you. And to be honest, I was still fighting it off until that night that I kissed you in the tent. I think what we felt that night was our mutual acceptance of the bond. You may had already accepted, but I had battled it the entire time. Once I was absolutely positive that I could no longer live another day without you, my heart acknowledged it and pulled us together. There was no denying it anymore. I was yours. And I'll never belong to another."

Light from our room reflected off of a single tear that fell down his face. It was the first time I'd ever seen him cry, and my heart skipped with nervousness at the sinking feeling that either I had just confirmed everything he already knew and he was that touched by it...or he was about to deliver terrible news and just wanted us to have an amazing day before he broke it to me. Neither possible outcome stopped me from reaching out to wipe it away. He laid his hand over mine and kissed my palm.

"Please tell me...what's wrong? Let me fix it," I pleaded, moving closer.

"My mother and father told me that I was to marry you when I was twelve years old. I was young and didn't really understand the concept then. But then I grew older, and when my friends began having their first real relationships, I decided to talk to my mother and get a better idea of everything. I asked her to find out as much as she could about you, and for years, I wondered what you looked like, what you were doing at random moments when I thought about you, and if you knew anything about me at all, besides the fact that you'd be marrying a stranger. I know that an arranged marriage isn't ideal to promote growth between two people, but I wanted so badly to make you happy...even if I never heard the words *I love you* come out of your mouth. Your father's reputation was enough for me to know that your trust would most likely take my moving a mountain to earn, and I spent a long time preparing myself for that."

"Luca..." I whispered. He took my hand from his face and held it with both of his.

"I've always understood that regardless of any female that came to my bed, my heart would one day be yours. I had never felt anything in my life more potent than how I felt when the moment I had waited for, all those years, had finally come and I laid my eyes on you for the first time. I didn't know how to react or how to keep breathing. You were so much more than I had ever imagined. Your beauty, your temper...the way your skin flushed when our eyes first met... I knew that the decision I'd made before we traveled to Valdaro was the right one."

"What decision?"

He lowered himself to one knee and kept my hand in his.

Oh my gods...oh my—

"I dreamt about this moment so many times. I remembered very clearly every detail about it. I never saw your face. But I saw this place. This balcony...and this." He pulled a ring from his pocket and slipped it over my finger. The band was crafted of silver vines and the stone was a massive teardrop shape, split in the middle—one half a brilliant diamond, the other a sparkling black sapphire. The diamond side had a blue topaz starburst where the band met the stone, and the black sapphire had a peridot on the opposite side. The entirety of the stones were crusted with tiny diamonds all the way around. My breathing grew rapid, and I fought back tears with all of my strength.

"Luca...it's...it looks like-"

"Cat. I know. I nearly lost my senses when I found you in the woods and saw him. And the meadow where you sat while I bandaged your ankle. I had this expertly crafted in Crona before we left to come meet you in the hopes that I could spend time getting to know you and take you to my home. I planned to ask you there, but your father had other plans. The ring wasn't ready yet. When I had corresponded with my father from Aeon, he insisted that he deliver it to me himself... to ask you when I was ready. When we got here and I saw this place...I remembered my dream. I was going to ask you last night, but when I worked up the nerve to come out, you had fallen asleep."

I laughed through my now frantic tears and he stilled, as he looked me in the eyes.

"I know that we're betrothed by royal responsibility and fated by the gods to be together. But aside from it all...I know that I love you more than anything, and as I continue to try and move this mountain, you deserve to choose for yourself. So...Arienne Genovese. Will you be my wife?"

I tried to keep my composure as I lowered myself to my knees, taking his face in my hands and kissing his lips. "It would be an honor, your Highness." He wrapped his arms around me and pulled me into his lap on the balcony, and the kiss that followed lasted a long while.

When we finally broke, he took me to bed and made no move to make love to me. He was more than satisfied with what he had asked of me in the tavern, and I fell deeper for him as he held me tight in his arms. Our bodies tangled in the same way they had the morning we woke up after our first night ravaging each other. I kissed his neck while he rested his chin on the top of my head.

"I love you, Luca," I whispered softly.

"I love you..." He moved his hand up and down my spine, and I relished in the moment until we both drifted into deep sleep.

CHAPTER 17

MERCY

A breeze from the balcony swept in with the morning light and I noticed a certain chill to it, which I hadn't felt the previous morning. I rolled over and squinted my eyes open and was met with empty space. I raised my head and looked to my other side but again...nothing. I sat up and looked down at my left hand, smiling at the ring Luca had put there as it glittered in the sunlight.

It really did happen.

"Luca?" I called, getting no response. I slid out of bed and padded to the entryway to the balcony finding that empty as well. Then I checked the only other place he could be...the closet... Empty. Confused, I walked over to the table, picking off a few grapes, and began wondering if perhaps he had gone to get us something more than fruit for breakfast. I figured he'd ring the bell for someone to bring it up, but maybe he wanted it to be more special after last night.

After waiting for over an hour, I began to pace the room impatiently. Another hour ticked by and my impatience turned to worry. I walked back into the closet and looked around to check if he had even changed his clothes. The only thing out of sorts was my bag lying half open in the corner, and I knew I hadn't left it there. I opened it and looked for the weapons. The knife was still there and so was Gideon's arrow...but my sword was missing.

Shit.

Luca wouldn't have gone into the city shirtless and barefoot with night pants on, and now my sword had been taken too. Something about this was way too peculiar for my liking. I pulled my robe on and wrapped it around myself as I hurried to the door and jerked the cable several times to ring the bell. I tied the belt together and nervously paced until a knock finally rang out at the door and Alister peeked in, announcing himself.

"Alister...please...come in." I panicked.

"Is everything alright, Mi'lady?" He asked politely.

"No, Prince Luca is missing. I haven't seen him since we went to sleep last night and some of my property has been stolen as well." Alister placed his hands on my upper arms.

"Your Highness, you can relax. The prince is safe. He was summoned around midnight to meet his grace at the temple of Nero and was carefully instructed to come alone, as he was, and bring him the sword he was to forge. My assumption is that Prince Luca is still there."

"I thought that we wouldn't be invited formally until tomorrow." I pressed, still feeling unnervingly anxious.

"He seems to have changed his mind." His eyes glanced down at the ring on my finger.

"Do you have any idea when Luca will return?" I asked.

"That, I'm not certain of. His grace will send word when he's ready to meet with you. May I suggest dressing formally for this gathering? When you receive your invitation, he'll expect you promptly. I'd advise you to be ready just in case."

"Luca wasn't dressed at all," I argued.

"As was his instruction. I have no answers other than what I've been given to deliver to you. I'm sorry, Mi'lady, I wish I could be of better use." He tightened his lips into an apologetic smile.

"It's alright, I'm sorry. I'm just worried. It's not like him not to say anything and disappear. Not at all. Something just feels...off." I pulled away and walked to the balcony looking over at the temple on the island and seeing nothing amiss.

"Don't fret, your Highness. I'll let you know as soon as he returns or if we receive your invitation. Until then, just be prepared."

"Thank you." I smiled politely. He dismissed himself and I crossed my arms, continuing to stare at the structure and wondering what the hell could be going on in it. I waited in our room for hours, hoping to see Luca come through the door. He never did and it unsettled everything inside me. I tried to remind myself that he was in the presence of a god and that we were the chosen two that the gods decided would save this world...though it was difficult to feel confident, especially after Elowen's warning about Nero being cunning and strong, nothing was wrong here. I prayed that Luca wasn't in some kind of danger. When the sun began to set, I got angry.

We've done nothing wrong. All we did was travel here to see him. I shouldn't be this worried. I refuse. I'm facing whatever this is and getting him back.

I prowled over to the closet and flipped through different fancy things, finding a long, shimmering black dress with a corset top. I assumed by the silver embroidery of a hammer crossed with a sword on the side of the corset that it was the one I was to wear for this meeting. I carefully stepped into the gown, sliding it over my hips and up my bust. The corset tied in the front with shiny black ribbon and the skirts were layers of sheer black with tiny gemstones tastefully scattered throughout. I slid into a pair of ankle-high boots with a small heel that matched my gown. I've never been good at doing my own hair, so I decided to brush it well and leave my natural curls to fall where they may.

Feeling satisfied with everything I chose, I stared into the mirror of the vanity and hardly recognized myself. I've worn gowns before and even had Paxe do that horrible job applying counter paints to my face...but this outfit was truly jaw-dropping. Something about it made me feel as if I could take on the entire world in a dress. Perhaps that was the idea.

I walked over to the table and poured a glass of wine. I hadn't yet gotten it to my lips before a knock sounded at the door. I sat the glass down and answered, Alister entered with an envelope addressed to me.

"He's sent for you, Mi'lady." He handed me the envelope and I quickly opened it, pulling out a fancy black and silver card.

His Greatness, Lord Nero, requests your presence immediately.
Arrive appropriately dressed.
You are to enter the temple alone and proceed to the main chamber.
Tardiness will not be tolerated.

I stared at the parchment and a small shiver of fear crawled down my spine at the way it was worded. I shook it off and handed the card back to Alister, looking at him with a fire in my expression that promised a world of hurt for anyone who would touch my betrothed. I'd had enough.

"Show me to the dock, please. Now." I spat, walking past him and into the hall. We didn't go down the elegant staircase, instead, he took me straight across, passing the stairs and opening a door opposite our room. He opened it and revealed a dark torch-lit passage with winding stone steps much like the ones at my home that I used to take from my chambers down into the corridors. We started down and my finger trailed the stone wall out of habit. The tail of my skirt swished across the steps as we continued and my heart pounded as we finally reached the bottom.

An opening that smelled of salt air appeared in front of us, and the violent sea became louder. A small dock with a large boat sat waiting for me, and Alister motioned for me to follow. An older male with a long white beard and shaggy hair met us at the entrance to the private dock and dipped his chin at me.

"This is Sir John. He's the boatman who will ferry you to the temple. Sir John can't speak, but you can mostly tell what he's saying through his expressions and body language. When you arrive on the island, he'll moor the vessel and wait for you. I wish you good fortune, Mi'lady," Alister said, bowing to me and making his way back up the stairs.

I looked at the boatman, who extended a hand to lead me to the bobbing vessel and smiled politely. "Thank you, Sir John," I said, taking his hand. He helped me onto the boat, and I took a seat in the middle as it thrashed against the pounding waves that hit the rocks of the cliff close by. He untangled the knot that kept us secured to the dock and took a seat facing me, grabbing his oars and starting us off toward the open water.

I looked around and noticed the rough ride became much calmer the farther we got from the cliffs. I had never been on a boat in my entire life and my stomach felt as if it could relieve itself at any moment. John slid a metal bucket from beneath his seat toward me as if reading the sudden paleness of my face.

"Thank you, sir," I said, taking it into my lap. He smiled and nodded as he continued to row. If I could manage just a few more moments, it seemed we'd be on dry land. I cursed my belly and closed my eyes, thinking perhaps it would help, but my urge to vomit only intensified. The boatman tapped my knee and pointed two fingers at my eyes, and then back to his. He repeated it twice as if telling me to keep my focus on something still and was offering his eyes as a focal point. I tried, and it did seem as if it were working. He then gave me a quick nod and smiled. I returned his smile and held tightly to the bucket. "I like you, Sir John." He smirked and looked over his shoulder at the approaching island.

He steered us toward a small dock, and we bumped against it a few short moments later. He tied the boat off and hopped onto it, extending his reach to lift me out. We walked to the beach and he tapped my shoulder before I set foot on the sand. He knelt down, dipping his fingers into the water and writing a message with it on the planks of the dock. I bent over and watched him while trying to make out what he was writing:

GOD MERCIFUL
STAY ALERT

We raised and he looked at me cautiously, patting my shoulder and nodding his head slowly. I put a firm grip on his shoulder and gave him a tight smile in thanks as I turned and lifted my skirts, stepping onto the dark-colored sand. It was surprisingly firm under my weight, and I headed toward the flickering torches that lined a stone path into the temple.

I gathered all the confidence I could muster and dropped the fabric to the ground, straightening my spine and holding my chin higher. With my shoulders back, I stormed forward across the stone, feeling stronger with every clack of my heels. The love of my life was in there and if he was harmed, it would take the wrath of this god to keep me from tearing this building down to get him back. Any sickening feeling of fear was gone as I pounded up a small set of stairs and pulled the massive hammer that served as a door handle. The great arched door creaked open and I stepped inside. The torches laid in iron sconces ignited with magic as I passed down a hallway along a crushed velvet black runner.

Ornate swords, axes and other fine weaponry donned the walls of polished volcanic rock, each one the size of a healthy stallion. I'd never seen such pristine work in such an enormous size. It was distracting as I continued down the long hallway, trying earnestly not to stop and admire them. The hall ended, opening up into a large chamber, the narrow rug ending and the floor continuing into a stone platform that extended over a half-circular pool of dark water. At the end of the platform was a worn stone altar, and on it, bathed in a light that seemed to originate from nowhere, sat my sword.

Behind the altar was a vast empty area that led up to a dais that took up the entire back wall. A painting, which covered most of it, depicted the god of strength bringing down a huge hammer onto a sword, fire and molten lava decorating his profession and filling any negative space in the artwork. In the middle of the dais sat an enormous throne cast from iron with two large pillars at each side. The top of the pillars housed large metal bowls with crackling flames raging inside. From what I could see, the chamber was empty and I was left with uncertainty about what I was supposed to do. The invitation read: "Proceed to the main chamber." I was sure this was the place as I never saw any other route to take after entering.

I paused on the platform surveying the quiet yet ominous dwelling before returning my attention to the sword that lay at the altar. Seeing no other option, I started forward and up three shallow steps, and the light from my sword glowed around my complexion. Wary of what would happen if I chose to touch the blade, I placed my hands against the stone instead. A low rumble echoed through the chamber as a booming, masculine voice spoke.

"Daughter of Valdaro...welcome." The bodiless voice greeted me. Startled, I looked around and still saw nothing.

"Your grace?" I called, my voice echoing through the chamber. "I received your invitation...I came to inquire about the prince's whereabouts." I went straight to the point.

"Your prince's whereabouts are not the reason you were to travel here. Why have you come?" His tone was warning and set off alarms in my chest.

"I accepted the quest of the gods and came here to present this sword for its blessing, your grace," I answered with feigned confidence.

"You insult me, youngling."

A chill crawled down my spine. "Your grace?"

"You accepted a task with great challenge after being warned of its consequence, and still you choose to insult a deity in his own temple by bringing this trash and indulging in my city?" His physical form appeared on the throne, and my heart pounded as his cold stare met my expression of panic and confusion.

"I—I don't understand. I was told by the goddess to present this to you, my Lord. Her instruction seemed clear. She blessed an arrow and told me this sword would receive a blessing from you and was to be used together to suppress my father's power. As far as my indulgence, the prince and I were informed that they were gifts bestowed by yourself. I don't understand my wrongdoing. I would never intentionally insult a god. I assure you, I'm faithful to my task."

"That is a lie." He said coldly, gripping the handle of a massive hammer that laid across his lap. His features were surprisingly human, with a long, dark beard that was framed and matched in color by long, deep brown locks. His eyes were glowing irises that resembled fire and war—they pierced through me like the great swords that lined the hallway of the temple. He wore nothing, save for a cloth to cover his groin and sandals that laced up his muscular calves. I shook my head in argument and confusion as he raised from his throne and pointed at the sword that still shined in front of me. "If you were faithful to your task, then you'd have heeded the warning from the goddess that sent you here."

"The only warning she gave was that you were a cunning sort, your grace." His face darkened and he sneered at me through lowered brows.

"Wrong again. That sword has spilled blood in hatred. Bringing this to me was a grave mistake—one you will pay a heavy price for. The goddess told you that hate begets hate and that you will never succeed in conquering evil with evil. Otherwise, the blessings bestowed upon these weapons will be rendered useless and your father will remain powerful and alive. You turned your back to your mission, youngling. The moment you took a life with this blade in a way that demonstrated the hate you feel for your father, you proved yourself undeserving of your destiny *and* my blessing. Take your tainted blade and return to your castle. Do not ever return. Your quest ends in Bolton." The muscles in his arm twitched as he twisted the hammer in his hand in a threatening movement. My body tensed, and my heart shattered as I recalled the words I had forgotten Elowen saying in the forest.

I had been so focused on what Nero could possibly test me with that I never considered what else she'd warned. He was right. The man I killed in Aeon may have deserved what he got, and he may have also planned to do terrible things to me or to my best friend. The gods only knew how many females had been subjected to his filth prior to my slaying him, but he hadn't yet moved to attack me. That kill was not as justified as we had perceived it. The worry I had when I took my anger out on Luca was only half correct. My father's blood ran through my veins and I had let that dark part of me escape the day I took that guard's life.

Luca...he's taking Luca. No.

"My betrothed...I'll do as you ask, but I want him back," I stated boldly. His lips curved into a cruel smirk.

"You are in no position to make demands from me, youngling. The prince will stay. Consider it mercy from me that I allow you to walk out of this temple rather than crawl. Leave. Our meeting is over." My breathing grew quicker as I tried to figure out a way to bargain with him, but I remembered the message that Sir John had written on the dock when we arrived.

GOD MERCIFUL. STAY ALERT.

"Mercy..." I whispered to myself, looking down at my sword. I raised my attention one last time to the furious god of strength. "I beg you. Give him back. I'll do anything you ask. I'll return to whatever fate my father has in store for me or renounce myself as queen. I'll accept banishment and live in the disappointment of my people if I must. Please grant us mercy. The gods have bound our souls...I'm as good as dead without him, your grace. I'll pay the price with my life if it means living without him..." I fought back a sob and asked again. "Please." My groveling seemed to appeal to him or give him a different idea as he quirked a brow at me.

"Are you certain about the bargain you're making, Princess of Valdaro?" He asked cooly.

"With respect, I've never been more certain of anything in my life than him, your grace. Name your price." I placed my hand lovingly over my engagement ring and a tear rolled down my cheek.

"As you wish." He snapped his fingers, and the glamour that had been hiding Luca disappeared, revealing his half-naked body slumped against the wall in the open space between the altar and the dais to my left. He had been badly beaten, blood staining nearly every inch of him. His arms hung above his head in heavy iron shackles on the wall and his chin rested against his chest as his hair fell into his face. He barely seemed conscious and my heart ached in a pain I'd never felt before.

"Luca!" I screamed, making to leap from the platform. The moment my feet left the stone, my body took flight and was hurled into the opposite wall, knocking the breath from my lungs and cracking my skull against the hard rock wall. Blazing hot iron shackles that were seemingly just forged from white hot metal secured themselves around my wrists and I cried out at the pain as they seared into my flesh. My arms were now chained above me and my body was hanging low enough to sit on the floor as I kicked and thrashed against the restraints. I heaved ragged breaths as I raised my face to look at Luca, warm blood beginning to trail from my head and running down the front of my ear. "What have you done to him?!" I growled, never taking my eyes off his broken body.

"The prince lives...for the present. Whether he remains as such, will be up to you." Nero walked casually to Luca's side, twirling his hammer and taunting me.

"Don't... Don't touch him!" I yelled, my voice threatening...as if I were able to do anything to stop a god. He raised the giant tool higher, stancing himself and bringing it down with mighty force across Luca's extended legs. My pleading screams and his wails of torture bounced off every wall in the chamber as Luca's head jerked back in agony. "Please!" I screamed. "Stop this! Take me!" The god of strength brought the hammer back, holding it at his waist and turning his attention back to me. Luca continued to gasp for breath helplessly as he groaned from tremendous pain and stared down at his shattered legs. I knew there would be no possibility of him ever walking again, even with white magic. The damage was too great.

"I will allow your freedom, only if you can manage to free yourself and take the sword from the altar. Your life will be miserable. More miserable than you imagined it was before the truth about your birth was revealed to you. You'll be disgraced by the world and will spend your existence tending to your broken prince. But...you'll be free. I do hope that what you feel for your mate is enough." I released a blood-curdling scream as Nero raised the hammer over his head and, to my horror, landed the blow to Luca's middle, crushing it beneath the heavy weapon and letting go of the handle. The shackles around Luca's wrists vanished and his arms dropped to the floor as he lost consciousness and the hammer pinned him where he lay, motionless and completely mangled.

"LUCA!" I cried, streams of tears tearing across my face. "Luca answer me!" He didn't respond. His body lay still and I was barely able to see spurts of shallow breaths as his chest struggled up and down. I beat the burning shackles against the wall, jerking every direction, and feeling nothing give as my face continued to jerk back and forth to his body, checking every few seconds to make sure he was still breathing. Nero lowered himself to sit back on his throne, tossing his ankle across his knee and watching me in entertainment as I made a complete fool out of myself.

Adrenaline fueled my rage and desperation as I tried eagerly to pull my hands through the iron cuffs. I flashed back to the image of the young, nameless mother that shredded the skin from her arm to hold her baby after my father had ruthlessly murdered them. The determination she had to mock his display of hate was no match for this life. I needed that strength, even if we died today. I looked at Luca and kept my focus on him as I took a deep breath and pulled one of my wrists with every bit of my strength. Nothing. I released a few heavy breaths as I clenched my teeth together and held the gaping last breath, pulling again. I groaned in pain when I began to feel my burned skin tearing a little beneath the restraint.

It's working. It's fucking working. Fight through it...fight.

I heaved ragged breaths and glanced at Nero, who watched with fascination as I tried again. I screamed angrily as I felt my skin rip another time, still not free from its shackle but now halfway across my hand. One more hard pull and I could get it out. I looked up at my arm, which was now painted with blood, as it trickled down from my wrist. I felt as if I could be sick, so I turned my attention back to Luca, who miraculously, was still breathing. I raised myself from the floor with my legs and clenched my jaw tight as Nero raised his brows in surprise. I dropped myself back to the floor, yanking my hand free from the iron and screaming loud enough to rupture my own eardrums.

My hand was mangled. Blood leaked from gaping wounds, and I could only look at it for a second or I'd be just as lifeless as Luca. Gods bless that poor woman in her cell. I can't imagine pushing through this while also delivering a child who was born dead and still finding it in herself to hold it close to die with her baby. But I understood it. Now, more than I ever had before. I wouldn't die here. Neither would Luca. I had to gather my remaining strength and will to free my other hand. Any life we had together was more than I could ask for if we could make it through this.

Nero leaned back on his throne, crossing his arms and smirking at me. I sneered at him and then looked up at my other hand, knowing full well I couldn't manage to peel my skin off a second time. I had to be smarter about how to use up any energy that remained in me. My well was nearly dry. I took a few moments to gather myself and breathe while keeping my eyes on Luca, and making sure he didn't die on me. My breath caught in my throat as I looked closer and realized his chest was no longer moving.

No...no, no, no...he isn't...

"Luca!" I called, becoming frantic and breathing as such. I was out of time. If I didn't act now, I may never look into those silvery eyes again. Without another thought, I stood again, grabbing my thumb with my mauled fingers and snapping it as I screamed again, perhaps louder this time and a mind-bending pain shot through my arm. I squeezed my fingers together in my freed hand and slid the last iron cuff off the other, holding it to my chest as I leaned my back against the wall and turned my face to the ceiling, growling back the intense pain.

I took a few rapid, steadying breaths and bolted across the chamber, keeping my broken hand close to my chest and hitting my knees to the floor at Luca's side. I leaned over him and pushed the hair from his face as I looked over him in desperation to find any signs of life. His gorgeous eyes which were once full of life and passion, were half open and starting to glaze over as he stared lifelessly at the ceiling. His skin was turning cold, and I pressed my bloody hand across his chest, feeling no pulse. The brand from my father's curse turned from the dark blue to an unsettling gray and something inside my soul broke. He was gone.

"No..." I whispered, my body beginning to shake with realization. "You can't." I sniffled as I pressed my open wounds to one of his. "How did you do it, Luca?" I said frantically. "How did you find me?" Our blood began to blend together, but this time, I felt no connection. "Don't leave me...come back! Come back to me! Please...Luca!" I cried, trying desperately to force a blood union and pull his soul back to mine. Nothing happened, and my bloody palm struck against his skin as grief sank its icy claws into my heart. I sobbed as I lowered my forehead to his and cupped his face in my hand.

"Your objective was to take your sword, youngling. The—"

"Fuck the sword!" I jerked my face to the god, briefly forgetting he was even here, as I shook wildly with heightened emotion. "Fuck your prophecy! Fuck my father, and FUCK YOU!" I screamed, jumping to my feet and grabbing the handle of Nero's hammer with both my injured hands. An animalistic growl escaped me as I tried to move the heavy metal object off Luca's precious body. Everything hurt, from my head to my shattered heart, my hands seemingly dull in comparison to the loss that I felt knowing he was no longer with me.

"What are you doing?" Nero asked, rising from his throne. I ignored him as I gripped the handle harder, pulling at it relentlessly. "It's no use, child.

Your kind ca—" He paused as the hammer moved slightly and my adrenaline took over. I heaved another loud growl as I lifted the monstrosity from my beloved and turned my entire body to thrust it into the pool of water to my left by the altar. It made a horrible thud as it crashed into the water and hit the stone bottom. Nero was frozen in awe as I fell over Luca's ravaged torso and wept uncontrollably.

"I can't live without you..." I sobbed. "I won't." I leaned over his face, kissing his cold lips, and made a promise under my breath. "Until death, my love...I'm coming for you. Wherever you are. Wait for me." I kissed him again, bringing myself to my feet as I ignored Nero and prepared to take my own life with my sword. The god of strength did nothing to stop me as I charged for the weapon at the altar, grabbing it by the hilt and turning the blade into myself. I barely flinched as I stabbed it into my chest and watched my blood run over the gleaming steel. My vision blurred as I looked one last time at Luca's body, fading to black as my body succumbed to a sudden peace and a bright light replaced the darkness.

...I love you...

The light retreated, and I found myself standing back at the altar, my sword still sitting upon it, shining and clean. Nero stood across from me at the other end of the stone structure, smiling and nodding his head. I looked down at my hands, turning them over and not seeing any sign of a wound. My eyes drifted to the spot where Luca's body had been and found it empty. There were no shackles on either wall, and nothing seemed out of place in the now quiet chamber.

"What happened?" I asked, looking up to meet his proud gaze. His arms crossed in front of him, and he grinned.

"You've passed. You...and your strong-willed prince. Though I've never had the misfortune of witnessing my pride being stolen from me as I watched you wield my hammer. There isn't another being in this world besides myself that can do that."

"Where is he?" My voice cracked as I dismissed his moment of weakness. His smile didn't fade as he inclined his head.

"I'm right here, love." A voice like an angel sounded behind me. I turned to see the love of my life...the love I had just speared my own heart for only moments ago, standing behind me.

His body was unscathed and he looked exactly how I'd remembered before falling asleep after he had asked me for my hand. Tears fell from my eyes as I thrust myself into his arms. He wrapped them tightly around me, and I buried my face into his neck, crying loudly and squeezing him nearly breathless. He tilted my chin up and I met his undeniably striking eyes that were once again full of life. He pulled me into a deep kiss, gripping my hair tightly into his fist and threatening to never let me go as I kissed him back hard. He broke away for a moment, pausing to look at me as he whispered into my mouth, "Don't ever turn another weapon on yourself. My soul ached for every drop of blood that left your perfect heart, Arienne." A tear fell from his eye, landing on my face. "You promise me. Right now." Our heads touched and his thumb slid down my jawline.

"I had to be with you," I whispered, closing my eyes.

"Not like that." He breathed. "Never like that. Promise me."

"I promise." I nodded, taking his lips again. Nero patiently waited as we came close to relieving each other of our clothes before a thought crossed my mind, bringing me to a pause. I felt this rage inside of me so, I pulled back to look at him and tried pushing him away but he didn't let me go. I knew he could feel the anger through our bond. "Why the hell did you not tell me you were summoned? I nearly lost my mind with worry," I asked, my tone harsh.

Before he had the chance to respond, Nero answered from behind me, "Because he was given careful instruction not to." Luca was still holding onto me as I turned to face the god that nearly destroyed my heart. I wasn't sure I was able to forgive everything that had just happened yet. "The prince's test of strength wasn't just in the physical sense either. Everything that you felt emotionally, he endured before you had even awakened in the safety of your bed chamber. I sent for him in secret and brought him here. I told him everything that would transpire before your arrival, and as much as it caused him grief as well as physical torment for you, he followed through with great strength. He understood what it would cost for you both to succeed in retrieving what was needed to stop your father while also learning a valuable lesson."

"And what lesson was that?" I asked firmly, still reeling from the trauma he'd caused us both.

"Love is a double-edged sword, youngling. It can be intoxicating and beautiful, but it also makes the deadliest weapon. Evil stands no chance against it. You must remember this. Let go of everything that you think you feel for your father and replace it with what is gifted to you both. You did not heed the warning of the goddess of nature. I urge you to take it moving forward."

"Did you not say that our quest ended in Bolton? That the sword I brought to you was now tainted and rubbish?" I asked.

"It is tainted no longer. You gave your own life with this blade to be with your soulmate. In doing so, it has been cleansed. It was a selfless act of love, much like your mother giving her life for yours. This weapon has been made worthy of its blessing. As have you. It would be my honor to forge it into its rightful glory." He pressed a fist to his chest. My mouth dropped open at the gesture and I couldn't help but smile. Not only had I won the favor of my people, but of the gods as well. There was no way I could be angry about any of it now. We had proved ourselves in ways that couldn't have been imagined. Luca and I put our fists to our chests in response and I bowed my head to the god of strength.

"Thank you, your grace," I said warmly.

"The sword will take time. I take great pride in my weaponry. I ask only that you truly enjoy yourselves while you await my next invitation. No deception this time. You have my word. The next time that we meet, we shall dine together like kings. I will gift you the finished sword and prepare you for your next destination...and you can confide in me how you were able to lift that hammer." He smiled.

"Perhaps by that time, I'll have a good answer, my Lord."

"Then I bid you both farewell. And if I may say so...fine work. I've never been quite that impressed by a being that wasn't immortal. If it isn't too painful, I'd very much enjoy discussing your tactics during our next gathering." He raised a brow.

"I appreciate that," I said, looking up to meet Luca's gaze.

"Let's go home." He said softly. I nodded and we turned to leave the temple. A loud sound cracked through the air behind us as we neared the entrance and I looked over my shoulder to find that Nero had vanished, along with my sword.

We exited the building and walked down the stone pathway, finding Sir John waiting by the dock. His expression was proud and he smiled graciously as we approached him. I broke from Luca's hold and pulled the old man into a hug that he seemed shocked I was giving, but reciprocated.

"Thank you, friend," I whispered. He pulled back and grunted as he nodded and pat my shoulder the way he did when I left him earlier. We all boarded the boat and John steered us back to Bolton. The way back didn't feel nearly as long and I kept my focus on my betrothed this time instead of our quiet ferryman. When we finally reached the dock to our residence, Alister was waiting to usher us inside. We waved our goodbyes to Sir John and followed Alister up the winding dark stairwell to our room.

"May I be of any assistance before I leave you for the night?" Alister asked as we entered the neatly cleaned bed chamber. I turned on my heel and gave him a side smile.

"Actually...yes. Can you make sure that the prince and I are not disturbed until we decide to come out? I don't care if the entire world is going to shit or you hear sounds of war in this room." Alister's face flushed red and Luca let out a bellowing laugh as he walked toward the bathing pool.

"I'll make sure of it, Mi'lady." He bowed. "Do enjoy your evening." He smiled bashfully as he backed away and slipped out the door.

CHAPTER 18

REVERENCE

Two and a half days had passed before we decided to leave our bed chamber. Time was of no importance to either of us as we slept long hours, ate occasionally and spent the rest worshiping each other's bodies. I was perfectly content with spending a few more days shutting the world out and continuing to live in the security of his arms, watching him sleep and paying closer attention to the motion of his chest and the drumming of his heart. I swore I'd never take a single moment with him for granted again, after what had happened in the temple.

Nero had been absolutely correct. Love *was* a double-edged sword. The sincerity of any decision I made to get Luca back when I stormed into the temple of a higher being, was fierce enough proof of what could build inside me without ever receiving any Ventus ability. I had given much thought to the surprise in the fiery eyes of the god of strength as he watched me toss his hammer aside after it had taken the life of the one I loved. I came to the conclusion that love was the source of my inner strength. It made me think a great deal about the first king and the loss of his beloved family. I understood now, everything he must have felt when he begged the gods to end him for the sake of the world. He wanted them back and couldn't bear to live without them. What burdened me most is that he did it anyway, taking another wife only to produce an heir to the power that he was gifted, to rule over the lands with justice and bring our people peace. There was so much sacrifice in it. I could only hope he was reunited with his wife and son upon his passing. I planned to ask Nero what he knew about that when he summoned us back to the temple.

It was early afternoon on the third day after we'd left Nero to his work, and I stood on the balcony under a partly cloudy sky that leaked rays of milky sunlight over the fjord. The air was salty and damp, with a slight chill, and the breeze was stronger. I had chosen a lovely black gown with a low neckline and long sleeves, the skirts just barely brushing against the floor. It was very simple, with no embellishments, and quite comfortable as well as warm against the drastic change of the weather. My eyes raked over the temple and I wondered when we'd hear from the god again.

"I wish someone could paint this moment so that I could look at it anytime I wished," Luca said softly from behind me. I turned to face him and he smiled as he leaned against the threshold of the entryway with his arms crossed in front of him. "You're the most beautiful creature I've ever seen."

"Care to join me, your Highness?" I smirked.

"If I do, then we'll likely not leave this room for another day." The buttons on his black shirt were only half fastened and the cursed symbol on his chest peeked out from beneath it. It seemed that whether or not any of our test of strengths was an illusion or actually happened and Nero shifted the universe, that damned symbol and its magic remained. The dark blue color had been returned to it as if even death couldn't break through its hold. His eyes followed my stare, and he looked down at it and then back at me. "What's the matter?"

"When you died...that...*thing*—it turned gray. It turned gray, but it didn't disappear. We never talked about what happened in the temple, Luca. I feel perhaps we should. If you're ready." I crossed my arms and leaned against the banister.

"I'm always inclined to be ready to do whatever my lady asks of me. I thought that since you hadn't mentioned any of it in the past two days, that perhaps *you* weren't ready."

"Perhaps, you're right. I had you here with me. I didn't want anything else to stain my mind...or yours. I just wanted to exist in this place with you. Safe and alive." I moved forward and our arms found their way around each other as I stared up at him.

"And exist we did," he smiled devilishly. "Would you like to talk over lunch at the harbor? Get some air, and take a walk?"

"That sounds nice," I said, leaning in to kiss him. I smoothed a hand over his thickening stubble. "You need a shave," I chuckled.

"You sound like my mother." He pressed a chaste kiss to the bridge of my nose and buttoned his shirt in the wrong holes.

"Your mother..." I swatted his hands away to correct them myself. "I wonder if everyone made it back. They should have by now, don't you think?"

"Mmh. Yes, in theory. Though, it may take a bit longer to get word here after they arrived. I suppose you did warn Alister not to make any moves to that chamber door...if they sent word, he probably has it downstairs."

"I did come off rather threatening, didn't I?" I giggled.

"You most certainly did," he grinned, straightening his collar and extending an arm. "Shall we?" I reached up, knotting my fingers around his instead and kissing his knuckles, dropping our joined hands between us.

"Lead the way, Prince."

We left the room and headed down the stairs into the foyer, and Alister's face turned up from a book he had been writing in at a desk. He dropped his quill and stood, bowing and giving us a shy smile as we cleared the last step.

"Good morning, my lord and lady. How are you both?" He asked, flushing a light shade of pink.

"Surprisingly, well rested," I grinned, following his eyes to a spot on my neck that Luca had bitten a bit too hard. I cleared my throat and covered it with my long hair, elbowing Luca for his snickering. Alister playfully laughed it off. He turned to his desk to fetch a small envelope and handed it to me.

"There were two of these. They came for you yesterday." He passed a second envelope to Luca. "If you're venturing out into the city, would you like me to fetch the carriage for you?" Luca started to decline, but I spoke up.

"Actually...yes. If it isn't any trouble, I'd like to read this on the way down into town." I looked at Luca, who nodded in approval and Alister dipped his chin, leaving us to arrange the transport. "This is Paxe's penmanship. I'd recognize it anywhere."

"My father's message was short and sweet. They arrived, and he asked if I'd given you the ring. Apparently, my mother is dying to know," he smiled. I opened the envelope and pulled out Paxe's letter, realizing she had quite a bit to say. I folded it back, deciding I should wait until the carriage was here before diving into it.

The wait wasn't long and Alister ushered us through the doors. I was happy to see both our horses pulling it, and gave my Alice a gentle pat and a kiss to her soft nose. Luca helped me into the open carriage and I took a seat. He climbed up, sitting across from me, and our driver asked where he would be taking us.

"Could you take us to a barber first? Do you know of a good one?" I asked, catching Luca's diminishing smile.

"Yes, Mi'lady. For you or for the prince?" He asked.

"For the yeti, sir," I cackled as my fiancé gave me an obscene hand gesture. Alister chuckled quietly from the side of the carriage as he clicked the small half-door shut.

"Enjoy your afternoon." He bowed, laughing softly as he made his way back into the foyer. The horses started forward, rounding the fountain in the courtyard and making their way through the garden entrance and into the city. I unfolded the letter, ignoring my griping future husband, and started to read.

My dearest friend,

I can't tell you how much I miss you and how emotional I was parting ways with you and Luca after your incredible address to our people. I haven't been able to get the image to leave my mind of how absolutely triumphant you looked waving that sword in the air and riding off with your prince. My heart has never been so hopeful and I'm so proud of you.

I'm continuing to wear your pendant and you'll be happy to know that it has served me well through our journey to Crona. We encountered no danger in our travels and I cannot wait for you to see Luca's home. The queen has been amazing company and I feel I have much to learn from Her Majesty in the months to come. I was reunited with Lakan and I've never been happier. I promise not to ever give you grief over your relationship with Luca again. We are safe and happy, though I'm also writing to warn you...

After the end of the first day of our trip across the continent, we rested in the village to the south in Valdaro. We stayed with a kind elderly female who was a white mage like Vetta. I fell quite ill that evening and vomited through the night. The king had almost chosen to halt our travel until I was feeling well enough to ride again...which, by the way, I'm much better at. Lady Galena offered her healing, but nothing seemed to help. She gave me a tonic to take with me that would settle my stomach and I used it sparingly until we reached Crona.

After I was reunited with Lakan, I met Queen Ayla and I'm ashamed to admit that she bore witness to my purging at dinner that evening. She confirmed what I never expected. It appears I am with child. The babe is safe and healthy, according to the royal mages. Your father somehow didn't detect it when he relieved me of my abilities. I may have been too early then. I know the look that must be gracing your features right now as you're reading this—excited and terrified for our safety. I feel the same. Should your father get word of my condition and the blending of our races, we could all suffer greatly for this. After you've finished reading this letter, I strongly urge you to destroy it. Luca's mother and father are offering their protection at all costs, as well as keeping this a

My heart flooded with battling emotions. She was right. I couldn't have
been more overjoyed that my best friend was going to be a mother, but visions
of that horrible night in the dungeon flashed in my mind. I had warned her to
be careful and she had assured me that she had been. But I do understand
that no matter how careful, these things can still happen. There was no way to
turn back now. I had to trust her and put my faith in the king and queen that
they would protect her and so would my mother, through her amulet.

"I can feel you," Luca interrupted my thoughts as he leaned toward me. I
folded the letter and shoved it safely back into its envelope, sticking it beneath
my leg and taking Luca's hands. "Something's wrong. Or right. Or both? I
can't tell which. Is she alright?" He asked, catching my stare.

"She is," I smiled. I motioned to the driver, whose back was turned toward
us, and Luca's expression turned understanding as he nodded his head.

"Later?" He asked quietly.

"In private," I answered, smiling at him. "When you don't look as much
like an ape." I laughed, bringing my hand to cover my mouth at his annoyed
reaction to my jab.

"You're wicked," he scowled as he leaned back in his seat. "I didn't hear
much complaining when I—" I cleared my throat loudly, cutting him off and
kicking his ankle. Our driver's shoulders bobbed up and down as he silently

laughed at our banter. The carriage slowed to a stop in front of the barber's shop and a sharp grin took over my mouth. Luca leaned forward, attacking my neck with his beard and relishing in my responding laughter as he raised his mouth to my ear. "Laugh now, Princess. When we get back, I'll make sure the inside of your perfect thighs are chafed from my stubble...among other things..." He whispered, his voice pure velvety seduction. My breath caught and a near-instant spark of desire began to ignite at the apex of my thighs.

For the love of the gods...can you do it right now?

"...And I'm the wicked one?" I whispered as I pressed my legs together. He nipped my jaw with his teeth and kissed over it before hauling himself over the side of the carriage, hopping to the street and giving me a promising look on his way into the shop. Locals around had started looking on and smiling at us as my face turned red from both bashfulness and need. My mind started to wander with all the things I wished we were still in our room to do before a loud rumble of thunder sounded from the harbor, breaking my filthy thoughts. I looked at the driver, who turned in his seat. "What was that?" I asked, startled as another loud rumble rang through the air. I looked at the calm, cloudy sky, wondering if a storm was brewing, but saw nothing particularly ominous about them.

"Lord Nero is hard at work, Mi'lady," the driver smiled, turning his attention back to the horses. "You'll likely hear it for a while yet, not to worry." The strange thunder continued as I glanced back at the fjord and the temple that seemed a good distance away, picturing Nero fashioning my simple sword into something as mighty as what hung on his walls.

"What's a good, quiet place to dine that offers a bit of privacy?" I asked, looking around.

"Annette's is a romantic spot, Your Majesty. Likely not as busy at this hour either. She serves delectable pastas and hot soups. Her recipes are unmatched here in Bolton. Perfect comfort food on a day such as this. Would you like me to take you?" He asked, looking over his shoulder.

"That sounds perfect. Thank you, sir." He clicked his tongue and tapped the reins, and the carriage moved further down the street, away from the sound of Nero's banging. We stopped in front of a quaint, but beautiful small restaurant and the smell of stewed tomatoes and fresh garlic filled my senses. The front of the shop was covered in green ivy and lined at the bottom with potted plants of different varieties. There were lovely flowers in an array of colors and a small window adorned with a ledge planter that was overflowing with daisies. I was wholly comfortable and hadn't even stepped through her front door yet. "Oh yes, this will do," I said as the driver helped me step out of the carriage. I reached back inside to swipe up Paxe's letter that had slipped down to the carriage floor when I exited.

"I'll fetch the prince and bring him to you when he finishes up at Mr. Joe's. Will you be alright on your own, Mi'lady?" He asked, a calloused hand resting across his round belly.

"Of course, thank you." I dipped my chin and turned to walk inside. A painted green door easily opened and nearly looked out of place from the rest of the city, which was as dark as the volcanic rock it had been carved from. This place reminded me more of Aeon as I walked inside, with more plants and wooden tables that were candlelit and tastefully spaced around the restaurant. Small rustic chandeliers with vines coiled around them hung from its wooden ceiling and offered the space a soft, cozy feel. A lovely red-haired female approached me as I closed the door and dipped into a curtsy.

"Mi'lady! What an honor. I'm Annette. I'm so very pleased to serve you."

"Thank you. I hear you're the best in the city. If it tastes as good as it smells, I'm excited to be here," I pressed my palms together, steepling my fingers.

"Will the prince be joining you?" She asked politely, looking around to be sure she hadn't missed him.

"He will. He's occupied at the moment. We were hoping for a private area, if you have one." I looked around, seeing only a couple of patrons sitting at a few tables.

"Yes, Mi'lady. I'll show you to your table. Please follow me." She led me across the dining room and made a left down a short hallway into a small room that bled romance. Another chandelier hung over the small table, and paintings of roses were placed on the walls. In the corners were tall braided iron stands that several gathered fat pillar candles burned in, another couple of those candles sat on a flat votive in the middle of the table. "Will this do?"

"Absolutely," I smiled, taking a seat at the little round table. I placed Paxe's letter in front of me and crossed my hands over it.

"Today, I have freshly made linguini with roasted chicken and red sauce. I can bring some toasted bread with herbed butter and olive oil for you. The soup for today is a tomato and cream base with fresh basil and roasted red peppers."

I nearly drooled on myself at the description of today's menu. "That sounds...amazing. We'll have both with a bottle of any wine... anything you're serving, I'll try," I smiled, excitedly.

"Splendid. I'll be right back." She rushed off and as soon as she was out of view, I turned to my letter and let out a long sigh. I looked up at the candles that burned in the corners of the room, realizing that they were perfect for what I was about to do. I stood, walking over to one of the iron stands and held the envelope over the flames. The parchment caught quickly, and I didn't release the corner I held until the last bits of ash fell into the wax.

Alright friend...your secret remains safe. As does the wee one growing in your belly.

I smiled to myself, dismissing any thoughts of danger for a moment and picturing her with a child of her own. I watched the ashes scatter across the melted wax and choked back emotion as I thought back on happier memories of Paxe and I as children. She was always by my side. I only wished I could be by hers now as she turned this chapter in her life. I wanted to protect them...to watch her baby grow. I wondered then if I'd ever have the chance to experience this with her, once the threat of my father's cruelty was gone. I would make that happen. She was right. There was a great deal more to fight for. With all the thoughts about her fragile, yet happy news came unwelcome thoughts of a similar sort.

She's been with child all this time...she didn't know. What if...I—

I looked down at my flat middle, running my fingers lightly over my womb. With everything that has happened in the last couple of weeks, I never stopped to think of the possibility that Luca and I have been in no way careful, and I could very well be...the same. We've been so lost in our rapture that I hadn't even considered the danger that being pregnant could mean. Neither Luca, nor I, were human, but that didn't mean my father wouldn't try to hurt me even if he knew I was carrying his grandchild. If what happened in the temple of Nero wasn't some grand illusion, then how would I know if our baby had possibly been harmed? Paxe's news cast a whole different light on so many real possibilities.

"Whatever it is that you're thinking about is radiating from you like a storm." I jumped, snapping out of my spiraling thoughts at Luca's voice, jerking into a spin to face him and grasping my lower belly for dear life. My reaction startled him too, and his attention went straight to my hand. He glanced back at me with a flash of deep worry in his eyes. "...What's wrong, Arienne? Why are you—" He moved forward, never taking his eyes from mine and placing his hand over my own. "Is there something I should know, love?"

"I–I'm..." I stuttered. Luca's eyes grew wide.

"You're...terrifying me," he continued.

"I'm sorry...I'm not. At least...not that I'm aware, but..."

"...But?"

"Paxe... Paxe is...with child," I whispered. He swallowed hard and looked down at my belly. His grip tightened over my hand.

"I see...and you're worried that we could be in that position." His brows drew together as he looked back up at me. "She's only been in Crona for a couple of days. How cou—" He paused and his expression went from confusion to shock. "Oh..."

"She didn't know," I said quietly. He took my hand and led me to my chair, pulling it out for me as I sat, and then dropped into the other.

"What else did she say?" He asked, seemingly shaken from thoughts that I knew had to be similar to my sudden panic attack.

"She said that they had arrived and that everyone was very happy and perfectly safe. She told me she was proud of me and that she missed me. She said that after the first day of traveling, she had fallen ill and retched all night. The woman they stayed with was a white mage, but nothing she tried had worked. Your mother apparently was the one who figured it out when they arrived in Crona, and Paxe got sick at dinner that evening. Both your parents are protecting her and keeping this quiet. She told me if I were to tell you the truth, I should destroy the letter and make sure to be careful of any interception of our messages from here forward."

Luca stared off, rubbing his fingers over his closely trimmed chin and getting lost in thought. "So, all this time...she has been pregnant. She's pregnant with a blended child." He gave me a relieved look. "Thank the gods she left that place. She'll be safe with my parents as long as we keep this nailed down. Try not to worry about her. My mother is a force to be reckoned with, I assure you."

"Here you are, dears. Welcome, Prince Luca," Annette cut in, sitting our plates down before us with a beaming smile. Another young female followed behind her with two bowls of soup and our wine. Luca popped the cork out and poured us both a glass.

"Thank you. It looks incredible." He flashed a smile at me, and I snorted into my wine.

"The bread will be out in just a moment...if I may say?" She paused and we both looked at her, urging her to finish. "Word around the city is that Lord Nero was quite taken with the two of you. That is no easy task. It's all anyone has talked about for the past two days. I wanted to wish you both good fortune. Bolton will support you on your journey, Mi'lord and lady. We are all in great debt to you both. It's truly an honor to have you," she smiled tearfully. I reached for her hand and she grasped it.

"Thank you, Lady Annette. It means a great deal to us. Truly." I squeezed her hand. She bowed and left us to our meal. I sipped my wine and tried a spoonful of the steaming soup and my eyes rolled back at its savory taste. "Gods...what an amazing lady."

Luca chuckled at my indulgence, trying a bite of the linguini and making nearly the same gesture. "You should try the pasta," he said over his food. We ate in silence for a few moments and the same young lady appeared with the toasted bread. She said nothing but smiled sweetly as she lowered it to the table, took our finished items and promptly left us to the rest of the food. "We should finish talking about this...are you truly worried you could be with child?" Luca asked softly.

"I suppose I never thought about it. I certainly did when Paxe told me she had bedded Lakan. I was concerned about her being...careful." I took another long sip.

"When was that?"

"It was the day I met you, actually. She was dressing me for the meeting. She can't be that far... she even said so in her letter. She mentioned that my father may not have detected it because of how early she had been when he depleted her magic. If he had known, I'm certain he'd have killed her."

"It was only a couple of weeks ago since we first laid together. I'm not sure if anyone we found to examine you would be able to tell if you were just yet."

"If I was, I have a feeling I may not be any longer," I said sadly. Our eyes met and Luca's expression turned absolutely heartbroken.

"Why would you think that?" He reached across the table for my hand and I gave it, locking our fingers.

"The temple, Luca. I'm pretty positive that we both died in there. We may be here and healthy now, but that wasn't the case two days ago. Even if it was only for a few horrible moments."

"But there was no sign of losing one either. You never bled or became ill. I told you my mother couldn't have any more children. I remember what it was like for her."

"She lost a child?" I asked, my heart breaking at the thought of Queen Ayla enduring such a thing. Luca nodded slowly.

"She was in terrible pain for several days and passed the child early. She was very sick. She nearly bled to death. The mages worked tirelessly to nurse her back to health, but she could no longer bear another. I haven't seen any sign of that in you," he said softly, looking at our hands and fidgeting with my ring.

"We may be grasping at nothing. I'm probably not even carrying a child. It was just a sudden thought that crossed my mind. Paxe had been pregnant for weeks, and had no sign of anything amiss." He nodded again in agreement. "We shouldn't make a fuss over something we can't possibly know right now. We still have a lot to discuss. I'm sorry I lost my senses."

"Don't be. You had good reason." He let go of my hand and poured more wine into our glasses. "You told me earlier that you were bothered about the mark...said it turned gray when..." I felt his eyes on me, but I didn't look up from my plate as I pushed my fork around, stressfully creating shapes in my pasta.

"When you died. I had hoped it would disappear," I answered, my tone melancholy and bleak. "Before Paxe left, I had come up with another idea, but I'm trying not to raise my hopes about it working. Especially now that your own death didn't even phase it." I looked up.

"Let's hear it," he said as he leaned back in his chair.

"Well...I had mentioned the idea of ending my father before the Ventus. Before the clock on your life stops ticking and we're faced with being ripped away from each other. Now that I know what that feels like, Luca...I can't bear the thought of keeping the promise I made to you and living like the first king had. I could never love another or take a husband...have a child that isn't shared with you. You're leaving me in an impossible position." I dropped the fork into the plate and placed my hands in my lap.

"And how would it make you feel if you were to watch me take my own life? To be helpless to do anything to stop you and watch you put a blade through your own heart?"

"You saw me?"

"I did. I saw everything. I was out of my body, screaming for you. I watched you break your own bones and tear your skin from your body to do exactly the opposite of what Nero had told you to do, just to get to me. I heard you kindly tell him to go fuck himself, too." He laughed for a moment, I did too, but the conversation remained tense. "I knew what you were trying to do, and I tried desperately to reach you through the blood union, but there was nothing. You couldn't hear me. I saw you lift that hammer and toss it like a stone into the pond...but when I watched you turn that sword... Ari... my soul was broken. I begged you not to, and then it was over. I could feel you just before the light consumed me and when it was gone, I was standing behind you."

"And that bastard curse was still branded to your skin," I added furiously. "If there's a chance that I could stop it by putting an end to him sooner, I'll take it. But now I'm second-guessing myself that it would even be fruitful."

"Then why don't we ask Nero at the next gathering? It's worth the risk...but you made a promise to me, love. Whether or not this works...I need you to live. If you are to die, I don't ever want it to be by your own hand. I can't bear to ever watch you hurt any part of yourself for my sake again. Please understand," he pleaded.

"Living without you is a much greater pain than any physical harm could ever get close to, Luca. My body won't last forever. We're not immortal beings. Even my father would eventually die if I never gathered these weapons and killed him myself. I cannot be in a world that doesn't have you in it. I promised you, but I need *you* to understand how steep a price you're asking of me. If this doesn't work...I—"

"We'll ask the gods. Until then...we continue this journey together...alright?" He stood and knelt next to my chair, turning me to face him and taking my hands. "Together, Arienne...until death," he whispered.

"Until death." I leaned forward, taking his face in my hands, and softly pressed my lips to his. "Shall we go?" I asked, no longer satisfied with being in public.

"Whatever my lady desires," he smiled. We rose from our seats, and although it wasn't necessary, Luca laid a handful of coin on the table and we made to leave. As we entered the dining room, Annette came to thank us and bid us goodnight. We thanked her in return and headed out the door to see every person in the city standing in the street, watching the harbor in silence.

The sound of thunderous banging was joined with a booming masculine voice that sang in an ancient tongue to the rhythm of the hammering. Luca's hand gripped mine, and we glanced at each other.

"Our driver said the banging was the sound of Nero forging weapons in the temple," I supplied. "I didn't hear him singing before."

"He had told me that too when he picked me up from the barber to bring me here. The banging wasn't even as loud when I got to the restaurant. Why are they all staring like that?" He asked as we turned our attention back to the people in the street. I raised my eyes to the higher levels and noticed hundreds more had gathered to look on... in silence.

"Luca..." I nudged, pointing to them. He followed my gaze and his mouth dropped open. We moved towards our waiting carriage and our driver stood next to it, gazing towards the fjord like the rest of the city. He turned toward us as we approached and bowed deeply. "What's happening? Why is everyone out here like this?"

"Lord Nero started singing a few moments ago, Princess..." He answered in a trembling voice.

"Has no one ever heard him sing while he's working?" I asked innocently. The driver straightened and looked at me with an expression most surprised.

"Mi'lady..." He started. "The god of strength has forged many a weapon...but no one has heard his grace sing for hundreds of years. It is your blade he's perfecting...the last blade gifted to any being that wasn't immortal...was that of the first king. It's the only other time Lord Nero was heard singing while he fashioned it. It is a sign of true promise. You and your prince...you are truly the light that is being given back to our world."

Luca and I stood in shock for a moment. My palms became damp with sweat, and my heart drummed along to the beat of the sounding thunder as Nero's voice surrounded Bolton in its entirety. His song echoed off of the cliffs, and the waves became loud enough to hear even where we now stood. The coachman gestured for us to enter the carriage, and Luca helped me in, closing the small door and sitting next to me this time, holding me close to him as we started forward. Annette and all her staff and patrons rushed out of the rustic green door of her shop, lining up along the street and kneeling near our carriage with a fist to their chests. I released a sharp breath as we traveled down the street and every person drew their attention to us, taking a knee and doing the same, in perfect silence.

"Mother of the gods..." Luca breathed as he held me tighter and watched with amazement. Nero's song became louder as we neared the harbor and made the turn up the first level. More bodies lowered to the ground as we passed. While making our silent journey back up the cliffside, we met eyes with a few as they knelt, and Luca and I pressed fists to our hearts in response. If I had thought Aeon was moving...this experience was deeper. More reverent. We finally made it through the garden entrance to the residence and rounded the fountain to see Alister already kneeling at the front entrance with his head bowed and his fist placed. We exited the carriage, and our driver smiled at me.

"It has been my honor, your Highness. Gods be with you both," he bowed. Alister rose, straightening himself and meeting my eyes.

"Welcome back, my lord and lady. Today is a day that will not soon be forgotten in Bolton or all over the world. Will you allow me to escort you? There's something you should see." We followed him warily into the foyer and I nearly lost my balance as I took in the sight.

In the center of the foyer now stood a massive polished black statue of me. It bore a striking resemblance to every detail of my face and hair, the dress I had worn in the temple and even had a ring carved over my finger that took the shape of the one Luca had given me. The statue had the chin raised to the ceiling, with blowing hair and skirts, and in my other hand was a replica of Nero's hammer. Luca gazed up at it, bleeding with pride as he slowly circled the sculpture.

"Ari..." He whispered, pointing to the bodice of the statue. I followed his direction and realized a thin necklace was carved into it that ended in a relaxed bow at its chest. I recognized it as Luca's hair strap. An indentation at the side of the bodice revealed the hammer and sword embellishment of the corset top from the dress. It was truly an extraordinary piece of art. It was as if I were looking at myself in a mirror of ink.

"Alister...who did this?" I asked, still not quite believing what I was seeing.

"Master Nero created this masterpiece over the last two days. He began to work on your sword this morning. I had tended to some matters of the residence and returned earlier to find it placed here. By his command, it is to remain here forever as a testament to your feat. He wanted to honor your wielding of his hammer and eternally capture it so that the world may know."

"I don't know what to say...this is...I'm speechless." I grasped at my chest, holding Luca's leather strap and watching him as he took in every inch of the sculpture.

"Can he make a smaller one for my pocket?" He joked, earning a snicker from our attendant and an eye roll from myself.

"You did mention this morning that you wanted someone to capture the moment so you could gaze at it forever," I laughed as he nodded happily from the other side of my onyx body.

"There's more," Alister offered, motioning for us to come upstairs. We followed him to our room, and he opened our door, revealing a floor full of gifts and offerings and an enormous bouquet of flowers that looked like the ones from Annette's restaurant. They were beautifully arranged and placed in a dark stone vase in the middle of the table that had been restocked with more food and wine and a fresh pitcher of infused water. "Lady Annette sent the flowers while you dined. She noticed that you were admiring them before you came inside."

"Where did they all come from? The city doesn't seem like an ideal place to grow much vegetation. Her parlor was also full of greenery," I asked as I thumbed across a handsome peach-colored rose.

"The lady's gift is her ability to grow most anything from nothing. She also sells her rare plants aside from her fine culinary talents. The rest of these gifts are for the two of you from all over the city. I had only finished delivering them before I heard the sound of Master Nero's singing. I had walked to your balcony and saw Bolton become still and I knew it was a sign that our people would remain safe. Please accept my deepest gratitude for your service to our world. I never dreamed I'd be the one, having the fortune of a lifetime, to attend to the chosen." He smiled and looked nearly ready to weep as he bowed and made haste to leave before losing his composure in our presence.

In our distraction from the shock of seeing a mirrored image of myself cast in polished stone and seeing all the clutter of gifts from local well-wishers, we didn't notice the thundering and singing had ceased. It was now late afternoon and the sun was beginning to set over Bolton as Luca and I stepped out onto the balcony to watch. He stood behind me, pulling me close and weaving our arms together across my middle as we studied the now silent temple.

"Every day becomes more strange. If someone had asked me five years ago what I thought my life might be like later on...I never would have imagined this," I admitted, watching the sun turn a deep orange over the water.

"Is that a bad thing?" Luca teased, mimicking my question from our trip into the city. He laid his chin on my shoulder. I smiled, turning my face and kissing his cheek.

"No, not at all," I said, facing forward again. "I'm just not sure how to balance it all. Everyone's expectations of us now...they're a tall order. I want to make them proud. Our people deserve this peace. They long for it."

"And they'll have it. So will we. When this is all over...the idea of helping you grow a child in this belly..." He palmed my middle. "I want it, Arienne. I want it all. If that makes me greedy, then I'll accept that. But thinking it was a possibility earlier, made me almost wish...." He paused. "I know that now isn't the right time, but I'm determined to *have* that time with you. We'll all be free to live when we finish what we've started. But you, love..." His firm hands slid further down. "You deserve it, just as much as they all do."

I leaned further into him as his hands continued to dip lower. I placed my own over them, pushing them further until he had finally reached the area I was hoping for. He gripped it firmly, moving his fingers across the fabric of my gown, and brushed his lips against my neck as my head fell back onto him.

"Didn't you promise me something before you went to the barber?" I whispered, closing my eyes. He crept up to my ear, taking the lobe between his teeth.

"I certainly did. May I take my lady into the bath?" He breathed, pulling us closer together. I could feel his bulge against my backside and a sharp breath escaped my mouth.

"Please do," I said, turning to face him and wrapping an arm around his neck as he hooked one beneath my knees and carried me inside.

CHAPTER 19

THREATS OF WAR

I woke in the middle of the night with the strange feeling that someone was watching us. Someone who meant us harm. Moonlight pooled into the room and I turned over to see Luca lying on his back, his breathing slow and even, utterly peaceful and sleeping quietly. I looked around the room, catching a familiar silhouette at the table against the wall, blocking the large bouquet of flowers that rested in the middle. My heart pounded as I slid silently to the edge of the bed and placed my bare feet on the floor. My black silk nightgown fell across my thighs as I stood, creeping quietly toward the closet.

"I advise against whatever you're thinking of doing, daughter," a voice promising death stopped me in my tracks, and every hair on my neck and arms stood on end. A low amber light flooded the room, illuminating the space only enough to reveal my father standing with his back turned to me at our table. "Make a move and it will cost you. You know, as well as I, that you're powerless to stop me. Don't be foolish."

"What do you want?" I asked, straightening myself and moving towards the end of the bed to stand between him and Luca. "You'd be the foolish one to leave the protection of your fortress and come all the way here. There's a deity in that temple below that isn't in your favor," I snarled. He slowly turned to face me, holding a rose in his fingers and plucking a petal off.

"You know...word travels quickly." He dropped it and it singed to ashes before it reached the floor. My heart thudded loudly. "It seems a great deal has changed about you. First with your boldness as you lashed out at me in my study..." He plucked another petal, never looking up from the blossom and tossing it away. My eyes followed it as it, too, hissed from its burn and fell apart. "Then you sent a threatening message to me in the way of a murder most familiar. I must say, I was impressed. I also heard that you made quite the speech in little Aeon, gaining the favor of every wretch that resides in it." He raised his face to meet mine, and a wicked smile graced his mouth as he looked me over.

"What did you do to them?" I shook, seeing Vetta and Frances' faces in my mind and hoping to the gods that they were safe.

"You look much like your mother did after she'd been well-ridden, only happier. It doesn't suit you. I much prefer your cowering. Seems your little prince is doing a fine job breaking you in," he grinned.

"Answer me," I growled between my clenched teeth. He tugged another petal off the rose and a sound flame enveloped it before it vanished into more ashes.

"I've no interest in that shit heap town. Burning a bunch of peasants would bore me. I'd much rather play with human filth. They're the most enjoyable. You needn't worry about your old nanny and her scum brother," he said coldly, taking a step toward me. I backed away, bumping against the ottoman at the foot of the bed. I glanced over my shoulder at Luca, who was still sleeping peacefully, and then back at my deranged father. "Don't bother. He looks as if you fucked him into oblivion. I doubt he'll wake for some time. Rumor has it that he asked for your hand. Was he good enough for you to give it?"

"He's more of a male than you'll ever be. Now get to the point. If there even is one. Why did you come here?" I spat.

"I know what you're planning to do."

My heart thrashed against my chest. If he was telling the truth, then he'd be expecting what was coming and our whole journey and quest to acquire these weapons would fail. I decided to use my trickery of feigned confidence again, straightening myself and pretending I was back in Aeon, playing a game of cards with Paxe on our bed. "Do you? And what's that? Aside from enjoying the freedom you never meant to give me and accepting my role as the queen you already knew I'd be."

"Don't play games with me, child." He took another step forward. "There's a pretty statue downstairs that looks very much like you...holding the hammer of Nero."

I raised my chin. "And? Are you not proud of one thing I've done? I told you I'd not kill anyone for you...and I ended up doing just that. I won a battle of strength with a god and wielded his famed hammer. According to his grace, I'm the only semi-mortal to have ever done that. Is none of it enough for you to at least tell me anything other than you're...*impressed?*"

He chuckled through his nose and gave me a smile you could almost call proud. "You're right." I drew my brows together.

"I'm right?"

"Yes. To tell you the honest truth, that news was the only news that brought me a bit of joy...and as odd as it is for me to say...yes, I'm proud of you. Greatly so." His face softened and for once, he looked like a father. I stiffened.

"Is this another one of your tricks?" I asked, my tone firm and threatening.

"No. I do truly mean it. Well done," he nodded.

"Why do you hate me? What did I ever do to make it so? Why do you wish so badly to hurt me? Have you ever loved me...even a little? As a child? An infant? I need to know."

"No...you don't. And it was never anything you did. I told you before...I do not believe in love. Love does not exist."

"It does exist. I've never felt anything close to the way I feel for Luca. Are you so evil, Father, that you couldn't accept love for me even once? What the hell happened to you?" I pulled my strength together and stepped towards him. His hand squeezed around the rose blossom, igniting it in a bright amber flame and crumbling in his palm.

"Enough." His eyes glowed with rage. I grew quiet, no longer as afraid. "You're rallying against me. You're traveling these lands to gather our people and turn them against their king."

Ahhh...he doesn't know the truth.

"Our people have never supported you. They surrender to you under fear. You cursed Luca," I returned. His eyes met mine and the cruel father I remembered was back. "Undo it." A smile crept across his face.

"I'm afraid I can't do that. Not when this is playing out so well. I knew you'd fall for that lie. You may have picked up that hammer, but you're still as weak as you've always been. I'll prove that to you if it costs me my life. And I'll take your handsome beau with me," he sneered. I closed the space and stood chest-to-chest with the monster.

"You'll release him from this, or I'll come for you. You only mistake love for weakness because you're consumed by evil...and it will be the death of you, Father. Make no mistake. I meant what I said. I'm not a helpless child anymore. I *will* fucking end you." I stared into his burning eyes and for once, I didn't feel hate. I felt sympathy. "You'll never have what I have. If you killed me this moment, you'd never take away what I've been given. The way I feel...the love of my people. I do pity you."

"If it is war that you seek, daughter...then consider this your warning. Bring an army to my door and I'll enjoy tearing the life from every last one of you. I'll keep you alive to watch everyone you love burn, and then I'll rip that heart from your chest and leave you to rot like your fucking mother." He grabbed me by the throat before I could say another word and squeezed tightly as he raised me off the floor by my neck. I clawed at his arms, struggling against his hold, and kicked my legs in panic. He smiled sinisterly at me. "Don't come back home unless you mean to make good on your promises. If you mean what you say, then I welcome you to try, little dove. Sweet dreams, daughter." He squeezed harder on my neck until darkness started to cloud my vision.

I jolted awake, sweating and gasping for precious oxygen as I sat up in bed and reached for my throat, startling Luca. I heaved in heavy breaths and looked around the moonlit room for my father but saw no one. Luca put a gentle hand on my back and another on my shoulder as I continued to breathe... as if I were drowning.

"What happened?" He soothed, rubbing his hand across my spine.

"My father!" I gasped. "My father was here. He nearly strangled me to death." Luca pressed his lips to my temple and brought his arms around me, pulling me close.

"Shhh...it was a dream, love. You're safe...breathe. Breathe with me." I tried to calm myself as he laid me on my back and leaned over me, placing a hand on my chest. "Your heart is pounding." It was no use. Panic began to overtake me and I couldn't catch my breath. He leaned in and kissed my forehead, and a familiar calm began to wash over my skin like a warm tide.

My lungs settled and I felt blissful, giving into his magic and relaxing my limbs. "Better?" He whispered, looking back into my eyes.

"Luca..."

"Yes, my lady..."

"I want you to use your magic..." I breathed, my lips brushing across his.

"I am."

My fingertips trailed up his back and I moved my hips to lay beneath his body, raising a knee on either side of him. "Use it and make love to me," I whispered.

"Are you sure?"

"Yes."

His hand moved from my chest down to my thigh, raising my silk nightgown up to my waist. The feeling of the material across my skin already seemed heightened under his influence, sending a shiver across my body and heat to my center.

"Give me your hands," he whispered, claiming my mouth. He interlocked our fingers and slid my arms above my head, holding them there and deepening our kiss. He broke away and looked me in the eyes, flipping his hair over his shoulder. "Last chance...if I do this, I'm pulling you out of the calm and into something more intense. Anything you were feeling before I shut it down could resurface."

"Then replace it with your everything. I'll never let him take you from me," I said, raising my head to latch onto his mouth again. He paused, looking deeply into my eyes.

"Is that what this is about?" He asked softly.

"My father believes love is a fable, Luca—a lie. I used to believe that too. You proved me wrong, and I want to feel every part of it. I want everything. Show me. Show me how far it can go," I begged.

"Ari..."

"You told me you'd only use your ability on me if you thought it was needed, or if I asked you to...this is me asking. I've never felt for anyone the way I do for you. If there's any chance we can dive deeper and get lost in what we have...then I want to be drunk in it with you. If you use it, you can feel everything I feel...right?"

"I can..."

"Then make it all disappear...until there's nothing left but us," I whispered, kissing him deeply. His returning kiss was burning, and in the time it took my head to fall back to the bed, the shift in his magic soared. My blood was like liquid fire, every nerve responding to any point of contact and intensifying every second. The tip of his length brushed against my core and nearly sent me to another world. He slid himself across me, breathing heavier at the response of my writhing body beneath him and slipped his tongue into my mouth.

He slowly pushed inside me and the wave of pleasure that tore through me was enough to think I'd finished before we'd even started. I felt him pull out slowly, our fingers locking tighter as every inch of him slid back inside, stretching me until our bodies met. The contact of our skin heightened every sensation and drove a shock through my limbs that felt like release at every slow, calculated movement. Luca didn't push harder or move faster. It wasn't needed at all, and I felt if he did, our time in this euphoria would be cut short, far too quickly.

The raw feeling of rapture, combined with pure adrenaline, desire and need, injected itself into every vein in our bodies that continued to move together like oil over water. Love grew deeper like rapidly curling vines, securing every one of those feelings in its rightful place. I'd never felt anything like it and craved more. Long, breathy moans freed themselves from both of us as the sheet underneath me became damp from my arousal every time he pushed back inside. My heart thundered to the point that I wondered if it was nearly audible as I arched my back from the bed and spread my legs further apart, offering him deeper. The dark sheet slid from his lower back as he rolled his hips into me, falling from his toned backside and dropping to the bed.

I wanted so badly to claw at his back but my arms remained above me, tethered by his strong hands. He tore his mouth away from mine and looked at me under lowered brows, completely consumed by our erotic connection. He looked angelic and, at the same time, godlike as silver fire burned his smoldering stare.

"Gods, I fucking love you, Arienne," he choked through a heaving breath, pushing and pulling himself slowly, in and out of me, with just enough force to leave me gasping for air. Our heads touched together and our lips hovered a breath apart. "Tell me..." he moaned. "Tell me... you're mine."

"I'm yours..." I gasped. "Forever." He released one of my hands and slowly pulled himself from my body, turning me over until my stomach was flat against the bed. I laid my cheek against its smooth satin surface and he brushed my hair from my face, raising my hips slightly and sinking his throbbing length back into me. I snapped my eyes closed, dropping my mouth open and gripping a handful of the sheet as my body greedily swallowed every last inch of him.

Cold metal slid between our joined palms and his fingers squeezed tighter as a quick sting of pain sliced across my hand. Warm moisture replaced the metal and my body jerked as our blood merged, and the bond between us became impenetrable. Every divine feeling we had up until that point became incredibly more powerful and a thousand times stronger as his magic bled into my body. His perfectly solid torso rested on my back and his chin grazed my shoulder as he smoothly pushed himself deeper with every thrust of his hips.

"Tell me you love me..." He whispered against my skin. "Tell me that you feel this, and it isn't just my heart bleeding for you..." His breathing was desperate and his voice longing as he kissed the exposed skin on my shoulder.

Every touch, every kiss and every fiber that made up my being responded in earnest, and tiny bursts of pure ecstasy erupted under my skin and began to gather low in my belly.

"I love you..." I whispered, breathlessly. "I love you more than anything...I *feel* everything." His body moved with mine, his thrusts becoming more forceful. His left hand caressed my side, sliding my nightgown higher up my waist and raising my hips higher as he pushed deeper inside. His hair fell around his face as he leaned back into my neck, tossing it over his shoulder and pressing his cheek against mine. I could barely breathe. Everything felt so incredibly good.

He moved faster and slid his hand between my legs, spreading them further apart and slipping his fingers over my slick, aching center. I gripped my fist tighter around the sheet and moaned loudly as he thrust harder and bit down onto my shoulder. I cried out his name as I plunged over the edge, release pummeling through me unlike anything I'd ever felt before, and he rode me through every wave. I thought my heart might explode as I felt him pulse inside me, hearing every sound he made and every deep groan of pleasure. My name left his mouth in a smooth rasp of breath as he came, sending me into another rush right along with him. His magic slowly seemed to retreat as we panted against each other for a few moments...but I wasn't ready for it to end.

I fed from the adrenaline I could still feel buzzing between us and turned my body, pulling him gently out and holding tight to his bloodied hand as I rolled him to his back. He watched me curiously, as I snaked a leg over, straddling him and leaning over his chest.

"What are you doing?" He whispered, his magic slowly building. I didn't answer, instead deciding to steal his lips and bring him into a kiss that was slow, sensual and devastating. It worked. I felt more of his magic feed into me as I slowly pulled away from his mouth and brushed my lips against the stubble of his chin. I tilted his head back with my free hand, lowering my head and grazing his neck with my teeth in the way he was accustomed to doing to me. I kissed down his neck, adding my tongue in some places and continuing down to his collarbone, searching for the place where our bond came together that night in Aeon, with my heart and my mind.

It didn't take long before I found it, and the tremble of his body told me that he knew it. I pictured his light that surrounded me and had brought me home to him that night and tried to will it all to heighten his emotion and everything he was making me feel. He took in a sharp breath with the next kiss I pressed to his chest...another indication that whatever I was trying to do was working.

"Ari..." he breathed heavily. "How are you doing that...?" I grasped at his hand a little harder, moving myself down and trailing kisses down his middle. "Dear gods..." he whispered as I neared his waistline, taking him into my free hand and stroking him gently. I ran my tongue from the underside of his base to the tip and relished in the way he moved as I closed my mouth over him. I willed his magic further and rolled my tongue around his head as my lips sank down his length and I tightened my grip. He jerked his leg, breathing hard and cursing under his breath.

His hand brushed against my hair, smoothing across it as I took him deeper into my mouth. He gathered it in his fingers, moving it away from my face and laying it over my shoulder as I sucked hard until I reached his head again. He moaned softly between rapid breaths as I continued up and down, slowly at first but getting faster as his grip in my hair became tighter. He got louder as I freed myself of the rest of his influence and used his own abilities on him, his body moving tensely and his back slowly coming off the bed. His cock pulsed underneath and I looked up, meeting eyes that I didn't realize were watching as I firmly stroked half of him, while I worked the rest with my mouth. His warm release filled my throat as his head fell back to the bed and a masculine groan left him while he scrambled for air.

I swallowed every drop, kissing the tip gently and raised myself to climb back over him slowly. I rested beside him and laid my head on the crook of his shoulder as I leaned my face over, kissing his neck softly. His free hand fingered through my hair and he slowly calmed himself. Our joined bloody palms gently separated, no longer actively bleeding, but sticky and damp. He turned on his side to face me, wrapping me in his arms and pressing his head to mine.

"How?" He whispered, brushing the tip of his nose against mine. I smiled and dragged my fingertips softly up his back.

"I'm not sure. I pictured your light...thought to will the magic to you...and it allowed me?" His stare was disbelief and amazement.

"So first, you wield the hammer of the god of strength...with no magic or abilities. And now, you figured out a way to also wield my own magic and use it on me? I'm sensing a pattern here," he said, a low chuckle leaving his lips.

"Is that a bad thing?" I mocked. He pulled me in tighter and his smile grew wide.

"Absolutely not." He kissed the bridge of my nose.

"What did it feel like?" I asked, hoping for an honest answer but knowing he was purely satisfied. He groaned as he recalled the last few minutes.

"I've never felt like that in my life. You're absolutely incredible."

"Has anyone ever...done that to you before?" This time, I wasn't as sure if I wanted to know, but I had already said it out loud.

"No. Never. I think I'm still in shock." He raised his palm over my shoulder, examining how deep the cut was. "I never considered the possibilities of joining our blood like this. It was impulsive, but...gods..." He paused. "What would you say to a midnight bath? We should clean these up. I'm sorry, love. I should have warned you or asked."

"Don't...the answer would have been yes, anyway. And another bath sounds divine. I have no interest in trying to sleep right now, strangely," I murmured.

"Maybe the magic?"

"Could be...and too much going on in my head." We laid there for a few long moments before finally deciding to move. Luca lit a few oil lamps while I disrobed and waited in the bathing pool for him to join me a moment later. He brought me the strap I usually wore around my neck and tied my hair into a loose knot on the top of my head. He took a seat in the corner near the closet and pulled my back against his chest, bathing me with a clean linen. I laid my head back against his shoulder and brought my palm out of the water, staring at the clean cut that mirrored his own. It wasn't as deep as the one Vetta had made and would heal quickly, but I became fascinated by how simple it was to be that close to him...as long as his precious heart was still beating.

"Did I hurt you, love?" He asked gently. I sank my hand back under the water.

"No, not at all. I'm glad you did it. I was just thinking, that's all." His chin rested at the base of my neck as he continued to move the linen over my chest and across my breasts.

"What did you dream about? You said your father strangled you."

"I don't think it was a dream. He was here. He was watching us." My voice became low and intimidating.

"He wasn't actually here. Do you suppose he used magic?"

"I do. He came to scare me...to send a message," I answered.

"What happened?" Luca paused, bringing our cut palms together and tracing around my raised fingers as I brought them just a few inches over the surface.

"It was really strange. He had taken a rose from Lady Annette's arrangement and kept setting petals on fire in an attempt to intimidate me...it would have probably worked, but something about him seemed..." I drew my brows together, pondering it for a beat. "Different."

"Different in what way?" He asked, raising a knee.

"I think he feels threatened by me, somehow. I almost thought he'd had us figured out, but he believes I'm trying to raise an army against him. He told me not to come home unless I planned to make good on my promise to come for him. He also threatened to slaughter everyone I love if I bring our supposed *army* to his door." I traced circles over his exposed knee, recalling my conversation with my father.

"So, he doesn't know about the weapons?"

"No. And I'm starting to wonder what really happened between my parents. Prophecy or not...I think he may have killed her, Luca." He shifted, lowering his knee back into the water and turning me to face him.

"He couldn't have. She exchanged her life for yours." His expression remained confused.

"I know...but I feel like there's something more. I don't think he was born evil. When I saw him tonight...I didn't feel my hate for him. I pitied him. He told me a lot had changed about me...he saw the statue in the foyer downstairs and heard all the chatter about the people honoring me. He actually admitted that he was proud. I've never heard him say that...ever. And he most likely wouldn't have had I not coaxed him into it, demanding answers. But I want to understand why he hates me. Something happened to cause him to be this way...he won't tell me. When he told me he'd kill every last one of you, he said he'd rip my heart out and leave me to rot like my mother..."

"Do you think he knows about the prophecy? Or your mother's sacrifice?" he asked warily.

"I'm wondering if, perhaps, he was allowed to believe that he did actually kill her so he *wouldn't* find out." His eyes grew wider with understanding. "She gave him an heir. He didn't need her anymore," I continued.

"That actually makes a great deal of sense. I hope Nero calls on us soon...I have a lot of questions."

"So do I," I frowned, tracing my finger around the mark on his chest. His wet fingers trailed down my jawline.

"There's something else you aren't telling me," he whispered. I met his eyes.

"I told him to undo your curse and he refused." Tears began welling in my eyes. "He knows how much I care for you...he's determined to take you with him." He pulled me in closer, hooking an arm around my back. "I didn't dare let on that I have this hope that ending him will end this curse...but I promised that if he didn't honor my request, I'd come for him. He's an evil piece of shit, but for the first time in my life...I see worry. I'm going to rain hell on him if it kills me." I pushed his hair back and leaned in to press my lips to his temple. He quieted, seemingly lost in his thoughts. "What are you thinking about?" I whispered against his hairline.

"He told you not to come home unless you were bringing your army?" He asked. I nodded, my lips never leaving his warm skin. "Then let's make him believe we're giving him one." I scrunched my brows again, leaning back to look at him. "If he knows how much you love me...we've proven all we need to prove. Let's go to Crona."

"What?"

"He's backing down on his own rules. What he asked us to prove, we've proven. You're not allowed back home. If memory serves...I can take you to mine. We can talk to my father...come up with a ruse. Make him believe this whole world is coming for him." My eyes lit up with hope.

"What about the last weapon? We still need to finish this, Luca."

"And we will...I never said leave tomorrow and travel across the world. But before we bring death to your father, I think we should consult with my parents and use his new weakness to create a diversion of some kind. He'll expect one thing, but be dealt another." He raised my wounded palm to his lips, tenderly kissing over it.

"I love you..." I whispered softly.

He sighed deeply into my hand and briefly closed his eyes. "I love you...more than you could ever know." He raised his face to mine. "We need to dig deeper into this ability you have. There has to be some kind of explanation. I don't think it's a coincidence, Ari."

"I wouldn't have thought to do it... had I not seen your light and heard you in my mind that night in Aeon. Perhaps it was only possible because of the blood union and our joined souls," I tried to explain it away and he shook his head slowly.

"That may be...but explain the hammer." I pursed my lips. "Let me have the hand that isn't cut." He held his out, and I placed my fingers into it. He looked into my eyes and a feeling of familiar magic made its presence known, although this time much softer and not as potent. "You feel me...I can sense it." I nodded. "Try to will it back to me without the blood union."

"I don't know how," I shrugged.

"What did you think about when you did it? You said you pictured my light...picture it again. Try to find me." His magic took a slightly stronger hold and I closed my eyes. I listened to the sound of his voice and recalled the image of the warm light and how desperate I was to get to it. "Come closer..." He whispered softly. I moved towards it and felt the tingle of his influence under my skin. "Push it back...try to manipulate it...control it." I tried, but couldn't feel any difference, other than a hint of his magic intensifying.

"It's not working, Luca," I said, becoming frustrated. I kept my eyes closed and focused on the pulsating light, moving closer to it.

"Keep trying. Don't give up on me yet. Fight me off. Use that frustration to throw it back at me," he pushed, tightening his hold on my hand. I held out phantom hands in my mind and pushed them forward and the magic eased off, respectively. He released a sharp breath, tensing under my legs and I realized I had actually done it...and without blood. "Do it again," he said, pacing himself. I sliced my arm through the air in front of me, in my mind's eye, and the magic burst away from me, causing Luca to nearly drop me from his hold.

The water splashed slightly and I tore my eyes open, letting go of his hand and palming each side of his face. "Are you alright?" I panicked. He simply smiled at me, tugging me close.

"I'm perfect. You did it." He pressed a chaste kiss to my lips. "This is remarkable." I put my arms around his neck, softly resting my head against his cheek. "Are you tired, Princess?" His hands moved up and down my back.

"I think I am, finally," I whispered, enjoying the feeling of his touch.

"Let me take you back to bed," he soothed, raising me up by the underside of my thighs and standing. I hooked my legs around him and he waded through the steaming pool, planting soft kisses across my shoulder. "Can I hold you?"

"Please," I answered, smiling as I closed my eyes.

We dried off and didn't bother finding clothes as we climbed back into bed. Luca held me from behind as I curled on my side. He pulled the top sheet over our waist and nuzzled into the back of my head, breathing in my scent. His arms were warm against the chill of the slight breeze coming in from the balcony. It was a perfect combination.

"Can I ask you something?" He breathed into my hair.

"Of course."

"Was it everything you thought it would be?" He asked, seemingly eager to hear my thoughts on what I'd spent weeks feeling curious about.

"It was undeniably the best thing I've ever felt. I can't imagine anything ever coming close to that. You were sensational...I can't believe you kept that from me," I smiled to myself. He chuckled softly and his breath fanned across the back of my neck, sending a shiver down my spine.

"I love you," he whispered. I ran my hand over the back of his, where it rested on my middle.

"I love you too..." I felt my eyelids growing heavier and gazed lazily at the full moon, peeking around the thick curtain at the entryway. Luca's breathing became deep and his arm slacked. I recalled the night I looked at the moon back home after the wager with my father had been made and his curse had taken hold, unbeknownst to me. I had seen that moon as a reminder about what little time would be left for me to live, having no idea that I'd instead be truthfully uttering those words to this male in my arms and meaning every syllable.

My heart ached at the thought that the moon I saw now wasn't a reminder of the countdown to the end of my life...but possibly his. I closed my eyes, blocking it from my view and pressed my hand more firmly against his.

"I want to marry you..." I whispered softly as a tear leaked from my eye, falling onto my pillow. I knew he didn't hear me and that sleep had taken him moments ago. But I meant it. I no longer wanted to wait to give death a chance to rob us again...and this was something we both deserved. I drifted closer to the peaceful embrace of deep sleep and slowly let go of my grip on my consciousness in the arms of the one I was now determined to call my husband.

CHAPTER 20

WORD OF MOUTH

A knock at our door woke us as thunder rolled outside and steady rain tapped against the stone of the balcony. My eyes crept open as another soft knock followed the first. Luca groaned from behind me, pulling himself to sit and grumbling under his breath. An amused smile tore across my mouth and I giggled softly, pulling the sheet up to cover my breasts. It was hard to tell what time it was because of the heavy storm that flashed outside, but it made it much harder to find the will to leave this bed. Luca pulled his robe around himself, tying it at the waist and rubbing an eye as he padded for the door. I listened without turning over and watched the rain blow harshly across the open entryway. The sea sounded angry this morning.

"Good morning, Mi'lord. I'm sorry to have woken you," Alister said politely, as Luca opened the door. "I normally wouldn't have, but I'm afraid messages from Master Nero take priority." Hearing that had me springing to sit, the tie in my hair loosening and my hair unraveling down my back. I glanced over at the door, only able to see a sliver of Luca and Alister's shadow cast on the wall through the opening of the doorway.

"He sent an invitation?" Luca asked.

"Actually, no. He sent word through Sir John. He was instructed to pass it along by word of mouth...or...rather, Sir John wrote it down at my desk when he returned from the temple this morning." Luca turned to peer around the corner at me and I wrapped the sheet around my body, nodding for him to let Alister inside. Luca invited him in and closed the heavy door as Alister stepped forward, glancing at me and flushing bright red, before turning away and shielding his eyes. "Oh...y-your Highness. Apologies," he stuttered. Luca walked past him, laughing quietly, smirking at me, and fetching my robe.

"It's fine, Alister. Just give me a moment," I snickered, feeling sorry for our poor attendant and taking the robe from Luca's hand. I wrapped up in it and tied it snugly as I stepped out of bed and fluffed my hair. My dashing fiancé was hardly a morning person today as he met me in front of the dark ottoman and slipped the hair strap around my neck, beginning to tie the loose bow. "It's okay to turn around now, friend," I smiled. Alister cautiously turned and watched the exchange between Luca and I, a puzzled look across his features.

"Forgive my curiosity...but Lord Nero featured your necklace on his statue and I couldn't help but notice you pointing it out when I revealed it to you. May I ask about its significance?" We smiled adoringly at each other as the bow fell lightly across my chest and I turned towards Alister.

"It started out as security for a bandage the day we met. Then my dearest friend tied it to my neck as a conversation piece," I grinned at Luca as he made his way over to the table behind where Alister stood.

"A trick I've been most grateful for," Luca smiled as he poured three cups of infused water and handed one to Alister, who accepted with surprise at our hospitality. He grabbed the other two and walked back to me, handing me one, and raising the other to his mouth.

"Ever since then, it's either been worn around my neck, in one of our heads, or on Luca's wrist. It's become something of a symbol of endearment," I smiled, taking a sip from my cup. Alister relaxed, sipping his own water and smiling softly.

"That's very interesting. Fascinating, really. Thank you for indulging my rudeness," he shyly smirked.

"Conversation isn't rude, Alister. We may be royals, but we're people too. We live and breathe in exactly the same ways. One day you'll see. No one will ever have to cower under our rule," I promised. His eyes turned glassy and sparked with emotion. He cleared his throat.

"You're two very special individuals. I'm eternally grateful for your comradery," he smiled sweetly. "I learn a bit more from you every day that passes. I'll be sad to see you go. Truly."

"Is Lord Nero kicking us out?" Luca asked, wrapping an arm around my back. Alister hummed into his cup, suddenly remembering why he stirred us awake.

"No, Mi'lord. Forgive me. Sir John relayed that he wishes you to join him for supper this evening. He gave no specification as to your attire, only that he's looking most forward to spending time with the two of you."

"Isn't it odd that he didn't send an invitation?" Luca asked.

"A bit," he nodded. "This isn't usual for Master Nero. He appears to be...how should I put this...less formal? More hospitable. Much like we are, currently. I believe he's grown fond of you." He inclined his chin. "As have I." My heart warmed. Lightning flashed, illuminating our room and thunder rolled shortly after.

"How are we going to get there without drowning?" I asked, looking outside.

"I doubt the storm will last all day, Mi'lady. But if for some reason it does, his grace will provide you a way to get to him...of that, I have no doubt."

"Did he specify what time?" I pressed, taking a deep swallow and finishing my water.

"At sunset." Alister turned, placing his emptied cup on the table. "I'll be changing the shoes on your horses in a few moments and primping them for you, in case you need to continue your journey in haste." He faced us again. "Maureen is attending downstairs, should you need anything. However, I'm not far. Thank you both...for everything." He bowed and smiled as he quietly walked out the door, snicking it shut behind him.

Luca and I exchanged glances. "He doesn't seem used to being treated like a person. It breaks my heart," I said, walking to sit my cup next to the one he had discarded. I started gathering meat and picking out a small loaf of fresh bread as Luca stepped up beside me. Thunder rumbled again outside.

"He may have other reasons than your father's rule. We don't know what he's been through. Oddly enough, Mr. Joe... the barber who assisted me in the city? He seemed the same when I tried to pay him for his services. He was really something as well...the male only had one leg." I looked over at him in shock.

"What?" I said, stuffing meat into the bread while Luca scooted a plate beneath it and picked off random fruits to add.

"He has an old, beat-up wooden peg where a leg should be. And he still refused to accept coin after doing a great job. That's another reason I didn't ask when I sat a handful on the table at Annette's." I cut the loaf in half and placed it on the plate. Luca refilled our cups and took everything over to the bed while the storm became louder outside. I lit a few more sconces, offering better light and pulling the curtains closed before joining him.

"Now that you mention it...Annette seemed to be a bit emotional at lunch that day," I said, sitting on the side of my thigh with my legs folded. "Strange..." I took a bite of my half of our sandwich and mulled it over in my mind as I chewed.

"Sir John can't speak either," Luca added, popping a grape into his mouth. My brows raised and I slapped a hand to my lap.

"You're right!" I said through my mouthful of food. Luca smiled as he chewed, looking at me the way he always does whenever I'm eating. I nudged him. "Don't start," I smirked, rolling my eyes.

"Better find those royal manners before dinner tonight," he grinned, taking a bite from his sandwich. A sudden loud crack of thunder sounded and I nearly jumped from the bed, yelping and covering my mouth with my hand. Luca nearly sent his mouthful flying as he exploded in a heaving laugh.

"Gods!" I yelled, pressing my hand to my chest. He continued to laugh loudly, running a hand through his hair and moving closer to me. "Shut up, you," I spat, slapping his upper arm.

"I'm sorry, love. Come here," he chuckled, extending his arms.

"Not a chance." I pulled away, shoving him back. He advanced anyway, grinning like a predator and crawling over our plate to wrestle me down onto my back. "Stop, Luca!" I laughed as he playfully nipped the skin at my neck and pinned my hands above my head. "You better back down...my knee is dangerously close to your bollocks." He raised his face over mine with his mouth gaped open.

"You would not..."

"Let me go or you'll find out," I smirked. "I want my sandwich, *your Highness.*" I moved my knee up a bit.

"I want your sandwich, too," he laughed, not being able to help himself. I kneed him in the stomach and he groaned through his teeth, scrunching his face and giggling through what breath remained after my assault. I threw my head back and snorted myself as he released my hands and fell over onto his side in defeat. "You're wicked," he grinned, staring at me as I turned to face him.

"You're filthy," I scoffed, leaning in and kissing his lips. He pressed his hand to his chest in feigned innocence.

"I don't know what you mean," he smiled.

"Finish your brunch," I laughed, sitting up. He growled as he sat beside me, stealing my food and biting a huge chunk from it.

"So we're clear, Princess..." He chewed. "This was not the *brunch* I was talking about." He winked at me and slid off the bed, dropping his robe and finishing off my sandwich as he stepped down into the bathing pool.

"And so *we're* clear...I'm eating your half of the sandwich...you bath-obsessed heathen," I sneered as I grabbed it from the plate and sank my teeth into it, eyeing his every overly-dramatic move. I got up and walked over to sit at the edge of the pool, kneeling down and lowering my feet into the water while he submerged and swam to the middle. I took another bite while I watched him resurface, and he gave me a look as he palmed his hair back.

Gods, he's beautiful...how is this mine?

My eyes snapped down at my engagement ring and I thought about what I'd whispered last night after he'd fallen asleep. I spun the stone around on my finger and had another mouthful of my lunch as thunder rolled again.

"Can I ask you something?" I started, looking back at him and realizing he'd moved closer. He wiped the water from his face and waded to where I sat, staring up at me with his gray eyes and crossing his arms over the ledge.

"If this is about your actual sandwich, then I'm sad to say that I'm not sorry...and am absolutely deserving of punishment," he smirked.

"You are such a fool," I snickered.

"Of course, love. Anything. Are you alright?"

"I am...it's about my ring," I said, turning it again and watching his expression fall slightly.

"Is something wrong?"

I tried earnestly to keep my tone convincing and my face straight as a pin. "Yes, actually." He glanced at the stone and then back at me and I almost felt bad about the look on his face.

"What is it?"

"You don't have one," I smiled. He gave me a well-deserved eye roll and exhaled sharply, briefly touching his forehead to his hands and then smiling back up at me.

"Yes, well...engagements don't typically require that," he grinned.

"But weddings do," I argued. His face turned into a combination of shock and absolute joy. I sat my bread down next to me and took his hands.

"What are you saying, Ari?" His voice quieted and he gripped my fingers tighter.

"I want to marry you. When we get to Crona."

Luca's mouth opened, and for once, my prince was speechless. "You don't want to wait?" He asked.

"Wait for what? For opportunity to pass us by? For death to come knocking at our door again? War? My poor sandwich to reappear?" I laughed. His face was unreadable. "I don't want to wait, Luca. I want to be with *you*. However long we have...I want to be your wife. Call me selfish or greedy, but I want it now. And if we're going to be in your home with the people we both love...then I feel like it would be the perfect time and place." He was silent for a long moment and lowered his face, pressing a kiss to my knuckles. When he looked up at me again, his eyes were welled with tears.

He raised himself up onto the seat of the pool until he was at eye level with me, keeping our hands locked and pressing his wet forehead against mine. The storm outside our room seemed to calm and low thunder sounded from the curtains. I released one of my hands and trailed feather-light fingertips across his dripping jawline.

"The idea of returning home and bringing you with me gave me such joy. Picturing you and my mother at our table giving my father and I, hell...seeing you happy with your best friend again. Showing you where I grew up? Making more memories there meant more to me than finding ways to stop your father. If anything, it was the best excuse to go. I've been given more than I ever deserved just having you, Arienne. Nothing would complete me more than seeing you in my home...meeting me at an altar and calling me your husband by the end of the day. I've always told you that I'd happily give you whatever you asked of me...but I don't think you realize what you're giving *me*." His smooth voice cracked and a slow tear started down his cheek. I kissed it away and shrugged my robe off. He moved back and put his arms around me as I slipped into the water and placed both hands on his face.

"So...that's a yes then?" I smiled. He scoffed and pulled me into a long kiss.

"It'd be an honor, your Highness," he whispered, softly.

"I love you, Luca Di Meo."

"Gods..." He choked, silently weeping as I wrapped my arms around his middle and pressed my face to his chest. I had never called him by his full name. He tightened himself around me and kissed my hairline. Thunder continued to fill the sky throughout the remainder of the afternoon.

After a long bath and a couple of hours back in our bed, evening crept up quickly and we found ourselves tearing through the closet, trying to determine appropriate options for our approaching dinner with a deity.

"Our first meeting, I had this elegant gown, and we ended up getting killed and resurrected while he wore a pair of sandals and a cloth that was smaller than our bath linens." I griped, placing my hands on my hips. Luca snorted as he dug through more clothes behind me.

"That might be true, but we're dining with...a god. Nero said we'd dine like kings. Don't you think we should choose something nice?"

"Well, Alister said less formal, more hospitable. Everything in here is *nice*...or flat-out formal. So what says *thank you for this gods blessed weapon and hospitality*...without being too much or too little?" Luca didn't answer and I turned to find him dressed in his Cronian uniform he'd worn the day that we met. His royal crest and silver buttons shined in the light from the sconces and the oil lamp from my vanity. "Wow...Luca you look..." I dropped my mouth open, looking him over and remembering the way my heart sped up the first time I saw him.

"Princely?" He grinned, pulling his hair behind his head. I loosened the strap from my neck and handed it to him. He tied a sophisticated knot behind him and smoothed the stray hair from his face.

"In every sense. Now I recall why it was hard to breathe when you escorted your mother through the Great Hall," I smiled.

"I suppose if we're accepting a gift made by a supreme being and sitting down to eat supper, perhaps I should represent my house." He straightened his collar and tugged the hem of his top. I frowned to myself, turning back to face my side of the closet and raked my eyes over the garments.

"I don't feel like I should represent something we're trying to take down." I dropped my arms in frustration and Luca took my shoulders, pressing a warm kiss to the back of my neck.

"Why don't you wear something that's yours? Something that makes you feel more like yourself? That's when you truly shine to me." I turned around, looking at him like the perfect soul that he was, and gently kissed him, knowing exactly what I'd now wear.

"You really are a gift, Prince. I'll be right out."

He gave me an intrigued look and I pushed him out of the closet doorway. "I just want to make it clear...I did *not* mean a nightshift...or nude." He pushed against me as I shooed him out.

"Calm yourself. It's neither of those things. Now *get.* I need...five minutes?" I shrugged.

"Just come down and meet me when you're ready. I'm going to talk to this *Maureen* and figure out how we're getting to the island. It's still storming like shit outside." He gave me a onceover and winked before finally slipping out of our bedchamber.

I plundered through my bag for a few moments, finally setting my hands on an outfit I knew well, and was nearly splitting open with excitement when I raised it up and looked over it.

"Nice to see you, old friend," I grinned, greeting my clothes like a deranged idiot. It took more than five minutes to get completely dressed. I also decided to let my long hair set my chosen garment off like a brushfire, soft curls cascading over my shoulders and down my back. Adding a touch that wasn't like myself, but more a bit of good fun, as Paxe had pointed out the day I met Luca. I stained my full lips a deep red and lined my eyes in stark, black kohl.

I was more than happy with myself as I stared at the female who looked back at me in my vanity mirror.

Look at that...she really has grown.

I flashed to the morning that I peered at my reflection in such deep thought and realized how much I'd found myself since then...since Luca—since I took some sort of control and decided to leave the monsters of my past in that castle with my father. It showed itself now. I was different. Older. Stronger. Loved... respected. I was breaking bread tonight with a god. I smiled at the queen in the mirror, giving her a proud nod, and turned to make for the door to meet my waiting prince.

CHAPTER 21

ANSWERS AND AMBITION

Buckles from my knee-high boots and from the straps around my thighs clinked as I walked down the short corridor towards the polished staircase. The sound of leather joined in with the first few steps down the stairs. My hand rested on the rail, gliding across, as I made my way down and caught sight of Luca, who had his back turned towards me while he talked with a pretty female with cropped blonde hair and a long scar that reached from her hairline, across her eyebrow, to the middle of her cheek. Her eyes raised toward me and her expression changed, from polite conversation to awe, as she took me in. Luca noticed her reaction and slowly turned, dropping his jaw open and closely watching every confident step I took.

Exactly the reaction I'd hoped for, Prince.

My mouth curved up in the corner as I made eye contact, and if his gaze could rip my battle leathers from my body, I'd be absolutely naked. I wished desperately I could hear every thought that was ravaging his mind as I neared the end of the stairs, but I also knew I could just about sum them up from the way he looked at me. Black matte leather with subtle dark threaded designs hugged every curve of my blossoming adult body. Straps and buckles lined my legs, and several more made up the top half of my flat-soled leather boots. A Valdarian insignia was carefully carved from the leather, lightly enough not to reach through the material and show any skin across the entirety of my bust. A snug, wide belt reached tight around my waist that was adorned with a large silver crest in its middle. I looked every bit the part of a seasoned warrior and a small part... a complete harlot. My curls swished against the material as I stepped to the floor and Luca was, once again, speechless. Maureen dipped into a curtsy and politely greeted me. I dipped my chin and returned my attention to my still gaping, future husband.

"Your Highness," I smiled, bowing to him, mockingly. "Are we ready?" I straightened. He said nothing, instead offering me his hand, and refusing to close his mouth. I placed my fingers into his palm and he raised my arm and started to turn me slowly in a spin.

"I—I'm not sure how to answer that, my lady," he gawked as I came to a stop, facing him again.

"You don't like it?" I pouted. He blinked too many times before resting a hand on my hip.

"Oh...on the contrary, Princess. But my mother, no doubt, would have already slapped my mouth with my unspoken impoliteness around company." His voice was as molten as the volcanic hidden secrets of Bolton's waters. "So this is what makes you feel most like yourself?"

"I spent most every day of my youth with a weapons master and training instructor. This feels as much myself as my own skin." I raised my chin and he cracked a proud smile.

"I thought you hated counter paints."

"That was for you," I grinned.

"I won't find you cursing and scrubbing your face by a river, will I?" He chuckled, softly pinching my chin between his fingers.

"Not today."

"Very well. Let's see what Lord Nero has to say about my queen being dressed to kill. Quite literally." His face hardened as if he were pulling every ounce of his strength not to say something inappropriate and I bit down hard on my lip under his stare. Maureen shifted on her feet beside us and I turned to face her, forgetting she was even there.

"I'm so sorry Lady Maureen. Forgive us," I blushed. She waved a hand in dismissal and shook her head with a tight smile.

"Nonsense, Mi'lady. I was just telling his Highness that when the two of you are ready to go, Alister had said he'd be waiting for you at the dock with Sir John." She inclined her head and gestured to the upper floor where the dark stairwell led out to the cliffside. Her jagged scar shined from the chandelier's glow as her face raised forward again. She was a soft-featured, lovely young female aside from that, and my mind wandered as I tried not to draw my attention to whatever misfortune had befallen her to leave such a nasty mark. "I'll be happy to tidy up for you and replenish any linens and food while you're out. It'd be my pleasure, Princess."

"Thank you so much," I smiled, taking her hands. "We should get going, but I do hope to see you again. It was lovely to meet you. We're very grateful and shall never forget how gracious everyone has been."

"If I may, Mi'lady...all of Bolton feels the same about you and your prince. I'm honored to have been in your service. Do enjoy your evening with Master Nero. He's truly a merciful being and a great deal of fun in leisurely company," she smirked. "I'll go get started on your chambers." She nodded slightly, releasing my hands and giving us both a bow. "Goodnight."

That's the second time I've heard Nero being described that way...and she's scarred.

I started piecing together a conclusion that I was certain I'd ask at supper this evening, as we parted ways and Luca and I headed upstairs to slide left and right back down another flight. When we were about halfway down the dark spiral steps, I slowed and turned to Luca, stopping him and whispering in case someone was nearby.

"Her scar..." I whispered, drawing a line over my brow with my finger.

"I know...another name to add to the list. I have a theory, but I suppose it will have to wait," he said quietly.

"I get the feeling you and I are thinking the same thing." He nodded in response and we continued down the stairs. When we reached the bottom, lightning flashed through the doorway and the moody dark sea crashed around the dock. Sir John was standing next to a slender, silver-haired male in attendant's attire that I didn't recognize, as we approached. Both of them faced the temple, watching the intensifying storm. My hair blew back violently as we neared them and I hooked an arm through Luca's extended elbow. Sir John turned to face us first, bowing and giving us a welcoming, closed-lipped smile. The other gentleman slowly turned, revealing bone-white skin and blood-red irises as he bowed.

"Good evening Mi'lord...Mi'lady," a very familiar voice said. He straightened and smiled while I narrowed my eyes and crept closer. His bright white hair blew into his face and my sudden realization hit, like Nero's hammer to my gut.

"Alister?" I asked in disbelief. His smile grew wider, and Luca's mouth dropped slightly open.

"Indeed, Mi'lady. My true appearance." He rested his hands behind his back. Luca moved closer and lightning flashed across the beauty of Alister's real complexion. Albinism. The once thin, dark-haired and flighty male was now a thing of incredible wonder and enchantment.

"How?" Luca asked, his tone soft and sympathetic. "More importantly...why?"

"Just a glamour, Mi'lord. I beg your forgiveness for my deception. I simply didn't wish to meet you this way. I never considered what keeping up with that version of myself may cost if you never saw the real me. I've long been ashamed of my appearance as it can be somewhat disturbing to some. But...I've grown to understand that the two of you aren't cruel...quite the opposite actually, and earlier this morning, when we spoke, you called me a friend. I don't think you understand how much it meant to me. I didn't want you to leave without knowing the truth."

My heart broke at the thought of such a kind spirit hiding behind what he considered a normal appearance. "Oh, Alister...you should never be ashamed of such a thing. That's not what counts. This would have never hindered a single thought we had about you." I didn't ask permission before softly putting my arms around his shoulders and hugging him tight. "And you're stunning," I soothed. He politely patted my back with one hand and smiled bashfully as we separated.

"I agree," Luca offered, clapping him on the shoulder. "Have you always been here in Bolton?" Alister looked at Sir John, and then back at us as he slowly shook his head.

"I'm afraid not. I was born in Irondale; the village that rests at the foot of the Horned Mountains. I spent much of my younger years being ridiculed for my condition. Once I was old enough, my mother told me that Master Nero had a fondness for those who suffer from abnormalities and ailments of all kinds, and she asked if I thought I'd be happy in such a place. She couldn't bear to see me unhappy. It was a hard choice, but I left her behind to start a life here."

"Did you ever see her again?" I asked.

"I did. After I was employed at the royal residence, I sent for my mother. She came and lived with me here for about four years. She sadly passed away... unexpectedly, almost a year ago now. But she was pleased."

"I'm so sorry," I whispered. He bowed his head, accepting the condolence. Luca turned to Sir John, who had been listening and keeping watch of the angry waves.

"Sir John...I assume that's why you came to Bolton as well?" Luca asked. John nodded and opened his mouth wide, pointing to a hollow place where a tongue should be. We both winced and Alister's laugh filled the small cavernous opening. We joined him shortly after and I wrapped an arm around Sir John's hunched shoulders.

"What about Lady Annette?" I chuckled, looking back to Alister.

"Lady Annette, to my knowledge, has no ailments. She's simply a passionate and heartbreakingly kind female who came here to bring joy to Bolton's citizens in any way that she could. She truly thrives on doing things for others and giving as much as she can to those in need. She's a remarkable lady. And an exceptional cook. Her flowers bring life to this dark city in her small corner. She designed the courtyard and supplied all its greenery. Some swear she's a gift sent to the weary by the gods. Much in the way we all feel about the two of you," he smiled softly. "Speaking of which...shall we get you both to the temple? Master Nero is waiting."

We inched towards the dock, looking bleakly at the rage of the sea and the side of the boat that loudly thrashed against the post it was moored onto. Luca drew me close and his expression revealed his thoughts about the impossibility of making it to the other side on the small vessel. A mousy voice called out to us from behind. We turned to see Maureen carrying our traveling cloaks and smiling when her eyes met Alister's gaze. I tried not to let on that I'd noticed the attraction she obviously felt toward him.

"I thought you may find these helpful. Doesn't look as if the rain will be kind tonight," she smiled while handing us the garments. We pulled them on and thanked her as she bowed slightly and turned to head back up the stairwell, giving our pale attendant an affectionate nod before disappearing into the darkness. Sir John chuckled under his breath and I shot Alister a look.

"Are you two...uh..." I started as I fastened my cloak.

"If you haven't made a move, I can tell you...she most definitely wants you to," Luca piped up from beside me, pulling his hood over his head. Alister rubbed the back of his neck and flushed.

"How can you tell, Mi'lord?" He asked.

"His...gift," I grinned, giving Luca a sultry look. He grunted in response, eyeing my painted lips. "The prince can sense and manipulate feelings and emotions."

"I would say that makes a great deal of sense," he giggled. "I'll ah...give that some thought, Mi'lord. Perhaps, you could give me an idea as to ways I can best express... *that.*"

Gods...how adorable.

"If we live through this journey across the fjord, I'll be happy to oblige," Luca laughed.

"Ah, yes...regarding that," Alister said, stepping into the driving rain and casually braving the storm as he walked down to the end of the dock. He took a fighting stance, anchoring his feet and bending his knees as he thrust his arms forward. An incredible passage of thick ice blasted across the water, creating an undisturbed path that ended at the small island. Luca and I stood back in absolute shock as Alister turned and smiled. "Make haste. It won't shield you from the rain, but you needn't worry about the sea." He stepped proudly from the dock and gestured for us to proceed.

"I'm a blasted royal and all I get is mind tricks?" Luca grumbled, still admiring the awe-inspiring magic that Alister had displayed.

"Trust me, Mi'lord, it was a struggle I had to learn my way around for a good many years. Anyone's gift can be both a blessing and a curse, I imagine. I hope you enjoy your evening. I'm looking forward to hearing what Master Nero has in store for you. Sir John will escort you across. I shall see you upon your return."

We thanked him and cautiously crossed the dock, stepping carefully on the impressive ice that glowed in the flicker of lightning around us as we followed closely behind Sir John, who had pulled a heavy hooded jacket over himself. It was difficult to speak as we made our way across the fjord, staring in amazement at the haunting river of molten lava that could be seen through the frozen, glassy surface. It was an unforgettable image of the beauty that was ice and fire and raging electricity, all in a perfect symphony with each other. We finally made it to solid ground and Sir John led us down the lit walkway, stopping at the entrance, where he communicated he'd be taking shelter while we dined with Nero. We pulled the great door open and started down the carpet, torches firing themselves up as we passed.

There were truly no other obvious choices other than to continue into what we knew would be the main chamber, the farther down we traveled. We dropped our hoods and Luca took my hand as we entered the chamber a moment later. The room lit up and looked nothing the same. The half-moon pool and the altar where I had last held the sword that pierced my heart were gone. The dais and throne were also missing, replaced by a long ebony table that was heaped with fine foods, wines, tasteful iron candelabras and succulent fruits. Nero sat in a huge chair that was ornately carved with mythical beasts in the center of the farthest side. A large fireplace that took up the back wall underneath the painting I had seen before crackled behind him. Only two other chairs were placed directly across from him. One for each of us. Around the expanse of the main chamber were dark plush rugs with huge leather chairs and a couple of well-arranged couches. The whole setting was completely different from the ominous feel from before. Now, it served as a hospitable gathering space that offered warmth and comfort, like being invited into someone's humble abode.

Nero stood, raising a giant silver goblet that sloshed over the rim with wine and smiling, as if he'd already had more than enough. He looked surprisingly ordinary in a form-fitting black tunic and accommodating trousers that were cut off by a pair of bulky leather boots that came up just under his knee.

"Welcome!" He bellowed, slapping a heavy palm to the table. "Forgive me, I've started without you." Luca and I exchanged sidelong smirks and started forward, unfastening our cloaks, while Nero pulled a sizable gulp from his large cup. I draped my damp cloak over my arm and he raked his eyes over my leathers, choking on his wine. "Fine choice of apparel, youngling," he grinned drunkenly.

I shrugged, making my way toward the table with a tight smile and Luca snorted at my side. "I thought you may appreciate my being dressed for battle, your Grace."

"I'm certain it's nothing to do with my poor taste in first impressions, either," he laughed, pouring two equally large goblets, in front of our seats, with wine while Luca pulled my chair out and I politely sat, dismissing the question. "I promise I'm not the monster I portrayed, Princess. I do hope you'll accept my *godly* apology and feel more at ease. I had hoped my gift would have been enough to appear worthy of your forgiveness." He dropped into his chair and leaned back, seeming more than relaxed.

"It was an unexpected surprise, my Lord. I'm truly grateful. While I do wish to relish in the idea that I've given a higher being reason to believe I'd come here with malicious intent, it was actually the Prince's idea that inspired my choice of attire," I smiled, raising the goblet to my mouth. Nero turned his amused and curious attention to Luca, who also appeared to have trouble keeping himself from choking on his wine.

"That—" He cleared his throat and tapped the side of his fist to his chest. "That's not entirely true, your Grace. I only offered for her to dress in what made her feel most like herself. Trust me..." His eyes caught mine and I rested a cheek on my hand, leaning on the arm of my chair in his direction. "It was a bit of a surprise to me, as well..."

You're welcome to peel them off, Prince.

"Save those thoughts for when I'm not present, if you please. I'm not the god of love," Nero chuckled, drinking from his chalice.

"Apologies, my Lord," I giggled, feeling a bit more comfortable. My limbs lost their tension, and the next hour was spent overindulging in wine and fun conversation while we ate. Once we had finished, Nero opened a fresh bottle of wine and we moved to an area near the wall where a pool of water used to be. He waved a hand, and a monstrous fireplace appeared on it, roaring to life. Luca and I took a seat on a dark leather couch that ran perpendicular to the hearth and faced a comfortable-looking chair that Nero plopped into heavily. Curious, I decided to ask some of my burning questions and started with the most obvious, "Is this the way your temple always looks, and perhaps the last time we were here, it was meant more for the purpose of your trial?"

He drank from his goblet and passed Luca the bottle. "Actually, it's the opposite. When there are priests or guests that arrive to pay tribute to me, it looks exactly as it did the first time you entered. There is only one way in or out. What you see now, is my home. You only see it because I will it so." He crossed an ankle on his knee and leaned further back. "There's a difference between guests of my own and guests of the *temple*." I accepted more wine from Luca and sipped it carefully, hoping not to lose my focus on what part of our reason for attending was.

"Do you have your own guests often? I imagine it can get a bit lonely," Luca asked.

"There's a bit more to that question, Prince. You can speak freely," Nero smiled. Luca shifted in his seat and relaxed himself.

"Alright...I couldn't help but notice most of the citizens in Bolton are impaired in some way. I'll be honest, it's very inspiring and curious. I was hoping you'd be willing to share the reason?" Luca asked. I pulled a knee up to my chest and hooked an arm around it, leaning in to anticipate Nero's answer.

"It may seem odd to you that a higher being would take interest in mortals at all. To put it simply, being blessed with power such as I and a long existence of immortality...it bores me. I find mortals fascinating. I'm the god of strength...power. I find mortals with affliction even *more* fascinating." He took a long drink.

"How so?" I asked.

"Consider this. Most of the people you meet in this city...they've suffered. They've lived mortal lives being tortured, disfigured from birth or other means. They've endured harsh words, been disgusted by themselves, or worse. Imagine the amount of strength it takes to confidently bare oneself to the world after having lived that way. That is a power like no other, which every being has, no matter their gifts. It pleases me to help them find that strength and wield it. Gives me a sense of purpose, rather than sit on a high and mighty throne and be the frightening *god of strength*," he smiled.

"That's very admirable, your Grace." I offered, really taking his words into consideration. Luca hummed and nodded in agreement.

"You may not carry your scars on your skin, Princess...but I see them. I was happy to see that you found your strength the day you raised the hammer. I have since found the answer." He stared into me proudly. My brows raised.

"You did? What's the answer?" I nearly begged. He was silent for a long moment and slowly shook his head.

"Sadly...I cannot be the one to reveal it to you. Some details of your quest must be saved for the right time. I can offer you another answer you seek, though the truth may not be pleasing to you." He turned his attention to Luca.

"Me?" Luca asked, pointing at himself with a thumb.

"Your impairment," Nero answered, inclining his head.

"The curse..." I said, narrowing my eyes. "You're saying there is no way to break it." My voice sank into a low, saddened tone.

Nero held up a finger and took another drink. "I didn't say there was no way, youngling. But I do know that you wanted to ask me if there was anything the gods could do about it. That answer is, unfortunately, no. The magic that binds you, Prince...it contains the power that was bestowed on the first king through her bloodline." His head nodded in my direction, but he kept his eyes on Luca. "That power was given by us. When you shook hands with the king and were in agreement with the terms...you agreed to *all* of them. Even the ones you didn't know about until it was too late. Think of it as a contract signed in blood, and sealed by the most powerful magic in this world. There isn't anything the gods could do to interfere now, although if it were possible, I'd gladly offer to. I am sorry." His face softened.

"I understand, my Lord. I do appreciate the sentiment," Luca said, resting a consoling hand on my raised knee.

"But there is a way?" I cut in, feeling a mixture of hope and desperation.

"Breaking something such as that would require something powerful enough to overcome it. All that I can offer is that you now know what your strengths are. Whatever liability dangles on the terms is often what can determine its violation, therefore eliminating it altogether. But it will be something you both have to figure out yourselves. I'm not able to hand you the key." I tried to fit the pieces together in my mind but came up short. This would take time. It was yet another matter of solving riddles that were carefully worded. I downed the remains of my goblet and stared into the fireplace. Luca's hand squeezed around my knee.

"It's a start, love. We'll solve this. Thank you, your Grace, for the information."

Nero sat his drink on the floor by his large chair and stood. "Perhaps, I can lighten your mood. Come. Both of you." He walked to the middle of the room and waved a hand where the altar used to be. It appeared, draped in a black velvet cloth. Luca and I discarded our goblets and stepped over behind him while he perched to the side, revealing a sheathed pair of swords. My eyes widened as I approached the altar, the strange light from before illuminating them in their glory. "You both demonstrated great power, not just on your own...but together. There is a weapon fashioned for each of you. My best. Please accept these as a token of my deepest gratitude for your courage...your bravery...and your choice to honor one another above all possible obstacles. That is what the world needs. Love. Strength in each other. Humility and acceptance. With those, we may all find our peace." He looked at Luca. "The light in the darkness." There was a long pause between all of us and Nero finally turned toward him. "Prince Luca...would you kneel?" He asked, gesturing to his feet.

I stepped aside and Luca lowered himself to a knee, one hand resting on the one that raised, the other fisted at his chest. Nero took one of the swords from the altar and held it across his palms. The pommel was polished white gold and took the shape of a roaring lion, matching the crest of Crona. In each of its eyes were sparkling rubies that reminded me of Queen Ayla's gown the day she visited Valdaro. The grip was finely made black braided leather, artfully crafted to fit Luca's hand. It was a thing of beauty to any weapons enthusiast.

"I, Nero...god of strength, beacon of power, bestow upon you, Luca Di Meo...Crown Prince of Crona, this weapon. Blessed by the gods, and given in honor of your service and your selflessness. Please accept this gift on behalf of our world. May it serve you well." Luca offered his palms as he bowed his head and Nero placed the sword into them. The sword sang as he unsheathed it carefully and the blade glowed a soft orange with a carefully engraved inscription on its fuller. "It features the language spoken by the gods. It reads '*Until Death*'."

"Thank you, my Lord. Truly. It's a masterpiece. The honor is mine," Luca said, sheathing the blade and standing. Nero clapped a hand on his shoulder and smiled, turning his attention to me.

"Princess...if you will?" He lowered a hand towards the floor and I stepped forward, taking a knee and placing my fist over my heart. He took the sword from the altar and presented it to me in the same way he had with Luca, who watched with deep pride and longing. "I, Nero...god of strength, beacon of power, bestow upon you, Arienne Genovese...Princess of Valdaro, and victor over evil by right of birth, this weapon. Blessed by the gods and given in honor of your service...your great courage, and your acceptance to conquer darkness and bring peace to us all. Please accept this gift on behalf of our world, as well as my blessing to be with you in spirit as you claim victory and bring the second calm. May it please and serve you well." I raised my palms and gratefully accepted the blade.

I had merely glanced at the two weapons at the altar, but now that it was in my hands, I was in pure awe of the art that used to be my simple piece of steel. My pommel was fashioned after the ring I now wore on my left hand. Instead of a teardrop shape, it was a striking likeness to a much more panther-like version of Hissifus. Every tuft of fur finely detailed with eyes that were represented by the same starburst gemstones Luca had chosen for my engagement piece. It looked as if Hiss had grown into a beast and was leaping with fangs, ready to sink into his prey. His moon side was intricately carved from a hunk of opal, and his midnight side the same rock Bolton was known for. Dark black and polished to perfection. The grip looked identical to Luca's and the same glowing symbols were etched on each face of its blade. I rose, unable to find words to properly express my gratitude.

"I may have taken inspiration from your prince's taste in jewelry and consulted with Elowen. She sends her deepest regards and wants you to know that she's grown quite fond of your companion," Nero answered before I could speak.

"Thank you so much, your Grace...I—" I held the pommel close to my heart. "You have no idea how much it means to me," I said tearfully. "It's beautiful." Luca beamed at me from Nero's side, his new sword secured at his hip. Nero placed a hand on each of my shoulders and looked me in the eyes.

"We shall see great things from you, Princess. The gods are behind you. You chose these leathers because they made you feel more yourself. It's because this is who you are. Who you were always meant to be. You will succeed. I'm honored to have done this for you." It was strange...Elowen was so creature-like in the forest and her voice otherworldly. Nero wasn't, at all, the frightening being he made himself out to be when we first came to Bolton. I felt as if an old friend was well-wishing me and it was tremendously comforting. "Would you both mind keeping me company for a little while longer? There's still more wine to be had," he smiled.

"Of course," I laughed, following him back to our spots on the couch. Before he reclaimed his chair, Nero spun on a heel and pulled something from his pocket.

"Oh! Luca..." He jerked his head in warning that he was about to toss something his way and Luca held his hands out. "I also made this especially for you. I understand what it's like," he grinned. I turned to my betrothed, curious about the small figure he caught in one hand, and Luca closed his fingers around it, an elated smile on his face as he raised it back to Nero.

"Did Alister tell you?" He laughed. Nero nodded and dropped back into his chair, pouring a goblet full of wine.

"I'd rather not know what you do with it moving forward," Nero chuckled loudly, taking a long drink. Luca and I sat, and I looked at his palm to see a tiny replica of the statue of myself. I couldn't stifle my giggle...or my eye roll.

"Males are so strange," I shook my head. Luca pocketed the charm and put an arm around my shoulder, seeming as though someone had just gifted him a small fortune.

"We think the same about you," Nero started. "I once tried courting Varuna...she loathes me. Elowen has also never much cared for me. I believe she tolerates me at best, but she, at least, converses with me from time to time. Especially now that we all have a common interest in making sure that you're prepared and protected. I do find females so lovely and their passion can be...phew...but make no mistake," he wagged a finger at me. "There is no difference in their difficulty, be that immortal or otherwise. You lot can be a bit savage," he laughed.

"Varuna? The sea goddess?" I asked. Nero raised his brows over his cup as he heavily drank from it, nodding. "You were together?" I grinned.

"For a time. She's a wrathful one. Great fun when she was happy, but a force to be reckoned with when she was mad...and she stayed angry with me often," he smiled. "Best I stay on my side of the world."

"Ari has a temper of her own," Luca chuckled, nudging me.

"So I've seen," Nero piped in, both of them laughing loudly. I shook my head and pointed a finger at Luca.

"Only when provoked. And you have a mouth too!" I snarled and poured myself some wine. "While we're on the subject of other gods...where are we to go next?" I asked, raising my cup to my mouth.

"Your next destination is the Horned Mountains. It will be a treacherous climb up the pass to the temple there. Irondale will be expecting your arrival, and I've arranged for you to be well cared for and prepared for the storm," he offered.

"The Horned Mountains...they looked like an omen of death when we passed through to Aeon. No one has lived that tries to brave that place," I argued, my voice lowering in anxiety and dread. Luca tightened his arm around me.

"The barrier that protects the mountain will yield to you. Those that have tried to reach the gods were damned. Those who entered in trials like the first king were allowed to pass through. You've been given permission as you've accepted a task from the gods themselves. You needn't fear. Elowen had already promised to keep you safe from elemental distress. Your goal is to present the last weapon at the temple. The rest of the gods reside on the highest peak...Mount Iren, but you'll only be meeting one. She will be waiting at the foot."

"She?" Luca raised his face.

"Yes...though I cannot tell you more. There are many gods and goddesses that occupy the mountains. This one has been assigned to assist you. She will have a trial of her own, and you are to give her your hunting knife, should you pass." We all sat quietly for a moment and I got lost in my thoughts. "Arienne...don't be afraid. Remember the strength and courage you showed here. You *will* succeed. I beg you...keep the stride you walked in here with tonight. Try to remember your mother's sacrifice. This has always been your destiny. You'll not fail," he soothed.

Mother...this journey...my father. Time to ask my last question.

"Your Grace...my father visited Bolton." I looked Nero in the eyes. The fiery stare was still there, revealing his immortality, but it was gentler.

"I know. I was wondering when this would be brought forward. While his body was never physically here, I sensed his power. Some of my own dwells within it. What was said?" He asked, crossing his ankle again.

"He thinks my intention is to gather an army to revolt against him. He challenged me, and I'm mostly sure he knows nothing about this prophecy or my mother's sacrifice. Which leads me to believe that you know the answer to my next question," I pressed, my expression more serious.

"I do," he answered simply.

"Did he kill her?" I asked, quietly. Luca gripped my shoulder, trying to ease the sting of saying the words out loud. Nero stared at us for a moment, swirling the wine in his cup. "Are you allowed to say?" I continued, watching him closely.

"The agreement was her life for yours. Dying from childbirth would have been ideal, but the king needed to believe that he had succeeded in ending her if the prophecy would be kept safe from him. So yes, your theory was correct. Though, there is more to the story that I can't give you, even if it pains me not to. I've said all that I can. I'm sorry. However, I do hope that it helps you. I feel you both are starting to uncover most of this on your own and only seek clarification at this point. You're doing well. Guard your thoughts, and move forward with strategy and caution. Before this all ends...you'll know everything," he finished, sipping his wine.

It almost felt like being back in my room with Vetta, at the castle on the day I left Paxe in that disgusting cell. A little more information, but not enough answers. Though, I was grateful for what he could give.

"Thank you, Lord Nero. I feel I might miss you a bit," I smiled sweetly. He scoffed.

"Youngling...when this is all over, we'll have plenty more days like this." He paused and looked to Luca, raising his cup to us both. "To new friends." We raised ours in turn and the three of us drank, watching each other and realizing no one would back down until we all competed for who would empty their goblet first. The chamber filled with more snickering and chatter, and we didn't leave his company for another couple of hours.

By the time we drunkenly stumbled out of the temple, the seemingly endless storm had finally quieted and the sea was not as angry. Alister's ice still held for us, and I was eternally grateful that I didn't have to travel across by a small boat, which would have undoubtedly made me retch. We slipped back and forth across the slick passage and Sir John was beside himself, failing to contain heavy laughter at our inebriated state. Alister wasn't much better by the time we reached the dock, snorting at Luca when he stumbled onto it and hit his knees. I burst out laughing, holding my middle and leaning forward trying, and failing, to help Luca to his feet as Alister approached.

"Oh, Mi'lord..." He chuckled. "My apologies, I should have warned you." He grasped Luca's wrist and pulled him up, holding him steady as we trudged forward. I gaped at the stairwell in the cavern and shook my head.

"Oh no..." I moaned. "Not these." A shadow flitted across the wall and Maureen appeared, covering her mouth and giggling.

"Let me help you, Mi'lady," she grinned, relieving Alister from the burden of carrying two obliterated royal asses up the stairs. I leaned onto her, slinging an arm around her shoulders and pushing at Luca's backside as he dragged up the steps in front of me.

"Nope...hands to yourself," Luca slurred without looking back at me. "Since you find this so amusing, no sandwich for *you*," he laughed. I squeezed my eyes shut in a silent heave of laughter, pressing my palm against the wall to steady myself. Alister and Maureen tried to keep their amusement to themselves as we painstakingly rounded up the stairwell.

"I told you he was fun," Maureen whispered as we finally cleared the top step and started across the short corridor to our room.

"I need to lie down," I laughed, my buckles clinking as I clumsily stammered around.

We finally made it into our bedchamber that was neatly organized and smelled of wisteria and citrus. Our bed was made and looked more than inviting as our attendants led us over and allowed us to plop onto it. My hair fluffed around me and I spread my limbs out, looking over to Luca, who was nearly ripping the buttons from his uniform, trying to get out of his top. Maureen cleared her throat and turned her face away as he finally succeeded, baring his chest and tossing the jacket across the bed, near the closet. He loosened his belt and handed it, along with his sheathed sword, to Alister, who nodded and walked over to fetch mine as I did the same. He placed them safely in the back of our closet space.

"Master Nero did a magnificent job, Mi'lady," he said, coming back around and helping Luca pull off his boots. Maureen remained quiet as she did the same for me, both of them taking the items back to the closet.

"He certainly did," I smiled with my eyes half open.

"Do you suppose you could stand a few moments, Mi'lady? I can help get you out of the leather," Maureen quietly offered, smiling as I winced at the thought.

"That's alright, dear. I suppose this is what I deserve," I snickered. "You're both so kind. Just leave us to waste and take that bottle of wine, over there, as my gift. You two go enjoy a night off together," I smiled, situating myself. They looked at each other, flushing a shade of pink.

"Mi'lady I—I don't thi—" Alister started.

"I'm afraid I must insist." I closed my heavy eyes, and dizziness set in. "You're adorable together." I heard a loud snore from Luca but couldn't manage to open my eyes again to witness the first time I'd ever heard him do it. I laughed through my nose and that was the last thing I remembered before the wine took me to a hard sleep.

CHAPTER 22

TURNING PAGES

"Ugh..." I groaned, turning towards the bright sunlight that seemed to taunt the unpleasant ache of my head through the open curtains of the balcony. I peeled my eyes open, squinting against the harsh morning and watching Luca as he snored quietly, both of us never managing to get under our blankets last night. He laid on his stomach, resting his face on his upper arms that were crossed above him. The stray hair that had loosened from his knot fell over his face, and I smiled as I brushed it away and tucked it behind his ear. He shifted a little and closed his mouth, smiling adorably in his sleep. I decided not to wake him and slid from the bed, wishing I had taken Maureen up on her offer to get out of this outfit before I fell asleep. I stood for a moment, pressing my fingertips to my temples and circling them firmly.

I turned to face my mirror on my vanity and was glad I hadn't woken Luca, staring at the smeared lip paint and smudges of black under my eyes. "Oh my gods..." I rolled my eyes and palmed my face, walking into the closet and stripping out of my leathers before promptly stepping into the bath. I scrubbed myself clean with the linens that were left for us and washed my hair, adding rosewater to it and floating on my back for a bit before smoothing velvety lavender oil into my skin and drying off.

Once back in the closet, I sifted through garments and opted to continue taking Luca's advice and find something comfortable of my own. I dipped into my bag, unsatisfied with everything I had, and so I pulled Luca's bag close to me. I smiled as I held up different items he had brought along with him. A small framed portrait someone had painted of his mother and father, a book about navigating, a small wooden box with letters from his father, two glass bottles of oils that smelled like him...I breathed it in and recalled the day he carried me down the path. He was intoxicating. I snapped the cork back into the bottle and put it back, pulling out the loose shirt he had discarded in the tent and slipping it over my head, hugging myself into it and pulling my damp hair from the neckline. I noticed a small, leather-bound journal and picked it out of the bag, turning it over and noticing his initials carved into the front. It was clasped shut with a small snap at the end of a little leather strip.

I looked through the doorway at Luca, who was still sleeping peacefully and wondered if I should open it. It seemed like an invasion of his privacy but at the same time, we were about to be married and my curiosity outweighed my reserve. I sat cross-legged and leaned against the wall of the closet and without trying to talk myself out of it, I snapped open the journal and laid it in my lap. The first few pages were drawings of different swords and weapons, some measurements and notes on attack strategy and form. I flipped a few pages and found where Luca had obviously been keeping score of a card game or some sort of gamble between himself, Michele, and someone named Leighton, that they referred to several times as "Fleck" and who seemingly lost the most coin. I smiled at unfamiliar scratchy handwriting that scribbled over different sums of currency and read: *'Dodgy lying brutes'*.

I flipped to the middle, passing something that caught my attention and turning the pages back...my breath caught in my throat. A perfect drawing of my engagement ring filled the page, and while it was colorless and grayscale, he had listed possible gemstone choices for the setting. I ran my fingers across the page and held my hand out in front of me to compare the two. Identical. I flipped the page and was equally shocked when he had drawn what looked exactly like the balcony of our room and the figure of a female from the chin down, who resembled me. I looked around the top of the pages but was unable to find a date.

I flipped to the back and worked backwards through blank pages until I found his last entry and nearly wept as I read it.

When I opened my eyes and realized it had all been real, I never wanted to let go of her.
She had come to me.
I'm not even sure if she wanted to at first, but she came anyway.
I had heard her tell me that she loved me before, but what I felt from her when she told me that even if she claimed she didn't, and chose to die in my place, she couldn't. She damned me by loving me...I felt it stronger than the moment she accepted the bond.
I only wanted to give her an out.
To stop her tears, reassure her...to touch her. I wanted to protect her from her nightmares.
But then she chose me.
Being inside her felt like coming home. Like some vital part of my body that was missing, had been replaced, and I was whole again.
The way she looked at me, the sound of her voice...how she moved.
Gods, I love her.
When I watched her sleep in my arms, I swore I'd rip apart anyone who would harm any part of her.
She's so perfect. How could anyone hurt her?
What did I do to deserve her?
How is she mine?
She loves me. I feel it.
I want to ask her.

A tear rolled slowly down my cheek and I sniffled, wiping at it as I turned a few pages backward. I skimmed across one and flattened it out, smoothing the parchment and reading it closely.

I smiled, turning the page forward instead of backward, and my eyes widened at the next bit. My stomach fluttered and the further I read, the more I remembered the night before the meeting with the royal family.

I couldn't stop the tears from flowing when I realized it hadn't been my imagination on the night he was writing about. Someone *had* been watching me, and it was the one that saved my life. I heard that twig pop, and I could have sworn I'd seen a rustle in the tree at the edge of the back courtyard. Hiss had thrown his attention that way in warning, and I had locked us in and blew my lamps out. I flipped to the next page and wiped at my face.

The next page had a rip at the binding, and I realized he had torn the parchment out to write the note he sent the wine with, the night we met. I covered my face with my hands and silently cried, sniffling and wiping and finally closing the journal. I snapped the strip together and carefully placed it back into his bag. Moving it back to the corner, I took a moment to gather myself and turned my face to the ceiling, a deep exhale leaving my chest. He had spent years pining for me before he had even known me, and I pushed him away. I may have had my reasons, but he didn't deserve what I put him through...and he loved me anyway. I made sure to clean myself up before I raised and padded out of the closet door, rounding the bed and sliding in on Luca's side, close to the balcony.

I brushed a hand across his shoulder, leaning into his back. He stirred and turned over to face me, smiling until he took notice of my puffy eyes. His brows drew together and he reached a hand to my face, pulling my drying hair behind my ear.

"What's wrong? Are you al—" I hushed him with my fingertips and his face drew up in more worry and confusion. I pulled back and moved myself down, unfastening the buttons at his waistline and pulling his pants down his hips. He raised himself on his elbows and watched with the same expression but didn't stop me, lifting his hips from the bed and allowing me to pull his pants the rest of the way off. I situated myself in his lap, thumbing over the mark on his chest and leaning in to press my lips to his forehead. His breathing became deeper as I guided him inside me and raised myself back up, pulling his shirt over my head and tossing it beside us. He reached a hand to touch me and I stopped him, slowly rocking my hips and pressing a kiss to his palm. I held his wrist with one hand and leaned my cheek into the other, riding him slowly and listening to him breathe louder. His eyes didn't leave mine and he seemed torn between letting me do whatever I was trying to do or stopping me completely and holding me until I explained myself.

I'm so sorry...I love you so much...I don't deserve you at all.

I cradled his hand between my cheek and my shoulder and closed my eyes while I continued my slow movements, warm tears falling down both cheeks. His labored breaths became shuddered and I opened my eyes to find his welling with tears of his own. I lost all composure at the sight of it and didn't fight the quiet sob that left me. Having no more control of himself, he sat up and his free hand took the other side of my face as he deeply kissed me. I wrapped my arms around him and cried harder, realizing he was too, as we moved together and our kiss grew stronger. The natural reaction of our bodies began to build and I slowly laid him back down, smoothing his hair back and dragging my fingertips across the stubble of his chin while our heads pressed together. His arms held me against his chest and our eyes locked, still shedding salty droplets, as his soft whimpers breathed across my lips and I felt him let go inside me. I tightened around him, trembling as I followed close behind. My limbs weakened and I rested myself against him, barely restraining more tears that were burning behind my eyes.

I closed them and laid my head beside his. He turned his face to mine and brushed the hair away from my face while I trailed a finger across his bottom lip. When I opened them again, he stared into me, and the knot in my throat seemed harder to swallow. When our breathing finally calmed, he looked as if he were waiting to speak or just had no idea what to say.

"I love you..." My voice cracked, another tear slipping out. His chest sputtered beneath mine and he swallowed, his jaw twitching as if he were fighting back more tears of his own. His arms squeezed tighter around me and I rested my fingers on his chin.

"I know..." His lip quivered. "I can feel you," he whispered, a single tear creeping towards the bed. "I love you too." I could feel myself slipping again and I moved my hand to cover my face as I let the silent cry free. "Baby..." he choked, turning us on our sides and pulling me in tight. His fingers buried themselves into my hair and I pressed my cheek to his collarbone, his lips resting at my hairline. "Please...tell me what this is all about."

"You came for me..." I whispered, sniffling.

"What?" He asked, leaning his face down and kissing my forehead.

"In the courtyard...the night before we met. It was you," I said quietly, flattening my palm against his chest. He tensed and was silent for a long moment, and I could hear his heart speed up and then slow again.

"Yeah...it was me," he breathed. I raised my face to look at him and he stared at me, tightening his jaw. "I had to see you..."

"Why didn't you say anything?" I asked. He wiped across my cheek gently and sighed.

"I ask myself the same question all the time. I wanted to. But I think I scared you off, and I guess it scared me too. By the time I thought I had the balls to get your attention, the light in your room was snuffed out and the guards at the corner were shifting. I had to find my way back out or get caught."

"You never told me."

"I didn't know if you'd think I was...insane. I wasn't sure how you'd feel if you knew, to be honest. Once we met, and everything happened the way it did, I thought you had made your mind up about me for a while. I figured... telling you then would only upset you." He swallowed hard. "Are you crying because that's exactly what it did?"

"No..." I whispered, placing my hand back on his face and slowly shaking my head.

"I'd rather die than hurt you. I only went because I felt...I felt like you needed me. When I heard you singing, it broke my heart. I suppose I'd always thought of you as proud, or perhaps ambitious...a princess with a court full of friends and males demanding attention from you, like most royals. But I felt you...and you were broken. I could hear it in your voice, and the sad song you chose about the moon goddess longing for her lost lover...it wasn't what I expected and I wanted to speak to you. I just didn't know what to say."

"I was terrified," I started. "Part of me knew you were close by and would be there in just a few hours, and I—I didn't know how to feel. One half of me felt drawn, and the other half was angry and afraid." I felt my eyes burning again and Luca smoothed his hand down my arm, resting it around my wrist. "I'm so sorry," I cried softly. He gripped my wrist a little tighter.

"I don't understand," he sniffed. "What could you possibly be sorry for? Please, Ari, I can't take this."

"You've loved me...you've loved me since before you even knew me and I—" I sobbed. "I was so cold to you. I pushed you. I screamed and fought and treated you so badly, all because I had been selfish and only wanted to see you as another male that was coming here to trick me into giving you my heart, so that you could squash it beneath your boot heel," I gasped and exhaled sharply, feeling so incredibly horrible about all the times I'd broken his heart. "All this time, you've been so patient. You just wanted me to be happy. It shouldn't have ever mattered what I'd been through...you deserve so much better. I'm so...so sorry," I heaved.

Luca's finger grazed over my lips, and our legs tangled together as he held me closer to him. "Shhhh...no," he whispered. "None of that matters anymore. We're together. You're going to be my wife. I'm far from unhappy, love. I'm the luckiest male alive," he soothed, wiping the back of his finger down my cheeks. "I'd have burned that damned journal if I'd thought it would cause you to feel this way. I wouldn't trade any moment we've ever had together for anything. Please don't cry...I know how much you love me, Arienne. My heart could have exploded with everything I just felt from you. You're my life's greatest treasure."

"And you're mine," I breathed. "I love you so much. Forgive me."

"I love you...more than anything. There's nothing to forgive."

"I shouldn't have gone through your things...it was wrong of me to read your private thoughts. They were closed up in a book for a reason."

He chuckled softly through his stuffy nose. "I couldn't give a damn if you'd brought it in here and read it out loud. It's just as much yours as it is mine." He leaned forward, and our lips met. Our bodies pressed closer together and our kiss became far more intense. I was just about to roll him back over and—

Knock, knock, knock....

We froze, opening our eyes mid-kiss and exhaling deeply as smiles cut across our faces. I couldn't help but giggle at his frustrated groan as he fell over onto his back and rubbed his eyes. "Just a moment!" I called, sniffing and grabbing Luca's pants. I dropped them against his middle and he started pulling them on while I pushed my arms through the discarded shirt and slid it over my head. I hopped over to the closet, snagging a pair of black leggings and struggling into them as I made my way to the door.

Maureen smiled as I opened it, carrying a tray with dainty teacups, fresh cream, sugar cubes and a massive urn of hot coffee. At the corner of the tray was a small envelope addressed to Luca and I. "Good morning, Mi'lady. Did I wake you?" She grimaced.

"No, no. We were just getting motivated...please." I stepped to the side and extended a hand to welcome her in.

"Are you alright, mum? You look as if you've been upset...or unwell. Was it the wine? I can fetch some peppermint for you. Or caraway?" She offered, setting the tray on the table. She glanced at Luca as he stepped out of the closet, tucking a thin tan shirt into his waistline. He smiled softly and she dipped her chin.

"I'm well, friend. Not to worry. I appreciate the offer. I see you come bearing something we desperately need this morning," I laughed. She held up the envelope and smiled.

"From Master Nero, Mi'lady." She placed it in my hand and I opened it, pulling out his signature fancy stationery.

IMMORTALITY HAS ITS PERKS.
I'M POSITIVE I FARE BETTER THAN YOU TWO THIS
MORNING.
THIS SHOULD HELP.
IF IT DOESN'T, FIND A MAGE.
I ENJOYED LAST NIGHT. SEND WORD BEFORE YOU TAKE
YOUR LEAVE.
I'D LIKE TO SEE YOU OFF.

I smiled and Luca stepped beside me to read the card, having the same reaction. "I'm going to miss him. We should come back soon," I muttered.

"When are you leaving us? I do hate to see you go," Maureen frowned.

"Probably tomorrow morning. We need to be well-rested and prepared to travel. I also have something I need to do in the city before we leave. Is Alister around today? Perhaps we could all enjoy the coffee," Luca answered, untying his hair and turning me to face him while he returned the strap to my neck. Maureen watched in curiosity.

"He...He just got in actually," she blushed. I jerked my attention to her, grinning and wide-eyed.

"Things went well?" I asked. She turned her face to the floor and smiled to herself.

"Very. Thank you, Mi'lady. I'll be happy to join you. I'm sure Alister feels the same." She looked back up at us and curtsied, gathering the tray and moving towards the door. "Whatever you said to him, your Highness..." She acknowledged Luca. "....I'm truly grateful." She bowed her head and started out to the grand staircase.

"Good for him," Luca said under his breath, nodding and retreating back to the closet. I left our bedroom door open and padded over to follow him, crossing my arms.

"What did you tell him?" I asked, leaning against the doorway while he dug out two pairs of boots. He passed me a pair and started pulling his on, smiling and shaking his head.

"Nothing..." He answered, fastening his buckles and tightening the straps. He straightened and gathered his hair behind his head. "I just took the small bit of his confidence he was feeling and...gave him a little push?" He smiled.

"Still think your gift is good for nothing?" I shook my head and pushed my feet into my boots.

"I never said that. But compared to that ice...damn. It was impressive." He tied his hair back loosely with a black leather lace. A piercing shriek startled us both, followed by a crash of broken glass and the sound of Alister's voice. "Fuck!" Luca panicked, grabbing our swords and tossing mine to me.

"Maureen!" I screamed, bolting for the door and tearing my blade from the sheath. I rounded the corner towards the sound of Alister's screams of rage and saw ice blasting surfaces all around the lower floor as a huge white blur darted this way and that, in an attempt to dodge his magic. When we reached the stairs, I nearly lost my balance. Maureen's slender body was trembling, clawed nearly in half as she fought to breathe, and her eyes stared in petrified fear at the ceilings. All the contents from the tray were lying in pieces around her. "No!" I screamed, rushing towards her.

Luca darted past me, securing a safe distance between her and whatever

Alister was fighting off, making to strike at any opportune moment. I knelt beside her and she grabbed at my shirt. "Is she alive?!" Luca called over his shoulder, swinging his sword towards the blur as it swept past him.

"Barely!" I yelled, gripping her hand.

"Get her under the stairwell!" He turned, making a small opening for me to pull her behind him and shelter her from the chaos. The blur halted by the statue in the middle of the foyer with a heavy thud, revealing itself as a massive pale-skinned beast with snow-white fur. It was monstrous and tall, and resembled a werewolf from the thrilling tales I was told as a child, the tales that had Paxe and I sleeping beneath our beds on nights when there was a full moon.

Maureen's blood stained its long talons as it panted, focusing its familiar amber-colored eyes upon me. Its gaping mouth was filled with fangs that were abnormally long for its snout, and it almost looked as if it smiled at me as it raised on its haunches and swung a powerful arm across the statue. It exploded into huge pieces of volcanic rock, Luca and Alister barely able to hurl themselves out of the way of impact. Part of the railing at the bottom of the stairs broke away, and I leapt over Maureen's body to shield her. Smaller pieces of the statue peppered my back as I glanced at her weak features. She was clinging to that thread of life and her eyes were glassy and wide as she mouthed words I could scarcely make out. I shook with adrenaline and tried to drown out the sounds of the beast whining in response to a blow from Luca's blade and the hiss of another blast of ice, leaning closer to her lips.

"Joh—" She faintly whispered. "Sir J—" Her body shook violently and I looked down at her abdomen as small bubbles of blood appeared and disappeared between the slashes through her flesh.

Sir John...

Understanding what she said, but not at all why she said it, I threw my attention to the battle between Luca and Alister and this monster that had ripped her apart. Alister used ice to stun the creature and Luca moved expertly, delivering his blade between its ribs, then again to its belly. It screeched and flailed, seeming to slightly weaken, but still strong enough to shatter the ice and charge again. I had only known Sir John to be in one place since we'd come to Bolton and hoped I'd be right as my eyes shot up to the top of the stairs. I raised up and used the edge of my sword to start a clean cut into my shirt and ripped it across my belly, tearing the fabric around my back and cutting the excess at the seam on my side. I profusely apologized as I slipped the material around her waist and tied it tightly, her moans of excruciating pain nearly more than I could bear.

I heard Luca cry out and glanced behind me in time to see Alister pin the beast within his ice against what was left of the statue's base. Luca was holding tight to his upper arm and blood bloomed across the material of his sleeve. The golden-eyed creature snapped its attention to me and I whipped around, using all my strength to carefully lift Maureen from the stairs and held tight to the hilt of my sword as I darted to the top and cut left. My foot met the door, busting it open and I heaved labored breaths as I hurried us down the dark stairwell, calling John's name at the top of my lungs. My own name was bellowed from behind me and a thundering sound followed it...I suddenly realized the beast was coming for us.

"Sir John!" I screamed, the shrieking of claws against stone drawing nearer. "John, help me!" My legs felt as if they were on fire and by the grace of the gods, Sir John appeared before me with his eyes bulging and his arms outstretched to take Maureen. "She said your name. Take her and run!" We leapt into the cavern from the stairwell and I turned sharp when my boots hit the stone surface. I bent my knees and straightened my back, and bloody talons scraped down the winding stone wall towards the exit. The beast lunged with its maw wide open and I bent forward, plunging my blade into its chest. I withdrew and blood sprayed my face as I hit my elbows against the steps and it roared over me, crashing head first into the cave wall. Heavy panicked footsteps tore down the stairs and Luca knelt before me, while Alister yelled for Maureen and blasted a shield of ice to hold the monster in place. It thrashed and somehow was still only heavily weakened, even with a strike to the heart.

"Arienne! Are you hurt?" Luca cried, pulling me up to sit and checking me over.

"No," I gasped. The sea, just outside the cavernous opening, parted with a deafening blast and Nero's hammer flew across in front of us, slamming into the beast and pinning it against the rocky wall. It fell silent as its strange limbs tried relentlessly to pry the hammer from its body, but it wouldn't budge. Nero appeared the way that he had during our trial in the temple, his eyes glowing bright with flame. He walked angrily across the small dock and his unbound hair blew around him, his lips tightly drawn with the promise of wrath. He turned his face to the other side of the cavern where Sir John, who I now gathered was a healer, was tirelessly and silently hovering over Maureen. Her eyes were closed and her head laid in Alister's lap as he loudly prayed to the gods to spare her. My heart ached and Luca helped me to my feet as we rushed to their side.

"Are you harmed?" Nero asked in an echoing boom. I slowly shook my head and Luca held his arm, offering Nero a glance that said he'd be fine. "Alister?" He asked. Alister raised his face, his crimson eyes pouring with tears. Sir John slowly lowered his hands to the ground and turned to look at Nero. His expression was grim as he shook his head. The cavern filled with loud sobs as Alister leaned over Maureen's face. Nero's body seemed to give off an orange light as his rage boiled and he stalked towards the scrambling creature.

I covered my mouth and held onto Luca as hot tears tore down my cheeks. They had only had a single night together as lovers, and she had been taken away. Alister's screaming chipped pieces of my heart away, bit by bit. Sir John put a hand on his back and rested his forehead on his shoulder. The sky darkened through thick cloud cover and Nero's hammer thudded against the stone as he moved it off the animalistic demon and raised it by the neck, throwing it like a stone into the parted water. I watched as the water came crashing down around it and its body disappeared. His thundering footsteps echoed through the space as he crossed the dock to its edge, where a mountain of hardening lava peaked from beneath. It encased the beast and trapped him inside, except for its snapping head.

"Arienne!" Nero bellowed, startling me. I looked up at Luca, who watched the god of strength as he waved a hand at me in summon. I hurried to the end of the dock and his eyes of fire met mine. "Look closely," he said softly, placing a gentle hand on my shoulder. I peered at the face of the merciless beast and it ceased its movement, staring at me with challenge. I saw my reflection in its eyes and realized then why it had come.

You heartless fucking coward.

"It can't be..." I whispered, conceding a step.

"It is, youngling."

"How is this possible?" I choked, my chest rising and falling rapidly.

"In the same way that he came the last time. His magic. He's outside of his body."

I shuddered as the bastard bared his teeth in a snarl of a grin that was straight from the depths of hell. I stomped down the dock, acknowledging no one and picked the hammer up with ease. Alister's cries quieted, and I felt eyes from all directions as I made my way back towards the swirl of molten rock.

"No mortal will ever dare to take life at my door. You mean to insult me and the power that was bestowed upon you by my own hand. Know this..." Nero leaned forward and stared into my father's eyes. "You believed an army would befall you...you believed you were stronger than even I. You are no king. You are no leader. You are no god. *But I am.* And you've sought destruction and fear. Allow me to give it to you...*Loren.* I will stand behind this queen and happily offer her my sword and watch you fall. Debts will be paid, and you will burn. A statue can be broken, but this image will live on in you until the world rids itself of your miserable existence...Arienne...take care of it." He stepped aside and my hair blew back as I approached the silent creature with the hammer at my side.

"Wherever you're hiding...I urge you to stay there. Your throne is crumbling. Your people despise you. You are alone. Your turn to cower now, Father." I raised the hammer and turned my body, thrusting my arm across me and ripping the wide-eyed head from the beast. It flew across the water, skipping like a stone, and disappeared into the crashing waves at the cliffside. The body was taken by the retreating lava as it hissed and steamed, sinking into the sea and boiling into nothing. A tear trailed down my cheek and I closed my eyes, wind whipping my face as I bowed my head.

A firm hand gripped my shoulder and Nero took the hammer from my hand. "Be strong, child. Making an enemy of me was unwise. He'll pay for what he's done today."

"She died because of me," I whispered.

"Turn around," Nero said softly. I opened my eyes and slowly turned and saw Alister and Maureen sitting in the cavern in a tearful embrace. I dropped my mouth open and ran down the dock, dropping to my knees at their side.

"Mi'lady..." Maureen said hoarsely, pulling me into her arms. I held her tightly and cried over her shoulder, pulling back when I felt her wince.

"Thank the gods..." I sniffled, leaning over to wrap an arm around Alister. Luca and Sir John stood and Nero approached. "How did she live?" I asked, looking up at him.

"It seems someone heard Alister's prayers," Nero smiled. "Sir John...please take care of that arm." He pointed his hammer in Luca's direction and John bowed his head and swatted Luca's hand away. A gaping slash peeked through a tear in his sleeve and Luca hissed as John's magic began to sizzle into it. "I shall go to the temple. All of you will stay with me in the main chamber this evening. When you're prepared, make your way and meet me. Tell no one what's happened. I'll see you soon," Nero gave a slight nod and vanished.

We all looked at each other, dazed and utterly broken, but happy to be alive and together. No one was ready to make a move to see the carnage in the residence. Maureen was weak, and Sir John convinced her to let him place her in the boat and offered to take her straight to the temple. Alister was hesitant to leave her side but insisted on helping us gather the important things. I had a feeling we had spent our last night in our chambers.

We watched until Maureen and Sir John had made it safely to the other side and then the three of us headed upstairs. The foyer was destroyed. The chandelier had crashed sometime after I had fled with Maureen; pieces of my stone form lay everywhere, and the once pristine surfaces were littered with ice and deep claw marks. Our bed chamber was untouched, and I startled when I took in my reflection, forgetting that I was covered in blood. My shirt was cut just below my breasts and spatter continued across the skin of my middle.

"Take a moment to bathe and decompress," Alister started. "I shall be waiting for you at the door when you're ready to pack. I'm in no hurry. Maureen is in good hands." I stepped in front of him, taking his hands.

"Alister...forgive me. He came here for me. It should have been my blood that was spilled, not hers. I'm so terribly sorry." He shook his head.

"No...no, Mi'lady. No matter his reason for the attack, you're not at fault. I'm grateful that the gods saw fit to grant me her life. Don't apologize for his evil. You're nothing like him. It was an honor to fight by your sides. Should you need me in the future...I do hope you'll allow me the chance to return this favor." His scarlet eyes burned.

"The honor is mine. You were a wonder." I smiled softly, turning my attention to Luca, who was closely inspecting his arm. "And you..." I kissed the faint purple line where Sir John had mended him. "I have no words." Our arms found their way around each other and his lips met mine.

"Would you perhaps be willing to think of some *after* we clean this off?" He smoothed his fingers over the dried blood on my cheek.

"I'll leave you to it," Alister bowed. "Ring me when you finish up. Take your time." He disappeared around the corner and we made haste to rinse off and dress. I tied my hair in a knot atop my head, and we opted for simple tunics of our own. Once packed, we gathered at the dock where Sir John was waiting to ferry us across.

I held a little tighter to Luca as the boat rocked calmly. My father has been reckless. It could have been any one of us that had met Maureen's fate today. I could feel the heartbreak in Alister's cries. I knew Luca probably felt it more intensely. He was no doubt thinking the same as I was, and I had no intention of letting him go tonight. Our large bags weighed down the hull and I remembered the way the morning started. I would have never guessed how quickly it all could change.

We docked and the four of us started up the walkway, cloudy afternoon light still lingering above. I looked back at the city across the fjord and thanked the gods its people remained safe...for now.

CHAPTER 23

ALLIES

Maureen rested on a couch near the massive fireplace on the western wall of the main chamber, Alister quietly watching over her with Sir John, who stayed by their side in case he was needed. She was still very weak and in pain, drifting in and out of sleep and drained of color. It would be a few days before she was well enough to satisfy Nero and return to the city. Luca and I took up a long couch on the other side of the chamber, where another fireplace roared. Nero paced unnervingly in a similar outfit from the night before.

"Why does he keep coming after me? Why challenge me the way he did and then decide not to wait to see what I'll do?" I asked, watching Alister tuck a heavy fur blanket around Maureen. Nero paused, bracing himself with his hands on the mantle and staring into the flames.

"The king is afraid. He's becoming impatient. Reckless. Impulsive. It's clear that he's losing control and has become increasingly aware of it. He knows his inherited power is now the only thing he has left over you. He's drawing you out."

I grew quiet and blankly stared at the floor. Luca leaned against the cushioned arm of the couch and pulled me to rest my back against his chest. We faced Nero, who slowly turned, crossing his arms and meeting my eyes.

"You have to finish this. Quickly. Tomorrow morning, you need to hurry to Irondale and prepare for the climb. We need to get the last weapon blessed before he decides to strike again," he frowned. "There is still much for you to learn."

Luca's arms tightened around me, but we said nothing. My mind drifted selfishly to what I pictured Crona to look like and the hopes of marrying Luca before facing my father for the last time. I had an overwhelming feeling of grief and I knew Luca could feel it, as he kissed the side of my head and sighed heavily.

"You planned to marry..." Nero raised his brows. We raised our attention to him and I slowly shook my head.

"It isn't as important as the lives that could be lost if we wait. We'll go and secure the last weapon. Perhaps, after this is over, we'll have a ch—"

"No," Nero cut me off. "That wasn't your original reason for seeking Crona. You were planning to conspire with the king and queen? What was your idea for a possible strategy?" He asked. Luca shifted behind me.

"Loren believed we were raising an army of his people to come against him. I was planning to ask my father for his help in making him believe there was one... but using that information as a decoy. A distraction. He'd be too focused on preparing to wipe out hundreds, but we invade his castle by ourselves. Take him out. I even thought..." Luca paused and it piqued my curiosity. I leaned forward and turned my body to look at him. His eyes were fixed on Nero for a long moment before he finally looked at me.

"You want to bring the castle down on him." Nero finished. My eyes widened and Luca's jaw tightened.

"It was just a thought," he answered in a low voice. My mouth parted and I turned my face to the floor. "Ari..." He started, placing a hand on my shoulder. "We don't ha—"

"Stop..." I raised my palm towards his face. "I never considered..." I trailed off. There was silence and I contemplated the events. "The guard that spoke to me in Aeon. The one that said he would be in allegiance to me when I'm queen...he was the same guard that let me in the dungeons to see Paxe before we fled the castle that day. Paxe told me that he used to fancy her when we were younger. I remember him telling me to be quick or it would be both our heads..." I recalled, returning my attention to Luca.

"What are you thinking?" He asked. Nero took a seat across from us and crossed his ankle over his knee.

"The guard I killed. He didn't recognize Paxe because of the amulet my mother left for my protection. Paxe had been wearing it and it disguised her only from the ones who truly meant her harm. All the others knew exactly who she was and said nothing. I think those guards would be our allies. They're under the king's employment but have no desire to be a part of his evil. If we can get word to Mischa somehow and convince him to allow us access...we could use him to help us evacuate the palace staff and infiltrate the castle." Nero nodded in agreement and Luca lowered his brows.

"That's genius," he whispered. "He could help set up traps in the castle too, if you'd rather keep it standing."

"No...let it burn. Let it all burn. If I am to rule...I don't want to stand where he stood. We'll rebuild." I looked at Nero. "We'll rebuild *everything*. Start a new world."

Nero's mouth turned up at the corner. "I'd like to assist you with this task."

"As would I," Alister's voice added from beside us. "And if I may..." He inclined his head to Nero, who gestured with his hand for him to proceed. Alister knelt in front of us, reaching for my hand. I placed my fingers into his palm and he squeezed them gently. "The two of you deserve happiness, Mi'lady. Give me the honor of keeping eyes on the king." He looked up at Luca. "Take this woman to your home, Mi'lord...make her your queen. You shouldn't have to sacrifice this for our sakes. It would give our people great hope to know that you married. I cannot think of a better distraction than a wedding," he smiled.

"I agree. An army would be expected...but a declaration of something he believes does not exist...and a statement that strong...that powerful? Would be all the diversion he'd need," Nero said as he leaned back in his chair.

"What if he tries to crash the wedding?" I asked.

"Varuna..." Nero rolled his eyes. "I told you she's a wrathful one. I suppose for you...I'll speak with her."

"Nero..." I whispered. He threw his arms out to the sides.

"They do say weddings bring people together," he grinned. "Perhaps she'll have second thoughts when she sees how well immortality has treated me all these years."

"You'll travel to Crona, your Grace?" Luca asked.

"To witness the marriage of the future saviors of our world? Absolutely." He slapped his palms to his large, muscular thighs. "I can't think of a better reason to leave for a while. I've not been away from Bolton since she and I..." He paused and his face drew up. "I look forward to it," he finished.

"Knightsfire," Maureen's hoarse voice echoed through the chamber. We all looked in her direction as she slowly sat up with Sir John's assistance. Alister stood and hastily walked across the room to her.

"Knightsfire?" I asked. Nero's brows raised.

"Knightsfire is a highly flammable, nearly explosive mud that gathers in a spring under Bolton's cliffs. The volcanic springs that feed the baths in the city hold a great supply. It's difficult to harvest it, but I agree...it would be perfect for sending the castle into rubble. That's brilliant." He looked at Maureen and they exchanged smiles. Alister brushed his fingers across her face and stared at her ardently.

"So, we figure out a way to extract it and smudge it into the castle walls? Then what...ignite it?" Luca asked.

"Precisely. I know how to extract it, but it will take some time. It has to be carefully stored. Even more carefully delivered across the country. Within the time it takes you to complete your tasks in the Horned Mountains and travel to Crona...I feel it should be enough to gather what we need. Let me handle that bit," Nero inclined his head.

"I can work out the small details with my father," Luca added.

"Then it's settled. We conspire against the king...destroy the castle, and I deliver the final blow." I raised my chin. Maureen slowly raised her fist to her chest.

"We're with you, Mi'lady," she squeaked. Sir John and Alister mimicked her gesture and faced us. I swallowed the knot that began building in my throat, and my eyes burned with unshed tears.

"I love you all," I choked, placing my fist to my heart. "I'll end it."

Nero raised from his chair and smiled, "We toast. And celebrate." He looked at Maureen. "In...moderation." Snorts and low chuckles flitted through the chamber. Nero filled goblets of wine and gave each of us one of our own. He raised his goblet in the air. "To our future king and queen."

"Here, here!" Maureen and Alister chanted, Sir John grunting with them. Luca and I smiled at one another and we all drank. The evening was spent in good company and food, and we savored the same warmth of family that we felt in Aeon with Vetta and Frances. I realized then how much better life was when I allowed love to take over. Not just with my soulmate but with my people—with my friends. Pity once again surfaced for my father, although I fought against any thought of him in that moment. He'd never know this. I wondered if he'd ever known it.

Sleep came quickly for all of us. All but Nero, who never had any use for it and kept watch over us through the night. We were safe here. When morning broke, Nero had prepared our bags and filled a sack with supplies, food and a letter stamped with his seal to give to the Innkeeper in Irondale for its finest available accommodations. We said our farewells to Alister and Maureen, and Nero cut a path across the fjord and escorted us on dry ground between walls of water. Sir John joined us and we climbed the winding stairs into the residence.

We stood in silence for a moment, surveying the damage in the foyer again and Nero shook his head. "I feel so badly about this, your Grace. Your statue...this place...Maureen," I shrunk in shame. He placed a strong hand on my shoulder.

"No, child. Maureen is safe now. It's only a building. I'm grateful it wasn't the whole city. This can all be replaced. The statue wasn't you. It only looked like you. That's the most important thing to remember. You're stronger than a hunk of volcanic stone," he smiled. "We're ready, John." He dipped his chin and Sir John nodded, carefully avoiding Maureen's blood on the stairwell and crossing the foyer to fetch our horses outside.

"Thank you again...for everything," I said, turning to face Nero and not giving him a choice when I threw my arms around his solid form. He winced in surprise but squeezed me back, raising my feet from the floor and setting me back down. He released me and clapped a hand on Luca's shoulder.

"See you both at the wedding," he winked. "Ride fast and you can make it to Irondale well before nightfall. Safe travels. We're watching over you." With that, Nero smiled and disappeared. He didn't seem very good at goodbyes. We headed down the stairs and out into the courtyard, where Sir John was waiting with Alice and Bjourne. He helped us load them with baggage and Luca waited to help me into the saddle.

I turned to face Sir John, who looked sad to see us go. "You're a remarkable person, John. I'm grateful to you for your friendship." I kissed his cheek and hugged him tight. When I pulled back, he was teary-eyed and patted my shoulder. He opened his mouth and tried earnestly to sound out words that wouldn't form, clutching his fist to his heart. I understood perfectly. "Until death, friend," I smiled, hugging him one last time and mounting my horse. Luca took his place beside me and we trotted off, rounding the fountain and turning back to wave at the garden entrance. Sir John waved back and we started our descent down the cliffside through the city.

"I have one thing I need to do before we leave, love. If that's alright with you," Luca called from his horse as we reached the lower level.

"Of course," I nodded. We rode down to Annette's and she greeted us from the little green door as we approached.

"My Lord and Lady..." She bowed. "Are you leaving us?"

Luca hopped down and smiled at her as she straightened. "We are. I wanted to personally deliver this to you, Lady Annette." He handed her a large bag full of gold. She grasped her bodice and stepped backward.

"Gods above," she gasped. "Your Highness...I can't accept that." Luca extended the bag further.

"Please. We want to help. We know that you do a great deal to care for those in need. I would be honored if you'd allow us to assist," he bowed at the waist. "On behalf of the crown." The morning light created a halo of near blue across his raven hair. I couldn't have loved him more. Annette carefully took the sack from his hand and held it to her chest as she dipped her chin.

"Thank you..." she whispered, raising her face back to meet us. "Thank you both...so much." Her eyes misted and she curtsied. "I look forward to seeing you again. Bolton will miss you a great deal." Luca nodded and pulled himself onto his horse. I reached for his hand and he grabbed mine. We smiled as we left her, riding close and exiting the city slowly, our swords clinking at our hips. I looked over at him as he stared forward, smiling to himself and squeezing my hand. He gave me a sidelong glance.

"What?" He smirked.

"I love you, Luca Di Meo. So damn much. You're an amazing male."

"Di Meo...when I marry you, do I take your last name?" He turned his face to mine, his brows drawn together. I laughed loudly.

"No, fool," I giggled.

"Arienne Di Meo..." He stared forward again, beaming. "My *wife*."

We couldn't keep the smile from our faces as we left Bolton behind us and made our way towards our next destination—Irondale.

CHAPTER 24

THE DARK

Irondale looked nothing like what its name suggested, save for the iron gates that opened to a city surrounded by darkness looming over the gloom of the Horned Mountains, where you could hear the whining of the storm that protected its face. You could hardly call it a city. Aged stone walls reached around a village covered in fluffy white snow. It reminded me what Aeon might look like during winter months, but instead of townhouses and outdoor vendors, there stood mountain cabins and cottages and enclosed shops with frosty windows. It would have been charming, aside from the fact that most all the sunlight was lost beneath the curse of its mountain base. What little street that was clear of snow was cobbled, and children played happily as if nothing were odd about the peculiar town. Snowmen lined the spaces between houses, and cozy light crept from every window as fires crackled in dens and kitchens everywhere.

It was hard not to think of Alister as we passed through in search of the inn we were to stay. This was where he spent his young life. I supposed that was what seemed so familiar about it, as I smiled and waved at a bundled-up young boy who stopped to stare. He dropped his mouth open and ran into his front door, returning with what I presumed to be his father. We slowed our horses to a stop, and I pulled my gray fur-lined cloak tighter around me.

"Good day to you!" The man waved as he stomped through the snow. He was of average height and build, and looked a bit like my father in the face. His hair and beard were neatly trimmed and brown, but his eyes a bright blue. "My son announced that the Prince and Princess have arrived. Would I be right to assume I've lost all manner of respect and courtesy, and he was correct?" He smiled, placing his hands on his hips.

I glanced at Luca with a smirk and he chuckled, pulling back the hood of his black fur cloak. "There's no need to be formal, sir. We are who he suspected. We've only just arrived. Would you know where we could find the inn?" Luca asked. The male bowed anyway, his son running to his side as fast as his little legs could carry him and mimicking his father as he grinned sheepishly. I put a gloved knuckle against my lips and chuckled softly.

"Yes, your Highness. The inn is down this street, all the way at the back of the village near the mountain pass. Shall I run inside to get my cloak and escort you?" He straightened.

"I can take them!" The little boy shouted, raising an arm in the air. His father tried to calm him, but the poor dear was desperate to do it. "I can do it! Please, Father! I'll use my toboggan!" He pleaded as he bounced on his heels.

"That would be wonderful!" I offered, giving his father an understanding smile. "I've never had the pleasure of being escorted by toboggan before! What's your name, love?" I asked as the little lad bubbled over with excitement.

"I'm Holt! This is my father, Benjamin," he pointed his little mittened thumb at himself, and then at his father, who shrugged and grinned apologetically. "I'm gonna go get my dog! She pulls my toboggan real good!" He exclaimed, running back towards the little cottage.

"Forgive me, your Highness. He's a bit excited," Benjamin scratched at the back of his neck. I shook my head and waved a hand across the air.

"Please, he's precious," I laughed, watching as the little boy returned with a large sled and a stunning wolf he considered a dog. It was an immaculate example of a canine. Beautiful and tame, with fur the same color as my cloak and eyes that were piercing blue. "Oh my, Holt. That's a beautiful pup!" I offered while the little boy harnessed the animal to his sled.

"Her name is Kyna. She's my best friend, but Mother doesn't like her much. She says her hair makes too much mess." He rubbed the top of the wolf's head gently and she took a readying stance as he climbed onto the toboggan.

"Thank you, Holt. That's quite enough. Back in before dinner, yeah?" Benjamin smiled. He then turned and bowed slightly. "Please let me know if I can be of any help while you're here. Our door is always open to you...and...thank you for giving Holt this opportunity. He'll not soon forget this. It means a lot."

"It's a pleasure, sir," Luca chimed. "Ready when you are, Holt!" The little boy gave us a nod and ordered Kyna forward, and we trotted down the cobbled path while he kept to the snow banks on the side. People took notice of us along the way; we waved and gave our royal escort his share of the attention. It wasn't long before the bright inn came into view near the pass.

Holt stopped and gave his wolf a proud scratch behind her ear at the covered entrance. I dismounted and met Luca between our horses as we led them closer to where Holt waited. We looked over at the ominous area across from the inn, and I felt incredibly cold and uneasy. It looked dark, treacherous and gave me a feeling of heaviness that made my bones ache, much like the way I felt when the mountains were far off in the distance when we rode through the grasslands towards Aeon. I dreaded going near it and fought my deep urge to put it off for a few days. We didn't have time to spend leisurely anymore. The little boy interrupted my bleak thoughts as he stepped between Luca and I.

"That's the forbidden pass. My mother and father warned me never to go there. No one crosses the wall. My friends said that if you do, you get dead!" He shot his attention up to our faces. "Kinda cool, huh?" He smiled.

"You should always listen to your parents, Holt. Never go there, okay? Besides..." I knelt down and flicked his nose. "If anything happened to you, then who would show us where to go?" I crossed my eyes and made a face, earning the cutest giggle.

"You're silly for a princess!" He laughed. "I like you. You're not like I thought you'd be."

"Oh yeah?" I poked him in the shoulder. "How did you think I'd be?" I asked. Luca chuckled at our exchange.

"Mother says the goddess has been waiting for you for a long, long time. She says sh—"

"That's enough of that talk, boy," an elderly woman cut him short, walking with a cane out of the heavy oak door to the inn. Holt startled and faced her as I stood, pulling my hood down and glancing at Luca, who seemed to have also wondered what the little boy was about to say. "Princess! I'm Hilda, the innkeeper. It's lovely to finally meet you." She struggled over towards us. "Holt, find another place for that mutt to relieve herself!"

"Oh! Agghhh! Kyna, no!" He screeched, bolting over to the animal who clearly had no intention of waiting to do her business. We quietly laughed through our noses. "Man...Ma's never gonna let you back in if she finds out what you did! Bad girl..." He scolded.

"Master Nero had asked us to give you this, Lady Hilda." Luca politely handed her the sealed envelope.

"Ahhh, yes. Prince Luca. You're a handsome thing, aren't you?" She smiled sweetly at him through her heavy wrinkles. Luca blushed, dipping his chin. "There was no need. I've got your rooms prepared. I'm afraid we don't have accommodations quite as fancy as Lord Nero expects, but I assure you, you'll be very comfortable." She leaned on her wooden cane.

"Pardon, did you say...*rooms?*" I asked as politely as I could manage.

"I'm afraid so, your Highness. I'm an old lady, and forgive me but...I'm set in my ways. While I'm delighted by the news of your betrothal, you are still unmarried. Under my roof, I cannot allow you to share a bed with one another. I hope you can understand." She bowed her head and I looked back at Luca, who sucked his lips into his mouth in an attempt not to laugh.

Is she taking a piss?

"It's quite alright, ma'am," Luca answered for me, still holding back his amusement. "She's an awful snore." I dropped my jaw and whacked him in the arm. Holt erupted.

"Really?!" He laughed loudly as the old woman snickered.

"Holt! Don't you have some dinner to get to, child?" She called over her shoulder.

"But—"

"You best mind me, boy. You'll see them again, don't worry." Holt humphed and led the wolf in the direction we had just come.

"Will you come visit? You're really nice," he asked, tugging at my cloak. I leaned down and rubbed some warmth into his small shoulders.

"You have my word," I smiled. "And thank you so much for being such an amazing escort. It's a big job. I'll have to tell everyone!" His little mouth popped open.

"You mean it?!" He gasped.

"Oh yes! But only if you're good and you do what you're told. Yes?" I inclined my head.

"Yes ma'am. I can't wait to tell Troy... He's gonna be so jealous!" He hopped onto his sled. "See you later!" He waved excitedly as Kyna took off. We waved and watched him until we were sure he made it back without taking any detours.

"Cute kid," Luca said, huffing warm breaths into his cupped hands. A young male hurried outside and approached us. He was tall and rail thin with a large nose and a pockmarked complexion. He bowed casually and his lips curled as he straightened, revealing his yellowed teeth.

"Evening! I'm Cragan. I tend to the horses. I'll also be attending to you while you're here, in case you should need anything. Lady Hilda has a hard time getting up and down these stairs nowadays." He reached for the leads and we handed them over as Hilda turned and gestured for us to follow her.

"Umm...would it be alright if I carried my own bag? I apologize if I seem rude. It's not that I don't trust you, I just have very personal belongings I'd rather not part with," I explained.

"I've got it, love." Luca didn't wait for any objection and promptly started unfastening the straps, shouldering my bag, as well as his own.

"Everything else can be brought in then? You sure you don't need the saddle too?" Cragan asked with an almost irritated tone. I nodded and Hilda cocked her head to the side.

"Use that tone again Cragan and you can sleep in that stable too. Off with ya," she fluttered her hand.

Good. What a pompous sh—

"I second that notion," Luca glared. Cragan chewed his bottom lip and made off with Alice and Bjourne around the back corner of the inn.

"Don't mind him. He's had a foul disposition since he was a child, but he's harmless. My apologies," Hilda said as we approached the large door. I stepped ahead of her and pulled it open, holding it for her and Luca, against his look of disapproval. "Gods above, child. Never thought I'd see the day where I received a courtesy like that from a royal. You really do break the mold don't you?" She cackled as she entered. Luca grumbled behind her as I steadied my hand on the door and followed them inside.

The inn wasn't very large but awfully inviting. Glorious heat warmed my rosy cheeks and nose as we stepped into the tiny foyer. Directly in front of us was a flight of wooden stairs with a corner landing and another short flight that went up left. To our right was a small counter and a wall with a few keys. To our left was a sitting room with a little round table and a few chairs. A good-sized fireplace was crackling on the far wall, and an old, comfortable-looking couch rested in front of it, over a fluffy fur rug. The whole inn was mostly wood paneling with various paintings of mountains and woodland animals, accompanied by mounted stag antlers here and there. It reminded me of a hunting lodge, though I'd never actually seen one for myself. I saw a door that was closed in the corner of the sitting room, but before I could ask, Hilda answered, "You're welcome to eat down here in the sitting room for your meals. I can come and let you know when I've got things prepared for you. There's always fresh coffee if I'm here, and my quarters are just beyond that door there if you need me. Come on up, I'll show you where you'll be sleeping." She started poking up the stairs a bit more quickly than I imagined she would. Luca made a face at me as we followed her up and I bit down on my lip. Hilda paused to catch a few breaths on the landing and started up the second flight. A few steps up, I overheard flatulence and nearly lost my composure at Luca's reaction. I had to cover my mouth. Hilda either had no idea she had done it, or just didn't care as she continued up the last few stairs.

She opened a door to her immediate right and walked inside, her cane thudding across the smooth wooden floor. We followed a safe distance behind. "This is your room, Princess. I had Cragan light fires for both of you...should be good and warm now. There are several lamps in here and a chest of drawers if you need them. The linens are clean and the pillows are crisp. That blanket on the bed will run you clean out of here, it can get so hot." Luca sat my bag on the bed and Hilda gave us a moment, trudging next door and opening the door to his room as if in an attempt to hurry us up.

This is so ridiculous.

He glanced out the doorway to make sure she was out of sight before bulging his eyes and grinning like an idiot. "I know I'm not the only one thinking she did that shit on purpose...quite literally," he whispered a tad bit too loud. I finally heaved the most silent laugh I could muster and he palmed his face. "Gods..." He chuckled.

"Stop..." I whispered through my laughter. "I can't breathe."

"Ari...she was so surprised a royal was chivalrous enough to hold a door open for her, but then she..." He made an exploding gesture with his hands in front of his face and I bent over to keep from completely losing myself. I put a hand on his cloak and gripped it tight, trying to catch my breath.

"Are you two about done with your goodnights? I promise it won't kill ya to spend one or two nights on your own," Hilda called from the other room. I finally gathered my wits and straightened, tightening my arms around him under his cloak and pressing my face to his chest. He squeezed me and kissed the top of my head.

"This is so stupid. I don't want to be separated," I said, quietly.

"Doesn't sound like I'll be far, and if she thinks I won't be checking in, especially with that little rat running his mouth downstairs, then she's mistaken," he spat. "But she's not wrong, love. We have to at least respect her for that." He pulled back and unfastened my cloak, straightening the bow on the leather tie around my neck. "Keep that close. I'll miss you."

I dropped the heavy cloak from my shoulders and tossed it over the bag on my bed, scowling at the impatient tapping of a wooden cane against the wall. "I'll miss you too," I said, giving him a chaste kiss. "You'd better go before she comes back to give you an eye infection," I giggled. He scoffed and rolled his eyes as he made for the door, turning back as he pulled it behind him.

"I love you," he smiled.

"Love you too, your Highness." The door snicked shut and I overheard him being the polite Prince for a few minutes before shuffling footsteps and more tapping slunk down the stairs. I resisted the urge to sneak over and started unpacking and filling the old drawers, hiding my weapons beneath clothes and hanging my cloak on a knob that extended from the wall by my door. I changed into a long-sleeved, short-cropped knit nightgown and pushed a worn chair from the corner up to the fireplace.

It was good and dark now, and thankfully, my window didn't face the mountain pass beyond the wall. I stood at the glass and stared out over the quaint little village that still seemed so out of place beneath this mountain and wondered, who in their right mind, would be comfortable living here? But it did have its own charm, and snow began to fall past the window. I had only seen snowfall a couple of times in my life, as it was usually warmer on our side of the continent during the year. The winter months could be brutal sometimes, but nothing like this. As children, Paxe and I were fortunate enough to be allowed to enjoy a dusting on the ground once and that was hardly enough to palm a snowball together, let alone create a person from it with twigs for arms. I thought of little Holt and how innocent he was, and I started to miss my best friend terribly. Soon she'd have a little creature of her own to chase around. I wondered how she was feeling and if her belly had started to swell.

No matter the thoughts that seemed to find their way into my mind, every strong feeling I had since coming here had me wanting to face this trial and whatever goddess we were meeting and get this over with. I didn't want to stay. Aside from the little boy and his father, the impression and heavy weight of this place just wasn't sitting well in my body. To top it all off, I couldn't even shove those feelings away in the safety of Luca's arms because a testy old woman was keeping us apart. She seemed nice enough, and it truly wasn't that I didn't care for her, but it was an obstacle I didn't want right now, and part of me missed home... Wherever home was. My breath fogged the glass in front of me and I sighed, turning away and dropping into the threadbare seat by the fireplace. I started to wonder if trying to curl up under the blankets and fall asleep would help, but before I could make a decision, my eyes caught a shadow beneath a crack in the wood paneling next to the fireplace. A folded bit of parchment and a small pen slipped through it. A smile crept across my lips.

I raised from the chair and padded over to the note, picking it and the pen up from the floor and unfolding it.

Feeling adventurous? I thought perhaps we could make this fun.

I breathed a laugh and scratched a message onto the paper, folding it back and sliding it between the crack as I leaned against the wall and pulled my knees up to my chest. A moment later, it popped back through.

If this is your idea of adventure, you're no fun at all.

I fancy a sandwich.

I snickered, and I could hear Luca chuckling on the other side of the wall. I rolled my eyes and wrote back, poking the note through again and smiling to myself when I heard him groan in frustration.

How would you like it? Stuffed with meat and folded over, or spread out so you can make it yourself?

You're absolutely wicked. I hope you're proud of what you've just done to me.

I felt heat in my cheeks that had absolutely nothing to do with the fire I was sitting next to. I jotted down another message, and he jerked it through the crack before I could push it all the way through. I heard the rustling sound of paper and then it appeared again, slightly wrinkled.

I am. Take him out and pretend I'm doing something worse. I dare you.

I will...if you do too.

My mouth went dry. The familiar feeling of a stampede roared through my stomach and I wrote something else, wedging the paper back to him. I felt the wall thud lightly against my back and knew there was no turning back now. I almost couldn't believe what we were about to do, but the thrill of it was exciting. Anticipation ate at me for a moment until the paper reappeared. I felt a throbbing ache between my legs when I opened it.

Lean against the wall...I want to hear you come undone.

I took a deep breath, my face flushed, and pressed my palm to the wall. I could definitely feel his influence over my body. I closed my eyes and imagined it were his hands instead. I did as he asked and parted my knees, reaching my hand slowly between my thighs and letting my head fall back against the wall as my fingertips touched my center. I had never done this to myself before, but at this point, I felt pretty well educated on how to please myself. I also didn't feel alone. My desire intensified and I used it to push back to him through his magic. I heard Luca take in a sharp breath through the wall, and the sound and mental image of what he must look like right now set me on fire.

My fingers smoothed circles over that bundle of nerves and I bit down hard on my lip. Luca sent through another wave of his magic and I wasn't sure where my pleasure ended and his began. His breaths became louder and more shallow. I arched my back and spread my legs open wider as I sank two fingers inside myself. I shot that intensity back to him and he groaned softly. My fingers moved in and out and a breathy moan left my open mouth. I pulled them out slowly and dragged them up to my center, breathing loudly and feeling release begin to burn low in my belly. I pictured the love of my life sheathing himself inside me as I plunged my fingers back in, moving faster and stifling my whimpering.

"Luca..." I whispered breathlessly. His answering groan and rustle of movement sent me over the edge and I gasped loudly, following it up with rapid breathing and I heard him do the same. A sheen of sweat covered my body and my knees quaked as I pulled them back together and turned to lean my side against the wall, panting and trying in earnest to calm myself back down.

Godsdamn...that was incredible.

I fanned myself with a hand and looked down at the open note, grabbing the pen and writing another message. I passed it through the crack and heard a breathless chuckle on the other side. I smiled to myself. It came back a bit slower than the last time.

I laughed a bit too loud, and he did too, shushing me from the other side. I wrote back and slipped it through as I raised myself onto my wobbling legs and crept over to the chest of drawers, peeling the nightgown off and changing into a sleeveless shift to cool down. The paper popped out of the crack and I grinned as I took the hair strap from my neck and tied a loose knot on top of my head.

I'm not ready to thank the dusty old hen just yet, but I should. That was unbelievable. I'd still rather have you.

You are truly incredible...I miss you. Try to rest. I'll see you in the morning.
Goodnight, my queen.

"Goodnight..." I whispered, kissing my fingers and lightly tapping the wall. He tapped back a few times and I folded the note and slipped it into a secure pocket in my bag that I dropped in the corner of the room near my bed. I blew out the lamps and slipped beneath the soft, heavy fur blanket. The glow from the fireplace offered a cozy, dim light and the crackle from the burning logs made my eyes heavy. Or perhaps it was the exhaustion that had been left behind the most erotic thing I believe I'd ever done. Either way, a new chapter had been flipped between us and whichever of those things gave me the comfort I needed, I welcomed it. It made the dark a lot less intimidating. In a rare turn of events, I said a silent prayer to the gods and thanked them for my future husband. I prayed for his safety and his comfort, and for the same to befall my friends. I snuggled into the deep pillow and closed my eyes. I had just about fallen asleep when—

"*Forgive me...*" A female voice I hadn't heard in a while spoke. I wasn't sure if I had been in between sleep and awake, or if it had been in my mind. I tore my eyes open and looked around the room, not willing myself to move. There was no one. I refused to give up the peace I had finally settled into and didn't reply, choosing to ignore it and tucking myself tighter into the blanket. I forced my eyes closed and begged my tired head to shut off. It didn't take too long. Once I was convinced I had just imagined it, I drifted into sleep.

CHAPTER 25

THE PASS

"Come all ye with weary bones, strained from battles over broken thrones. Come all ye who yearn to be blessed...come...and let thee find their rest."

I jolted awake, breathing heavily and throwing my blanket from my legs. The voice was singing...loudly. My heart recognized it, but my mind refused to believe it. Her voice was angelic...ethereal and soft. It was welcoming and haunting at the same time—like a siren that drew you near but didn't have the intention to harm.

"Where are you? What do you want from me?" I whispered, a cold sweat trickling down my spine.

"Come all ye with hearts untamed, seek my arms and call my name. For through the darkness shall I be...come...I humbly welcome thee."

I flew from the bed, firing my lamps and stripping out of my shift. I pulled a pair of ivory, fleece-lined leather leggings up my waist and secured the laces. Nero had gifted us warm clothes for the climb, and they were perfect. I wouldn't wait anymore. Even if it was the middle of the night. I wrapped a gray fur-lined tunic around me, tying the leather laces on the side, and slid into matching boots. A soft knock at my door startled me and Luca appeared in the doorway.

"What's wrong?" He asked as he closed the door quietly.

"Do you hear that?" I whispered as I met him in the middle of the room. He looked half asleep and completely confused.

"Hear what, love? Are you alright? Why are you dressed like you're about to go do something crazy?" He ran his eyes up and down my body.

"Luca...she's singing. You don't hear singing? It's deafening." I looked around the room.

"Who's singing? I don't hear anything. Are you sure you didn't dream it?" He cupped my shoulders.

"Come all ye who answer the call, to bring the calm and peace to all. For with your love shall you succeed...come...I wait to honor thee."

Luca's eyes widened and he suddenly seemed very awake. "Gods above..."

"I think...Luca, I've heard her before. I know who she is," I trembled. His brows drew together and he stilled.

"What are you talking about? Who is she?" He asked, shock still etched on his face.

"We have to leave. Now. Get dressed and grab your sword. We need to go through the pass. Tonight." He nodded once and kissed my forehead, rushing to his room to change. I slung my leather belt around my hips and fastened my sword to it. I slipped the hunting knife into my boot and took my hair down, loosely braiding it down my shoulder and tying it off with the leather strap. I hurried to my bedroom door, throwing my cloak around me and fastening it at my neck, as Luca met me fully dressed and armed at the landing of the stairs.

"Come all ye who seek the light, to vanquish evil within the night. For as it dwells inside of me, so shall it burn inside of thee..."

We were frozen in each other's stare and my heart pounded at the words she sang. I needed no other sign that my suspicions were right. Luca's chest rose up and down and we said nothing as we tore down the stairwell. We barreled through the heavy oaken door and snow blew harshly past us. We pulled our hoods over our heads and slipped our hands into woolen gloves, giving each other a nod and bolting towards the stone wall that guarded the entrance to the pass.

Luca hoisted me up and I grabbed the snowy ledge, pulling myself on top and reaching down to help him up. We landed in a deep snow drift on the other side and kicked through it, approaching the darkness of the pass. Deep down, I knew that what Nero had told me about the barrier yielding for us would be true, but my heart thrashed against my ribs and I was shaking with fear. I could feel death only a foot away from where we stood, and if I could feel it...I knew Luca felt it more. He took my hand and squeezed.

"Come all ye who suffer with fear, who sacrificed much to wander here. For within these peaks shall you be freed...come...embrace thy destiny."

We stood closer together. I looked over at Luca and the silver in his eyes sparked. He leaned in and kissed me deeply. "Together," he whispered. I nodded and he clutched my hand. We raised our free hands and stepped forward, reaching out until a jolt of powerful magic struck our palms and a loud cracking sound thundered all around us. Luca threw his arms around me and I held onto him for dear life as we were pulled through what felt like a heavy ocean of darkness and flickers of starlight. It was as fast as a flash of lightning and we landed on our sides, tangled in each other and gasping for precious air, as we locked eyes and realized that somehow, we had survived.

We raised up and our lips crushed together in a devastating kiss that ended in a strong embrace and a string of curses before we finally looked around and took in our surroundings. A perfect, cloudless day...soft green grass littered with flowering plants and wildlife. Songs of birds and a calm, serene mountain lake lined with evergreens. It looked lush and enchanting. Colors seemed more vivid, sounds and light more vibrant. The air was a pleasant balance that was neither too warm, nor too cold. Snow capped the mountain range and on a path that led a short way up Mount Iren, perched a small temple. It was pure white and gleamed in the sunlight, beckoning us from where we sat, utterly astonished in the grassy meadow.

"I can't believe what I'm seeing," Luca said, gaping at the sight.

"It was a ruse? A trick?" I added, turning my body to look around.

"A glamour like no other...I should think we'd have expected that after Nero. But I can safely say that I didn't." He stood and offered a hand to help me to my feet. "Are you alright?" He checked me over, taking his gloves off to touch my face.

"Yeah, I'm fine. You?" I asked, doing the same. He nodded, kissing me again for good measure.

"Come ye brave who traveled far, to find the place in which you are. Your trials for your quest are through...come...I'm here. I wait for you."

My eyes welled with tears and I choked them back, swallowing hard and refusing to acknowledge yet what I was now positive I'd find to be true as soon as I walked into that temple. Luca gave me an understanding smile and gently took my hand as we started down the path in silence. Every step we took forward made me more emotional. My prince steadied me, never rushing and, as always, leaving me in complete control of the pace. He was here for me...the way he was meant to always be here for me...the way the goddess, inside the temple that we were about to approach, decided it to be.

I was about to cross a boundary in my life that I thought had always been lost. My heart thundered like the squall in the forest. This was why Nero couldn't tell me. This was the reason that Vetta and the older generation of Valdaro had mentioned that one day I would understand...and know everything. It all led up to this moment. We took the first step onto a small set of pearlescent marble stairs and I halted. I suddenly became extremely hot and unfastened my cloak, dropping it to the steps. Luca removed his as well, his clothes nearly the black opposite to my gray and white. I fixed the stray hair around my face and smoothed over my braid, tugging the hem of my tunic down and straightening my spine.

"Beautiful..." Luca whispered from beside me. I looked at him and took deep breaths through my nose and exhaled through my mouth as I flexed my fingers at my sides. He smiled and offered his hand again and we interlocked our fingers as we started up the stairs and pushed open a set of frosted glass doors.

The inside of the temple was stunning and simple. Shining white marble was everywhere. The floors, pillars...the walls. Iridescent light reflected from the surfaces between swirls of silver. The ceilings were high and arched, with a massive crystal chandelier hanging from the center. Narrow arches of frosted glass lined the sides, and the back wall was taken up completely by a dais of the same marble...and in the center of that dais was a blinding orb of white light. It was utterly silent, save for the sound of our footsteps, as we slowly walked to the middle of the chamber. A blurry silhouette formed in the middle of the light and I stopped. A figure of a woman in a flowing white gown stood in the middle with her back turned towards us. My heart pounded when I took in her shining cinnamon hair that flowed like waves of magic down her back. She slowly turned and I stopped breathing. Luca's hand squeezed tight and I widened my eyes as I stared into the face of a woman I had only seen in a portrait beside my bed.

"Mother..."

She smiled softly and stepped barefoot down the two stairs of the dais and the light behind her dimmed, allowing me to see her more clearly. My chest bobbed up and down as I met a pair of emerald eyes that matched my own. She stopped and stared into me and my lip quivered. A tear crept down my cheek and she opened her mouth.

"Arienne..." She said hoarsely, her green eyes lining with tears. She started to raise her arms to reach for me and hesitated, holding them slightly in front of her and watching me closely. Luca let go of my hand and caressed my back before he lowered himself to a knee and bowed his head. I choked on a broken sob and ran to her, falling into her arms and gripping beneath her shoulders as I buried my face into her soft hair.

"Are you real?" I whispered as tears ripped down my face. Her arms held me tighter before releasing me and pulling back to look me over. The painting that had haunted my dreams since I was a child did her no justice. She was flawless and breathtaking.

"Yes..." she nodded, tearfully. "You are more beautiful than I'd ever imagined. I've watched over you...but having you before me, I—" She paused and her gentle fingers touched my face. "Forgive me, my daughter...I beg you. Please forgive me." Her tears sparkled like brilliant diamonds and I couldn't speak. It was clear that she was my mother, of that, I had no doubt...but she also wasn't. She was something else entirely. A goddess...an immortal. And it showed. I found myself letting all my questions drown my mind until I felt nearly suffocated. I almost asked her why she was begging for forgiveness, but in that moment, I understood.

"It was you tonight," I started quietly. "Before I fell asleep." She took my hands and stared into my eyes.

"Yes."

"And outside Aeon? You're the voice I heard?"

"Yes...and the star you saw. I've caused you deep pain. Please understand...it was never my intention. I've loved you from the moment I realized I carried you. I had never known such love."

"Why did you leave?" I asked. I didn't even think to stop myself. Her expression grew despondent and she clung tighter to my hands.

"Would you like to take a walk?" She responded softly. I couldn't hide the surprise on my face. "There is much to say...and I—some of this will be difficult to hear and accept. I don't want you to feel as if the world is collapsing around you. Please, allow me to give you comfort. I know that I don't deserve it, but...it would please me if you—"

"Yes. I'd like that," I smiled. "Would you like to meet Luca?" We both turned our attention to my betrothed, who remained benevolent on his knee. She moved towards him and I followed slowly behind. A soft smile graced her lips as she approached him, kneeling and lifting his chin with a finger.

"Do you know who you are, child of the light?" Luca swallowed as he took her in. "You were chosen to help deliver this world...you shall bow to no one. Rise. Let me look at you." They slowly stood and he looked nearly ready to weep, but said nothing. "You are more than I ever prayed for, young prince. Your heart is so pure...and you love her so fiercely."

"I do, your Majesty. More than anything." He glanced at me and I smiled. "I once told her how badly I wished I could thank you...and now I find the words difficult. I could never truly express my gratitude for choosing me to be here for her." His throat bobbed and she rested a hand on his shoulder.

"I heard you." Her smile grew wider. "Hear *me* when I say, I thank *you*. I'm honored to call you a son." I stepped beside him and he took me by the waist, nodding at my mother and blinking back his emotion. "Come. I'd like to hear about your adventures together," she gestured toward the entrance.

"Don't you already know them?" I asked politely. She nodded.

"I'd rather hear them from the two of you. It would give me great joy. I don't wish to start our relationship with heaviness. Please...spend some time with me? Tell me about yourself. Your joys, your childhood. Whatever memories conjure a smile."

She led us back outside and we walked, talking together and trying to make up for nearly twenty lost years. I found her incredibly easy to converse with and so did Luca. The main reason we had come to her loomed over my mind, but I fought it back relentlessly. I couldn't bring myself to ask her if I'd ever see her again after today for fear of an answer I'd not easily bear. I finally had a mother to cry on, speak to, confide in and trust. The thought of losing her all over again hurt. I knew I couldn't stay here with her. My father had to be stopped. We would have to go back...finish what we had been born to do. After what seemed like a long while, we stopped and sat near the crystal clear mountain lake that looked as if someone laid an enormous mirror before us. We all grew silent, each one of us most likely knowing what we had to address now.

She leaned on her hands in the grass, watching us, as Luca raised his knees at my sides and leaned my back against him. Her white gown pooled around her like a velvet cloud. "You're truly beautiful together. I never expected such a perfect pairing." Her smile faded and she dropped her eyes to the ground. "One day, I hope that you can find it in your heart to understand my reasons for abandoning you and little Paxe." She frowned but jerked her attention back up to me. "But I suppose I can no longer say that. She's also grown into a strong young female and—"

"Wait...abandoning *us?*" I interrupted.

"She was just a small child. I cared very much for her. She was innocent and pure. I knew that making that bargain with the gods would leave her just as exposed to your father's evil as you were. It gave me comfort to know that the two of you would be cared for and that you'd have each other to grow with. She needed you just as much as you would grow to need her. So many details about the decision I made were difficult for me to balance," she explained.

"Start from the beginning. And please don't spare anything. I need to know, Mother."

She took a deep breath and slowly nodded. "Very well. Before I met your father...I loved another. The marriage between he and I had not yet been arranged, and that was a time when humankind wasn't enslaved or oppressed. When my mother and father revealed their intention of marrying me into royalty, it broke my heart. While I tried earnestly to end things and suppress my feelings with my lover...it was never something I could do."

"He was human?" Luca asked.

"Yes. We had grown together since we were children. I had given him my heart without any hope of getting it back. I was never able to, and I didn't *want* it back. After meeting Loren at the castle a few weeks later, I told my lover that we could never pursue a future. My marriage was not in my hands, and I needed to give my best to the prince. It wasn't a horrible match. Your father was charming in his youth. He gave me everything I could have ever wanted...but try as I may, I—" She paused.

"You weren't in love with him," I finished.

"No," she breathed, hanging her head. "No, I felt nothing. Nothing except shame. He deserved my love, but I had given my heart away, and I longed for the one I *truly* loved. Every day became more grueling and my disposition more grim. I knew it had started to become more evident to him months after we had married. Your father adored me. But I became distant and spoke less. I pushed him away, more often than not, when he would try to lie with me. Things became worse as time went on. One night, I was restless...I couldn't bear it any longer. I snuck out of the castle and went to my lover. When we weren't caught...I figured out other ways to see him. Eventually...Loren found out and intercepted a message I had sent by a servant. He found us that evening...and the pain I caused him. The heartbreak. Something inside him awakened. Something that was pure evil," she sniffled and wiped a stray tear from her cheek.

I felt nausea beginning to take in my stomach. This was why he didn't believe love existed. The reason he couldn't look at me without seeing her and bore me such hate. He loved her and she had broken his heart. I had the sinking feeling that what she was revealing was about to get far worse.

"I know what you must be thinking, and you'd be justified. I deceived him. I had broken him and made him into a monster. I'm the reason humans suffer at his hands. Truthfully, the suffering of all our people started because of my selfishness. His hate for their kind began that night. He beheaded him. He locked me in my chambers for days, and when he finally let me out...he led me to the castle gate where he had impaled my lover's head on a spike..." She began to cry harder. "He forced me to look at his severed head while he raped me. And in the weeks that followed, he began enforcing new laws that forbade the blending of our races. Humans were subjected to torture and servitude.

The Midlands were created to keep them contained, and Crona was forced to comply. The king was never the same. The treatment I received was what I had deserved, but...others were receiving it too. Others that did nothing wrong." She calmed her breathing.

"He needed an heir. He reminded me every time he came to bed me that he'd wished I were dead, but I needed to first *make myself useful* and give him a child. For three years, I worried myself sick that one of these times would prove successful and my child would be ripped away from me while he had me burned. It terrified me. But then...one evening I overheard that one of our servants had been badly beaten by Loren...and I sought her out. She had worked for us for years and I knew she'd had a child. I feared for her and the babe, and I wished to protect them. So, I gave her the position to be my aide. I felt responsible for the way he had mistreated her, and then later that month, I discovered I was pregnant with you." She looked at me and her face paled with worry. "What I'm about to tell you will change everything. I won't continue unless you feel ready."

Luca reached down and interlocked our fingers while I started to fight the vomit that wanted to creep up my throat. "Tell me," I said simply, terrified that what I suspected may be true.

"The king..." she started as she glanced for a moment to the ground and then back up to meet my stare. "The king had been raping Isabelle. For months. Isabelle did have a male that she had grown close to, but the situation had scared him off. Loren was aware that she was already with someone, and he's truly oblivious to the truth. After Paxe was born, and he learned her male had fled, the king started beating her again...among other things. I didn't know any of this was happening until Paxe was nearly half a year old. I wish I had known before."

I jumped to my feet and started to struggle with my breathing. Luca stood and I put a hand out to keep him back. "Wait...go back. You just said that Father was oblivious to the truth." I spat, breathing harder. "What you mean to say...is that Paxe...Paxe is—"

"Your sister. His firstborn and heir. And he has no suspicion at all." My mother slowly stood. I started to hyperventilate. Luca steadied my shoulders and I began to feel lightheaded.

"Paxe..." I whispered to no one. "So, when...when I kill him. She'll..."

"Yes." The queen resolved. "His power will pass down to her." I couldn't look at my mother. I couldn't look at Luca, who was rendered speechless behind me. My chest heaved up and down as I turned away from them both and stared over the water.

"She doesn't know about this. Does she?" I gripped the back of my neck.

"No, she doesn't. Isabelle and I agreed that she'd tell her when she was old enough to understand, but we found it difficult to keep her protected if the king found out Paxe was his daughter. Neither of us were certain what he'd do to her, or to you once you were born. His behavior was so unpredictable. We finally decided to keep the truth from all of you until the time came for your Ventus. My mother and father settled in Aeon and I sought out Vetta. I was becoming further along in my pregnancy and wanted to make sure that you and Paxe would be safe and that Isabelle wouldn't have to raise you both on her own if your father chose to kill me." I spun and stared at her.

"And he did kill you..." I breathed. She was silent for a moment and slowly nodded. "What did he do to you, Mother?"

"Loren never tried to bed me while I carried you. He began demanding Isabelle to him in spite. To make it obvious to me that even though I had taken her as my aide, I couldn't stop him from having his way with her. After a while, she revealed to me that when I delivered you, she was to poison me. To taint my water with hemlock and make it look as if I died during childbirth." She swallowed. "I tried to comfort her. I wanted her to know that I accepted my fate and I never blamed her. If she refused or failed in what he wanted her to do, he'd kill her and, possibly, slaughter little Paxe, and you would be alone. I told her that it must be done. On the night that she had revealed his plans to end my life, I laid in bed and I felt you move in my womb for the very first time." Her eyes welled with tears, and she smoothed a hand over her middle, recalling the memory.

"Your kicks were so strong. You were a powerful, tiny little blessing that came out of a nightmare. I wanted so badly to protect you. I had gone to the window and hit my knees...I begged the gods to hear me and tell me what I could do to stop him and..."

"You made a bargain," I finished.

Tears crept down her lovely face and she softly smiled. "I did. I offered the gods my life to right the wrong I had caused. To secure your future...to be sure that you were never alone. To protect your sister. I understand how selfish it seems, and I know that it has caused you deep grief...But Arienne...I felt you. I knew that you could survive this. I knew you could make it. I knew that Luca would show you what real love felt like and that it would strengthen you to allow this warrior for peace to awaken inside." She moved towards me and I backed away. She winced and another tear fell from her eye. Luca stepped forward and took my hand gently, and I met his stare. I felt his magic, and a subtle calm let me know that he was here and that no matter what else we heard next, he wasn't going anywhere.

"I've accepted what I am. I'm having difficulty accepting what I'm not," I choked, staring back at her. "Our people believe I'm their *queen*. They depend on me! If what you say is true...I'm not their queen! *Paxe* is their queen, and you don't know her! She doesn't want that life! She deserves to be *happy*. She deserves to live in peace and raise her baby without fear. What am I to do with this? Do you know what you're asking of me?" I cried. "How can I tell her this? How can you put this responsibility on me? Why am I to be the one to take her joy from her? She just got her hands on it!"

"You're right...." She whispered. "You *all* deserve happiness. I never said that you had to tell her, Arienne. It is your choice to confide in her or let it reveal itself on its own. Paxe wasn't born into royalty as you were. In our people's hearts...you *are* their queen. It is your right by birth. Paxe has always deigned to choose her own path and live as she wishes. I know that she's told you as much. If she doesn't seek to rule, then the crown belongs to you. You may not have the inheritance of power, but you and Luca will be rewarded with something much greater."

"And what is that?" I shook.

"Immortality."

Gods above...it all makes sense.

I thought of the story of the first king. The choices that were given to him and to the others who failed their trials. Immortality, or power. The first king chose power and brought peace to our world. My mother...she chose immortality. She became the goddess of light. Luca was the *bringer of light.* What was I in all of this? I could lift Nero's hammer...I was able to use Luca's abilities, but other than that, I'd proved nothing. Luca's arms pulled me close and wrapped around me. I broke my spiraling thoughts to look at him, realizing the things that my mother was revealing also had a great impact on him.

"I don't care for any immortal life if you're not in it," he said firmly. "I'll follow you down whatever path you choose to take. I'll be your throne. I'll be your light. I'll be your wings if you need to fly away and leave this all behind. I'll see this through with you or stand beside you if you choose to walk away." He placed a hand on my face. "As long as whatever choice you make includes me."

"He is right. You have the power to relieve yourself of this. But if that is what you choose to do, there truly is no other way to stop your father's tyranny. You'll have one another, but he will never cease. Paxe will never be safe. Her child will need to be protected and live its life in secret. The threat will always be there...for you, and for your people until the king no longer lives. It is your choice to make," she warned.

"Nero told me that he found the answer to the mystery of why I was able to wield his hammer. Is it because of you?" I asked.

"Because I live an immortal life...and your blood is shared with mine."

"And Luca's abilities? I can use them."

"You can use them because you are bound to one another spiritually. You both have accepted and secured your ties to each other. You have witnessed the light within him and recognize that light as the home in which you belong. It is the most powerful sort of love that exists."

"How do I break his curse?" I demanded.

"I wish I knew. Although, Nero was correct about the liabilities of agreements sealed with great magic. In my experience...it would be wise to warn you that should you find the answer, breaking it may cost you. While I cannot confirm such a thing, it is something that could be a real possibility. I know nothing more than that. I'm sorry."

I leaned my cheek against Luca's chest and listened to the drumming of his heart while I stared at her. This situation was so complicated. As badly as I wished to tell her to take her dealings and shove them up her ass, I also deeply loved her. I had finally been reunited with the one person I longed to meet my entire existence and yet...I was so angry with her. She was right to beg me for my forgiveness. All of this was her fault. But then, the other half of me that had found love, completely understood why she was unable to leave it behind. I knew that I'd tear the world apart for Luca had that choice been made for me, and he would do the same. Love and death were similar in the sense that neither cared who or what you were.

I also knew that regardless of what decision I chose to make, Paxe was going to inherit overwhelming power. Power *I* didn't even want. What if she didn't want it either? What if she never used it at all and let it rest in her body until her child one day received it while Luca and I rebuilt Valdaro and set things right? She deserved to know the truth but I didn't deserve to have to be the one to give it to her. Mother was right. My father would never stop coming for us. He made that clear enough. We'd never be safe, and my people longed for that. I promised them that. I couldn't walk away from them. Whether she was at fault for what my father became or if it was because of his inability to overcome her rejection...it no longer mattered. This was why I was born. I knew that. Isabelle was probably overridden with guilt and pain. She chose to walk away and never be hurt by my father again. But she left Paxe alone in an impossible predicament. I couldn't do that to her. I wouldn't. If I didn't fight for them, then who would?

I turned my face up to meet Luca's and placed my hand over his mark. He covered my hand with his palm and pressed firmly. "Until death," I whispered. He smiled ardently and slowly nodded.

"I'm with you. Together, love. Until death." He leaned forward and pressed his lips to mine. I softly pulled back and bent over to pull the hunting knife from my boot, straightening and laying the blade flat against my palms while I stepped towards her.

My mother stiffened and her jade eyes misted as she smiled. "I'm so sorry," she breathed. "You should have been allowed a normal life. I hope that one day you can forgive me. I shall bless this for you. Are you certain this is what you choose? It cannot be undone," she warned. I raised my palms to her. I knew who I was. I knew my purpose. I straightened my spine and lifted my chin.

"My name is Arienne Genovese. Princess of Valdaro, daughter of Lucinda....Goddess of Light. Descendant of the first king and deliverer of the calm. I vow to stand with my soulmate and end this suffering. No matter the reason...*and I forgive you, Mother.*"

The queen did her best to hold back her emotion, grazing my cheek with the back of her finger and taking the large knife by the handle. She nodded once and pointed the end towards the skies as she raised it above her head. She recited something in the ancient tongue and a bright light surrounded us. Her voice echoed through the blinding white space like the song she sang when we rushed for the pass. Luca's arms found me as my mother disappeared into the light. I held tight to his body and heard her whisper before we were violently pulled back through the barrier, to the mountain pass.

"I love you, Arienne." Her whisper sounded all around me. *"I shall be with you."*

"I love you too," I whispered back.

The harsh plunge of gravity and darkness roared around us and small flashes of light passed my vision before we landed in a deep drift of snow, our fur cloaks fastened around us, once again.

We stood on unsteady limbs and dusted the snow from our clothes while we kicked out of the drift. The driving snow and bitter wind howled around us near the entrance to the pass and it looked as if we'd never left. Luca and I breathed heavily and looked at one another in confusion.

"We're back?" He huffed, looking around for any sign of the realm we had just left.

I staggered around in a spin, unintentionally doing the same thing and craning my neck to look up at the stormy darkness of the mountain. I felt the firmness of metal in my boot when I turned my foot and looked down to see a shining silver pommel glinting in the dim light from the village.

"Luca..." I called quietly, as I bent down and slowly pulled the weapon from my boot. He stood beside me, and we both gaped wide-eyed at the beauty that used to be a weathered hunting blade.

I now held a masterpiece of a dagger with a depiction in white gold of the North Star on the pummel and a straight, narrow blade that came to a deadly point with ancient runes that glowed white on its flat side. The grip was polished pearlescent marble like the build of my mother's temple and it, eerily, seemed to hum with a faint sound of her angelic voice. Our trials were complete. We had been gifted the last blessed weapon.

"We should take it back to the inn and put it somewhere safe," Luca said, softly.

"I want to leave," I breathed. "Get me out of this place...please." His hand brushed my face and he pressed his head to mine. He didn't bark at me about needing to rest up or try to get me to talk about everything that was on my mind. He simply smiled and nodded his head. He had sworn to be whatever I'd needed and right now...all I needed was for him to be close to me and for us to put some distance between ourselves and this town. I wouldn't be forced away from him tonight. Having this last piece of the puzzle meant that the only thing left to do was take my father down. But before any of that...I was marrying this male. I was ready to go to Crona. Ready to become his wife...and ready to see my *sister.*

CHAPTER 26

TAKING OFF

The inn remained unlit inside, and quiet. There was no sign that the old woman had heard anything at all, which was surprising given the fact that in our hurry to leave and follow my mother's voice, Luca and I had practically broken the stairs. We threw ourselves over the stone wall near the pass with the stealth of a couple of assassins. When we neared the entrance to the inn, Cragan stepped out and eyed us suspiciously.

"A bit late for a hike," he stared, crossing his arms in front of him. "You're lucky I didn't wake Lady Hilda." His greasy hair fell forward over his brows. I stalked towards him, Luca hot on my trail, and made to open the door. He moved himself to block me.

"Let me pass. Or I'd be happy to wake her myself," I growled.

"You're a demanding thing. And so rude. Typical of a royal. Tell me what you're really doing here," he demanded. Luca gently moved me aside and stood close enough to the slick bastard that their noses nearly touched.

"You have two seconds to apologize to my wife and remove your scrawny ass from this door, or so help me, I'll filet you like today's fresh catch," Luca snarled through his teeth. It made my skin heat.

His wife...Gods...

I adored the way it sounded coming from his mouth. Especially when that mouth was spouting off the promise of a swift gutting in my defense.

"Cragan!" Hilda hobbled out the door, her cane knocking against the wooden threshold. She raised it slightly and whacked the back of his legs. He winced and let out a groan, but kept his stance against Luca, who stared him down like prey. "You must have completely lost your wits. Get inside. Now." Cragan backed away and slowly turned into the doorway.

"Just a moment, asshole," Luca added, stopping Cragan in his tracks. The fool didn't turn back to face him. "I didn't hear an apology." Hilda kept quiet and found just about anything else to look at as Cragan turned and tossed the hair from his eyes. He sniffled through his large nose and raised his chin.

"My apologies, *your Highness,*" he bowed mockingly at me.

"What is your problem?" I finally piped up, shoving Luca aside. He chose not to answer and turned into the doorway, walking quickly into the inn and making a right to sit behind the counter. He wasn't quite fast enough. Luca pushed in and jerked Cragan by the back of his tunic, turning him around and shoving him against the side of the counter.

The sliver of a male gaped at him, eyes bulging and his back nearly snapping against the edge of the wooden countertop. Hilda rushed inside as fast as she was able and screeched for mercy while Luca held him by the collar of his shirt and leaned into his face.

"I—I told her I was sorry! Get the hell off of me!" Cragan sniveled.

"You're going to mean it first and then answer her fucking question. You've been a prick ever since we got here," Luca growled.

"I told you, he's a harmless fool! Let him go. He'll answer for his smart mouth. I'll not have this violence in my house." Hilda put a hand on Luca's shoulder. "Please. Calm down and let me explain."

Luca loosened his grip but didn't take his eyes from the male as he stepped back, and Cragan straightened his shirt, his face contorted with rage.

"Lady Hilda, if it's all the same to you, I think I'd rather hear Cragan explain *himself*," I said, leaning against the doorway with my arms crossed.

"Of course...you *would*. It must be nice to travel from place to place, being who you are. To have everyone fawn over you just for being born with a title. If all that isn't enough, you were born privileged as well as attractive. Both of you, in the favor of the gods, just because a pretty crown sits atop your head. Meanwhile, people like us suffer while that head gets bigger and bigger." Cragan's anger seeped through his voice—a voice that rattled with hate.

"Is that what you think?" I asked, pushing myself off the wood of the doorway. "You think that we're privileged because we were born into royalty? That's your reason for—"

"Yes!" Cragan yelped, slapping a palm against the side of the counter. "Yes...I most certainly do. Don't try to tell me it isn't true. You haven't lived like I have."

"You think because I'm a princess that I haven't known suffering?" I snapped.

"Ari...you don't owe him any explanation." Luca put out a hand to stop me. I ignored him.

"No, I think he should know. What reason do I have to be ashamed? I didn't choose this life any more than he chose his. Pathetic though he may be, he's still one of my people. I'll ask you instead. Would you like to know? Or would you rather hold onto that hate?" I moved past Hilda to stand next to Luca, stepping closer to the shaking male.

"My hate is all I have," he trembled. Luca and I bore the same confused expression. "I was never given abilities. The gods found me unworthy. I once traveled to your castle to plead for an audience with the king. I begged to see him after days of travel. He refused. I would have done anything he asked of me to be given power. But he wouldn't give me five minutes of his precious time. Before I submitted to my defeat and traveled back here, I went back to talk to you instead. You wouldn't see me either." He looked into my eyes, and my brows drew together.

"That's why you hate me?" I whispered.

"Isn't that enough? For five years now, I've vowed to one day seek audience with you when you're crowned queen...not to beseech you for the only thing I wanted, but to spit on your throne.”

Five years...

I lowered my head and Luca shook next to me, realizing what I just had and hardly containing his rage. “Arienne...don’t,” Luca seethed.

“It’s alright. He deserves to know why,” I whispered. Hilda shifted on her cane.

“He deserves nothing,” Luca gritted between his teeth.

“Cragan...I wouldn’t have known you were at the castle five years ago...” I slowly raised my face and put a hand against my betrothed, seeking his magic and willing calm into him. I could have sworn I felt him fight me off for a moment but then gently retreat, and his trembling stopped. “I was either locked beneath the castle in a dungeon or up in my chambers alone. No one would have told me you were there to see me even if I had been healthy enough to meet you.” I met his eyes and his brows lowered.

“A dungeon?” He asked. I nodded slowly. “Is this some sort of trick?”

“Shut your mouth Cragan, and listen to her. She’s already giving you more than you deserve to know,” Hilda spat from behind me. Luca faced her.

“Do you know?” He asked.

“Sadly, yes. I’m an old woman. I know more than I desire to. Please don’t feel obligated to tell him more, Princess. While his story seems just...there’s a reason he was denied his abilities.”

I stared into the male whose shoulders tensed at her words. “If you want my honesty, Cragan...I require yours,” I said, raising my chin. He sighed deeply and crossed his arms.

“I’m a bitter person. I always have been. I—” He glanced at Hilda and then back at me as he slowly shook his head. “I’ve always had the misfortune of looking this way. My own mother was ashamed of me. I had little in the way of friends and have never known a single person to love me in any way. I took that out on many. Growing up...I was a horrible person, who was hated by everyone. I even ran a boy off, and to tell you the truth, I felt no remorse for it. None, whatsoever.”

Luca’s head snapped to him in surprise. “Alister?” Cragan’s brows raised.

“You know him?” He asked. Luca didn’t deign to answer and instead slammed his fist into Cragan’s jaw, startling both Hilda and myself. Cragan slumped against the counter, wiping a bit of blood from his mouth and rubbing at his jaw as he stared back at Luca. “I see...” He started, his voice broken while he breathed raggedly from the blow. “So, he did go to Bolton. If you know him, then he must have been successful there. I’m glad. I deserved that...but you didn’t let me finish.” Luca stepped back a few paces and leaned against the wall, rubbing a thumb firmly across his knuckles. “I felt no remorse then. When his mother left Irondale to go be with him...that changed. I felt badly about everything. Terrible, really... even worse when word got back that she recently passed. Alister’s mother was a lovely person. He himself was much like her. But the gods denied me my abilities for the way I treated others." He licked his split lip.

"It's what you deserved," Luca growled, glaring at him.

"You're right. But what does one have to do to redeem himself? I was never given a chance. No one would hear me. No one would let me apologize. At this point in my life...who would care? Or believe me? All it does now is fuel my anger."

"Ha!" Luca laughed loudly. "You don't know anger. I grew up with a mother whose ability is pure, undiluted fury. Even she had to learn to control it. She's the most level-headed person I know. Your rage is not an excuse."

"If you want to seek penance Cragan, you may have to confront that head-on. Alister lives in Bolton. Lord Nero has a genuine love for those with affliction. He also was a great help in teaching me to resolve my hatred for my father. Perhaps, seek audience with him instead? Face Alister...he's a wonderful person. He deserves to hear the words from you," I offered. "Had you been able to meet with me, I assure you...I most likely could have done nothing to restore your abilities even if I wished to. I'm not as privileged as you believe me to be."

"I'm going upstairs. I'll pack our things. I can't bear to hear you give him this." Luca's jaw twitched, and he stepped over, pressing a kiss to my temple and stomping up the stairs. I finally saw Queen Ayla in her son and couldn't stop the slight smile.

"You don't have to tell me anything. I get the feeling I was wrong." Cragan pampered his jaw.

"You were. I'll spare the details. Five years ago...I did something stupid. Something I knew I shouldn't have. I paid a heavy price for that. Aside from that...my father has been just as cruel to me as he has to all our people. For my entire life. You wanted to know the reason I'm truly here? I just met with a goddess who ended up being my deceased mother...who told me things that turned my life upside down and gave me the means to stop him because that is my entire reason for drawing breath. My life's purpose is to right a wrong that wasn't even my fault and save our people. You think I'm privileged? Spoiled? Five years ago, when you came to the castle...I could hardly walk or sit. I was broken in unimaginable ways, both physically and emotionally. My scars run deeper than you know. I have more reason to hate than you do. But instead..." I paused.

"You're sticking your neck out for scum like me," he resolved. We stared at each other for a long moment. "Forgive me."

"Forgive yourself, Cragan. You must first learn to do that before you can start earning it from anyone else. If there is one thing I can understand where you're concerned...it's that letting someone in is incredibly difficult when you feel the way you do. Justified or not, your life will remain this way until you decide to do something about it. I wish you the best of luck." I nodded once, and turned to start up the stairs.

"Princess..." Cragan called. I looked over my shoulder. "...Thank you..." I gave him a side smile and nodded again as I slowly climbed the flight. When I reached the landing at the top, Luca was mostly finished packing us up and met me at my bedroom door. His eyes met mine, and his shoulders sagged as he sighed deeply.

"Do you know how much I love you, Prince?" I smiled, leaning against the door frame. He said nothing and looked at me, dropping the bag on his shoulder to the floor. His expression was so sorrowful and the way he stared into me felt as if I could hear every word he was thinking. Everything he saw the night of our blood union when he rescued me from my darkest place...every time he's ever had to hear about what I had been through. It deeply hurt him.

I closed the space between us and wrapped myself around him, laying my ear against his pounding heart. His arms tightened around me and I felt his warm breath in my hair. "I'm okay, Luca," I whispered against his chest. He squeezed tighter and I returned it, closing my eyes as he exhaled loudly.

"I'm not. I don't know if I ever will be." He kissed my head. "I wish I could have known...to be there and protect you. A part of me dies every time I think about someone hurting you," he breathed, his voice shaky. "It fills me with rage..." I chuckled softly against him and he scoffed. "Why is that funny?"

"I'm sorry," I whispered, pulling back and craning my neck to look up at him. "I just realized only a moment ago that you're equal parts Tidus and Ayla," I grinned. He rolled his eyes.

"Gods..." He smiled slightly and then quirked a brow as if forgetting to tell me something. "Gods! I forgot..." He pulled away quickly and walked to my bed, picking up a folded piece of parchment that was sealed with wax and a stamp of the North Star. "This was here when I came up to pack." He handed it to me, and I flipped it over to see my name written in silver, in flawless penmanship. It was no doubt from my mother. Beneath my name, it read: *Do not open until you are ready to leave Irondale. Open this outside the gates. My wedding gift and my blessing. Congratulations. I love you both.*

I looked up at Luca, whose curiosity matched my own. "Until we're ready to leave? I've been ready to leave since we arrived here," I frowned.

"We could go now, or we can wait and try to sleep. If we leave without visiting Holt, I fear the poor lad will never recover," Luca said, tightening his smile.

"Holt..." I stared at the wall, picturing that sweet little face. "You're right...I promised. Do you think Benjamin and Holt's mother would be angry if we knocked on their door in the middle of the night?" I glanced back at him.

"Not sure...but he did tell you that their door was always open. We could give it a try, if for no other reason than to say goodbye."

"Let's go," I nodded, placing my mother's letter into a pocket inside my cloak. We grabbed our bags and walked downstairs. Cragan and Hilda were sitting quietly by the fire in the small sitting room. We stopped in the doorway and peered in. Cragan was holding a cloth with some ice on his bruising jaw. I fought back the urge to smile. Hilda raised on her cane and clinked toward us with a heavy frown.

"You don't have to go. I'm deeply sorry about all of this," she hung her head. I placed a gentle hand on her shoulder.

"Don't apologize. We did what we came to do. We have an incredibly long journey ahead of us. We appreciate your hospitality, but..." I looked at Luca. "I'm ready to marry. I don't want to wait any longer." I faced her again and she smiled. Cragan raised from the small couch and softly nodded at Luca.

"I'm sorry. Truly. Congratulations to you," he smiled. I nudged Luca in the ribs and he grunted, dipping his chin and thanking Cragan. "Should I get your horses saddled?"

"If you don't mind, Cragan. We have a stop to make first...we'll come back to the stable and meet you. I appreciate your help," I said softly.

"Going to see the boy?" Hilda asked. I nodded. "Don't expect to leave until the morning, child. Benjamin and his wife Mora are gracious hosts. You'll be fed and offered a warm place to sleep. I wouldn't turn their offer away."

"I'll prepare them, Princess, and sleep here in case you decide to wait until dawn," Cragan gestured to the couch.

"Thank you, both." I politely said, smiling as we pulled the heavy door open. I decided not to look back and ignored the tightness in my stomach as we stepped outside into the blustery snow. A small part of me felt bad about how ungrateful I must have seemed to them, but I wasn't sure how to convey the way this whole place had weighed me down since we first entered the gates. I felt even heavier now, knowing the truth about everything that had been a close-kept secret all my life, and I hoped that she understood why I couldn't stay, if she was being honest about knowing more than she desired to.

I found myself walking faster than I had realized through the empty street as we neared the door to Benjamin's small cottage. Without thinking, my knuckles peppered the wooden door and the light from a lantern moved across the window. The door creaked open and Holt's father stood warily behind it, rubbing his eyes to make sure he was seeing correctly.

"Sir Benjamin? I'm so sorry to wake you," I said softly, placing a hand to my buckle on my cloak.

"Princess? My Lord? Is everything alright?" Benjamin opened the door wider and looked around us.

"Everything is fine. I know that it's late and I do apologize. We're leaving town and I was hoping to see your son before we do."

Benjamin appeared shocked but stood aside to usher us in from the cold. "Holt? You came back to see him? Has he done something?" He asked, closing the door.

"Nothing further than making an impression on me. I promised him that I'd say goodbye, and I'm one to keep my word. He's truly a fine young boy," I smiled. Luca pulled an arm around my shoulder.

"Forgive me, I'm in a state of shock. I never expected to meet you, let alone have the two of you inside my home. Please...come inside and warm yourselves. I'll add a few logs to the fire and fetch my wife."

"You're too slow, Ben," a soft female voice sounded from a hallway to our left. "Mend that fire and light some lamps, would you?" Her lovely face appeared out of the darkness of the hall at about waist height to Luca and I. We were standing in a small kitchen that extended out into a family room with a small couch placed against the wall on the left, a fireplace on the back wall, and a deep armchair near the wall on the right. It took a moment to realize she was in a wheelchair before she was finally exposed to the light of the fireplace. She had high cheekbones and a slender jawline with beautiful blue, almond-shaped eyes and blonde hair that was braided into a coronet. "Your Highness...my Lord...it's an honor to have you. I'm Mora," she bowed her head. "Please, make yourselves at home." She waved a hand towards the living area where Ben was nervously poking at the fire and brightening the oil lamps around the room.

"Thank you so much," Luca smiled as he led me to the couch. We sat and waited for Mora to move to a place by the armchair that I soon realized was the reason the furniture was placed this way. She faced us and tossed a blanket over her bare legs as she made herself comfortable in the wooden wheelchair.

"Holt told me much about his experience with you today, Mi'lady. He'll be very sad to know you're leaving. Though, if I may, I'm a bit surprised to see you leave us so soon. Unless..." She paused and cautiously looked me over.

"Unless I met my mother?" I finished for her. Her face grew pale and Benjamin stopped fidgeting, straightening himself and staring at us as if begging to spare her life. "It's alright, you can relax. I'm not my father. I'm growing very accustomed to surprises since leaving home," I smiled sweetly. "But yes...I met her. I believe you knew. Holt had almost slipped up at the inn before Lady Hilda hushed him."

"Did he?" Benjamin's mouth dropped open. "I'm so sorry...what did he say?" I waved my hand back and forth in front of me.

"No, no...he's perfectly fine. I'm alright. Really. I think part of me suspected before I even got here. Holt had just mentioned that his mother told him the goddess had been waiting for me for a very long time."

"I did tell him that, Mi'lady. I apologize. When we learned that you were coming, he got very excited. Too excited really. He's always been that way, but I mostly wanted him to know that you weren't coming to visit *him*...and that you had very important matters to take care of with the goddess in the mountain. Of course...Holt has a great many questions," she laughed. "But yes...I did know about your mother. I used to live in Aeon and knew her personally."

She looked sympathetically at me and had I not just been blindsided by so much, where my mother was concerned, I would have probably asked her questions about what my mother was like before she was forced to marry my father. I felt as if I owed Mora some sort of explanation so that she wouldn't think of me the way that Lady Hilda probably did right about now. "Perhaps you can tell me a bit more another time. I'd be interested to hear all about her. I'm afraid I've been overstimulated for one day, though. I'm sorry." I gave her a half smile. She returned it in kind and softly nodded.

"You both look thoroughly exhausted. Did you not wish to rest before venturing back out again?" Benjamin asked. Luca chuckled through his nose.

"There were some slight complications at the inn," he laughed. Benjamin gave him an understanding grin.

"Lady Hilda separated you?" He glanced at Mora, who giggled. "She can be a testy old bat, but I promise, she's all bark. It's a shame you didn't stay long enough to have some of her cooking, though. That may be the only good thing about an old woman who's set in her ways," he laughed. A shuffling of more than one set of footsteps sounded from the hallway, and Holt appeared with Kyna through the darkness.

"Ma? I heard—Princess!" He shouted happily, rubbing both hands across his sleepy little eyes and running across the room to hurl himself into my lap.

Oh, my heart...what a little doll.

His small arms wrapped around my neck, and he snuggled into me like he'd known me all his life. Luca watched with an expression I'd never seen before, and a part of me melted at the smile that etched his face. I could just about guess what was on his mind. "Hi, love. How is my little escort?" I beamed as he pulled back to look at me. "Did you make sure everyone saw you when you came back home?" I giggled.

"Yeah! Are you staying here? I thought you were gonna stay with *Miss Hilda.* Did she say she was gonna whoop ya with her stick? Sometimes sh—"

"Holt..." Mora smiled. "Settle down. You know better." Her voice was soothing but firm. His little muscles slackened as he nodded cautiously and returned his attention to me.

"Sorry..." He shrugged. Luca fought back a laugh. "Did you go see the goddess?"

"I did, actually." I repositioned him across my lap and covered his little bare feet with my cloak. His eyebrows shot up and Kyna nudged Luca's leg for attention.

"So you crossed over the wall? And you didn't get dead?" He looked over me for injuries.

"I did, yes...but..." I held up a finger. "I only crossed that wall because I was asked to. You still have to promise me that you'll never go there, okay? Prince Luca and I can safely say we never want to go there again."

"That is correct," Luca added, giving Kyna a good scratching behind her ears with both hands. "I'm big and strong, and still wouldn't go back."

"Wow...yeah, I promise. What did she look like? Was she nice, like you?" He went on, his little fingers fidgeting with the clasp of my cloak.

"She looks a bit like me, but with red hair. And yes, she was very nice. I came to see you because now that I've met the goddess, it's time for us to leave. I made you a promise too, remember?" He looked up at me and the light in his eyes dwindled. It tugged at my heart.

"Aww, I don't want you to leave yet...you just got here! I wanted to show you the snow castle I built for you. I worked real hard on it!" He frowned. Luca and I glanced at each other.

"Won't you stay for the night? Let us make you a hot meal, at the very least, before you cross? It's a dreadfully long way to your city, my Lord," Mora pleaded.

"Yeah! Stay here with me! Ma's such a good cooker. But you gotta clean your plate, or she'll make you sit in the corner," he folded his arms. I couldn't help but bite my lip as all of us laughed.

"Holt...son, please," Benjamin chuckled.

"She'll stay, little lord," Luca snickered. "I'll make her." I didn't even argue as I pressed my cheek to the little boy's head and rocked him back and forth. Luca and I talked quietly to Ben and Mora until Holt had fallen asleep in my arms. We had taken our cloaks off as well as our boots, and I had nearly dozed off before Luca covered us with his cloak like a blanket. I stretched out and laid my feet into Luca's lap, wrapping an arm around Holt to keep him from falling off the edge. He laid his little head in the crook of my shoulder and Luca leaned over to rest against me. It felt strangely perfect.

Benjamin and Mora thankfully allowed Holt to stay put and didn't move him as they added another log onto the fire and dimmed the oil lamps before returning to their room for the night. They asked several times if we were sure there wasn't any way they could convince us to take their bed instead, but if they only knew how absolutely content I was for the first time since coming here...I closed my eyes and quickly fell asleep, clutching the sweet little snoring child.

We awoke a few hours later to the smell of bacon and coffee. None of us had really moved an inch since we had fallen asleep. Holt had an impressive puddle of drool on my tunic and when I raised my head, Kyna had climbed onto the couch and was snuggled up against Luca, who was hardly able to keep his eyes open. I glanced over at Ben and Mora, who were busily preparing things in the kitchen, surprised at how well she managed everything in her chair. It didn't slow her down a beat, and she moved with such grace that one wouldn't believe she was impaired at all. I envied her confidence and general disregard for her disability. I needed to be a bit more like that.

"Good morning!" Mora called from the kitchen, wiping her hands off on a towel and wheeling over to the side of the couch. "Were you able to sleep with him suffocating you like that?" She teased as she brushed the little boy's hair from his face.

"He's a joy. You're very fortunate. I appreciate you letting me snuggle him all night. I know that may have seemed a bit unorthodox," I smiled.

"Not at all. He adores you. Holt is a champion snuggler. Although, I am surprised you're not bruised from the waist down. He also kicks like a mule," she laughed. Luca sat up and the wolf promptly licked every inch of his face. "That one you can take with you, though."

"Ah, she's a good girl," Luca soothed, petting her soft coat. "You're kinder than my mother. She never allowed me to have a dog."

"If it *were* a dog, I'd not mind so much," Mora chuckled. "That beast was never meant to be indoors. She's a sweet one, but she's huge and her hair covers the entire house."

"Holt mentioned that," I laughed softly. "Where did she come from?"

"He brought her home one afternoon after being out near the woodline, just outside the gates? He and his friends found her by herself and she was barely alive. She may have been a couple of months old. For whatever reason, her pack abandoned her. I didn't have the heart to turn her out, but I soon regretted that decision. She got so large so quickly. Holt loves her. She's devoted to him, so I suppose it's a bit late to turn back." We looked down at the little boy who had started stirring in my arms. He peeled his eyelids open and looked at his mother and then at me, smiling.

"Ma made bacon," he said sleepily, wiping at the side of his mouth as he raised up. "That smells good!"

"Better hurry, I love bacon," Luca said with a wink. "Might not be any left if I get there before you do." Holt looked back at me with drawn brows.

"You're gonna marry him?" He asked with complete sincerity. Mora and I burst into laughter and Luca's mouth dropped open before he wedged a finger under Holt's arm and mercilessly tickled him. Adorable cackles ensued and the little one begged for mercy. Breakfast was delicious and reminded me of Vetta. I felt as if we were back at the little table in Aeon, laughing over food and sipping coffee from warm mugs. The comfort this little family offered was everything I didn't realize I'd needed. It seemed Luca felt that way too, and before we were finished eating, Holt's loyalty to me was divided evenly between the two of us. I felt sad that I'd have to see the frown on his little face and prayed he wouldn't cry when we left.

Mora allowed me to help with dishes and cleanup. After breakfast, I followed Holt outside to see the snow castle he'd built, which we were forced to reconstruct after last night's fresh covering of snow. He introduced me to several of his equally tiny friends and they convinced Luca and I to build our first-ever snowmen. Once they were satisfied with the sorry excuses for snow people, we were taught how to make snow angels as well. The townspeople gathered to enjoy the spectacle, and the heaviness I felt when we had first come here virtually disappeared.

When the clock tower in the square rang nearly noon, I passed out affection to each one of the children and shook hands with their families. I saved Holt for last, and try as he might, he couldn't hide his pout as I picked him up and hugged him tight.

"Alright, little royal escort. Time to be brave, yes? You don't want your friends to see you weep." I tried to take my own advice as his little lip trembled and he nodded. "This isn't goodbye. We'll see each other again soon, okay? Until then, you have to keep your promise and do as your parents tell you. No going over the wall. Take good care of Kyna and watch out for Miss Hilda's stick," I smiled.

"I will, Princess," he sniffled. I flicked his pink nose.

"You can call me Ari. That's what my dearest friends call me. And you're definitely that." I glanced at Luca, who reached his arms out for a turn. Holt leaned over and grabbed onto him, leaning his head on Luca's shoulder.

"Ahhh, don't worry. We'll come back, lad. You mind your Ma and Pa. I'll be checking in on you." Holt raised and looked at him. My heart ached in the warmest way.

"Will you write?" Holt asked.

"I sure will. You be looking out for my letter. And..." Luca reached into his pocket and pulled out the charm that Nero had made him. "Here. This is *very* special to me. You hold onto it, alright?" I pressed a hand to my chest.

"Is that you, Ari?" Holt asked, holding the tiny statue up and comparing it to my face.

"It sure is. Lord Nero made that himself. You're very lucky. Prince Luca must think very highly of you to give you that." He held it close to his heart and blinked back tears. I stepped closer and hugged them both.

"I love you guys," he sniffled. I had to swallow the lump in my throat to keep from bursting into tears.

"You mean to make me look less of a male today, don't you kid?" Luca smiled with glassy eyes. I pressed a kiss to Holt's frozen cheek.

"We love you back, little guy," I whispered. We looked over to Ben and Mora, who were watching from the steps of the back stoop. Luca walked toward them and placed Holt into Mora's lap. "Ben...Mora. Thank you both so much. We'll never forget your kindness." Ben stepped forward.

"Princess...you and your prince have changed lives all over this town in a matter of hours. Please. Thank *you*. Both of you. We look forward to hearing all about your nuptials. Congratulations to you, and safe travels." He extended his hand and I took it, shaking gently. I bent over and hugged Mora, who was becoming a bit emotional, and had to quickly pull away before I found it any more difficult to leave.

We shouldered our bags and pulled the hoods over our heads, and as we walked out front, Cragan met us in the street with our horses. His jaw was good and bruised now and his lip had closed up, but was puffy at the side and darker in color. I felt a twinge of guilt, but it was short-lived when I thought of Alister, and I smiled politely as we approached.

"Lady Hilda packed a few things for you to eat on the trip. They should keep for a while. I hope you both find your way safely," Cragan smiled genuinely and handed us the leads.

"Thank you," I dipped my chin. Luca followed suit.

"Sorry about your lip, brother." Luca patted his shoulder.

"No, don't be. I kind of like it. Makes me appear tough, yeah?" Cragan grinned, wincing and licking the split on his lip. I laughed loudly as I mounted my horse. The gate tenders turned the cranks to let us out and Luca hopped into his saddle.

"Good luck in Bolton. You'll be fine. Alister's a good one. Lord Nero makes one hell of a friend." Luca nodded and we waved at Holt and the townspeople as we trotted out of the gateway. Holt was full-on crying now, and it took everything in me to turn away. Once the gates closed behind us and we weren't far from the wall, I waved an arm to get Luca's attention and pulled my mother's letter from my cloak.

"Should we see what this is all about?" I asked, my fingers eagerly tapping the seal.

"Absolutely. Crack her open."

So I did.

A bright light flashed all around us and the hiss of magic and the townspeople's yelping filled my ears. We were completely blinded and I panicked for a moment when I could no longer see Luca or his horse. I heard my mother's voice singing through the light.

"May your marriage be blessed, and your travels be swift. May your dreams be fulfilled as you cherish this gift. For I know how you wished to be able to fly, enjoy life together as you tear through this sky...I love you."

The light receded and I refused to breathe as I took in the sight of enormous white wings that spanned across Alice's muscular frame. I jerked my attention to Luca, who was equally shocked as he sat atop Bjourne, who now had raven-black feathers that fluttered against Luca's legs. Every single body within Irondale ran through the gates as they slowly opened up to allow them past the wall to witness it.

"I—I can't believe it," I gaped, trailing a finger across the immaculate white feathers. The horses huffed and trotted in place, nearly bursting with the need to leave the ground.

"Are you ready to taste the sky, love?" Luca beamed as he made sure everything was secured tightly on his horse. I twisted around to do the same and let out an excited squeal as a tear escaped my eye.

"Thank you, Mother..." I whispered. I could have sworn I felt the warmth of a phantom embrace as I gave Luca a nod and we tore across the snow, gaining speed and riding as fast as our horses could manage before they spread their wings and gave a strong leap from the ground. We took flight beside each other and I yelled in joy as Irondale got smaller beneath us with every thrust of Alice's wings. I looked over at Luca, who couldn't stop smiling.

His arms raised to his sides and he whooped loudly. I did the same as we sailed through and over clouds. It was what I could imagine the heavens to look like, and I breathed deeply as I let my head fall back. My arms caught the wind and I moved my fingers through it. It was more than I could have ever dreamed of.

"I love you!" Luca called from beside me. I looked over and smiled wide.

"I love you!" I shouted.

We embraced the sun and made to leave Valdaro behind as we sailed across an ocean of clouds...

To Crona.

CHAPTER 27

HOME

Flying wasn't anywhere near as exhausting as dredging across terrain. Bjourne and Alice seemed as if they were no closer to tiring than they were when we left, and it had been hours. When the castle I used to call home had appeared below, we had flown higher into the safety of the clouds. If my father had sensed my presence, it didn't show. I desperately wished I could swoop down and visit Hissifus, or at the very least, steal him away from his new companion and take him with us. Although I doubted very seriously that he'd be much for flying.

The Midlands seemed bigger than they appeared on the maps I had grown up seeing. It still didn't make me feel any less terrible for the humans that were enslaved and contained in them like a prison. My skin crawled at the thought of a child like Holt being subjected to torture, or someone like Ben or Mora. We didn't venture close enough to make out the way that the humans lived. I wasn't sure I could stomach it. I felt horrible for not making an appearance, but Luca also reminded me that it was a risk we couldn't afford to take just yet. In time, the Midlands would be no more than a place to settle and rebuild between Crona and Valdaro. Somewhere safe that people could *choose* to live rather than be forced.

The vast grasslands between the Midlands and the city where Luca lived were much like the ones we had traveled across, only greener. I caught a familiar scent in the air, and the humidity increased. I looked over at Luca, who had leaned forward, and his face and body changed completely. He turned that lovely face towards me and the joy that swept across him, I felt from yards away. He was home. We descended beneath the towering puffs of white clouds and the Crimson Sea came into view. It was peculiar to be called such a thing as its color was anything but crimson. A large, beautiful city was nestled into the curve of the shore, and the water matched the turquoise color of circular, dome-shaped rooftops that sat atop round white buildings covered in ornate windows. Luca pointed north and I looked over. A massive white castle stood high over the city. It looked like a much more gargantuan version of the snow castle Holt had built.

It glittered in the sunlight that reflected from the beach, like a beacon guiding us home. The people inside it were as close as one could get to feeling exactly that way, and knowing I'd walk through those doors with this male at my side, filled me with warmth I never thought I'd come to know. Luca sported a smile that showed all of his teeth as his dark hair shone in the sunlight, blowing away from his face and making him appear as if that light he carried inside him had somehow burst from his skin.

"Welcome home!" He shouted over the roar of the wind. I grinned and nodded into the direction of the castle. He leaned left and guided Bjourne down towards it and Alice followed close behind. As we neared the white cobbled streets at the edge of the city, Crona's denizens stood and watched us in awe. Luca's name was shouted by nearly all of them as they waved us in. Children gaped at the mythical beasts that we flew in on. As far as I was aware, no one had ever experienced the sky. Creatures like Alice and Bjourne didn't exist...until now. It did cross my mind a time or two, on our journey here, that the sea monsters from our books and Nero's paintings could possibly exist as well.

Hooves clacked against the street as we touched down and Alice's wings fluttered a couple of times more before she rested them at her sides. Everyone stared and chattered, most of them standing back. Luca ran a hand through his windblown hair and waved at several who he recognized on the street. I overheard a few loud whispers around us and could barely make out that they were talking about me. As I'd never been anywhere other than the castle all my life, I half expected as much. Nothing I heard was derogatory, but more surprised that we were here. We never sent word to Luca's parents or to Paxe, and I was eager to see the looks on their faces as well. Luca moved closer and reached for my hand with a proud smile. I took it gingerly, and the crowd cleared a path for us as a large, white stone archway stood before us; its enormous gate already lifted to invite us into the long castle entrance.

We rode side by side, and several of the guards standing watch saluted Luca after the shock had worn off at what they were seeing...and who. Luca raised a finger over his lips for the guards to keep our arrival quiet. We stopped at the open, sunny entrance to a small courtyard that led into the castle and finally dismounted. Luca helped me down and I unfastened my heavy cloak, laying it across the saddle. It was warm here.

"I guess this is the last of me having you all to myself," he snorted, pressing against me as his hands took my waist. I put my arms around his neck and leaned into him, our heads touching. "When Paxe and my mother aren't demanding your attention, what would you say to sneaking around the castle in the dark?" He smiled.

"That sounds...devious," I grinned. "I don't want to get on your mother's bad side." He laughed through his nose and pulled me closer.

"I don't think you'll have to worry about that. I finally have you...here. In my home. I've waited for this my entire life, Arienne. Everybody knows it. And, when we do actually leave Crona..." He closed his eyes and sighed.

"I'll be your wife," I breathed.

"We're so close." His lips pressed against mine. "So close, love." A guard shifted on his feet close by and we paused. Luca smiled against my mouth and hissed. "Let's go make a scene," he chuckled. We pulled back and I untied my unruly hair, fluffing it out of my braid and combing through it with my fingers. I handed Luca the strap, which he, of course, tied around my neck. He dropped off his cloak and we strapped on our weapons, deciding that even though they were safe in Crona, it would still be a better idea to keep them close. Luca motioned quietly for the guards to help with the horses. The two that came over were a bit apprehensive as they approached the gorgeous creatures, but we assured them that they were docile and safe. Luca flipped a piece of silver to each one and they agreed to take them to the palace stables and bring in our belongings.

We crossed the courtyard, which was beautifully maintained with odd-shaped coastal trees and crescent pools lined with turquoise tiles that gleamed beneath the water in the sunlight. Around the expanse of the courtyard were open hallways lined with stained glass windows that depicted Varuna in a siren form. Others were decorated in colored glass that looked like ocean waves. Balmy, warm light shone through them, casting colorful reflections on the white stone floors. We walked hand in hand through the halls until we reached a large chamber with a pearl white staircase. Huge conch shells decorated the ends of the banister and castle attendants scrambled about. Several of them gasped at the sight of us, and Luca silently begged them for secrecy. One older gentleman smiled and pointed up the stairs at a set of turquoise double doors that stretched from the floor to the ceiling.

"That's my father's study," he whispered as we climbed the first few steps. "Mother calls it his sanctuary. I'm not surprised that he's in there. It's where he spends almost all his time."

"What does your mother do in her spare time?" I asked curiously. He smiled.

"I'd rather show you. Let's go make his day first, and then he'll take us to see her." We reached the landing at the top of the stairs and Luca quietly pulled one of the doors open to peek his head inside. He tugged at my hand, and I followed him into the doorway as he shut it softly behind us.

The study was, in fact, an entire library. One that put ours to shame, to be honest. Everything about my castle in Valdaro was dark and miserable. This palace was absolutely the opposite. Bright, clean and teeming with life and different hues of aqua and blue that blended so well with the white castle. It was so inviting...and this library. I didn't have words. Luca gave me a moment to take it in as he walked us slowly down a deep blue carpet. Instead of rows of shelving, all the books took up space on built-in shelves on the walls. Every wall in the circular room was covered in different colored tomes until it reached an upper level where more books reached to its glass dome ceiling. The glass was the same color as the rooftops in the city. At the back of the study was a large fireplace that was unlit, with a mantle that housed more books and an enormous painting of the royal family that included an infant Luca perched on the queen's lap. I couldn't stop smiling at it.

A beautiful mahogany desk stretched across the front of the fireplace, and in the middle of the desk, King Tidus bent over, his back facing us as we crept quietly across the room.

"What a gorgeous backside. I know a few females that would pay top coin for those fresh baked buns," Luca said loudly, grinning from ear to ear as the king startled and spun around. I covered my mouth and giggled softly.

The king's mouth dropped open in a huge smile as he clapped his hands together and threw his arms out, rushing towards us, almost tearfully. "Gods be damned. You're home!" He said as he and Luca embraced. He slapped Luca on the back and took his shoulders as he smiled at his boy. I felt envious for a brief moment of their relationship. "Don't talk about my buns in front of the lady, fool," he laughed, turning his attention to me. "Princess..." He grinned, wrapping me in a tight hug. "Welcome to Crona, lovely girl. It's good to see you again."

"It's good to see you too, your Highness. It's so beautiful here," I said, pulling back.

"Different world, isn't it? I'm so happy you were able to come." He looked wide-eyed at Luca. "Your mother is going to *shit*...I apologize, Arienne. I'm a bit too comfortable in this room."

I laughed and shook my head. "No need. I've quite the vocabulary myself."

"Understatement," Luca argued, pulling an arm around my waist.

"Why didn't you tell me you were coming? And how the hell did you get here so fast? Did you even go to Irondale?" The king asked, crossing his arms in front of him.

"We did...we're finished," Luca answered. Tidus raised his brows. "With everything. We wanted to surprise you and Mother...and as for our transportation..." He glanced sidelong at me, and we both smiled. "That you'd have to see to believe. We've got a great deal to talk about."

"Very well. Can't wait to hear about it." He looked between us as Luca pulled me closer and grinned. "You look happy. Something's changed." My face flushed, and I brought my left hand forward. Tidus looked down and pressed his palms together as he raised his eyes to the ceiling, as if in thanks to the gods. "I won't weep."

"You're getting soft in your old age, Pop," Luca laughed.

"Perhaps," he chuckled, hugging us both. "We need to celebrate."

"Not just yet...we should talk first," Luca smiled. The king conceded a step. "Let's wait for Mother." Tidus nodded and clapped him on the shoulder.

"Are you ready to go give her heart failure?" He laughed.

"Lead the way," Luca grinned.

We followed the king down hallways and bright staircases until we reached a single red door at the end of a long corridor. Outside the many windows, I could tell that this part of the castle overlooked the sea. It was also much brighter than the other spots we'd traveled through. On the other side of the door, there was a loud crash and an impressive string of loud curses. I stepped back, tugging on Luca's hand. He and the king looked over their shoulders, smiling.

"Not to worry, Arienne. This is a daily occurrence," Tidus smirked, pushing open the scarlet door.

"Fucking pile of horse sh—"

"Darling!" The king interrupted. "Take a breather."

Queen Ayla didn't turn around as we quietly stepped inside a small studio filled with pottery, paintings and a giant unfinished sculpture of a roaring lion that she was chiseling at as she leaned over a small ladder. "Get out! Don't tell me what I need to do!" She barked.

I crossed my arms and watched her in fascination. What an extraordinary female. Her red short-sleeved tunic was dusted around the smock she wore with powdered bits of white stone and there were handprints on her dark leggings that suggested she'd been in here for quite a while. I smiled in admiration as she tediously hacked away at the sculpture. Luca stepped behind me and wrapped his arms around my middle.

"Amazing, isn't she?" He whispered in my ear, resting his chin on my shoulder as we continued to watch her.

"Incredibly," I whispered back. "I'm in love," I giggled quietly. He laughed through his nose.

"Ayla..." Tidus called. She jerked her chin over her shoulder and opened her mouth, to no doubt lash him again, before her eyes stopped on Luca and I. The tools in her hands clattered to the stone floor.

"Luca?!" She cried, leaping from the ladder and running to us. Luca stepped to the side and caught her in his arms and she wept loudly. "Oh, my gods...oh my gods..." She pulled back and put her messy palms on each side of his face. "What the hell are you doing here?" She kissed his face repeatedly. Tidus crossed his arms and stepped beside me.

"I think she still believes that boy to be five years old," he smiled.

"He doesn't seem to mind," I laughed.

"Arienne!" She wiped at her face and jogged over to me, pulling me into a powerful hug. I wrapped my arms tight around her, even though I had only met her once. I felt like I knew her already, as much as Luca had spoken about her, and she embraced me like she was the happiest she'd ever been. "Darling girl..." She didn't let go as she looked me over. "What a surprise! Look at you!" She sniffled. "Forgive my obscenities...I wasn't expecting—"

"You don't have to do that, Mother. I already explained to Father tha—"

"Oh, you mean she has a mouth like yours, boy?" She glanced behind her at Luca, whose clothes were now covered in white dust.

"Precisely," he beamed.

"Well...doesn't make it acceptable. I'll work on that while you're here. That being said...why are you two here? It's certainly not that I'm not completely ecstatic, but the last I heard was that you were headed for Irondale." She released me and stood next to the king. Luca returned to his spot behind me and pressed me close to him. She watched the movement and her eyes lifted in happiness.

"They've already been, apparently...and your son has something to tell you," Tidus answered for us, nodding at Luca, who pressed a chaste kiss to my neck and slid his hand down my left arm to raise the engagement ring to his mother. Her mouth fell open, and her eyes bulged as she placed a hand over her chest. She jerked her attention back to us and tears lined her eyes.

"You asked her!" She gasped. "Ohh..." She hugged us both and smiled at me. "I told you, it's not always so bad."

"That you did, Mi'lady. I do want to apologize for my tantrum when I last saw you. It was terrible of me...I'm so sorry," I lowered my head.

"I'd hardly call that a tantrum. You, no doubt, heard me through that door. No apologies. I'm so happy the two of you found love. That's the most wonderful news. We should throw an engagement ball!" She looked at Tidus.

"I thought the same, but I believe there's a bit more." They both looked back at us.

"Correct. If you'll give us some time to wash up and change, we'd like to discuss everything at dinner," Luca offered.

"Yes, that would be wonderful!" Ayla clapped. I grew quiet at another thought and looked at the queen in earnest. "What's wrong, cherub?" She asked sweetly.

"Paxe...is she—she's here, right?" My voice shook.

"Oh, yes, of course. She should be with the healer at the moment. Shall I take you to her? She'll be so happy to see you." She placed a hand on my shoulder.

"A healer? Is she well?" I panicked.

"Yes, yes. She's doing very well, actually. The healer checks up on her at the end of every week to make sure that she and the child are progressing as they should. She hasn't been sick as often and she's feeling much better. Come, I'll show you."

"No..." I gently brushed my fingers to her arm. "I'd like to surprise her. Don't let her know that we're here, just yet. We'll come in late to dinner," I smiled. It wasn't a lie. I did want to surprise her, but I also was incredibly nervous about what I would say or feel when I faced her again. I'd been missing her so badly, but now that I knew the truth...I was still warring with the decision of whether or not I should tell her *everything*.

"Very well. That's a great idea. We'll keep it a secret," she winked. Tidus nodded and looked at Luca.

"Why don't you show Arienne to your chambers? You only have about an hour before supper," he gestured to the window.

"Is that alright with you, Mother?" Luca asked. The queen crossed her arms.

"Luca Di Meo. You know very well what I find appropriate and what I do not. I should hardly think you would believe that I'm unaware of what the two of you may or may not have done." My face heated and I knew I had to be as red as her tunic. "But this isn't some infatuation. She is to be your wife. I've absolutely no problem with you sharing a bed. Unless, of course, you'd prefer to have your own chambers, Princess. I can certainly arrange that for you." She smiled.

"Oh no, Mi'lady. I do appreciate it. I'm a bit out of my wits when he isn't close." Luca squeezed and laid his chin back on my shoulder.

"I'm very happy to hear that." Her smile grew wider. "I'll have a few gowns sent to his rooms for you. Get going, Luca. You really need a wash, child."

Luca scoffed and I bit down my laugh as we dipped our chins and turned to leave. Luca's chambers weren't far from the queen's studio and were twice the size of mine back in Valdaro. His door was tucked at the end of a private corridor, and as we entered, it was dark inside as his deep blue curtains had been drawn while he was away. He led me inside and closed the door, pulling the curtains back to reveal an incredibly tidy and spacious bed chamber. His bed was bigger than the one we shared in Bolton and was lined up against the back wall. The paint on the masterfully carved headboard matched the color of the curtains as it towered above the mattress. His bedding was a lighter blue, and there were several large pillows that were neatly placed against the back. Long, narrow windows took up both sides of the bed and a small table sat in front of each one, with lamps resting on both. A large rug ran across the white marble floor at the foot of his bed and a huge bookshelf filled to capacity took up the wall to my left.

On the right wall, between two doors, was a good-sized desk with miscellaneous trinkets and a fat, stubby candle that had been half destroyed. He opened the door to the right of the desk and showed me into an equally large bathing room with a washing basin and a claw foot tub big enough for two people. He pulled the curtain open to a modest stained glass window and then showed me to the other door to the left of the desk. This was a comfortable sitting room with a fireplace to the right, a circular rug that rested beneath two large leather armchairs, and an assortment of weaponry. Framed drawings of different weapons hung on the walls between sconces. The back of the room opened to a small area with two armoires on each side and a set of windowed double doors. He unlatched them, propped them open and led me out onto a small white balcony that overlooked the sea. The sun was beginning to set and the clouds became a band of gold over the bright water. It was breathtaking.

"I really love it here, Luca. It's so calm and peaceful." I stretched my arms and breathed in the warm salt air. He stepped beside me and looked out over the ocean.

"Now you understand why I was so intrigued by the forest?" He laughed.

"I do. Though, I'd trade that forest in a heartbeat for this. Why don't we just demolish that castle and let it grow over?" I watched the sun touch the water. "I'd be happy to never see that place again."

He turned me to face him and brushed the hair from my face. "My kingdom is your kingdom, Princess. Always." My throat bobbed and I swallowed hard.

"I love you," I whispered.

"Mmhh," he grunted, kissing my forehead. "I love *you*. I felt you in my mother's studio. You're worried. Feel like talking about it?"

I trailed a fingertip down his neck. "I can't tell her. I'm nervous about seeing her again. It's going to weigh so heavy keeping something like this from her. It feels wrong," I sighed.

"I can understand that. Would it help if I reminded you that she's in a fragile state? Perhaps, it would be better for her not to know, at least, until after she gives birth." I looked up at him.

"I underestimate you way too often, Prince," I smiled. "You're truly amazing."

He shrugged. "I know." I slapped his upper arm and he chuckled. "I'll draw you a bath. We don't have long before dinner." He pulled away, kissing my temple before turning back towards the sitting room.

"You're not joining me?" I pouted. He turned to the side and his eyes raked over me, stopping on my mouth.

"Don't do that," he muttered. "I'm trying to behave myself...at least, for the first few hours." I untied the laces at the side of my tunic and gave my best impression of his voice as I started toward him.

"I'm sure I don't know what you mean," I side smiled, pulling the tunic over my head while walking past him into the chambers. I discarded it on the floor and loosened the laces in the front of my pants, lowering them enough to tease him with a glimpse of my rear. I looked over my shoulder to see him nearly chewing through his lip and both hands clenched into fists at his sides.

"Yeah...alright. Gods." He swept a hand through his hair and turned back towards the balcony, bracing both hands against the doorway and shaking his head. "Wicked creature."

I drew the bath myself and tried not to soak too long in the deep tub while a shirtless Luca trimmed up his face. I stole glances every so often and he smiled back at me from the large oval mirror above the basin.

"Enjoying the show?" He grinned, scruffing the blade of his razor across his chin. I snickered from the tub, sinking down into the water, where I could still keep eye contact with him in the glass.

"This feels incredibly domestic," I laughed. His responding chuckle nearly cost him the rest of his facial hair. "I'm watching my future husband shave while I keep him company in a bathing chamber. Not to mention, the absence of anything remotely sexual," I snorted.

"Perhaps, for *you*," he smiled, washing the razor in the basin. "I've quite enjoyed the eyeful from my corner over here."

"Oh? A shame you missed the *eyeful* from the other side of the wall at the inn," I grinned devilishly. The razor dropped from his face into the basin and he growled at me in the mirror.

"Arienne Genovese...you keep that up and you'll not see anyone else until morning...two days from now." He pointed at my reflection.

"You wouldn't," I challenged, wringing out my hair and rising slowly from the water. He turned around to face me, his gray eyes ravenous.

"Oh, I would. How badly do you wish to see her?" He licked his lips and the corner of his mouth curved up. I stepped onto a soft rug on the floor and wrapped myself in a large towel. He eyed my every movement as I stalked towards him and closed the space between us. His knuckles turned white from his grip on the edge of the basin stand.

"Tell me something, Prince..." I trailed my fingertips down his toned stomach and tugged the laces of his pants open. His eyes locked into mine and his breath fanned across my mouth as I leaned in. "Which one felt better? Your hand..." I palmed the bulge in his pants that hardened at my touch, and his breath caught. "Or mine?" I smiled.

"Godsdamn..." He whispered, turning his face to the ceiling and nearly cracking the wooden stand in his grip. I lowered myself to my knees, taking his pants down with me and he kicked the door shut. We didn't come back out for several minutes.

I dressed while Luca bathed and was surprised to see how well the gowns fit that the queen had sent to his room. I opted for a sea green silk gown with flutter sleeves and beaded embroidery of various florals. The bodice raised my bust slightly but was still modestly cut, and the skirts barely swept across the floor. I was unsure what to do with my long hair and given that I had no styling talent to speak of, I curled the ends and pinned them back to drape over my shoulder. I toed into the matching flat slippers and inspected myself in a gilded mirror in the sitting room.

Luca appeared behind me, already dressed in a more relaxed version of his royal garb and smiled over my shoulder in the mirror. "You're dripping with Crona. It's unbelievably satisfying." He dangled his hair strap in front of me. "Mind if I borrow this?" He smirked.

"I suppose I can go without it for one evening." I turned my face to his, and he gently kissed me. "Doesn't exactly go well with this dress." He tied his damp hair back in a knot and raised a finger, turning to one of the armoires and digging something out. He returned with a gorgeous string of pearls, and I moved my hair to allow him space to fasten them around my neck.

"I found every single one of these throughout years of exploring this sea. Before I left, I had them commissioned for you by the same craftsman that fashioned your ring. I was going to wait to give them to you until our wedding day, but..."

"You did this for me?" I fingered the shining beads.

"I did." He trailed his lips up my exposed neck and kissed below my ear. "But don't think because you have them now that I won't be returning this strap to its rightful place," he smiled against my skin. I twisted around to face him and kissed him deeply.

"You really did think of me all the time, didn't you? You didn't even know who I was or what I looked like." I fought back my urge to cry. He brushed a thumb across my lip.

"I knew exactly who you were, love. I planned to dote on you whether you deigned to like me or not," he whispered, smiling proudly. "Shall we? It's time to get my parents excited again." He offered his arm and I hooked mine around his elbow.

"Is it odd that I feel nervous?" I blushed as we walked into the bedroom and neared the door.

"If it is, then you're not alone. I imagine I'll piss myself when I see you in a wedding gown," he chuckled. I tucked myself closer to his side as we closed the door and started down the corridor. The elephant stampede made its return to my stomach with every step, and I couldn't decide whether it was because we were about to announce the biggest news of our lives or that I was a few moments away from facing Paxe as a secret sister...and my heart pounded.

CHAPTER 28

DINNER

Two guards stood at every door leading into the large dining room. Luca kept them quiet while we listened beside the door to the soft chatter inside. We kept out of sight, and I caught Paxe's sweet voice as I pressed into Luca and craned my neck to listen closer.

"She said things were moving along very well."

"Any chance she could figure out how big he is?" I recognized that voice as Lakan's. I had almost forgotten he was here.

"Not just yet...and I already told you, it isn't a *he*." I could hear the smile as she said it.

The guard closest to us nodded into the room and glanced in our direction to indicate that the king knew we were waiting. I heard his voice next.

"Have you received any word from the Princess?" Tidus asked. There was a pause, and I assumed she was chewing before she finally answered.

"No, actually. I'm not even all that sure if she received *my* letter. It worries me a bit. About interception *and* their safety. Have you heard from them?" Her voice had turned melancholy.

"Yes, now that you ask." A utensil clanged against a plate. "It seems they've completed the trials and mean to travel here," the king offered.

"Really?" Another pause. "Do they have safe transport? How long until they arrive?" Paxe asked with a shudder of excitement. Luca smiled down at me and I returned it, nodding and grasping his hand as we slowly emerged from the hallway and into the dining room.

The king sat in a large chair at the very end of the long table, his queen around the corner to his left. Paxe dropped her fork as she sat utterly astonished next to the queen and across from Lakan, who turned in his seat to see what caused her reaction. Every worry I had about seeing her again vanished when she slapped her palm to her mouth and quickly stood, brushing a hand down the tiny pooch of her belly and almost running around the royals to get to me. Her scarlet gown swished across the marble floor and I stretched my arms wide as she slammed into me. She squeezed around my neck so hard that my pearls left indentions in my skin.

"Ari..." She wept soundly. I felt warm tears fall from my own eyes as I held onto her. "Gods, I've missed you." She pulled back and put her hands on my face. "Not that I'm upset, but what in the world are you doing here?" She wiped at my face and I sniffled through my smile.

"We have a few reasons," I swiped under my eye. "I did get your letter. Let me see?" I looked down and she tugged the fabric tight across her middle.

The tiniest bump protruded from it, and I smoothed my hand across, crying again and kneeling down to talk to the little creature. "Hi there, big surprise..." Paxe laughed, and soft chuckles sounded around us. I laid a palm against it. "I'm your Auntie Ari..." I swallowed, feeling guilty about my choice of words. "You grow those strong arms and legs quickly so I can show you how to whoop your Mama and Uncle Luca, yeah?" Luca snorted behind me. I kissed the little bump and raised to find them all misty-eyed and grinning. Even the servants waiting against the wall looked emotional, especially the females. Paxe took my shoulders and positively glowed. She wore her motherhood so well.

"We've much to catch up on, friend," she smiled tearfully.

"That we do," Luca added as the king gestured for a couple of plates to be added to the table. Lakan moved down a chair and Luca pulled that seat out for me. I lowered myself into it as Paxe went back to her spot and my betrothed took his place between myself and his father. Two nimble young servant ladies brought us both a plateful of steaming food and an older male that I'd recognized from the stairs by Tidus's study poured us some wine. I leaned to my right, smiling at Lakan as he bowed his head at me.

"Good to see you, Lakan. Congratulations," I whispered, patting his shoulder.

"Thanks, Princess. It's good to see you too...and if I may?" His soft brown eyes bore into mine. "Thank you...so much for protecting her. You'll never understand how grateful I am. Truly. For everything." He looked over at Paxe, who dipped her chin and reached for his hand. He took it and thumbed across her knuckles as his attention returned to me. His dark hair fell into his eyes. "I know that things would be very different had it not been for you and Prince Luca... and these amazing monarchs. I'm undeserving and forever in your debt."

"You owe nothing...to anyone. There shouldn't have ever been a cost this great to live. You can repay me by treating her well and being here for your precious baby," I smiled sweetly. He nodded in response and I reached for my wine glass. Paxe nearly choked on her food as I lifted it to my mouth.

"Excuse me?" She gaped. My brows drew together and I swallowed down my wine. What is that?" She pointed at the ring on my hand and I couldn't stop the wide grin that crept across my face. Luca cleared his throat and the king chuckled through his mouthful.

"Oh, do tell her," Ayla giggled, taking a sip from her cup.

"Father...Mother. If you thought that our family meals were interesting before these two came to Crona, you're about to be a great deal more entertained," Luca laughed, shoveling a scoop of potatoes into his mouth. Paxe waited impatiently for me to explain while she placed her elbows on the table.

"Your dear prince asked me to marry him in Bolton...and I graciously accepted," I grinned.

"What do you mean? You were already betrothed!" She cackled, leaning over the table and reaching for my fingers. "Oh, my gods...Look at this!" She palmed her mouth and looked as if she could start crying again. "Luca, did you design this? It looks just like Hissifus!" Ayla choked into her glass.

"Hissifus?! What is a Hissifus?" She laughed. Tidus joined her.

"I did," Luca snickered. "And Hissifus is Ari's cat. He's two-toned." Paxe sat back down, staring at me adoringly.

"He's a chimera. One half of his little body is white, the other black as midnight. He was one of the most important beings in my life, aside from Paxe...that is, until I met this one." I pointed my fork at Luca, who turned his face to me and opened his mouth to show the wad of food inside. I elbowed him and giggled.

"Luca Di Meo...act like a child and I'll be happy to treat you like one!" Ayla laughed. "Whatever possessed you to name that animal such a thing? It's hysterical."

"I couldn't tell you." I forked a bit of steak into my mouth. "It just left my lips and stuck. Paxe and I were just kids, there's really no telling what I was thinking," I smiled.

"I quite like it," Tidus added.

"I just call him cat," Luca smiled. "But to answer your question, Paxe...this was something I planned to ask her when the time was right. Regardless of our arrangement. I would have rather asked for her hand as a male in love. I felt she deserved that too."

Paxe pressed a hand to her chest and pouted as if it were the sweetest thing she'd ever heard. "Gods, Luca. I never expected you to be so damn romantic." She picked up a grape and hurled it at Lakan. It bounced off his shoulder with a thwack, and I snorted. Lakan's face flushed red and he covered it with his hands.

"Are you ready to explain why you refuse to let us celebrate this engagement?" Ayla swirled the wine in her glass and tapped her fingernails against the ornate dining table. Paxe looked over at the queen and lowered her brows.

"Wait...you mean we're not?" She asked.

Luca raised from his chair, earning attention from everyone at the table. "No...we're not throwing an engagement ball..." He smiled ardently at me and took my hand. "I brought my soulmate home to marry her." The room erupted. Even the servants and guards jumped and squealed in excitement. Tidus slapped the table and stood, jerking Luca into a hug and clapping his back with an almost tearful grin. Ayla and Paxe wailed and jumped from their chairs to tackle me. Poor Lakan slumped dumbfoundedly in his seat. He knew he'd be saving his coppers to prepare for a wedding next.

"Why didn't you write?! I could have been planning this for you!" The queen cried, releasing me from her firm hold. Paxe nodded in agreement.

"No kidding! There's so much to be done! I can hardly breathe. I'm so happy! A royal wedding!" She bounced up and down on her toes.

"We wanted to surprise all of you. We only just decided this in Bolton. So much has happened and...we don't want to wait. There are so many things we need to discuss. But, I'm eager to let the two of you take over with wedding plans," I smiled. Everybody found their way back to their seats and Ayla cautiously stared between Luca and I.

"So, now that we know what brought you home," she gestured for more wine. "Are the two of you comfortable talking with us about everything that's been happening? How did you get here so quickly?"

Luca and I exchanged glances and smirked. "Winged horses," he offered.

"Son...we're trying to have a serious conversation," Tidus said into his glass.

"I know. And I was serious." Blank faces peered at us from around the table. "The horses we left Valdaro with...are goddess blessed. They now have wings. If you think me a liar, then you're welcome to go check the stables," he grinned and forked a carrot into his mouth.

"Is that the reason you told me I'd have to see it to believe it?" Tidus gaped. Luca nodded.

"It was a wedding gift," he started, but Paxe cut in.

"A wedding gift...from the goddess. A goddess who happened to know what Ari's oldest desire was?" I looked at her and guilt stabbed at me again.

"Paxe...I—" I cleared my throat and Luca put his hand on my leg. "Maybe we should start from the beginning?"

"Please do. Spare nothing." Ayla said. Lakan seemed a lot more interested too, but kept quiet. Luca and I took turns telling them about everything. I started with what happened with Paxe and the guard I killed in Aeon, then our departure in the rain when Tidus took Paxe to Crona and we all parted ways. Luca explained most of the details about Bolton until he reached the part about my father threatening me in a dream that wasn't really a dream. Paxe shifted a bit in her seat during that bit, obviously feeling uncomfortable, and placing a protective hand on her belly. It caused an ache in my chest that I couldn't shake off for a while.

Lakan had finally spoken more than I'd heard him since we sat down, when we discussed Nero and had tons of questions about the God of strength. Which was understandable, given that they had the same profession. We told them about our last night with Nero and the plans that we made. About the Knightsfire and the distraction that the wedding would cause. Lakan was pleased to hear that Nero would be attending said wedding, and Ayla mentioned that Varuna would most likely rage. Tidus was eager to study up on possible strategies for sneaking into the castle, and Paxe assured us that Mischa was trustworthy enough to use as an ally in that regard.

When we finally reached the trials of Irondale, Luca let me take over. I supposed that he felt as if it weren't his place to tell that part of our story, although I wouldn't have minded a bit. I found it rather difficult to put into words...words that were carefully chosen so as not to reveal that Paxe was indeed my blood. Every person in the room was still and quiet. Luca squeezed my knee when I finally finished, and I drew a long breath, exhaling loudly.

"And...now we're here, and everyone is caught up." I took a long drink of my wine, emptying it. Luca smiled and waved over the male to refill my glass. "I apologize. It's still a bit overwhelming even for me," I sighed.

"Ari..." Paxe called quietly. Our eyes met. "I'm so sorry...I didn't realize." Her eyes filled with tears and she hung her head. "So, that was the reason that my mother left the way she did." I froze with fear, anticipating her next statement. I was almost certain she'd pieced it together and I wouldn't have been surprised at all. Everyone had always underestimated her. "She killed your mother."

"Paxe, no...my father is the one responsible for both our mother's deaths. Don't put that on yourself. Please. My mother knew he'd find a way to rid himself of her, one way or another. I'm not wholly convinced she didn't poison herself just so that Isabelle wouldn't have to. Whatever the reason...it was never her fault. Paxe, look at me." She raised her face back to me, tears spilling down her face. Ayla rubbed her shoulder. "None of this was anyone's fault. While my mother had a great deal to do with the state the world is in, even that doesn't completely fall on her. My father is a monster...one we're going to extinguish. One way or another. You keep your focus on your health and that child you carry. Do you understand?" I leaned towards her.

She gripped her gown in the middle and cried as she nodded. "You're right," she sniffed and wiped her cheeks with her napkin. "I do have another question," she straightened.

Luca drank from his glass and tensed. He felt something. Or perhaps, I was feeling him through our bond. I couldn't be sure. "Alright," I urged.

"You've barely a month and a half until the night of your Ventus. Did either of the gods tell you how to break Luca's curse? Is that why you're marrying now and going after the king earlier than originally planned?" Her question was innocent, but I quickly realized why Luca paled, and tension soared across the table when Ayla stared daggers into him from across the table, and Tidus leaned forward, doing the same.

"What curse?" She asked with a fire in her dazzling eyes, so powerful even I was short of breath. "Luca? You had better answer me...now."

"Luca..." Tidus whispered, looking as if he were about to be sick. Luca looked at Paxe, who covered her mouth and shook her head in shame. She didn't know. Hell, I didn't know that he had never told them about it either, but I did understand his reason.

"Leave us...all of you. Arienne, you stay," Ayla spat. All the servants hastily fled the dining room, and the guards stood on the other side of the door, out of sight. Paxe and Lakan moved from the table and she looked back at Luca and I on her way out the side door, mouthing an apology as Lakan took her gently by the elbow and led her out. "What did that bastard do to you? Tell me now...I'm about to lose my temper and I do not wish to terrify your fiancée."

Luca pinched the bridge of his nose and let out a deep sigh. I took his hand, interlocking our fingers, and squeezed. "I—I didn't want you to worry. I thought we would have this figured out before you even had to know about it," he said quietly, dropping his hand to the table and leaning back in his chair.

"And how long have *you* known about it?!" Ayla shouted.

"Since the day we went to the castle. He snuck it into the deal that we sealed in magic. I felt it and glared at him until you spoke to me." He looked up at his mother. I remembered that pause...my father had looked at him with a smug expression and Luca had looked ready to kill him right there. I was too angry to even realize that was the moment it had happened. And the queen had broken their interaction when she put a hand on his arm. She must have just realized that too. Her body trembled with rage. The calm she had at that meeting was nowhere in sight right now.

"Felt what exactly?" Tidus interrupted. Luca let go of my hand and unfastened the first few buttons at the collar of his shirt. He pulled it open and the king and queen leaned in to inspect the mark on his chest.

"Fucking senile piece of shit!" Ayla screamed, slamming a fist to the table. "What does it mean? What does it do?!"

"Do you remember the terms of the deal we agreed on?" Luca asked. They nodded.

"You had to prove that she loved you by moonrise on her Ventus..." Tidus recalled.

"He's taking you with him, isn't he...?" Ayla breathed. "How could you not tell us this?" Luca swallowed and his jaw feathered as he looked into her eyes. Her breathing grew frantic and she spun around, releasing a deafening scream and everything on the table flew off, crashing into the dining room walls. Glass shattered everywhere and Tidus looked to Luca, who leapt from his seat and threw his arms around her, holding her back to his chest and releasing his magic. They slowly slumped to the floor as she calmed, crying softly and turning in his arms to hold him. I gripped the arms of my chair, shaking from the shock of what I had just seen, and Tidus stepped around to soothe me.

"I'm so sorry," he whispered. "Are you harmed?" He looked me over.

"No," I shook my head. None of the items on the table seemed to have hit any one of us. "Should I leave?" I whispered.

"No, no...please. I'm sorry. It's just—" Tears began to line his eyes. "We'll never have more children...Luca is all we have. There has to be a way."

"I know...I understand. I've been trying for weeks to find something. The only thing we have left to go on is that Nero said to focus on liabilities of the agreement. He told us that sometimes it can be the key to its undoing. But I have no idea where to go from here." I looked over to the floor where Luca was still rocking Ayla back and forth. "I'm so sorry...I never expected to love him, Sire. I surely never expected to love him as deeply as I do." Luca turned his face to me and a soft, reassuring smile rested across it.

"It's not your fault, Arienne," Ayla whispered as Luca helped her to her feet. She wiped her eyes and faced me while Luca rested a hand on her back, keeping contact and making sure she was calm. "Remember what you just told Paxe. The king is responsible. My son has likely loved you long before you knew him. I would know. He spent a very long time learning everything he could about his future wife. You make him happy. I can see it all over the two of you. There isn't a more precious thing in this world than your love. As much as this pains me..." She looked at Luca and brushed her fingers over his cheek. "I'd never want anything less for either of you." She returned her attention to me. "I meant every word I said to you in the Great Hall. You were strong and brave enough to do exactly as I said...all the while enduring such pain. What you have together was hard earned by both of you, and gods help me...I'll find a way to stop this. You'll not be torn apart by this tyrant."

I swallowed down the knot in my throat. "Thank you, Mi'lady." I offered softly.

"I'll start researching both this curse and our strategy. There has to be a book somewhere in that study that can help. Darling...until then, you and Paxe plan them a wedding that will be talked about for centuries. If they can find happiness through this obstacle, so can we," Tidus said with a tight smile. Ayla nodded and looked around the dining hall.

"Forgive me, Princess. It's rare that I lose my control in this way. I never meant you any harm and I'm sorry if I scared you," she pressed her hand to her chest.

"Don't apologize. It was actually magnificent," I grinned. Everyone chuckled in response. "Really...I—I'm fascinated by you," I blushed.

"Luca..." She faced him and took his chin. He stiffened. "If you ever keep something like this from me again..." She shook her head.

"I'm sorry, Mother." He pulled her into an embrace, and she breathed deeply.

"Don't be angry with Paxe...I know she must feel terrible about outing you. You have no one to blame but yourself," she scolded, pulling away to look at him again.

"I'm not. It isn't her fault."

"I'll talk to her, Luca. Let me speak with her alone and I'll find you after," I said.

"She spends a lot of time on the beach around dusk. I'll be happy to take you," Tidus offered.

"Thank you," I replied, taking his arm. We stepped carefully around the mess on the floor and neared the doorway when Luca called from behind me.

"Ari..." I looked over my shoulder. "I love you." His tone made me blush and the king and queen definitely didn't help matters as they gushed. I knew he genuinely meant it, but he probably did it on purpose, knowing full well how I'd react.

"I love you too, *your Highness,*" I smiled bashfully.

I walked arm in arm with the king in silence until we were out of earshot of the dining room. The white hallways were lit with sconces at every turn. The castle was bright even in the darkness of night, and it was a comforting notion, considering my existence being contained in the prison of the place I used to call home.

"He really does, you know," Tidus said, finally. "I knew he was captivated by the thought of you for a long time before we finally made the trip to Valdaro...and I may be saying too much, but did you know that he snuck out the night before he met you?"

"Yes. Yes, I did. I learned that recently."

"His mother still doesn't know, and to be truthful, she'd probably have his ass for it. But I was waiting for him when he returned. Whatever he saw that night had truly broken him. I had planned, of course, to scold him for being a damned fool, but when I saw him...I couldn't." I grew quiet. "He convinced himself that he had to get you out and that you needed him. I knew he had sensed it, somehow. He told me that he hadn't met you and still wasn't able to see your face."

"Did he tell you anything else?" I asked.

"No. But the excitement from the trip there had turned into determination. And the moment he saw you in the Great Hall...I could tell that he'd fallen for you. The way that he gave himself to the king...it was the way I felt for Ayla the first time I'd laid eyes on her."

"She's an extraordinary person," I said.

"So are you," he glanced sidelong at me, and I bowed my head.

"I know what happened to you, Princess. You have the strength and courage of the lion that represents our house. Perhaps you've always been meant to be a Di Meo. I'm honored to have you join our family." He stopped and turned me to face him, taking my hands and nodding his head slowly, "Honored."

"Thank you, your Highness...." I whispered, trying not to become emotional.

"Thank *you*. For letting him in...for giving him joy and purpose. You're truly all my son ever wanted," he smiled. "And please...call me Tidus."

He led me to an open hallway that emptied itself into a small outdoor patio that was partially covered, and small tables and chairs scattered about. There was a short stone ledge that jutted out the side and stopped where sand began to cover the stones at the floor. It was a small access to the beach. A short ways away, near the water, I caught a glimpse of my sister sitting on the sand and staring at the rising moon over the water as she leaned back on her hands. Lakan wasn't with her, and I wondered why.

"She comes out here at dusk? Is she always alone?" I asked.

"She likes watching. She says it's too warm during the day and prefers to watch the stars come out around this time. It's been a sort of comfort to her, I believe, especially when she was ill. I think that she comes alone to unwind and perhaps just...breathe. We don't bother her; we just make sure that she's carefully guarded. You may not ever see them, but trust me...you're safe here. I have eyes everywhere to protect my family," Tidus winked. "If you need anything at all...please don't hesitate to ask. I'll leave you to it."

His family...

The king had said it and truly meant all of us. My heart warmed, and for once...I really did feel safe. I felt as if we had always belonged here. If I didn't have that blasted clock ticking away the seconds of Luca's life and a world full of people to rescue...I'd let my father live out his miserable existence alone. Perhaps, only deal with ending him when he struck. Whether his heart had been broken or not...he had no reason to do this to everyone. He ruins everything good in this world.

Gods...I just want to live. I want us to live.

I took a deep breath and slipped my shoes off, lifting my skirts and stepping into the soft sand. It was cool beneath me and felt wonderful. Another first for me. I glanced up at the sliver of the moon and made my way to the golden-haired mother in the red dress.

CHAPTER 29

HALF TRUTHS

"You know how to spice up a banquet, huh?" I called as I approached Paxe and spread my skirts out to sit next to her. She looked over at me, her mouth open and shook her head.

"I'm so sorry, I—"

"Stop...you didn't know. And I didn't either. It would have come out eventually. You know he refused to even talk to me about it, and I asked when we were half naked and alone." I scoffed.

"Floozy..." She rolled her eyes and smiled. I shoved her in the shoulder and we giggled for a moment before looking out over the water. "I am sorry, though. You just got here and Ayla's angry. How bad was it?"

"Ah..." I cocked my head to the side without looking at her and squinted one eye. "A few broken dishes. But...no fatalities." I smirked.

"Luca probably hates my guts," she sighed.

"No...he doesn't. It caught him off guard, but he's not even angry. At least now he doesn't have to build up the gall to tell them. We can move past it."

"How, Ari?" She turned her face to me. "How can you move past something that big when it hovers over your happiness like an asp about to strike?" Her voice held a hint of frustration and pain. I looked at her and lowered my brows.

"Do we have any other choice? Paxe, I watched him *die*. I watched the light go out in him...and that *fucking* mark was still there. I've thought of everything. If death can't fix it, and the gods can't make it disappear...then what other choice do we have but to keep trying and enjoy what time we have while we do?" It came out more forceful than I meant it to. "I'm sorry..." I hung my head.

"No...you're right." She leaned back on her hands, and we looked back at the sea.

"Is this about the curse, or is this about your mother?" I asked, my voice low and sympathetic. She breathed deeply.

"It's about everything. I come out here every night when it isn't raining. I look at these stars and I think back to what you told me about when your mother reached out to you. I don't remember mine either. I'm carrying a child that grows more each day...a child that is just as damned as Luca. It—" Her face drew up and she wept. "It breaks my heart. Why is everything so incredibly sad? She killed herself. She'll never know me, she has no way to ever speak to me...or see her grandchild. She was tortured and forced to murder her only friend. It's not that I blame her, Ari...but—*fuck*," she sniffled hard and placed a hand over her belly. "All this happened because of a *crown.*"

I put an arm around her. "I know..."

"Your mother was forced to marry someone she didn't love...if it weren't for a fucking hat made of precious metal and an ungodly amount of power...none of this would have ever happened. To any of us. Your mother and father can't have been the only ones who suffered from the lovelessness of an arranged marriage. People's hearts should belong only to those who they wish to give it to. It may have worked out well for you and Luca...for the king and queen even. But...I know there were others. It shouldn't be this way."

She calmed herself and grew quiet. I counted the number of heartbeats as she spoke, where I almost told her the truth, but I still couldn't. So, instead, I pulled her to my side and she rested her head on my shoulder. "What would you do, Paxe?" I asked, staring up at the glowing crescent in the sky.

"About what?"

"What would you do with the crown? With my father's power?" I tread carefully. "If the roles were reversed, I mean."

"I'd end it. I'd use that crown and that power to heal this land. Heal our people. I'd marry for love. Not advantage. And I'd make sure that no one ever had to be forced to do anything else against their will. No more ripple effects...no more war," she paused. "No more pointless death."

"Do you feel that's something you'd *want?*" I added. She raised her face to me.

"Why?" Her brows scrunched. "Don't you?"

My heart sped up, and I found it difficult to breathe. I looked into her sparkling, puffy eyes. "No..." I whispered, shaking my head slowly. "I don't."

"Ari..." She leaned back and peered into me deeply. The breeze from the bay blew our hair. "You've waited your whole life for your Ventus abilities alone..."

"Do you miss it?" I asked.

"If I'm being honest...I don't anymore. Especially the more time I spend with Lakan. He's non-magic folk, you know. My abilities were...great. But it came with so much responsibility and became so much more of a hindrance. I realize now how much I prefer ignorance. No one should know the things you don't wish to tell them until they feel ready to do so."

Damn it...just...damn it.

The weight of the guilt I felt was so heavy. "Maybe I feel the same. Maybe never having that power and still doing so much more taught me that I never needed any abilities to make a difference. Paxe...I have *everything* I've ever wanted. I don't want the crown or the power. I have love...I've had adventure enough for a lifetime already. I have a family now, and I've experienced the joy of riding wings through the skies. I find myself not wanting to rule...now I simply... just want—"

"You want to live. You want that simple life that we talked about the day that I left Aeon." She finished for me. "I saw that look in your eyes before...and I told you that it suited you. But I also reminded you then, and I'll remind you now. You...you are the world's future, Ari. You're our queen. Sitting on that throne doesn't have to be a burden. It will be whatever you make it to be. If you're asking me what I'd do if I had no other choice...then my answer would be simple. Live that simple life on the *throne*. Be the peace...let Luca be the light. Share it. Enjoy it. That's what I would do. I would make this world a safe place for Lakan...for our baby. For all the families out there that have so much to lose. Isn't that what we fight for?"

I pressed my hand to her little bump. "Yes...yes it is." I smiled.

"Don't let my hormonal emotions discourage you. I'm sorry. It's so difficult to control them these days," she laughed. "That's why I come out here at night. I have to dismantle just so I'm able to sleep. I never meant to make you think that your responsibilities to your crown are meaningless. They're not. I'm just..." she sighed loudly. "Pregnant."

I laughed and leaned down to kiss her belly. "You're absolutely adorable." I grinned, leaning back on my hands.

"You'll find out one day how *un*-adorable it is...and this isn't even the worst part. Ayla told me that when she was pregnant with Luca, she was hardly able to walk near the end. Apparently, I can also look forward to wetting myself every time I sneeze or laugh too hard." She rolled her eyes when I bursted out laughing.

"I can't wait to witness that," I heaved.

"Shut up..." She nudged with a grin. She narrowed her eyes and looked back over at me. "Are you...taking any kind of contraceptive? A tonic? Anything?" I promptly stopped laughing and met her stare. "Arienne!"

"No...I—" I struggled to find an excuse. "We...talked about that after I got your letter. I burned it, by the way. I got nervous after reading it and I think I scared Luca out of his wits, but...then later that night, he actually said that whether it was selfish or not, he wanted it all. I think I do too."

"Right now? Do you even know if you are?" She nearly shouted.

"Shhh...keep your voice down. No, I don't. And I don't mean right now, no. I'd like to enjoy being married for a while first, but...there was a little boy named Holt when we went to Irondale." I smiled, recalling his little face. "Paxe...we fell in love with him. He was precious, and he fell asleep in my arms on his parent's couch. Luca had laid with us and this huge wolf, which the kid insisted was a dog. We built snowmen and played with the other kids in town, and I—it felt so right. I've always been so terrified of what kind of mother I would be, but...I do want it. Someday."

"Someday, yes. But you know that if there's a child growing in that belly, Luca would never let you anywhere near Valdaro. Neither would the king...or Ayla, or me for that matter. Your father wouldn't hesitate to hurt you again. I doubt knowing you were with child would even stop him. He'd use it as another way to destroy you and everything you hold dear." She bit down on her lip, and I tapped my fingertips over the bridge of my nose, knowing she was absolutely right.

"I know," I whispered, squeezing the spot where my fingers rested. "You're right."

"I'm summoning my healer tomorrow. You need to at least make sure it isn't already too late. I know damned well you're not being careful. Not the way you two ravage each other." Another eye roll. I scoffed.

"You're telling me you and Lakan haven't been rocking a bed since you were reunited?" I swiveled my head back to her and grinned.

"Oh, have we ever. But you know...I'm already pregnant...so what harm could it do now?" She smirked at me. "You want a bit of advice? And I mean this with all seriousness..."

"Alright, let's hear it."

"If you and Luca can control yourselves, hold off until your wedding. I mean everything. No touching below the waist at all."

"And why would I ever want to do that?" I asked, intrigued.

"The time that Lakan and I spent apart?" She shook her head and smiled devilishly. "Our first time bedding each other after I got here was better than the night I conceived." She laughed.

"Really?"

"Yes. Gods... yes! And every other time that night, sick or not. I'm telling you...try it. What's a week or two? I know it won't take long for the queen and I to cook up this wedding."

"Paxe, I kissed him, fell head over heels, and bedded that male within two weeks of meeting him. Do you know how difficult it is for us not to...not to—"

"Not to be buried in each other's insides?" She laughed loudly. "I understand, and it must be that much harder with the binding that holds you two the way it does. But just think about it, would you? Talk to Luca and see if it's something he'd be interested in. Not only does it make things more passionate for your wedding night, but I do feel it would be such an endearing commitment between you. You'll have tons of things to keep you busy while we're planning this wedding."

"It's actually a very good idea. I just don't know how long we'll be able to stick with it," I said. She didn't look at me when she responded.

"How long has it been since the last time you slept together?" She asked with a tone that suggested she wouldn't believe me even if I had told the truth.

"Are you counting anything other than actually..." I started, refusing to look at her.

"Should I?" I saw her eyeing me from the corner of my vision and smirked. "Alright, fine. When was the last time you did anything sexual? Not including an intense kiss or two." When I didn't respond, she leaned her face around mine to force me into looking at her, clearing her throat loudly. "Arienne Genovese. You've only been here for a few hours! What did you do?"

"Nothing *you* haven't done!" I cackled.

"Oh my gods!" She slapped my arm. "When? Before dinner?" She gaped.

"Perhaps..." I grinned, dodging another blow to my shoulder.

"You're deranged." She snorted. "If we find out you're not pregnant tomorrow, it'll definitely surprise me. I have never." She shook her head. "I do understand, though." She fell silent and looked ahead. "Love is strange, isn't it? Sometimes, I think I could kiss Lakan until my lips were too swollen to speak...other times, I would love nothing more than to scratch his bloody eyes out. But if anyone ever tried to take him from me again...or hurt him in any way I—"

"Yep. I completely understand. I lifted a god's hammer. Plunged a sword into my own heart because I could never live without him. I didn't even think about what I was doing. Only that I needed to be wherever he was, Paxe." I looked back up at the moon and imagined a clock face peeking from its dark side. I shivered.

"I can't imagine what it must have felt like to see him like that. I don't even want to think about it."

"None of the physical pain that I endured that night held a candle to the way my heart ached. A part of me died with him and I couldn't find him when I tried to join our blood. When it was clear to me that he was gone, I—I was ready to die. I felt more ready then than I had in that cell five years ago." My head hung and Paxe took my hand.

"It's over. Tidus will find something to get rid of this. Let him work on it. I can't wait to see you marry your prince. You both deserve this." We smiled at each other and her mouth went wide in a yawn.

"Alright Mama, come on." I stood and pulled her up. "You and little bump need to rest. Let's get you back. I slipped my fingers between hers and forced her to show me to her room instead of Luca's. Lakan was waiting when we entered and I pulled him aside to ask him for a small favor before saying goodnight. I found a guard down the hall who was happy to lead me to Luca's private corridor, and finally padded into our room with my fingers hooked into the heels of my slippers.

I crept in and found Luca sitting upright against a pillow and the headboard, fast asleep with an open book in his lap and a finger beneath the page he looked as if he were about to flip. He wasn't wearing a shirt, and loose strands of his hair fell against his face that was slightly turned toward the lamp beside the bed. I smiled and dropped my slippers by the door, walking quietly over to the side of the bed and sitting carefully on the edge. It felt strangely familiar to the first night we—

Damn, you're beautiful...

I brushed the hair away from his brow and tucked it behind his ear. He inhaled deeply and stirred, catching my eyes and smiling lazily. His hand smoothed across the silk over my thigh until he found purchase on my fingers that rested in my lap.

"Must have been an interesting read," I whispered, smiling. He softly chuckled and looked down at the book.

"Actually, I did find something interesting that I never knew. But I think I may have worn myself out calming my mother." I raised my brows, the sudden realization that using magic to calm unbridled fury would definitely be draining. Even his voice sounded strained. I reached for the aged book, and he let me have it. I stared down at a page and noticed a drawing of a male that looked oddly similar to Nero, and on the opposite page was a picture of a raging storm over the sea.

"Is that?" I drew my brows together.

"Nero. Apparently, long ago, he and Varuna had fights that would cause the worst storms Crona had ever endured. The last one sank twelve ships. Crona has yet to see another storm like that since he left."

"That's why he stays away...he feels responsible." Luca nodded. "Wow." I folded the corner and closed the large book, sitting it on the bedside table. "Are you reconsidering his invitation?" I smiled.

"Nah. I think if it impacted him that strongly he's most likely learned his lesson. How is Paxe? Is she alright?" He sounded completely exhausted.

"Yeah, she's fine. Just pregnant." I snorted. "Actually, I—need to talk with you about something." I raised from the bed and he turned his body slightly, watching me with intrigue as I walked into the sitting room and fumbled through my bag for a nightshift.

"Is something wrong?" He asked, his eyes only half open. I slipped out of my gown and laid it over one of the armchairs, and his eyes opened a bit wider. I gave him a smirk as I pulled the short blue shift over me.

"No, nothing's wrong. She suggested that I see her healer tomorrow. The one that's been keeping up with the baby." His expression was unreadable.

"Why? Are you alright?"

"I'm fine," I assured him, pulling the duvet back to climb in next to him. He moved over and reached his arm over the pillow so that I could rest on his body. "The healer is going to check to see if I'm..." I paused, looking up to meet his eyes.

"Ari..." He ran a hand through his hair. "You think—"

"I don't. But I certainly could be, for all we know. We should probably make sure of that before we start deciding on how we'll take my father down."

"You're right." He sighed deeply and moved a hand down my middle. "We haven't given that much thought since Bolton. What if you are?" I looked down and placed my hand over his.

"Let's cross that bridge when we get there, yeah? And if I'm not, then I think we should consider using a contraceptive tonic until we're ready. Until this is over, at least." I turned my face back to his. "Luca, if I were to live and you weren't here. If we never found a way to break this curse...I don't want to think of raising our child without you."

"I know." He breathed, kissing my forehead. "I think it's a wise choice." He pulled me in closer.

"There was one more thing Paxe suggested," I said, brushing my lips against his neck.

"Mmhmm?" He hummed. I paused for a moment.

"She asked if we would consider waiting until our wedding night before doing anything else." He stopped breathing momentarily and pulled back to look at me.

"What?" His face was contorted into a mixture of disbelief and near grief. I tried earnestly not to laugh and sucked my lips into my mouth. "Why?" I snorted a little.

"I felt the same way until she explained it," I said.

"You're not actually entertaining this, are you?" My poor fiancé looked ready to weep.

"Just listen," I chuckled, placing my hand on his cheek. "She said that reuniting with Lakan after their time apart really intensified their passion. She swears that the first time they made love after she arrived in Crona was better than their very first time. She also mentioned how meaningful a commitment like that would be for us... Which, unlike her, the next time we make love...we'll be husband and wife. I can definitely see the appeal. Although it would take every bit of my self-control." His brows shot up.

"Yours?" He palmed his face and flopped over onto his back. "So, I suppose we need to figure out a way to have this wedding tomorrow then?" He pouted. I leaned over him and pulled his hand away from his face, grinning and showing my teeth.

"Why don't we think of it in the way you did the night you asked me to be your wife?" He looked into my eyes and traced my jawline with a finger. "I could let you hold me that way every night for the rest of our lives. This could be a good thing. I'm eager to see how it feels." He exhaled deeply.

"I'll do anything you ask of me, Princess. Anything. If it's what you want, I'll do this with you. You know that. And neither of you are wrong, I just..."

"I know. If we decide we can't hold out...we make that decision together. Agreed?" He nodded slowly and poked his lip out. I laughed through my nose and gently kissed him. "It won't be that bad. We can do it."

"Alright," he whispered, kissing me back. It deepened quickly and his hands instinctively roved beneath my rear. I broke from his mouth and gave him a look. "What?"

"It hasn't even been a whole minute!" I laughed.

"I can't even—"

"No, fool." I giggled. His eyes rolled back and he gripped both hands in his hair, swearing under his breath and growling. "I'm not sure what's more adorable to me at the moment. Paxe's little belly, or the way you look right now." I cackled, pulling the pins from my hair and tossing them on the bedside table.

"Can I hold you at least?" He frowned. He looked truly pitiful, and I felt bad. I leaned over and blew out the lamp, snuggling into his arms with my back against his chest. He tucked me in close and nuzzled into my neck, breathing me in and pressing his lips to my skin. I draped an arm around his and squeezed.

"This isn't so bad," I whispered, pressing in closer. He tightened around me and sighed in deep satisfaction. We lay quiet for a few long moments until I felt him slack. I smiled to myself and brought his knuckles to my lips, kissing them tenderly.

"I love you," I whispered in the dark.

CHAPTER 30

ANNOUNCEMENTS

Soft knocks sounded at Luca's door that morning and I felt his arm around me, pulling tighter as if begging me to ignore it. So, I did. We shuffled around, tangling our legs and suffering from days worth of exhaustion and an overhaul of heavy truth and information. Neither of us had been fortunate enough to have a full night's rest in what seemed like days. Nothing needed to be said for me to understand exactly what he wanted, and I couldn't have agreed more. I curled in closer to him and felt a brush of a kiss on my shoulder.

After a few more moments the knocking grew a bit louder and a male's muffled voice sounded from the other side of the door. "Prince Luca?" Another knock. "The queen wishes to see you, my Lord." Luca didn't budge. I nudged him with my elbow and he groaned miserably. The guard knocked yet again. "My Lord?"

"Tell her I'll be down shortly. And please, for the love of the gods, get away from my door," Luca answered, tucking his chin back into the column of my neck. A low laugh escaped me, but I refused to open my eyes.

"Someone is cranky," I whispered. He grunted next to my ear and tightened around me.

"We're not leaving this bed right now. If he'd knocked again, I might have given him the Cragan treatment." His voice was tired and hoarse. I giggled softly.

"What about your mother?" I asked, eyes still closed.

"She'll be fine. Whatever it is, it can wait."

I wasn't sure how long it had taken, but we both fell back into the deepest sleep. By the time another knock sounded at the door, the light in Luca's room suggested that half the day had crept by. Neither of us had moved an inch and our skin was practically glued together from body heat and a tight embrace. "I know you're in there! Get your lazy ass up and cover your bollocks! You're not going to sneak into town and make an announcement like that without seeing this gorgeous face, prick!" I snapped my eyes open and raised my head from the pillow staring at the door with a confused scowl. Luca rolled onto his back, rubbing his eyes and laughing soundly.

"Gods, no..." He dragged his palms down his face. I sat up and pulled the duvet up to my chest, looking down at him and pressing my lips into a thin line.

"Wakey, wakey!" The male banged on the door.

"Come in, bastard," Luca called. The door burst open and a very handsome, tall male appeared in the doorway. He grinned widely with a mouthful of straight white teeth, dazzling blue eyes and dark brown hair that was shaved into whirling designs on the sides and long enough on the top that pieces of it dropped attractively over his brow. His facial hair was cut like Luca's...closely trimmed and enveloping his mouth and chin. He quickly bowed at me, winking as he bolted for the other side of the bed and leapt on top of Luca, nearly knocking the wind out of him.

"Ohhhh, I missed you!" He dramatically laid over him, rolling back and forth as Luca fought him off. "Look at my darling prince! You bulked up, you dashing son of a bitch." He grinned, pinching at Luca's bare torso. I couldn't help but laugh at the exchange as I scooted farther over and pulled the cover higher over myself.

"You—bitch!" Luca grinned, snarling through his teeth and wrestling with the towering individual that looked like he was carved from pure muscle. There were several playful pops and slaps between them before the male finally backed off and slipped off the side of the bed, chuckling. "I apologize, love." Luca smiled at me breathlessly. He waved a hand toward our guest. "This rude piece of work is Michele."

Michele rolled his hand in front of him and bowed again. "At your mercy, Mi'lady. Forgive me, but I'm a creature of habit. I couldn't pass up the opportunity to rough up your...*fiancé*." He wagged his brows at Luca. "I am sorry though, he's absolutely correct. I wasn't thinking. For whatever reason, I thought he'd be in here alone. My apologies."

"It's quite alright." I smiled. "I'm Arienne. Luca has told me lots about you. It's a pleasure."

He raised his brows and looked at Luca who sat up and leaned against the headboard. "Oh? You told her all about how positively sinful I look?" He straightened his tight fitting turquoise tunic and grinned.

"You're still as insufferable as you were when I left," Luca said, stretching an arm around me and tugging me to his side. "What brings you over so early to torture me?" He laughed.

"Early? Fool, it's nearly one in the afternoon. Are you so special now that you're not required to be present for important shit?" Michele crossed his arms and leaned against the bookshelf, crossing an ankle over his boot.

"What do you mean?" I asked, looking at Luca for clarification. Luca shrugged and we brought our attention back to Michele.

"So you didn't know that the king and queen made a formal announcement about your wedding a few hours ago?" He smirked.

"They didn't," Luca snapped, eyes wide.

"Oh, they most certainly did. The whole city erupted. My wife is so excited she just went and likely emptied our bank account for something to wear to this shindig. I was surprised when I didn't see you up there. Everyone was looking for you."

"Gods." Luca buried his fingers in his hair and pulled. "That's why she wanted to see me this morning." I stared off at the wall, lost in my surprise.

"I'm sorry, Ari. I didn't know."

"No, no...it's alright. It's probably a good thing." I looked back at him. "News like that will spread fast, if you catch my meaning." His eyes deepened in confirmation that he fully understood what I meant. *My father will catch wind of our plans and the distraction will be set in place.*

"Is everything okay?" Michele interrupted.

"Yeah. All is well. Sorry I didn't make it. How is married life? It's odd to think of you settling down," Luca probed.

"Ha! Better than I ever imagined. The kid is a handful too. Best oopsie I ever made," he laughed. I jolted forward with a sharp inhale.

Shit...kids...oopsies.

"What's wrong?" Luca leaned forward, placing a hand on my back.

"The healer. I completely forgot. I have to go." I kissed his cheek and hurried into the sitting room, closing the door behind me. I heard Luca excuse himself and slip into the door as I changed into a simple navy gown with silver thread and half sleeves that fit close and flowed smoothly to the floor. The front of the gown was a mock corset, laced with silver ribbon. It didn't suffocate me, instead allowing me a snug fit under breathable material that only gave the illusion that my chest was supported by one. My favorite gown thus far. I fingered through my hair and wiped beneath my eyes with my forefingers, as Luca slowly approached.

"Will you let me know as soon as you find out?" He asked in a low voice, his hand brushing against the flat plane of my belly. His eyes looked longing and I hooked my arms around his neck.

"Careful, Prince. You almost look as if you're hoping I am." He gripped my hips.

"I know I shouldn't hope that. But you know I'd hardly be upset if you are. I want to know." He pressed his head to mine. I nodded softly and kissed his lips.

"What manner of hell are you about to get into with your friend there?" I smiled. He groaned in irritation.

"If I had to guess, a trip into the city and probably a few ales with a couple of my other friends who I haven't seen for a while. They'll most likely wish to celebrate. But first...I suppose I should go and face my mother and accept a sound lashing." He laughed, untying his hair and reaching the strap around my neck. I leaned back while he tied it in place.

"You're not—going to the tavern are you?" I asked, recalling our discussion in the forest about the female he'd first lain with. I felt a stab of jealousy, gods only knew why. I knew damned well I was, and always had been the only one he truly wanted. But if I found out some harlot's ambitious hands were anywhere on his body, I knew I'd find my inner Ayla Di Meo and rip her bloody throat out.

"You do realize there's more than one in the city, right?" He flicked my nose and smiled with knowing as he watched a flame ignite in my stare. "You have nothing to fear, love. If it bothers you at all, I'll stay far away from that side of town. Besides that, I've not seen her for years. I'm not even sure she's still around."

"Good," I spat, dropping my arms to my sides. He laughed loudly.

"Do I detect jealousy?" He bit his lip.

"No. You detect a dragon...guarding her treasure. Your past is your past, bu—"

"My *future*...is you. My whole life is you. And don't worry, I don't think any female would be daft enough to try and test you, my queen." He grinned and leaned in to kiss me again. I kissed him back harder than I meant to. I tasted his tongue and my body reacted. What started out as a playful argument turned into a fire so strong, I could have burned us both alive. I had no idea where it came from but I suddenly needed to claim him as mine. I backed him into a small alcove in the wall and our mouths savagely devoured each other. I gathered his hair in my fist and pulled his head back, biting hard into the skin of his neck. He hissed through clenched teeth and pressed the lower half of his body into mine.

"You have to stop," he growled, his grip tight on my hips. "If you don't I'll throw my will out the fucking door and take you right here." It took me a moment before I realized what he meant. I paused my assault and breathed heavily into his neck, my body trembling with the desire to have him bend me over and do unspeakable things. It was then I remembered the proposition I stupidly extended last night before we fell asleep. No more before the wedding day.

I forcefully cursed through an exhale against his skin. "I'm sorry." I kissed the angry red marks from my teeth. "I forgot." I slumped against him and his chest heaved up and down, his hand brushing down the back of my head. Michele loudly cleared his throat on the other side of the door.

"You guys are terrible hosts!" He yelled from the other room. Luca and I both snickered quietly. I raised my face to his and his deeply frustrated expression made my knees weak.

"Hey, Michele?" Luca called.

"Yep!"

"Did that announcement this morning happen to include a date?" Luca's other hand pressed firmly against my back.

"Damn, Prince. You don't even know the day of your own wedding? That's bleak. It's two weeks from tomorrow." Luca's eyes closed and his jaw tightened. "Everything alright in there? You know I'm not letting you off that easy! Get dressed, let the lady breathe!"

"Ha!" Luca laughed, giving me a truly feral grin. "You got it all wrong, brother. I'll be right out." Michele chuckled from the other side of the door.

"I'm sorry." I scrunched my face.

"Two weeks..." He breathed.

"I'll do better." I promised. "And I don't care what tavern you go to. In fact, I'm encouraging you to go." I pulled back with a smirk.

"Oh? Why the sudden change of heart?" He purred.

"Wear your hair back today." I winked, making for the door. He stepped over to the mirror and laughed under his breath.

"Well played, Princess...well played." I opened the door to find Michele sitting on the edge of the bedside table with his ankles crossed in front of him. He caught sight of Luca behind me and the red ring of teeth marks on his neck and whistled with a proud smile. He nodded at me and I dipped my chin. "I love you, heathen!" Luca called, as I passed the desk in the bedchamber.

"I love you too," I giggled.

"I like her, man. I like her *a lot.*" Michele beamed as I walked out the door. I made it down the corridor and surprisingly turned a few corners in the right direction when I found Paxe hurrying down a hall, apparently on her way to get me. She looked disinterested in whatever excuse I had for making the healer wait, but I was grateful she'd found me before I inevitably ended up turned around in this castle.

"Alright, you," she started, reaching for my hand as she stalked toward me. "If I don't have the luxury of sleeping all day, then neither do you. We're late." She grabbed my hand and tugged me along. "I suppose you already had the pleasure of meeting Luca's obnoxious friend?" She smiled as we hastily walked, taking several hallways and short flights of stairs to the other side of the castle.

"Michele? I kind of like him." I smirked. She scoffed and rolled her eyes. "What? Is he that bad?"

"That male is so full of himself that I wouldn't put it past him to occasionally tongue his own reflection." I burst out laughing as her assumption was likely very accurate. A nearby guard apparently thought it was amusing as well.

"Does he come here a lot? I assumed he'd be busy with his family if Luca wasn't here for him to visit with."

"On the contrary, he's here at least twice a week. Tidus is very fond of him. They're working on a project together in the southern bay. Michele has been commissioned to design and build a university. The first and only in Crona. He's rumored to be one hell of an architect."

"Luca mentioned that before. That's really admirable. Was it his idea?" I asked. Paxe stopped dead in her tracks and looked over at me.

"How did you not know?" She asked, puzzled. My face must have looked the same.

"Know what?"

Paxe's mouth turned up in the corner. "That university was Luca's idea. Ayla told me that years ago, he had been spending a great deal of time designing weapons and teaching human youths in Crona how to defend themselves since they had no magic. The queen had become worried that it would stir trouble for them if King Loren found out. So, apparently sometime later he talked to his father about the idea of building a university that all could attend. Then they could be taught anything from defense, to business or anything else they could use to better themselves." My heart was so full it nearly ruptured. He wanted to help them. That could have also been the reason for all the sketches in his journal and on the walls in his sitting room.

"Gods, I love that male." I shook my head and stared blankly at the stained glass window, unknowingly palming my middle.

"Arienne..." She broke my train of thought and I looked at her. Her blue eyes were on the placement of my hand. "Is there something you need to tell me, or did I just scare you last night?" She raised her eyes to meet mine.

"No, no...I'm sorry. Let's go. I just need to know now that it's back on my mind."

"Did you talk to him about...?" She cocked her head.

"Yes. He agreed we should use a contraceptive if I'm not. And the other...phew. He agreed to that too, but Paxe—that's going to be so damn hard. I forgot about it already this morning and now—"

"Now you have to wait two weeks? Oh, how horrible." She grinned and rolled her eyes, tugging me forward again.

"Who do I have to thank for that nonsense this morning?" I griped, nearly tripping over my skirts to catch up with her. "You couldn't have come to warn me that they were going to make that announcement?"

"Someone did! You two refused to get up this morning and the guard told Ayla that Luca threatened him if he didn't get away from the door." She snorted. "Anyway, she originally had said one week, but I needed at least one more for a good reason."

"And what pray tell, would that be?" I humphed.

"That I can't tell you right now. It's a surprise." She stuck her nose in the air and we slowed to a white door with a lion's head carved into the middle. I opened my mouth to retort but she hushed me and turned the knob, leading us inside a clean, white chamber that was stocked to the brim with dried herbs, salves, jars of different colored liquids and a small cot against the back wall. A small framed older female greeted us as we walked inside. She wore attendant's attire, with a head covering, a pale blue dress and a white apron.

"Lady Bethel, this is Princess Arienne. I'm so sorry for the delay," Paxe apologized. The old woman smiled sweetly at me and bowed at the waist.

"It's quite alright. The poor dear looks tired. It's an honor to meet you, Mi'lady." She turned to the side and gestured to the cot. "Please, come in and have a seat."

Paxe softly shut the door as I smiled and stepped over to the cot, sitting nervously. "Thank you for seeing me on such short notice, Lady Bethel. I'm assuming she told you what brought me here today?" I asked.

"She did, Your Highness. I'm happy to help." She pulled a small wooden chair up to the cot and sat. "Can you tell me the day you last bled?" I drew my brows together and looked at Paxe.

"Your courses." Paxe whispered, smiling. I remained quiet, staring at her.

"Princess?" Bethel started softly. "Do you not remember? I can still examine you if you can't recall. It's no bother." I turned my face to the healer and felt incredibly stupid. My cheeks heated and I struggled to form a single response.

"I—" My mouth hung open and I shook my head. "I'm sorry, I—I don't understand what you're talking about." I looked back to Paxe for help. Her face was suddenly unreadable.

"Ari, have you...have you never bled before?" Paxe asked quietly.

"No?" I continued to shake my head and looked between the two of them through lowered brows. "I don't know what you mean."

Lady Bethel smiled kindly. "It's alright dear, lay back for me would you?" I did as she asked and awkwardly let my hands fall to the cot at my sides. The healer moved her chair closer and placed her hands on my lower belly. She gently felt around and pressed and poked. Her facial expressions gave nothing away. I looked over at Paxe who leaned with her arms crossed against a small table with a concerned look. "Would you mind if I did a physical examination? Have you ever had one before?" The old woman asked. I shook my head.

"That's fine. Will this hurt?" I asked nervously.

"No, it won't hurt you. Just a bit uncomfortable for a moment and then I'll be using magic." She replied softly. Paxe stepped over and knelt down to take my hand while Bethel moved her chair to the end of the cot. "Alright, Princess. You're just going to raise your knees and I'll do a quick check and we'll be all finished." I breathed deeply and complied, wincing as she did what she had to do, and while she was fast, she was also thorough and it felt as if it had taken a lifetime. I gripped at Paxe's fingers until she finished and she gently lowered my legs and covered them with my skirts. "Remain there for just a moment, dear." She called over her shoulder, moving across the room and washing her hands.

When she returned she scooted the chair back to my side and looked at me with something I could have sworn was pity. "Am I with child?" I asked.

She slowly shook her head. "No, Mi'lady. But I do need to ask you something." Paxe looked at her and then back at me.

"Alright?" I grew worried.

"Have you been through some kind of trauma? Something that would have caused damage to your reproductive organs, or deep scarring?" Paxe's face paled and she tightened her fingers around mine. I swallowed hard.

"Yes, ma'am. When I was fourteen...I was attacked," my voice cracked. "Why do you ask? Is something wrong?" The knot in my throat got bigger and I felt as if I could choke. Paxe's eyes were lined with tears.

"Princess...I—I'm afraid the injuries you sustained have caused you to be sterile. It appears that you'll not be able to conceive. I'm so sorry." She rested a hand on my arm. My body began to tremble and I stared at the ceiling, my breathing becoming rapid.

"Ever?" I choked, my lip quivering and hot tears escaping my eyes.

"I'm afraid so." She rubbed my arm consolingly and Paxe rested her head on my shoulder, softly crying. "Should I summon the prince for you?"

"Oh gods..." I sobbed, covering my face with my hands and losing my composure completely. "No...no, please don't." I turned on my side to face the wall and curled in on myself. All I could think about was Holt. His sweet little bubbly disposition. The way it felt to hold his small body all night while the love of my life tucked in close. I'd never be able to give that to him. I'd never be able to have it for myself. Yet another thing that my bastard father has stolen from me...from both of us.

Paxe laid behind me, pulling an arm over me and holding me close as I sobbed and wept uncontrollably for a solid half hour. So many of my dreams shattered. The ache and hollow place that had invaded my heart was more than I could bear. I knew only one person that could understand how this felt. Once I was finally calm enough to speak I wiped at my face and turned over to face my sister. Tears continued to fall from her eyes onto the cot and she brushed my hair away from my face. Bethel patiently sat with us, offering comfort however she could.

"I need to speak with the queen..." I whispered. My voice was hidden somewhere far away.

"Okay," Paxe replied, running her fingers through my hair. "Do you want me to bring her here? Or would you feel more comfortable talking to her in her quarters? I can go request a private meeting."

"I want to go with you." I sniffled. "We need to make sure Luca's gone into the city. I can't tell him yet. It'll break him." I bit down on my lip and squeezed my eyes closed, crying again. "Take me...please."

Her lip wobbled and she nodded, kissing my forehead and slowly raising from the cot. She and Bethel helped me to sit and I took another few moments to gather myself. Bethel brought me a small cup that smelled of lavender and something else I couldn't place and told me to sip it and that it would help with my nerves. I finally put on an impossible mask of bravery and stood, hugging the kind woman and thanking her for her help.

"I'm always available if there's anything you need, child. You're certainly not alone. Everything will be alright. I know that it may not seem that way now, but in time...you and the prince will mend. One never fully recovers from grief. We only learn how to manage and accept it. You have people here that love you deeply. Lean on them." She squeezed my shoulder.

"Thank you, ma'am." I breathed. Paxe and I held hands as we left the chamber and were mostly silent as we took our time down the halls. Thankfully, I didn't see any sign that Luca was still in the castle. When we finally approached the doors to the queen's quarters, Paxe spoke to one of the guards quietly outside the door. He told her that the queen had just recently entered and that she was alone. We waited outside while he sent for her and when he returned, Ayla came with him.

"Arienne?" She called from the doorway. I raised my face and her eyes softened. "What's happened? Come inside, both of you." She waved us in and we entered. As soon as the door closed behind me I could only stare into her face and see Luca. Which must have been enough by the time I was able to speak the words out loud.

"I—I just saw Lady Bethel and—" I choked on a sob. "I'm so sorry...I'm so—" My chest rose and fell and my jaw shook. She braced my shoulders and tried to steady me as I finally said, "I'm barren."

The queen's eyes were filled not with the scrutiny that we'd have no heir, but with the sympathy and the understanding that I knew she'd have as they welled with tears and she forcefully pulled me to her. I collapsed into her shoulder and she tightly held me as I wept. After nearly an hour of sitting down to cry, talk, and regroup, she had finally convinced Paxe and I both to rest in Luca's room until dinner, which she was having sent to the small dining hall in the king and queen's shared chambers. Paxe decided the four of us should dine alone and that she'd press Lakan to take her into the city for their supper so that Luca and I would have some privacy to weather our news with his parents. Michele had apparently been obligated to his own family this evening, and had promised the queen that he'd return Luca before the dinnertime hour. This of course, gave me little time to prepare for this conversation, dress, and try to appear less like the withered sack of skin and grief that I currently was, as I curled against my sister on the large bed.

"Ari, you do know that Luca would never love you any less," Paxe whispered, stroking my hair. "I know that the idea of raising a family may have been new, and that you both felt more strongly about what you wanted...but his heart," she lifted my chin. "You were always first."

"I know," I breathed.

"I feel horrible."

I lowered my brows. "Why? Because of the babe?" I pressed a hand to her belly. Don't you da—"

"No...no not that. Although, yes a little. How could I have never known that you never bled? I was to be the one to look out for you. To grow with you, and share these things in our lives. I shed my first blood when I was thirteen," she softly shook her head. "I'd had it for a few years before you ended up in that dungeon."

"I never knew that. This isn't your fault, Paxe. I knew *how* to create a child...I never was told about the rest. The only blood I shed from that part of my body was after..." My breathing shuddered. "After they did that to me. I was in the bath chamber alone. I thought perhaps I might die. It didn't stop for two days. Every time I washed it off, all I could see were bodies. Bodies forcing themselves and other objects into mine. Bodies lying mangled on the floor. Somehow, I wasn't dead...and I wanted to be." I cried silently and Paxe pulled me close, tears escaping her sapphire eyes. "Perhaps this is what I deserve, Paxe. I lived when they couldn't. That baby in his mother's lap...I—"

"Stop." She pulled away. "Don't you ever say that again." Her tears continued to fall. "No one in that dungeon deserved that. Least of all, you. *You were a child too.* What you did to end up down there wasn't any less criminal than when we stole pastries from the kitchen. Or when we switched the maestro's sheet music for the royal banquets. You kissed someone, Ari. Someone who wanted you to. Someone who cared deeply for you, and died to protect your virtue. The only person who should suffer is your father. Do you understand?" I nodded and wept quietly. "Sit up," she whispered, helping me to raise myself.

"What are you doing?" I asked, wiping my eyes.

She slid off the bed and walked into the bath chamber, returning with a handheld mirror. It was placed into my hands and I held it face down and shook my head. "Hold it up and face yourself."

"I can't," I whispered, another tear falling from my eye.

"Yes, you can. Hold it up. Do it now." She sat across from me and covered my hands with her own around the handle. "You're not alone. I'm here with you. Hold it up." She slowly raised the mirror with me and I kept my eyes on hers. "Look into it." I held her gaze for a long moment and then stared at my reflection and fell apart. She refused to let me put it down. "Take a deep breath and talk to her, Ari. Tell her why she's strong."

I've never grown used to the love-hate relationship I have with mirrors. The way that they make you think too much, or threaten to have you longing for something...or someone. It can bring a smile to your lips, or a tear to your eye. Then there's that awkward feeling of catching that glimpse of a scar or two in your reflection that has your mind swimming in all kinds of memories. The good and the bad.

"You look just like your mother." I started, my fingers gripping the handle as I spoke to the same flourishing young female I had seen the morning that I met Luca. "She was broken too. She loved fiercely, and died honorably. It wasn't your fault," I wept. Gideon's face flashed in my mind.

I need you to forgive yourself and let me go.

"Let them go," I whispered. "You made a promise. You survived for a reason. You are Arienne Genovese, Queen of Valdaro, deliverer of her people. Daughter of Lucinda...Goddess of Light. You are the wife and soulmate of Luca Di Meo, the bringer of light. You are the wielder of ancient weapons, and the blade of justice." My voice grew steadier and my spine straighter. Paxe's lips curled into a smile as tears pooled in her eyes. "Your purpose isn't to create life...but to give it back. Your purpose is to love, and to live for the other half of your soul. You will stand beside him as his equal and continue to survive...*Until Death. I forgive you.* I forgive *them.* I forgive that broken king, and his frozen heart. You'll hold that head high, and you'll wear that crown. You'll govern these lands without that sword. You'll heal them with your heart. You'll do these things with him at your side. You will *survive.* Not because of your past...but because of your *future.*"

I stared at that face in the glass. I took in every word, every scar. I smiled at her and she smiled back. And with strength I didn't realize I possessed, I looked into those deep green eyes that were lined with tears and said; "*I love you.*" As the words left my mouth, something deep inside my body—no—my *soul* snapped free. It was as if a link to my chains were broken and a small sliver of freedom escaped, and a tear fell to my lap. The mirror seemed to pulse beneath our hands and we released it as it fell to the bed. Paxe and I looked down at it, moving away and glancing up at each other in surprise.

"What the hell was that?" She asked, turning her hands over and causing me to feel the need to do the same. Our palms looked unscathed and we returned our attention to the mirror that laid face down on the duvet.

"I have no idea." My hand shook as I held it over the handle. I didn't feel any buzz of strange magic, or dark feeling that touching it would harm me. I carefully picked it up and turned it over and we both audibly gasped at the large crack across the face.

"What do you suppose?" Paxe whispered, staring at it with caution and palming her little bump. A knock sounded at Luca's door and I shoved the mirror beneath the pillow.

"Yes?" I called. A guard spoke on the other side.

"Prince Luca has returned early, Princess. He's looking for you." His muffled voice replied. Paxe and I looked nervously at one another and I rushed to the door, opening it only a little.

"Where is he?" I asked. The guard bowed his head.

"The prince is in the dining room with the king and queen. He's asked to see you urgently."

"Do you know why?" My stomach flipped.

"I do not, Mi'lady. He's not even told them the reason as of yet. Shall I escort you upstairs to their shared quarters?" He asked politely.

I looked over my shoulder at Paxe, who darted into the sitting room and began searching for something to dress me in. I turned back to the guard. "Would you mind waiting for me? I'll just be a moment." I smiled thoughtfully.

"Of course, Your Highness. I'll be right here at the end of the corridor when you're ready." He bowed and began making his way down the hall.

I met Paxe in the dressing room by the armoire and she helped me into a gorgeous deep purple gown that was nearly identical to the one I was wearing. Where my previous dress had silver thread, this one had gold. Paxe brushed through my hair before braiding it over my shoulder and tugging the plaits to make them fuller. She retrieved a small box that the queen had no doubt sent with the gowns, and started decorating the braid with pins that were adorned with small violets. Before she let me go, she softened the puffiness of my face with a cool, wet linen and I was amazed at the difference it made. I *almost* could have passed for a maiden that had spent a leisurely day about the castle had it not been for the redness in the whites of my eyes.

"Paxe...what if he knows?" My fingers twisted around each other.

"He'll know soon enough anyway. I don't think his parents will tell him something like that before you have the chance to. It has to be something else."

"But what? Could something have happened?" I bit down on my lip and the churning in my stomach grew stronger.

"I'm not sure. Maybe it has something to do with the wedding? There's only one way to know. Let's get you out of here. You're ready. Everything will be fine." She handled my shoulders and leaned her face into mine. "Go to him."

I nodded and we made for the door. We started down the corridor to meet the guard who was dutifully waiting at the end. "I'm nervous. I feel as if I'm about to vomit...or cry. Or perhaps both." I breathed deeply.

"You just stand tall, and remember what you said to that queen in the mirror. Understand?" She slowed and turned me to face her. "I'm so proud of you." She smiled.

I hugged her tight. "As usual, you know best. I can't thank you enough for forcing me to do that. I should have done it a long time ago." I drew back and kissed her cheek. "I love you, Paxe."

"I love *you*. More than you could ever know." Her belly grumbled loudly and she gripped at it. I laughed for the first time since we'd left Lady Bethel's workroom and patted the bump.

"Go feed my niece," I smiled softly, turning to the guard.

"Your *niece?*" She called from behind me as I followed the guard down a hallway opposite from where she was headed. "Ari! How do you know?" Her voice echoed down the hall. "We're not done talking about this!" I smiled to myself, smoothing my hand down my bodice and dropping my mouth into a frown as my fingers brushed over my middle. I swallowed hard and straightened my spine as we continued to trek through the halls.

"Are you alright, Princess?" The guard asked from beside me.

"I will be," I whispered.

CHAPTER 31

OF JOY AND SORROW

I stood before the tall, turquoise double doors to the royal family's shared quarters, and my heart thudded loudly in my chest as the guard reached for the handle of the right one and pulled it open to announce me. I raised my face from its lowered position in time to see Luca with an extraordinarily potent and elated smile, rushing to meet me at the entrance. That smile faltered as he took in the state of my eyes, still teeming with evidence of my grief and he slowed to a halt. His brows lowered as he stepped slowly toward me, the king and queen standing in front of their chairs at the small dining table behind him. My eyes met Ayla's for a heartbeat and she dipped her chin, as if to assure me that neither had breathed a word to him about my news. Luca's gentle hands cupped my face when he approached and I sank into his touch as he peered into my swollen eyes.

"You look overjoyed about something." I smiled softly. He closed the space between us and stared down at me, as I eased my arms around his back, almost instantly comforted from his proximity alone.

"And you look absolutely devastated. Tell me what's wrong, love." His stare was pleading. "Was it the healer?" I closed my eyes and leaned forward until our heads touched. "What happened?"

"I'd rather hear what's made you so happy before I break your heart, Luca." I whispered, choking back the new knot in my throat. I didn't have to open my eyes to see the look I knew was on his face.

"You know I can't do that now. Do we need to be alone?"

"No," I breathed. "That's why we're eating in here tonight." I opened my eyes when his breath shuddered. He leaned up and kissed my forehead, and then cradled my head into his neck. I pressed in closer and we stood there for a long moment, before he finally led me in silence to the table.

The small dining table was designed to only seat the four of us and was no bigger than the one at Vetta's house in Aeon, but very elegant and sturdy. There were no servants in the room as they waited to be called on outside the delicately, but ornately decorated space. The room was not at all large, and very private with a single doorway leading in or out. The king and queen smiled sweetly at me as they lowered themselves into their seats; Tidus heading the table, and Ayla seated to his left. Luca pulled the chair at the other end out for me and turned it sideways before sitting me down. He knelt in front of me and gently took my hands into his own, seemingly struggling to control his breathing, as he stared up at me in anticipation.

"Luca..." The queen started. "I want you to know that your father and I are here for both of you. When you're ready to talk about what she needs to tell you, there's nothing we won't do to help you through this as life partners. Neither of you are alone, as I assured Arienne earlier today." The king nodded. Luca never took his eyes from mine.

"I'm here, love. Take whatever time you need," he said softly. I thought of the female I spoke to in the mirror that was still buried under our pillows and took a steadying breath.

"You remember the things that you witnessed during our blood union. The one in Aeon." He tensed and his fingers gripped tighter around mine. He slowly nodded and I scraped up what dignity and strength I had left. "You remember seeing what those men had done to me, and how badly injured I told you I was the night we fought in the woods by the fire?" He stayed silent. "I saw Lady Bethel today...and she examined me thoroughly. I'm not with child, Luca." I paused and stared into his silver eyes that were lining with tears as I continued. "And because of what happened that night...I never will be." My lip quivered and my eyes burned. "I'm sorry."

The muscles in Luca's jaw feathered and his breaths became shaky as a single tear fell from his eye and broke as it raced down his cheek. His fingers firmly wound around mine and the room was utterly silent for several moments, until he brought my hands to his mouth, squeezing his eyes closed and kissing every one of my knuckles until he broke into heavy sobs and dropped his other knee to the floor. I lost control of the hold on my emotions, and so did the king and queen as he laid his head into my lap and cried harder. I pulled a hand free and brushed his hair back as I leaned over him and pressed a kiss to his temple.

"I'm sorry...baby, I'm so sorry." He wept into my skirts and I laid my cheek over his as I smoothed my hand down his spine. It was clear to me then that he wasn't as upset about not having a child as he was about what I had been through, and what had brought us here. I allowed us both a moment to release every following emotion, and the sound of his sobbing tore my heart into scraps. I flattened my palm and searched for his magic. He jerked slightly when I found it and gripped my hand tighter, as we both eased the pain away...together. Breathing became a little easier and our bodies weren't as tense. I could feel the beating of our hearts fall into the exact same rhythm and I smiled tenderly against his skin.

"Luca, *I love you*," I whispered. "I spent the day realizing that this changes only a small part of our future. I know...I know how badly this hurts. As long as you're willing to stay with me, we can get through this together." He shifted and I sat up slowly as he raised his head. Our heads met again and we both swept fingers across each other's faces before he leaned in with a kiss that ran deeper than any we'd ever shared.

"I've spent my life waiting for you, Ari." He spoke into my mouth. "There will never be an obstacle in this world to keep me from you." I kissed him again and my very soul ached for him. When we broke away his arms wrapped around me and his cheek rested on my chest. I held him close for a few moments and the king and queen sat silent, save for the occasional sniffle. "I love you," Luca breathed.

"We grieve tonight. We push forward tomorrow...alright?" I kissed his hair and he nodded against me. There were a few more moments of silence before he finally spoke again.

"I have something to show you," he whispered, forcing himself to stand. He faced the three of us and took a deep breath. "Something happened a while ago."

"Is this why you returned early?" Tidus asked.

"It is. I was halfway up the palace entrance after I left Michele at the gates. I felt a jolt like I'd been hit by lightning." My eyes widened as I put the pieces together. The pulse we felt, and the cracked mirror. It had been about that time. I felt something deep down that seemed off. "I nearly tripped, it hit me so hard, and a snap of light flickered under my shirt." He started unbuttoning his collar. "I'm not sure what happened or how..." My heart raced and both Luca's parents leaned forward. "But I think some part of this curse has just been broken." He pulled the material apart and the blue mark on his chest had turned a dull gray. Much like the gray color from when he'd lost his life in Nero's temple, only a shade lighter, and somehow weaker in comparison.

Ayla leapt from her seat at the table and rounded it to inspect the mark. "How do you know it isn't just starting to take its hold on you? There aren't but a few more weeks left." I stayed pinned in my seat and I felt the king's eyes on me.

"I don't know for certain, I suppose. But when it was over I felt as if an enormous weight had been lifted...not...*from* me, but deeper. Like something incredibly dark and heavy had been removed from my soul, and the mark looked different. *I* feel different." Luca held his shirt open as his mother traced the mark with her finger. His eyes caught mine and I could tell by his stare that he knew there was something I wasn't saying. "Ari...are you alright?" Ayla turned around. I now had the attention of everyone in the room and my breath quickened.

"It was me," I said hoarsely. "I think it was me."

"What?" Ayla asked, watching Luca as he moved around her to get to me.

"What do you mean, love? Did something happen?" I slowly stood and looked at his chest. His hands smoothed down my sleeves.

"I came to see your mother after I left the healer. We talked and I realized some things. Paxe took me to your room to lie down a while before dinner. She wouldn't leave me and we had a strong conversation. She held a mirror in front of me and forced me to talk to my reflection and—" I paused and looked up at him. "I forgave her. I forgave the men that hurt me. I forgave my father...I reminded myself of the things that make me strong...for my people, but most of all for *you*." His hands squeezed around my arms. "I told the girl in the mirror that I loved her...and it pulsed and the glass cracked. If you were almost in the castle then the timing is right." Luca exhaled sharply as if he were about to cry again and pulled me against him, pressing his mouth to my hairline and breathing hard.

"I'll be godsdamned," Tidus whispered from his seat. "It's no wonder I'm not finding anything in these books. That's one clever son of a bitch."

"What are you talking about?" Ayla asked breathlessly, near weeping with relief.

"I'm talking about the tangled threads he put into this curse." We all faced him now. "He broke her. He put her through enough torment that he knew without a doubt would subdue her and cause her to be just like him. That's all he wanted. Less like her mother, more like the husk of evil that he embodies." His finger pointed in my direction. "He knew that she'd blame herself. He knew she'd nearly succumb to pain and guilt. He also knew she'd hate him for it. He said at the meeting that he wanted her to kill him, remember? I had asked just to clarify it. He wants her to grow a spine. He's forcing her to be something she'll never be. She'd never love. No one could convince her. She wouldn't love herself, and she sure as hell wouldn't risk loving someone else." A smile crept across his face and he looked at Luca. "But he didn't expect *you*, son. He's never known love like you have for her. Like you have for each other. That's the answer."

"But it isn't fully gone," I argued. "What would be enough?"

"I don't know. But it's likely woven together so complex that he's made sure you never find out. Look how much you've proved him wrong so far. Look at that damned thing." We stared at the mark that seemed to gleam in the lamp lights. "All these weeks, when had it ever changed other than when Luca's heart stopped beating? And even then, didn't you say it remained there and was back to normal right after?"

"Yes," Luca answered. "If death couldn't do it, then what would break it altogether?"

"It isn't life. Because if it is, this curse will never break. He's taken that from us too," I stated sadly. Ayla looked at us with the deepest sorrow.

"We need to put our heads together. We have a month. If this curse has broken even the slightest bit, then I've no doubt the king knows it too. We need to be prepared for anything. Arienne...I—" The king's voice cracked. "I can't imagine how difficult this is for you both. To have so much joy and hope while also feeling so much pain. When the queen fell ill...we at least had one child. I can't tell you how sorry I am." His eyes softened and he rubbed at the corner of one with a finger.

"I—" Ayla followed. "I just don't understand it. I always believed that the reason I was only able to give birth to one child was because Lucinda and I were the bodies that were destined to carry this world's deliverers. I still believe that. But why would the gods join them this way and give them the power to conquer, but not give them a way to produce an heir?" She slowly walked back to her seat as she spoke, lowering herself into the chair and taking the king's hand.

"Because..." I whispered, gaining their attention...and Luca's. "I was never meant to carry the heir." I met Luca's eyes, which conveyed the support he offered in telling his parents the truth.

"What do you mean?" Tidus asked quietly.

"We didn't tell you everything the night we returned home," Luca offered. The queen's face hardened.

"If you're about to cause me to tear this room apart, Luca..." She warned.

"It's not that. It has nothing to do with me. But what we're about to tell you has to stay in this room until it's time. And I'm only starting to realize now why my wife is handling this so well." He tugged me close to his side.

"Go tell the staff to bring the dinner in and leave us. If it's that serious, no one needs to be near that door." The king inclined his head. Luca nodded once and stepped out the door as I sat back into my chair and scooted it closer to the table. The attendants made quick work rushing in and out and placing our plates before us as Luca finally took his seat. Once they had left and we were sure no one was listening, the queen leaned over her plate.

"Why do you believe such a thing, Princess?" She asked. Luca took my hand and I drew a long breath.

"The heir already lives, my queen." I fought back tears. "In Paxe's belly." Both their mouths dropped open and they were quiet for a long moment.

"Oh, my Gods..." she whispered, staring off in shock. "She's his daughter." Her face turned to me and she placed a hand over her chest. "Your sister."

"Yes, Mi'lady."

"And she doesn't know?" Tidus asked finally. Luca and I both shook our heads.

"My mother told me in the immortal realm. I haven't been sure how to tell her, but I fear for her state if she takes it badly. We wanted to wait until she's safely given birth."

"But that's months off, Arienne. If the king dies in the next few weeks, then she'll—" The queen's face grew pale. "Are you waiting until she receives your father's power?"

"I considered it. I don't know." I propped an elbow on the table and pressed a palm to my forehead. "I felt her out when we talked on the beach. I just...I don't know what to do."

"Whatever she decides, Mother...that's Arienne's decision to make. No one can take it upon themselves to tell her this truth. It's difficult enough just knowing." Luca gripped my hand and spoke directly to his mother.

"He's right, darling. This isn't our place. Paxe is strong too. She's also a survivor. You know that." Tidus looked at his wife, but she didn't take her eyes from me.

"And what of your crown? What of this marriage?" She asked. Her tone was more worried than angry and I understood both.

"This marriage will happen regardless of anything else. She's the half of my soul that was missing. Crown, or no crown...I'm marrying her," Luca snapped.

"Luca, you know that isn't what I meant. The crown has been a birthright for both of you since the day you were born. But if Paxe is the heir, how does this work? When you marry, you'll be the waiting king and queen. If she doesn't know the truth..." My hand fell to the table.

"I will rule until she's ready. I made vows to my people that I intend to keep. My sister is included in that. She deserves to live her life without the weight of a crown. The people don't have to know who she truly is until she decides that she wants them to. That's her right. I want her to have the chance to raise her baby without the world watching. I don't need magic to rule, or to free our people. All we truly need is your support. Knowing that my father's magic is in safe hands is good enough for me."

Tidus offered me a proud smile and nodded slowly. The queen's mouth turned up in the corner as she looked me over. "You truly are a queen," she said softly.

"Yes, she is," Luca added, his voice smooth as he smiled at me.

"You have, and always will have our support, Princess," Tidus dipped his chin and I smiled sweetly.

"I want to say this to both of you..." Ayla started as her attention flickered between Luca and I. "The loss and the pain that you feel...it is devastating. We don't know why the gods do what they do, and it isn't our place to ask such a thing. Should they will it...you may wake up one morning to find you've been blessed with life in your scarred womb. You may not. No matter which of those things happen, do not allow this to hinder you from sharing everything else together. There are many others that share our grief in this way. It never made me love your father any less, Luca. If anything...it brought me closer to him, and to you, my son. Live. And love one another. Find your strength and your will in each other. There is great healing in it."

"Thank you, Mi'lady. I promise...you've nothing to fear." I looked over at Luca who watched me with longing, and I wanted nothing more than to leave this table and return to our bed. I ached to hold him. I ached to *be* held. I wanted to give him comfort, and to have our time to be alone and mourn together.

"You must be famished," The king said. "Please, eat something. The two of you have a great deal to discuss tonight. You'll need that strength." We all began quietly eating, but it wasn't long before the queen broke the sound of clanging utensils with something to lighten our moods.

"Luca...did you get too close to a rabid animal while you were out?" She forked fresh greens into her mouth. He cleared his throat, and I pressed a napkin to my mouth and choked for a moment. The king chuckled into his wine glass.

"You could say that. But it was before I left, and I suppose I was just as rabid." He grinned as he chewed. I kicked his ankle beneath the table and he winced. "That was all that happened, I assure you."

I looked toward the wall and raised my glass to my lips. "Right." The queen laughed.

"It's absolutely true. My darling fiancée has proposed that we...wait...until the wedding." He raised his brows at me and took a drink.

"Ha!" Tidus bellowed, wiping his mouth. "Is that right?" We both nodded miserably.

"So...you left a little reminder before he left of what's yours?" Ayla grinned at me, drinking from her glass.

"Precisely." I raised my glass to her.

"Clever girl," she snickered. "A queen indeed."

"Well, this will be a long two weeks." The king smiled, taking a bite from his fork. "You'll need something to keep you occupied, my friend. Did Michele take you to see the foundation for the project today?"

"No, but we did talk about it. He showed me some of his other work around the city," Luca said, taking a small bite of a dinner roll. I didn't let on that I knew about the university and we all continued to talk amongst ourselves, avoiding the painful subject that had brought us together tonight. When we finally bid each other goodnight, Luca led me out the door and it snicked shut behind us. We took a few steps away and he turned me to him, pulling me close and holding me tight.

"You're the strongest...most incredible person I've ever met," He breathed, taking my chin in his fingers. "Don't call me a jackass." He smirked.

"Why would I call you a jackass?" I asked under scrunched brows. He said nothing as he slowly reached behind my knees and scooped me into his arms. I smiled as I recalled the day we met, and he had carried me down the path. My arm slipped behind his neck and my other hand rested on his chest as I pressed myself against him and breathed in the scent at the base of his neck. I closed my eyes and he laid his head against mine, as he took his time carrying me the entire way back to his room.

Once we had finally made it, neither of us bothered to disrobe or even pull the blankets back. We laid on top of the bed, took turns crying, kissed, talked very little and after a while when I had no more salt water left to leak from my eyes, I laid on my back and stared at the ceiling. Exhaustion and a pounding headache took its toll on me and I could hardly stay awake as I ran my fingers through Luca's hair. His head rested on my lower belly, one arm tightly wrapped around me and the other tucked beneath him, his fingers clinging to mine. I could tell by the way he was breathing that he had chosen his spot for the night. Tomorrow would be a new day, and one day less to count down until the rest of our lives. As deep as it hurt, I refused to let it consume us, or the joy and excitement of helping plan the happiest day of our lives.

I suddenly heard my own voice, involuntarily humming the tune of the song Luca had heard me singing the night he'd snuck out to seek me. I didn't question myself and continued, silently apologizing to the small baby that we'd never know, with my hair and Luca's eyes. I pictured tiny fingers gripping around one of his, and my lips stealing a kiss from a little button nose. One last tear fell toward my hairline as I hummed the rest of the song, finishing it by singing the last line.

"And when I fill the dark with light...drowning the stars as they say goodnight..." I closed my eyes and sniffed. *"They'll never understand the way....my heart will long for thee..."* My head fogged and our infant blurred away, leaving me in darkness as I let go and fell into sleep.

CHAPTER 32

THE BEST LAID PLANS

Three days passed and I already had enough to keep me occupied with only a bit over a week left until our wedding. The pain I had been pushing aside became more dull, and my nerves more unhinged, as the time for me to walk to an altar and finally claim Luca as my husband drew closer and closer. Paxe and Ayla were happy to provide any distraction to take my mind away from my mourning, and the obvious tension between my betrothed and myself as every day became more difficult for us both to keep our hands to ourselves. We found it easier during the day to separate and stay busy with everything else than to be in close proximity, although nights and early mornings were spent close enough to one another that even excusing ourselves to use a chamber pot was put off longer than needed.

We didn't talk about our loss anymore, as it was perfectly understood through silence and the reality that neither of us were going through it alone. Oftentimes it was enough just to stare into one another and have those conversations without any words. Today, Michele and Luca were meeting with contractors and hiring extra hands in the southern bay to help plan and construct the project that the king had been all too happy to throw himself into, now that his boy was home. More distraction. I was grateful for it. We both needed this kind of support, and they all were working tirelessly to provide it. We were surrounded by amazing individuals.

The west wing of the castle's second floor had an exceptionally large and breathtaking ballroom with a large balcony that overlooked the sea. This is where I now stood with the queen and my sister, and several hired planners and assistants, who were taking notes on Ayla's ideas to convert the back half into where we'd exchange our vows, and the enormous half Paxe and I were standing in to accommodate festivities after the ceremony. The room glittered with crystal chandeliers and silver sconces, nearly every wall was covered in stained glass windows that reached from the floors to the ceilings. Like most banquet halls or royal gathering spaces, there was a raised platform near the back wall that was large enough to fit us all for the ceremony, along with a choir that Ayla insisted was necessary. I overheard her conversation with one of the planners about spreading a turquoise runner down half of the room to divide the congregation. Her hands splayed about as she talked and pointed, and then, she walked over to the location of where she wanted it placed.

"Need an out?" Paxe asked as she crossed her arms and glanced sidelong at me.

"I'm not sure if that's—"

"You haven't left this castle since you got here. Let's go into the city today. You need to go check in with Lakan about his little project anyhow. She's got this handled, we're just standing here."

"You're right...should we at least tell her?" I asked, looking sympathetically at the animated queen.

"I'll handle it. Come on." She grabbed my hand and led me to the ballroom doorway, speaking to a castle attendant and tugging me down the halls, until we found ourselves traveling down the long walkway to the gates.

"Does Lakan have a shop of his own here?" I asked as we started into the city.

"Yes! His very own, and he's thriving. I've never seen him so...content." Paxe smiled as we dipped our chins to passersby that waved in the street. She glowed in the warm coastal sunlight in her rose colored gown. She had chosen a similar gown for me today that was the exact color of the rooftops in the city. I wondered if she'd planned this trip out of the castle all along.

"What can we do after? Are there any places you like to frequent around here?" I asked, taking in the beauty of this place.

"Oh, yes. After we visit Lakan, let's go to the shopping district...oh! There's a tailor that assists in the castle as well, I need to take you to see her before we go back this evening. I want to make sure I have your measurements right. Her shop is close to the smith."

"I suppose it wouldn't do well not to have a wedding gown," I laughed. "I find it so strange that I've yet to even think about that part of my own wedding. These things really do rattle your mind, don't they?" She smirked and kept her face forward as we walked.

"Well, it's a good thing you don't have to worry about that." I looked over at her curiously.

"Did you and the queen already get one?"

"Oh yes...months ago." She giggled.

"I don't understand."

"That was your surprise. The extra week was to make sure Perla was able to send your dress from Valdaro. The one we were having made for your Ventus. I needed time for it to get here and make necessary adjustments for it to be used for your wedding instead." I pulled her arm and we stopped.

"Are you kidding? Paxe that's—" I hugged her. "Thank you...so much."

"I can't wait to see you in it." She cupped my cheeks. "Surprise." We both laughed and started to continue down the street, passing rounded white buildings and clutching hands. "I'm glad that you never got around to seeing the progress. It's exciting."

"When will it be here?" I asked excitedly.

"I'm hoping by the end of this week so that we'll have some time to add a few things."

"Like what?"

"Like a veil? And a few finishing touches so that it's more like a wedding gown and less like a Ventus garment." Her smile was bright and heartwarming. "You know, a couple of months ago it was hard to convince you to explore a forest with Luca, let alone speak to him. You two have come a long way in such a short time. This is bittersweet for me. Thank you for letting me be a part of this." She slowed at a door that had a hanger above it with a hammer that was crossed with a sword. We faced each other and everything inside me wished to tell her my biggest secret. But her smile and disposition knocked me back. However she took the news, I didn't want to risk ruining this day.

"I'd never be satisfied with anyone else, Paxe. I truly mean that," I smiled. She nodded and pushed the door open. A blast of stifling hot air rushed out as we entered Lakan's shop. We only stayed long enough for me to approve of his favor, before it became too sweltering inside for us not to be drenched in sweat. I also had no intention of talking too long with my sister's shirtless lover. We relished in the fresh air as we left and headed down the block to the tailor. "I can see what you found so attractive about him," I snickered, fanning myself and dabbing at my damp forehead.

"I find it difficult to visit his shop while he's working," She laughed. "Brings fond images to my mind and he's a professional here."

"You're adorable together," I pecked, nudging her with an elbow.

"Thank you, friend. Let's get you measured up and then we'll go spend some coin, yeah?"

"Yes. Gods yes." We strode into the tailor, which took longer than I wanted. The old woman looked very human as well, but insisted on showing us a hundred different swatches of material as if she were going to be making this dress from scratch. We gave our opinions on what she offered and I finally gathered that my Ventus gown was already white and silver with a lot of embellishments and would be the perfect substitute for a wedding gown. I was nearly bursting to see it. We were still talking about it after we'd finally left the tailor, who everybody referred to as 'Gran', and strolled down Crona's bustling shopping district.

It wasn't a surprise that Paxe's first order of business was to drop into the confectioner's shop. We tried several different things at the counter and left with a bag full of sweets which her hormonal, pregnant hands dug into as we peered through the windows of different stores on the strip.

"Oh, my Gods...yes! We're going in here," Paxe said through a mouthful of chocolate, as we approached a storefront with window dummies draped in provocative lingerie. I blushed and turned my face away, walking quickly past it. Her arm hooked around mine and she spun me around and dragged me to the door. A little bell sounded as we entered, and I could have died of humiliation.

"Paxe, for the love of the Gods..." I whispered loudly. "I do *not* wear things like this, and you know it." My face was on fire as I looked around at a display of lacy underthings, spread across small tables throughout the store. "I can't do this." I tried to pull away and bolt back out of the door, but she was having none of it.

"You never had a reason to! Look, you're spending the next week and a half holding out until your wedding day. Why not make this even more exciting and let Luca salivate while he takes that dress off, and you spend your first night together as husband and wife?" Her voice was not in any way quiet, and it caught the attention of a very heavily made up employee who stared in our direction with a smirk. I politely smiled back and mouthed an apology as Paxe dragged me from table to table. The female approached us a few minutes later, obviously realizing I refused to touch a single item and felt very much out of place.

"Can I offer some assistance?" Her bright red lips pulled back and the little beauty mark above her top lip raised with it. She was a pretty girl, with sensual curves and tight fitting clothes. She carried herself with a great deal of confidence as she fluttered her false lashes and twirled her finger around her hair, which was a much lighter shade of blonde than Paxe's. I swallowed hard and cleared my throat, trying and failing to present myself in any other way. I wasn't able to come close to matching her level of self-assuredness.

"Yes! What would you suggest for a bride with a rather...*special*...taste in bedroom habits?" Paxe grinned, clutching her bag of goodies in her arm. I covered my face with my hands.

I just want to die...right here. Someone put me out.

"Special?" The female giggled. "Can you give me a bit more?"

"No." I dropped my hands and sneered at Paxe, who pretended I didn't exist.

"She and her prince are known to break things and draw each other's blood. They're animals. That about covers it," Paxe said without a shred of remorse. I smacked her upper arm. The large breasted woman dropped her mouth open in surprise and gaped at me.

"Oh!" She sank into a quick curtsy. "You're the Princess? I'm so sorry, I didn't realize...I suppose I didn't expect you to be so...simple?" She smiled.

"I'm sorry?" Paxe lowered her brows. The employee waved her palms at us in apology.

"No, no I didn't mean it in a harsh way. I only meant that your beauty is so natural and that you seem so...normal. As if you wear your title only because you have to. I really admire that. I'm not at all that way, although I wish I were." She darted her attention between the two of us. Paxe watched her closely and I decided to be the polite one and reassure her.

"It's alright, I've been told that in a few different ways recently." I smiled.

"I think I have just the thing. Follow me," she said, turning and heading for a table near the back. Paxe and I looked at each other as we followed and she glared at the back of the girl's head, as she bit into a small pastry. She chewed angrily and stalked toward the table.

"She didn't mean any harm. Calm your pregnant nerves," I whispered. Her eyes rolled as she finished off the flaky chocolate bread.

"I think this would be perfect," The blonde chirped, holding up a deep crimson two-piece set. It was really something, and though I wasn't comfortable even looking at things like this, I wasn't inclined to deny that I really loved it. There was definitely not much to leave to the imagination. Both pieces were nothing but sheer red lace. The top was cut to barely cover the whole breast, and plunged into a deep V in the center that was embellished with crisscrossed red ribbons. The entirety of the upper piece looked to cover half of my torso, and the bottoms were mostly just a single strip of lace held together by a thin scarlet strap. She handed it to me, and I raised it, turning it towards Paxe who squealed with glee.

"I actually like this a lot," I grinned. "Thank you."

"Oh, you're welcome. I hope Luca loves it." She smiled, very pleased with herself. I caught Paxe's eyes as soon as his name left that woman's mouth and both our heads jerked towards her.

"What did you say?" I asked, narrowing my eyes.

"I was just saying...I hope Luca enjoys what you picked." Her face showed a bit more malice.

"I may be from a different side of the world, but is it customary here for a citizen to refer to their prince by their name? Especially in front of his future wife?" My adrenaline began to spike.

"I meant no disrespect. He and I used to be great friends a long time ago. Though, I don't remember him being so...*adventurous* in his bed." She smiled and showed every last one of her teeth. I wanted to smack them all out of her over-painted face. I had been so worried about the tavern girl that I'd completely forgotten about the one that snuck into his room. The one that used to work in the castle that the queen had dismissed. Before I could say another word, or act on my rising anger, Paxe's paper bag dropped to the floor and her fist loudly connected with that whore's mouth.

"Say that again!" Paxe yelled, as the woman fell back against the wall, stunned and bleeding down her chin. The little harlot felt across her top teeth.

"Bitch! You chipped my tooth!" She screamed, looking as if she were about to put her hands on my pregnant sister. I lunged for her, grabbing her by the hair and handing the garments to Paxe. I pinned her to the wall and leaned into her face, as I hissed between my teeth.

"I don't care what you think I'm supposed to look like, or how great your one night in my husband's bed was. But let me enlighten you on a few things, wench. I've killed someone for a lot less. You lay one finger on her and I'll gut your cheap, tasteless body the way I did the male you'd probably sell yourself to. Perhaps the queen wasn't as clear as she meant to be when she threw you out of the castle. Pack your shit and don't ever let me see your face in our kingdom again...or I'll be all too happy to finish what she started." I nodded toward Paxe, who smiled with challenge.

I released her and she breathed heavily, saying nothing and not moving a single inch as we grabbed the bag of sweets and headed for the door. I looked over my shoulder before we walked out and tossed a couple of gold coins that I was certain she knew was too much. They bounced off the floor and scattered toward her.

"Here. There's some extra for a dress that covers your tits. And I just wanted you to know...Luca thought your previous position, before you were a palace aide, was in a *brothel.*" Her eyes widened at my words and I realized that she had thought I was never told about their tryst. "Oh yes. He told me about you. You should be more conscious about how you carry yourself. It makes you dreadfully unattractive. To be honest...I would have expected someone that my husband found worthy of lying with him to behave differently. It's a shame. *You never knew him at all.* Have a nice day."

"Don't look so glum, puppet," Paxe smiled through a mouthful of cake. "If anything, your little mishap is an improvement." We turned and walked out the door, snickering quietly. "Thanks for the help!" Paxe raised an arm as the door dinged shut behind us.

We laughed about the exchange for a few blocks, and Paxe dipped into a small shop to ask for a bag to hide my purchase from Luca, and any other wandering eyes along the street. She talked with the shopkeeper for a moment, and I browsed around while she excused herself to use the facilities and wash the lip stain from her knuckles. I soon realized as I poked around that we had unknowingly wandered into a magic shoppe. There were assortments of stones used for practically anything; blessed jewelry, supposed spell books, religious tapestries, dried herbs, and a small round table with two chairs in the back corner that was covered in a strangely embroidered cloth. In the middle of the table was a shining clear globe set in a hand-carved, gold-painted base.

A crystal ball? Really? What kind of foolishne—

"Care to have your fortune read, Princess?" A withered voice asked from behind me. I was startled at her intrusion and turned to face her with a hand on my chest. "Apologies, your Highness. I didn't mean to alarm you," A robed, dreadfully aged woman bowed.

"You know who I am?" I asked, looking her over.

"I know a great deal more than that. Won't you let me share it with you?" She gestured over to the table with scarred, bony fingers.

"Ahh...that's alright, I've seen enough magic in my day. I'll just wait for my friend. Thank you." I started to move past her and wait outside, suddenly feeling too heavy, but the tired figure placed a cold hand on my arm.

"So your friend...she still doesn't know that she's your kin?" She side smiled. I glanced at the back where Paxe was still in the bath chamber and then glared at the pretentious woman.

"I don't know what you're talking about," I lied, shrugging from her grip. My heart began to sputter under her strange stare. Her eyes looked as if they held thousands of years worth of secrets and mystery. They seemed to swirl with the fog of magic. I had seen that familiar stare in my father's amber eyes. Hers were the deepest blue, like an ocean that was angry and wanted to crush you beneath it.

"I think you do. Spare me five minutes. Have a seat." I felt as if I disobeyed, something ill-fated would consume me. So, with another quick glance at the chamber door I slowly slumped into a seat across from the witch. "Have you any idea who I am?" She asked.

"No."

Her skeletal hands hovered over the crystal surface and the same fog I had seen in her eyes began to take shape in the globe. "Good. Don't look into the glass. Look at me. Keep your eyes on mine." Her hands moved around the sphere as I met her stare.

Paxe is taking an exceptionally long time.

"I should go check on—"

"Silence, youngling," She interrupted. "She's perfectly fine. Control your breathing. Concentrate on me. Clear your mind and pay attention."

I shuddered, not liking any of this at all. "Pay attention to what?" I leaned as far as the back of my seat would allow.

"You took your own life for your prince," She started. "Why?"

"Because...I refused to live without him. He's my soulmate."

"You hadn't completed the task given by the gods."

"The God of strength refused my weapon at that time. When I took my life, my fiancé was already dead. I had been told to leave and never return. That was until..." I paused.

"Until he gave you what you had come to him for. And restored your lives." She stated.

"That's right."

"Should anything happen to your prince before you've successfully delivered your people, what would your action be?" She asked.

"I made him a promise to never turn another weapon on myself. I made a promise to my people. I would find a different way to him...after I ended my father and put a stop to his torture."

"When that time comes...do not be distracted by anything. Do not yield to your deeply rooted feelings. Do not stray from the task you accepted. Doing so will cost you the one you love most. I sense in your heart that there are two in your life that fit that description. Three, if you count the child growing in your sister's body."

"Stop." I stood quickly, and the chair tipped over behind me. "We're done here. I'm devoted to saving my people. I'll never let anything happen to the ones I love. I know my task, and I'm not going to fail in it." I turned and charged through the shoppe. I had my fingers around the handle, when she called from behind me.

"Should you find yourself left with no other way to keep your vow...search for the light. The light will guide you home." I glanced back at her and a chill crept down my spine. I pulled the door open and stepped out into the street.

Refusing to acknowledge her again, I leaned my back against the storefront window and crossed my arms, as I watched the busy city folk. Paxe finally emerged, oblivious to everything and rubbing her knuckles. "I have no idea how that trollop ever gets that shit off of her lips. She must sleep in it and reapply it every morning." She looked over at me. "What's wrong?"

"Nothing. Just some stupid fortune teller," I growled.

"Fortune teller?" She asked, a puzzled look on her face. "Where?" She looked around the street, seemingly interested in having a reading of her own. There was no chance I was going to let that happen.

"In the magic shoppe. She's a fraud. Let's go, I don't want to be here anymore." I pushed off of the glass and started to walk, before Paxe's next words stopped me in my tracks.

"Magic shoppe? Have you hit your head?" I turned and she stood in front of the window with her hands on her hips. Behind her I could see patrons dipping in and out of a small cafe. A cafe that should have been the shop I had just exited. The sudden smell of coffee, and fresh baked goods wafted into my nose.

"What the hell?" I stormed past Paxe and threw open the door. A young cafe worker greeted me and bowed her head, excited to see that I'd visited.

"Princess! Welcome! Congratulations, I'm counting down the days until your big day!" She smiled sweetly. "Can I get you anything? Would you like a table?" Several of the occupants noticed our one sided conversation and bowed at me, but I was too confused to react.

"Umm...no, I—perhaps another day. Thank you." I rushed back out and Paxe was munching on yet another truffle.

"Are you alright?" She asked.

I grabbed her hand and started walking us across the busy street, needing to get away as fast as I could. "Do you mind if we go home? It's nearly dinner time and I still need to bathe and change my gown."

"Okay, but...what was that back there?" She freed her hand and had another bite. "Is something wrong?"

"No, I think...perhaps I'm just tired."

"Yeah, me too. I'm getting a bit hungry as well," she said through a mouthful. I cackled and she looked at me as if she didn't understand why.

"Paxe, you've been eating all day. How is there room enough in that body for anything else?"

"I'm sorry! Look, don't pass judgment. Everything I eat goes straight to this child. It's as if I have a worm or something." She rolled her eyes and seemed desperate for another treat from her bag. I threw my arm around her as we walked.

"You're the most adorable...violent creature I've ever seen," I laughed.

"That bitch had it coming," She chuckled. "You think she'll rat us out?"

"Nah. I'm pretty sure she doesn't want anyone to know what happened, and she sure as hell wouldn't want us to pay her another visit...or the queen for that matter. I think we've seen the last of her. I wonder what her name is?"

I pondered, trying to get the seemingly nonexistent old hag off my mind.

"She looks like a...Jezabelle...or a Sasha," Paxe sneered. I threw my head back in laughter.

"Claudia?" I added.

"I think I like *Bitch* better." We cracked back and forth, laughing the entire way back to the castle.

CHAPTER 33

A PICKLED SITUATION

Luca didn't make an appearance at dinner. Neither did the king. Ayla, Paxe and I did a swell job of making Lakan feel uncomfortable, as he was the only male at the table. He cowered in his usual bashfulness, and as curious as I was about the female that had shared a bed with Luca, we had agreed on the way back that if we'd ever ask the queen about her...it wouldn't be tonight. It was a monumental effort to keep her face from my mind, as well as the face of that withered old woman in a magic shoppe that seemed to never have been real, and all the things she'd said. Ayla was in a lovely mood this evening and I planned to keep it that way, so we kept our conversation light and she talked about all the wedding plans that were coming into place and everything that had so far been completed.

It sounded as if the ceremony would end in a grand celebration that would last well into the night, with a great many in attendance. Subjects from my side of the continent were also sending word about their desire to travel for the event. Paxe and I were happy to learn Vetta and Frances would be two of those, as well as Alister and Maureen, who would arrive with Nero.

"Arienne, I also wanted to ask about the plans for where you'd like to spend your wedding night. Would I be overstepping my maternal boundaries?" Ayla smiled.

"Not at all." I blushed. "I assumed we'd remain here. I hadn't really thought of leaving, if that's what you mean."

"Would you like to? I'm happy to make arrangements if the two of you would like a bit more privacy?"

"You may want to give them their own castle with a limited amount of breakable items...and at least a good mile from here if you'd like to get any sleep," Paxe chuckled.

"Do shut up." I palmed my face, as Lakan and the queen joined Paxe in her giggling.

"I suppose both you girls are a bit more like me than I expected then, Paxe." Ayla snorted as Paxe's red face darted toward her, hushing her snickering. "I drowned out your noise in my studio for several days after you arrived here and were feeling better." She drank a proud sip from her wine. Paxe and Lakan gulped and I howled from across the table.

"I'm sorry, Mi'lady," Paxe croaked. Lakan scooted his chair back, wiping his mouth politely and raising from his chair.

"Your Majesty, if I may be excused...I—I..." He cleared his throat.

"You may," Ayla laughed loudly. "My apologies, Lakan." His face glimmered with a sheen of sweat as he bowed while excusing himself. Several of the wait staff smirked as he walked past, and Paxe laid her head against her forearms in shame. A couple of booming voices rang out from the hallway outside the door where he had just left and I recognized them immediately before they stumbled through. "What in the name of—" Ayla slapped a palm to the table and glared at Luca and the king as they drunkenly swayed into the dining room, an arm draped over each other's shoulder.

"What did you all do to the poor blacksmith? He looks thoroughly wrecked," Luca slurred, his eyes half open and his disheveled hair covering half of his gorgeous grin.

"Ah...it appears he's not the only one," Paxe laughed from her seat.

"We forgot to hydrate..." Tidus grinned. "And...eat." He nearly tripped over the toe of Luca's boot, as they failed miserably to support each other's weight. The king stumbled and Luca snorted loudly, heaving over in silent laughter. I smiled to myself as I raised from my chair, Ayla slowly shook her head in amused disappointment. I stepped around the table to help them find a chair.

"Ari..." Luca's fingers reached up, and I assumed he was trying to touch my lips. His fingertips nearly went up my nose instead and I scoffed. "You're so b—beautiful." His compliment broke into a hiccup.

"Tidus, you should be ashamed of yourself, you fool," Ayla hissed from the table. "Tell me your people didn't have to see their king behaving like a—"

"Ohhh Ayla, stop your fuss...I just wanted to celebrate." Tidus clumsily waved a hand in her direction, while smiling at both Luca and I. "I'm a father first...and I'm happy. You can rough me up later, I need to sit down first."

"You can s–sit. I want to lay." My incredibly inebriated fiancé started to lower himself to the floor before I stopped him and tried desperately to hold him up. Ayla snapped her fingers at two guards by the door and they were at my side quickly, helping the king to one chair and turning Luca who started laughing hysterically, to the doorway opposite the room.

"Gods have mercy," Ayla snapped under her breath as she straightened the king in his chair. "You reek." She waved a hand across her face. The king smiled at her adoringly and I caught her smacking his hands away as we passed behind his chair. Paxe giggled quietly from the other side of the table. I followed suit as Luca stumbled between me and the guard, an arm thrown over each of us. "I apologize, Arienne. Will you be alright?"

"I'll be fine," I chuckled. "And to answer your question...I wouldn't wish to be any place else. If that pleases you." Paxe and the queen both smiled sweetly at me, as I continued to lead Luca toward the doorway.

"Understood, dearest," Ayla nodded. "It pleases me just fine. Yell down the hallway if you need me to beat him after I finish with this one." She pointed at the king who was almost asleep in his chair. I gave her a nod and said goodnight as we drudged down the hallways and struggled up the flights of stairs. I had never seen Luca quite this intoxicated, and was well beyond exhausted when we finally made it to his room. The guard smiled as we got him situated in bed. I pulled his boots off and Luca pointed at the guard, smiling deliriously.

"You need a hike in your pay, friend," He slurred.

The guard only chuckled under his breath, bowing to Luca and then to me. "Can I help you with anything else, Princess?" He smiled kindly.

"No sir, you've done more than he deserves." I breathed heavily with my hands resting on my hips. "I'll see to it that you're given something for your trouble."

"Many thanks, Mi'lady...but I'm privileged enough just being in service to this family. I'd have it no other way. Should you need me, I'll be at the end of the corridor this evening. Goodnight." He fixed his hands behind his back and dipped his chin before seeing himself out the door.

"Please don't be angry with me," Luca whined playfully from the bed without moving a single inch of his body. "I've never passed a bottle with him before. I didn't want him to think I couldn't keep up." I looked at him and realized his eyes were closed.

"I can't tell which of you has it worse," I said, smiling as he grunted in response. I slowly began coming out of my dress and making my way to the sitting room to find a shift. The moment he heard my dress drop to the floor his eyes opened and he slowly turned his face to me, a deep frown marring his lovely face. His eyes raked over every inch of me as I bent over completely naked and retrieved my gown.

"It's me. Godsdamn...It's me, I have it so much worse." He seemed to struggle to find any strength left to move anything but his head, as I laughed loudly and he watched me all the way to the armoire. I quickly changed and slid into bed, brushing back his hair and kissing his temple as soft snores sounded from his nose. I could feel how big my grin was as I looked him over and said a silent prayer to the gods, thanking them yet again for this male.

"Poor Prince," I whispered against his skin. "I love you." I pressed one more kiss to him and covered us with the duvet, snuggling into his warmth. I realized there was no place that would compare to where I was at this moment when we closed our eyes on the night of our wedding. The peace and the safety of his arms...being surrounded by the ones we love. This was home, and I couldn't imagine that even the most elegant of suites would amount to it. This was where I wanted to exist. He sensed my emotion even in a drunken sleep and with whatever was left of his energy, he wrapped his arms around me. I breathed in the smell of lavender, salt, hard liquor and leather and my smile never left me as darkness blanketed us both.

Morning came swiftly the next day, exceptionally bright and warm. The sound of gulls outside the windows seemed more excited, the churning of the sea more welcoming. Luca's snoring had ceased and he slept peacefully beneath my cheek, as I found my eyes opening rather easily this morning.

Something felt different. Better. Easier, and...normal. Though I could still feel a tinge of grief from the past week, my heart felt lighter. There was no pain, no worry. There were no traces of lingering specters of my brutal past. I couldn't keep the smile from coming back, as I lightly kissed the soft skin of Luca's neck, trailing them up to his jawline and causing him to shift softly beneath me. He groaned as if it were terribly painful to open his eyes or move, and I softly pressed my lips to his.

There was an entirely different groan as he kissed me back tenderly, then a bit more passionate. I relished in the feel of his mouth moving over mine and the way his fingers wove through my hair. His sleep riddled eyes finally met mine as he smiled softly up at me.

"There he is," I whispered.

"I'm sorry." His voice was barely audible.

"Oh no, it was very entertaining. How do you feel?" He grunted and I grinned wider.

"I should have been here. I'm a bit jealous."

"What?" I drew my brows together. "Why?"

"I wanted to be the one to show you around the city...but I—" He frowned. "How can I make it up to you?"

"Well...first, I'm drawing you a hot bath," I laughed.

"Do I smell?" He raised his arm and turned his head, sniffing beneath it. I snorted and rolled in laughter as my hands turned his face back to mine.

"No. But it will make you feel better. Then, if you still wish to make it up to me, then let's go spend the day out. Just the two of us...I miss you." His fingers grazed my cheek, reaching up slowly and tucking my hair behind my ear.

"As long as you and Paxe left some trouble for me too...sounds perfect." His smile made me weak, but my eyes grew wide under the weight of the word *trouble*. The bloodied face of the girl from the shop flashed in my mind and I suddenly wondered if somehow he'd found out. "What is it?" He asked, sensing my nerves.

"You...you didn't hear anything odd about us did you?" I asked carefully. He raised his brows and sat up to look at me, his attention pegged directly into my soul.

"Odd?" He grinned. "No, I didn't but you certainly look worried." My stomach churned, but a sag of relief graced my shoulders. "Ari...?" He raised my chin and smiled, waiting for an explanation.

"There were two reasons we went into the city yesterday, besides getting out of the castle. I can't have you poking around. You'll spoil wedding surprises," I lied bashfully. His features relaxed and he leaned back against the headboard. I immediately felt horrible about my decision and offered a smirk as I slipped out of bed and padded into the bath chamber. As I filled the bath, and added oils to the water, the heaviness of keeping the truth from him began to crush me. I wondered how upset he'd be and if it would ruin our day together, or cause him to choose not to see me at all, but my conscience overpowered my thoughts when I heard him walk in behind me. I moved my fingers through the water as it filled the tub, staring down into it and feeling too ashamed to look at him as I spoke. "Luca..."

"Mmhmm?" He hummed, sounding as if he were undressing. I hesitated, and nervously continued blending the bath oils.

"I can't do this," I breathed.

"Do what?" He asked softly, his tone full of worry. "The wedding?" He knelt half naked beside me, placing his hand on my shoulder and causing me to feel even more horrible for being the reason he would assume something like that first. The water splashed as I jerked my hand from it and turned to face him.

"What? No...no, no no." I placed my wet hand on his cheek and my heart fluttered at his deep sigh of relief. "This wedding is most likely the one thing in my entire life that I'm not second guessing."

He blew out a breath and smiled. "Thank the gods...then what is it?"

"I—I lied." I lowered my hand and he caught it, smoothing a thumb over my knuckles. His expression showed concern, but he remained that steady support he'd always been as he waited for me to continue. "Not about the reasons I went out...but—there was one small incident yesterday. I can't keep it from you."

"Did somebody hurt you?" His jaw tightened and a small fire ignited in his eyes.

"No...no, we—*we*...hurt someone." I bit down on my lip and his mouth turned up slightly at the corner.

"I'm intrigued." He half smiled. "Did they deserve it?" I closed my eyes and pinched the bridge of my nose.

"Yes, but...I'm sorry. I didn't know it was her at first, and then..." I sighed. Luca moved my hand away from my face and forced me to look at him.

"Who, love? What happened? Look, if you're telling me you were provoked and acted on it there's no way I could be angry with you. I can tell you're holding back. I could tell before you left the bed." He stopped the water and sat on the edge of the tub.

"I don't know what her name is, I'm sorry. Paxe and I were doing some shopping and one of the employees at a place we went...made a comment about you, and being in your bed and..." Luca's brows nearly reached his hairline.

"Lydia?" He leaned forward, crossing his arms and staring at me in shock. "Blonde? Mark on her lip?" I felt a hint of nausea hearing his description of her. It threatened to send me into rage, but I calmly nodded.

"How did you know which one?" I asked, crossing my arms as well.

"Because there was only one of the two I've been with that had ever slept in my bed." He pursed his lips. "What did she say to you?"

"She was merely doing her job and offering her help at first, but when she realized who I was...she called you by your name and it sat wrong with me. I asked her why she spoke of you with such informality and she said that she didn't remember you being so adventurous in your bed. Paxe laid her out, and I—I may have threatened to beat her skull in if I ever caught her around here again." Luca howled in laughter before I got the last few words out, leaning over his knees and slapping one with his palm. I lowered my brows. "I have to be honest, Luca. This was *not* the reaction I expected." I admitted, as he wiped at the corner of his eye with his forefinger.

"Did you honestly believe I'd have been upset with you for this? Ari, if she was bold enough to try and get a rise out of you like that, then I'd say she deserved what she got and then some. Just because we laid together doesn't mean I ever had any deeper feelings for her. I thought I'd been clear about that when we talked about it in the forest that night."

"So, you're not angry?" I squeezed my arms and he knelt back down in front of me, still laughing softly and shaking his head.

"Not at all. In fact, I hate that I missed it." He pulled me to him and chuckled. "There's nothing you could ever say to me that would change the way I feel for you, you know. Don't ever feel as if you have to keep anything from me."

"Well...since I've told you about that, there is one more thing," I said with regret in my voice. He scoffed and pulled back.

"Arienne!" He laughed. "Did you also trip an old woman or something? On purpose?"

"No, it's nothing like that. It was just something strange that I have absolutely no explanation for."

"Something bad?" He asked, standing up and unfastening his pants. I stared at his waistline, distracted by it completely and swallowed. "Ari?" He grinned. My eyes darted up to meet his.

"N–no. Well...I don't know. Do you know of a magic shoppe in the shopping district? One with a fortune teller that wears black robes?" He looked utterly confused as he stripped himself bare and stepped into the bath, lowering himself into the water and shaking his head.

"I've never known there to be anything like that in the shopping district, or anywhere in Crona. Why?" He went under and then resurfaced, palming his hair back and sending a flare of heat to my lower belly. It was an effort not to join him and crawl into his lap.

I cleared my throat and pressed my thighs together, leaning against the side of the tub as he started to bathe. "We stopped by this shop so that Paxe could relieve herself, and this old woman with the most bewitching eyes practically forced me to let her read my fortune in a crystal ball. Of course, I found it completely ridiculous at first, but she knew that Paxe was my sister, and that I hadn't told her about it yet."

"What?" He started, lathering his hair. "Was that all?"

"No. She asked me why I took my own life in Bolton, and why I had done it before making sure I'd kept my vow to our people. It was almost as if she didn't believe that I took this task seriously, or doubted me. I decided I'd had enough when she said..." I paused, shaking my head.

"When she said..." He urged.

"She said that if I became distracted by my feelings when the time came, that it would cost me the one I loved most. She said she sensed there were two that fit that description, and three if you counted Paxe's child. I cut that short. I walked out to wait for Paxe and when she came outside, I had turned and the shop was a cafe. Like I had imagined the entire thing."

"Cafe Pentola?" Luca asked, quickly rinsing himself off.

"That's the one." I confirmed.

"That's the only cafe in that district. There's never been any kind of shop like that. We may need to let my parents in on this bit. It's strange, yes...but with the tricks your father has pulled on us thus far, I wouldn't trust that this isn't some way he's using magic to gain information from you."

"Strangely, I didn't feel that at all. She didn't seem malicious, nor did she seem familiar. She did feel powerful, but if my father had anything to do with it then it would also mean he already knows too much. He knows about the weapons, the god's plans, and the fact that Paxe is his daughter. I think we could rule that possibility out."

Luca was quiet for a long moment before he said, "You're right. Let's tuck that away for now. There's still a great deal we have to think about before we make any moves on him, yeah?" He smiled.

"Yes." I smiled back, leaning over the tub to kiss him. "I'm going to get dressed." I stood and he watched my every step, as I backed through the doorway and into the bed chamber.

"Right behind you, Princess." He raised himself out, water trailing down him in rivulets, and dripping from anything still. I paused outside the door and we stared at each other for what seemed like an eternity. His lips curled into a sultry smile as he teased a hand near his length.

Godsdamnit, Luca. You're killing me.

My mouth went dry and my skin incinerated as he held himself and I nearly choked. I cursed quietly and tore my eyes away, making quickly for the sitting room. I could hear him snickering from the bath, before I slammed the door behind me.

We dressed for leisure and comfort, wearing simple knit tunics. Mine was a pale gray, and Luca's a soft blue that made his eyes stand out like the water gleaming with sunlight by the bay. I let my hair fall where it may, and Luca tied his back. The longer we spent struggling to keep from pawing at each other, the more beautiful that male became to me. I was starting to fully understand what Paxe meant when she explained this concept to me. By the end of this week he'd be my husband, and the most precious thing I'd ever had in my life. It was becoming a hell of a lot more clear as the days went by. It seemed Luca was feeling the same effect. He held my hand tighter, stared into me longer, pulled me closer. As we walked down the hallways of his castle, I found myself feeling less of a queen...and more like a wife. Like a lover, and a best friend. Something genuine and pure. Something effortless. I was unapologetically happy.

Luca was rambling on as we made our way, hand in hand, through the castle entrance and down the long walkway to the city gate about gods know what. I leaned into him, glancing up occasionally and suddenly realizing then that this was the reason waking up this morning had felt completely different.

I'm happy. And I'm not sorry.

He was my existence. He was my whole heart, the other half of my soul. He shared everything with me from the moment we'd met, and years before I had ever seen him. Every emotion, from anger to the deepest grief. Now we're finally allowed our happiness. We earned this. We've earned this and so much more. In a few short days, I planned to put these feelings as well as my gratitude into words. Vows. Devoting my entire life to him, mind, body and soul. Who would have ever thought...five years ago? Who would have ever imagined that I'd ever make it to a point that I was able to feel something as precious as this? Without meaning to cut him off, my words erupted from my mouth.

"I love you, Luca." He stopped mid-sentence and stared down at me. We stood in silence for several moments never breaking that gaze and his answering smile turned my heart into slop.

"I love you too, Arienne. More than you could ever know."

Making our way through the streets of the city was more difficult than I expected while on Luca's arm. Many stopped to speak to us, human and non-human alike. Luca and his family held a completely different kind of respect from their subjects, and it showed...it showed a great deal. The king, queen and prince were adored by their people. They showed the same courtesy to me...a princess they didn't even know, save for the reputation of my father who showed kindness to no one. If they thought ill of me in any way, I certainly wasn't able to gather it. It was a far cry from the way the people in the marketplace at my previous home behaved toward me, although my situation regarding Gideon had given them a rightfully placed foreboding. I was welcome here. Everything seemed so absolutely perfect.

We browsed several shops that Paxe and I hadn't walked into yesterday, every shopkeeper thrilled to have us and offering half the store, which we both declined at every turn. We weren't there for handouts, or gifts. Luca had me wait outside his jeweler's storefront, insisting he check in on the progress of a wedding band he was having made to fit together with my custom engagement piece. I was not allowed to peek, but he never said I wasn't allowed a glance through the window at the way his face lit up when the craftsman presented it to him. The slop turned molten and dripped its way slowly through my ribcage.

A few blocks down was the bustling cafe and even when I found myself hesitating, I couldn't deny Luca his chance to go inside. He had practically begged, and had I known his true reason I'd have run the whole way back to the castle. I followed him inside and the same female from the day before welcomed me back. The cafe owner whom everyone called '*Pat*', stepped through the commotion beaming, and offered Luca and I congratulations, as he hugged my prince and gave a delighted backslap. He scooted around the back of the counter, reaching beneath it and plopping a large jar of what looked to be boiled eggs in a pinkish liquid, down on the top in front of Luca.

"Oh no....what is that?" I slowly pointed at the jar, wide-eyed as Luca held it and turned himself around with an excited grin.

"You don't already know?" His pretty white teeth gleamed in the store light. He sat himself on top of one of the small tables and tugged me to stand between his knees as the jar rested in his lap.

Pickled pelican eggs.

"I think I do, but I'm hoping like hell I'm wrong." I winced, grimacing at the jar and its contents. He chuckled at the look of disgust on my face, and snapped the lid open, twisting it off and setting it down beside him on the table. The smell hit my nose like a coiled fist and I covered it with my hand. "Oh Gods," I gagged. "Are you really going to force me to watch you eat these? It smells absolutely dreadful."

"Of course not, love." He pulled one of the eggs out of the jar and sucked the rank liquid from the surface before popping the entire thing into his mouth. "You're trying them too." He gargled through his mouthful.

"Like hell!" I tried backing away, but his arm reached behind me and pulled me closer, his grin reaching both ears as he locked his legs around me. "Luca, no. I'm going to vomit." I threw my palms up and he leaned in and playfully bit one of my fingers. Several patrons giggled around us, stopping to watch our interaction.

"Please? You promised you'd try one." He smiled, reaching in for another egg.

"I promised no such thing! I distinctly remember telling you the opposite." He raised the evil little oval shaped monstrosity near my mouth. "Ugh..." My face paled, and I waved my hand across my nose as my face wrinkled in refusal. He snickered hard through his nose.

"Do it for *me*." He gave me the stare and knew damned well I wouldn't say no to that face. "I have a surprise for you if you'll try just one bite." Again with the grin.

Bastard.

"If I can't actually eat it, do I still get the surprise?" I pouted, trying desperately to prepare myself for the humiliation of emptying my stomach on this floor, in front of everyone in the cafe.

"Come on, love. You broke your own bones to get to me, and beheaded an unnatural creature with a god's hammer. You can handle a little *egg*." He wiggled the stinking thing between two of his fingers and I scowled at him as several more giggles spread across the room. I feigned a pitiful whine, and turned my face to the ceiling, taking a deep breath and shaking my hands at my sides, as I lowered my attention back to him and squeezed my eyes shut. A few of the patrons cheered me on as I slowly opened my mouth and waited for something foul to enter it.

A cold, slick tang replaced the taste of stale air as the egg slid between my teeth and I reluctantly bit into it. My eyes popped open and my face drew up as Luca burst into laughter with the rest of the cafe. I made truly distressing sounds as I bounced on my heels and tried my best to chew the spongy menace. Luca ate the other half, continuing to laugh and setting the jar down beside him, while his hands took my waist and his head pressed against mine.

"Swallow it," He chuckled.

"Mmm-mm." I chewed, my face turning red as I shook my head and squinted. He laughed harder and people hooted around us in encouragement.

"Come on. Pat's got your surprise." He grinned.

"You've got this, Princess! Make him eat crow!" The chubby shopkeeper called from behind me. I breathed deep and choked back the vomit that threatened to creep up my throat and swallowed, pulling back from Luca's face as I jerked my head back and forth and stuck out my tongue. Everybody whooped in my victory and Luca placed his hands on my face, planting a massive kiss on my mouth.

"That wasn't so bad was it?" He laughed hysterically, kissing all over my cheeks.

"That tasted like tangy old cheese, and dirty socks!" I complained, giggling a little. The girl from the entrance appeared at my side with a mug of fresh coffee and a huge slice of Panettone. I squealed at the sight and wrapped my arms around Luca's neck. He broke off a piece and fed it to me, flicking my nose as I chewed. He started chatting up a few of the employees, thanking them for their help while I rested against his thigh and polished off my bread and coffee. I looked up to the shop window and noticed a familiar face watching us as she held a large box in her hands.

She was lovely. Blonde hair pinned back from her face, a simple blue dress with a cream colored shawl draped over her chest and shoulders...and a small beauty mark above her unpainted top lip.

"Lydia?" I whispered to myself. As if she'd heard me, she nodded and smiled sweetly. She looked at Luca, and then back at me and mouthed a *'thank you'*. I raised my mug, sliding my arm around Luca's back and smiling back at her as I dipped my chin. She winked and turned to load her box onto a cart full of other crates and personal items. She was leaving. She'd taken what I'd said to heart and seemingly wished to start a different life. I almost stopped her, but realized that perhaps that's exactly what she needed. The way that I needed to leave Valdaro, and didn't know it until I ended up here with my home, in the form of an unnervingly charming prince at my side. Everybody deserves this kind of happiness. I sent a prayer up to the gods that she'd find hers too.

We ended our day walking barefoot in the tide while the sun set over Crona, painting the bay in hues of gold and fuchsia, as gulls squawked overhead. The peace I felt as I held onto him stayed with me well after we'd crawled into bed that evening, as I marked out another perfect day until the beginning of the rest of our lives.

CHAPTER 34

THE COUNTDOWN

The side of my neck felt warm. A gentle kneading nearly put me back to sleep until a warm, wet...bristled sensation grazed my cheekbone. I smiled, knowing exactly who was responsible, and without opening my eyes, I reached a hand over my shoulder and scratched behind the fuzzy ears that tickled my skin. Loud purring ensued, and the speed of the kneading picked up. That was the moment I realized...

Wait...

My eyes snapped open, and I turned my face to see two mismatched eyes and a fluffy face of black and white...in Luca's bed. "Hiss?" I nearly wept, raising myself to sit and cradling him to my chest. Tears began to well in my eyes as my attention caught Luca sitting cross-legged at the end of our bed, grinning as his cheek rested on his knuckles.

"Happy *almost* wedding day, love."

The pads of Hiss's paws batted my lips, as I cried through my smiles and smothered his peculiar face with kisses. "Luca...how did you—" My voice cracked as I nuzzled my little bundle of floof.

"Don't worry about how. I had help. I couldn't think of a better wedding gift for someone who deserves the world. There *are* some things that riches can't buy." Luca's hair glinted blue in the morning sunlight from the window, but it didn't compare to the light in those gray eyes that teemed with the deepest affection and joy. I reached out an arm, nearly begging him to come to me. He leaned forward, crawling on his hands and knees across the duvet until his soft lips met mine. Hissifus smooshed his tiny nose between us and we laughed softly through our kiss. Luca's hand smoothed over the top of Hiss's head and he turned his face to him. "Hey cat," he smiled. "Can we share?" His voice was light and playful, as if he were talking to an infant.

"I don't have words for the way I love you, Prince." Luca's head rested against the crook of my shoulder and I pressed my cheek to his hair as he slid a hand beneath the blanket. Hissifus purred against my neck, watching Luca in curiosity.

"When have we ever needed words?" He breathed. His body leaned against mine and the blanket popped up and down, catching my cat's attention while Luca skittered his hand beneath the covers, jerking it this way and that. Hissifus pounced with his claws out, determined to dig out whatever creature was dodging him beneath. I snickered as I watched until a sound knock rang from the door and Paxe's excited voice followed close behind.

"Ari, it's here! Get up!" She rapidly knocked a second time and Luca winced and cursed, as Hiss's claws locked onto his hand through the duvet, sending me into a flurry of giggles.

"Come here, Paxe!" I called, hardly registering a thing she'd said. The door burst open and she rushed in, winded and flushed as if she'd raced down every hallway.

"Get up, get up, get up! Your dr—Hissifus!" she shouted, making her way quickly towards us. Hiss leapt from my lap, brushing Luca's face with his tail and darting for her. He was quick to get his sugar as she sat on the edge of the bed and allowed him to nuzzle every inch of her face. "What are you doing here, Floof?" She glowed as her fingers fiddled with his soft ears.

"My wedding gift from Luca." I beamed, wrapping my arms around him as his face buried into my chest. I snickered from the tickle of his stubble against the skin between my breasts.

"Luca, I underestimate you. I'm going to get Lakan to follow you around with a stack of parchment and a quill." Paxe teased, rising from the bed and picking Hiss up for a snuggle.

"Tell him not to jot down this part!" I cackled as Luca pinned me down and relentlessly tickled me. "Stop!" I yelped. He didn't. Instead, he laughed like a hyena as he held my arms above my head and tortured me with his chin on the sensitive part of my neck.

"Fight back, you wuss," Paxe laughed as she scratched Hiss's neck and enjoyed every moment of my torment.

"I can't!" I panted, my confined legs wiggling pitifully beneath Luca and the blanket. He snorted against my skin as my teeth clicked together near his ear. I was utterly useless.

"You don't actually believe I'd make that mistake again, do you?" Luca laughed, raising his face above mine while I continued to struggle. "Last time you got me in the bollocks."

"You ate my sandwich!" I hissed. His smile was devilish.

"Oh, I certainly did. Devoured it...and it was *delicious.*" My core heated at the tone in his voice and I immediately ceased all movement.

Godsdamn this blanket.

"Oh, good gods." Paxe rolled her eyes and sat Hissifus down on the bed, smacking Luca in the behind. He chuckled and pressed a chaste kiss to my forehead, releasing me and flipping onto his side as he threw an arm behind his head. "Get dressed, heathen. We've got to go," She grinned.

"Why?" I whined, smoothing a hand over Luca's bare chest and earning another eye roll from Paxe.

"Because...for one, you two still have a couple more days before you're allowed to rain hell on the castle. And two... Gran is in the queen's private dressing room with your wedding gown!" She squealed the last few words and hopped from one foot to the other, clenching her fists in excitement. I shot up.

"Really?" I asked, clapping my palms together. Luca's fingers trailed my spine and he looked ready to tear up as I climbed over him and stepped onto the floor. He offered a wide smile.

"You're going to be devastating," he whispered, staring into me as I leaned in to kiss him. "I can't wait." He loosened the hair strap and his long locks fell down his shoulders. He tied it loosely around my neck and kissed me one more time before letting me follow Paxe into the sitting room.

"Oh, that...*other thing?* Is ready as well. Lakan is bringing it to your fitting," Paxe said, braiding my hair behind me, as I laced the sides of my pale peach gown.

"Yes...perfect." I smiled, adjusting my bodice. We paused and looked at each other in the mirror.

"I can't believe this is happening." Her eyes went misty and she perched her chin over my shoulder, wrapping her arms around my middle. Tears started to threaten their way into my own eyes and I turned myself around and held her.

"Save it for the wedding day," I laughed through a sniffle.

"He looks so ready to call you his wife, Ari. I remember braiding your hair like this the day you met him. It was such a different sort of day." She brushed her hands down my sleeves. "Now it's....I'm so glad to see you happy. You're my sister in every way that matters. Forgive me, I just—I'm..." She wiped at the corner of her eye and my throat bobbed. I wanted to tell her right then and there.

"I love you," I breathed. "So much." We hugged and remained there for a moment. When we were finally able to gather ourselves, we marched back out to the bedchamber, where Luca and Hissifus were back to battling each other with the blankets. It was quite possibly the most adorable thing I'd ever witnessed. "Who's winning?" I grinned, slipping my feet into some flat shoes.

"Cat." Luca griped, laying on his stomach and jerking his hand back as Hissifus struck again. His dainty paws tapped the tip of Luca's nose and he flicked a finger at them. I laid over Luca's back, enjoying my victorious feat of stealing the wind from his lungs as he groaned and leaned his face back over his shoulder. I kissed his temple and patted Hiss's head before heading for the door with Paxe. "What are you doing today?" I asked, looking back.

"I have a fitting to go to as well, then most likely meeting Michele at the site. No drinking this time...I promise." He winked. Paxe laughed her way out the door, and I smiled as Hissifus slid his white side across Luca's cheek and they both stared at me.

"I love both of you," I winked back, resting my palm on the door jamb.

"We love you too. See you at supper, wife." It was all I could manage to put one foot in front of the other, as I slowly shut the door and those perfect faces disappeared behind it. It was even more difficult to continue down the hallway, and had it not been for Paxe pulling me along, I might have gone back. But...I was just a *tad* bit excited to see this dress.

Ayla's private dressing chamber was already fitted with three full-length mirrors placed alongside each other to provide a view from every angle as you stood in front of it. My breath caught as Paxe and I entered the room with the guard who escorted us inside. It was the same guard, I realized, who had helped me take Luca to bed the night he and the king stumbled into the castle. His expression was as proud as if he himself were giving me away while Gran and the queen stepped aside the mannequin and revealed the truly breathtaking masterpiece that Perla and her mother had crafted. Ayla tearfully covered her mouth with her hand and stared at me as I approached the gown slowly, with my fingers placed over the bow of Luca's hair strap on my chest. The room was silent, save for Paxe's hormonal weeping at my side.

The bodice was constructed in various shades of silver, white and pewter. Halter cut, with intricately beaded embellishments of thorny roses that sparkled as I moved around it. Two delicately placed cutouts donned the sides of the backless gown with a gossamer overlay that was studded with tiny diamonds. The skirts were of the same shimmering material, dyed in a gradient that started in the pewter color of the top half and lightened into the silver that resembled Luca's eyes, ending in a bright white. Gray patches of rose embroidery scattered throughout the skirt, gleaming in the light with silver threads. On a small table placed beside the mannequin were a matching pair of heels, in the same gradient and design. The roses were to rise and coil around my ankles like vines. I'd never seen a more stunning ensemble.

"I'd have little trouble creating a veil to match the skirts, Princess," Gran started, fluffing the lower part of the gown. "I could remove part of th—"

"No." I breathed as my forefinger trailed across the sparkling beading on the bodice. "Don't take anything from it. It's perfect. I think I may just wear it without a veil. I don't wish any part of this gown to be covered. If that would be alright with you?" I turned my face respectfully to the old woman, who smiled in agreement.

She placed her soft, wrinkled hand on my shoulder and leaned in. "This is *your* gown, Mi'lady. Your day. It will be exactly as you wish it." I slowly nodded, looking back at the dress and hardly able to contain my emotion. "Shall we help you into it then, dearest?" She smiled.

"Yes! Gods yes!" Paxe cried, wiping her eyes as we all tearfully giggled. The queen pulled me into a swift embrace as Gran began removing the gown from the display. She then led me into a side room with the tailor, and the emotional guard excused himself.

"We'll be right out here, my darling." Ayla sniffled, leaving me to disrobe and closing the door behind her.

It was difficult to describe the way I felt as I finally stepped into the dress with Gran's assistance. There were no parts of it to fasten, or tighten. It fit perfectly over my body as if Perla and her talented mother had fashioned all the pieces of it over an exact mold of myself. The skirts felt incredibly smooth against the skin of my legs, and the inside of the bodice was lined in silk to prevent itching or being stuck with beading and other uncomfortable snags.

The bones of the top were supportive and only tight enough to uphold my bust, allowing me to move freely with it. It was a flawless work of art. I worried for a moment if the bottom hem would be too long and have to be adjusted, but even that was taken into account in its design. I slipped my feet into the custom heels and the entire problem was resolved.

"How does it feel?" Gran asked, adjusting my flowing skirts and straightening parts of the embroidery that laid on the exposed skin of my back.

"Surprisingly comfortable," I answered, as I smoothed a hand over my middle. "Do you see anything amiss back there?"

"Nothing, actually. You're certain its crafters didn't use magic?" She chuckled as she continued to circle me and shift parts around.

"No, ma'am. They're human."

"Even more admirable. We non-magic folk can be exceptional at some things." She looked up and winked. I stopped her fidgeting with my hand and leaned toward her.

"I want you to know, Gran. I've no more magic right now than you. I have never...and would never...think any less of you or any other human. You have always been my people, and I need you to understand how much I admire and care for all of you. I'm so honored to be able to wear this on the most important day of my life. This gown was originally made to be worn in celebration of acquiring magic that humans will never possess. That used to seem so cruel to me. I understand now how beautiful this is, just knowing that gifts and abilities like the ones that dwell in the hands of people like you...and people like Perla, and her mother...they're just as special and just as powerful as the ones I'll soon receive." The old woman was quiet for a moment and stood to look me in my eyes.

"My dear...you are a queen in every way. Truly. The prince is a very fortunate male. The two of you will do great things, of that I have no doubt. We're all so incredibly grateful for you...and for your sacrifices." Her eyes welled, and I choked back the knot in my throat.

"Thank you," I whispered. She opened the door and nodded, gesturing me forward. I raised my skirts and slowly walked out, trying earnestly not to cry as Paxe and Ayla gasped. I made my way to the mirrors and stepped onto a small circular platform in the middle where the mannequin had been. Gran adjusted the skirts to flow and fall delicately over the toe of my heels. The sounds in the room faded into complete silence as I slowly raised my face and found the female in the mirror that I'd come to find somewhat heroic and...*incredible.*

Look at you...look at that. That...is a survivor. That is a small taste of the way he sees you. This is the woman that the gods had foreseen nearly twenty years ago. Look how far you've come, Arienne Genovese.

I smiled at her, and she returned it. Her eyes raised in happiness...genuine and pure. I tightly squeezed around my arms and bowed my head, snickering bashfully while Paxe bounced around my skirts in childlike delight. Ayla stepped up behind me, fidgeting with my braid. She coiled it and raised the plait over the back of my head, holding it there and looking at me through the mirror.

"Hair up or down, darling?" She asked, hardly containing her tears. I turned my head from side to side and shrugged softly.

"Is there an elegant way to do both?" I asked, bringing my attention to Paxe, who was still carefully examining the fit of my gown.

"Oh, yes." She snapped her face to me and pressed her palms together. "How do you feel about flowers in your hair? I have such a lovely image that would go so well with the embroidery in this dress."

"Minimal. I think that would be perfect, but in moderation. Do you think you could come up with something that wouldn't take too much attention away from the gown itself?"

"I do."

Ayla dropped my braid over my shoulder and slowly turned me around to face her. "You know that the only thing he'll be paying any attention to is you, don't you?" She smiled softly. "You know that he's waited for this moment for a very, very long time?" I nodded and we both began to choke on unshed tears. "In a lifetime spent controlling my rage...learning to get a handle on my fury. I've only ever been this happy two other times in my life. The moment I realized how much I love his father, and the moment that boy's eyes found mine for the first time as I held him in my arms." Her voice broke into a quiet sob and she went on. "I've never met anyone more deserving of something so precious to me than you, Arienne. I love you both...so very much." The queen pulled me into a tight embrace and Paxe lost all control over her emotions as Gran softly patted her shoulder.

"I love you too. I'll make him happy, my queen," I sniffled.

"You already do, my love. You *are* his happiness," She whispered into my ear. "Whatever happens...I'm so glad the two of you have each other." She pulled away and wiped my tears as she smiled through her own and turned me back around to face the mirror. "Take a good look. The next time you see yourself in this gown...you'll be mere steps away from becoming a Di Meo." We all grinned ridiculously, chattering like young girls for the rest of the fitting.

After I'd gotten dressed again and bid my wedding gown farewell, the four of us enjoyed a small lunch in the downstairs dining room. Ayla went over the finishing touches of the wedding plans, and we promptly made our way to the ballroom for a quick rehearsal. Luca and the king weren't present, as their parts in the ceremony consisted mostly of standing there like statues and doing as they were told. As my father wouldn't be invited anywhere near my wedding or anyone I loved...I was to walk myself down the aisle alone. Thankfully, the walk wouldn't be long, and Paxe would be flanking me every step of the way. I tried desperately to calm my sudden nerves in the empty ballroom that was beginning to look more and more like a temple of reverence, with rows of seats meticulously placed on the sides and the runner Ayla had requested lying beautifully in the middle. We spent nearly two hours there and once Paxe had decided an afternoon nap was in order, I found myself needing the same.

"Before you go, I wanted you to see one more thing." Ayla clapped, retrieving a thin box from the dais. Paxe and I stood close and peered over it as she lifted the lid to reveal a lovely, long silver bit of material with the Cronian crest embroidered at the ends. It resembled a sash and I didn't want to appear ungrateful or downright stupid, as Ayla seemed excited to gift it. I had absolutely no idea what it was. "It looks nearly identical to the one the king and I were hand-fast with at our wedding. I had it made for you."

Ohhhh...

"It's beautiful." I smiled, staring too long into the box. She missed nothing.

"What's wrong?" The queen asked, leaning forward to look at my face. I chewed my lip and Paxe waited silently next to me, most likely thinking the same thing. I had started out not wishing to appear ungrateful and stupid...now I was hoping I didn't appear ungrateful and rude.

"Nothing is wrong...it's stunning. I just—I had something special in mind that I was hoping to surprise Luca with...for this particular bit of the ceremony." Ayla's expression was neither offended nor angry. Instead, she studied me in curiosity and there was a long pause that was finally broken by Paxe's loud gasp and the sound of her hand slapping her mouth.

"What is it?" Ayla demanded.

"Ari...are you trying to use the hair strap?" Paxe placed her other hand over her heart and looked as if she could cry...again.

"What?" The queen placed the box on a small table and rested her hands on her hips. "A hair strap? You can't be serious! Why in the world—"

"I never thought in a millennia that this would be such an important thing between you two. You have to do it. You *have* to." Paxe took my hands and bounced on her heels.

"Is anyone going to explain this madness to me?" Ayla waited impatiently with a smirk.

"On their first outing, I tied Luca's hair strap around her neck as a conversation starter. It was a joke. But apparently, ever since then, it's been a symbol of endearment between them. One of them is wearing it at all times. In some way or another. It couldn't be more perfect," Paxe explained. Ayla softened and stared at the leather bow on my chest.

"So that's what this is? I wondered about that ever since you got here." She stepped closer and inspected the simple strap, smiling from ear to ear.

"I don't want to upset your plans...I kno—"

"Nonsense." She picked up the box and tossed it over her shoulder. It clacked to the floor somewhere far behind her and she grinned. "That's precious. Let's do it. We'll keep it quiet until they bring it out during the ceremony." With that important detail taken care of, I saw myself back to Luca's room to rest and hoped he wouldn't be too long.

Hissifus had made himself completely at home in our pillows, with all four feet raised in the air. He only saw fit to spare me a lazy head turn and deep rolling purr as I softly shut the door behind me. "You are a spoiled rotten sack of floof, Hiss. Don't mind me. It's not as if I haven't seen you in weeks," I complained, crossing my arms. He responded with a dramatic yawn and snuggled himself back into the pillow. I rolled my eyes as I slipped out of my shoes and padded toward the bathing chamber, stopping short when my eyes caught Luca's journal left open on the desk. His quill rested in the spine and I placed it in the small inkpot in the corner, picking the book up and admiring his drawings.

Only they weren't just drawings. They were plans. I lowered my brows as I turned the journal this way and that, realizing his true reason for devoting all his spare time to this project at the bay. Notes about the structure were scrawled out in Luca's handwriting and someone else's. Most likely Michele's, as he was the architect helping to build this masterpiece. The floor plans were elaborate, and sketches of statues in the main foyer lined the walls. One looked similar to Nero, and behind it were dotted lines indicating a hidden chamber. I flipped the page over to find plans for a sublevel that was to take up the entire lower floor, with compartments made to fit two people comfortably lined throughout the space. There was a place set up for food storage and another for weapons. Bunks were drawn in to fit as many as possible in case...

Oh my Gods...Luca...

Around the entire expanse of the site was a thick-layered wall of apotropaic stone—stone that could only be supplied from the Horned Mountains. He was building this place to function not only as a place where humans could learn but also as a safehouse. A place with magic wards where they could take refuge from my father should things go terribly wrong. I supposed I couldn't blame him for having something like this in place. I had no intention of failing them, but we both knew full well that the possibility of something happening was always there. I felt my eyes stinging and my heart nearly breaking at how selfless and perfect he is. I also wanted to throw myself against a wall for how I'd never given him the attention he deserved when it came to something like this. He had probably been dying to talk to me about it. I decided to go and see it for myself. I tossed the journal down and the pages fluttered, landing open on something else... Something I hadn't seen yet that he must have written recently. I reached down, smoothing over the parchment and brought it back up to my face.

Tick...Tock...That moon is her clock.
The ballad she sings as she's silently mocked.

Her heart...Her sin...Bewitched by his pen.
Bleeds the ink of her life, as he hurts her again.

I didn't even realize I was crying until a tear splattered the ink on the parchment. Folded bits jutted out of the side a few pages further and I tugged it out and opened it. He'd found the note I'd saved that we'd passed back and forth through the wall at the inn. I smiled tearfully to myself and tucked the paper back into its place. My sudden need to see him was so strong that I barely registered sliding my shoes back on and making it halfway through the city. All things considered, it was a long walk, but I'd been so eager and so lost in his words that echoed through my mind that I found myself at the bay in what seemed like mere minutes.

The construction site was busy. Workers scurried about like ants in a mound. I spotted Bjourne relaxing near the shore, but no sign of Luca. As I neared closer, I did find Michele going over blueprints with one other male at a thrown-together table that leaned against a large pile of stones. One unfamiliar face turned toward me and bowed at the waist. Michele noticed the exchange and turned to face me.

"Princess!" He grinned, running his fingers through his damp hair. "What brings your royal tuckus out here?" His arm reached out and slung around my shoulders, and the male next to him gawked as if shocked at the informal gesture.

"What is wrong with you?" The timid male asked, punching Michele in his other arm. He was tall and thin, didn't have a great deal of broadness to his shoulders and hardly any muscle to speak of. His brown hair was pulled back and didn't quite reach his shoulders as he sneered at Michele through hazel eyes. "She's not Luca. You need to be more respectful."

"You worry too much. She likes me. Don't you, pet?" Michele's lovely white teeth gleamed in the sunlight, as he continued to grin at me.

"A pleasant surprise, Michele." I snickered, easing out of his hold. "Though I can't say the same about Paxe."

"Oh, no. She hates my guts. I think I'm too pretty for her." He laughed, rubbing the back of his neck.

"Don't flatter yourself, stupid." The brown-haired male jabbed, reaching a hand to shake mine. "I'm Leighton. Honored to meet you, Princess." I gently shook his hand and Michele slapped him on the back of the shoulder.

"We call him Fleck. He's a mathematical genius. Don't feel obligated to call him by his real name. None of us do." Leighton rolled his eyes and gave a decent effort to shove Michele into the table. Michele's body didn't move an inch.

"Are you here to see Luca?" Leighton asked, smiling politely.

"Yes, although now I feel a bit like I'm interrupting. Perhaps I should have just waited ba—" A pair of soft lips hushed mine as I was abruptly turned around and pulled into a salty...absolutely divine kiss. I melted into Luca's arms, ignoring the whistles and laughter from Michele and some of the workers around the site.

"Well...hello beautiful." Luca smiled against my mouth, his arms tightening around me as I leaned into him. I placed my hands on each side of his face, kissing him again once. Twice. At least half a dozen more times, before finally pulling back to look at him fully. "Did you walk all the way here?" He asked as his head darted around, searching for a horse or any other transportation.

"I did. I needed to see you, and I couldn't wait...so. Here I am," I shrugged.

"Is everything alright?" He asked nervously, checking me over.

"Everything is perfect. You...left your journal open. I haven't been here yet, and I wanted to see it for myself." I smiled as I glanced over at the foundation that was beginning to look like a building.

"Really?" Luca grinned bashfully, a proud expression gracing his features.

"Yes. I want you to give me a tour." I hooked my arm through his, waving back at Leighton and Michele, who watched us as I tugged Luca toward the structure. He was more than happy to show me around, excitedly going on and on about this and that. He pointed at different areas and explained all his grand plans, showed off a trunk of weapons that were his own design, and once we'd found his father, he even placed poor Tidus to stand in several spots alongside the half-constructed wall where the statues from the drawings indicated they'd be placed. I happily listened to them both talk ambitiously about what would be built in the next few weeks following the wedding and before I knew it, the sun began to paint the sky in its trek beneath the horizon. "I'm so proud of you," I breathed as we walked back towards Bjourne, who was sitting comfortably on the bank of a dune. "Luca...this is the labor of a true king to his people. You're amazing. I have no words for how I feel." He stopped us, bracing my shoulders, as the workers around us busily packed up to go home for the night.

"Hey..." He started, lifting my chin. "You know that you're just as much a part of this place as I am, right?" His thumb grazed my jawline.

"I understand what you're saying, yes. But I can't take credit for this. This undertaking...you deserve all the recognition the world could offer, Luca. Do you realize how many lives you'd be saving if something happens and I can't..." I trailed off, looking at the building that was beginning to glow in the light of Crona's sunset.

"You know I'm not doing this because I doubt you..."

"I don't think that at all," I smiled. "I just wanted you to know how much I love you...how much *more* I love you because of this. As if I needed any more reason." My eyes locked with his and my heart fluttered at the presence of his magic.

"This isn't just about the plans, is it?" He smirked.

"No. Not a chance. Though...it takes up a great deal of it. I had already decided to come down here before I ended up reading other pages." I snickered. He lowered himself, scooping my thighs up in one arm and throwing me over his shoulder. I yelped and several chuckled, Michele and Leighton included as Luca popped my backside and carried me to his horse.

"You said I could read it!" I laughed, swatting at his rear.

"I know I did. But the last time you read that thing you broke me. If I can't have you for two more days, then you'll have to take this whoopin'." He laughed softly through his nose, slapping his palm against me again.

"You...ass!" I squealed, getting him back and apparently well enough to earn a groan as he chuckled through a hiss. Tidus waved his hands silently behind Luca's back to get my attention, gesturing for me to gnaw the sensitive part of his ribs. I did and he nearly dropped me wailing and turning back to find his father's head thrown back in howling laughter.

"Pop!" He yelled as I cackled on the other side of his back. "Who's side are you on?!"

"Hers!" Michele, Tidus and Leighton all called in unison. I raised my arms, victorious as Luca rolled his eyes, clicking his tongue to get Bjourne to his feet. He hurled me up onto the horse's back, those mighty black wings fluttering and stretching after a long rest. Luca climbed up behind me, taking my waist in his arm and pulling me close, as he playfully nipped my neck.

"Let's go for a ride," He whispered into my ear, sending a chill down my spine. I didn't respond, nor did I wait while my fingers found the reins and I tapped my heels against Bjourne's sides. The winged horse sprinted off toward the shoreline and we leaned forward, Luca holding me tight as we picked up speed. Water began splashing around us as we eased into a strong gallop through the tide and became a black smudge against the long stretch of the bay. Bjourne pushed hard off the ground and leapt into the sky, his wings gloriously shining in the golden sunset. The view of the castle, the city and the sea from our altitude was something to behold. Wisps of clouds misted around us as we settled into a glide above the water, and the wind threatened to tug my braid loose. Luca reached around me, resting his chin on my shoulder and untying my hair on the other side. It unraveled and flew freely behind me.

After a few moments, we were completely surrounded by swirls of magenta, gold, deep orange and purple, with the glowing ocean only a short distance below us. Bjourne's wings flapped every so often and Luca's broad hand pressed me closer, his other hand turning my face to his. "I love you." I couldn't hear his voice, and didn't need to as his mouth met mine. I turned my body just enough to comfortably settle in for a long, deeply satisfying kiss, as we owned every moment of that sunset until the world became dark and studded with starlight. I caught the glint of a bright star tearing its way across the night sky as if in approval and my mother's face flashed across my mind as I smiled to myself and kissed him again.

CHAPTER 35

THE GATHERING

Fresh coffee and buttered bread had been brought up this morning while Luca and Hissifus snored softly together in our bed. The little traitorous fluff practically laid across his face, and I couldn't figure out for the life of me how Luca was even able to breathe. I didn't wake either of them. I filled a dainty mug from the tray and swayed through the sitting room, opening the doors to the balcony and stepping out into the gray morning. It was the first time since being in Crona that I'd ever seen the sun hide behind endless layers of dark clouds, and the ocean itself looked malicious, as it had turned from the lovely turquoise of paradise to the deepest blue. A blue I had seen before but couldn't place where. My eyes traveled over the churning sea as I sipped my black coffee and I savored its warmth. A shiver crawled down my spine like a snake slithering unnervingly from the gathering storm over the water and thunder rumbled in the distance. The wind caught the tail of my long silk nightgown, the deep teal material blowing back and exposing my bare leg in the thigh-high split. I chewed my bottom lip nervously and stared at the streaks of lightning, both my palms warming on the porcelain mug at my chest.

A pair of strong, warm hands slid around my abdomen from behind me and Luca's scent filled my nose as he leaned his chin over my shoulder and lightly kissed my neck. "That looks ominous," he said, following my gaze over the water.

"Something doesn't feel right about it." I breathed as I studied the view. "It makes me uneasy...like it's directing its attention to me."

"Maybe Varuna's a bit salty." He grinned, coiling his arms around me and pulling me against his warmth. "Maybe she's feeling a little intimidated about how absolutely divine you look in that nightgown." His teeth nipped my earlobe and he chuckled softly when I nudged him with an elbow.

"I'm being serious...heathen." I snickered, setting the mug down on the stone railing.

"So am I." His breath fanned across the tender skin in the column of my neck and I ached to take him back to bed. "You're in trouble tomorrow night, love. You'll be lucky to make it back down that aisle before I jerk you up and carry you all the way back up here." I turned in his arms until my chest was flush against his bare torso.

"You've done so well. I'm absolutely shocked at your restraint." I laughed, reaching my arms around his neck. The wind blew our hair between our faces and he brushed the fluttering strands behind my ear. "I'm proud...and jealous.

You've handled this a lot better than I have." His smile was downright guilty.

"I wouldn't assume that. Michele and my father have dealt with a great deal of my shit out at the bay for the past two weeks." Our foreheads touched and we both grew quiet. The thunder rolled a bit closer, and his fingers brushed down my cheekbone. "Tomorrow..." He started. I couldn't stop the gaping smile at that word and my eyes fluttered shut for a short moment. "Tomorrow, I get to call you my wife."

"You already do." I giggled.

"But tomorrow, it will be real. I can't tell you how long it feels like I've waited for this." He paused and I met his gaze. It was as deep as the ocean beyond that balcony and lined with silver. "How long I've waited for you..." I brushed his hair back and held both sides of his face.

"Kiss me," I whispered against his lips. Thunder cracked at the exact moment those lips crushed into mine, and it didn't do anything other than fuel my burning need for him when his tongue slipped into my mouth. The strap of my nightgown dropped down my shoulder with the aggression of our movement around that kiss, and I almost asked him to agree that we'd waited long enough. But it was just one more day—merely hours. We could survive it. I just had no desire to. The wind suddenly felt stronger...more urgent. Lightning flashed bright, followed by another deafening rumble, every touch of his hand against my skin as electrifying as if I'd been struck. The sting of large raindrops carried by the wind started to pepper our skin and Luca's breathing turned purely feral. My hands dropped between our bodies and I curled my fingers around the laces of his night pants. His body tensed and heated when I started to tug the thin strings apart and—

"Don't the two of you have a bit of shame?" A familiar voice boomed from the sitting room doorway, stopping us both in surprise. "Are you not worried at all about anyone bearing witness to this tryst, or are you simply trying to make a very *memorable* spectacle of a damn good way to die?" Nero laughed loudly as he crossed his massive arms across his chest and leaned on the door jamb.

"Gods above...don't you knock?" Luca laughed, grabbing my wrists in frustration as I reluctantly let go of the laces and leaned against him.

"I did, bastard." Nero answered. "However...if it's indeed the latter, I'm certain I chose a fine spot to watch." Luca and I both shook our heads in laughter and made to walk inside. The storm began to rage as Nero stretched his arms wide and I hopped into them. He hugged me tight and lifted me off the floor, shaking me back and forth. "Hey there, youngling." My toes touched back down and he clapped Luca on the shoulder, pulling him too into a brotherly embrace. We ducked into the large sitting room as the rain fell harder and began blowing through the open doorway.

"When did you get here? Are Alister and Maureen with you?" I asked, closing off the doors. Nero waved a hand across the fireplace close by and it lit with his motion in a roar. I handed Luca his hair strap and we padded over as he tied his hair back.

"Actually...no." Nero cracked a side smile as he leaned against the mantle and faced us. I frowned deeply. "Maureen isn't well enough to travel. Alister didn't want to leave her behind. He offers his congratulations and wants you to visit soon."

"She still hasn't healed from the attack?" Luca asked, a pointed stare directed at the god of strength. Thunder clapped loudly outside the glass doors.

"On the contrary. She's recovered beautifully." Nero's smile grew wider. My mouth dropped open and I stepped forward.

"Oh gods...she's with child!" My hand slapped against my mouth. Nero nodded. "That's wonderful!" I nearly wept. Images of her blood bubbling through the horrific gashes across her midsection flashed in my mind, and for a split second...I felt the green monster of jealousy. Her wounds nearly killed her. They *did* kill her. She was spared by Alister's answered prayers from the gods to bring her back to him, and after all of that...she was able to conceive. Luca appeared at my side almost instantly, feeling the mixture of emotions I was putting off. His fingers brushed down my spine and I felt the warmth of his magic settle the sudden intrusion of grief.

Nero's eyes narrowed and he turned his body to face us fully. "Something's happened." Not a question. A demand to reveal who would suffer his wrath if either of us had been harmed. Ironic as that notion may be, it comforted me. We both raised our eyes to him and his attention darted back and forth between us, as he used his immortal mind to piece together what neither of us wanted to say. His fiery eyes softened and he stepped closer, taking my hands. His calloused fingers squeezed on mine and Luca rested his own hand on the small of my back. "Oh, Arienne. Luca, I'm—I'm so sorry. I didn't—"

"It's alright." I smiled sweetly. "I'm overjoyed about the news. Please extend our congratulations as well and let them know we'll make plans to get to Bolton following the wedding."

"Damn...that's going to be one beautiful child," Luca breathed. His hand rubbed at the back of his neck as he stared into the fireplace. I hummed in agreement, picturing a moon pale, silver-haired baby with scarlet eyes. How anyone could ever think Alister's condition was anything but extraordinary still baffled me. Between that and Maureen's dove-like features, that babe would grow into something stunning regardless of its gender.

"I did bring someone along that I think you'd be happy to see." Nero offered, trying desperately to lighten the sudden drop in mood. I perked up. "Lady Annette is with the queen as we speak, offering her gifts to help with your wedding decorations for tomorrow. I hope you still enjoy flowers." He chuckled.

"Ohhh, that's perfect!" I smiled genuinely. "I do hope she was able to make good use of what we left her. Is she well?"

"She is, yes. And your gratitude went a long way. She insisted on taking

Alister's place to give you something in return." The sound of driving rain was loud enough against the doors that I wondered if I'd closed them well enough to hold against it. Nero's attention went right for them and a knowing expression flashed on his face.

"You alright?" Luca asked, noticing his change in disposition.

"I apologize for the storm," He answered simply, walking over to wiggle the handles and check their security. Luca and I glanced at each other in confusion. "I told you...she's a wrathful one. She knows I'm here. I know this weather. There are only two reasons it gets like this in Crona." He peered out the glass and a bright bolt of lightning hit dangerously close to the balcony; the sound similar to an explosion as if in reply to his affirmation. I jumped and Luca steadied me.

"Varuna." Luca confirmed. "She's pissed at you." I remembered the night I had found Luca sleeping with the book in his lap and what he'd been reading about Nero. The truth about why he really left. I thought it wise not to pry or bring up painful memories. Nero nodded slowly without turning around, seemingly unfazed by her show of disappreciation.

"What would be the other reason?" I stupidly asked without thinking. Nero glanced over his shoulder with a smirk. "Oh..." I bit my lip. "Forget I asked."

"The thighs on that—never mind. You'll see when you meet her." Nero spoke against the glass while the doors rattled as if in rage. He chuckled under his breath. "I'll leave you two. Clearly, I...interrupted something." I couldn't help the flush of my cheeks.

"It's no bother. We aren't supposed to be doing anything anyhow. Not until tomorrow night." Luca complained. Nero abruptly turned, his face twisted in amusement.

"You can't be serious." He purred, planting both hands on his strong hips. "It's no wonder. And whose bright idea was that?" He laughed loudly. Luca glanced frustratedly at me and I opened my mouth, unwilling to fully accept blame. "Why?" He roared.

"Paxe...my—my best friend. She encouraged me to try to hold off until the wedding night. Before you judge...I do feel that it's worth it. Or...well—it will be. Tomorrow." I crossed my arms and stared at Luca, who cleared his throat and shifted around in discomfort. I didn't miss the slight bulge below his waist but wished I had when Nero's laughter grew increasingly loud.

"Didn't seem at all to me as if either of you had any intention of waiting until then...considering the display I walked in on." Nero chuckled.

"I sincerely hope he's taking a piss, Arienne Genovese." Paxe's voice trailed from the short hallway as she made her way into the sitting room with Hissifus curled against her on her arm. Nero's eyes went wide and so did his smile as their eyes met.

"Well..." He started, giving her a respectful once-over. "You must be the best friend." I watched as an immortal god bent over at the waist to a semi-mortal. I couldn't keep the surprise from my face. Luca seemed to feel the same way, fluctuating his attention back and forth between them. "My name is Nero. It's a pleasure to meet your acquaintance."

Paxe flushed a shade of rose that matched her flowing gown, her little bump seemingly more noticeable this morning as she dipped into a curtsy and smiled at Nero. "Paxe, your Grace. An honor to finally meet you. I've heard fantastic stories." Another loud crack of thunder sounded from outside and Hiss leapt from Paxe's arms, scurrying beneath the small sofa near the fireplace. Nero rolled his eyes and glanced out the window and I had to suppress my giggle with a few fingertips to my mouth. The goddess was not having any of his charming behavior.

"Prince, does your father have a wine cellar in this fine establishment? Or perhaps a collection of hard liquor?" Nero asked.

"Yes, and yes. If it's raining, you'll probably find him in his study. I'm sure he'll be happy to oblige. Be wary of my mother. You get him too drunk and we'll all be suffering for it." Luca laughed.

"Bah." Nero waved a hand at him and dipped his chin in farewell, sparing another suggestive look at my sister and smiling before excusing himself. I stood, staring a hole through Paxe with my hands on my hips, finding her staring off in the direction Nero had disappeared. Luca chuckled softly behind me and crossed his arms.

"Ahem," I cleared my throat, breaking her distracting thoughts. "Something on your mind, friend?" I raised my brows. She looked at me with a surprised expression and bashfully hurried herself to the armoire, trying her best to appear rational as she fumbled through my clothes.

"Sorry, umm...V-Vetta and Frances are here. I came to get you dressed, and Luca, your mother wants you. She's not pleased with your fitting and wants Gran to do your measurements instead. She told me to ask you if you'd be so kind as to meet her in your father's dressing chambers." She fished out a lovely deep blue gown with long sleeves and hidden bust support.

"Gods." Luca cursed under his breath, turning to his own armoire and randomly selecting a tunic. "I'd just as easily get married in these night clothes."

"Luca..." I grinned.

"You wouldn't care either way, I don't know why she's making such a damn fuss over it." He griped, pulling the shirt over his head.

"Let her. It's our wedding day. She's been waiting for this as long as you have, you brute." I stepped over and straightened his tunic, tying the front laces. "And you're right. I wouldn't care. However...I'm not going to be overdressed...so, on with it." He pressed a chaste kiss to my nose and started to turn to leave. "Umm..." I called.

"Hmm?" He looked over his shoulder. Paxe giggled softly into the door of the armoire on the other side of the sitting room.

"Are we planning to stroll about the castle in our undergarments?" I laughed. Luca glanced down and rolled his eyes again, stalking over to a chest of drawers and grabbing a pair of dark gray pants. He grinned mischievously and winked at me as he darted down the hallway and into the bedchamber. I heard rustling as he quickly changed and flung the night pants onto the bed on his way out. I swiveled and looked at Paxe, who was holding up the gown and waiting for me to come dress.

"Say it." She tensed under my stare.

"Could you have been any more obvious?" I laughed, walking towards her. "What's gotten into you?" I disrobed and took the gown from her.

"Nothing... I—" She huffed out a breath and turned her face to the ceiling. "I don't know if it's my hormones or just...I don't know, alright?"

"Liar." I smiled, stepping into the gown and pulling it up. "What is it, really?" I slipped my arms into the sleeves and turned my back to her. She promptly began lacing up the back of my dress, her movements answering my question before she spoke.

"Lakan refuses to lie with me right now. He...he's afraid something will happen to the babe. But my *body*. Ari, I need to be touched. I need him to put those hands on me." She breathed deeply, seemingly feeling the same urgency that Luca and I were weathering. "I can't blame him, but...I also can't control this—*this*."

"Need?" I finished, smirking to myself.

"Yes!" She forcefully pulled the laces with her reply and I jerked backwards. "Sorry..."

"I understand." I snickered. "You need to be careful."

"I wouldn't do anything to hurt him. I would never. But you can't blame me for reacting to a look like that, holy gods." I could hear the heat in her voice.

"I understand that too. Nero is captivating, to say the least. But you need to keep a tight check on those...*reactions*." I smiled. "Just be glad Vetta wasn't up here to witness that exchange."

"*He* should be glad. He practically undressed me with his eyes." She finished tying me off and started brushing my hair.

"You looked at him like you'd let him do it." I buckled, covering my mouth. She slapped my arm and chuckled softly.

"We're not having this conversation, *Mi'lady*." She teased. Her nimble fingers braided my locks into a loose plait, and she coiled it around into a coronet, pinning it behind my head.

"You mean the conversation about how you seem to have a type?" I jabbed. She grew quiet and I felt her pause behind me.

"Shit." She whispered. I cackled at her sudden realization.

"You've got a taste for blacksmiths." She gripped her flowing golden hair and paced around the room. "Relax, there's nothing wrong with that."

"I need...I need *relief*, Ari." She flapped her hands almost angrily at her sides as she continued to pace. I stopped her and braced her shoulders.

"Good gods. It's that bad?" I asked, trying to understand how she must feel without having much control over what her body was going through. She nodded. "Have you considered..." I quirked a brow.

"Considered what?" She urged me to finish.

"Doing it yourself?" I whispered as if someone other than Hissifus was around to hear us. She looked shocked that I even mentioned it.

"What? No. I've never—I don't think I could do that." She pulled away and waved me off. I stayed put and she quickly turned and looked at me under her brows. "Wait a second...are you saying you have?" I shrugged and her face ignited in shock. "Are you kidding?" I shook my head and gestured for her to follow me into the bedchamber. Luca's journal was still lying on the desk and I flipped around until I found our note folded into the pages. I opened it and handed it to her. I grinned ridiculously as her face started turning different shades of red and her hand blindly found its way to her chest. She giggled at the lower half of the page and when our eyes met again, she gaped at me as she handed it back.

"I'd be lying if I told you it didn't seem strange at first, but I don't have a single regret. If you don't want to try it alone, then what if the two of you...you know...together?" She leaned in and kissed my cheek.

"You're brilliant." I placed the journal back on the desk and slid my feet into my shoes. "I can't believe—well...yes. Yes I can. Clever. That was incredibly clever. But have you done this since the two of you started holding back?"

"No. Well, I haven't at least. If he has, I wouldn't know." She took my hand and we started through the doorway. As I shut the door, I could overhear voices at the end of the corridor. Vetta's and a guard I didn't recognize. Paxe and I looked at each other and smiled adoringly as we started toward them.

Vetta's round form took shape around the corner, and the poor guard she was scolding cowered in front of her. She raised her face and stopped dead. She looked so different. Her silvering hair was neatly pinned and her dress was more formal than I'd ever seen her deign to wear. Simple, but elegant. A deep green velvet that flattered her shape. She took us both in and I could already see the emotion flaring up in her soft eyes when she spotted the little bulge in Paxe's middle. She opened her arms and sniffled. "My girls." We practically ran to her, all of us huddled together in a heap as if we hadn't spent only a few weeks apart. But I understood that everything was different now. I wondered for a moment if Vetta knew the truth about Paxe's relation to me. I wouldn't jeopardize that truth any time soon, but I tucked it away for later.

"I've not felt it move yet, but the queen believes I'm close," Paxe said tearfully as Vetta's hand cradled her belly. She gave it a loving pat and pinched Paxe's chin.

"A girl." Vetta grinned.

"What? How do you know that?" Paxe exclaimed, looking at me as I nodded in agreement.

"I just have a feeling. I've also never been wrong." She laughed. The guard snorted, to which Vetta sneered over her shoulder. He straightened and backed toward the corner, eager to mind his own business. "You..." She cupped my cheek. "You look just like your mother."

"I know." I beamed, giving her an understanding stare. She gave me a soft nod as if to tell me she had promised I'd know everything and knew I now did. "Thank you. For everything."

"I'd have it no other way, child." She looked down at my flat stomach. "I won't be expecting one from you too, will I?" She looked back up at me with that grandmotherly scold in her eyes. It was an effort to keep my emotions on a leash, but before Paxe could give me away, I smiled and shook my head.

"Not yet." I laughed it off. I decided not to travel down that road with Vetta yet, and Paxe either understood exactly why I'd said it or knew it wasn't her place and mirrored my grin.

"They still maul each other like animals, if that's what you mean." Paxe rolled her eyes. The guard shifted on his feet, trying and failing to be disinterested in our conversation.

"What in the world ails you two?" Vetta shook her head, turning and taking our hands on each side of her as we started down the halls.

"You'd not ask if you gave it a try." I dared, earning a bellowing laugh from Vetta that I'd never heard before. Our conversation was animated the entire way to the ballroom. Every step through the castle, Vetta would stop and admire the beauty of this place that was nothing like the dark gloom of the home I'd left behind. The peace in her eyes told Paxe and I enough of the joy she found in knowing that we were finally safe and that she'd done her job well...and wouldn't need to worry about us any longer. She was free to comfortably live her life and allow us to grow up on our own.

As we stepped inside the enormous ballroom, she surveyed the placement of seats and decorations for our ceremony and her eyes filled with tears. The queen was quietly talking with Lady Annette near the altar and they both turned to acknowledge the three of us. It seemed that Annette had already used her magic in a few places around the space. There were flowered vines draping down the panes of the windows and hanging down from the chandeliers, soft romantic light peeking around white blooms and flickering around bright green leaves. It was such a lovely example of someone's abilities and I almost envied her for it. The two females approached and Annette curtsied as she stood before me.

"Mi'lady...it's so good to see you." She smiled and waved her hand at the vegetation. "How do you feel about the flowers? Will they do?"

"Oh Annette, they're beautiful. It was the touch we didn't realize was needed. Thank you so much." I held her hands and Ayla brushed a hand across my shoulder.

"This will be the last you see of it until tomorrow, dearest. The rest will be a surprise." She proudly looked around the room as castle attendants hurried around with everything from dishes and flatware to vases for more flowers.

"You're kicking her out?" Paxe chuckled, leaning in to smell some of the small white flowers near the window.

"I suppose I am," Ayla replied as she reached a hand out to Vetta. "You must be Lady Vetta. I owe you thanks...for raising such wonderful females. They're a great joy in my life."

Vetta accepted her hand and bowed over it. "No lady...just Vetta. And you needn't thank me. It was I who was blessed with such a task. I thank the gods every day for that. I thank *you* for allowing me to bear witness to this moment in Arienne's life. I can hardly believe it's happening. Your prince is a fine male."

"I'll not argue that...but don't let the lovely face fool you. He can be quite the wretch." She laughed. I scoffed and forcefully nodded my concurrence. "He's much like his father." She faced me fully. "I'm afraid that's not all though, little dove."

"This should be interesting." Paxe grinned, crossing her arms. I drew my brows together and Annette smirked.

"I'm afraid to ask," I admitted, glancing between them all.

"You and the handsome wretch will be separated tonight," Ayla said apologetically. My shoulders sagged and I could feel my frown of disappointment beginning to creep over my mouth. "I'm sorry. It's customary. But don't worry," she and Paxe exchanged smiles. "You'll be in good company and so will he.

"You're rooming with me." Paxe squealed. "Luca will have Lakan and Nero."

"Will they be in Luca's room?" I asked.

"No, we're—having the room tidied up and your bedding cleaned and changed. The males will be in the king's chambers doing whatever males do for the evening." Ayla smirked and rolled her eyes.

"What about Hissifus? He'll be alone." The queen's brows nearly touched her hairline.

"I'm sorry?" She leaned toward me as if in surprise. "Is there an animal in the castle?" I suddenly felt myself cower under her tone. I hadn't realized she wasn't aware.

"Your Majesty, that cat is only an animal by its confinement to his body. He's nothing more than an obese, lazy child who eats too much." Vetta offered, trying to cut the tension in the queen's body.

"I'm sorry, my queen. I didn't know that you weren't told about him. Luca surprised me with it a few days ago." I wrung my fingers in nerves.

"He *would.* I told that little shit ever since he was young...it doesn't matter, dear. I apologize for my forcefulness. Animal dander upsets my sinuses. If he's kept from around the castle, I can manage. We'll make sure he's taken to Paxe's chambers for you."

"I could be of assistance with that." Vetta raised a palm. "I wield healing magic. Should you need it." The queen nodded and thanked her.

"If you'll excuse me, I must go see to my son and his poorly tended wardrobe." The queen bowed in farewell. She pointed at me as she walked past. "Take one last look, Princess, and find something to do. No peeking until tomorrow!" Her smile was lovely as she headed out the doors. We could all tell she was nearly bubbling over with excitement.

Thunder echoed through the ballroom and I glanced at the stained glass windows, wondering how long Varuna would rage at Nero's presence. I couldn't think of a single thing to do in the castle to settle my nerves about the fact that I only had a few hours left until I walked through this room in that gown, and married the most incredible male in front of our entire kingdom and two very hot-headed higher beings. I wished I could go into the city and clear my head.

"The reflecting pool...come to me. I wish to see you, and I don't have much time." A soothing voice echoed in my mind. I felt a slight tug within my body as if it were trying to direct me toward the voice. I looked at the females chattering happily amongst one another around me and couldn't hear a single word they were saying as the voice spoke again. *"Hurry, daughter."*

"There's something I need to attend to...alone. Could I meet you all in the dining room in a while?" I asked no one in particular. Vetta quirked a brow and Paxe peered into me as if she were trying to remember anything we'd forgotten to check off the list of things that still needed to be done before tomorrow.

"Are you well, child?" Vetta asked, taking my hand.

"Yes, I'm fine. Just something I need to do by myself." I assured her. She smiled sweetly and Annette stood wholly confused.

"Go then." Vetta's eyes showed a hint of knowing. I nodded and hastily left the ballroom, walking quickly down the hallways and stairs until I reached the open area of the courtyard where the reflection pool sat, undisturbed and oddly vacant. Not a soul around that I could see. Not even a guard.

I approached the side, peering down into the still water and admiring the colored glass that sparkled beneath. I lowered myself to sit on the edge and my finger drifted involuntarily to the water's surface. I dipped the tip of my forefinger into it and ripples began traveling away from my hand, spreading themselves out across the pool. Soft light slowly enveloped me until the only thing I could see was the few feet of the water I sat alongside. A familiar face began to take shape in it, my reflection replaced by my mother.

"Arienne." She smiled.

"All these years I've longed to see you...and it was this simple the entire time?" I half-heartedly joked, earning a motherly scowl.

"It's good to see you too." She grinned. *"And no...you'd not crossed the barrier to the immortal realm then. I can only spare a few moments. Doing this from my realm is frowned upon by the gods, but it was the only way I could see you before you marry."*

"Is there no way to leave the immortal realm? Live the way Nero and Elowen do?" I asked curiously.

"Not for the ones who agreed to live out their immortal lives here. One day you'll understand. It binds you much like the way you and the prince are bound to one another." Her eyes seemed to glow within the water.

"I wish you could be here with me tomorrow, Mother." I frowned.

"I will be. I'm always with you. I've never left." My eyes pricked with the invasion of tears. Her hand raised before her, seeming desperate to reach for me. *"My beautiful girl. I'm joyous of your marriage. I wanted to tell you myself. This is all I ever wished for you."*

"I know." I smiled, choking back emotion. "It pains me that you have to live your immortal life alone. I wish you had someone with you to give you the love he gives to me."

"I knew what I was sacrificing to atone for what I've caused. I've long since accepted that. Do not pity me, my darling." The ripples shifted and her face faded slightly but then reappeared. *"My time is nearly spent. I need to warn you."* Her voice was pleading and I leaned closer.

"What's wrong?" I panicked.

"Love him, Arienne. Love him, and keep him close. The prince is strong, and though he may not ever show you...he is also fragile."

"I don't understand. Is it the curse?" I asked.

"His curse has shown him a good many things he'll never reveal to you, Arienne. He withholds it to protect you...but I fear..." She faded in and out. *"Choose—in the end—eternity."* The light around me quickly disappeared and so did her face. I was left staring into the pool, the water just as still as when I'd come to sit by it.

"Mother?" I braced both hands on the side and leaned over the pool. "Damn it." My breathing quickened and I struck the surface with my palm, splashing the water across the expanse of the pool. "Luca...what the hell?" I couldn't tell if I was hurt, or angry...or just plain terrified. Every single time we had ever been close to being this happy, something always went wrong. So very wrong. I had managed to release part of this curse by choosing to love myself. Forgive myself. I began to feel like we'd wasted precious time putting this wedding together and trying to steal a few moments of peace when we should have been tirelessly finding some other way to break this damned spell my father had over my husband.

All that I did know, without any doubt, was that all signs led me to believe it could be done. I just didn't know how.

But I'm willing to bet someone else does...

I lifted my skirts and raced upstairs, barreling through Luca's bedroom door and into the sitting room. Hissifus startled from his spot on the small couch by the fire and trotted over to slide his body around my bare legs as I changed out of my dress and into a tunic and leather leggings. I gave him a quick pat on the head and pulled a heavy cloak around myself, raising the hood over my head and hurrying back down to the castle entrance. The rain pummeled me as I ran past the guards outside without a word and down the long walkway to the city gate. The streets were empty and I clutched my cloak together at my chest as I quickly made for the shopping district toward the imaginary magic shoppe.

CHAPTER 36

THE NIGHT BEFORE

The rain didn't slow, nor did it lighten up as I walked into a near jog through the flooding city streets. Patrons that had braved the storm yelped as they ducked from door to door, covering their heads in everything from bags, to books and freshly purchased garments. I passed what used to be Lydia's lingerie shop, its darkened windows empty and a makeshift sign on the door indicating the space was available for hire. I hurried down a couple of blocks and to my shock and relief...was a dimly lit window where I knew a cafe should be. I marched toward it and peered inside. I knew I hadn't been insane. There it was, a dodgy-looking place with 'blessed' brick-a-brack and dried herbs...a tacky, stupid table tucked into the back corner, with that ridiculous glass globe perched atop it. I couldn't see anyone inside.

I looked around and saw no one in the streets to test the theory that I had indeed lost my mind. Finding myself becoming more irritated, I yanked the door open and the little bell above it chimed in my arrival. I dropped my hood and slowly crept around the shoppe, careful not to touch anything.

"Hello?" I called. No response. Not a single sound, save for the rain still battering the window. I rolled my eyes and turned back to the door, nearly making it with my hand outstretched to grab the handle, when a loud boom of thunder startled me enough to wail and jerk back. I grasped my chest, my heart thudding loudly beneath my palm.

"You've returned." An ancient voice croaked from behind me. I turned toward the sound and met the cloudy, unsettling gaze of the old crone. Her robes were exactly the same as they'd been before, and this time, her presence seemed even more cold. A spider-like sensation trickled down my spine and I shuddered. "Does this mean Her Highness doesn't find my truth-telling to be all that comical after all?" Her bony fingers curled around a short walking stick and she took an unsteady step toward me.

"Why am I the only one that can see this place? See you?" I asked, lifting my chin in feigned confidence. "Even the prince has never known you or this shoppe to exist, and he's lived here his entire life." She copped a fierce smile.

"You don't ask the right questions, Princess. What is it that you truly wish to know?" My heart sped up at her dismissal, and the thought of what I truly wanted to know...to be left unanswered as it always had been. "You wish to save your prince." She answered before I could voice it myself.

"Of course I do." I breathed, my heart heavier with every thought. "He's everything to me. He's my heart and soul...my *life.*" My voice broke with heartbreak at the thought of his lifeless body at Nero's temple.

"And your people? In what order have you placed them on the list of what you care for most?" She narrowed her dark eyes and I felt as if she'd wrapped her hands around my throat.

"My people still have my honor. And my promise to deliver them. You speak to me as if you doubt my will. What is it about me that leads you to believe I'll not do what I was born to do?" I snapped.

"I do not doubt your will, youngling. Nor do I doubt your heart. I know the life you've lived. The suffering that was bestowed upon you. I respect you for everything you've given and your desire to make it right."

"Then why do you insist on making me feel as if that isn't true?" I lowered my brows.

"That isn't my intention. I only wish to inquire about *yours*." Her voice was grave.

"And what right do you have to question me, witch?" My tone lowered in authority. The old hag's cane dropped to the floor in front of her and her robes seemed to flutter in wind I could neither see nor feel. They began to change in color, and shape. The homespun black material turned into a satin blue that matched the color of her eyes...the color of—the color of the sea this morning...before the storm approached.

Gods above...

Her entire form began to change, spiraling around her from the bottom of her skirts to her shapely hips. An enchanting female now stood before me with long silver hair, and skin that was so pale white it nearly looked blue. Her face was fluid and flawless, a radiant beauty that was equal parts gentleness and rage. I was so aghast at the realization of who I had just mouthed off to that I hit my knees and bowed before her.

"Varuna...I'm—I'm so..." I stammered, wondering if she'd smite me right here.

"Stand up, Princess. You bow to no one." Her voice was as simple as my own, yet entrancing and intoxicating. I raised on wobbling knees and tried earnestly to straighten myself and hide my shame. "Do you still not realize who you are, youngling?" She asked.

"I know who I am. That doesn't mean I'm exempt from reverence toward a being such as yourself," I replied.

"I do not have the answer you seek. None of us do. I approached you in this way to find out the truth about the things that distract you. Things that could bring you to failure...even when you believe you're safe." Her lovely face reminded me of a statue made of polished marble from Ayla's studio.

"I understand if you believe that Luca is a distraction. But it was the gods themselves that bound us this way. *You* chose us for this task. *You* were the ones who decided we would do this together. Why is it selfish of me to want to protect him? How could I not worry about the male I'm fated to love this much?" I choked back my sob and sniffled. "Do you have any idea what it took for me to allow myself to feel this way about someone? Do you not understand that my need to even make love to him was a battle I had to fight just so I wouldn't think about the two men that had been inside my body before him?" Varuna's expression was unreadable. I wept softly and went on. "We'll never share the joy of having a child of our own. We'll always only have each other. I don't want to have the only thing that completes me to be snatched away when I free my people. I don't want to be left alone...without my soulmate. The way the first king had been. If that is my price after all we've been through...it seems unfair to me, your Grace."

"I understand," she said simply. "I understand what it's like to love that way. But I also understand what it's like to be so lost in that love that you cause irreparable errors in your judgment. Errors so great that the cost can never be paid." Pain flared across her features and her dark eyes softened.

"Nero..." I whispered, almost to myself. She nodded softly. "The storms...the people that were killed."

"Because of our passion and our foolishness, we were blinded and too selfish to realize that we were endangering mortals...until it was too late." She turned herself away, her movements ghost-like and graceful as she stared down at the floor. "We loved each other so fiercely, but our quarreling was relentless. There were children on that ship that fateful night. When I recall the reason for our bickering that evening..." She faced me again. "We all have choices, Princess. And we all suffer consequences for our actions. Be them honorable, or otherwise."

"I understand."

"What is your reason for not telling the heir about her true lineage? Of what it means for the child she carries?" Her shoulders balanced and she appeared more like a goddess then, rather than a jilted lover. I drew a long breath.

"I fear for her. I fear for her happiness. The weight of the responsibility that comes with the crown. I feel as if having my father's power within her brings safety to our world. Her heart is pure, and strong willed. She'll not abuse it. I have no desire to wield that power, but I'm more than capable of governing our lands. I just haven't decided on a good time...or a good way to tell her the truth. I must have considered it thousands of times since learning it myself. I know that her child will be the heir I cannot give my crown. I suppose I thought that when the time is right...she'll be ready to rule, and I can step down. Live my life with the prince, and just..."

"Just be at peace," she finished for me.

"Yes, your Grace." My head bowed and I closed my eyes.

"Do you know the visions that your mother speaks of where the prince is concerned?" My head raised at that and I knotted my brows. I shook my head slowly.

"She told me that he's been keeping things from me. He feels he's protecting me." I breathed. Varuna dipped her chin.

"When you've traveled from place to place. When you've met your subjects and they address you as their queen...have you beheld your betrothed?"

"Yes. He's been supportive. Proud." I started reflecting back on all the times I could remember, fists against chests and knees on the ground. All the cries for hope and freedom from my father's rule. I had never thought to consider how Luca felt about it all.

"He always will be, youngling. The love that he has for you...it cannot be tamed. It cannot be extinguished. It burns and rages within him and grows stronger with each passing day. The prince desires nothing more than to give you that love. He desires to give you happiness. It is admirable, and precious. But he also has seen for many years now...glimpses of his future. The prince understands that he shall never be king, youngling." I stiffened at her words. I felt the sting of them in the same manner that I'd felt the stab of that healer telling me I'd never have a child to call mine.

"Are you saying...are you telling me he's accepted death? He's going to die?" I recalled flashes of moments I hadn't given a second thought to. When we first met Frances and he had called Luca his future king...Luca had looked as if someone had slapped him in his face. The night that he'd given me that ring...his expressions had looked so utterly broken. I had foolishly thought that it had been because for whatever reason he perhaps thought that I'd say no. Or that maybe he'd known what was going to happen later that night when he died for me in that temple. I would have never guessed that he'd been holding this back all this time.

"It is clear to me knowing what you did to yourself in Nero's temple, that you'd give your life to be with the Crown Prince. I suppose my question is...if it came down to giving your life for your people and this cause...would you be willing to accept that fate as the prince has done for you?" Her stare was like stone. Hard and unyielding. I was surprised at the lack of hesitation when I answered.

"Yes," I choked.

"May I offer you a word? Something to comfort you in regard to your struggle with your sister?" She stepped forward. I didn't respond, instead looking into her eyes. "Peace." Her mouth turned up in the corner.

"Peace?" I echoed, my face drawn in confusion.

"Her name...means peace." My limbs slackened and my body slumped. "You should consider that the gods also took her into account for the rescue of our world. Do not doubt her ability to support the weight of your crown, youngling. When you find a way that gives you comfort...tell her the truth." Her hands were surprisingly warm as they took my shoulders.

"What—" I cleared my throat. "What does my name mean?" I almost regretted knowing the answer...until she said—

"Holy."

She held me steady as the rest of my body went limp. Anything holy...*anyone* holy. They were considered as such by death. By death...or through an immortal being. My mother. Together...Luca and I were...*Holy Bringer of Light.* I couldn't breathe.

"Do not be afraid, youngling. We will never allow you to be separated from one another. The choices you make in unity are your own. But again, the task you've accepted is the only way to stop the king. We promised your reward would be great. The curse is a thorn, but I have faith that between the two of you...you'll find a way to break through it. We all wish that there was a way to banish it...but I'm betting that neither of you have considered the small blessing it's given you by accident."

"There is no blessing in that *thing.*" I said between clenched teeth.

"Look at how much you both have grown. As partners...and individually. All because of this. Would you have been so inclined had he not been marked by the king?" A fair question. And a completely foreign thought as far as I was concerned.

"We're going to die...aren't we?" I whispered. The goddess was quiet for a long moment. "This was always the true plan wasn't it? All of you gods...you have a way with your words. You tell us what we need to know, but never reveal too much." I smiled to myself and refused to look up at her. "Elowen explained that the power would be passed down to the heir. She was careful not to say that it would be passed down to me. Nero danced around his explanation of the goddess in the Horned Mountains. He'd been careful not to tell me I'd meet my mother. You're giving me that same courtesy now. Being careful...only telling me a small part of the truth. So that we'll continue to press on and save it all."

"If you knew everything...would it change anything?" She asked. I met her stare.

"Only that I'll never take another moment with him for granted." I replied. She smiled softly and slowly nodded her head.

"Then go live, youngling. Own the rest of your lives. Make it something wonderful, despite all that's against you."

"I should go," I whispered. She released my shoulders and I straightened, turning away and noticing the beams of sunlight piercing through the clouds like mighty swords from the heavens. The promise of silver lining. The storm was over. I looked over my shoulder as I gripped the handle of the door. "Your Grace...if I may?"

"Yes?"

"You should consider taking your own advice...he still loves you, you know." Her face went taut and her body shifted, but she said nothing. I smiled and opened the door, stepping out into the street. The bell jingled above my head. "See you at the wedding."

As soon as the door closed behind me I peeked over to look through the window. The cafe was again teeming with patrons. Pat, the shop owner waved at me and I waved back before turning and taking a longer route back to the castle to gather all the thoughts I now had swimming through my aching head.

No one bothered to stop me or speak to me as I walked down street after street.

I thought back several times to what my mother had said at the reflection pool. *Love him, Arienne. Love him and keep him close.* If there was a possibility that neither of us would make it much farther in this mortal life…then I planned to do just that. They said our reward would be great. It already was. The greatest thing in my life. *'My greatest treasure'*, as Luca had once said. I thought of the moment I had decided to let him in. The moment I'd decided that even if I'd only known him for a few days, then that amount of time with him wouldn't be wasted. I fully surrendered my heart that night, and suddenly felt so glad that I had. My people would be free. And maybe we would die. Maybe this curse would never be broken. But my father would be. Gideon and that nameless female with her tiny baby wouldn't have died for nothing. My imprisonment and torture would be given new meaning. But above all else…my remaining time with Luca would be blissful. We'd stop living a life that raced a clock. Starting tomorrow, as soon as I stepped into that ballroom and claimed that male as mine. *Forever.*

However long our forever would be.

My cloak felt like the weight of a body as it draped over my arm, still wet from my escape into the city before the storm had subsided. I nodded once at the guards by the castle entrance and they both dipped their chins at me as I entered to find Paxe waiting impatiently, poised with both her slender hands on her hips.

"Where in the hell have you been? You look a dreadful mess!" I smirked and walked past her toward the staircase and she fell into step behind me, catching up quickly and continuing to nag. "I searched everywhere for you to see if you were alright, and then I finally got word from the guards that you'd gone out into that storm in a hurry. Have you—"

"Paxe!" I turned abruptly, startling her as we halted on the stairs. "I'm fine…just relax." I gripped her shoulder to ease the sudden sting of my outburst and softly pat her little belly. "Don't fuss. She's sleeping. Let her dream." I smiled. Her face softened and she laid her hand over mine.

"I'm sorry…" She whispered. "I just—I was worried."

"I know. I'll tell you all about it later tonight. I need to see Luca. Do you know where he is?"

"Yeah. He's in Tidus's study with Frances and Nero. Lakan couldn't keep up with Nero's drinking tolerance and passed out already. It's not even late afternoon." She rolled her eyes. I chuckled under my breath and we started side by side back up the stairs. "The damned fool was so excited to meet his idol that he took it upon himself to make a fool of us both. His human body was no match for that male."

"Paxe, he's a god." I laughed as we turned down a hallway. "It was hard for Luca and I to keep up with him. Give Lakan a little credit. Not many can say they shared wine with a deity." Her throat bobbed as she swallowed and I could have sworn she blushed a little.

We approached the study doors and the sounds of masculine laughter were muffled beyond it. I shook my head. "I've already been in there once to take my fiancé somewhere to sleep it off. This is where I leave you," Paxe scoffed.

"I'll just be a moment. Do you think you could go snatch my dress from Luca's room? I'm freezing." She took the wet cloak from me and held it up to examine it.

"Absolutely. You're not allowed back in there right now, anyway." She winked.

"You lot are killing me. If you're turning that bedchamber into some kind of—I don't even want to know." I placed a hand on the door handle and she giggled as she strode off. I raised my other hand and softly knocked at the door. It opened swiftly a moment later and Tidus stood before me, seemingly in mid-laughter about something Nero said.

"Arienne?" His face drooped at my weathered appearance and the door opened wider. "Are you alright?" He waved me inside.

"Yes, my Lord. I just needed to see Luca for a moment if that's alright." The door closed behind me, and Luca stepped around the ornate desk at the back of the study when he spotted me there, rushing past Nero and Frances who both gave me pointed looks.

"I'll give you two some privacy," Tidus smiled, reaching down and squeezing my fingers before calling over his shoulder to his guests. "I'll be back in a moment!" Nero threw his hands up in disappointment while Luca jogged to a stop in front of me and placed both hands on my shoulders, thoroughly looking me over. Tidus slipped out of the study doors without making a sound.

"What's wrong, love?" He asked softly, leaning in to look into my eyes. "Why are you cold and wet?" His hands moved up and down my shoulders as he tried rubbing some warmth into them. My arms found their way around him and I laid my damp head against his chest.

"You don't have to shoulder anything on your own anymore, Luca. You've been hiding things from me." I breathed. His arms had come around me and paused at my words for a moment. I didn't need to look up to see the expression I knew was on his face. He pulled me in tight and I felt a deep sigh slither out of his lungs.

"I'm sorry. I—I just didn't want that to be the only thing on your mind every time you look at me." He rested his lips in my hair. "I just wanted us to be free of it...happy."

"And how happy are *you* when you see yourself die every night in that meadow?" I argued. He stilled and I heard the thrumming of his heart grow faster in his chest.

"You already torture yourself with the weight of this curse every day, Ari. I won't be a reason that you feel more pain. Please don't be angry with me...I just want to protect you. I need to be the cushion you fall back onto." His voice shuddered.

"Why won't you let me be that cushion for you?" I asked, pulling back enough to look up at him. "We're equals, Luca. We're meant to hold each other up. Brick by brick...remember?" I traced his bottom lip with my thumb. He looked as if he were about to break, when I recalled what Ayla had said at the meeting in my father's castle.

"How did you find out?" He dared ask, reaching a hand behind my neck.

"Never mind how I found out. Promise me before we make these vows tomorrow that you'll never keep another thing from me. No matter how painful you think it is. Tomorrow, we'll be husband and wife. We live the rest of this life for each *other*. We get through it *together*. I won't ask you to tell me the details, but I want to know. I want to know every time that you're plagued with something awful so that I can chase away the demons that haunt you...that haunt *us*."

He slowly nodded and half smiled. "I promise."

"Tomorrow...when I see you again," I started, brushing my knuckles across the stubble of his chin, "We start doing things differently. No more racing against time. No more what-ifs. No more worrying about moonlight and violets in forests that are miles away. It's just us. Just us and whatever we face together. Deal?" His arms tugged me closer and his eyes were piercing when he said—

"I'll make that deal."

My heart nearly burst. The phrase that started everything. The words that bound him to this game...this curse. My fellow pawn on the chessboard. I wasn't sure which one of us moved first, but our mouths found each other and I wondered then which kiss would be deeper. The one we were having now, or the one that waited for tomorrow in that ballroom.

I tore myself away, both of us strangled with need. "I love you," I rasped, sliding my fingertips down his chest as I backed toward the study doors. I crept backward until I met the wood and he stared into me, trying to regain his composure.

"I love you," he whispered. "I'll see you at the altar, wife."

"Yes. Yes, you will." I smiled as I pushed down the handle and opened the door. Our eyes locked until I had fully shut the large door and I breathed heavily on the other side of it, feeling the strong pull of his magic intensifying and knowing he hadn't moved a single step. Nero bellowed something behind the door, distracting Luca enough that the tinge of his abilities began drifting slowly away. It was only then that I was able to turn around and walk away from the study and find my way to Paxe's room.

I turned corners and shuffled down hallways, gripping my arms and shivering with cold from the heavy damp tunic, as I slowly realized I had absolutely no idea where I was going and couldn't find a guard or castle attendant anywhere in sight.

Of course...when I need one, they disappear.

My brows spiked when I heard faint whispering from around a dim corner and I made my way toward salvation. I stopped short when the whispers sounded more like…I silently crept to the large pillar at the end of the hallway and peered around it.

Oh, Gods…

Tidus and Ayla were backed against an alcove in the empty hallway, her red skirts pushed up around her waist and her bare leg thrown around his hip as he pushed and pulled himself in and out of her. I turned away quickly, my hand over my mouth concealing my shock and 'get it, girl' smile.

"Take them off," she whispered breathlessly. Tidus groaned.

"Someone could walk down this hallway any moment."

"And to whom does this hallway belong?" Ayla asked. I heard rustling and a soft moan, and couldn't resist the urge to glance one more time. The king's embroidered black tunic hit the floor, his muscles in his back rippling, as he hoisted her higher up with one arm, and coiled his hand around her neck. "That's a good boy." She grinned, her head falling back against the wall, as he thrust himself inside her.

"You love me," he grunted.

"I adore you."

"Scream, Ayla." Tidus growled into her ear. Her teeth dug into her lip and she dropped her head back down, until their noses touched.

"Make it so," she whispered, her scarlet lips tearing into his. I turned and smiled down the hallway in which I came, her demand quickly fulfilled when I started down a set of stairs. Her cries echoed down the second flight I took and I giggled to myself. When I was confident I was a safe distance away from the king and queen, I found myself in a familiar part of the castle, and thankfully, I spotted Vetta's plump form inching out of a room near the end of the corridor.

"Where have you been, child?" She asked, walking toward me as I quickened my steps. "You look like a wet dog." Her lips curled into a smile and she gestured to Paxe's bedroom door.

"I got lost." I shrugged, ducking into the doorway. I met Paxe's stare upon entering her quaint, rose-colored bedchamber. Sheer white curtains swayed in the breeze from her open windows and she smiled as she waved a hand toward a long, narrow table against the side wall. It was piled with sweets, wine, and candies.

"As soon as you go bathe, we can start tearing through all this." She grinned. "We could start at this end and work our way back." Her slender finger pointed at a slab of chocolate cake and trailed down the table.

"So your idea is to either have me retching in a chamber pot the night before my wedding, or cause me a struggle to fit into my dress?" I laughed, taking it all in.

"You'll be fine. Come. The water has been ready in here for twenty minutes," she said, pulling me into a bath chamber on the other side of the room. I looked around the steamy room to find it eerily similar to my own at the castle in Valdaro but bathed in white instead of dark stone and inverted to a mirror image of what I remembered, with the sunken tub built on the far-right wall. A bottle of wine and *three* large goblets sat at the edge of the bathing pool. Hanging from a ribbon on the neck of the bottle was a small note and Paxe smiled almost tearfully at me. "That's for you."

I pouted a smile, knowing full well who'd sent it and picked the bottle up to read the scribbling on the parchment.

This morning was an adventure…tomorrow will be better.
Enjoy the wine…and my stupid letter.

Also…run down the aisle tomorrow…my arms are empty.
I love you more than anything, wife.
-Luca

"You two have come a long way since then, child," Vetta offered, choking on emotion behind me. I wiped a stray tear from my cheek and handed the note to Paxe.

"Put this somewhere safe. I want to keep it," I whispered. She took it from me and nodded, excusing herself from the bathing chamber. I turned to face Vetta and she reached for the bottle in my hand.

"I believe I'll start, before my old lady sobs beat me to it." She sniffled, smiling and uncorking the wine. "I couldn't be happier for you both." She filled a goblet and took a deep drink. Paxe re-emerged a moment later with Hissifus in her arms.

"Don't start without us!" She nagged. I kissed between his ears and he purred loudly. "Get in. Relax. Let's enjoy your last night as an unmarried female, yes?"

"I still can't believe this is happening." I grinned, unlacing the side of my tunic and pulling it over my head. I finished disrobing, and Vetta took my discarded clothes while I stepped into the bath and waded over to sit at the edge closest to them. They both sat on folded towels, and Paxe let Hiss rest in her skirts. Vetta only allowed Paxe half a glass and poured a good amount into my goblet.

"Why did I get so little?" She frowned, staring into the cup.

"Because, you foolish girl. You're with child." Vetta rolled her eyes.

"You're allowed wine when you're *with child!*" She argued.

"In small amounts!" Vetta shook her head. "Since when did you become such a fish?" Paxe didn't deign to answer her, looking away and sipping from the goblet as I chuckled softly.

"Is there room for one more?" A smooth voice sounded from the doorway. The queen sauntered into the bathing chamber, her crimson skirt swishing over the floor. I nearly choked on my wine.

"Your Majesty!" Vetta stammered, making to rise from the floor. Ayla put her hand out to settle her and shook her head.

"No, no. Please. Stay seated." She smiled, dropping another towel between them and lowering herself.

"I'll go fetch another goblet," Paxe started, Hissifus stirring in her lap. Ayla winced when she beheld him, but her eyes widened at his unique coloring.

"No need," Ayla said, picking the bottle up and drinking straight from it. "So, this is the famed Hissifus?" She reached a hand near him and he sweetly sniffed and nuzzled her fingertips. Her answering smile was genuine.

"Where did you run off to earlier? I was looking for you," Paxe asked the queen, her brows puckered. Ayla flushed, and I turned my face away, downing the remains of my cup.

"I went upstairs to attend to something important. Took a bit longer than I anticipated." She drank again from the bottle, and Hiss stepped over Paxe's leg and pawed tenderly at Ayla's lap. "Ummmm...uhhhh..." She leaned back, raising the bottle into the air and making an uncertain face at him as he began making himself comfortable in the crease of her thighs.

"Awww, he likes you," I grinned, reaching my goblet up toward her for more wine. She handed Vetta the bottle, who promptly refilled my cup.

"Shoo, kitty." Ayla poked him in his fluff. He stretched himself across her lap and rolled onto his back, his two-toned paws kneading air. "Oh my gods...you may be right about this one, Vetta. I've never seen an animal behave this way." She held in a sneeze and Vetta laid a hand over her, stifling the next. "Thank you." She smiled. Her attention returned to Paxe. "Why were you looking for me? Did something go awry in the ballroom? Please, say no."

"No," Paxe giggled. "I went to get Ari some dry clothes and I wanted to see if you approved of Luca's—the changes made to their chambers." She winked.

"Ah." Ayla grinned, nodding and taking a long swig from the bottle. "I'll be sure to check on that on my way out."

"I'm officially terrified." I put my forehead down on my extended arm over the edge of the bathing pool and all three of them snickered softly to themselves.

"You're the one who insisted on staying holed up in your own chambers for your honeymoon, dearest," Ayla chuckled, filling my cup. "I'll not let any son or daughter of mine miss out on anything *fun*." She wagged her brows at me as I lifted my head and glared at her.

"I hope you didn't include anything breakable." Vetta teased from beside her. "Frances spent two weeks repairing our bath chamber." She drank from her goblet and Paxe nearly spit out her wine.

"I said I was sorry about that." I rolled my eyes. "And so we're clear about the reason for all the destruction...that was more rage than...than..." I stuttered.

"...Than clawing at each other and grunting like pigs?" Paxe jabbed, earning heavy laughs from the queen and Vetta. I sank under the water in humiliation. When I surfaced, Vetta leaned forward, unpinning the braid that was coiled around my head.

"You and Luca are more like the king and I than you realize. Don't be ashamed. It's perfectly healthy." Ayla smiled.

"Healthy?" Vetta scoffed. "I was sure the prince alone was left with permanent scarring in some places when I saw his back that evening."

"And that was just from the night *before* they brought down the bath chamber!" Paxe added. My face had to have been as red as the queen's gown. She looked down at me, nodding in approval and raising the bottle in toast. I snickered, raising my goblet in turn and we both drank heavily from them.

"If I'm being perfectly honest..." Ayla started. "I recognized that similarity the day we met at that meeting. It was another reason I countered your father and tried to explain the benefits of being forced to be in the company of someone and get to know and see them for who they truly are. Bound or otherwise...I still believe that had you both met under different circumstances, you'd probably still have been drawn to one another. I'm happy to admit that I've never seen two individuals more compatible. It gives me great joy." I could have sworn her crystalline eyes lined with tears as she smiled down at me.

"To our future king and queen." Paxe raised her nearly empty goblet. The words stung—ached...deep into my chest. But I put on my best mask and raised my cup with the rest of them. "May their union inspire us, their love live on forever, and may their bodies recover swiftly after tomorrow." We all laughed softly and clinked our glasses against the bottle.

"Here, here!" Ayla grinned. We drank and laughed about this and that, the queen told us more embarrassing tales of Luca and his playmates. Paxe offered a few of our childhood memories, to which Vetta consistently corrected. After my pruned skin had soaked enough, I dressed and we moved into the bedchamber to partake of the vast layout of confections, until we all thought we could be sick.

It was well after midnight when Paxe decided her maternal body could give no more, and Vetta and the queen left us to our slumber. My sister fell into a snore first, Hissifus tucked under her chin. I squeezed in beside them, watching them both and trying to silence my head from nerves about the ceremony, and the information I couldn't stop stewing on. I gently kissed them both on the head and slid my arm around Paxe. The perfect ending to my last night as an unwed royal.

CHAPTER 37

PREPARATION

A warm breeze fluttered across my skin and the smell of coffee filled my nose as I laid still, eyes closed and wholly comfortable. Gulls were loudly quarreling over their breakfast outside the open windows, and the sounds of the sea close by left me to almost forget what day it was. I slowly lifted my lids to find Paxe in her nightshift, sitting cross legged and smiling at me with a mug of steaming liquid in her palms. Hissifus stretched his entire body and flopped onto his side against my pillow.

"Happy *wedding day*, Mi'lady." She glowed, her generous smile showing all of her pretty teeth. Her hair was unbound and swaying slightly in the tendrils of wind, whispering about the bedchamber.

"Gods, Paxe...I'm getting married in a few hours." I swallowed. Her smile grew wider as she nodded excitedly. I laughed to myself, covering my mouth and burying my face into my pillow. She scooted closer and I raised to sit, disturbing Hiss's position and earning a curt look from his mismatched eyes. She handed me the mug and I carefully sipped from it.

"Nervous?" She asked, chewing on her lip.

"Very." My hands gripped around the mug and I stared off across the room.

"I wonder how Luca's faring. I asked the guard down the hall about him this morning, but he was utterly useless. Wouldn't reveal a single thing."

"Where is Lakan?" I turned my face to her.

"With the king. They're picking out ceremonial swords for Tidus to wear today. Just for show, but you know how males are about their weaponry. They wear them sometimes like fine jewelry." She shrugged.

"I would have assumed Nero would jump at that task."

"He may be there too, I'm not sure. I know Michele's arrogant ass arrived bright and early this morning. I'd jump ship in his company too." Her eyes rolled back and she crossed her arms in front of her.

"You really don't like him, do you?" I chuckled.

"No. He reeks of narcissism. It evades me how anyone could stand to be around him."

"I hear he's a doting father." I nudged her, raising a brow.

"It would take a great deal more than that to change my mind." Her hands lowered to the swell on her lower belly and she shifted uncomfortably as she went on. "Ayla told me that he once spent nearly two hours readying himself for a royal dinner in Luca's bath cha—" She lowered her brows and looked down, pressing her palm against her middle and jerking her face back up toward me, her mouth dropped open in shock. I leaned forward in concern and placed a hand over hers.

"Are you alright? What's wrong?" I panicked. Her mouth turned up on one side and those blue eyes teared.

"I feel her." She breathed. "I didn't realize it was—she's moving." She grabbed my hand and pressed it firmly against her bump. "There. Can you feel it?" My brows drew together and I concentrated, but could feel nothing.

"I don't." I shook my head. "Perhaps she's only big enough for you to feel her." I smiled and lowered my face to her stomach. "Bumpus! Can you hear me?" Paxe chuckled and nodded as if to let me know the tiny babe was responding. "Are you ready to go to a party? Dance with your auntie?" I poked at it, kissing it softly and bringing myself back up to look at my sister's lovely face.

"If she looks like you, I feel for you both." I chirped, flicking her chin. We grew quiet and my heart weighed down. I thought it was as good a time as any to ask her what I'd been hoping to ask her last night, but never got a moment alone when she was awake. "Paxe, I need to talk to you about something."

"Is something wrong?" She asked warily, her finger coiling around the ends of her hair.

"I've thought a great deal about this, and I need you to be open minded, but completely honest with me...alright?" She nodded and repositioned herself. "I've no heir to pass the crown to. Unless the gods decide that there is some way that Luca and I can bear a child, I fear for the future of the throne."

"But that's a long way off." She placed a hand on my knee.

"No one could ever know that for sure." I took her hand gently and squeezed her fingers. "If something were to happen to me, gods forbid...or to both Luca and I...who would take the throne then?" Paxe's face paled and she dropped her eyes to our joined hands.

"I don't want to think about that, Ari."

"Neither do I. But I have to be certain that should something happen to us, there's someone in line to do the right thing. I need to know that if I'm not here...our kingdom, and our people have someone left to protect them. I won't ask you, if I know that your heart truly wants nothing to do with it." I tilted her chin up. "But there's no one else I'd trust more with my kingdom than you." A single tear fell from her eye and I wiped it with a finger.

"I'm not afraid of that crown, Arienne. I would gladly uphold what we fight for. I'll protect our people and maintain a bright future for all of us. I must. Not just to honor you and Luca, should it come to that...but for Lakan. For this child. For Perla, and for Gideon and all the others that suffer. My vision is the same as yours. I'll do that for you. You have my word."

"Until death?" I whispered, choking back unshed tears. Paxe placed her fist over her heart and dipped her chin.

"Until death, Ari," she smiled.

"I love you so much." I finally broke. Our arms tangled around each other's necks and we cried softly over our shoulders for a moment.

"I love you too." She sniffled, pulling back. "That mug is blazing against my back." She laughed through tears. I cackled, wiping at my eyes with my other hand and turning to set the mug down on the bedside table. "We can continue this later. We've got a wedding to get to." She ducked off the bed and tiptoed to her vanity on the far wall, pulling from it an ornate silver box and coming back to sit on the edge of the bed.

"What is this?" I asked with an incredulous look. "You weren't supposed to be getting me gifts. You have a baby to prepare for."

"Hush, now. Just open it." She nudged, placing the box in my palms. I unlatched the rim of the lid and inside was my mother's emerald pendant, polished and reset, perched beautifully in white crushed velvet.

"Oh, Gods." I lifted the large stone carefully out of its confinement and raised it up to my eyes. Roses and thorns were crafted in white gold around the emerald and the gold chain was replaced by a stunning new one that resembled the setting. It had been remade into a work of art. "Paxe...this—" I sat the box in my lap and covered my mouth. "This is beautiful. I don't know what to say."

"The chain is shorter. I had it made to sit nicely and compliment your gown."

"What happened to the other chain?" I asked, still admiring the craftsmanship and detail of the delicate leaves and vines of the chain.

"Lakan smelted it and fashioned your commission for Luca. What he gave you the other day at your fitting is everything left over from your mother's heirloom. Now you both have a part of her with you." She grinned.

Tears once again fled from my eyes and I reached my arm around her again, pulling her into a tight hug. "Thank you. So much." A knock at the door interrupted our embrace and Vetta cracked it open, peering inside.

"Arienne?" She called, wobbling inside. She softly closed the door behind her and palmed her cheeks, pouting as if it took all her strength not to cry. "It's your wedding day."

Paxe and I both smiled at her and I placed the necklace back into the box, adding it to the bedside table and walking over to hug my caretaker. She squeezed around me, sniffling. "I'm so glad you're here with me, Vetta." I whispered into her soft gray hair.

"Me too, child. Me too." She patted my back. "Are you ready?" Feeling much lighter after the talk with Paxe and the thoughtful gift she'd just given me, I was only left with one other missing piece. Luca.

"Yes." I nodded as she braced my shoulders and brushed my cheek with her fingers.

"Very well. Get yourselves into a robe and let's go meet the queen. She and the king are beside themselves with joy. There's a woman called Gran waiting for you in the queen's dressing rooms. We'll be getting you prepared there."

The next two hours were a blur. I hardly registered them. I didn't even distinctly remember how we found ourselves at the queen's dressing room, or chewing the toast and fruit I was given before two hired attendants I didn't recognize began applying cosmetics to my face and weaving my hair into a masterpiece of soft braids and sweeping curls. I sat quietly in a chair by the cracked window in Ayla's small study, sipping more coffee and gathering a hold on my nerves per the queen's request...alone. A bit of quiet, and time to myself before I was to start the process of getting into that gown and adding all the finishing touches. Outside the window, waves crashed and glimmered on the shore, and rays of balmy sunlight shone over the water like pillars in a heavenly temple. It was an absolutely gorgeous day and the air was warm and comforting. A dark figure appeared a few minutes later wading along the tide and I raised from my chair to get a closer look.

Nero's unbound hair blew behind him as he paused in the water. He held a large wine goblet in one hand, the other was shoved into his pocket and he stared out over the ocean longingly. The sea gave no response. I couldn't clearly make out his features, but I could almost feel the heartache he tried so eagerly to hide. He was indeed still in love with Varuna, and it showed. I wondered how that reunion would play out at the ceremony, and when she would decide to present herself. I only hoped that it wouldn't be painful for them and that perhaps seeing each other again would spark some kind of forgiveness. It made a bit more sense to me now why the gods and goddesses were so inclined to push me away from the hate I felt for my father. It does this world no amount of good.

My thoughts were broken by a commotion outside the study door, followed by Ayla's muffled voice in argument and two heavy sets of footsteps. "Do *not* open that door! You can't see her until the ceremony!" She squawked.

"Relax, Mother. Give me just a few moments. I need to hear her voice."

Luca. Thank the Gods.

I rushed to the door and placed my hand against the wood. "Luca?"

"Arienne, don't you dare!" Ayla hissed.

"Shhh...she's not. Ari?" Luca's voice neared closer.

"I'm here." I smiled. "What are you doing up here? Shouldn't you be getting ready?" I heard him chuckle under his breath and a thud sounded against the door.

"I've been ready for this for far too long. I just wanted to be close to you before everything starts. I think—I think I needed to." I heard Tidus's voice softly convincing Ayla to leave us and she reluctantly complied.

"You two have five minutes." She scolded. Then silence. I leaned my forehead against the door and listened for movement.

"Are you afraid I'll leave you waiting at the altar?" I joked. He scoffed.

"No. It's not that." I felt magic, and then my heart sped up. No—not mine. I felt...*his.* Echoing mine and then beating in time as if he were trying to match my energy. "You're nervous." He whispered.

"Only about the bit where I'm concentrating on successfully making it to you without stumbling over this gown." I smiled.

"Crack the door." He begged, the handle jiggling in challenge.

"And suffer her wrath? I think not, Prince." I snickered.

"I promise I won't look. Just crack the door and take my hand...please?" I pushed the handle and the door creaked open. My fingers drifted around the side of the door until they were met with his and we twined them together. "There she is." He whispered. I could hear the smile in his voice.

"It's only been a night. One would be right to believe we're absolutely ridiculous." I leaned against the door.

"I suppose it's a good thing that we couldn't give a shit less what anyone believes." He laughed. "I came for two reasons. Two other than to get us in trouble."

"The first?" I breathed, smiling. His fingers left mine and I was left holding my hand out beyond the door. "Luca?" A smooth, worn sensation gathered around my wrist and I didn't need to look to know what it was.

"It may not be fine jewels, but I couldn't let you walk down that aisle today without it. I don't care what my mother or Paxe say about how stylish it is...but my only request is that you tell them both to bugger off and wear it anyway." He chuckled, tying off his hair strap. I laughed softly to myself.

"I'd have it no other way. The second?" I asked as our fingers weaved back together.

"I made a bargain with you yesterday. I came to make good on it."

"What happened?" My smile fell, and I knew he'd sensed my change in mood. His magic fluttered back to me, calming me as if warm hands caressed my very soul.

"I dreamt about you last night. You were more beautiful than I'd ever seen you, and surrounded by light. You ran to me and I wrapped my arms around you. I'd never felt so close to you. It gave me a peace I didn't know existed."

"Like the blood union in Aeon?" I asked, sliding my thumb over his skin.

"Stronger than that. Better. Like the world could fall to ruin around us and neither one of us would care. I've dreamt about you for a very long time. Some good, some bad. Some devastating enough to keep me awake for the rest of the night...but that... That was the first time I've ever dreamt of you this way." I squeezed his hand and he squeezed back.

"I love you, Prince."

His lips pressed against the back of my hand. "I love *you*, Princess. Don't focus your attention on the gown. Don't pay any mind to how far the walk is. Look at me. This will be the only time you'll ever see me impatient...hurry home."

"I promise." I grinned. The sound of a door flying open was nothing compared to the wailing of the queen as she stormed inside the sitting room.

"Luca Di Meo! I knew it! Out!" She yelled. I felt a quick peck to my fingers and he shoved my hand back through the door, slamming it quickly and laughing through the impact of Ayla's palms, while she smacked him a good many times in gods know where. "I should string you up by your bollocks, child. Go get dressed." She cackled. Tidus mumbled something similar that I couldn't make out aside from the word *'Idiot'* and the door shut forcefully as they escorted him out.

I traced the wraps of the hair strap tied around my wrist and padded back over to the window, looking out to find Nero gone. As I lowered myself back into the chair, pulling my knees up against my chest, I thought back to every moment I'd spent alone like this before I'd ever met Luca. How alone I felt in the world. How hopeless everything had seemed. The scars that had run so deep that no one could have ever known were there, unless they truly knew me. Those scars were fading now. They had been fading since the moment he'd climbed into that tree the night before our meeting and chose to rescue his princess from her tower.

"Hurry home."

Nothing had ever been more true. He was my home in every way. My mind raced back to the moment he patched me up in the meadow, carrying me back to the castle even when I'd tried in all ways to insult him, kicking and screaming the entire way. He never gave up on me, and never would. A sudden intruding thought crossed my mind then, something I had never considered. Before I'd ever been given an explanation of his abilities...he'd sensed everything I felt. Most likely *felt*...everything I felt. The moment we'd arrived back at the castle with my injured ankle. That horrible fight in the woods when I was at war with myself about kissing him and promptly backed down. He knew exactly what I wanted to do every single time and had still been so patient...even without knowing the extent of all the abuse I'd suffered.

"This will be the only time you'll ever see me impatient."

I was ready. Time to go. I snapped up from my chair and barreled for the door, jerking it open and briskly walking back into the dressing room, meeting the eyes of everyone in the room who stopped busying themselves when I entered.

"Arienne? Are you alright, darling?" Ayla asked. She was absolutely stunning in her usual crimson, donning a ball gown truly fit for a queen such as herself. Her hair was curled and braided, loose pieces framing her pale face and accenting her red pout. Three handsome blood red roses were gathered in her hair against a sparkling diadem.

"I'm ready. Someone help me get into this dress." The queen's smile was more beautiful than I'd ever seen it, and she nodded softly as she turned to summon Gran.

Paxe stood from her seat, interrupting the timid attendant who was fussing over her hair. She was equally captivating. I nearly wept at the sight of her. She bled royalty in a shimmering turquoise gown with capped sleeves, and a revealing bust that didn't do a thing to give her swelling breasts any modesty.

Her little 'bumpus' was cleverly hidden in the design of the gown and the skirts flowed like rushing water around her hips. Her blonde strands were swept back in elegant matching hair combs on each side of her face, the rest fell beautifully over her shoulders.

"Oh, Paxe." I steepled my fingers over my mouth and held back tears that I knew would ruin the effort the attendants had put into these counter paints. "Look at you." I whispered.

"Does this please Her Highness?" She giggled, mocking a curtsy and swishing over to pull me into her. I held her tight and noticed Vetta over her shoulder in a lovely deep violet gown. I scrunched my face in another desperate attempt not to cry.

"All of you will outshine me, I fear," I choked, as I smiled at my caretaker.

"Alright, Princess. Your turn." Gran smiled from beside her, waving me into the hallway I'd stepped into during my fitting. Paxe released me and I happily followed the tailor through the doorway.

It took a great deal longer to perfect every detail of the fit during this round. Gran spared no effort in making sure all of the delicate parts were pristine, unwrinkled, unsnagged and falling into place precisely as they should. She helped me secure the roses that coiled around my ankles above the heel of my shoes and double checked that the skirts wouldn't catch on them as I walked. When she was satisfied, we walked out to the gasps and mouth coverings and handkerchiefs wiping beneath eyes and noses. Vetta especially, who had no shame in her weeping. Paxe stepped behind me as I gazed over my reflection and was still coming to terms with the bride that stood before me. She smiled over my shoulder and strung my mother's pendant around my neck. It gleamed in the sunlight and a faint voice sounded through my mind.

"Beautiful. I am with you, my beautiful girl."

I nodded in the mirror and Paxe dipped her chin, her eyes catching the hair strap on my wrist. "Clever prince." She laughed.

"What in the world is that?" Vetta asked, pointing at it.

"One of the most important things in this ceremony," Ayla answered, smiling. "When the minister presents the other one...you know what to do."

I nodded in reply.

"I've two more surprises for you. You'll have to wait until the ceremony begins." The queen beamed. A knock sounded at the door and one of the attendants opened it only a little, peering out and then allowing our guest inside. Michele, dressed to kill, entered a moment later. He bowed at the waist and then looked up at me first through the strands of his hair, buckling slightly as he took me in.

"Well..." He pressed a hand to his chest. "If you don't look every bit a queen." We smiled at each other and he gave me a wink of approval. "Luca is going to lose his princely mind...the poor bastard." His attention fixed on Paxe next who glared at him through thick lashes, crossing one arm over the other and shuffling her weight to one hip. "Paxe." He tossed his head in her direction.

"Michele." She growled.

"You look almost as lovely as I do." His sly grin clearly indicated he knew exactly which nerves to strike where my sister was concerned. I couldn't help but admire him for it. I snorted loudly.

"Thanks?" She replied, rolling her eyes and turning away from him to face me.

"Sorry to interrupt, but I was tasked to let you lot know that we have a bit less than thirty minutes left. The king has suggested preparing to make your way to the receiving room."

My stomach flipped. "The receiving room?" I gulped.

"It's the suite across the hall from the ballroom where you'll wait until it's time to walk." Ayla offered. Michele bowed again slightly and to Paxe's relief, excused himself to let us gather ourselves.

"This is it, Ari," Paxe smiled, watching me with disbelief. "Half an hour left before you're his wife."

"This may be a bit forward, but humans use this time to help give us a little push." Gran said, holding a tray full of tiny glasses filled with amber liquid. "And of course, to congratulate." She half smiled. "One for each of us...that includes you all." She gestured to the attendants who helped get us ready. We all took a glass and waited as Gran placed the tray down and held her liquor in the air. "To the prince and princess. Happiest of wedding days to you both."

We knocked them back and the whiskey burned, oaky and yet sweet. Just enough to warm my insides and leave me aching for more. Paxe and two of the attendants swore, shaking it off as if it were the worst thing they'd ever tasted, and the queen cackled alongside Vetta who asked for another.

"Let's get married!" Paxe yelped, swaying her hips suggestively all the way to the door and opening it wide. My heart thundered as I raised my skirts and began to walk forward. Ayla stopped me with a hand.

"Ah, ah...drop them. If you can't walk to the ballroom without carrying them then it isn't time to leave just yet." I released them and walked a few steps until she approved. It only made me keenly more aware of every step I took from that room to the hallway where the ballroom was located, and I nearly vomited at the sounds of music inside and about a thousand voices I'd never heard before.

Some guards nodded their congratulations on the way, some stood like statues. Some like the kind one that helped Luca to bed that night nearly cried at the sight of me. Servants from around the castle gathered against the walls to offer their well wishes, and when we approached the ballroom, two of them closed the doors to shield me from view. We stepped into the receiving room and I took a seat on the small couch in the center. My hands shook and I took deep breaths in and out as Vetta and Paxe knelt in front of me.

"This is where we leave you, my dear." Vetta sniffled. "You're mere steps away from being an adult. My job here is done." She gripped my fingers tight and leaned in to kiss my cheek. Paxe lifted a gorgeous bouquet, no doubt crafted by Lady Annette and placed it into my hand.

"Break a leg, *Mi'lady.*" She brushed her fingers against my jaw. "Bumpus and I will see you on the other side." Her eyes began to well and she quickly hugged my neck before tugging Vetta away. Ayla stepped forward and leaned down to kiss the top of my head, adjusting the small rosebuds that decorated my braids.

"Deep breaths, darling. The hard bit will be over before you realize it began." She smiled. "See you soon." She patted my cheek and turned to meet Paxe and Vetta at the door. They all looked toward me one last time.

"I love you all...thank you for everything." I choked. Nods. From each of them. Handkerchiefs were back out, and Ayla shooed them out the door, closing it quietly behind her and leaving me to await my turn.

I sat for a few moments, shaking uncontrollably, and then decided to stand up and pace instead. I could have sworn I had started making trails in the pristine carpet before a soft knock had my heart thrashing and stealing my breath. I expected a coordinator, but—

"Is there a lonely female in here with a fine dre—" Nero stepped through the door and stopped short when I turned toward him. "Oh my...hello, youngling." He stuffed his hands into the pockets of his slacks. His hair was combed back into a slick knot behind his head and the rest of him filled out a waistcoat and jacket, leaving little room for much else with his broad shoulders, and massive arms. He looked very...mortal.

"Nero...shouldn't you be at the ceremony?" My voice stuttered under my nerves and the flowers in my hands shook.

"Not without my escort." He smiled.

"Your escort?"

"I don't make public appearances without the prettiest one on my arm." He winked. "It's my right as a god, after all."

"Oh, thank the gods." I exhaled sharply, rushing over and throwing my arms around him. He squeezed tight and kissed my cheek and I was instantly more at ease.

"You're welcome." He grinned, showing all his teeth. I nudged him in the rib and looked him over. "In all honesty though, thank *you.* Varuna will be extremely jealous." Another devious grin.

"You clean up nicely, your Grace." I smiled.

"As do you. Truly. You're a vision."

A guard leaned into the open doorway and nodded toward us. "It's time, your Highness." He stepped aside and I straightened out my skirts, hooking my arm into Nero's extended elbow. I stepped out into the hallway, between two lines of posted guards holding their swords with their blades upright between their breastplates. Two others stood at the ballroom doors and awaited their cue to open them. I began to tremble again and Nero placed his fingers over my arm.

"Breathe, Arienne. Just keep your eyes on the prince." He whispered. I nodded as we took a few steps forward and the music and chanting of the royal choir grew louder within.

Deep breath in...and out...

And then the doors slowly opened.

CHAPTER 38

THE CEREMONY

Faces and music swallowed my vision from every corner—some familiar, some completely foreign. The royal choir was giving their best performance, and I tugged tightly against Nero's solid arm as my eyes darted back and forth across the room. Subjects from my lands and from Crona were standing in any available space throughout the ballroom. Several elated children pointed and smiled while their parents tried to calm them. To my left, I caught one child in particular, who waved vigorously at me from his mother's lap as she sat in a wooden chair with wheels, her well-dressed husband standing happily beside them.

Holt!

I smiled sweetly at him, waving with my forefinger and relishing in his beaming grin. Mora and Benjamin nodded toward me, smiling. To my right stood Varuna, a spacious circle around her as no one seemed to dare get that close to her. She too, nodded respectfully at me and glanced at Nero before turning her face away. He huffed at my side. We moved in time through the sea of bodies until we reached the blue carpet that Ayla had fussed about for two weeks and I knew exactly how many steps it would take before I reached the altar. I lifted my eyes, meeting the silver ones I'd come to adore so dearly, and my breath caught sharply.

"Luca..." I breathed involuntarily.

There. Standing alongside the king on the second step of the dais. I paused, Nero halting with me and locked eyes with him. His shoulders dropped in his crisp, highly decorated royal apparel and he breathed heavily, swallowing and reaching for Tidus, as he stumbled sideways at the sight of me. The king held him upright and patted his back as they both looked at me with glassy eyes. Luca pinched the bridge of his nose, cunningly wiping his tears from the corners of his eyes as I started forward again. I found it difficult to choke back my own as Nero and I inched closer, each step making Luca more emotional. He'd waited so long for this. My heel caught slightly on the runner and Nero steadied me, my trip almost unrecognizable and Luca and I chuckled at each other through tears as we made the last few steps and stopped. Soft laughter around us died out with the choir as they finished their last notes.

"What would you do without me?" Nero whispered in my ear. I elbowed him and he snorted through his nose. The priest stepped down from around the king, speaking in the ancient tongue and waving his hands in sacred tradition. There was silence throughout the room as we all bowed our heads, all but Nero, who nodded toward the holy man and accepted a reverent bow.

The robed figure retreated and Tidus stepped forward, as Nero offered him my hand. I placed my fingers into his and he led me up to the step Luca stood on. Paxe appeared from behind Luca and reached for the bouquet with a smile of deep affection. I handed them off and the king placed my hand in Luca's.

He took my other hand and we both squeezed, smiling widely. Luca brought my fingers to his mouth and kissed them gently, dropping them back down between us, as we faced each other. Tidus made his way to the left side of the dais, greeting his queen and they sat first. The priest motioned for the congregation to be seated following their sovereigns and stood a step above us to begin the proceedings.

I hardly listened to anything he said in the beginning, my eyes wholly devoured by Luca's, and every ounce of the tension I'd felt melted away in his stare. Everything he'd said behind the door this morning rang in my ears. The world truly did fall to ruin around us and I couldn't bring myself to care. The world disappeared *entirely*. Every single thread of my being that could feel was amplified and without a single hint of magic. I heard bits about the first king's sacrifices and the journey and tradition of the royal bloodline. The priest went on about the bettering of our world, to which the congregation interacted. Finally, he announced the moment for Luca and I to exchange our vows. Our hands trembled and our breathing shuddered when the priest requested our rings be brought forth.

We waited for a moment in silence until my attention was broken by the coos of the congregation and soft chuckles all around. We turned our heads to the aisle to see young Holt carrying Hissifus in his arms and wearing a wide grin as he adorably marched down the blue carpet, Michele strolling supportively behind him. Luca and I both laughed and as the boy neared closer, I realized Hiss had been adorned with a small bowtie with two rings dangling from its center. I pressed a hand to my chest.

Oh, my heart.

Holt came to a stop on the step below us and bowed slightly, grinning from one ear to the other. I leaned down, pressing a kiss to the top of Holt's head and scratching behind Hiss's ear, while Luca opted to fluff through the boy's hair...much to Holt's despair. Paxe stepped forward, leaning in to remove the rings from the collar and handing them to the priest. Holt reluctantly followed her back to her post at the side of the dais as she gently guided him away, his little fingers fumbling to put his ruffled strands back in their rightful place. The priest stifled his chuckle and we faced one another to join hands again.

"The joining of crowns. A tradition upheld for centuries. Bound by blood, and by right...but also by love. A promise to serve our lands and our people, but also to serve one another. At this time, Prince Luca..." The priest placed my wedding band into his hand, "Will you proclaim your vow to Princess Arienne Genovese of Valdaro...to her people and to her lands?" Luca's eyes lined with tears and he smiled at me, breathing deeply and shaking slightly as he slid the ring over my finger. I could hardly contain myself.

"By the gods in the peaks, within the earth and its seas...by blood and by bone..." His voice cracked and he paused. *"Your heart is my home."* He swallowed. "Arienne...I was chosen by the gods to love you. I've spent my life waiting for that chance. I didn't realize how much it truly meant until the moment you chose me for yourself. To be cherished and adored the way I know that you do every time you look at me...I'll spend every day of my life eternally grateful for this gift. My greatest treasure. My soulmate...*my wife.* I love you with every fiber that holds this body together, and I vow to continue to love you. Forever. *Fino alla morte."*

Until death...

A tear raced down my cheek and he gently swept it away with a finger, pinching my chin as one also fell from his eye. I could hear sniffling from around the dais, and couldn't stop my soft giggle when I heard Holt whisper, "What's that mean?" As he tugged at Paxe's skirts. There was a soft rumble of snickering and after a moment, the priest gathered himself and repeated his question to direct toward me. He placed the ring Lakan had carefully fashioned into my hand and Luca looked down at the engraving around the glinting gold surface that read exactly the words he'd just spoken. *"Fino alla morte."* He looked up at me and I knew it was taking all of his self-control not to pull my face to his right then. I carefully slid the smooth, polished metal over his finger and held his hand tight, staring deeply into those intoxicating eyes.

"By the gods in the peaks, within the earth and its seas..." I didn't make it farther than he had before stopping to cry. He thumbed away my tears as I continued. "By blood...and by bone. Your heart is my home." I sniffled and our heads pressed together. The priest didn't object and murmurs of our onlookers, lost in emotion as they watched us, filled the room. "Luca...I—when we met...I was hollow—a shell of a person that I didn't know. I was broken...angry. I didn't wish to live." I cried softly, lifting my head to stare into him again. "Until you." I smiled tearfully. His lip quivered and I ran my thumb over it. "You loved me through it...loved me anyway. Even when I pushed and fought. You filled every empty space within my mangled heart and you did so without question. You devoted yourself to me. You showed me what real love feels like. How life could be when you have someone to hold your hand as you weather every storm, battle through every war...I'm honored to be a pawn next to you on this chessboard." He huffed a laugh through his tears. "I'm honored to be your wife. I love you, Luca Di Meo. I love you so very much. I didn't believe that someone like you could truly exist...and I vow to love you this way until I no longer draw breath. We've traded the pieces of our souls. And one simply cannot live without the other. You are the tether that binds me to existence. *Fino alla morte,* my love...forever."

"Forever." Luca breathed, tracing a finger down my jawline as if there weren't a single other soul in this room. The priest sniffed and waved a hand for an acolyte to bring a long, narrow box forward, taking it and presenting it before us. I cracked a side smile and Luca furrowed his brows.

'The hand fasting ceremony is a tradition among the royal family, signifying the eternal bond between husband and wife. King and Queen. It is with great honor that you accept these roles in unity. At this time, Prince Luca…Princess Arienne…will you join your left hands at the wrist?" We complied, and I smiled knowingly at Luca as the priest lifted the lid to the box and grunted in confusion. His elderly face teetered this way and that, searching for an explanation for the absence of its contents. Luca looked on and I glanced toward Ayla, who winked at me. Tidus looked over at her and then at me…all of them puzzled and panicking. "I—I'm sorry, we seem to have lost—" The priest watched as I tugged the end of the leather strap toward the painted ceiling. Luca's eyes went wide and his mouth dropped open, his heart no doubt combusting, as I held the worn hair strap in front of the priest with a grin.

It dangled above our joined hands and the speechless minister carefully took it from me, passing the empty box back to the acolyte while Luca tried and failed not to visibly weep at my gesture. Tidus clapped his palms together, steepling them over his chin and leaning back in his ornate chair next to Ayla, who nodded proudly as she dabbed at her eye. We held tightly to each other's wrists as more ancient verses were recited over the seemingly insignificant strip of leather. The priest's knotty fingers wound the strap around our wrists, binding them together and tying it snugly…and as he finished reciting the last line, our eyes locked.

A snap of powerful magic hissed through the leather, humming against our skin and glowing in coils of amber and blue around our wrists and up our arms. We jolted backward, stopped only by our arms that were still tightly bound and the king and queen leapt from their seats. The congregation gasped in shock and Michele threw himself in front of Holt *and* Paxe. I heard Nero curse loudly and a bright flash of light was all I could see then, as Luca's horrified face blurred from view. When the light receded back enough to take in my surroundings, familiar dark stone took shape around me and I saw my father. He was stanced, as if he too were overtaken by the force of magic and trembling in waves of undiluted rage. He tore open his tunic and gaped at his chest, and the scream of bitter anger that followed was deafening. Sconces and ornamental decorations on the wall began to shake and the walls themselves cracked under his tantrum. He threw objects around his chambers without touching them, glass and porcelain shattering everywhere as he screamed and screamed. His arms thrust out around him and ice tore across the floor, gathering on the walls and the chandeliers. Candles snuffed out, and the crashing of more broken things sounded as I backed away, not realizing that somehow my physical body wasn't there. I searched for Luca, not finding him anywhere in my sight, and the light began pushing inward again, overtaking everything around me.

"Luca!" I screamed into the void. I turned my soul in every direction. *"Luca, where are you?!"* I started running.

"Ari!" His voice sounded in front of me. I still couldn't see him. I ran faster. He finally appeared, arms outstretched in the same clothes he'd been wearing and I could still hear my father's screaming as I bolted for him. He ran for me then, his left hand reaching and I panted desperately as another deafening roar rang out around us. I threw my left hand out and Luca grabbed my wrist as I leapt into him, our other arms clinging around each other and throwing our souls back into our bodies.

The light flashed again, blinding us and then was forcefully sucked into the strap around our wrists. It sizzled, and we both hit our knees against the dais steps. The strap disappeared, leaving ancient script inked and coiled up and around our wrists in deep blue. We both gasped for breath and Luca's eyes were wide, as he unbuttoned the top of his formal jacket and shoved his dress shirt open. I covered my mouth with my hand when I realized what had just happened. He peered down at the flesh of his chest...now free of the mark that was my father's curse.

It was broken.

Ayla cried out, Tidus restraining her as the entire ballroom fell silent.

"Arienne..." Luca's voice broke and he sobbed softly, raising his face back to me. I thrust myself forward, grabbing each of his cheeks and crying loudly in elation as my lips crashed into his. His arms wrapped around me and he gripped behind my head. It was a kiss that could shatter the world.

"YEAH!" Nero's fist pumped in the air, startling everyone as we rose from the floor, never breaking our kiss. Varuna had appeared beside him, looking at him and shaking her head as if he were the biggest fool. Tidus and Ayla tearfully joined, clapping and cheering while our congregation erupted. The poor decrepit priest threw his hands up and smiled, clapping with them as Luca and I pressed closer, continuing to devour each other at the altar. Paxe and Lakan cried in joy, covering Holt's eyes and Hissifus trotted over to weave himself around Luca's legs. Vetta's old lady sobs indeed overtook her as she held onto Frances and leaned into his shoulder.

Luca scooped me into his arms and the crowd grew louder. We grinned at one another, our noses touching, and he carried me back down the aisle through the roaring congregation. Hiss followed us close behind. Lady Annette raised her arms and showered us all in petals of all different colors as we passed. Two guards graciously opened the ballroom doors, and two more guided us into the receiving room to allow us both a few moments of privacy to collect ourselves and come to terms with the reality of everything that had just happened.

He kissed me again, twirling us around while the door closed softly behind us.

CHAPTER 39

A CAUSE FOR CELEBRATION

"Let me see it again," I whispered, leaning into my...*husband*...while my skirts draped across his lap as he held me close on the small couch in the receiving room. We'd been in here for nearly fifteen minutes, our lips becoming puffy and swollen and our small bit of self-restraint wearing thinner after finally becoming husband and wife. Luca pushed the lapels of his jacket aside and I slid my newly tattooed hand beneath his shirt, opening it and gazing at the skin that held no sign that any brand had ever been there. "Did you see him?" I asked, meeting his stare. His jaw clenched and he nodded slowly.

"The way he had torn open his clothes leads me to believe he bore a mark the same as mine. I can only assume he'd known it was half broken when it faded days ago too."

"His rage. The way he destroyed everything. I'm afraid he's going to do something reckless. He's been unnervingly silent since Bolton." I bit my lip. Luca took my hand from his chest and pressed his lips to my palm, gently kissing every inch of the ancient script that traveled up my wrist.

"I refuse to think of that right now. Not today..." He kissed again. "*Definitely* not tonight..." Another. "And not for at least the next few days." His voice was smooth and promised fire. My skin tingled and heated beneath his touch.

"I just married you," I breathed.

"Yes, you did." His fingers brushed down my cheek. "You are without a doubt...the most beautiful creature I've ever seen." The corner of his mouth turned upward. "Made me cry in front of our entire kingdom. How dare you?"

I huffed a laugh. "Well, before the dramatics, how did you enjoy my surprise during the hand fasting ceremony?"

"You might as well have held up my bollocks for all to see and squeezed them like a vise." He chuckled. "I lost every bit of my senses. I'm a bit sad the strap is gone, but I quite like the new additions to our hands. Do you?" He raised his left hand from around my back and we compared them.

"I love them." I grinned, admiring the detail in our skin. The blue shone in the light from the sconces the same way Luca's brand had. We grew quiet and I stared at him for a long moment. "You're safe, Luca," I whispered.

"*We're* safe. One day soon...that bastard will be a distant memory and the world will be safe right along with us." His jaw tightened again and I lowered my brows.

"Are you alright?" I asked.

"I'm more than alright." He reached up to stroke my hair. "I saw you...like this. Last night, in my vision. The light, and the way you reached for me." I slackened in his arm, recalling what he'd said this morning. "The peace you give my soul, Ari...it's unmatched. You free me. I absolutely adore you."

"And I adore you...husband." I grinned, kissing him softly. He smiled against my mouth.

"I love that." He kissed back. "Just don't forget my name now that we're joined in marital bliss." He chuckled.

"I would never." I tugged his lower lip with my teeth, and he sighed deeply.

"I'll make sure you don't. You'll be screaming it later." His voice was barely a whisper and my mouth dropped open.

"You're filthy," I smirked.

"Don't pretend you're not." He purred. I eased from his lap and stood between his knees.

"Perhaps I'll show you just how filthy I can be, Prince." I adjusted my bodice and fluffed my skirts. He watched my every movement and chewed his bottom lip. "We'll see who's crying out for whom later." I winked, backing away toward the door.

"Where are you going?" He pouted, leaning forward.

"There's still a wedding going on in there. Rumor has it they're pretty important people who have a habit of disappearing." I laughed, pointing with my thumb toward the ballroom. Luca eyed every inch of me and swore, raising from the couch and smoothing his hair back. He stepped forward and I buttoned his shirt and jacket, smiling to myself at how handsome he looked.

"What is it?" He shrugged, matching my smile.

"I didn't get an opportunity to tell you how...princely you look today." I laughed.

"Only when necessary."

I straightened his collar and we stared at each other for a moment. "You stole my breath. When I saw you, I—I couldn't breathe. I had to stop the world for a moment just to take you in." He took my waist and pulled me into him.

"At least you didn't need assistance to stand on your own legs...wouldn't that have been humiliating?" He grinned.

"Everything was perfect." I reached back to grip the handle of the door. "Will those legs cooperate long enough for the prince to dance with his wife?"

"Oh, allow me," he said, reaching behind me and closing his hand around mine as we pushed the handle down together. The door opened slowly and the sounds of armor shifting from outside was enough indication that we were steps away from being announced. Luca extended his elbow as I straightened beside him and smiled down at me. "Shall we?"

I pulled his arm loose and slid my hand down the length of his limb until our fingers interlocked. The gesture nearly brought him to tears. "Yes...let's." I nodded. We walked closely beside one another between the royal guard and listened as our names and titles were loudly spoken beyond the ballroom doors. They opened slowly and music poured out of the crowded space as we entered.

Every person aside from the king and queen, Nero and Varuna, were bowed with fists against their breasts as we strode forward. The space was cleared in the center of the ballroom and we strode to it, stopping and facing each other and allowing our congregation to ease. Luca took my waist and raised our joined hands, pressing me close and waiting for the maestro to start the next tune. It started soft and slow, and neither of us could hold back our grin as we swayed. It began to build and we stepped in time with it, turning and snickering when he raised our arms and twirled me around.

For a few precious moments, we were back in that kitchen in Aeon, the rest of the world disappearing again and the perfect memory surfacing and filling us both with comfort and joy. He sank his arms around me and pressed my back into him, keeping our pace with the rhythm of the music and transporting me back to the night in the tavern...the night he gave me the ring that sparkled on my inked hand. Our steps were feather light and swift, my skirts flowing around my legs as we both moved like whispers around the congested ballroom. He lifted me gently by my middle, bringing me back down and spinning us delicately around until the music began to die down. His strong arm lowered me backward and I extended my ankle...the ankle now scarred with an eternal reminder of the day I met the male that changed my life in every way.

I raised slowly to meet his face, placing my hand on it and pulling us as close as our garments would allow as our lips met, and the ballroom filled with cheering and applause. The blurred faces began to reappear around us, Tidus and Ayla joining the floor. Paxe and Lakan followed, along with Vetta and Frances, Michele and his lovely wife, and a dozen other couples, who gathered around us in formation for more fast-paced, lively dancing and celebrating. Luca smiled and his attention flashed over my shoulder in the corner, where I glanced to see Nero offering Varuna a hand to lead her into the throng of bodies, patiently awaiting their cue to begin sprawling about. She glared at him for a heavy moment, but I was pleasantly surprised to see her hand reach for his and the slightest hint of a smile on her lips when their fingers touched and they made their way to the floor.

"Alright, Nero," I whispered under my breath, nodding as I watched them join the ranks. There wasn't a great amount of space around them then, as if the gods were accepted more as good company than higher beings. It speared my heart and my face began to cramp with my ever-present smile. I faced Luca again, who watched me with an expression that bled the deepest love and contentment one could ever hold. I felt like a puddle beneath that gaze.

"You look so happy," he muttered, holding me close.

"I can't remember a happier time in my entire existence, Prince." I beamed.

"If I died this very second in your arms...I would have fulfilled every single thing I've ever wanted to accomplish in this life." His head pressed against mine.

"I love you, Luca Di Meo." I breathed.

"I love you...*Mrs. Di Meo.*" He grinned.

"Oh, Gods!" I cackled. "That's right." He quirked a brow and nodded happily.

"Mmmhmm." The music started and everyone began moving. "Oh, yes. Here we go." We shuffled quickly and spun around, Luca laughing as he handed me off to Tidus. Ayla switched off, taking Luca's extended hand with a broad smile. They danced off behind the next line and I hurtled around quickly in the king's arm.

"Welcome to the family, Princess!" Tidus bellowed over the music and the sounds of gleeful chatter as dancers around us paired off with one another, switching partners and hopping from one foot to the other in rhythm. I barely had time to thank him before Michele appeared in a spin to take my hand.

Everyone was lost in music and exhilaration. Everyone, including myself, who I no longer recognized as the broken, tormented soul from months ago. No...this—this was a wife. A queen, a sister...a friend, an ally. An individual who survived everything she'd been through to reach this moment. A moment that allowed undiluted happiness, fun, laughter and, above all things...love. Not just the kind that bound me to Luca but the kind that freed me from my chains. These were my people. My family.

"Keep up, youngling!" Nero laughed, twirling me around to meet Lakan. I left the god of strength with a very impolite hand gesture as I took Lakan's hand. Nero's booming laughter faded past the weaving dance line and Lakan chuckled breathlessly as we danced. I took the small window of opportunity to say a few words.

"You look very handsome!" I called, trying to handle my skirts through a sharp turn.

"Thanks, your Highness!" He huffed, switching arms with me.

"When you're ready...raise a glass to me!" I wheezed, hopping to the other foot. "I'll make sure you have some privacy." His face flushed and he nervously nodded. I glanced over at Paxe, who was glistening with sweat as she laughed and twirled around Frances close by. "Make sure she hydrates before you knock her on her ass, yeah?" I giggled.

"You got it." He spun me around twice and I winked at him before making off to a partner half my size. I bent over and picked up Holt, bouncing him on my hip while he wailed in delight.

"My favorite guest of honor!" I grinned, taking his pudgy hand and keeping time with the dizzy arrangement. "We missed you!"

"I missed you too! Guess what?" He squealed, hardly able to contain himself.

"Tell me!" I replied, spinning us around.

"Ma and Pa said we're moving! I get to play with you all the time!" He flung his little arms around my neck and tightened himself around me.

"Really?" I gaped, looking around for Mora and Ben. I wasn't able to find them through all the merriment. "Oh, Holt, that's wonderful!" I squeezed my arms around his middle and Paxe fluttered by to reach for him.

"Oh, Gotta go!" He waved over Paxe's shoulder as she scooped him up. "I love you!" His hair bounced in and out of his face while he blew a kiss my way and my heart nearly burst.

I love you too, little guy.

I stared and stilled a bit too long and a heated body bumped into mine. I stumbled forward and was caught from behind by an arm and a familiar scent filled my nose. I smiled to myself the moment I was turned around and whisked away by my beaming husband.

"Oh, Mi'lady...I'm terribly sorry. How ever could I make it up to you?" He danced us around and nuzzled playfully into my neck.

"Water." I laughed, following his lead around the sea of unending dancers. He snorted and hoisted me over his shoulder, dancing his way to the edge of the floor toward the buffet. I eased down to the ground and fanned myself while I tried to catch a breath.

"Drink up, love. This party is far from over," Luca chuckled, handing me a large goblet. I sipped before I sniffed and winced, looking up at him over the rim.

"This isn't water, your Highness." I rolled my eyes.

"No, it is not." He mused, raising a cup of his own. We both drank deeply, somehow making it a competition and emptying our goblets. "Are you hungry?"

"Very." I surveyed the long table, filled to its capacity with everything one would expect at a royal wedding. Luca held a plate in one hand and our empty goblets in the other and followed me down the table while I piled it with various foods. I stopped and smiled wide when I spotted something in particular. "Oh, look," I said, picking up a good-sized sandwich and turning toward him. "Your favorite."

"Ha!" He laughed, making to set down the goblets and reach for it. I raised it to my mouth and slowly took a bite, watching him stop dead and eye every chew...every flick of my tongue across my bottom lip. I side smiled at the expression on his face and placed the remains of it on the plate. "Wicked..." He growled. "Just plain...wicked."

"It's *delicious.*" I smirked, nudging his rib and taking the empty goblets from his other hand. "Have a bite." He gave me a truly sinister smile.

"Oh...I plan to, Princess." He picked the sandwich off the plate and bit off the end, his promise of naughty things thwarted with raised eyebrows. "Godsdamn...that's—" He nodded in appreciation. "That's actually really good. It's got to be one of Pat's." I threw my head back, laughing at him, as he continued to eat.

"You damned fool." I cackled, holding our goblets steady as a castle attendant filled them with wine. Luca grinned as he chewed, adding more things to the plate as we moved along to an empty table near the end. We sat and watched our family and friends, laughing while we dined from the same plate, swooning at some of them and how wonderful it was to see everyone together and enjoying themselves.

Several songs filtered in and out, some people taking short breaks for wine or food and others continuing to dance with each other. Luca pointed out Nero and I nearly spit out my wine. I spotted the now-intoxicated lord, raising an entire bottle of liquor in one huge arm. The other dropped down by his side, his dress shirt half open while he wiggled his hips around in circles next to Varuna, who seemingly was no match for his charm tonight. She cheered him on, dancing suggestively and drinking from his bottle...a far cry from the distant, reserved goddess I had seen in the city. She looked like a woman in love, having the time of her immortal life with her mate. I was elated to witness it.

Paxe was doing her very best to humiliate poor Vetta, who cowered behind her as she ground her lovely hips against her round belly. I couldn't hear a word she was saying but knew them by memory nonetheless. We laughed ridiculously at them, along with Lakan and Frances, who encouraged Paxe to prolong our caretaker's torture. Lady Annette was close by them too, having a lighthearted conversation with a very handsome older male I didn't recognize while they sipped wine and took in her immaculate talent around the room.

Tidus and Ayla stood on the dais in the back, laughing with Michele and his wife, Wrenn. Holt was dancing on the lowest step, Mora and Benjamin watching on in amusement as the little lad tried desperately to get the attention of an adorable brown-haired Cronian girl in a fluffy blue dress.

"I wish this day could last forever," I said, leaning my cheek against my hand while continuing to watch them all. Luca scooted closer, wrapping an arm around my back.

"So do I." He drank from his goblet. "We'll have many more days like this one, love." I turned toward him and clinked my cup against his.

"That we will." I smiled, coiling my arm around his. We raised our cups to our mouths and drank, again racing each other to the bottom and laughing while I wiped a drip of wine from my chin. I started to feel pleasantly lightheaded. "We should go exchange pleasantries with our subjects before I start slurring my words." I chuckled.

"Before?" Luca laughed, lightly tipping me to the side with his finger on my shoulder. I leaned back up in my seat and threw my palms up in surrender.

"I don't want to give them a foul impression." I sighed deeply. Luca leaned over, turning my face to his.

"Royal event or not...they wouldn't be here today if they ever had a foul impression of you, Princess. And if one of them did, I'd be the first to throw them out. I could care less if it sounds selfish, but this is *our* day. Ours and no one else's. This isn't just a political joining of houses. Your only obligation today is to enjoy being happy and have the time of your life...mine is to give that to you.”

“You give that to me every day, Luca. What about your happiness?”

“You *are* my happiness.”

“Don’t think I’m letting either of you slip out to finish whatever I walked in on yesterday.” Nero stumbled into the table. “Up. Both of you. Time to dance!” We both watched him finish the remains of his liquor bottle in one swift gulp and then turned it on its mouth to shake it, pouting when he found it empty. The maestro began another arrangement and the fire in Nero’s strange eyes roared. He slammed the bottle to the table and threw his arms into the air. “I love this one! Get up! Let’s go, let’s go!” He clapped, sloshing himself quickly back to the dance floor.

Paxe waved us over excitedly and I turned my attention to Luca, who was already raising from his chair with a sly smile. He offered his hand and I took it, raising myself and letting him lead us back out. There weren’t many left standing against the walls or sitting at tables after the first hour that we joined everyone. Many of our guests found it difficult to decline and those who watched, seemed drawn toward the commotion the longer they sat it out. Ayla passed us glass after glass of various wines, and before any of us had time to look, the sun began to set on our wedding day.

“I’ve never had so much fun in my entire life.” Paxe gasped, slinging an arm around my shoulders. “I’ve never been so *exhausted* in my entire life.” I held her steady and glanced over at Lakan and Michele, who were talking quietly to each other and looking in our direction every so often. Luca came to stand beside us and turned Paxe’s back to the males as a distraction.

“Don’t tell me you’re forfeiting already, *piccola madre.*” He grinned, bumping her with his hip.

“Ha! When you males are graced with the anatomy to grow an entire person in your bodies, *then* you may come and speak to me about it, Prince.” Paxe laughed, bumping him back. “Would either of you happen to know the reason Lakan feels the need to be in constant conversation with your guard dog this evening, Luca?”

“Actually, I do,” I answered before Luca could speak. “He was very grateful to Michele for throwing himself around you and Holt during the ceremony earlier. There is, after all, another someone in that belly that not many others know about that was protected as well.” I raised my brows and waited for a cheeky remark, but Paxe bowed her head in submission.

“I suppose I didn’t think of it that way.” Her mouth quirked to the side. “Perhaps he isn’t completely self-absorbed.” She snorted.

“Oh, he most definitely is.” Luca countered. “But aside from that…there is a truly amazing male in there. You know that I wouldn’t trust anyone to be Hand of the King if he weren’t the most respectable one I know.” He shrugged.

Paxe’s mouth dropped open. “Michele is the King’s Hand?”

Luca nodded. “He has been since before I left home for Valdaro.”

"I had no idea. So, that's why he's always around." She shook her head. "I'm sorry...I—" "Don't write him off just yet. Besides...I think they're done now." Luca finished. I looked back over my shoulder to see Michele clapping Lakan on his back with a side grin as the trembling male raised a goblet toward me and nodded slightly. Paxe turned to face him and I gestured behind my back for Luca to go clear the balcony.

"Not off to bed already, are you?" Michele teased as he approached us. His hands curled into his pockets and he flipped his stray strands over his brow.

"Perhaps not just yet." Paxe shuffled. I nudged her with an elbow. "Ah—thank you, Michele. For earlier. I suppose you've earned yourself a bit less of the grief I give you."

"You would have done the same for me." He winked, patting her shoulder as he strolled past us. He leaned down before he left our peripheral and looked her dead in the eyes before he whispered, "Take care of him. He's a good one." And disappeared into the crowd. Lakan nervously crept forward and stopped in front of us, reaching for Paxe's hand.

"Could we talk?" He asked, his voice slightly hoarse.

"Right now? What's wrong?" Paxe inquired, taking his hand. I swiped the goblet out of his other hand and stepped away from my sister as he led her to the balcony doors that overlooked the golden crested sea. She only looked back at me once, as if in apology for leaving me alone on the dance floor.

"That's going to be a familiar sight," Nero said from beside me. "I remember a young prince asking a feisty princess a similar question on a balcony by the sea." He winked.

"Yes. Right before some mighty deity summoned him from his bed and tortured him in a temple." I rolled my eyes and side smiled.

"Hmm...always the romantic," Varuna chirped, turning a fresh bottle of liquor to her full lips. "Don't worry, youngling. I'll not do any such thing. I'm certain they'll sleep soundly tonight...after a great deal of lovemaking." I huffed a laugh and Nero turned toward the goddess, an inquisitive expression on his face. Luca appeared next to me and slid an arm around my waist.

"Is that all I was to do to get you to—" Nero started, reaching for the bottle in her hand.

"Hush." She jerked it away and took another drink. Nero folded his chiseled arms in defeat while Luca and I snickered quietly beside them, all of us patiently watching before Lakan finally lowered himself before Paxe on his knee.

Paxe, of course, burst into tears, extending her hand while he slid a ring onto her finger and I heard Vetta's gasp from across the floor. The queen was next and then the entire congregation stopped what they were doing to look. Clapping and delightful cheering filled the ballroom as Lakan gently kissed her carefully hidden bump and then lifted her and spun her around. Warm tears trickled down my cheek and Luca squeezed around me from behind.

"You think she suspected?" He whispered near my ear. I shook my head.

"Not at all." I sniffled, smiling. "I'm sorry, Luca."

"Sorry for what?"

"I know it was to be our day." I turned my head toward him.

"Shhhh...it's perfect. Everything is perfect. I don't think it could have gone any better." He kissed the corner of my mouth.

"It isn't over yet," Varuna whispered from beside us.

"Psh..." Nero hissed, turning the bottle up that he'd swiped from her fingers.

"I'll be taking my leave, younglings. I wish you the happiest of days." Her stormy eyes fixed on mine for a bit too long, but we smiled at one another. She turned back toward Nero, who watched her carefully. "If you're not coming, then I suppose the night *is* over for you, little lord." She snapped, smirking as she gracefully stomped toward the ballroom doors.

"Little?" Nero growled, handing Luca the bottle and charging after her.

"Where is Varuna's temple?" I asked as we watched the two of them bicker the entire way out the doors.

"Under the sea." Luca laughed, pressing his chin on my shoulder. I giggled hard.

"Why do I get the feeling that we're all in for a long night?"

"Mmm...well, *you* certainly are, wife." He purred. I swiveled in his hold, hooking my arms around his neck.

"*We*...certainly are, *husband.*" I corrected, kissing him softly.

"Need an out?" Ayla cut in from beside us, taking the bottle from Luca's hand. It dawned on me that Paxe had asked me the same thing the day we watched the queen fuss over the carpet for the ceremony...and somehow, she'd known.

"Shouldn't we wait for the exit to be announced?" I asked, clutching Luca against me. The king stepped around his wife and cut us a knowing smile.

"Not if that isn't what you both wish. We didn't." He shrugged.

"You'll find that the guests will make the most of a royal event, and linger well into the night. They'll hardly recognize that you're missing. If you're ready, I'll have the maestro begin another set. They'll all be so consumed that you'll be able to slip out unnoticed. And—" The queen lifted her forefinger, "I've asked Lady Bethel to be on standby should you...need her for anything." Luca huffed a laugh as I cleared my throat. We looked at one another, and the way his eyes shone, said enough.

"Will you extend my congratulations to Paxe and Lakan when they decide to come back inside?" I asked, looking toward the balcony. I lowered my brows to find it now dark and empty. My attention shifted back to the king and queen. "Where did they go?"

Tidus and Ayla both chuckled softly.

Ohh...

"Luca, before you both run off...I'd like to share a drink with my son on his wedding day. We'll go cue the maestro. You two head for the doors." Tidus requested, pulling Luca aside while the queen and I inconspicuously started for the exit. She took my hand and I gave one last look at the ballroom and its occupants, all the decorations, the sound of laughter and music...our friends and family.

"It was magical, darling," Ayla uttered. "The heaviness of that curse lifted from you both must be as much of a relief to you as it is to us." She stopped us and placed her gentle hands on my shoulders. "Although it wasn't intentional...either time, I—I want to personally thank you, Arienne. For saving my son's life. In so many ways. I'm eternally in your debt for it. I love you...very much." My eyes went misty and we embraced.

"I love you too," I whispered, offering a reassuring rub to her back. "You owe me nothing. You and the king have given me the comfort of what a true mother and father are supposed to be. Something I've never had. You'll never understand what it means to me. *Thank you.*" She squeezed and as she pulled back, the music and tempo changed. It was time to go. I looked over as Tidus and Luca began creeping past our guests toward us, the king stopping him for a short moment to hug him and exchange a few words.

"Now that you're married...would you allow me to lend a word of advice?" Ayla grinned, raising a brow. I was intrigued and we hooked arms, walking slowly toward the doors.

"Absolutely." I smiled. She leaned in as we moved forward.

"There is great power in words, dearest. When spoken from the mouth of a queen...in the right tone, it will surprise you how quickly you can bring a king to his knees." A devious slash crept across her mouth.

"Ah...so. Be a bit demanding?" I asked, recalling the way she had Tidus falling all over her in the hallway.

"Tell him what you want. Males aren't always as hesitant to obey when they're being told what to do if it comes from...a different place." She glanced sidelong at me.

"I understand exactly what you mean." I nodded, grinning.

"Good girl." She laughed. Luca and the king slipped up quietly beside us. "Ready?" She asked, leaning into her king lovingly as they both smiled at us. They looked as if they were trying earnestly to hold back tears. Luca and I grinned at each other and nodded eagerly.

"Go. Have fun you two." Tidus winked.

Luca grabbed my hand and we hurtled through the doors, startling the guards on the other side as we raced down the hallway, laughing. Our steps echoed down the space and they chuckled behind us. Two flights of stairs, and a few more turns and we'd finally make it to our corridor. My cheeks flushed, and I was nearly spent for oxygen as I tried to keep up with him after too much wine and the overuse of my legs. I nearly tripped, cackling at him when he turned a corner and ran into one of Ayla's statues against the wall. He yelped and sped up, dragging me down another hallway.

I got halfway up the next flight of steps before catching the material from my skirts on my heel and stumbling forward, jerking Luca back and causing him to fall sideways on the step in front of me. We sat there howling in laughter, unable to breathe for a few moments and I miserably made an attempt to crawl over to him as he slumped against the railing.

"Luca…" I heaved. "Are you—are you alri—" I lost myself in my giggles and placed my hand on his knee.

"What the *hell* was in that bottle?" Luca huffed, still laughing and wiping at the corner of his eye.

"I changed my mind." I snorted. "Let's just sleep right here."

"Oh, absolutely not." He rasped, rising from the step and scooping me into his arms. He stole kisses from me from the landing of the stairs to the corridor and stopped when we finally reached the door to *our* room. Thunder rumbled through the empty hallway and we looked at each other.

"Sounds as if things with Nero and Varuna are either going very well…or very badly." I snickered.

"Are you ready to brew up a storm of our own, Princess?" His eyes glinted in the flash of lightning across the hall.

"As ever." I breathed, hushing him with my mouth.

Luca opened the door, carrying me inside and never breaking our kiss as he kicked it shut behind us.

CHAPTER 40

UNION

We stood by the door with our mouths dropped open; both of us finding it difficult to acknowledge that this was the same room we'd been sharing—and Luca had occupied his whole life. The entire room had been redecorated. The desk was no longer between the bath chamber and sitting room doors. It was replaced by a fancy breakfast table with two chairs. A bottle of aged wine chilled in a decorated silver bucket of ice, fruits and sweets shared halves of a serving dish alongside it. A large pitcher of water and an arrangement of cups sat near the back of the round table.

Luca's bed had been stripped and replenished with a handsome black duvet, pulled back to reveal deep crimson silk sheets. Several enormous, fluffy pillows peaked against the headboard in accommodating hues. Candles were lit on any available surface, gathered on the new dark-stained bedside tables, offering a romantic glow around the room. Lightning lit up the space, followed by deep rumbles of thunder and my skin prickled. Paintings of abstract figures hung on the walls, taking the shape of bodies tangled in passionate embraces. Dark red rugs sprawled over the floor and flower petals had been scattered about. We stepped forward and Luca sighed deeply.

"It looks like...someone came into this room and vomited my mother everywhere," he admitted, shaking his head. I covered my mouth and snorted back heavy laughs, walking further in and looking around. I smoothed my hand over the soft duvet and nodded in approval.

"This feels amazing." I smiled, turning my head toward him and realizing the next new addition to the room that he'd just found. A massive mirror, ornately framed and taking up the entirety of the wall directly across from our bed. Luca's smile was ridiculous.

"I might like this." He pointed with his thumb.

"You would," I giggled. We stared at each other from across the room for a long moment and then grew quiet. My stomach churned...the familiar feeling of the elephant stampede that I hadn't felt in a long while. Luca's mouth turned up in the corner.

"Nervous?" He asked gently.

"I'm not sure why...but...yes." My breathing shuddered and I fidgeted with my mother's pendant. Rain began to pound the windows and my heart echoed the thunder that rolled outside. He moved closer and my pulse raced.

"You're trembling," he whispered, easing his hands down my shoulders...my arms. "We don't have to—"

"No. I want to. I've wanted little else for two weeks...I don't know what's wrong with me. It feels...it feels like the first night we..." I trailed off, sliding my fingertip down the front of his shirt.

"Well...it's the first time since we became husband and wife. Since this curse was broken. The first time we've had to think of nothing else but the two of us in a long time. Want to know a little secret?" He tilted my chin up. I nodded. His hand pressed over mine and flattened my palm to his chest. His heart was thrashing.

"You too?" I smiled.

"Ever since I turned down the corridor." He huffed a laugh.

"Would it be alright if...could you give me just a moment?" I asked, chewing my lip. He pressed a kiss to my forehead and smiled sweetly.

"Take all the time you need, love. I'll be right here."

I backed away, our fingers lingering until we parted, and I disappeared into the sitting room. I cracked the door, but he made no move to follow me. I heard him plop down onto the bed and he groaned from the other side of the door.

"My body just got lost in this damned blanket. I could get used to it, I think." I smiled to myself, making my way down the short hallway and unclasping the pendant as I walked. Several things in the sitting room had been rearranged to make room for Luca's desk and other items that had been replaced in the bedchamber. The armoires were still in their usual places and I opened mine, tucking the necklace into the box that Paxe had presented it to me in. I carefully tugged off my heels, dropping them beside me on the floor and starting the process of easing the gown off my body.

I didn't hear another sound from Luca and glanced every so often at the door, which was still cracked and unmoved. I draped the gown over the back of an armchair and pulled out the bag I'd hidden, with the garments from the lingerie shop inside. It did nothing to calm my nerves as I held them in front of me and looked back over at the door. Thunder clapped beyond the balcony doors as if in encouragement and I tried not to give my rattled stomach another thought as I slipped the red lacy pieces onto myself. I adjusted the bust and fluffed through the curled ends of my hair, turning to face the gilded mirror and stopping dead.

Oh, Gods...

It was a flawless fit. Lydia knew her naughty underthings well. While a small part of me still wanted to hate her, I thanked her silently as I looked myself over in the mirror. I wondered if breaking that curse had done a damn bit of good...Luca's heart would likely stop the moment I step out of that door. I found myself panicking for a bit, wondering how in the hell I was to present myself. I paced on bare feet around the sitting room, shaking my hands back and forth for a few moments, and then paused to stare at the doorway.

Just go, stupid. Listen to Ayla...tell the male what you want. Stop being squeamish.

I padded slowly down the shallow hallway and stood quietly behind the door, listening closely and hearing nothing. I closed my eyes and pressed my tattooed hand to my heart...searching down the bond we shared for Luca's magic. I felt him and pushed it gently.

"Ari?" Luca's voice croaked from the other side. I heard him sitting himself up and I opened my eyes, straightening my spine and slowly opening the door. He paused, sitting on the edge of the bed, wholly stunned and his mouth parted, with his bare feet on the floor. I think he tried to speak, but all that came out was a faint choking sound.

The way his eyes devoured every inch of me filled me with confidence I didn't realize I had. I took a step forward, softly closing the door behind me. He gaped at me and I decided I'd rendered him speechless as I took another step toward him...stopping barely a foot away. I didn't feel nervous anymore.

"Are you alright, *Prince*?" I whispered, smoothing my hands down the front of my top. His throat bobbed, and he inhaled deeply as if he'd forgotten how to breathe. All I got in response was a dumbfounded nod and a slow blink. The side of my mouth curled up. "Do you need the healer?" I slyly smirked, slowly turning myself around and raising my hair to give him a fair view of the back. I finished my slow circle and watched him blink twice, shifting around the discomfort of the bulge below his waist.

"I—" He swallowed. "I need a priest."

"Are you dying?" I raised a brow, hooking my thumb around the scrap of material around my hips.

"I think I already did."

"Lie back...unbutton your shirt. Slowly." I breathed.

The queen had told me the truth. The command in my voice, my tone...the fire I knew was in my eyes. It moved him quickly. He retreated to lean back on the pillows, half sitting and did exactly as I asked. One button popped open at a time and his bare skin slowly revealed itself beneath. He raised one knee slightly, his other leg thrown out in front of him...he never took his eyes from mine. So many unspoken things were being fired off between us. Things I never would have deigned to say nor even consider before meeting him. His chest moved up and down and I eyed his leather belt. I didn't even have to ask...he noted my stare and unbuckled it, pulling it open. He unfastened his pants and started to raise his hips from the bed.

"Stop," I said, heat spreading through my veins. He relaxed and we stared at one another for a moment before he patted his lap with one hand and waved two fingers toward himself with the other. A silent demand of his own, beckoning me to come closer. Lightning flashed through our room and I eased onto the bed with a knee, slowly crawling between his legs and over his hard stomach. I trailed my mouth up his middle, spreading his open shirt further apart and breathing the softest kisses over his heart...over that damned mark that was no longer there and thanking the gods again for giving us more time.

He breathed heavily, gathering my hair in his hand and claiming my mouth without another word when I raised myself over him. He pulled me closer with his other arm and we moved against each other in all the right places, my fingers reaching behind his head and releasing his hair from its binding. We stayed in that moment, sharing breath and tasting the tang of wine on each other's tongue, until the need became too much. We both trembled then, not from nerves but from our well of restraint, now empty and bone dry. He released my hair, dropping his arms and gripping me by my thighs. I was reluctant to break my hold on his lips, but he raised my body higher, moving himself lower until I was straddling his face. I could feel the heat from his breath along the strip of lace that barely covered the most intimate part of me, and my core burned with desire.

Strong arms hooked around my thighs and the warmth of his palms spread up my backside. I felt the sting of his nails in the bare skin of my lower back and I curled my spine. His lips brushed against the thin material and I suddenly found it difficult to breathe.

"Grab the board," he demanded hoarsely, lightly kissing me over the lace. I shivered and gripped the wood with both hands, straightening myself and trying hard not to move. He kissed me again, slightly harder and the material began to feel moist. His hands traveled up my sides as he continued to tease, kissing everywhere except the spot I needed him to.

"Take them off," I rasped, growing impatient and biting a hole through my lip. "Please." His fingers curled around the thin strips and in one swift movement, he ripped them apart, pulling the remains away and tossing them to the floor. His tongue swept through my center and I gasped, feeling the reverberations of his hum against my skin through the entirety of my lower half. His hands gripped the underside of my rear, spreading me open and my back arched as he continued to make a personal feast out of me. I whimpered, letting my head fall back and losing control of my hips while I slowly began to ride his mouth. My grip on the headboard tightened right along with my insides as I grew closer and closer to ecstasy.

"I want every drop of you, Arienne," he growled against me as he sucked the swelling spot gently and rolled his tongue over it. My breaths staggered and I shook with broken moans, moving with the ministrations of his tongue and the hands that had me ready to sob with release. My skin was on fire and I cried out, feeling close to suffocating and tightening my thighs. "Call out for me," he whispered, digging his nails into my skin and flicking his tongue expertly through me.

"Luca..." I attempted breathlessly, looking down between my legs as he devoured me. Our eyes locked and his tongue slipped inside me, sending my body into a wave of blinding pleasure. I shook violently, nearly cracking the headboard and every muscle in my body reacted to it. He pressed a palm to my stomach, sending magic through me, heightening every sensation and I nearly lost my mind. I screamed his name while he drank greedily from me. I rode wave after wave of that high until I could no longer move. I braced myself against the board and he wrangled himself out of his pants before easing me back down into his lap. His hair fell around his face and down his back, his shirt the only thing still clinging to his skin besides myself.

I continued struggling to catch my breath as I dragged his shirt down his broad shoulders and was relieved to finally be held in his bare arms. He traced the lines of my top with his finger, taking in every part of me. My breasts, my face...my eyes...as if he couldn't get enough.

"Did you get a proper look at yourself before you came into this room?" He whispered against my mouth. I kissed him, dragging my nails lightly across the stubble of his chin. I was still short of breath. "Turn around. I want to show you something."

I twisted in his arms and we faced the mirror on the wall at the end of our bed. He raised to his knees and backed me against him, moving my hair and dropping it behind my shoulders to expose my entire front. The outer edges of his naked body were immaculate from behind me in the mirror, glowing with the candlelight around us. His fingertips grazed down my neck and across my collarbones, then down the length of my arms.

"Look at my wife," he started, softly kissing the column of my neck and gazing at me in the glass. Our fingers interlocked on our right hands and his inked left hand traveled back up across my middle and between my breasts, his gold ring glinting in the dim light. "Look how absolutely beautiful you are. Your perfect body..." He kissed the place where my neck met my shoulder and my eyes fluttered. "The way your skin flushes when I make you lose yourself..." Another lingering kiss. "The way your eyes shine the fiercest green...especially when you're pissed." He snorted, kissing my shoulder and sliding his hand gently up my throat. I smirked at him in the mirror and reached behind me to stroke his bare thigh. His eyes met mine in our reflection. "I love every part of you."

I turned my face to his and our lips hovered a breath away from each other. "I love you. So much." We were lost then, our lips at war with our tongues and our teeth. Our joined hands snaked across my middle and his fingers gripping slightly harder around my throat. I moved my other hand from his thigh, and he flinched when I found his rock-hard length against my back. I tightened my fingers around him, stroking up and down until deep groans started to creep up his throat. Raising myself higher, I moved our hands further down my body and spread my thighs apart, letting him release my fingers and hold me up against him by my right leg. My wrist turned and I stroked him harder. He grew restless and his mouth left mine, searching for any available oxygen while I continued. "Look at me, Luca."

He did, and I could have burned alive. I moved faster and he gripped at my throat, pressing into me and raising me higher. He breathed hard and I held his gaze while I brought my arm up around the back of his neck and spread my legs wide, moving his cock between them to rest against my sex. "Tell me," he begged, his voice barely a whisper between ragged breaths. I brought the other arm up and hooked it around his neck.

"You wanted every drop of me. I want every inch of you." I panted. "Fuck me, Prince," I said, crushing our lips together. He growled, raising me by the neck and kissing me deeply. He turned my chin to face the mirror and we both watched as he sheathed himself inside me, sliding in and out until every last inch of him disappeared within my body. His arms crossed around me and he thrust harder, both of us shaking and gasping for air. Every instinct told me to drop my head back and close my eyes, but neither of us could stop watching that mirror and it made everything more intense...raw. The skin of his length glistened with my arousal every time he slammed it back into me. The storm raged outside the windows as if in challenge and we accepted graciously, screaming the paint off the walls and ending up on our sides. Luca coiled around my back with an arm hooked beneath my knee and a tight squeeze on my throat while he ravaged me from the inside out.

"Gods, you fucking feel incredible," he moaned through his teeth, pounding faster with every sound I made. I felt him throbbing inside me and he whined softly at my ear, nearly sending me over the edge.

"Let me see it." I gasped, earning his attention. "I want it all over me." He cursed under his breath and bit down on my shoulder, thrusting hard and readying himself. I eased onto my back and he draped my legs over his shoulders, sliding back into me and tearing my top open down the middle. I flung my arms over the edge of the bed, moaning loudly as release claimed me, my body quivering around him while he drove deeper. Luca pulled himself from me and groaned as he held himself in his hand and gave me every last drop. I slid my left hand up his waist and across his middle, relishing in the satisfaction on his face. Warm drips of his release settled between my breasts, the flat plane of my stomach...the crease of my hips. His hair blew in and out of his eyes with his sharp breaths and I didn't think my husband could be more attractive. Something like surprise...and triumph burned in his eyes when he lifted them to mine. His thumb wiped over the tip of his length and I caught the movement as he attempted to speak.

"I was wrong..." He trembled, staring at the remains of his arousal on his thumb and flashing his eyes at me.

"About?" I huffed, still caressing his midsection and carefully watching his fingers.

"I didn't believe anything could be more stimulating than seeing your mouth around me...but the way you look right now..." His other hand slid down my leg, still hanging over his shoulder. All things considered, I wasn't sure either of us felt like ourselves since we'd stepped into this room. Perhaps even after we'd stepped off the dais after the ceremony. It was clear that everything between us was twice as potent, and somehow, becoming his wife...securing ourselves to one another forever...we were different. We were closer and more comfortable sharing things we may not have normally. I moved my hand and gripped his wrist, raising myself and guiding his thumb into my mouth, sucking it clean while his eyes widened at my audacity. "Dear

Gods..." He whispered, grabbing my chin with his thumb hooked between my teeth and pulling my mouth to his. That kiss was positively sinful, which was saying plenty after the way we had just spoken and what we'd done to one another. What I'd very happily let him do to me.

A spark of white-hot flame lit up inside me and I channeled it into him, forcing him to resign onto his back and mounting him like a stallion. He gave me absolutely no argument. I jerked what was left of my top from my shoulders and dominated over his body, leaning myself back and supporting my weight with my hands on his legs. In all the moments we'd shared in a bed, I'd never heard Luca make sounds like the guttural ones he was ushering now. My nails broke the skin of his muscular thighs and I anchored myself, rolling my hips and tightening around him like a serpent constricting around its prey. We'd somehow managed to tumble to the floor but never missed a beat and I continued my assault. He did indeed call out my name—several times. The last time being more of an animalistic growl while he violently came, grasping his hair in both hands and swearing impressively. By the time we had exhausted ourselves enough to rest for a while, we realized neither of us had enough strength left to climb back onto the bed. So we laid there facing each other, a familiar position. Legs tangled, bodies heaving rasped breaths. Pressed close together and staring into one another, my fingertips trailing lazy strokes down his side...his own fingertips toying with my lip.

"What are you thinking?" I whispered, reaching up to smooth my hand across his face. He smiled lazily, tracing my bottom lip with his finger.

"We've been like this before," He breathed. "Sometimes with exhaustion...sometimes with tears." A pause.

"What's wrong?" My brows drew together.

"Sometimes I saw us this way...in my visions. Before the curse was broken. Under that moon...in the meadow."

"You never have to think about that again, Luca."

"I know. I just need you to know...I would have been perfectly happy with it." He tucked my hair behind my ear and tugged me closer.

"You would have been happy to die and leave me without you?" I choked.

"I would have been happy to die that way. To have your face being the last thing I ever see...those eyes."

"One day...a very long time from now, I hope the gods grant us both that much. But for now...especially on our wedding night, could we refrain from speaking about such things?" I nudged him in the shoulder and he huffed a laugh, wrapping his arms around me and pressing a kiss to the bridge of my nose.

"You're right."

"How did those words taste coming out of your mouth, Prince?" I chuckled, holding him close.

"Not as delicious as your name." He grinned.

"Ah." I raised my face to meet his stare. "Did I earn his Majesty's seal of approval on my promises in the receiving room?" I smiled, awaiting his answer. His eyes were half closed as he barked a laugh.

"You most certainly did." We quieted, eyes closed and nearly falling asleep when rumbles of thunder began to stir up over the sea again after hardly an hour of silence. We looked at each other in disbelief and Luca softly shook his head. "You've got to be kidding me."

I ducked my forehead into his shoulder and lost myself in exhausted giggles. "To have the strength of immortals."

"I mean..." Luca threw up a hand and lowered his brows.

"You dare to try another round with me, *Luca?*" I propped my head up on my hand and wagged my brows. He raised himself on his elbow and looked at me as if I'd lost my mind. "Or is my prince tuckered out?" I smiled. He rolled me over, towering over me with an arm beside each of my shoulders and tossed that head of thick, gorgeous hair over the side. I adjusted myself so that he could settle between my legs.

"I'm sure I don't know what you mean...*Arienne.*" He chirped, grazing his teeth across the skin of my neck. "I remember someone saying that we were both in for a long night."

"I seem to recall that being in response to someone say—" My retort was stifled with his mouth and I twined my fingers into his hair.

The rest of our wedding night was slow...deliberate. Passionate. The world stopped. It was no longer a race against time or figuring out which one of us could come up with ways to test our boundaries. There were none anymore.

That curse was broken.

All that was left now was the two of us. The feel of his body...free of its bind to the dark. The warmth of his light and the way it beckoned me home. The breath in his lungs that gave me life with every uttering of the words '*I love you*'. The ancient script on our hands that promised the peace we'd fought so hard to find. The faint scars on our palms that were our gateway to each other's souls. Only the gods themselves could understand how much we loved one another. How two beings could weld so perfectly together...handpicked and joined, our union like a supernova...the birth of something higher. Something greater than us. Greater than everything.

There was something about the way my name left his lips tonight. Something that sounded like my name, but more like a prayer sent up in earnest. It left me feeling as if I were nestled deeper into his heart. Protected and cherished. We were reforged into vital parts of each other...forever.

Fino alla morte.

Luca's breathing was deep...even. Perfect. Our bodies melted into the soft rug on the floor, limbs twined around each other. I couldn't do a thing other than smile at him. His eyelids were still as stone. Most likely in the deepest sleep I'd ever seen him. I tucked myself beneath his chin and breathed him in deeply, settling myself into sleep. I wasn't certain if it was the dizziness of every emotion still running rampant through my mind and body, the amount of wine we'd consumed...the overkill of exhaustion in my limbs, or the small fear that lingered in the outskirts of my mind; that our dangers weren't as far away as they seemed...but I found it more difficult to relieve myself of consciousness. The notion that it could all be ripped away from me seemed to crawl up my spine. As if he'd been aware, even in sleep, Luca tightened his hold around me. So I banished every intruding thought, kissing his neck softly and losing myself in his embrace. Sleep finally found its way to me instead, consuming us both entirely.

When I awoke, the sun was harsh and bright. Most likely mid-morning, and the air in our room suggested it was warm out as well. I heard the steady thrumming of Luca's heart as I laid on his chest and smoothed a hand over him. His own hand found mine and our fingers interlocked. When I raised my face, I found him staring with his brows drawn at the three large paintings on the wall where the worn chest of drawers used to be. I snorted.

"Morning?" I croaked, half smiling, when he finally looked at me. His answering smile was surprisingly vivid. Awake. As if he'd been staring up there for a while now.

"Morning, Mrs. Di Meo."

"Why are you staring at that thing like it's going to leap from the canvas?" I chuckled. His face jerked back up to the triptych, brows knotted again as if he were at a loss for words.

"I—" He started. "They're really just..."

"Yes?" I laughed, wiping the corner of my eye and glancing between the paintings and his expression.

"Ari, they're fucking hideous," he sighed deeply. I barked in laughter and dropped my forehead into his chest. "They are! Look at them!" He pointed up at the artwork, and I raised my head again, biting back another giggle and trying to seem supportive. "That one there...where are their legs? Why do they look like that? And that one..." He moved his finger over, continuing to point at them as if they offended him. "I feel like they're watching me. Who kisses with their eyes open? It's creepy. I can't take it." I grinned, easing over him and drawing his attention to me instead of the wall.

"I adore you." I breathed, brushing his hair back and nuzzling his lips with the tip of my nose. His hands trailed up my sides and he pulled me into a deep kiss. It took him a moment to realize I'd kept my eyes open and he abruptly stopped, our mouths making a harsh sucking sound as he jerked back. I exploded in laughter.

"Oh my Gods! Stop it!" He barked, shaking his head and popping my backside. "Just...wicked."

"Well, I suppose I know now what makes you unsettled." I cackled.

"And what's your plan for resettling me?" He pouted, rubbing over the spot he'd just smacked.

"Hmm...a bath?" I raised a brow. He nodded pitifully, his eyes shining like a scolded child. "Alright. I'll draw it. Poor prince..." I kissed the bridge of his nose and raised from the floor. "All flustered over a smudge of paint." He raised on his elbows and watched me walk bare across the floor to the bath chamber. I heard him chuckle and I looked over my shoulder to see half his face peeked over the edge of the bed. "What?" I shrugged.

"Go back to the mirror." He snorted. I backed up a few steps and examined myself. I couldn't help but giggle and heat graced my cheeks as I took in the perfect outline of his fingers on my right buttock. I noted the accompanying marks of his fingernails from the night before, several on my lower back and on my shoulders, bite marks in other spots...light bruising where he'd sucked my skin. He stepped up beside me, biting down on his lip. "You know I'd never deign to harm you in any way...but I find that extremely arousing."

"So do I." I winked. "How bad are yours?" I looked him over, turning him around. I'd left several long scratches down his middle, drew a small bit of blood from his thighs and his back didn't look nearly as bad as it had in Aeon.

"I think you've given me worse." He grinned, pulling me to him and pressing our heads together. "But last night was..."

"Incredible," I finished.

"Yes."

The scent of intimacy was all over us. All over this room. My body heated and I pulled myself away gently. I wanted to take him again. Right here. He must have felt that in me...my eyes flickered below his waist. I swallowed. "Open those windows," I said hoarsely. "I'll get the bath ready." He smirked and nodded softly and I reluctantly turned from him and padded into the bath chamber. The sweet smell of jasmine and lavender filled the steamy room as I blended the oils into the water, checking the temperature again before pausing to gape at my husband on my way out the door. His naked backside was flexed as he struggled on the tips of his toes, draping his discarded dress shirt over the middle painting on the far wall. "Luca!" I pressed a hand to my hip and shook my head. He startled and turned around.

"I can't take it." He shrugged, turning back to the painting to finish covering the other side.

"You are ridiculous." I scoffed, rolling my eyes and laughing my way back to the tub.

Pins and small flowers littered the marble floor next to the large bathtub that I'd painstakingly removed from my hair as the water sloshed over the lip and the sounds of our lovemaking echoed through the space. We stayed in that chamber for nearly two hours, our bathwater mostly cold when we finally emerged. My body felt limp and useless after I'd gotten myself dressed and found him on his back on our bed, tossing and catching an apple repeatedly. I leaned on the door jamb, arms crossed and staring at him.

Just when I thought I couldn't love you more, Prince.

A smile crept across my lips. "You look comfortable." He'd dressed himself in a light gray, half-sleeved knit shirt and dark pants and his hair was damp, unbound and softly beginning to curl in the warm breeze coming in from the open windows. He caught the bright green apple in his hand and sat up, taking a large bite out of it and smiling at me while he chewed.

"You look beautiful, wife." He patted his knee and I stepped forward, taking a seat on it and accepting the apple when he offered it to me. "There's an orange or two over there if you'd rather take a half hour eating that instead." He grinned, earning himself a soft punch in the shoulder.

"There may be some bread I could dirty up for you as well, wretch." I chuckled, biting into the fruit.

"Dirty up how, exactly?" He quirked a brow.

"And you call *me* the heathen." I shook my head, passing the apple back to him and straightening my teal tunic. My loose braid draped over my breast and he toyed with it for a moment.

"What would you like to do for the rest of the day? Is there anywhere you'd like to go?" He asked, kissing the exposed skin in the vee of my shirt.

"Hmm...what do married couples do all day?" I hummed, grazing a hand up his back and leaning into his touch.

"I can think of a few things." He whispered against me, burying his face in my chest. I almost considered it...again. "We could venture downstairs if you want. It's nearly dinner. Get some real food? You should probably eat." I fumbled my hands through his hair and pressed my lips to the top of his head.

"They'll likely be surprised to see us out so soon." I kissed.

He huffed a laugh between my breasts. "They will."

I stood and lingered between his knees, gathering his hair and twisting it back into a loose knot. My eyes searched for a familiar leather strap, but I quickly remembered it had vanished and I peered down at the script on my hand. I pouted. "It is rather odd not to have that damned strap, isn't it?" He raised his face to me and stuck his bottom lip out. "I do miss it a bit."

He looked around, his attention stopping on the floor and eyes brightening as a devious smirk graced his face. "Pardon me, Mi'lady," he chirped, leaning down and snatching the pair of ripped undergarments from the floor.

"Luca...no." I barked, covering my mouth with my hand.

"Oh, yes. This is happening." He twisted the scrap of material into a small rope and I gaped as I watched him tie off the knot with it. "I won't be sharing this one, love. Sorry." A wide grin and a sultry look.

"And what exactly do you plan to say when someone asks you about it?" I asked, mortified. He stood, pulling on his boots and smiling triumphantly.

"Oh, I'll be telling the truth. And be damn proud doing it."

"Oh my Gods..." I griped under my breath, sliding into a pair of flat slippers. His arms wrapped around me from behind and he tucked into my neck, chuckling.

"No one will even notice. Relax."

"I'll bet a large amount of coin that you're wrong." I snickered.

"Bet something else, and I'll accept that bargain, Princess."

"You're insufferable."

The guard at the end of the corridor startled when we started out of our room and straightened himself against the wall. We walked hand in hand, nodding at him as we passed and noting the disbelief on his face that we'd decided to come up for air. I didn't think too long about how long he'd been stationed there or how much he may or may not have heard. Similar expressions appeared on the castle attendants busying themselves with their daily tasks as we made our way downstairs. A few smiled and congratulated us. The palace was mostly quiet, save for the ins and outs of the usual commotion.

"Something smells amazing," I said, my stomach grumbling as we neared the dining room.

"Oh...I forgot to mention..." Luca stopped us and faced me. "You and I head the table now. Along with my parents. It's customary after we wed." He jerked his head toward the doorway. "Are you alright with that?"

"Oh...yes, that's fine. I wasn't aware of that."

"I just wanted to tell you before we wander into the snake pit." He laughed. "We can generally do whatever we like, but while we still have guests staying in the castle, my mother will likely keep up with traditional practice."

"For show?"

"Precisely." He winked.

"Very well. Let's eat."

He grinned and leaned down to peck my cheek, twining our fingers together and pressing them to his chest as we made the last few steps and entered the dining room.

CHAPTER 41

SURPRISE

"Gods above!" Tidus beamed as we stepped into the room. Everyone at the long table turned their attention toward us, as expected.

"Princess!" Holt exclaimed, leaping from his chair beside Mora near the end of the table. Benjamin sat next to her wheelchair to her left, Vetta and Frances across from them. Lady Annette was a seat down from Benjamin, accompanied by the same elegant male she'd been chatting up at the wedding. Paxe and Lakan took up chairs across from them, nearest to the king and queen. The two empty seats near the sovereigns had small vases with white rosebuds at their place settings, indicating who those chairs belonged to and why they were vacant. I was suddenly very grateful to Luca for explaining the change in royal dinner etiquette, as I'd have been otherwise confused about the symbolism. Holt's small body crashed into my legs and I scooped him up into my arms.

"Holt! By the gods..." Mora pinched between her eyes and shook her head.

"It's alright," I whispered over to her, squeezing the lad tight.

"Guess what?" Holt whispered into my ear. "Your cat likes me. Look under my chair." I glanced over to find Hiss patiently awaiting more of whatever the little boy had been feeding him, his bristled tongue lapping at the edges of his mouth.

"Where's Kyna?" I asked.

"She can't come in the castle. Ma said I was lucky we even brought her here. But the people at the horse stable are taking real good care of her. I like your house, Luca," he replied, looking over my shoulder to speak to Luca.

"Thanks, lad. Come here." Luca picked him up and hauled him over his shoulder, tickling his legs while he walked him back over to his seat. Two of the serving attendants against the back wall hurried over to the table to remove the vases from our spots, and replace them with plates and flatware.

"I certainly didn't expect to see you two at dinner this evening." Ayla smiled, pouring our wine as Luca pulled out my chair. I sat and he took his place to my right, next to his mother. "Not that you'll hear any complaint from me, of course." She sat the bottle aside and the same two ladies began piling hot food onto our plates.

"We were starving," Luca said, gathering vegetables onto his fork. "Perhaps missed you lot...a little."

Tidus chuckled through his nose and chewed.

"Things went well?" She pressed, smirking as she politely bit the meat off of the end of her fork. Paxe leaned forward, smiling at me from down the table. I snickered into my plate and my face heated. "How did you like the new bedding? Is it not wonderful?"

"I knew you had to be responsible for that. Our room looks just like your wardrobe." Luca huffed, drinking from his glass. Ayla's mouth parted.

"Go ahead and try to tell me you didn't sleep like a king on those sheets. It doesn't matter what color they are." She rolled her eyes. I nearly choked on my food, and Luca on his wine. Her fork paused in front of her mouth and she drew her brows. "What?"

Paxe was giggling from down the table and I covered my mouth with my napkin.

"We haven't slept on them yet, Mother." Luca cleared his throat. Vetta and Lady Annette both joined Paxe in their soft laughter. Tidus grinned silently, shaking his head as he stabbed a few carrots. "But the rugs are nice," Luca added, earning a hearty laugh from Lakan.

Ayla's eyes widened. "Oh...oh, I see." We all tried to be mindful of the child that was present at the end of the table. It seemingly became a challenge of wits when the queen spotted the strip of crimson in Luca's hair. "You must not despise the color too much. I've never seen you elect to wear red before." She grinned, raising her brows at him and lifting her glass. I dropped my fork, eyes wide and snapped my head to my husband, praying he'd come up with a good lie. Paxe swiveled in her chair, craning her neck to see what the queen had noted and covered her mouth with her hand.

"It's truly a lovely color on you, son." Tidus laughed, wincing when Luca's foot connected with his shin beneath the table.

"*Thank you*...Pop." Luca's face flushed. "It's a trophy. And that's all I can deign to say about it...for now." He winked. I loosed a long breath.

"A trophy? I want one!" Holt squealed.

The dining room erupted. Even the servants lining the walls couldn't help themselves. Benjamin got a handle on his composure, and tried not to continue laughing as he scooted his chair back and took Holt's little hand. "I think it's time for your bath." He chuckled, leading the boy from his chair.

"Why? I didn't get to eat dessert yet!" Holt whined, Hissifus following behind him.

"Someone get that kid the largest hunk of chocolate cake you can find," Luca ordered. Holt bounced on his heels. Mora wheeled herself behind them, mouthing a thank you to us as they hurried him into the hall. Once we were sure he was out of earshot we all resumed our dinner.

...Or attempted to.

"That new hair strap looks vaguely familiar. Perhaps I'll wind up being the deliverer of fine ideas." Paxe jabbed, snorting into her plate. Luca wagged a finger at her in approval with a huge grin.

"Wait...so they are?" Lakan asked, leaning over to get Luca's attention.

"Yes." Luca laughed. "I'm considering it as a permanent accessory."

"Like hell, Prince." I snapped. Ayla giggled. "Oh...did you ask Luca what he thought about the artwork?" I smiled, turning up my wine. He snapped his face to me, his coy smile gone. "Do tell her, husband."

Ayla's eyes flickered and Tidus gulped. "I'm assuming you don't mean the new mirror." She said with a tone. Luca wiped his mouth with a linen and I could hear low laughter down the table, as he covered his lap with both hands.

"No, ma'am. We quite enjoyed that." He croaked.

"Is something wrong with the paintings? I did those when you were in Valdaro." She straightened herself in her chair.

"They're yours?" Luca winced.

"They are indeed."

I couldn't let him suffer any longer. I gripped his knee beneath the table and offered up feigned praise. "He found it difficult not to keep staring at them. The largest one in the middle was his favorite." I lied. His fingers squeezed around mine in defeat. We locked eyes for a brief second and his stare promised punishment I was all too eager to accept.

"Oh. I'm so glad." Ayla grinned. "That room has looked so bland for so long, I have plenty more things we could add now that it belongs to the two of you. Give it a touch of romance."

"Why don't you let Arienne decide?" Tidus asked, pointing toward me with his fork. "Now that they're married, perhaps she'd like to add her own flare to the space?"

Vetta scoffed. "That room will be full of cat hair and empty wine bottles." Luca giggled from beside me.

"Your dear friend here, prefers anything and everything covered in any shade of pink." Lakan mused, Paxe dropping her mouth open at the remark.

"And what's wrong with that?" She pouted.

"Nothing, dear." He shrugged, sipping his wine. Paxe palmed over her growing bump, her rose pink dress smoothing beneath her hand.

"How is the babe?" Vetta asked, Frances peeking over at the question.

"Strong and well. Beginning to give me very little rest." Paxe glowed.

"Luca... Ari? Now that you two have officially become husband and wife, I'll be expecting news that all my hard work was put to good use, mending wounds of passion when you announce your own bundle of joy. Have you decided if you'll wait very long?" Vetta asked innocently. Clangs of silverware and movement grew silent and I felt several pairs of eyes on me as I stared blankly into my plate. Luca's hand rounded the small of my back and he cleared his throat.

"We haven't discussed it very much yet. We wanted to wait until all the fuss dies down from the wedding," he offered.

"That's smart," Lady Annette cut in. "The way the two of you look at one another is inspiring. You should allow yourselves time to enjoy being married."

"Thank you, Lady Annette." I smiled sweetly.

"The celebrations yesterday were lovely. It will be talked about for a long while. Congratulations again." She raised her glass.

"Here, here." Frances agreed, raising his own. Everyone did the same and we all drank, hardly finishing the swallow when a stirring from the hallway drew the attention of the entire room. Michele rushed in, gasping for breath, two unfamiliar guards flanking him. All three of them huffed as if they'd run the entire way here. The look on his face was gaunt...especially the moment he saw Luca and I sitting next to the king and queen at the table. Something like pain flickered beneath the strands of golden hair in his eyes and he dipped his chin respectfully at Luca.

"Brother." He rasped, forcing a smile. Luca lowered his brows and started to raise from his seat in concern.

"What's wrong, Michele?" Tidus asked, cutting a hand toward Luca to remain seated. Two more figures quickly entered behind them without announcing themselves.

Nero and Varuna, their faces grave.

"We should speak in private, sire. I apologize for the intrusion." Michele bowed slightly and glanced at me...only for a second. I bristled and grabbed Luca's hand.

"Go." Ayla whispered to the king. He nodded and looked at us before leaving the table and hurrying out the doorway. Nero's eyes burned wearily and he said nothing before turning and following them out. "Clear the table please," the queen ordered, waving a finger over the plates. Servants from every corner silently began collecting everything and we all sat in deafening silence.

"Should we excuse ourselves, your Majesty?" Lady Annette asked nervously.

"Not until we've been given clearance that it is safe." Ayla shook her head. Her tone was soothing and she willed herself calm, which was more than I could say for myself or Luca who gripped my hand and stared impatiently at the doorway, his knee bouncing unnervingly beneath the table. The king reappeared a moment later, alone and approaching the middle of the dining room.

"Paxe, I'm sorry. Lakan...I need you to go with the guards. Hurry, please. We're moving you to the compound." Tidus waved him forward. Paxe shot up, as did Luca and I.

"The compound? What's he talking about?" Paxe's voice shuddered and she grabbed her belly. "What's happening?" Lakan's face paled and he turned her to face him, pulling her to him and shamelessly kissing her as if he'd never see her again. My heart began to crack. "Lakan?" Tears welled in her eyes.

"I love you," he whispered, leaning down and pressing his lips to her middle. "And I love *you.*" He tore himself away and Vetta came to Paxe's side, holding her steady as she quickly started losing her composure. Lakan moved as if he'd already known to be ready and what he'd need to do, should the king ask him such a thing. I'd put it together by then that he was being taken to the barracks beneath the university. For protection. Something had happened. I felt as if I'd be sick.

"Luca..." Tidus's voice was low and he waved a hand toward himself. Luca breathed deeply and turned toward me, taking my face in his hand and thumbing my jawline. His eyes were pleading and I shook with nerves. I nodded once. He nodded back and rounded the table, following his father to the study. Ayla placed a hand on my shoulder and Paxe's soft sobs grew panicked. Vetta and Annette whispered words of comfort to her, but it did little to calm her. Deciding that I couldn't take much more, I stalked to her side and wrapped my arms around her shoulders. The little bumpus was nestled between us and no one breathed a word. There was nothing to say...nothing to do but wait. No one knew any more than the other.

A few moments later, shouting sounded from down the hall. Muffled curses and three male voices. I recognized the loudest one as Luca's and my spine curled. All attention darted toward the dining room doorway. Breathing became difficult and heavy footsteps neared closer. Paxe stiffened beneath my hold and we all froze in anticipation. Luca appeared in the doorway, leaning against it; Nero close behind him, steadying him with a firm grip on his shoulder. Strands of his hair had been pulled from its knot and his face was red and splotchy, eyes damp and full of pain and rage. His breathing was ragged and choked. I was about to run to him when—

"Leighton is dead." The last word hoarse and barely audible. "The Midlands have been sacked, and Aeon..." He looked beseechingly between Vetta and Frances. "Aeon...burned last night."

I wasn't sure I was breathing.

Vetta stumbled back in shock and devastation, Frances catching her with an arm. I eased Paxe aside, as she stood pale as death with her hands covering her mouth, and hurried around the table to Luca. He swallowed hard and fought back his tears, holding me tight. The muscles in his jaw feathered against my cheekbone and I met Nero's hard stare over his shoulder.

"My father?" I whispered, shame and utter heartbreak threatening to overtake me. Nero nodded gravely.

"Leave us." Ayla shuddered, waving off the petrified servants. Tidus, Varuna, and Michele entered another doorway in the back of the dining room a moment later. The queen traveled heavy-footed across the floor, heels clacking across the pale stone. "Explain."

The king addressed us all, Nero stepping around us to be part of the conversation. "King Loren has murdered nearly two hundred humans in The Midlands. Men...women, *and* children. Fleck—*Leighton*...was among those dead. He had fought for the life of a human girl he'd been courting. Neither made it. The markets outside the castle have been demolished. About fifty were taken prisoner and placed in the castle dungeons." Paxe and I exchanged horrified glances.

Perla.

"The king ordered the destruction of Aeon to serve as a warning to any town or city that renders aid to the Princess's *army...*" He paused and lifted his eyes to me. "His threat was clear. He'll burn every city and execute prisoners every day, until she and her prince face him themselves."

"No." Ayla spat. "Enough." Her body trembled and the king placed his hands on her arms.

"Ayla..." He soothed. She jerked from his hold and trinkets around the dining room began to clatter and shake.

"I'll not offer my children up like *fucking* chattel! Damn him!" A tear raced down her cheek. "Damn him! And damn you!" She turned toward Nero, burning a hole through him with her eyes, which she then directed to Varuna, who stood stone faced by the king's side. "Damn the gods who find us all to be so disposable! If you've so much power, how could you not have stopped this in the beginning?" She cried. The clatter became a rattle and Luca clung tight to me. "Why does *one* person who is no more an immortal than I, have so much fucking power? I can no longer sit here and pretend to be in agreement to a prophecy to raise my son to be a lamb for slaughter! Alongside his *wife!* Has she not been through enough? They've barely been wed a full day, and they couldn't even get through their first meal without this?!" Tears burned my eyes. Ayla thrust her arms toward both the silent gods. *"Tell me why!"* Glass cracked beneath her anger and I could tell she was clinging to her self-control desperately. She wasn't only angry. She was a mother devastated for her only son. Devastated for me.

Luca released me, taking his mother's extended hand and overpowering her with his magic. She sagged into his arms and wept. Sniffling from our guests became a roar in my ears and the room began to spin with my thoughts and anguish. I felt myself slipping back into that dark place I'd been in Aeon...Aeon that was nothing more now than a heap of ash. Nero pulled me to his chest, embracing me as sobs tore up my throat.

"Your Majesty..." Varuna started, her voice calm and sympathetic. The goddess swayed silently toward the queen and Ayla turned her face from Luca's chest. "We may be immortal, but even we have laws to abide by. Boundaries that cannot be crossed. I understand your frustration. That power was gifted by us to restore stability to your lands...your people. It was placed by unanimous decision, into the hands of one who was worthy. It is only by unanimous decision alone that it can be taken away."

"What sort of being agrees to such cruelty?" Paxe shuddered, tears pouring from her eyes. "Who among the gods would decide against interference in something like this? And for so long?"

"You misunderstand, youngling," Nero answered. "None of us agree or support what he does. The first king was the start of a bloodline that would *govern* the people. Before him, there was chaos. Much like what we see from King Loren...but those responsible *were* your people. The conflict of interest among the gods isn't about who thinks this is acceptable. The conflict is about leaving the responsibility of mortals to mortals. Therefore, when there is no unanimous vote...we are only able to decide for ourselves who we aide, what we do, and in what way we assist."

"You went around them," I stated hoarsely. "You couldn't all agree and so some of you devised a course of action." Nero nodded softly.

"It began with the bravery and sacrifice of your mother," Varuna offered. "At that time we knew we'd been given a way. To assist one who would be courageous enough to stand against him. We could end it. Without the help of any gods that refused to be part in it. We chose the two of you. Bound your souls, and gave you *each other*. So that in the end...what you found in one another would be worth the risk."

"Pawns," Paxe whispered. Luca and I looked at one another, a slight smile exchanged.

"If you choose to perceive it that way. Mortals are not disposable to us. They are quite the opposite." Varuna's eyes met Nero's and it seemed the only understanding in her admission was held between Tidus, Ayla, Luca and myself.

"Mortals are not the only ones who make mistakes. The gods are far from perfect. We suffer loss as you do. We pay heavily for the shortcomings in which we're responsible. I've spent a very long time striving to account for blood that stains my hands." Nero's chin dropped.

"*Our* hands," Varuna corrected. They met each other's stares.

"I constructed Bolton to allow refuge to mortals with affliction. I've fought to protect both human and non-human. The bastard king rides for Bolton next. I cannot leave them open to attack." His arms trembled around me. "Your people are our people too."

"I wish to go, my Lord," Lady Annette stepped forward. Her new beau braced a hand at her back. "I may not have much to offer in the way of magic but I should like to continue to offer my help to Bolton. I've known no greater peace. Please take me with you." Nero nodded to them both and I felt so ashamed of myself. Annette could cook meals, and grow flowers...she spent her life bringing joy to others. She didn't have weapons that were gods blessed. She could slice a tomato, but didn't know how to properly handle a sword. And yet, here she was, offering herself to the cause. For whatever good she could do.

"I'm going." I pushed out of Nero's arms. Luca's jaw tightened and he gently released his mother, grabbing my hand.

"Ari, no. Please," Paxe pleaded, Michele holding her steady.

"He wants me, Paxe. This is about me. This is about his pride. He'll keep taking innocent lives until I stop him. The way I was meant to." I faced Luca and we stared into each other, his throat bobbing. "We didn't go through all of this for nothing. They didn't die for nothing. We knew this time would come, Luca."

"Wait...you don't even have a plan!" Ayla wept.

"We do," Luca breathed. "We always have."

Tidus swallowed. "Luca..."

"This is our destiny. She's right. Perhaps I'm selfish." His eyes lined with silver and he traced the line of my lips. *"I just wanted more time."*

"Your destiny..." Ayla sniffled. "Your destiny was to be a beloved king...a loving husband."

"A father?" Luca cut his eyes toward Ayla, the entire room going silent. "We both know that isn't true, Mother. My destiny was *her*. It's always been her. It's always been *us*. Where she goes, I go. We end it together."

"You speak as if you won't come back." Paxe shoved Michele's arm from her and straightened her spine. "You speak like this is the end. I won't accept it."

"Paxe—" Vetta croaked.

"I won't!" She yelled. "You'll come home. You both will. Promise me. Promise me this...right now." A tear fell down her cheek and she lifted her chin. "I can't go with you in this state." She palmed her swollen belly. "I don't give a damn about destiny. You'll survive. We'll all survive. Promise me."

I swallowed down the lump in my throat and glanced toward the tray sitting on a buffet against the wall. I silently walked toward it, taking a rosebud from one of the small vases and making my way to her around the table. We faced each other, choking back tears and I took her hand, raising it between us and placing the rosebud into her palm. Her lip quivered and she broke, collapsing into my arms and weeping loudly. I gripped her tighter against me, silently crying with her while Michele looked on, firm and solemn...doing his best to control his emotion.

"What can I do to help?" He asked, his usual cocky demeanor wholly defeated. Tidus stood beside Luca, sounding every bit the commander when he spoke.

"We fight." He raised his head to Michele. "Send soldiers south. Divide them. Half to the Cronian territory beyond the river, the other half to Valdaro's southern lands. Prepare them for any possible attack from the king. Spare as many as we can. Send an order for every human in our city to be evacuated and taken to the shelter of the university's lower levels. Do not seal the door until they're all accounted for."

"The Knightsfire?" Luca asked, facing Nero.

"I'll transport the urns in route to Bolton. My contacts within the castle will know what to do." He crossed his arms.

"Mischa?" I asked. Nero nodded.

"He and several others are prepared to assist you when you're ready to infiltrate the castle. Once breached, trust only the guards you see wearing an iron cuff with a hammer. The rest may put up a fight, so be prepared. You're familiar with his father, Byron...the weapons master?" I nodded. "He's constructed a master key for the cells within the lower level dungeons. There is only one wall near the end of the hallway that isn't underground. You'll have to be quick. Blow out the wall by the gate across from the stairwell into the dungeon, and let Mischa and his father evacuate the prisoners and any palace staff.”

“And then?” Luca asked.

“Take it down. Arienne, take the western wing of the castle starting from the upper floor. Smear the Knightsfire into the walls, on any scored surface that it will stick. It’s a thick, gritty paste, and highly flammable. Drop an urn in any place that you wish to level completely. Luca...you’ll take east. Once you’ve made it to the lower floor, ignite the trail. The king will know you’ve come for him and I’ve no doubt he’ll be waiting for you. Strike hard and true. End it. Be mindful that to fully suppress him, you must use all three weapons. Once he’s dead, leave him and get out. Set off the urns in the Great Hall and run like hell.” He paused and looked at me. That immortal flame burning bright in his eyes. “Valdaro will fall.”

“You make this sound so simple,” Ayla whispered, hanging her head. Tidus took her waist. “They’re only children. This is madness.”

“With all due respect, your Highness...” Nero stepped toward her. “I’ve seen how resilient and stealthy the two of them are. What they’ll do for each other. They may be younglings...but they are not children.”

“What about Bolton? Irondale?” I asked.

“Leave Bolton to me. Irondale is protected...” He half smiled. “By your mother.”

“I will be responsible for Crona,” Varuna announced, straightening herself. “The sea will protect your city, sire.” Tidus dipped his chin in gratitude.

“Lady Vetta...” Nero called. Vetta wiped her nose. “Aeon yielded no casualties. Your homes can be rebuilt. Bolton welcomes all of you until that time.”

Paxe and I sagged in relief. Vetta and Frances embraced.

“Luca...Arienne,” Tidus started. “Take the night. Rest. Be husband and wife. This can wait a few more hours.” Luca’s mouth opened in retort but Ayla fired up.

“That was not a request.” Her lips pursed and she and her son held each other’s gaze for a long moment. “Take your wife back to bed, boy. Give each other just a few more moments to be young and in love. Go.”

“Michele...go collect your wife and child. Bring them here until it’s safe. Everyone back to their rooms. No one leaves unless approved by myself or the queen.” Tidus finished.

“Lady Annette...” Nero extended his elbow, exchanging glances with Varuna who nodded. He looked between Luca and I, as he escorted her and the gentleman toward the doorway. “See you on the other side, younglings.” Varuna followed them out. Vetta and Frances slowly trudged arm in arm around the table and out into the hall. Michele excused himself next, slapping backs with Luca on his way through the door.

“I’ll walk you,” I said, taking Paxe’s hand. She wiped at her cheek and sniffed, allowing me to lead her out. Luca stayed behind to have a moment alone with his parents.

We didn't speak the entire way to Paxe's room. I don't think that either one of us could think of a single thing to say in comfort. We decided that it was comfort enough to be close to one another and have a few minutes to digest everything we'd been dealt in the past hour. I didn't have the will to promise her something that I was unable to know for certain I'd be able to keep, and she didn't have the will to let me leave her side when we finally approached her bedroom door.

"Come inside," she whispered, opening it and stepping in.

I followed close behind her and snicked the door shut.

CHAPTER 42

PROMISES

Paxe stood silently with her back turned to me, staring out of one of the large windows that overlooked the city. I couldn't help but think about its citizens...the human ones who were scrambling to gather what they could and haul their children from the safety of their beds...their dreams, to flee from their own homes and shelter themselves between walls of magic-warding stone. All because my father was a monster. My heart shattered at the thought of Paxe being one of those mothers. If that small baby inside her belly was already here, she'd be among them. She'd be running too.

Now no one was safe. Even magic wielders and semi-mortals were being butchered, or their lives burned to rubble before them just for being in allegiance to me. Just for desiring to have a brighter future where they'd not have to worry about the danger of falling into forbidden love, show too much talent to better themselves, or simply breathe the same air as someone of a different race. I wanted to vomit.

"Why did you give this to me?" Paxe asked, her voice merely a devastated whisper. She held out the rosebud between her forefinger and her thumb and didn't turn around to face me.

"Because it was easier than making you a promise that I may not be fortunate enough to keep, Paxe. You know why." I breathed, sitting myself down on the edge of her blush-colored bed.

"Lakan used to leave these for me as a message. A message that we'd be together. Or that we'd see one another...again."

"I know."

She turned and hung her head. "So...you gave it to me so that you wouldn't have to promise it out loud." Not a question. I sighed deeply. "When we were on the beach, you asked me what I would do. If the roles were reversed and I wore the crown."

"The fucking hat made of precious metal?" I laughed.

"Don't joke, Ari."

"I'm sorry." I rose from the bed and walked over to her, taking her belly in my hands. "You know that I've never been easy to talk to about the difficult things. I either lash out, shut down or completely lose my senses. You've always been the tough one."

"How can I make this easier for you then, Arienne?" She raised her bleary face to mine. "Do you want me to pretend that you didn't ask me that because you're not confident you'll live through this?" Tears streamed down her face.

"We broke that curse."

"That curse would have only killed you if you didn't love him. And you do. There's something you're not telling me." She drew her brows and her face crumpled. "There's something you haven't been telling me. For a while...and I wish like hell I hadn't given up my abilities if for no other reason than to force it out of you. Because whatever it is...must be so terrible that you can't find it in yourself to hurt me with it."

My teeth were bearing down on my lip so hard I was sure I'd break through. My eyes burned and my mouth was dry—every word echoing in my mind and every part of me wanting to blurt it out.

You're my sister...my sister. My blood.

But I just couldn't. Not this way. Not if there was any part of her that rejected what I may very well have to leave her responsible for. What her child's future would be, as heir to the throne if Luca and I, gods forbid, didn't make it.

"Don't make me, Paxe. Please. Just trust that no matter what happens...you're the only one I would ever deem worthy of that crown. You're the only person with a heart strong and just big enough that this world can be saved should I no longer be in it. I can't make you a promise that we won't die because curse or no curse, it's been a real possibility throughout this entire ordeal. We've already died once. Even that seems odd to say. But it happened. It could happen."

"And if it did, I couldn't take that crown anyway, Ari. I'm not of the royal bloodline. Without you...there is no bloodline. It would end with you. The king and queen have no other children. If you and Luca lose your lives...it's over. Tidus and Ayla will rule until they live out the rest of their lives...and there will be no more royalty. There is no one to leave the crown to without you both."

"There's no one to leave it to should we *live*." I argued. "I'll never have children, Paxe. If Luca and I could grow old together, ruling this kingdom, then I'd be wholly satisfied with that. But there will be no heir. After we're gone...the world will be left with the same option. Appoint new blood or have no sovereign."

"So, you mean to appoint me in your stead?" She asked, eyes weary.

I looked at her for countless moments before I could answer. "Not if it isn't what you want, Paxe," I whispered. My hands peeled away, and I went back to sit on the bed. She turned back to the window, arms crossed and we were both quiet for what seemed like an eternity.

"I asked you if that was what you wanted too. You said no," she finally said.

"I remember."

"Is that still your answer?"

I pondered that for a moment, recalling that conversation and all the others before it. I had yearned for the simplicity of life without the weight of a crown...but I hadn't yet realized how rewarding having the power to change could be.

"No." I breathed. "No, it isn't."

"Good." She smoothed her hands down her bump. "Because I feel the same." Her head turned over her shoulder and we locked eyes.

"Do you?" I asked, seeking reassurance.

"Yes."

"Even if your child is born into royalty?"

She stilled and looked back toward the city. "Imagine our world ten years from now. Imagine me as queen. Think of how different it all would be...my sitting on that throne...beside a king who was human, and a child who was both? For it to be perfectly normal. Legal...forgiven. When I think of a world like that, Arienne...it seems as if royalty is a very small price to pay. For that kind of peace and equality." She turned to face me. "So, yes. I do. And I understand your reason for feeling like making a promise you can't keep would be fruitless. So let me offer you a promise that isn't."

"Paxe..." I whispered. She knelt in front of me and squeezed my fingers.

"If this doesn't end the way we wanted it to." She paused, choking back tears. "I vow to wear that crown for you. For what you sacrificed to make that possible. And I promise you that I'll carry on that peace for all of us."

I nodded tearfully.

"I need you to promise me something in return."

"Anything."

"Promise me that whatever path you decide to take...no matter how long or short our lives may be...you choose the one that brings you joy. Choose the one that makes you happy, Arienne. That's all that I want." We both broke. "That's all I've ever wanted for you. Is that a promise you can make?"

"Yes." I closed my eyes and nodded. "I promise, Paxe."

"Could you do something for me?" She asked.

"Of course."

"Will you lie here with me for a while?"

I didn't even reply. I eased back across the bed and extended my arms, reaching for her. She curled in beside me and I held her while we faced each other, my hand coming to rest across her womb. Bumpus adjusted herself beneath my hand and although I felt my heart breaking...I smiled. Paxe's mouth turned up in the corner, another tear sliding toward her temple. We laid there silent for a long time.

"I'm scared..." I whispered against her hair.

"What frightens you?" She breathed.

"I've been trained my entire youth to fight. And these weapons, they—I know it will be easy to subdue him. It's just something I feel. I'm not afraid of the battle."

"Are you afraid of dying?" Her eyes were puffy as she raised them to meet mine.

"No." I shook my head gently. "I'm afraid of killing."

Her brows knotted.

"Paxe, I—when I was suffering...when I was in the kind of pain that could have easily made me into the monster he is...no one could help me. I know that you tried. I know Vetta tried, and if it hadn't been for the kind of love Luca gave me...that patient, indestructible kind of love that withstands that sort of darkness...I'd have never made it."

"What are you saying?" She folded her hand over mine.

"What if I can't kill him?" I wept, my words a whisper in the quiet of the room. "He's a horrible person. He deserves to die. But knowing what caused him to be this way...knowing that there was no one to pull him out of that dark place. What if I can't deliver the blow? What if the person that I've become...can't do the one thing I was entrusted to do?"

"Ari..." She scooted closer. "Whatever good that was left in him died a long time ago. You have to keep telling yourself that he's gone. He's lost. The man that could be a father to you? You never knew him. And he never existed. Remember that your mother was pregnant long after he became this...evil. He expected evil from you from the moment your heart started beating. You're nothing like him. You're pure. Good."

"Good, pure people don't murder." I sighed.

"You're not murdering him. You're *freeing* him. Arienne, his heart knows no other way. Think about it. He's baited you to end his life for a very long time. He told you on multiple occasions that he wanted you to be the one to do it. He's taken life from you; he's beaten you...he's waged war on your heart in ways that he knew would drive you to hate him enough to carry this out. He's begged you...your entire life, Ari. He's begged you to end it. And he's shown you that if you don't...he'll only continue to destroy everything. He knows that he's never earned the right to ask you for anything else."

Holy Gods...

I couldn't speak. Everything she'd just said was beyond what thoughts my head could manage and I was being swallowed by it. Years and years of memories...of torment and tears. The look in my father's eyes. The ice that left him every time I'd asked what happened to make him this way or why he hated me. She was right. It had always been there...had always been this. Perhaps that was the only love he could show me. The only kind he was capable of.

I wrapped my arms tight around her and she tucked her head beneath my chin.

"I love you," I said, stroking her hair. She didn't speak for a moment, clutching me closer.

"I love you, too. Always."

I didn't leave her until she and the babe became still. I watched her sleep and took in every detail of her beautiful face. Her golden hair, her long eyelashes. My thumb swept over the slender fingers that weaved countless braids into my hair. I thought of every time she exploded into heaving laughter, every time we shared a moment that wasn't stained with heartbreak. I thought of how much better cookies tasted when they were stolen. How swollen her knuckles were when she chipped Lydia's front tooth without an ounce of hesitation and still finished an entire bag of chocolate croissants afterward.

My sister...my best friend. A light of a different sort. The first one I was given to fight the dark.

It took every bit of my will to ease myself off the bed. I pulled off a soft blanket that was draped over an armchair and covered her with it, kissing her temple and aching all over with every step toward the door.

Then I stepped through it, softly shutting it, and cried the entire way down the dark hallway.

CHAPTER 43

FLIGHT AND FIGHT

I entered our bedchamber after purposefully taking the wrong hallways and declining assistance from guards who thought I was lost until the need to feel Luca's arms around me was suffocating. It felt wrong to be so consumed in these thoughts when he'd just found out a childhood friend had been killed by none other than my own father. I didn't know how to face him. I argued with myself the entire way back to our room, until I finally decided to face it head-on and be the wife he needed and deserved. Any words I had planned to say left me when I walked in and saw my battle leathers and all our weapons in a heap on our bed.

"Luca?" I called, getting no answer. I shut the door and paused at the bedside, running a finger across the sheath to my sword. A light breeze drifted down the hallway from the sitting room, and I turned toward it, walking slowly into the dim light and finding the glass doors to the balcony open. When I peered outside, I saw his figure...bathed in full moonlight and his hair unbound and blowing across his naked back. His hands gripped the railing, and one foot was propped against the base as he stared over the dark ocean beyond. If he'd heard me calling his name or approaching him from behind, he didn't let it show.

My fingertips brushed across the back of his shoulders and down his sides until I slid my arms around him and pressed my lips to the claw marks I'd left. He twined our left hands together and anchored me against him with his arm, loosing a long breath.

"I'm so sorry," I whispered, holding onto him and resting my cheek against his spine. He said nothing, instead tensing beneath me and holding my hand tighter.

"The moon is full enough to light the way to Valdaro," he finally said in a low, broken voice.

"Talk to me," I replied, squeezing my arms around him. He didn't. After a long pause and uncomfortable silence, I came around to stand in front of him. I had never seen his eyes so hollow...void. Grief radiated from him in waves as if he'd sent it through willingly to share how he felt without having to say anything that would rip him apart. It ripped me instead. How he had dealt with my pain this entire time, loving me the way he always had...must have been so devastating for him. I tapped into his well, taking it all into myself. It was the only thing I could think to do.

"Don't." He choked. "I have to face it myself, Ari. Let it go." He took my hands and I could feel every tendril of his magic ease back from my veins.

"Give me half." I pressed, willing it back. It was like a tug of war. He was so willing to take my burdens on himself but unwilling to let me carry any of his. "Please, Luca. I want to help you."

"Not like this," he whispered, pulling me to his chest. "You think I don't know what you're doing?" His arms settled around me and we stood close enough to share breath.

"We're equal. Your grief is my grief."

"Until you start blaming yourself for what happened." He pressed his head to mine. "This isn't your fault." My throat bobbed with every word.

"Isn't it?" I palmed his chest, blinking back tears. "The wedding was meant to be a distraction. Not a death sentence." He grew quiet.

"Do you regret it, love?"

My mouth dropped open. "Marrying you? You must have hit your head." My brows crumpled.

"Perhaps it was meant to be a distraction, but I meant every word."

"Luca..." I placed a gentle hand on his face. "You think I didn't? There was never a happier time in my entire existence than the moment I became your wife. Do you understand?" Tears lined his eyes and he slowly nodded.

"I'm sorry." His lip quivered and my heart cracked open as a tear left his eye. It crept down his cheek and I caught it with my mouth, softly kissing it away. I continued kissing my way to his lips and he let himself break, collapsing into my hold and fiercely claiming my mouth as he wept.

"I'm here, my love," I whispered into his mouth. "I'm right here." Something within us snapped. I felt it the moment he did. Our bodies reacted to it in any place of contact and it was as if our souls were pulling from our own skin to be closer to the other. We shared the same rhythm, our hearts thundering together. Warm tears continued down his face, his kiss salty...deep and perfect. I broke from it only long enough to pull the shirt over my head and bring him closer to me. The firm feel of his hands across my back, set me on fire. I wanted to give him everything. Whatever I had left. Anything to help him find home again.

We freed ourselves of everything but our own skin and he raised me up onto the railing, the lady of the moon the only witness as his body sank into mine. There was nothing but raw emotion in the way we made love on that balcony. Every touch from our hands, every breath that was shared...every single time our eyes met or our lips touched, I could feel us. A strong, steady...unbreakable thing. Neither of us were sure how long we'd made it as we sat, still joined together, on the cool stone. He leaned back against the rail and I laid against his chest, still heaving from enervation. I drew lazy circles across his skin and his hands moved up and down my spine as we lay there in silence.

"I love you," he whispered, his fingers gently stroking my hair. I raised to lean my face against his shoulder and stared up at him. "Even if it all goes to shit, Arienne...I love you. And I want you to know how grateful I am that you're in my life. How whole I feel just because you're in it. If Fleck felt even a fraction for that girl of what I feel for you...he went down a hero, as well as a damn lucky male. I'd want nothing less for him."

I softly kissed his collarbone.

"You're my everything, Luca Di Meo. I don't think I'd be here if not for you. You saved me...in every way, you saved me and I love you more than anything in this world. I vowed to love you until death...but I think I'd love you *in* it. *After* it. *Beyond* it." I reached up to brush the hair from his face as it swayed in the wind from the sea. "You're everything that is good in me."

His palm smoothed over the back of my hand and he held it to his face, turning into it and kissing the faded scar across it gently.

"Do you think our souls have a mind of their own? Their own consciousness?" His breath was warm against my hand.

"I wondered that myself, actually. Do you suppose sharing each other's blood strengthens the binding?"

"I'm not sure if it has a single thing to do with our blood anymore. I think it's you. It's me. It's what we are to each other. When we wed...you told me that we'd traded part of our souls. That one couldn't live without the other." He interlocked our fingers and brought his face down to mine. "I think you were right."

I smiled and he kissed me. Long and gentle. The ocean breeze roared past my ears and I breathed in his scent, wishing we could exist in this moment together, forever.

"Do you truly mean to sneak out of the castle tonight?" I reluctantly asked. He sighed deeply.

"Yes."

"I'm going with you," I said, both of us staring up at the moon.

"I know."

"Do you think we'll ever see them again, Luca?"

"I do." He caressed my hand against his chest. "But I made my peace with that being the last time...in case it was."

"So did I."

He pulled me closer.

"I want to sleep next to you again...before we leave," he said softly.

"Just in case?" I asked.

"Just in case."

He raised us up, holding me against him while I wrapped my legs around his hips and he walked us back into our room. We finally pulled back our new bedding and slipped into the smooth sheets. He kicked everything from the bed and it clattered to the floor as we tangled our legs together. We held each other as if we'd never let go and let the darkness take over, sleeping soundly in each other's arms. When I awoke, silver moonlight painted the lines of his face...his body. I laid there staring at him for a while, unable to move.

I thought about Paxe being in that bed alone tonight. How she must be feeling should she wake and not have Lakan beside her. Something inside me tugged and I felt as if there was too much unsaid between us.

Just in case.

The words kept splintering my mind and I quietly slipped out of bed, carefully...so as not to wake Luca. A silk white robe hung from a small hook just inside the doorway to the sitting room. I plucked it off and shrugged it around myself, padding into the breezy room and starting to pace around it. Filtering through all of these thoughts was hard enough without the weight of what had happened, but now that people were dead—dead and imprisoned—spending the night waiting for execution in the same cell I had been tortured. The same cell that Gideon bled to death. The place where a mother and her child took their last breaths. We had to go. We had no other choice.

After I ended my father...Paxe would receive that power. She'd receive that power without knowing the truth, and I wouldn't be here to explain or to apologize. The cost of keeping it from her...I deserved it. But she deserved better from me. My eyes stopped on Luca's desk. I stepped over to it, pulled out the wooden chair and sat down. His journal was tucked into the small drawer beneath and I pulled it out, tearing off a couple of blank pieces of parchment and grabbing a quill. I ended up crumpling several and starting over. When I was finally satisfied with what I had managed to say to her, I tri-folded them. I lit a candle on the desk and pulled out the sealing wax and Luca's house stamp. I opened the armoire, fetching the silver box containing my mother's pendant and the small drawstring satchel with the pearls that Luca gave me and collected them all in my hands.

I slipped out of our bedroom barefoot and tried not to acknowledge any guard I saw perched at corners or down hallways until I'd made it back to her door. I listened closely behind it before creaking it open and found her exactly where I'd left her. Truthfully, aside from her hand now cradling her belly, she hadn't moved at all. I left the items on her bedside table, tucking the letter beneath the silver box and pausing to look at her again before forcing myself back into the hall.

"Gods protect her. Protect her and protect that child. Grant me the strength to do what needs to be done to save them all." I prayed quietly, my eyes burning as I closed the door. "I love you, Paxe," I whispered against the wood.

By the time I got back to our chambers, the room was lit with every candle available and Luca stood by the window like a lion...the pride of his house, ready to strike at any threat. He wore leather of his own, expertly crafted and hugging every line of the steel body beneath. His belt was weighed down with his sword, and a twin set of old-fashioned daggers crossed around his left hip. I caught a glimpse of scarlet red in the tight knot that rested at the base of his neck and my mouth curled at the sight of him.

"You still amaze me, Prince," I said, closing the door behind me. He turned and half smiled. "Still a fine example of a male."

"Paxe?" He nodded toward the door.

"Yes. Asleep. The castle is quiet," I replied, walking toward the bed where he'd laid everything back out.

"Where the moon is positioned in the sky, we look to have about five hours or so until dawn. The ride will take at least one...nearly two." He peered back out the window to the skies.

"I feel once we arrive there, everything will move quickly. I think we can get them out before morning. End this all before the sun rises."

"Mmh," he grunted, nodding once as he turned. I dropped my robe and he watched, taking in every inch of me as if memorizing my entire body. "I know time isn't on our side tonight...but dress slowly." He sighed. "Please," I smirked and complied, allowing him to help me get into the suit, fasten the belts around my waist and tighten straps around my thigh. My hair cascaded over my shoulder as I turned to face him. "I don't know that it wouldn't snatch the breath from my lungs every single time I saw you like this." He said, studying the intricate design on the leather of my bust. "You're going to be a distraction when I see you fight," he chuckled.

"Don't make me lock you in this room," I warned, flicking his chin.

"You wouldn't."

"You need to be fully focused. You know that." I straightened his belt.

"I won't disappoint you." He smiled. I leaned in and kissed him softly.

"You couldn't even if you tried."

I fastened my weapons to myself, making doubly sure that Gideon's arrow was in my quiver, when I suddenly heard scratching coming from the bedroom door. My body sagged and my heart felt heavy. Luca went and opened it. Hissifus skittered through, hurrying to the security of my legs. He pawed up at them as if he were completely aware that we were leaving. I reached down and scooped him up, burying my face in his fluffy coat and letting him drag his nose back and forth across my cheek.

"Hissifus, you smell like dinner." I huffed, trying earnestly not to cry. "If you aren't just the most worthless...amazing—" I paused and choked on my words. "I love you, Floof," I whispered, kissing him all over and savoring his rough tongue on the tip of my nose. "You're a very good boy. Thank you for always being so good to me." He cocked his head to the side like a dog and peered into me with his mismatched eyes. I could have sworn he knew exactly what I was saying. "You can't go this time. You have to stay and take care of Paxe and Holt for me." Luca came to my side and scratched behind Hiss's ears.

"Hey, cat." He smiled sweetly. "If my mother refuses you chicken, I want you to rub some fluff on her. She'll reconsider." He walked two fingers across my arm and Hiss swatted at them. "Keep her busy while we're gone, alright?"

It took a great deal of strength to set him down on the pillows. Luca wrestled him with a hand onto his back and Hiss snuggled into the soft pillowcase, his usual position with all four legs in the air and his head thrown back, nearly looking upside down at us. I leaned over him and kissed his belly, rubbing it for good measure and slowly retreated backward. We made it to the sitting room doorway before he flipped himself over and stood at the edge of the bed, his green and blue eyes pleading.

"Stay here, Hiss." I whimpered. Luca gripped my hand in support. "I love you."

I tore my eyes away, wiping them with my other hand and we closed the sitting room door. I followed Luca down the hallway and out the balcony doors, shocked to find Varuna standing outside, waiting. Gone was the elegant dress she'd been sporting these past few days. They were replaced by iridescent armor that covered her entire body like fish scales. Her silver hair whipped around her in the wind, and her eyes glowed like a festering storm about to annihilate the world. For the first time since I'd seen her...she appeared more godlike than in her sophisticated form.

"Princess." She nodded softly. "I must admit...I prefer you this way." She looked me over proudly.

"I'd have to say the same about you," I smirked. "I wasn't expecting to see you out here."

"I summoned her. She's helping us get out of Crona unnoticed," Luca offered. "We can't exactly walk out the front door."

"Ah. I hadn't considered that."

"Are you both prepared to leave? Nero has sent word that he was successful in placing what you needed. It lies in wait at the castle," Varuna said. Luca and I looked at each other and then back into the sitting room before dipping our chins to her in reply. "He requested that I inform you...that should there be any complications, he's left something for you just outside the western wall. It will remain in your possession until the king has drawn his last breath."

The hammer.

I smiled to myself. Luca chuckled beside me, Varuna smiling at both of us.

"Very well, then. Join your hands...step forward." We did, huddling close as the goddess placed her moon-white hand on our shoulders. Soft blue light and a rush of water surrounded the three of us, and my stomach dropped as I felt solid ground disappear from beneath me. It was merely a flash of weightlessness and movement, but enough to make anyone nauseous before the swirling wave receded and the earth returned. We were transported to the shoreline where Bjourne waited, unfazed and seemingly oblivious to the impressive display of magic that delivered us to the beach.

"Where is Alice?" I asked, looking around.

"She'll be easier to spot coming, and I feel it would take less time for you both to travel on the same steed. Better to have only one creature to hide than two," Varuna said simply.

"Thank you, your Grace." Luca extended his hand. She looked down at it and then met his eyes. Her pale fingers gripped his hand and she folded her other hand over them.

"Thank *you*. Both of you. Your courage and heroism shall never be forgotten by the gods. We are with you. Be strong." She patted her palm against their joined fists once and turned toward me, offering a firm grip on my shoulder and dipping her chin. I smiled and she conceded a step, gesturing for us to mount. Luca helped me into the saddle and nestled behind me a moment later, holding me to him with one arm and taking the reins with the other. I rested my hands on the saddle horn.

"Ride like the wind, Bjourne," Luca said, clicking his tongue and tapping his heels on the horse's sides. Bjourne nickered, starting down the sandy beach and turning himself toward the tide. We rode into a gallop when he reached firmer ground. I looked over and lifted my hand to Varuna in farewell. She lowered her chin and essentially vanished into mist. We tore down the beach and Bjourne spread his midnight wings, leaping forward and carrying us into the open sky. There wasn't a cloud in sight and the moon sparkled on the water like a sea of diamonds.

We circled Crona as we ascended higher, and neither of us could speak while we watched it become smaller behind us. Luca finally turned his face forward, resting his chin on my shoulder and tugging me close. I understood everything he was putting off. I could feel him in my blood. It may have been the last time we would ever see home. I snaked an arm over his and reached up to stroke his face with my other hand, determined to bring Crona's prince back in one piece. The ride was mostly silent. Both of us were too lost in thought to say anything. After a little more than an hour, Bjourne descended to fly beneath a blanket of smoke. We'd reached the western end of the Midlands.

The charred remains of human homes were smoldering, and I couldn't let myself think about the bodies that were no doubt among the ruin. Luca stiffened behind me, urging Bjourne higher. Leighton and his lover were somewhere down below. My heart grew heavier with every forced breath of Luca's lungs. I gripped his thigh and attempted to offer him comfort, but he remained the steel male who feigned a heart of stone. Valdaro came into view shortly after and we rounded the Aegan wood, searching for a discreet place to land that would be safe for Bjourne to remain when the castle went up in explosive flame. We found a place among the rubble of the marketplace.

Buildings and vendor carts were left in shambles. Nothing seemed burned, but rather just destroyed, as if it had been the aftermath of a catastrophic storm. I ached in my chest as I surveyed it all, Luca dismounting and reaching for my hand. My eyes didn't leave the destruction when I grabbed it and let him take my waist and hurl me down.

"This pains me," I whispered, anger seething in my veins. "It was hardly anything to begin with and now..." My fingers curled into fists at my sides. A soft breeze swept through the wreckage, shuffling my wind-strewn hair across my face. Luca turned me away from it and pressed me to his body, holding the back of my head and peering down into me. His eyes gleamed like fine crystal. "We have to get them out." I shuddered.

"We will, love." I felt the twitch of magic whisper through me. "Take it. Clear your head. I'm here with you. We don't need to move forward until you're ready to fight." I let him will me to calm and fed off of it, sinking into his arms. "Better?" He purred, nuzzling my cheek with his nose.

"Better." I breathed, inclining my head to brush my lips against his. "Kiss me," I begged. My arms found their way around him. "Kiss me the way you wanted to the last time we were in this gods-forsaken place." His mouth melted into mine, breathing hard and squeezing the air from me. I imagined the two of us at the castle entrance each time we'd been interrupted and before I could register the thought, Paxe's voice sang in my mind. She wouldn't be here this time to cut in and give me a shameful look. Vetta wouldn't be here to mend any wounds. We were on our own. My prince and I, against the world. Against the evil that consumed it. The last time I'd kissed a man in this marketplace, we'd been beaten half to death afterward. The last time I'd been in this forest, I'd told Luca the staggering truth about my past.

So...the last time that I stood in this place that haunted me with nightmares and rage...with the deepest heartache and the ever-present smell of blood...it would be with the one I loved. The one who gave me life. It would be a memory that wouldn't cause me to shudder in fear. It would be this kiss—this kiss that we finally had in this disaster that I used to call home.

"Thank you," he choked, his breath ragged as he held me there.

"For what?" I asked, leaning my head against his.

"If you only knew how many times I'd thought about that kiss since I first saw you...I—"

"Me too." I huffed. The silence of the ruined marketplace felt cold around us, and the area seemed to darken. We stilled and didn't take our eyes off one another.

"I think it's time to go." Luca trembled, his firm grip slowly easing.

"Together." We stared into each other's eyes and he nodded softly, taking my hand and leading me down the southern wall toward the brooding castle. Clouds began to gather, shrouding the moon as we silently crept down the pathway. We reached the entrance and hid behind the stone wall, Luca counting the guards on the east wing while I scoped left.

"Three on the east," he whispered, searching for Nero's cuffs. "Unfriendly."

"There are only two on my side. I don't see cuffs on either of them. Do we shoot?" I knelt in the tall grass against the wall.

"Save as many arrows as you can to set off the Knightsfire. We're going to have to sneak up on them. If we shoot one, they'll spook and everybody will know we're here." He crouched over, moving himself further away from me and picking a large stone from the ground. My heart slammed against my ribs with every step he took and a different sort of stampede began to roll my stomach. When he finally reached the far corner, he turned toward me and signaled for me to make my move when he tossed the stone over the wall. I nodded once and readied my dagger. The rock thudded against the ground and the guards threw their attention toward it.

I nearly laughed at how pointless it seemed to have so many thickheaded idiots under my father's employ as I watched every last one of them leave their post to investigate the noise.

They're making this far too easy. What if this is a trap?

I didn't have time to consider it. Luca's steps were feather-light as he jumped the wall and snuck up behind them. I sprinted stealthily past the entryway, cornering the rest. None of them even had a chance to squeal on us. I moved, bouncing up from behind one guard and making quick work of slashing his throat before jabbing the dagger through the neck of the one next to him. Blood sprayed as Luca's blades sang, crossing over each other and tearing through flesh, stealing the life essence from the others. Within seconds, we were stepping over bodies and running toward the gated entrance that was wide open. We stayed close and eyed every possible vantage point of attack.

"Something feels wrong, Luca," I whispered.

"Too simple?" I nodded in reply and he checked the right side. "I thought the same thing. Stay alert. Be ready for anything."

A glint of armor shone, catching my eye as a lone guard peered from the castle entrance. I reacted quickly, nocking an arrow in my bow and lowering myself next to Luca against the iron gate. I took aim, and Luca put a steadying hand at my back. The guard called like a bird and raised an arm to reveal a cuff.

"Friendly." I huffed out as the male inched further out into the moonlight. I recognized him then. "It's Mischa." I lowered my bow, quivering the arrow and we raised from our spot to show ourselves. I made to step forward and Luca stopped me with an arm.

"Wait." He snapped. "If we walk out there and this is a trap...we're fish in a barrel." My body stiffened and Mischa waited, his eyes drawn in confusion and nerves. Luca waved an arm for him to come to us instead.

"Nero told us only to trust those wearing the cuffs. Shouldn't we have a bit more faith in him?" I asked quietly.

"I have faith in him, but he's immortal and also not present. If he steps out into the open to come to us and nothing happens, then we move."

"That's fair." I nodded, gesturing Mischa toward me. He looked around for a split second and started walking to the gate. Once he'd reached the center of the dusty courtyard, Luca tapped two fingers on my back and we made our move. Mischa bowed slightly with a fist to his chest as we approached.

"Princess," he whispered. "It's good to see you. Congratulations to the two of you. I'm sorry to have missed that."

"Thank you." I smiled.

"We should stick to the shadows as often as possible. Lord Nero left everything you need, and there's a huge hammer hidden against that wall over there. He said to make sure that you see that first," he said, pointing to the darkness along the wall to the entrance. We tread light-footed into the security of night and leaned against the wall, checking all angles. Nero's hammer, indeed, sat against the dirt. "Once you're inside, you'll need to move fast. I'm sure you've been briefed on your roles, but if you feel like I do..." He shook out his hands and flexed his fingers.

"Nervous?" Luca asked.

"Nervous...excited...a little scared? I'm not really sure." Mischa's eyes fluttered and his voice was laced with adrenaline. I laid a hand on his shoulder.

"Mischa...we'll get through this tonight. Tomorrow, I'm hoping to make your life as a royal guard the most boring thing possible." He calmed and looked at me, gripping my forearm and smirking as he nodded his head.

"Paxe?" He whispered.

"Safe."

It was hard to imagine being infatuated or longing for someone who was very much alive and knowing you'd likely never be with them the way you wished you could. But I found it so admirable and the male beneath the royal armor that reeked of this place began to shine through in Mischa. It built a trust that I knew we needed walking into what Paxe once referred to as the dragon's mouth.

"I'm going in first," Mischa began, jerking his head toward the entrance. "I'll signal you the all-clear, then you'll need to split up. Prince Luca, head right. Keep right until you reach the library and take the stairs up to the attendant's dormitories. Evacuate them from the service entrance. They'll let you know where. There are four urns of Knightsfire at that door. Once they're out, take the urns back upstairs and start laying it on thick. Leave two to blow the east wing. A half hour. That's all we're going to have, so keep up with your time." He turned his attention back to me. "Princess, you know the way to your chambers. You know the castle better than anyone. Head there and do the same. Your urns are in your room by the fireplace. Again, leave two. When you're done, be quick and meet me at the gate to the dungeons, where I let you in to see Paxe. My father should be there to help us free the prisoners and we'll take care of the back wall at the end of the hallway."

"And then?" I asked.

"I'll make sure they get a safe distance from the castle. You'll head back up to the main floor, and hopefully, we'll all time this just right. Blow it. After that..."

"The king," Luca finished. Mischa nodded once.

"The king's chambers are above the Great Hall. He's there. He's been there all day and hasn't come out even to eat. The castle has been frigid since he brought the humans to the dungeons. You know how he gets."

"I do." My eyes were distant and I stared at Nero's hammer.

"Everyone ready?" Mischa asked. Luca and I exchanged looks. I stood, picking up the hammer and the young guard's eyes went wide with awe. I twirled the massive tool in my wrist as if it were no more than a simple blade.

"Amazing, isn't she?" Luca grinned, nudging Mischa and preparing his weapons.

"Gods above."

"Let's go," I said, stalking from the shadows and moving with purpose toward the entrance. The two males shuffled behind me, catching up and matching my pace. Mischa entered first and we stood on either side of the entrance, awaiting his signal. It took several moments and my heart thrummed with every passing second. This was it. No turning back now. Mischa finally reappeared, beckoning us inside and I swallowed hard. My throat was dry and my face tingled. Luca pulled me to him in the middle of the threshold, holding my waist.

"I love you," he breathed, nearly gasping with nerves.

"I love *you*." I kissed him deeply and we tore apart, Luca quickly heading right while I hung left. We looked back over our shoulders only once before disappearing into the cover of darkness.

CHAPTER 44

RETRIBUTION

The sconces on the walls leading up the stairwell and on the second floor were unlit. They looked as if they hadn't been used since I'd been gone...and why would they? No one had occupied this level for months now. It was eerie and ghost-like.

Cold.

Haunted.

A chill crept down my spine as I coiled my fingers around the handle to the door, the bedroom I'd had my entire life just on the other side. What was once so familiar now felt so foreign and uninviting. A half hour. That's when Luca's side of the castle would go up in flames. I didn't have time to be sentimental. I pushed the handle down and the door silently opened, tendrils of dusty moonlight illuminating the dark room. The bed was unmade, ruffled and littered with different items I had decided not to take when we fled the castle for Aeon. I leaned Nero's hammer against the door jamb and stepped inside.

Four urns of Knightsfire sat near the hearth by my bedside and I felt like a thief lurking in wait as I slowly walked towards them. The comfort of being in my own space was completely absent. I grabbed two of them and remembered to handle them carefully, per Nero's warnings about how dangerous they were to transport. I hoped like hell that Luca had remembered it too. A single leather glove laid on the corner of my bedside table and I slipped it on, setting the urns on the table surface and twisting the lid from one of them. I winced at the strong, sulfuric smell of its contents and dipped my gloved hand into the clay jar. It was thick and heavy.

I smeared a trail across the floor and out the bedroom door, going back and securing the urn in the crook of my arm while I continued to run the putty down the wall like a fuse. It wasn't until I found myself halfway down the stairwell that I realized what I was doing. My finger trailed through familiar cracks in the stone, a habit I'd had since I was a child...the thick paste being left behind everywhere I touched.

Shit...I'd been unwittingly preparing for this moment my entire life.

The shock of every recollection of my finger making this journey down these steps hit me like a fist to the gut. I gathered myself and continued on, reaching every so often into the jar and slapping more generous amounts of the Knightsfire into the walls. I had nearly made it to the lowest landing of the stairwell before I ran out. I set the urn down and traveled back up, grabbing the next urn from the table and picking up where I'd left off. Once I reached the hallway that led to the Great Hall, I clutched the urn in one arm and kept a steady hand on the pommel of my sword with the other, searching around the quiet space for any threat.

Silence…only deafening silence.

Something curdled in the pit of my stomach and I hurried along the expanse of the wall until my finger stopped on the mortar that jutted out between the stones. The little accidental figure of a cat that reminded me of Hissifus every time I saw it. I tried to ignore the ache in my chest as I lathered the Knightsfire around it. A clink of armor sounded from behind me, followed by the drawing of a sword. I stopped dead.

"Turn around," a male voice, strained with the promise of death said. "Drop whatever it is in your hand and turn around slowly."

I squeezed my eyes shut for a moment, lowering the urn to the floor and peeling the glove off my hand. I heard the male adjust his stance as I rose and slowly turned to face him. His mouth parted and he bent his knees in a defensive position, his sword poised and ready to strike.

"Princess Arienne?" He croaked, his brows knotting.

"Yes," I whispered. I slowly pulled my sword from its sheath.

"I'm ordered to kill you on sight." He swallowed, throat bobbing as he stared at me.

"You can try." My mouth took a wicked curl upward.

The guard looked at me as if he'd never seen me before. I recognized him. He'd been in my father's service for years, although I never learned his name. He was also in the Great Hall the day that Luca and his parents met me. I distinctly remembered checking him with my shoulder when I'd stormed out. He seemed like an honorable male—but—I didn't see a cuff on his wrist.

"Why did you come back to this place?" He asked, almost sounding as if it were an apology. "You were out. You escaped. What are you doing here?"

"Others weren't as fortunate," I said, bringing my sword in front of me and taking its hilt in both hands. "I'm not leaving them here."

"You can't stop him." He shook his head. I glanced toward the castle entrance, remembering that the clock was ticking and I had little time for this.

"You can either watch me, or you can die here. I'm on a bit of a tight schedule. The choice is yours, but make it now," I warned, repositioning myself.

"I've served your house and its king for many years, Princess. I took an oath." His sword shook.

"You can serve me, or you can die for *him*. Which do you choose?" I repeated, cocking my head to the side. He paused for a moment, considering. I thought about what Nero had said about trusting *only* those with the metal cuffs and decided against being lenient. It wasn't worth the risk. "Time's up," I said, rushing toward him and spinning into an attack. Metal sang against metal as our swords clashed, his strength surprisingly brawny. He was skilled, but not as fast. He thrust forward and I dodged, using that split second to swing my blade. It clanged against his again and again. We danced through battle until he seemed to begin to tire, and a small part of me dreaded taking his life. But I saw my opportunity as his heel met the wall and the sweat on his brow glistened in the light from the sconce above him when he realized I'd backed him into it and there was no other way to go.

I turned my blade across him and he blocked it, blood seeping from his hand as the metal bit into his bare fingers. Our swords crossed between us and I pushed with everything I had. His teeth clenched and an exhausted growl escaped him as he fought back. He was much older than me, and his eyes revealed that he knew this was over. I forced my knee up into his groin, his arms going limp from the impact and his sword dropping between us as I brought mine back and swiped...his head rolling clean off his shoulders. The crumpled look of defeat was still etched across his face as it looked lifelessly at me from the floor. I closed my eyes, chest heaving, and turned away.

Furious.

I was furious.

Why would anyone fight for him anymore? Why give it a second thought? You could have lived, you helpless fool.

I wiped my nose with the back of my wrist and shook my head. There could be more like him. I had to move. I ran back down the hallway and hurled myself up the stairwell, sheathing my sword and grabbing the hammer from the bedroom doorway before racing back down and scaling the darkness of the walls that led down into the dungeons. The sound of fighting rang in my ears as it echoed down the damp, musty tunnel. Mischa had run into trouble. I hurried further until I caught a glimpse of shadows on the wall. Three of them. Just outside the gate at the end of a short flight of steps. Prisoners from down the hallway wailed, some of the voices belonging to children, and I thought I'd be sick.

"Mischa!" I called, racing toward the commotion. I raised the hammer and drew my dagger, my boots scraping against the stone floor.

"In here!" He yelled, grunting as his weapons collided with theirs.

I rounded the corner and swung Nero's hammer into the skull of the first guard. There was little flesh left on his now unrecognizable face and he slammed into the floor. I doubted he felt anything. That would be the only mercy I'd give tonight. The second guard staggered back, gaping at his companion, his eyes growing wider as they fixed on me. I grinned, blood spatter on my face as I stalked toward him. He backed away, dropping his weapon and raising his hands. Mischa stooped to the floor to tend to someone who'd fallen in combat, though I couldn't decipher who.

"P-Please..." The guard begged.

"Did any of you answer my pleas for mercy when I was tortured down here?" I whirled the hammer and the dagger simultaneously in circles at my sides and continued to move on him, the buckles on my belt and boots clinking as I walked. "Or was my screaming not loud enough for you to hear?"

"He said he'd kill us!" He cried. I didn't even recognize my own voice when I replied.

"Now, I get to." I slammed the hammer into his side and he screamed in agony as his body was pinned against the bars of one of the cells that was filled to its brim with humans. They piled up, standing as far back as they could manage as I rammed my dagger into his open mouth. It jutted through the back of his skull, and the gurgling sounds of his choking filled the silence while every soul trapped within these walls stood dumbfounded and shocked. I retracted my blade and released his meaty body. It slumped against the cell door and the pleading faces of my father's victims met mine.

"The key!" One woman said hoarsely. "Get the key!"

I snapped my head toward Mischa and hurried back to him, soon realizing that the male that laid before him was Byron...his father.

Fuck.

"He took a slice to the gut," Mischa said as I approached them, his voice wild with worry and emotion. I knelt down and met Byron's eyes. He smirked at me, his face paling and his breathing labored.

"You look like a bloodthirsty savage, kid," he groaned, clutching the wound on his belly. "There's more outside. Remember everything I taught you."

"Let me see," I whispered, folding my hand over his. I moved it away and it may as well have been as bad as Maureen's when my father had practically killed her. I closed my eyes and bowed my head.

"It's over, Princess. Move me over there and leave me," Byron gasped, jerking his head toward the stairs.

"Father!" Mischa wept.

"Stop your sniveling, boy. You're gonna be alright. She needs you to help get them out. We've still got work to do. Take this." He raised a large skeleton key into the air and I took it, nodding respectively. "You're running out of time and goodbyes are too hard. Move me and get out of here. Blow this place to hell. Do it now."

I grabbed beneath Byron's arms while Mischa took his legs and we laid him against the steps by the gate. He groaned in pain but smiled with bloody teeth at his son as he placed a hand on Mischa's face. I let them have a moment alone and sprinted down the hall, unlocking one door after another and directing everyone to the way I'd come from.

"Don't panic! Everybody remain calm. I need all of you to focus. Any child small enough to carry, hold them. Work together, make two lines and clear as much space in the hall as you can. Let's move!" I ordered, continuing to free the locks from each door. Once they were out, they fell into line and backed over to one side. I checked the cells for anyone left behind before quickly making my way past the trembling humans. A rogue arm reached for me when I was halfway through and I turned to meet Perla's face. She was scratched up and dirty, but mostly unscathed.

"Perla!" I exhaled in relief, forcibly pulling her into an embrace. "Thank the gods." I leaned back and she wiped a tear from her face. "Your mother?" I asked, bracing her shoulders. She slowly shook her head and her lip wobbled. My face hardened and I could feel the molten stabbing of my anger beginning to boil beneath my skin. Before I could say another word, the ground quaked and the walls shook. A deafening explosion sounded, nearly causing my ears to bleed and bits of dust and stone fell from the ceilings. Shouts and cries from the women and children echoed with the passing of the thunderous aftermath and it was then that I realized Luca had blown the east wing.

"Princess!" Mischa yelled from the end of the hall. I jolted backward, releasing Perla and raced to him. I was out of time. "The wall!" He pointed.

"Get back!" I thrust my hand to the side, still running and everyone pulled away as Nero's hammer flew from my hand and obliterated the wall beyond me. Two guards on the other side were hit and unmoving, the rest skittered across the ground. Some wore cuffs, others didn't. Mischa took one last look at Byron, who cursed loudly and screamed at him to go. The heartbroken son motioned for the long hall of refugees to follow him and we all tore out of the castle. "Get them as far away as you can! I've got this!" I called when Mischa shot me a pleading glance. He nodded once and stood defensively beside the line of pouring humans that fled alongside the western wall.

The guards were brawling with each other. Between the darkness in the stable yard, the matching uniforms, and the chaos that ensued as weapons clanged everywhere, it was difficult to determine where to strike. That was until I was kicked from behind and thrown to the ground. I rolled onto my back, drawing my sword in just enough time to block the plunge of a spear into my chest. The guard's eyes were wild with bloodlust as he bore down against me, his body lowering with his weight as he tried forcing my own blade to my throat. I wrestled and kicked, hardly stirring a ripple in his assault. My heart raced.

No. Not yet.

The pristine edge of my sword nipped at the skin of my neck, a trickle of blood sliding down toward my shoulder as I willed more adrenaline into my arms. It was enough to push it back a little farther. He looked as if he were about to spit some filthy insult at me, but those thoughts were cut short as Luca's daggers ripped his neck apart from behind, nearly severing his entire head. I heaved in gaping breaths, kicking the body off me and springing to my feet. Luca grabbed me, his fingers roughly caressing my cheek as he checked me over for injury.

"Are you alright?" He panted, his hair disheveled and strands of it sticking to his face and neck with blood and sweat.

"I'm fine, it's just a scratch," I said, my voice breathy and strangled. "I have to ignite the west wing." He nodded and kissed me hard.

"Go. I'll help them," he said, releasing me and rushing into the ongoing battle. He moved like he'd been a soldier all his life. Fearless...savage. Heroic.

I leapt back through the hole in the wall, pausing to thank Byron. He sat lifeless, his empty stare fixed on the stone wall across from him. I cursed and stepped over him, running as fast as my tired legs could carry me. I smelled smoke up ahead and prepared myself for the onslaught of heat and flame as I hurtled through the tunnel and into the main level of the castle. It was a sight I could never have imagined. A wall of fire and rubble raged where half a castle used to be. The stairs to my father's chambers were still intact and made for a perfect cover for me to blow the rest. I headed for them, reaching for one of my arrows and dipping the head into the urn I'd left by the wall. I held it out to the flames and it hissed when it caught. I ducked into the stairwell and drew back my bow, aimed for the tiny sculpture of Hissifus and—

Ping...swish...boom.

A perfect line of bright flame raced down the hall and up the stairwell. I crouched against the wall, covering my head with my arms as my bedchamber and everything around it exploded. If my father was anywhere but his chambers up ahead, he was no doubt dead already. I dared a peek beyond the Great Hall and if I could have guessed what hell looked like...that was it. Clouds of smoke, dust, embers and fiery hunks of stone were falling and crashing everywhere. My eyes stung and I coughed uncontrollably, forcing my way up, up, up. I made it to the first landing, turning left and climbing the next flight. Then, the second. When I had finally made it to the third, I halted at the massive oak doors in front of me. Beyond these doors was the man who'd ruined my life. The man who slaughtered so many. The evil that was in the world. The darkness that had to be banished from it. Beyond these doors was the ending to someone's story.

The ending to a prophecy that had been the purpose of my existence.

...Now I had to find out which one of us would live...

CHAPTER 45

LONG LIVE THE KING

The roar of my former home falling to ruin was all around me. It drowned out the sound of the fleshy muscle hammering like a drum inside my chest...my chest that was rising and falling in anticipation and panic, godsdamn revenge and pain. Paxe's words echoed through my head, reminding me that the king imprisoned by the darkness of begrudging hate and a broken heart waited on the other side of these doors...and he was ready for this. But was I? I remembered the way he looked that day in the Great Hall. The way that the room chilled and the color of his eyes when he looked at me. How they darkened a bit when he realized how much I favored my mother.

My mother...

The woman who never loved him. The woman who never meant to cause him to be this...*thing.* I remembered all the moments sitting at the end of that long table and thinking about how much I wanted to watch him die. How I would enjoy every second of it. But that was before I knew the truth. Before I'd learned how it all came to pass. Before I found out that Paxe shared our blood...and he had no idea. With everything that's happened and the woman I'd become...the only truth that remained now was that the sands of time had run out. Come dawn...one of us would be dead. There were no longer any seconds left to think about the past, or to linger at these doors, wondering if either of us could have done something different. It all had come down to this moment. I had a job to do. A prophecy to fulfill. And I had all the working parts to finish this.

Be her. Die for it, if you have to. Don't let him take anything else from you. End him.

End him...I had promised.

"You don't understand now. But you will. Promise me that you'll give him a chance. If you don't do it for yourself, then do it for me. Do it for our people. Deliver us...promise me."

Gideon...I'd promised him too.

"Come all ye who seek the light, to vanquish evil within the night. For as it dwells inside of me, so shall it burn inside of thee..."

Mother...she is with me. They're all with me.

I pulled Gideon's arrow from my quiver and nocked it, taking a deep breath and pulling back the string. Without another distracting thought, I put every bleeding memory into the strength I willed into my leg and kicked open the right door to his chambers. The room was dimly lit, but the bright glow from the raging fire outside his windows allowed me to see plenty. It was a mess. There were pages of ancient books strewn everywhere, broken glass and busted heirlooms littering the floor. Paintings were ripped open, hanging crooked from the clawed remains of the stone walls—but—no sign of my father in the vast expanse of the chamber.

This chamber was more of an enormous foyer or sitting area. A door on either side near the back would reveal where he slept and bathed. They were both closed, one of them—his bedchamber door—looked nearly ready to fall from its hinges. I tried not to think too long about how long it had looked this way. Had he been throwing tantrums the entire time I'd been gone? When I'd sent back a promise of his demise with the body of the guard I killed in Aeon? Or when I ripped the head from the creature he embodied when he attacked us in Bolton? Perhaps all this destruction had happened when Luca and I found a way to sever the bond of that damned curse...

Not the time...focus. End it.

I took slow, calculated steps. My eyes searched every shadow in the room. It was so eerily quiet, save for the sounds of our castle continuing to burn around us. My sword felt heavy on my hip and too far from my hand as I held the string of my bow with vigor.

"My beautiful daughter...come home to have her way with me at last?" My father's disembodied voice filled the space. I looked everywhere, pointing my arrow wherever the sound bounced from every wall. My arms trembled and I blew a calming breath through my lips.

"This isn't my home." I breathed, continuing to aim around as I crept farther into the room.

"I always knew you'd say those words one day. When it came time to finally prove yourself," he drawled.

"I've nothing to prove to you." I spat.

"I thought you'd bring an army of vermin with you...raising their torches and pitchforks like the peasants they are. What is it that you wish to save, daughter?" I turned on my heel, aiming for the voice that now sounded as if it were to my left. Another deep breath in...and out.

"Perhaps I did have something to prove. I never needed an army to bring Valdaro to its knees." My voice strengthened, adding an edge of arrogance to my tone and trying to coax him out. A sinister laugh...to my right. I snapped toward it, aiming.

"Kingdoms can be rebuilt, Arienne Genovese. But you can't bring the dead back to life. How does it feel to have failed them all?"

"Di Meo...my name is Arienne Di Meo."

A chuckle. Straight ahead. I aimed.

"Right. Your clever prince. I suppose congratulations are in order. Do his hands feel as good as the ones I chopped off that young beau of yours in the dungeon?"

"Come out, bastard," I growled between clenched teeth. The evil that laced his breathy laugh made my spine curl. It sounded as if it were coming from everywhere at once and I frantically followed it with the tip of my arrow...until—

A quick flash of light caught my eye in the center of the room. I poised, aiming straight for it and my brows raised. Gideon's form stood. A specter of the brave human boy I used to love, smiling and holding his fingers in a circle over his chest...the way he used to do in the woods. A bullseye on a target. He nodded once. I exhaled, letting go of the string and listening to the whip of his arrow slicing through dead air...finding its mark into flesh. Gideon disappeared, my father's figure replacing him as he looked down at the red hawk feathers glowing green in his abdomen. The ethereal light of magic infused within the cedar twig seeped into his body, the visible parts of him sputtering in and out of view as he tried to fight off the effects of the god's power. It was clear to me...the moment that he realized what I'd hit him with. What was happening to him. He raised his cold, amber eyes to me slowly.

"I see," he seethed, gripping the shaft and grunting in pain as he forcefully ripped it from his body. He held the arrow out, the bloody weapon transforming into a delicate rose in his hand. Handsome...peach colored. Like the one he'd held in my room in Bolton. I watched it catch fire in his hand, limited to ashes within seconds and crumbling to the messy floor. My stomach churned and bile threatened to leave my throat at the notion that as powerful as my father was...it was going to take much more than Gideon's arrow to stifle it. All three weapons. Although these chambers were blanketed by fire and smoke, bitter cold began to surround me. It bit at my skin and the darkness within my sire began to fester. He drew his sword, holding it in front of him. Blood trickled in a wide rivulet down his middle, the stain blooming across his tan shirt.

I tossed my bow to the side and it clattered on the stone floor. My father smirked, lowering himself into position. I put a hand on the pommel of my sword.

"Don't tell me you're scared now. Take it out. I'm eager to see that I've done at least one thing right where you're concerned." His eyes lit up with excitement.

"Don't flatter yourself, Father." I started, unsheathing my weapon and gripping its hilt before me. "You never did a damn thing right."

His eyes flickered and he glanced at the blade. At the glowing runes that ached to spill his blood. "Isn't that pretty." His lips curled into a vicious smile. "I suppose the question is...can you use it?"

"Why don't you finally shut that mouth and come find out?" I smiled back, hatred and bloodlust boiling.

"As you wish, *queen.*"

He rushed forward, eyes like a demon on fire and I sprinted toward him. Our swords met and sparks flew from them, the sound a metallic screech that rang in my ears. He deflected, turning to his side and I parried, distributing my weight and sweeping across from my left. He blocked and I spun, dodging his next blow and striking his blade again with my own.

"Not bad, Princess," He grunted. "I should have trained with you." His breathing was beginning to quicken with exertion and I wondered when he'd last had a fair fight without magic.

"You should have done a lot of things," I growled, sparring and concentrating on my form and precision. "But I know now...I was never more than a card to play in your games." I struck, his arm turning and guarding me off again. He pushed hard with his blade and I stumbled back, falling into a more defensive stance and meeting his eyes as we began circling each other.

"You know nothing. Always whining about what you've been through, but never learning how to be above it," he huffed, wiping the sweat from his brow with a sleeve. I barked a laugh.

"Oh, I know *everything.*" I purred, turning my feet and carefully continuing our circular path through the clutter on the floor. "And you're one to talk about learning or being above *shit.*"

He quirked a brow and cocked his head. "Oh? Do tell me."

"I've always asked what happened to you. I begged you to tell me the reason why you hated me." I watched the smugness in his face turn to dark bitterness. "Still want me to tell you? Or is seeing the woman you *long to forget* in my adult face enough?"

"*Fuck you,*" he growled, charging for me again. Frost sparkled over broken glass and stone as our boots scuffed across the floor. The clanging of our swords grew more hurried...louder. His brute strength seemed more intense. The king was angry.

Tire him out...take your time.

"Why couldn't you have moved on?" I spat, lunging forward while he dodged. "You could have been happy with someone else. You had the power. You had the ability to enforce any rule you wanted." The edge of his blade screeched across mine, scraping in a circular motion until we pushed off from each other again. "Instead, you chose to force her to have me. Then you chose to hate *me* instead. Tell me why!" I howled, bringing my sword down across him. He blocked with his sword in one arm, his other hand clutching at his stomach. His shirt began to stick to his skin with his steady loss of blood and he peeled it away before returning his hand to his hilt.

"I gave your whore mother *everything!*" He said through his teeth. "I gave her my castle...my crown..." Our swords clashed. "You say you were only a card to play in my game...she played *me!*" He swung again, and I met it, breathing through all the exercises Byron had taught me and letting him do what he did best...talk. "She chose a lowly human stable boy with nothing to offer her except his filthy *cock!*" The last word was labored in a hard thrust toward my face. I dodged the blade, but not his fist. My head rocked to the side behind the force of his knuckles against my mouth. I hurled myself back, clearing mere inches away from the swipe of his sword. He breathed heavily, his arms shaking as he jerked his head to beckon me back to him. "Shake it off, Arienne. You're better than her," he panted. "Come on."

"You murdered her!" I wailed, kicking up half of a broken vase toward him and spinning into another blow. He turned, dodging the glass and weakly stopping my blade from taking his head. I threw my knee into his injured stomach and he flinched in a guttural growl. I slammed my pommel into his temple and kicked the sword from his hand. He raised it toward me, gripping his wound, now heavily bleeding, with the other. I felt a phantom set of fingers wrap around my throat and they squeezed until I began to choke. They seemed to react to the way he was now clenching his own outstretched fist. He raised it higher and my feet began to lift from the floor. I gripped my sword and sliced across his side, the ancient symbols humming against my blade and Nero's fiery light was sucked into his gaping wound. My father cried out, his magic growing weaker, and I hit the ground.

"She knew," he admitted through ragged breaths. Sweat dripped down his face, marrying the trickle of blood from his temple. "She knew about it." I stood, spitting blood from my mouth and holding my sword steady while he looked up at me. "She had known the entire time that I was using her little confidante to kill her. She never tried to stop it. I didn't give a shit about what happened to her anymore. I wanted *you*. I wanted to train you up to be something the gods couldn't knock down...but you..." He heaved exhausted breaths and shook his head. "You were just like her. You sang...when you were little. You sang and it sounded just like her voice. You got older and you looked and walked...even *sat* like her. And then when I caught you in the marketplace with that fucking boy," he trembled with rage and disgust. "You knew too. You knew what I'd do. Neither one of you cared." He straightened, his shirt now torn open and almost fully crimson with blood. "But both of you spent your whole lives crying over what you forced me to do."

I shook with anger. "You fucking bastard," I shuddered. My moment of weakness cost me. He kicked the sword from my hands and charged at me, both hands around my neck and we fell to the floor. He strained on top of me, his blood and sweat dripping into my face while I fought for air.

Think stupid! You trained for this! Fight back!

My thumbs hooked into his eyes and he growled as I clawed at them until he couldn't stand it anymore. He drew back and I hooked him as hard as I could in the jaw. I gasped for precious oxygen, squirming to relieve myself of his weight and he backhanded me with a sound *thwack* across my face.

Keep him talking. Get that damn sword.

"Did you know you have a grandchild?" I groaned, my face throbbing. He leaned over me, pausing and looking into my eyes. He fought to keep me pinned when I tried wriggling away—his face was arguably stricken with something like pride.

"Lies," he grunted, steeling his posture.

"I'd never lie about something like that." I spat...quite literally. Bloody saliva hung from his cheek and he eased off of me, wiping it away and making to stand. I stayed low to the floor, using the time that it took him to steady himself to slide nearer to my sword. I noticed his breathing had become more shallow, his strength giving out. I feigned exhaustion and wobbled onto my legs, making sure to inch closer to my weapon.

"How long have you..." He stared at my belly and I looked down at it, my next words carefully considered.

"Did you know...that the night you killed Gideon. The night that you let those demons into my cell...you stole something from me that I could never get back?" I breathed, wiping my bloody nose on my wrist. He said nothing and I raised my face back to his. "Did you know that they hurt me so badly that I could never bear children of my own?" My lip quivered and my eyes burned.

"You just said—"

"I know what I said!" I screamed. "If that had never happened...if I were pregnant. Would it make any difference to you?" I sidestepped. "Or would you slaughter my baby...your own blood, the way you slaughtered so many others?"

"I'd not seek to harm the heir to our throne. But as that isn't the case..."

"So...no apology? Nothing? No filthy insult about how worthless I am? Don't you even want to know about the true heir to the throne?" I countered.

"I killed those fucking imps! It was never to be as severe as it was! And you just told me there was no heir. *You lied.*"

"*No...*" I smiled. "No, I didn't." Another step closer to the sword. "And you killed something far more important. You killed my *future!*" I cried, tears fighting their way out. "You killed *Valdaro's* future when you let them hack my body apart that night, you *fucking coward.* But..." I gathered my dignity and steeled myself. "Luckily for you...for all of us...your ruthless carelessness *did* yield something greater...you have a grandchild. And you want to know the best part? She's half human."

My father's eyes were the darkest hue of gold I'd ever seen them. Even crueler than the night he had stolen life from me. "More lies. Just like your fucking mother," he coughed, spitting up blood and grasping at his side.

Just a little more.

"Did you ever wonder why my *mother*...took such close care of Isabelle?" His head jerked forward at the uttering of her name. I raised a brow. "Did you ever suspect that the baby that grew in her womb was yours? You should have. You raped and beat her enough times to impregnate her." His body began to shake with realization.

"*No...*"

"Yes," I grinned. "Paxe is your daughter. And what you heard about her relationship with Lakan Fauci was true. They both are safe and protected...and when I kill you..." I stomped my heel on the end of my pommel and my sword sprang up. A faint figure of Paxe's mother stood proudly behind my oblivious father and she nodded her head, encouraging me to strike. I caught it by the grip, charging forward and burying the point into his gut. He fell backward, grunting and wide-eyed. I fell on top of him, twisting the sword with my wrist and peered into his eyes. "When I kill you...she'll receive that power. She'll take that throne with a human as her king, and their child will carry on this bloodline," I whispered, close enough to his face that we shared breath. Blood leaked from his mouth and he strained, every vein in his neck protruding out and the magic remaining in Nero's sword diminishing his power.

"And you?" He gurgled, struggling to breathe.

"What about me..." I lowered my brows, my voice cracking and my eyes filling with tears.

"You did have something to prove..." He choked. "Did you find the love you sought?" His face was strained with death...hatred...fear...heartbreak. "Was it worth it?"

"Lie to me, Father..." I wept. "Tell me there's nothing good left inside you. Tell me there isn't one thing left to save!" My heart pounded and his eyes were sorrowful. I couldn't stop the tears as they tore from my own.

"Finish it," he croaked, his face beginning to pale and his stare hardening. "Grow a fucking backbone and finish it." My face crumpled and I reached a hand to my thigh, pulling my mother's dagger from it. I sniffled and my chest ached. His hands dropped to his sides, his chest rising and falling in short breaths. My mother's immortal face appeared behind his shoulder. Her blurry eyes were pleading, urging me to finally end it.

"Ari!" A voice cried from the open doorway. I shot my attention toward it and found Luca, his eyes widened and hurling himself through the door. "Ari, watch out!"

I looked down to see my father's fingers, coiling around a large knife he'd hidden at his waist. I thrust myself backward and the bastard smiled...*smiled at me*...as he threw it with all his remaining strength toward the love of my life. I watched in horror as it flew through the air, Luca running too fast to see it coming for him...and it landed with a sickening sound...embedding itself between two of his ribs. A bloodcurdling scream left me and Luca stopped, staggering back and looking down at the handle of the blade in the left side of his chest.

"NO!!!" I screamed, looking back at my father's face, every inch of it revealing exactly why he did it. He knew what it would take to get me to make the kill. He smirked and I saw red clouding every corner of my vision. I raised the dagger in my hands, screaming so loud that my voice cracked and stabbed him in the heart. Once...twice. Over and over. Blood began warming my face and I stabbed him again. Again. It wasn't until I heard metal sing that I looked over. Luca threw the knife to the floor and drew his bloody sword, his face full of Ayla's fury as he stormed toward us. I jumped to my feet and he bent over, lifting my father's mangled body by the collar of his shirt and hacking his head off his shoulders. It rolled a good ways with the force of the blow and Luca dropped his body like a sack of grain, along with the sword in his hand.

Panic and raw adrenaline, combined with every emotion one could possibly feel at once, ripped through me. I wiped my face with my palms, slowly realizing they were covered in my father's blood. My leather sleeve did nothing to free me from it. My breathing became frantic and sobs tore up my throat. Luca's body clashed with mine and I collapsed into his arms, crying hysterically against his chest.

"Shhhh....it's over," he whispered, stroking my hair. "It's over, Ari." I gasped and looked up at him.

"The knife! You—"

"I'm fine." He hushed me with a gentle finger on my lips and redirected my chin when I tried to check his wound. He pulled a cloth from inside his lapel and wiped my face with it, kissing my forehead gently. "We have to go. Are you hurt?"

"No." I shook my head, wiping my hands and face. I glanced back down at the body on the floor.

"Don't..." He turned me away and we hurried across the room toward the doors. Luca bent down, grabbing the bow and a single arrow from the quiver and reached for the cloth in my hand. I handed it to him and he wrapped the point with it. "Let's move."

We ran out the door and down the stairs, a wall of thick smoke meeting us at the very bottom. I could barely see anything in front of us. I spied bright moonlight spearing through and knew it had to be the castle entrance...or what was left of it. Our only way out. Luca guided me through the rubble, kicking the door open to the Great Hall and igniting the end of the arrow. Eight urns sat in the middle of the room, stacked together on the hideous orange carpet.

"Run!" Luca yelled, pointing to the entrance. I darted for it, and Luca took the shot. The sheer force of the explosion nearly cracked our bones as we ran blindly out of the castle and through the courtyard. More booms continued to sound from behind us and massive chunks of debris and ash fell from the sky. There was fire everywhere we looked. "Keep going, Ari! Run!" Luca's hand gripped mine and we ran faster, dodging every burning piece of what was left of the castle as they fell and crashed around us. "Don't look back! Go!" We headed east, gasping for air and were still not far enough to be safe by the time we reached the rubble of the marketplace.

Not seeing any other option, we cut through and took the path into the woods...praying the cover of the Aegan would be enough.

CHAPTER 46

FINO ALLA MORTE

The thick brush of the treeline was overgrown since I had last seen it and was difficult to spot. We nearly tripped over it as we hurtled through and panted, coughing from exhaustion and the inhalation of smoke. It wasn't long after we'd made it to the slight curve of the path that we realized embers had stopped falling past the canopy of trees and swatches of moonlight were shining through. I heard the roaring of the waterfall close by and slowed as we finally reached the riverbank. Luca gently let go of my hand and I bent over, bracing my hands on my knees and gasping for breath.

"Are you alright, love?" He heaved, caressing my back. I tried to nod as best as I could manage, my hair tangled and flopping toward the ground with the movement.

"Yes," I panted. "Just out of shape...you?"

"Damn proud," he huffed breathlessly. "I love you, Arienne."

"I love you too, Prince." I closed my eyes and tried to level my breathing. He coughed and sounded as if he'd turned away to do it.

All I could think about was my father's face. The once proud and ruthless king...had fallen. In all the years that I'd looked upon that face, never once had I seen it seem so...defeated.

Defeated...I killed him. He was no longer in our world.

I'd driven that dagger into his chest...so many times I'd lost count. Luca took his head. And then we limited him to nothing more than ashes in that castle. No more now than the ashes he'd left behind in Aeon. As dead as all those innocent humans he'd butchered. And that meant—

Paxe...Paxe has most likely learned the truth I could never tell her.

But his face...

When he'd thought I carried a child. The flicker of...*pride*...in his eyes. I'd never seen it before. The pause he had given. The sudden change in his will. For once in this peculiar darkness of my life, I realized...there may have once been a sliver of good in him that yearned to live. But in the end...he still chose to murder that too. And he had—

Luca...he had hit Luca with that blade.

Once I'd rested my burning lungs enough to register the thought, I eased my spine straight, my eyes catching a figure across the river in the misty dark. It was watching us...eyes a faint glow and its body unnaturally large and tree-like.

Elowen...

I stepped closer to the bank and she didn't move or speak. My eyes narrowed and my hair fluttered in the humid air from the waterfall. Luca coughed again.

"Luca?" I said, turning around. He stumbled into the moonlight that illuminated the meadow in the circular grove of trees, holding his chest as his knees hit the ground. "Luca!" I cried, rushing toward him and hurtling over a rotting log. His tattooed hand covered his wound on his ribs and blood leaked from his mouth as I dropped onto the bed of violets before him and raised his chin. *"Shit!"* I panicked, steadying his face. His eyes were bleary and distant, fighting consciousness, strands of his hair blowing in and out of his face from his labored breaths.

"I'm sorry...I—I'm sorry I lied to you..." He raised his other hand to my cheek, thumbing across it and blinking slowly.

"No...no, you're alright," I sniffed, pulling him close to me. "I saw Elowen...she'll fix it." I nodded frantically, looking back across the river at the goddess who went wholly still and watched...doing nothing. "Fix him!" I begged. "Please!" My lip wobbled and my voice broke, holding him tighter as he began to lean on me with a bit more heaviness...less control.

"She can't, baby..." He breathed, turning my face toward his. He huffed a strangled cough and I moved his hair from his face. "The prophecy is fulfilled...they can't help us anymore." His eyes turned up toward the moon, its face shining bright over us. I sagged the moment realization hit me.

His visions...no. No...

I looked around at where we'd unintentionally found ourselves. It wasn't a coincidence. It didn't matter that we'd broken his curse. All this time we'd fought to find a way to sever that bargain and save his life...just because I loved him. This was his fate. He'd seen it for months. We'd thought we were safe...I never thought to ask him if he'd dreamt of it since.

"Love is a double-edged sword, youngling."

I fought back frustrated screams, squeezing my eyes shut and forcefully shaking my head.

"When that time comes...do not be distracted by anything. Do not yield to your deeply rooted feelings. Do not stray from the task you accepted. Doing so will cost you the one you love most."

I'd hesitated. This was my fault...and the cost was...the cost was—I felt like I was drowning. My chest moved, breath catching on a sob and a sharp exhale. Another...Luca's forehead leaned against mine and a deep heavy cry found its way from me, hyperventalative and desperate. I couldn't breathe.

"Hey..." He soothed, his bloody, inked hand raising to tuck my hair behind my ear. His gold wedding band glinted in the ghost of moonlight. "Do you remember...your first words to me?" A smile curled his lips as they brushed mine. I tried to smile back.

"Yes," I whispered, nodding softly. Tears tore down my face and he chuckled, wiping at them with the back of his forefinger.

"You were so pissed." He grinned. "So pissed, but that green in your eyes told me there was hope. You hadn't given up yet." His lips kissed away another rogue tear and I felt magic...faint and struggling. He was trying to ease me with whatever he had left. "You can't give up now, Ari."

"I wasn't angry with you," I admitted. "I never wanted to drag you into this."

"You didn't."

We met each other's stare.

"How can you say that?" I asked, lip quivering.

"*You are my life.* I chose this life...I chose *you.* And I'd do it all again just to be near you." I gripped his forearm and leaned into his mouth, his lips taking mine and the tang of blood dancing on my tongue.

"Promise me that whatever path you decide to take...no matter how long or short our lives may be...you choose the one that brings you joy. Choose the one that makes you happy, Arienne."

Our kiss broke when he suddenly coughed, his strength leaving him and his skin paling. His magic began to fade and his limbs weakened. I held him steady, but he felt heavier...

"Luca..." I begged, leaning with him as he sagged to the ground. Blood flew from his mouth when he coughed again, and I wiped it from his chin. "Stay...stay with me, please." I cried softly, laying him half on his back on the carpet of soft grass.

"It's gonna be alright," he whispered, his eyes flickering in the light. "I promised you I'd never leave you, Ari...and I won't. Whatever distance there is, I'll cross it." His breaths were shorter, his voice more quiet. *"Fino alla morte..."*

"Luca, please!"

"Come here." He breathed, reaching for me. I laid down next to him and he turned on his side, my head resting on his upper arm. He brushed my hair over my shoulder and pulled me closer, our legs tangling and our heads touching. "Tell my mother I'm sorry...don't let her level Crona with her fit." He forced a smile.

"Stop." I sniffled. "Don't say your goodbyes."

He tried to manage a deep breath, but choked and I raised slightly off his arm. He brought it to his chest and coughed hard, the rattle of his lungs heavy and suffocating. When he gathered himself, we rested our heads on the velvet petals and pressed closer.

"My father..." I started, holding his hands. "My father asked me if I'd found the love I'd sought." Luca stared at me, his eyelids heavy. "I once believed he was right. That perhaps there wasn't such a thing...like what we have together. Now, I can't imagine that emptiness or remember how it felt before you. *Before us.*" He swallowed, gently trailing a fingertip down my jawline. "*I love you...*so much." My face drew up and I fought back my tears, if for no other reason than to relieve him of the need to take my grief. "Luca, this world is nothing to me if you're not here. I *have* nothing without you beside me."

"You have to live," he whispered.

"I can't." I whimpered. *"I won't."*

His brows knotted and he tried earnestly to shake his head. "You promised me...in Bolton. You promised me you'd never hurt yourself."

"You still don't get it, do you?" I wept. "A few hours ago, you said that you thought I was right. Part of my soul *lives* in you. Part of you lives within *me.* One cannot live without the other, Luca. You said I hadn't given up yet...you said you didn't want me to give up now. I'm not. I'll never give up what we have...I'll never be without you."

"Arienne..." His voice shuddered with the iciness of death.

"You once told me that you wanted no part of an immortal life if I wasn't in it. You said that you'd follow me down whatever path I chose to take. You'd be my throne...my light. My wings if I needed to fly away and leave it all behind...do you remember?"

"Yes." His eyes welled with tears.

"Then be those things. If you meant it...take me with you. We're supposed to be *together* and I'm ready to die with you. We're pawns, remember?" I heaved a silent sob and his finger grazed my lip, stilling it as it trembled beneath his fingertip. "The king is down. The queen is standing...we're done. We've given this world everything, Luca...they can give us each other. You chose me..." I slipped a hand around the hilt of one of his daggers on his hip and slowly pulled it out. His breathing was weak and a tear fell from his eye into the grass as he smiled. I slid the blade between our joined palms and we gripped tighter around it. We both breathed heavily, staring through our tears and silently agreeing on our ending. The one we decided for *ourselves.* The last chapter in this story...and the beginning of a new one. "I choose you too..." I smiled tearfully against his finger. *"Fino alla morte."* I jerked the blade through our flesh and our blood merged.

"Should you find yourself left with no other way to keep your vow...search for the light. The light will guide you home."

A quick glimpse of his face and a soothing green glow was all I could see before darkness enveloped us both. The familiar feeling of being absent from my body overtook me and I stood in the silence. Something was different this time. I felt warm...peaceful. A faint heartbeat sounded around me...slow...dying.

"Ari..." Luca's voice whispered.

"I'm coming," I breathed, walking into a jog toward his voice. His heart beat again...strained...weak. "I'm coming, Luca!" I ran faster, a melody creeping its way into the corners of my mind. I hummed it...a flicker of light flashing just ahead.

"I hear you..." He said, the light burning a little brighter.

Another beat.

I sped up...drawing closer to it.

Images played across my vision, given life by the light I raced for. I saw my mother...sweaty and exhausted...the sweetest smile on her pale lips as she lay dying next to Isabelle at her bedside. Warm candlelight flickered across the sheen of perspiration on her forehead as she drew her last breath.

She saw me.

Thump-thump...

The image faded, and I hurled myself faster.

"And when I fill the dark with light...drowning the stars as they say goodnight..."

I sang, another image blurring into view. His light became my beacon...the force that brought me home. I saw Paxe and I as children, her golden hair bouncing as I gave chase through the hallway of the castle. She turned back with a toothless grin. A flash of light...and then her sapphire eyes tearing with laughter as I stood at my mirror howling at her failed attempt at applying kohl to my eyes.

I saw Ayla...Vetta. All of us snickering over wine goblets and bottles in my bath chamber. Frances...singing and dancing with us in that little shabby kitchen. I saw Holt...sleeping soundly against my chest and Luca's head resting on my hip on a tiny couch in a dim living space in the mountains. Nero. Squeezing me in the sitting room...walking me down a little blue carpet. Hiss's affectionate gaze of different hues...nuzzling my nose with his. And then there was this...male—

"They'll never understand the way...my heart will long for thee..."

Another beat...barely sounding. I could see him.

A chubby, dark-haired infant...his mouth wet with slobber, tiny flat feet slapping across pale stone and running toward a young queen in a crimson gown...her moon-white arms outstretched.

Thump-thump...

An image of a journal...of a quill scratching across parchment and Luca flicking stray hair from his brow...of my silhouette in a dimly lit window, and his breath catching as he sat in a tree. Trees...rain. His face dripping in streams of water as it hovered a breath away from mine in a storm born of malicious magic. His silver eyes reflecting firelight, begging to hold me in the woods.

Thump-thump...

A tin cup full of stew and a puny campfire. That kiss...that *night.* The moment that my heart knew he was its reason for beating...for pumping life through my body. Thick wooden beams on a ceiling above our bodies as they lay there, breathless from experiencing each other for the first time. The way I fit into his arms in the gray light of dawn. Dancing in a tavern...watching him drop to a knee. That moment I plunged a steel blade into my chest to be with him in that temple. A stolen bite of a sandwich and a playful knee to the groin.

Thump-thump...

Sailing through clouds on the back of a horse that had little business having a pair of mighty wings as they carried us home to Crona. His arms outstretched and jubilant as he proclaimed his love for me across the sky. A strap of leather.

A jar of eggs. A smile that took my breath every single time I saw it. Interlocked fingers on another side of a door. The stumble he took on the steps of an altar, where we made the vow to never be apart. A broken curse...

"I love you," he breathed.

Thump-thump...

I smiled, running faster and reaching for him. He opened his arms just as the last beat of his precious heart sounded and I leapt—*thump-thump...*

...Life...

Life was strange...beautiful. Painful and brutal...hard and unforgiving. So precious in its fragility. So easy to take for granted.

Death was simple. It was gentle and silent. Peaceful and unwavering. It took no prisoners, and it held no scales of justice. Death came for everyone. Kings...peasants. To evil, it was eternal darkness...the cost of living a life of malice. To the rest...peace. Joy...*love.*

I awoke...my cheek resting against the brush of smooth grass. My hair blew softly against my bare arm that was stretched between myself and a chest that moved steady and even beneath a crisp white shirt. The air was pleasant, and the smell of familiar blossoms filled my senses as we lay in warm sunshine. I slowly raised my eyes, looking forward to see a pair of bright gray eyes staring back at me, unscathed and brilliant with life. The back of his fingers grazed my cheekbone.

"Luca..." My palm smoothed across his face and he smiled, raising us both to sit. The silk of my sleeveless ivory gown slid across a body that didn't feel like mine. A body that was in all ways the same...but different. Stronger...godlike. Even the touch of his hand felt more intense as he took mine and we stood. He looked even more like the stunning example of a male that I always teased him about. A god in his own right. His hair shone in its deep hue of blue from the sunlight and blew gently in the light breeze that surrounded us.

"You found me," he breathed, taking my waist in one arm and raising our joined hands in the other, cradling them against his chest. "I hope you're ready to spend an eternity looking at this face." An insufferable grin.

"You wanted more time." I smiled, touching our heads together.

"I want forever."

I reached up, hooking my arms around his neck. "Then take it, Prince. As long as it includes me." His arms wrapped around me, holding me tight. "What do we do with all of it now?" I asked, brushing my lips against his.

"That's simple," He whispered against my mouth. *"I get to love you."*

I kissed him. A deep, slow...immortal thing. He lifted my bare feet from the ground and spun...effortless and graceful. We were no longer mortal beings. The feel of his soft lips against mine was enriched...the breath in my lungs felt unnecessary. We'd spend eternity this way...*together.* Gone only in the mortal realm...but very much alive in this one. The corner of my acute immortal vision caught a glimpse of a figure standing on a path leading up to a pearl-white temple. Her cinnamon hair swayed in the warm wind sweeping across the blooming plain. She smiled at us and I beamed, returning my attention to the face that was *my* forever.

He was bathed in his own light, which seemed to seep into my very soul...every fiber of the person I now was...because of *him*. He smiled at me...his eyes flickering and swirling with eternal promise. As I leaned into his kiss, that light embraced us...

...and we were home...

CHAPTER 47

-PAXE-

GODS SAVE THE QUEEN

There was nothing peaceful about the way I had fallen asleep across this bed. The way I looked my best friend in her mossy green eyes and knew...just *knew* somehow that...this was the last time I would ever see her...knew that somehow...even *knowing* that, she was keeping something dark and painful from me. And the only thing that stood between me beating it out of her, begging on my knees, or simply telling her that something in my gut felt as if I already knew that secret too...was the fact that I'd paid for my ticket to freedom with my abilities and couldn't just pilfer it from her mind. So, I gave her the only gift I had left to offer. That promise. The promise that...should I be right...I would take care of what she left behind. Protect and cherish it. Let the metamorphosis of our new world...the peaceful, just, *safe*...world that we dreamt about slowly come to be.

I'd meant every word I'd uttered to her before the changes that my body had made to accommodate the growing miracle in my womb stole the consciousness I tried earnestly to hold tight to. My heavy eyelids slowly closed and her lovely features were replaced with dreams about Lakan...nightmares really. His kiss goodbye still felt wet on my mouth, the brisk draft of the distance between his body and mine chillier with every step he'd taken out of the dining room doorway. Sleep had found me and swept me deep into its current, the pull like the tide outside this castle. As the child within me followed me to my rest, the urge to open my eyes again burned like acid...no— not an urge. My body was...igniting.

Lakan's face blurred into a white light that surrounded me everywhere I looked. Every muscle in my body felt as if they were being ripped apart and threaded together again with something...powerful...untamed. I tried to scream but found I wasn't able to breathe. My veins seemed to buzz and vibrate beneath my skin, and I could swear I heard it hum with a thousand voices as they met in the middle, where my heart thrashed in my ribs. My ribs...my *bones*. Everything felt like fire and ice, my unborn baby turning flips within my belly. I panicked, fearing for her life. A life that hadn't even truly begun yet. Were we dying? Had the king found his way into this palace to claim his revenge for my treason? The molten licking of pure fire slithered up my throat and I grasped at it, finally feeling the savory recompense of precious oxygen and snatching the deepest breath of it into my searing lungs.

My body arced off the bed and I screamed, pure white light tearing from my mouth and eyes until every bit of that gaping breath was gone and I slumped back into the mattress. The room was still—still and eerily silent, my eardrums throbbing with the rhythm of my thundering heartbeat...and a faster roaring of a tinier heart taking up the space between. My fingers clutched my wriggling belly and I nearly wept when I felt the movement of little limbs beneath. It wasn't until the agony of whatever had just happened to my body subsided into a trembling wave of strength and raw energy that I realized I was damp with sweat beneath a blanket that had been draped over a chair before I'd fallen into my slumber.

I shook, peeling it off and raising to sit...my short breaths shuddered and unsteady. As I gently eased off the edge of the bed, I noticed a letter on my bedside table...nestled beneath the silver box that I had fashioned for Ari to gift her the pendant her mother left her. Beside it was a small satchel made of crushed blue velvet with a short drawstring puckering its opening. Dazed and confused, I pinched the bridge of my nose and lowered my bare feet to the floor. It was unusually cool, and seemed more textured or...

Gods, what is happening?

I stood, padding to the mirror in the corner of my room and winced when I saw myself in it. My eyes...my eyes were near glowing. Swirling in every shade of blue and...flickering with—my head jerked behind me at footsteps that seemed too light to be close. Several sets, if I was to be correct. Was he here? The Valdarian royal guard? Crona's royal guard? I panicked, searching for anything I could use as a weapon, my little unborn fluttering in my belly. A combination of muffled voices hummed in my ears...also sounding distant and frantic. The familiar feeling of nausea churned my stomach and I held tight to my middle as I raced toward the bath chamber. I'd barely made it to the wash basin before hurling up my dinner. I wasn't sure if it was the strain of my retching or the violent consumption of whatever was now overtaking my body that caused a flicker of...*lightning* in my fingertips. I jolted back, wiping my mouth on the back of my hand and flexing my fingers wildly.

"What the f—" I whispered to myself, heaving heavy breaths. My brows drew together and I stormed back into my bedchamber, swiping the letter from the table and breaking the seal. I read one line...two...by half the page, I'd nearly lost my balance. My palm found its way to my mouth when the realization of what had happened only moments ago finally sank in. My eyes burned, and a sob tore from my throat...half from the truth that what I'd suspected was accurate, the other half from relief that...she'd done it. If I'd received the king's—*my father's* power...he was no longer alive. This war was over before it had a chance to begin. She saved us all.

Oh, gods...Oh, gods...

"Ari..." I shivered, my voice barely above a whisper, as a tear raced down my cheek. I pressed the letter to my heart and squeezed my eyes shut, raising my face to the ceiling and breathing deeply. I looked down at the table. I knew what was inside that silver box and why she'd left it. But the satchel...

I pulled it open and dug out a string of pearls fit for a queen. *"For Bumpus..."* Ari had said. My lip wobbled, and I dropped them back into the bag, tying it off and plunking it back down onto the table along with her letter. Without another thought, I ran barefoot out of my bedroom door and down the hallway with impressive speed. My legs and body felt foreign. I clutched my skirts and sped up, winding my way down halls and up flights of stairs until I reached Ari and Luca's private corridor. I'd somehow managed to avoid any servants or guards who were likely rushing for the king and queen a level above. There was an abundance of light shining beneath the door to their room and I didn't announce myself as I barreled in, calling their names and knowing damned well they weren't there. Hissifus yelped and leapt from their bed, quickly reaching my legs and pawing at me as if he had a great deal to say.

"What happened?" I asked the distressed cat, picking him up and cradling him to me. I looked around the room...the bed had, by all accounts, been slept in; although they had made it very clear at dinner that they hadn't yet. There were discarded clothes around the space, a shirt hanging over a painting on the far wall, and a bag...Ari's bag...lying empty beside the bed. I recognized it as the one she used to hide the weapons they'd acquired and traveled with. Hiss struggled from my arms and darted to the sitting room door, scratching at it and looking back toward me. I rushed for it, jerking it open and charging down the short hallway into the room where the balcony doors had been left open. When I reached the open doorway, Varuna stood gazing at the moon by the railing with her back turned toward me.

"Hello, youngling," she greeted me in a low voice. I took a careful step forward, but she didn't turn around. Her shoulders slumped and she didn't appear at all like the proud goddess she was known to be. Her silver hair danced across her back in the breeze from the sea.

"Where are they?" I demanded.

"You already know the answer to that question. Surely, you've learned the truth by now. I can feel your power. I could feel it before you even set foot near this hall." Her tone was...melancholy.

"No one would have been able to leave this castle tonight. It's heavily guarded. How did they get out?" I took another step.

"I helped them," she said simply. I turned back to face the doorway at the sound of someone entering the bedchamber. Hissifus hid beneath the small couch near the fireplace. A moment later, Tidus and Ayla stormed in wearing their nightclothes, eyes wide and breaths staggered.

"Where are my children?" Ayla panted, stalking toward us, Tidus flanking her. His bare chest rose and fell, and it seemed to me that they both knew before they'd even burst in. Varuna slowly turned to face us all. "Where?!" She asked again, growing furious.

Tidus placed a hand on her shoulder and stared at me in awe, his mouth dropping open when he'd realized—

"Let go of me!" Ayla spat, jerking from his hold.

"Ayla!" He bit back, gripping her again and meeting her eyes. "Look." He said, nodding toward me. Her face slowly turned towards mine and her mouth parted. A huff of breath escaped her and tears welled within her crystalline gaze.

"No..." She breathed, staggering backward into the king's chest. "They didn't."

"You knew?" I narrowed my eyes and crept toward them, shaking from anger.

"We did," Tidus replied quietly, making to stand in front of his queen.

"How could you not tell me?" I asked, a single tear rolling down my face.

"Because she asked us not to. She wanted to tell you herself. It was made very clear to me that it wasn't our place," Ayla offered. I paused, turning back to face Varuna, who stood silently behind me.

"How did they get there...?" I asked, meeting eyes that now looked like my own.

"Bjourne," she said, "I transported them to the beach, and they flew out from there."

"And Alice?" I pressed.

"In the stables."

I walked to Arienne's armoire, flinging it open and pulling a dark blue tunic from it. I grabbed the first pair of leggings I could find—a rich brown—and looked around for her boots.

"What are you thinking, Paxe. You can't—" Ayla started, coming from around the king and following me to the couch.

"I'm going and you're not going to stop me," I spat, not giving her another glance. "I'll find them...bring them back home."

"The baby..." She said softly.

"Well, you and I both know that I have the means to protect us both now, don't we?" I looked up at her that time as I pulled on the leggings and secured my belly beneath them. Tidus turned away and the queen bit down on her lip. I stepped out of my gown and shrugged on the tunic, tossing the dress on the floor and sitting to pull on the boots.

"I'm coming too," she said, turning toward the armoire.

"She'll make better time if you stay." Varuna cut in from the doorway. "If you want to help, I feel a better use of your authority would be to let the humans know they're safe and can go back home."

Lakan...

"My Lord—"

"I'll get him," Tidus said, nodding toward me and rushing back down the hall to the bedchamber. I hurried to the mirror and made quick work of braiding my hair before rushing past the queen and following Tidus out. Hissifus raced past us and lingered by the bed with longing and unspoken pleas filling his mismatched eyes. I paused, my chest aching as I looked down at him.

"You...should stay here, Hiss." I ground out. He cocked his head to the side and pawed forward near Ari's discarded bag. "I don't think you'll enjoy flying."

"Put him in the bag," Ayla said from behind me.

"They locked him in here for a reason," I replied.

The queen quieted for a brief moment and then laid gentle fingers on my shoulder. "It seems that reason has since changed. Take him with you." I turned slowly, looking at her in shame for the way that I'd spoken to them. She was obviously hurting and afraid, and all I could manage was my anger. "Arienne and Luca will never bear children of their own...but you will. Very soon, you'll realize, Paxe...that being separated from them is the most terrifying thing for a mother. If something—" She swallowed and blinked back tears, "...if something went terribly wrong, she'll want him with her. Take him." I stared at her for a moment and then nodded slowly, opening the flap of the canvas bag and placing him gently inside. Hissifus curled up, making himself comfortable and I shouldered the strap. Vetta appeared in the doorway of the bedchamber, looking around the room and then fixing her eyes on mine.

"Dear Gods..." She muttered, covering her mouth. She pulled off her nightcap and inched toward me warily, raising a palm toward me with trembling fingers. "You're..."

"Did you know, too?" I asked, my voice cracking. She shook her head and tears fell down her round face. Her fingers grazed my cheek and I swallowed down the lump in my throat. "I have to go to her. I have to get them home. They may be in trouble and I'm not leaving her there, Vetta."

"Get them here as fast as you can manage. If they're injured, I'll prepare a bed for them and work with Lady Bethel. Go...make haste." She nodded. I dipped my chin, looking back at Ayla as she tightened her arms around herself and then hurried out the door.

My legs didn't tire, even when I'd practically leapt down the stairs and out of the castle. I rounded the cobbled walkway to the stables and Varuna waited by Alice's stall. The enchanted horse was ready and saddled, and she nickered at the goddess as she led her out of the stable. Two guards looked on, keeping their distance and bowing their heads.

"You'll fly her west. She'll not need much direction. Try to communicate with her. The power that you've inherited can do much. You don't need to be an experienced rider," she said, handing me the reins. I secured the bag to the saddle, making sure that Hiss couldn't fall to his death and then stared at her.

"It pains me that no one has enough faith in me to tell me the truth. I've been kept in the dark about everything and now that I have this power...knowing what I am. Knowing that she's been my *sister* this entire time...it's unfair."

"She—"

"I don't care," I growled. "You know more than you're willing to tell me now, don't you?" The goddess said nothing. Her eyes grew dark, her face

sagging in shame and sorrow. I silently prayed that at least for one time tonight, I'd be wrong about something. I hauled myself up into the saddle and adjusted the reins as Varuna stepped back. I didn't deign to say another word to her and clicked my tongue, tapping my heels against Alice's sides and leading her down the long walkway to the castle gate. The muscles rippled in her strong legs as she picked up speed and tucked her wings closely. I leaned forward and gripped the saddle horn, closing my eyes and trying to get a feel for the unfamiliar power strumming in my veins. "Find them, girl," I whispered. "Take us to Valdaro."

Alice's wings nearly shimmered in the moonlight as she thrust forward and spread them out, taking us into a steady glide toward the starry heavens. My stomach flipped, or perhaps it was the little babe inside and we soared higher. I looked down at the castle and gasped at the beauty of the city below. When my eyes raised forward again, we were ascending into wisps of milky clouds. It was magnificent...liberating. Free. I ached at the thought of not being able to experience this with my sister and wanted to kick myself for not doing this while we still had time. I struggled to think of what I would do if we never had another moment together. So many thoughts eddied around my cluttered mind and I forced them out, smoothing my hand over Alice's coat. Arienne's voice spoke within my head as I recalled every word of her letter.

My dearest friend...

I must have ripped about a hundred pages from Luca's journal trying to start this letter...to try to write down everything I couldn't say. To share our secrets the way we always have and to tell you my biggest one. Only the gods know how badly I wanted to...so many times. Only they know how many times I almost did, and still couldn't find the courage to speak it for fear of what that would mean for you...for us. For Bumpus and Lakan. For the world. I never wanted to ask anything of you. When you told me that when it came time to choose my path, you wanted me to choose the one that brought me happiness...I only want the same for you. Revealing the truth may have put a damper on that happiness and I couldn't bear to be the one to do that.

But...you deserve better from me, Paxe.

You are my sister. My blood.

When I found out the truth...our past and our bond became so much clearer. Everything fell into place. Before Luca, I had never cared so deeply for someone. It was always you. I know that when I leave this letter...bad things could happen. When you finally read it...you'll already have our father's power and will have figured it out by now. I want to tell you that I'm sorry, Paxe.

I'm so sorry that I kept this from you and that I was such a coward that you had to find out the truth this way. I hope that you can find it in your heart to forgive me. Know that I love you...I love you more than anything, and for the darkest years of my life...it was you who was my light. It was you who saved me. Without you, I'd have been mere scraps for Luca when it came time for the two of us to meet.

I don't know what the future holds for us, but I want you to thrive. I want that child to grow up safe and happy with a mother and father that love her...the way that Tidus and Ayla love him. I want to witness that future...but should things go...wrong... Should it end tonight as I leave you, I wanted to tell you to be strong. Be the queen you were always meant to be. Guide our people. And don't worry about me. Wherever I end up, just know that I chose, Paxe. I chose happiness in the end. And a part of me will always be empty without you. But I'll be watching. We will see each other again...in this life or the next. We'll be together. I'm leaving my mother's pendant to protect you and the baby should I fail and our father comes for you. Either way...I'd like you to have it. Inside the blue bag are pearls that Luca found and strung himself as a gift for me. Give them to Bumpus. Tell her that I love her, although we never met. I

Tears stung my eyes as we sailed through the moonlit sky. Dawn would break soon. If they were alive but not on their way back...then they needed me, and time was running out. It was as if Alice could read it from me. She flapped strong, bearing down into the roaring winds faster...more eager. Hissifus mewed from the bag. I tried to picture the magic that flowed inside me...tried to will it into Alice's strong frame. It worked...the world around us became a blur and she whinnied as we charged forward.

"I'm coming, Ari. Just hold on," I whispered into the night. Barely an hour later, the glow of a great fire spread through towering plumes of smoke and ash and my heart thundered as we slowed, Alice searching for a way around it. My breath caught in my throat, and a lump as big as a lemon gathered there, choking me. "Oh, Gods..." I said hoarsely, taking in the destruction of the place we'd inhabited our entire lives. We rounded the burning aftermath of Valdaro, and I finally spotted figures down below. I sank into the saddle in relief. They had to be down there. Alice descended, squealing when she saw Bjourne among the throng of survivors a safe distance away from the remains of the castle. We landed near them, small children—human children—pointing in awe at the winged horses. I dismounted, and a familiar male ran toward me.

Mischa.

"Paxe?" He called, eyes wide in surprise as my feet hit the ground. I turned toward him and he looked me over, his gaze stopping on the bulge in my middle. "Are you alright?" I nodded.

"I'm fine. Crona is untouched. The humans there are safe. We should gather any means of transportation and take them all through the Midlands...what's left of them. The king and queen will welcome these people."

"Alright. I'll gather any able men to help." He smiled, making to turn back. I grabbed his shoulder.

"Where are Ari and Luca?" I asked frantically. A young woman pushed past him to get to me and gasped at the sight of my face.

"Paxe!" She cried, throwing her arms around me. I pulled back and took in her scraped, dirty features.

"Perla!" I nearly wept, pressing her close and gripping tight around her shoulders. "Oh my Gods...thank the gods, you're safe." I drew back again. "Lakan is alive. He waits in Crona. I'll take you back with me." She tearfully nodded, lip quivering and we hugged again. "Where is your mother?" I asked, realizing I hadn't seen her and Perla hadn't mentioned her yet.

"She didn't make it," Perla croaked, sniffling against my shoulder. I closed my eyes and rubbed at her back.

"I'm so sorry..." I whispered. "I need to find Ari and Luca. Do you know where they are?" My head darted back and forth, looking through the weary faces of the rescued and finding neither.

"No one has seen them since the blast. Their horse found his way here, and we've been awaiting orders on where to go. We've not seen anyone since the castle came down." I glanced at Mischa, who nodded in confirmation. A chill went down my spine and I released my friend, stumbling toward the burning rubble of the castle and wondering if they had even made it out. I don't know how long I stood there...watching it burn and thinking of their faces.

Hissifus scrambled within the bag that was still secured to the saddle and wailed to be let out. I turned, quickly pushing past Mischa and Perla, and flipped open the flap. He leapt out, landing with feline grace on the ground and took off toward what was left of the eastern wall that surrounded the palace.

"Hiss!" I called, sprinting after him. "Hissifus!" But he didn't look back. I dodged massive chunks of smoldering stone, trying not to lose sight of him through the smoke and devastation. I heard Perla call my name from behind me, but I ignored her, picking up my pace as we neared the ruined marketplace. He darted right...past splintered parts of vendor stands and shabby workshops toward the overgrown brush that I knew too well.

Shit.

I ran faster, my heart thrashing, and Hiss disappeared into the Aegan. "Ari!" I cried, hurtling over the brush and running down the narrow path. "Luca!" My power hummed within me, growing wild with desperation and the tug of a horrible feeling deep in my gut. "Arienne!!!" I screamed, tears threatening to break through as I rounded the curve of the path. The sounds of the waterfall roared as I cleared the end and I finally saw Hissifus paused atop a rotting log near the grove. I skidded to a stop, staggering back and losing my breath when I saw what he had been staring at.

There...in the spears of moonlight shining through the canopy. Ari and Luca lay cold and pale...tangled together in an embrace on the bed of violets and yellow flowers, their bloody hands joined...a dagger lying close by. Luca's fingertip still rested on her parted mouth...their eyes stared lifelessly at each other, glassy and distant.

I staggered forward, a broken sob catching in my throat. Hissifus hopped down from the log, circling around Ari's body and leaning his head down to sniff her ear. I stumbled another step, unable to tear my eyes away from them both. Hiss pawed at her shoulder, looking up at me in question and then did it again. I broke...the deepest pain surging up through my chest and my heavy weeping took over as I dropped to my knees. I clutched my chest, took another deep breath and screamed as I wept...deafening and utterly wrecked. Another deep intake of air...another broken scream. My eyes squeezed shut around the tears that poured out, rivulets of salty water racing down my cheeks.

A large, firm hand gripped my shoulder in comfort. One I didn't recognize or acknowledge as I continued to wail. I cradled my belly with my other hand and the small infant beneath seemed to still as if even she knew they were gone and was consoling me.

"They are not lost, youngling." A choir of voices echoed from a single throat, ethereal and otherworldly. "They chose to be together. The Prince and Princess are safe. Alive...in the immortal realm." My head hung and tears continued to splatter the lush ground beneath me. I struggled to breathe.

"How?" I wept. "How did this happen?"

"It was their gift. The gift they received for fulfilling their duty to the task they agreed to by the gods. One refused to live while the other survived. But they both would survive with what they'd earned together. So, we bestowed them their immortality."

"Immortality..." I breathed, my palms pressing to the ground. "You...did you...*kill her?*" The words were like splinters leaving my mouth.

"No. The prince was dying. I gave her what she wished...a direct path to find him should she truly wish to go." A pause. "She did."

"What happened to him?" I sniffled, finally raising my face to see her. I don't know what I'd expected...but I flinched when my eyes met hers. The eerie green glow of them would have been enough to know that she was a goddess without hearing her voice...but she looked as if the most beautiful tree in the Aegan had grown legs and arms. Her strange hand held steady on my shoulder.

"The king fatally wounded him. As the prophecy had been fulfilled...I was not able to lend any aid in saving his life."

I looked back to where Hissifus was now visibly mourning the loss of both Ari *and* Luca. He didn't seem to be able to choose which one to lie next to, and he nestled between their bodies. Soft feline moans were the only sound, save for the rushing water, and each one sounded more heartbreaking than the next. As if my heart couldn't shatter anymore. I didn't look back to the goddess as I trembled in grief. I could do nothing but stare at them. At their faces...frozen forever with the same look I'd seen them give each other since

Arienne had fallen for him. Those were the faces of deep, indestructible love. Tragic and beautiful...eternal. But I couldn't think of a single thing to do. It seemed wrong to separate them...or even touch them. Luca's wedding band glinted in the light breaking in from the trees...their markings still visible from their wedding day. Both of them looked as if they'd put up the fight of their lives, dried blood flaking away from any exposed skin.

They really had fought for this. For each other. Who was I to pull them apart?

"What do I do?" I asked, crying again. "How do I...*what do I do?*" My chest shuddered with the sobs that followed behind my burning question. The thought of Ayla finding out that her only son was dead nearly shattering my soul. Footsteps sounded from behind us and a soft gasp as they halted. I turned to see Perla and Mischa standing at the end of the path, her hand dingy and smudged with dirt...covering her mouth. Mischa stood in shock, bowing his head in reverence with a fist to his chest.

"Rise... Your Highness," Elowen said, offering a hand to help me to my feet. I had to take a moment to let what she'd said register in my mind.

Oh, Gods...

Shaking, I accepted it and stood on wobbling legs. Mischa lowered to a knee and Perla looked on in utter disbelief, her mouth open and her eyes bulging. She slowly lowered with him.

"On this day...I crown before these witnesses..." She lifted her hand and within it, a crown of violets and small mecardonia weaved together in vines. The goddess looked at me, silently requesting the name that I was to be called. I stammered, looking back down at my sister's body.

"P-Paxe...Paxe...Genovese," I muttered, my voice straining above a whisper as a tear fell from my eye.

"Paxe Genovese. Queen and rightful heir to the throne of Valdaro." She gently placed the crown on my head as I bowed it. "Will you accept this role and protect these lands and its people?"

"I will." I wept.

"Long live Queen Paxe," Mischa and Perla whispered, heads bowed, and their fists clutched to them.

"Come, creature..." Elowen called to Hissifus, who paid no mind to anyone other than the two he dearly loved. He watched her, his head resting against Arienne's breast and made no move to get up. He wanted no part in a life without them. "You can stay," Elowen continued, Hiss's ears turning at her offer. "Stay here with me. You don't have to leave them." She dipped her chin at the heartbroken animal and he finally raised his head.

"What are you going to do to them?" I asked, my anguish seemingly deeper with the power I now harbored. Hissifus rose, slowly padding toward us and stopping at Elowen's feet. He sat as if he were a knight awaiting honor. I supposed he was. Her long fingers reached toward the fallen lovers and I watched...audibly crying, as flowering vines began to coil around them, twisting and twining...protecting them and holding them to each other in their eternal embrace. Their legs disappeared beneath the foliage. Then, their torsos...their arms. Their joined hands. Luca's ghostly touch against her lips. Their faces slowly began to be consumed by them. I looked at Luca, shuddering with soft sobs as he disappeared first.

Then I looked at her.

My sister.

My dearest friend.

Her beautiful features sank beneath green and yellow...purple. First with her chin and then her nose and ears. Perla's arms slid around me from behind as I sobbed, truly inconsolable as the last of her...those jade-green eyes faded away. A green misty glow surrounded the thick meadow that now encased them. Their tomb. The trunks of the trees around them grew wider, protecting them from the outside world. There was space enough between them to peer in. Space...enough for her only true baby to come and go as he pleased. The magic extended, circling around Hiss's small frame and seeping into his body, changing nothing, it seemed, except the strange new glow to his eyes. As if he were obeying a silent order, he turned and slowly walked to the grove. A flat rock lay near it and he perched there proudly. I understood then what the goddess had given him. An eternal life. To be their guardian. To stand watch at their grave and protect them forever.

"I love you, Arienne," I breathed, wiping my cheek and heaving a deep breath. "I'll keep my promise." I slowly walked to the edge of the grove and rested my head against the trunk of the nearest tree. "I'll see you both again...take care of her, Luca."

As I smoothed my hand across the bark, stepping away and leaning down to pet Hissifus, my heart nearly stopped as I beheld a small gift. A gift that hadn't been there a moment before. There, sitting next to him on the rock...was a white rosebud. I knelt down, covering my mouth as tears returned to my eyes and picked it up. I nodded generously to myself as a silent reply to my sister and kissed the top of Hiss's soft head. I stood, backing away and joining Perla and Mischa, who stood silently by.

"Should you ever find yourself in need...we shall be here for you. *They* will be here for you. The Aegan now belongs to you. It welcomes you at any time."

"The king and queen?" I asked, tearfully.

"The burden of this news has been brought to their attention. It is not yours to bear," she replied.

"I don't understand."

"Varuna is with them. Return to those that need you, youngling. They completed their journey...yours is just beginning." And with that, she vanished.

Perla took my hand, interlocking our fingers, and I looked toward Mischa, who watched her every movement. I noticed it, a slight smile turning my mouth up at the corner. A Valdarian captain of the royal guard and a human dressmaker. Their future could blossom into something as beautiful as what

Ari and Luca had...what Lakan and I have.

And they were free to have that future...because of *them.*

I smiled at Hissifus, who watched me as if to say he had everything under control, and turned with Perla toward the path, walking slowly past Mischa, who allowed us by and then followed behind us. I paused, looking over my shoulder one last time at the grove of lush trees and smiled.

"Goodbye, *Mi'lady.*"

Walking away from them was the most difficult thing that I had ever done, but as dawn broke and the sun began to peek out over our lands, turning the darkness into a hazy gray morning...we emerged from the forest—one of us as queen. And as I looked at the faces of the people who waited...that longed for their chance to finally live, my heart felt full. Aching...truly. Devastated...but full. Two winged horses stood among them as they all watched me. Fists raised to chests in reverent silence. A weathered older man stepped forward. The butcher. The father of the young boy who had given his life for my sister and had crafted the first weapon that would change our future and livelihood forever.

In his hand was a sword. The pommel was fashioned into the shape of a mighty cat...a cat that resembled the one that would spend eternity protecting the most courageous lovers the world had ever been blessed to know. The man knelt before me, raising the blade in his palms and bowing his head. I accepted it, raising it to my puffy eyes and closing them as I pressed the flat side against my chest. I breathed deeply, silently recalling the words I'd promised and lowering the sword to my side.

My eyes scanned the smoldering remains of Valdaro around us, glowing brighter in the incandescent light of the sunrise. The first day of our new lives. I lifted my chin high.

"Let's go home."

EPILOGUE

Two years have passed since I've become queen. The life that seemed so strange at first and yet...unusually simple, has seemed to pass me by quickly. The ruins of Valdaro have been cleared and reconstruction well underway in the time it has taken the world to heal and rebuild their lives in freedom. Our people are no longer divided. The Midlands no longer exist. Crona is growing and expanding...flourishing in the wake of the banishment of darkness and fear. Michele was appointed to design a truly magnificent castle to tower over our lands. Appointed by myself, which I hope made Luca proud. His university is thriving. A statue of my sister and her brave prince has been crafted by Queen Ayla and raised in its courtyard to honor their vision and sacrifice. People from all over the continent flock here to learn the arts of weaponry. Of healing and medicine. To learn how to hone their Ventus abilities and magic. King Tidus is a frequent visitor, pushing forward through the loss of his son by educating our youth.

Through these passing years, I've since learned to delegate... and also learned what it's like to be a mother and a wife. I've been given help from Ayla on the ways of royalty and consider her in every way a mother to me. We've grown closer since losing Ari and Luca, sharing our grief and growing as a family. It's helped us all. The queen no longer weeps as much, and while she still spends long hours in her studio that overlooks the sea, her time...she feels...is better spent with my daughter. My beautiful, vibrant daughter whose temper is often unmatched even by a queen who embodies fury itself. Lakan has taken a very long while to adjust to being a king. His quiet, reserved nature...except in times where we still sneak off like unruly adolescents...often presents him as the cowering human he was accustomed to being. Perla gives him tease about it every chance she gets, and they bicker like the siblings they are every moment of every day. I've named her my lady in waiting, though she prefers to be called a noblewoman. She and Mischa are now expecting their first child.

Nero and Varuna have finally agreed that even upon trying...they still can't live together. They decided it was best to take turns swapping seas and allowing Crona its rest from the raging storms between their visits. Vetta and Frances returned to Aeon, which was rebuilt—bigger than it had been before. She has since thoroughly enjoyed her retirement. Young Holt is studying at the university, training beasts of all kinds. Kyna is now twice his size. Our days are...peaceful.

This day, in particular, has been unseasonably warm. It's midsummer now, and since I peeled my eyes open to the bright morning sunlight...I could think of nothing else. Today is Arienne's birthday. Today, she would have been almost the same age I was when I'd become queen. Although that age would be older than twenty...I still thought of this day, and perhaps would always think of this day as her Ventus...as she never got the chance to celebrate it. I visited their tomb in the Aegan a week after I'd given birth. I went alone. I had needed to tell her everything. Today, we are all traveling there to visit her and Luca. Tidus and Ayla were never able to bring themselves to go, but we had agreed that when the day came that they felt ready, we'd do it together.

While talking amongst ourselves and admiring the ongoing construction of what would soon be my new home, I felt a relentless tug in my gut. It pulled at me to make my way into the woods. The king and queen followed me, swinging my daughter between them and we made our way down the path that is becoming overgrown with greenery. A small rabbit darted across as we walked and my child squealed with excitement, rushing forward toward the sounds of roaring water.

"Ari!" I called, stomping after her. "Slow down! Wait for the rest of us!" Her ash blonde hair bounced around her as she paid me absolutely no heed. Tidus and Ayla chuckled behind us as we reached the clearing. On a flat rock near a grove of trees that rustled with a warm wind, Hissifus stretched and mewed. Standing beside him with his large arms crossed against his broad chest was Nero, smirking and nodding in greeting.

"Well, isn't she something," he laughed, watching her as she gaped in awe at the waterfall a short distance away. I threw up a shield with my magic, knowing full well that she'd make a break for it and ruin her new dress.

"It's so good to see you," I smiled, approaching him and hugging his neck.

"And you, youngling. Motherhood suits you," he squeezed. We broke, turning toward the king and queen, Ayla's eyes filling with tears as she beheld the place where her son was laid to rest. Hissifus nuzzled her skirts in comfort and she smiled down at him.

"Hello darling," she whispered, leaning down to brush her fingers across his head. Tidus's eyes lingered in the space between the tree trunks as if he could see them both lying there. Nero and I stepped aside, deciding to distract little Ari and give them a moment alone with their children. They knelt close to the trunks and whispered in private conversation.

Nero picked up my curious toddler and she took in his familiar face. She reached a chubby finger to his nose.

"Boop." She grinned, poking him playfully. We giggled back at her and he kissed her soft cheek before returning his attention to me.

"You miss them," he said, not in question.

"Every day." I replied, sighing deeply.

"Perhaps it's time to take a short leave from your royal duties and pay them a visit." He quirked a brow.

"Yes, well...that's why we're here." I shrugged, not catching his meaning.

"Not here..." He reached a closed hand toward me and I offered my palm cautiously. He pressed a tiny white rosebud into my hand and my eyes misted as I looked down at it. I raised my face back to meet his fiery stare and he gave me his infamous half smile. "They want to see all of you." My mouth dropped open and hope filled my every pore.

"What?" I gasped. "Are you saying...that—"

"Pack your bags, youngling. And pack warm," he grinned.

"Nero..." I was at a loss for words.

"The only way through the pass in the Horned Mountains is by invitation. They wait for you."

My heart sped up and I wept with joy. I turned back toward the king and queen, nearly tripping over roots to get to them. Ayla met my eyes first and I handed her the rosebud.

"Do you want to see him?" I asked tearfully. She stared at the white petals between her fingers and then back at me, her crimson lip quivering. "Let's take a trip," I breathed.

"Where?" Tidus's voice shuddered, every bit of it laced with desperation.

I smiled and looked down at the purple and yellow blooms between the trees.

"To Irondale."

About The Author

H.B. Elliott is a simply-dressed, coffee-obsessed, book heathen and aspiring author from North Carolina. When she isn't writing stories that rip hearts out, while also piecing them back together, she's spending time with her husband, and two children.

She started writing when she was barely in her teens, and grew to love literature and art. She was inspired by romanticism projects and moody writers like Edgar Allan Poe. Aside from her work as an author, she also creates digital art, and loves photography and music.

She firmly believes in the Savior, and credits her success to Him and to the most important piece of literature in the world.
After all...He is the one that told her she could do all things.
He still reprimands her on a regular basis for all the smut she continues to read.